I0760746

THE COMPLETE SERIES

THE DRAGON DIARIES

USA TODAY BESTSELLING AUTHOR

DEBORAH COOKE

The Dragon Diaries Omnibus Edition
By Deborah Cooke

Hardcover omnibus edition 2024

Omnibus cover design by Mulan Jiang.

DEAR READER

Fifteen years ago, I was in the middle of writing my paranormal romance series, the **Dragonfire Novels**, and I had an idea. In the world of Dragonfire, the dragon shifters called the *Pyr* are all male—with a single exception. There can be one female *Pyr*, known as the Wyvern, who has additional powers. She's a bit mysterious, but known to be a prophetess with the power to send dreams. In book three of the series (**Kiss of Fate**) the current Wyvern, Sophie, sacrificed herself for the good of the *Pyr* and their quest to save the earth. Each of the *Pyr* may experience a firestorm, which is the sign of encountering his destined mate, or the human woman who can bear his child. Each book in the Dragonfire series is a romance, featuring one dragon shifter warrior and his firestorm with his mate. Usually, that child is a son. But the child conceived in **Kiss of Fate** was a girl, named Zoë, raising her father's hope that she would be the next Wyvern of the *Pyr*. Zoë and the other young Pyr appeared in the series in cameo roles, and when I was writing **Darkfire Kiss** (book six) it occurred to me that it would be fun to write Zoë's coming-of-age as the new Wyvern.

The Dragon Diaries trilogy is the result of that idea. There are three books in the series—**Flying Blind, Winging It** and **Blazing the Trail**—and the series takes place over the year of Zoë's sixteenth birthday.

With only one Wyvern at a time and past Wyverns being even more secretive than the rest of the *Pyr*, there's no reference guide for Zoë. She expects to come into her powers at puberty, like the male *Pyr*, but beyond that, she's on her own. When she senses a new threat to her kind and all other shifters, she and her friends—human, *Pyr* and other shifters, too—have to work together to save the day.

The Dragonfire Novels are set in real time, since solar eclipses influence the firestorms of the adult *Pyr*. As a result, we know that Zoë was born in 2008. When I wrote this series, it had to be set in 2024. I could look up eclipses that would occur in this year, but otherwise, I had to speculate on the future. I guessed that handheld devices would become more powerful than the phones we were using them. Zoë and her friends covet one called a messenger in this series, but we'd call it a smartphone. I failed to anticipate Covid-19 and its effects on our society, but beyond that, I think the story holds up pretty well. As a result, I chose not to make any changes to the original version for this new print edition.

The books have been out of print for a while and available only in used print copies as well as ebook. It's exciting to give them a new life with these three new editions. The Illustrated Hardcover Omnibus Edition is a luxe edition, with gold foil on the dust jacket and case laminate, printed endpapers and color illustrations in the interior. It's available only via Kickstarter or directly from me in my online store. There is also a Hardcover Omnibus available at the online portals: the dust jacket and case laminate have the same design but no foil on this edition, and the interior is black-and-white, without the illustrations. There is also an ebook version of the Illustrated Omnibus available from my online store, **Deborah Cooke's Books**.

I hope you enjoy whichever of the editions you choose and that you have as much fun reading Zoë's story as I had writing it. You can learn more about my dragon shifters and future books at my website, Deborah Cooke.com. Thanks for reaching my books!

All my best—

Deborah

FLYING BLIND

THE DRAGON DIARIES BOOK ONE

Zoë Sorensson is perfectly normal—well, as normal as a girl obsessed with drawing dragons can be. The thing is, she's always been told she's special and destined for great things. It's not just because of her good grades, either. Zoë is the Wyvern of the *Pyr*—the one female dragon shape shifter with special powers. But Zoë is at the bottom of the class when it comes to being *Pyr*, and her powers are AWOL. Worse, there's no reference book to consult, and the last Wyvern is dead...

Everything changes when Zoë's best friend is bullied and Zoë reacts. Before she can blink twice, her inner dragon is loose, she's suspended from school and she's headed to a shape shifter boot camp with guys she's known all her life. But soon she's doubting her powers—and even some of her friendships.

Zoë quickly realizes she has to master her powers yesterday—there's danger ahead and boot camp is a trap. A secretive group, the Mages, wants to eliminate all shifters and the *Pyr* are next in line—unless Zoë and her friends can solve the riddle and work together to save their own kind...

I

Thursday, April 4, 2024—Chicago

There was a guy in my bedroom.

It was six in the morning and I didn't know him.

I'm not much of a morning person, but that woke me up fast. I sat up and stared, my back pressed against the wall, sure my eyes had to be deceiving me. No matter how much I blinked, though, he was still there.

He seemed to think my reaction was funny.

He had dark hair and dark eyes, and he wasn't wearing a shirt, just jeans—and he had one heck of a six-pack. His arms were folded across his chest and a smile tugged at the corner of his mouth.

But he seemed insubstantial. I could see through him, right to the crowded bulletin board behind him.

Was he real?

I was going to try asking him, but he abruptly faded—faded and disappeared right before my eyes.

As if he'd just been an illusion. I jumped from the bed, then reached into that corner. My fingers passed through a chill, one cold enough to give me goose bumps. Then my hand landed on a pushpin holding a wad of drawings and everything was perfectly normal.

Except for the hair standing up on the back of my neck.

I took a deep breath and looked around. My room was the pit it usually is. There were some snuffed candles on my desk and bookshelves, a whiff of incense lingering in the air, and the usual mess of discarded sweaters and books all over the floor.

No sign of that guy. If I hadn't seen him, if I'd woken up two minutes later, I wouldn't have thought anything was wrong at all.

I shuddered one last time and headed for the shower. Halfway there I wondered, had Meagan's plan worked?

The visioning session had been my best friend's idea. Her mom calls herself a holistic therapist, which makes my mom roll her eyes. I was skeptical, too, but didn't have any better ideas. And Meagan, being the best friend ever, had really pulled out all the stops. She'd brought candles and mantras and incense for my room, and even though I'd felt silly, I'd followed her earnest instructions.

When the candles had burned down and she'd left—and my mom had shouted that I should open a window—I'd been pretty sure it hadn't worked. Nothing seemed to have happened.

But now I didn't know what to think. Who had that guy been? Where had he come from? And where had he gone?

Or had I just imagined him? I thought that if I were going to imagine a guy in my bedroom, it wouldn't be one who thought I was funny when I wasn't trying to be, never mind one who kind of creeped me out.

I'd have imagined Nick there.

In fact, I frequently did.

I heard my mom in the kitchen and my dad getting the newspaper and knew I had to get moving. I did my daily check in the bathroom, but nada. No boobs. No blood.

Four more zits.

At its core, then, the visioning session had failed.

I'm probably not the only fifteen-and-a-half-year-old girl who'd like to get the Puberty Show on the road. Even Meagan got her period last year, which was why she was trying to help. But my best friend didn't know the half of it.

That was because of the Covenant. I couldn't confide in Meagan because I'd had to swear to abide by the Covenant of our kind. I come from a long line of dragon shape shifters—*Pyr*, we call ourselves—and we pledge not to reveal our abilities to humans on a whim.

That would include Meagan.

The Covenant goes like this:

> I, Zoë Sorensson, do solemnly pledge not to willfully reveal the truth of my shapeshifting abilities to humans. I understand that individuals may know me in dragon form, or in human form, but I swear that I shall not permit humans to know me in both forms, or to allow them to witness my shifting between forms without appropriate assessment of risk. I understand also that there will be humans who come to know me in both forms over the course of my life – I pledge not to reveal myself without due consideration, to beguile those who inadvertently witness my abilities, and to supply the names of those humans whom I have entrusted with my truth to the leader of the *Pyr*, Erik Sorensson.

Do humans know we exist? Sure. Humans always have–thus the dragon stories they tell. But knowing dragons exist, believing that they are actually dragon shape shifters and being convinced that your neighbor is one of them are entirely different things.

That's probably a good thing.

The Covenant came about pretty recently. During the Dragon's Tail Wars, some *Pyr* decided they wanted to be more active and visible. My dad, though, remembers when we were hunted almost to extinction. The Covenant is a compromise, between putting it all out there and living in secret. So, humans might see Sloane on the news, appearing at the scene of natural disasters to help–he's the tourmaline dragon–or Brandt–the orange dragon–making another daring rescue, but they don't know their names or where they live in their human lives.

We teenage *Pyr* had to pledge to the Covenant after Nick tried to impress the twin girls living next door, and his dad caught him.

I still thought it was funny that they hadn't been impressed.

I, in contrast, was awed by Nick in dragon form.

The fact is that most humans don't believe they could personally know a dragon shape shifter. Those twins thought Nick had pulled some kind of illusion to make himself look more cool than he is.

So, in a way, we might as well be a myth.

Which is funny, if you think about it.

THE TRICK IS that the dragon business is all theoretical when it comes to me. I'm the daughter of a dragon shape shifter, so I should also be a dragon shape shifter. Sounds simple, doesn't it? Except it's not happening. Nothing special has happened to me. I can't do it and I don't know why—much less what I can do to hurry things along.

Dragons are by nature patient. That's what my dad says. He should know, seeing as he is about twelve hundred years old. That's supposed to reassure me, but it doesn't.

Because dragons are also passionate and inclined to anger. I know that from spending my life around all those dragon shape shifters who are my extended family. And the fact that my dragon abilities are AWOL—despite my patience—is seriously pissing me off.

The *Pyr* are all guys—men and their sons—except for me. The story is that there's only one female dragon at a time, that she's the Wyvern and has special powers.

Yours truly—I'm supposed to be the Wyvern.

The issue with there only being one female dragon shape shifter at a time is that the last one died before I was born. And it's not like anyone has her diary. Zero references for me. Zero advice.

Zero anything.

Just an expectation from my family and friends that I'll become the font of all dragonesque knowledge and lead the next generation to wherever the heck we're going.

Sooner would be better.

No pressure, right?

My dad says I was a prodigy, that I was already showing special powers before I could walk. Then I started to talk and all the Wyvern goodness went away. *Poof.* Instead of being special and a prodigy, I was just a normal kid.

I'm still waiting for the good stuff to come back.

No sign of it yet.

Some incremental progress would be encouraging. It's one thing to be a disappointment to everyone you care about, and quite another to just sit back and accept that inadequacy. In fact, I was starting to think that those dragons who believed I wasn't really the Wyvern might have it right.

Thus Meagan's session.

An act of desperation.

Because the one thing I did know was that the other dragon teenagers like Nick had come into their powers with puberty. Their voices cracked and bingo, they were shifting shape like old pros. So being a late bloomer has bigger repercussions for me. Meagan thought we were doing the ritual for my period to start. She didn't need to know I was after a little bit more than that.

Instead I got a guy mocking me in my own bedroom at the crack of dawn.

Like I said, it wasn't the best way to start the day.

THE DISSOLVING GUY was at my school.

Still shirtless.

Still mightily amused by me.

He was leaning against the brick wall, away from groups of other kids, gaze locked on me as I walked up to the school. I could still almost see through him. I felt a blush rising from my toes. Would he talk to me here? Would he tell me what the deal was?

What exactly would be the best opening question to get him talking?

Meagan caught my shoulder and I jumped. "Well?" She pushed her new glasses up her nose, almost bouncing in excitement. "Did it work?"

I glanced over at the smug half-naked dude. "Who is that? Do you know?"

"Who? Mark Smith?" Meagan rolled her eyes. "Be serious, Zoë."

"No, the other guy. The one leaning on the wall."

She gave me a stern look. "There is no other guy, Zoë." She nudged me. "Come on, tell me. Any *results*?"

"Nothing." The guy waved at me, smirked for a moment, then sauntered away. He had to be freezing without a shirt on. It was even starting to snow lightly. I watched Meagan follow my gaze, scanning the schoolyard.

She couldn't see him.

Neither, apparently, could anyone else.

Bonus. I was delusional as well as a failure and a disappointment. I'd lost my powers at the ripe age of two, and some thirteen and a half years later was losing my mind.

"Nothing?" She wrinkled her nose. "No change?"

"None."

She exhaled heavily and fell into step beside me. "Not even a cramp?"

"New pimples. Does that count?"

"It could." Meagan bumped my arm and whispered, "Did you have any dreams, at least?"

It was on the tip of my tongue. I wanted to tell her about the guy, and I would have, if she hadn't been unable to see him. When you're going crazy, I think it's better to keep the news to yourself for as long as possible.

"Nope." I shrugged and smiled.

I felt like seven kinds of a rat for lying to my best friend.

"I really thought it would work," Meagan said, so disappointed that the whole session might have been for her benefit. "Maybe we should try again."

I could do without more strangers showing up in my bedroom while I was asleep. "Maybe it just takes time." I smiled. "See you in gym?"

Meagan groaned. "Highlight of my day." She rummaged in her backpack and nearly spilled textbooks all over the floor. "Hey, draw me a dragon on my new notebook?"

Now she was trying to cheer *me* up. "Sure. Any preferences?"

"Whatever you want. Surprise me."

I took the book and tucked it in with mine. "Don't scare them with your brilliance in math class."

Meagan laughed, flashing a mouthful of hardware. She was good at math. Truly genius. Meagan's destiny was in the realm of the brainiacs.

Mine? Apparently in the land of liars and losers.

I was thinking that my day couldn't get any worse.

• • •

I HATE GYM CLASS. Nothing like ending the day with a reminder of your inadequacies. The only good thing about having it last period is that I can skulk home after the ritual humiliation. That day, I wanted to be anywhere else in the world, but cutting class isn't really an option for me.

My dad isn't just a dragon shape shifter and leader of the *Pyr*. He also has the talent of foresight. If you think your dad always guesses when you're going to do something wrong, imagine if he really did *know* it. It's not an accident that I'm a goody-two-shoes, solid-B-student, color-within-the-lines kinda chick: I've got a dragon watching over my shoulder.

I changed and followed the others to the gymnasium, even less motivated than usual. Then I froze in shock. That guy was lounging in the bleachers.

Watching me.

He gave me a salute with two of his fingers and seemed amused.

Once again, no one else seemed to notice him. Those abs should have distracted every female in the class, even Coach O'Connor, but they were all oblivious to his presence.

"*Unktehila*," he whispered, and I heard it clear across the gym. I had no idea what that meant, but no one else even heard him. I turned to stare at him and he grinned.

Then the basketball hit me in the shoulder.

And I remembered—not getting injured in gym—or doing injury to anyone else—requires all of my concentration.

Suzanne taunted me and I focused on the game. I'm tall, but being tall is not an advantage in basketball when you're a complete klutz. Artistic skill gets you nada on the court. Basketball is for the coordinated girls.

Like Suzanne.

Suzanne scored a three-pointer immediately. We had ended up on the same team, her and me and Meagan. Suzanne complained about having to carry the whole team, getting louder when Coach O'Connor wasn't looking.

(I suspect, actually, that O'Connor looks away on purpose.)

I was thinking Meagan and I would just mark time, get out of there relatively unscathed, if humiliated.

As usual.

But when the seconds were counting down, Meagan actually caught the ball.

Meagan would prefer to *never* get the ball. We're in sync on that. This time, though, it was passed to her so hard that she couldn't help but catch it.

And then she didn't know what to do with it.

That would be the hazard of never having caught the ball before. The fact that our side was behind by two points and the game was in the final minute didn't help.

I knew it would go badly. I saw Meagan's shock change to terror. I saw her hands shake, and if she had tried to say anything, she would have stammered. That's what always happens when the focus of attention is on her.

Unless she's calculating a hypotenuse or the area of an ellipse, right in her head. She is a human computer.

"Shoot already!" Suzanne shouted.

The second hand swept past the six.

Meagan's lips set and I knew she was going to try. Okay. I was with her. I managed to block one guard, Anna. Meagan defended her possession of the ball from another guard; then she eyed the net.

Calculating. I dared to hope geometry could help. Something had to go right on this day.

Meagan stepped back, her form perfect, and threw. The ball sailed through the air. Perfect! My heart pounded. The trajectory looked good.

Really good.

Oh, my God. We all stared.

The ball sank toward the net and I crossed my fingers. I heard Meagan catch her breath. O'Connor lifted her whistle to her lips.

The ball bounced off the backboard not six inches above the net, rebounded, and missed.

The whistle blew as our entire team groaned in unison.

Game over.

I hazarded a glance at the bleachers but the mystery guy was gone.

Just as well.

"Twenty-eight to twenty-six for Team Blue," O'Connor shouted. "Good game, girls! Five minutes to shower."

"Nice try," Fiona said to Meagan, and Meagan had time to blush a bit before Suzanne turned on her with a snarl.

I knew we had big trouble on our hands.

I HATE the showers almost as much as gym class itself, but Suzanne's expression had me dreading it. Everyone crams into the tiled space together, checking one another out, comparing bra cup sizes. That's bad enough without the most popular girl in our class looking to get even. Meagan and I stuck together instinctively.

"Gonna need a bra anytime soon, Sorensson?" Trish sneered at me when I pulled off my shirt.

"At least mine won't be sagging before I'm thirty." Like I knew anything about it. My mom gave me that comeback. She's a teacher and knows how girls are.

"Hurry up, girls." O'Connor made her ritual stroll past the shower area.

"Jameson will be blind by the time she's thirty," Suzanne mocked.

It was a cue and I saw it too late.

"She's blind now." Yvonne, one of Suzanne's pack of cool friends, snatched Meagan's glasses off her face.

"Hey!" Meagan protested.

She was defenseless and we all knew it.

Yvonne tossed the glasses across the shower room to Suzanne, who put them on and made a face. The lenses made her eyes look small and beady. "Seriously defective eyeballs." She pulled off the glasses, then tossed them into the air. "Oops!"

Suzanne snatched them out of the air in the nick of time, laughing. Her followers gathered closer, Yvonne and Anna and Trish. All the other girls stepped back, avoiding the confrontation as they showered quickly and disappeared.

Meagan had found the wall and was feeling her way toward Suzanne with a determination I'd seen before. "Give me my g-g-g-glasses back, please."

"G-g-g-glasses," Trish mimicked. That made me mad. It wasn't as if they were perfect.

"Puh-leeeeeeeeeeese," Yvonne said.

"Or what?" Suzanne taunted. She leaned closer to Meagan. "Whatcha going to do to me, Four Eyes? You can't even find me." She backed away suddenly as Meagan snatched in the direction of her voice, and they all giggled when Meagan missed. Meagan flushed but she kept after Suzanne.

"Give them back to her," I said, knowing they'd turn on me.

They did. "You gonna make me, Sorensson?" Suzanne spun the glasses by the ear wire as she taunted me. She pivoted to face me, bouncing a bit on the balls of her feet.

Ready to fight.

Confident that she could win. But she wasn't bargaining on my anger. I was mad enough to take her dare.

Maybe mad enough to win.

"You can only win if you don't fight fair," I challenged, and saw her surprise. "Give her the glasses."

"So, you want to fight, Sorensson?" Suzanne took a step toward me. Her team laughed and circled behind me.

Meagan took advantage of their distraction. She lunged for Suzanne, but Trish body-checked her. Meagan slipped on the wet tiles. She slammed her back into the wall and caught her breath, blinking rapidly. I knew that had hurt.

They laughed.

And I saw red.

A shimmering heat began to boil inside of me, feeding on my anger and becoming stronger. I knew what it was, what it had to be, even though I'd never felt it before.

If I'd been thinking, I would have shoved it back in its jar.

I wasn't thinking: I was mad.

"As if *you* could take me," Suzanne whispered to me. Her eyes were dancing. She was so sure she'd win.

For once, I didn't step back. For once, I didn't back away. For once, I was ready to challenge expectations.

The red tide of fury seethed, and I let it.

"Maybe I *will* take you." I took a step closer, noting how her gaze flicked. I had a new sense of power. Dangerous power. "Maybe you'll be surprised."

"Oh, I'm so scared!" Suzanne said in a falsetto, and her team giggled.

"Leave it, Zoë." Meagan had the resolve that got her perfect scores on math tests every time. "I'll g-g-g-get them myself."

Suzanne pitched her voice higher. "Oh, so brave! Come on and g-g-g-get your glasses *all by yourself* then. Look! Here they are!" She waved them in front of Meagan, who lunged toward the shiny lure.

I knew what would happen right before it did.

"No!" I shouted, and snatched for Meagan. Yvonne was faster. Trish blocked me with an elbow in my ribs. Yvonne hooked Meagan's ankle with one foot, jerking it hard. Meagan fell quickly, cracking her jaw on the tile floor.

She didn't move.

And there was blood running toward the drain.

I was right there beside her, on my hands and knees.

"All those expensive toothies getting smashed," Suzanne said in her fake baby talk. "But I thought she was the smart one."

"Meagan?" I put my hand on her shoulder. I felt her shaking.

"I'm okay," she whispered, but I knew better.

She wasn't okay.

And it was Suzanne's fault.

I felt the strange crimson strength growing inside me. I knew it was my dragon finally awakening, but I didn't imagine for a moment that it would take shape.

And let's be honest—if I had, I wouldn't have cared.

"Better make your shot next time, Jameson," Suzanne hissed. "I don't *like* losing." She tossed Meagan's glasses carelessly toward her, probably hoping they'd break when they hit the tiles.

I snatched them out of the air, surprising both of us by how quickly I moved.

"Bitch!" I snarled. I had Suzanne cornered in a heartbeat, moving faster than I ever had before. It shocked both of us. I thought I was just finally mad enough, but soon learned different.

Because when I raised my hand to slap her, I saw that my thumbnail had become a talon.

A long, sharp white claw.

A dragon talon.

Holy frick. It's finally happening.

Suzanne turned as white as a ghost, her eyes wide and her pupils tiny as she backed away from me. She even hit her head on the tiled corner; she was that anxious to put space between us.

"Your eye," she whispered. "What happened to your eye?"

I wished I had a mirror. I knew what she had to be seeing. Maybe Meagan's session hadn't been a bust after all. I didn't actually care. I smiled at Suzanne, awed by my own body's power, and she cringed.

Before *me*. Zitty Zoë.

This was the good stuff. Suzanne was hyperventilating, staring at me in horror. I felt powerful and huge, an avenger against bullies and bitches—for exactly four seconds.

"O'Connor," murmured one of Suzanne's friends, and they melted out of the shower like wraiths.

"Meagan slipped," Trish said with feigned concern, and O'Connor's footsteps became louder.

"What a klutz," Yvonne added as she headed to the dressing room.

That was when I realized what I'd done.

I'd broken the Covenant.

Uh-oh.

"Just what's going on here, girls?" O'Connor demanded from behind us. "Meagan! When are you going to be more careful?"

There was a flurry of activity, commands that Suzanne and I get dressed, first aid for Meagan, and bunches of fast lies from Suzanne's troop. O'Connor decided that I was wanted in the principal's office.

But Suzanne was freaked. She remained pale and she kept her distance from me. It would have been funny if I hadn't been so worried.

I wasn't afraid of the principal. Whatever happened in her office wouldn't be fun and it wouldn't be the truth, but I had bigger problems.

My dad, you see, is the one who created the Covenant. He's the one who made all the other dragon shifters swear to the Covenant.

And he was the one who enforced it.

That would be the Covenant that I had just broken, even though I should have known better.

Even though I *did* know better.

Actually, I had time to realize while waiting on the principal that I'd broken the Covenant twice: once by revealing myself, and the second time by not beguiling her into forgetting what she'd seen.

Oops.

I had bigger worries than what the principal might say.

Maybe the fact that I had let loose in defense of someone else, someone weaker, someone human, would persuade my dad to cut me some slack.

Or maybe not.

2

My mom picked me up from the principal's office. Her face was expressionless, which was not a good sign.

"Suspended." The word crossed her lips in a low hiss of fury, one that made me wonder whether I'd been afraid of the wrong parent.

I knew better than to argue my case.

My mom never drives well—it doesn't hold her interest enough—but that day we used up a good half dozen lives getting home. She cut off a tractor-trailer, went the wrong way on a one-way street, ran a crapload of red lights. I couldn't believe we made it home alive. Her knuckles were white on the steering wheel the whole time, and my nails were dug into the upholstery beneath my butt.

There was no way I was going to distract her with a plea for mercy.

She hit the fender on the wall when she parked the electric Toyota in the garage beside my dad's beloved Lamborghini, then got out of the car without saying anything. She slammed the door so hard that my teeth rattled. She headed for the entry to our building, not even stopping to look at the damage. She rattled her keys as she walked, as if she couldn't remember which one unlocked the door.

I'd never seen her this angry.

This was so not good.

I followed, trying not to attract attention to myself. It was admittedly a bit late for that.

My mom held open the door and glared at me.

"When did you learn?" she asked when I was right beside her.

I shrugged, startled by the question. "I didn't know I could. She was picking on Meagan and I just...reacted."

My mom wasn't buying it. "Bullshit." I froze and blinked—my mom never swears. None of us do. House rules. "Even if you never did it before, you had to know what you were feeling. You had to know what it was."

I couldn't hold her gaze. I wasn't going to make this worse by lying to my mom.

Because she was right.

"You chose to let it go," she added.

I stared at my shoes, no confession necessary. The worst part was that I knew I'd do it again, exactly the same.

No, the worst part was that I was still excited about it.

My dragon powers were *back.*

She knew it, too. I could tell by the way she sighed.

"Well, your father will be pleased, at least."

Really?

I might live to tell about this, after all. I glanced up in time to see her turn away in disgust.

"I thought it was my destiny," I dared to say.

My mom was impatient with the idea. "Well, you can't blame me for hoping that destiny might pass you by, that you might just be a normal teenager."

"But you're the one who studies stories..."

"Not every story has to come true, Zoë." She pinched the bridge of her nose briefly, then shook her head. "Here's another one for you. You know all those medieval stories about Saint George conquering the dragon? Do you know why they were so popular?"

I shook my head, knowing she was going into lecture mode and that there was no escape until she was finished.

"Because the dragon was a metaphor. The story was about overcoming a challenge. There are some scholars who believe that paganism was the force being defeated by Christianity in those stories, but I think it was even simpler than that." She put her hand on my shoulder and her voice dropped low. "I think that in conquering the dragon, Saint George was overcoming his own base instincts."

"The dragon within," I murmured.

"Or the anger that feeds the dragon. You can react in anger, or you can think before you act. Everyone has that choice. There are just bigger repercussions for you now."

But my fingernail had shifted shape only because I'd been angry. Did she mean that I should ignore what I could do, or control it, for the greater good?

Locking my dragon in the closet sounded like a losing proposition to me. I liked the idea of becoming a dragon—and yes, maybe roasting people once in a while.

When they deserved it. I could compile an Incinerate Now list on the spot, with Suzanne in the number one ranking. What was not to love about the ability to mete out justice?

My mom squeezed my shoulder. "I thought it might be easier for you if your father was wrong."

I wasn't sure what to say to that.

"Homework, *now*. I don't care how much you have—you'll find more to do until your father has time to speak with you." Her eyes got that glint, the tough look of a woman who had survived as the partner of a dragon shape shifter for almost seventeen years, and her voice hardened. "Move."

I ran to my room.

Two disciplinary intervals down, one to go.

If nothing else, my dad knew how to pick his moment. You might think your parents know how to play mind games, but trust me: they've got nothing on my dad.

My dad made me sweat.

He left me to worry.

He gave me lots of time to imagine dire scenarios, each in glorious detail, each of which ended badly for yours truly. He has more patience than anyone I've ever known.

He's definitely got more patience than I do. I didn't dare pick up my pencils, even though it would have settled my nerves—drawing dragons clearly was not homework and would have only gotten me in more trouble.

But there's only so long that nineteenth-century English literature can hold my undivided attention. There's only so much I can read about the wind on the moors even on a good day, before my thoughts wander.

On this particular night, they wandered in several (very predictable) directions.

1. Could I shift without getting pissed off? I tried, in the privacy of my room, without success.
2. What color would I be in dragon form? Mine had been a nice pointy talon, but I was disappointed that it had been white. I mean, really, if you're going to be a dragon, what color would you want to be?

I'd always thought I'd be a flaming orange dragon, maybe with red and gold details. Like Smaug there, framed on my wall, immortalized by both J. R. R. and the Brothers Hildebrandt.

I could even go with black. Maybe a nice zingy lime green. My wardrobe is what my mom calls "oil on water," so any of those colors would work for me. Purple. Electric blue. Lime. One of ten zillion shades of gray.

My dad is an onyx-and-silver dragon, very impressive-looking. Big and dangerous. It works. Or Donovan—my friend Nick's dad—is the blue of lapis lazuli in his dragon form, with gold edging his scales.

Nick is a yellow so bright that it's as blinding as the sun. It turns to shades of gold on his back. Yum. It works for him.

But my talon had been so white that it was almost clear. I was pretty sure it hadn't even had any glittery bits in it.

I wanted more flash.

Nick's eyes went all amber and radiant when he shifted, for example. Very hot. Just thinking about them made another flame light inside me.

A different one.

3. I thought about Nick. This was a habit of mine. Not only had Nick razzed me since forever about my inability to shift, but he was *Nick.*

All that almost-big-brother stuff went out the window when he'd gotten those broad shoulders, that deep voice, those hot amber eyes.

He's the guy I've always known, my best friend since forever, but now with way better packaging.

The other thing is that there's this story, one no one will really tell me, about Nick and the Wyvern having a destiny together. Now that it looked like I was actually going to be the Wyvern, I desperately wanted to see Nick and show him what I could do.

Maybe, just maybe, he'd stop acting like a big brother toward me when I was a real live dragon girl.

His *destined* dragon girl.

I switched to my history homework, but all the battles of the Civil War pretty much bled together in the face of such interesting questions. I didn't even care whether Meagan's visioning session had been the trigger, whether patience had finally won out, or who that shadowy guy was. Not having caught a glimpse of him for a few hours made it easier to forget him.

Everything had begun, and I couldn't regret a thing.

I just wanted more.

My dad ensured that there was enough time to get my homework done—the homework for this week and the next month—and I would have, if I hadn't been playing around.

As it was, I nearly jumped out of my skin when he finally confronted me.

Maybe because he challenged me in old-speak.

"*Why?*" he demanded, the single word cracking like a whip within my own thoughts. I sat up, halfway thinking it was my dragon again, and spun from my desk to face him.

He looked grim.

That was so not good.

So much for American history.

Maybe *I* was history.

My dad was leaning in the doorway of my room, arms folded across his chest. His eyes were vividly green—not a good sign—and he was shimmering blue a bit around the edges.

That's a warning sign. Dragon shape shifters on the cusp of change shimmer a bit. It's always a blue shimmer and I usually love how it looks. But I was thinking we'd have a more reasonable discussion if he stuck with human form. Things tend to get dramatic when anyone breathes fire.

I tried to think of something clever to say.

In old-speak.

Uh-huh.

It's spooky, old-speak. It throws me off my game. It's the way dragons have communicated for millennia. It's like human speech, but lower, slower, deeper, at a frequency well below the range of human hearing. Although technically, it's just like any other speech–but low–you feel it more than you hear it. It's guttural and primal, and when you've mastered it, like my dad has, you can merge your words with the thoughts of the person you're addressing. You can make your words sound like their thoughts.

Like he'd just done to me.

I hate old-speak.

And yes—big surprise—I'm terrible at it.

But it would have been rude—if not asking for major trouble—not to answer my father in kind. It's not that hard to believe that dragons have protocol, is it? And I could do without pissing him off even more.

He was plenty mad already.

"She was making fun of Meagan."

Probably the longest string of old-speak I'd ever uttered. No, it definitely was. It exhausted me.

My dad was impressed. He tried to hide it, and he was fast about that, but we are of a kind. Dragons are all super observant. We hear things that humans don't, see things that humans don't.

Actually, I thought it was pretty cool that I'd noticed my dad's reaction.

The longer he stood and considered me, though, not moving, not blinking, the more I began to doubt myself—or how likely it was that I could persuade him to go easy on me. I had still broken the Covenant.

I didn't know how long he stood there, just thinking, before he unfolded himself and stepped into the room.

"How much did you reveal?"

"I don't know." I frowned, concentrated on forming the words. *"She said something about my eye."* I swallowed, feeling myself break a sweat from the effort. *"I saw my talon."*

He studied me. The room felt full of his presence, full of his strength and intensity, as if there weren't even room left to breathe. I realized the magnitude of my mistake.

And there was nowhere to run.

Big, big screw-up, Zoë. Epic.

Would I live to tell about it?

Would I even have a chance to show Nick?

"Have you done it before?"

I shook my head.

"Since?"

I looked down, not wanting to admit that I'd been less than racked with guilt since being confined to barracks. I hadn't had any success, anyhow. I shook my head.

His old-speak slid into my mind again in a dare. *"Do it now."*

You'd better believe that I tried.

I threw everything into it, sensing that this could save the day. I tried to change just my nail, but no luck.

In fact, I couldn't find one speck of dragon awesomeness in my guts. Maybe my dragon had bailed on me—again.

I even tried to get pissed off to invoke the change.

Zip.

My dad gave me time. There was no pressure beyond his bright unblinking stare and his presence—okay, that wasn't an insignificant force, but he is my dad. I should be used to him.

He watched and he waited, and I'm sure he was aware of the sweat trickling down my back. He could probably smell my anxiety rising when my nail stubbornly stayed as it had been for fifteen and a half years.

Human.

My dad's hand landed on my shoulder, the contact making me jump. "You can't force it," he said softly, speaking aloud. "Remember the hurdles?"

Oh, I remembered. I'd been signed up for a track-and-field event in sixth grade. (You know that a gym event like that wouldn't have been my choice to join, and it wasn't. And my performance had been predictably pathetic.) I hadn't been able to jump the hurdles at first, even the low ones, instead always knocking them over. It had been mortifying, and yet more proof that I'd never, ever be an all-star.

"You said I was thinking about them too much," I said. "You told me to think about running and jumping, not about the hurdle."

"To look at the goal instead of the obstacle," he agreed.

I'd been able to do it about every third time after that, when I'd managed to follow his advice.

He crouched down beside me. "Within you, there's a trigger to the change. It's in some corner of your mind. You found it once in anger, and you will find it again. You can't force it, but you do need to learn how it feels to find the trigger and touch it—when you *aren't* angry."

"What happens if I try to change when I am?"

"No control." It was clear he disapproved of that.

My dad stretched out his hand and I saw the blue shimmer dance over his flesh. I watched it with awe.

And yearning.

"I know where to find this light," he said very quietly. "And when I need it, I summon it. I let it grow. I encourage and coax it." While he was saying this, the shimmer got brighter and brighter. "Until it claims me completely. I *choose* to invoke it. I choose when to let it run its full course. It doesn't run me."

"I saw red."

He smiled at me and tapped the tip of my nose with one fingertip. "It was running you. You have to change the balance of power so the shift is your choice."

"Otherwise I'll never be able to do it again?"

His intensity doubled. Maybe tripled. There are times when I catch glimpses of his dragon, even when he's in human form. This was one of them. "Otherwise, you won't have control of your abilities. You'll only be able to retaliate. You also won't be able to manage the timing, to ensure that you have the chance to hide your clothes."

I nodded, and proved that I'd done my dragon homework. "So no perceptive human can snatch them up and refuse to give them back to me unless I fulfill three wishes."

My dad smiled a very reptilian smile. "Three wishes would be the least of your worries. They might ask for more than that."

My dad, in case I haven't mentioned as much, is Mr. Super Logic. Sometimes he seems like an android, completely lacking in feelings. My mom says he actually feels too much, but keeps it all contained. I think she likes shaking that emotion loose, kind of like tickling the dragon's belly, but I understood his point. Acting in passion wasn't a good plan.

My mom had said pretty much the same thing, in a different way.

"What does your mom say about things worth having?"

"That they're worth working for?"

My dad smiled a little. I have to say that he didn't seem overly concerned about the whole thing, as if he weren't taking me seriously.

Or maybe he knew something I didn't.

I would have asked him more but he was already turning away.

"I'll talk to Donovan tonight," he said.

I sat up, instantly intrigued by whatever my dad's plan might be. He kept his gaze averted, watching his own hand slide down the doorframe.

I felt a sudden certainty that he was going to announce something big. Huge. My heart skipped.

"I want you to go to boot camp this year, with the younger *Pyr*. The competition might be just what you need." My father spoke so quietly that I didn't dare shout with joy. "All I have to do is persuade your mother that I'm right."

He smiled, quick, conspiratorial.

And then he was gone.

I flung myself on my bed with a hoot of glee.

Boot camp! Yes!

Boot camp is an annual competition for the younger *Pyr*, one week of trials and tests, with prizes. It's run by Donovan, who is huge on training, and so far only Garrett, Nick and Liam have been allowed to go. It's top-secret, although there's always a kick-ass prize.

In short, boot camp is gym to the thousandth degree.

It should have been my worst nightmare. The other dragon guys would eat my liver with their experience and power and just raw knowledge of their capabilities. I would lose on every conceivable level.

But I still bounced on the bed. I wanted to squee, even though that's not my style. Because Nick would be there, and we would be forced to spend a whole week together, being dragons.

Wrestling, maybe. The prospect made me dizzy.

I would get to see Nick's fab new packaging up close and personal.

Maybe *really* personal.

I'd learn more about my abilities as Wyvern and my secret destiny with Nick. It was a score on every possible level, and I couldn't wait to go.

And that was when I realized something astonishing. I had broken the Covenant. Twice. I had ditched my usual goody-two-shoes game plan, broken the rules, yet I *was being rewarded.*

Just as I'd always suspected, the return of my dragon powers was changing everything.

3

I woke up suddenly in the middle of the night, as if someone had tapped me on the shoulder. It was cold in my room, colder than it should have been, and the hair was prickling on the back of my neck. I had the feeling that I wasn't alone.

You know who I was expecting to find watching me.

I rolled over, keeping my eyes squeezed shut, telling myself that I'd find everything just as it should be when I looked.

Except it wasn't.

The walls and floor of my bedroom were gone. Sort of. But if I squinted, I could still see them. I could see the framed posters of dragons—drawn by me and others—and my crowded bulletin board. The bare-chested guy wasn't there.

But there was a large tree. It grew where the doorway normally was, one big root snaking across the floor to disappear beneath my bed.

Plus I could see the sky through my ceiling—but it was filled with stars, as if I were far out in the country. It certainly wasn't the sky over Chicago, the stars dimmed by the ambient light of the city. That's what should have been on the other side of my ceiling.

But that wasn't even the weirdest bit.

The weirdest bit was the old woman sitting in the corner of my room—

well, the corner of my room that looked more like it was under a huge tree. She was knitting.

The hairs on my neck had it right—I wasn't alone.

She didn't seem to be aware of me, so I had a good long look. She was more substantial than Buff Boy had been, which was a reassuring sign of sanity on my part. (All things being relative.) She was old, but not in a creepy way. Think Mrs. Claus. She had white curly hair and little round silver glasses. Her cheeks were rosy and her lips were pursed. She was soft and plump, as if she'd been sampling cookies she made daily from scratch.

She could have been the grandmother I'd never had.

My mom knits, but with my mom, knitting is an Olympic event. My mom knits with furious speed, needles and elbows flying. She's usually talking at the same time—no, lecturing—and she's not above making her point with, well, a needle point. She knits as if she's got something against the yarn. Or she's on a deadline.

This woman knit quietly. She was almost motionless, only her right index finger dancing back and forth, moving so fast that it was a blur. Like a hummingbird. Instead of the ferocious clack of steel on steel that accompanies my mom's knitting, Granny's knitting made only a faint clicking sound. Like the ticking of an old clock. She was knitting something white, something that seemed to grow faster even than she was knitting.

I was going to ask her a question—whether she was real, why she was in my bedroom, where the tree had come from, just how crazy a person had to be to have these kinds of visions—but no sooner had I opened my mouth than she shot me a look. There was something dangerous about her expression, something not quite as fluffy as the rest of her, and I shut up fast.

She smiled a bit. *Good choice.*

Then she held my gaze and shut her left eye.

She opened it again, then shut her right eye instead.

With both eyes open, she smiled at me again. She returned to her knitting, concentrating on it as if I weren't there. As if I were the imaginary friend. Ha.

Message received.

I shut my left eye and Granny disappeared. My room looked exactly as it usually did, right down to my dirty clothes that I'd tossed in the corner by the door the night before.

I opened my left eye and she was back. Sort of. She looked ghostly, as did the tree, and so did the walls of my room. I had the same dizzy sense of things overlaying each other in irrational ways.

I shut my right eye and Granny was as clear as could be. I was in the same place as her and the tree, and there was no sign of my room. I was lying in the snow, and when I looked back where the wall and window should be behind me, all I could see was endless tundra.

It was a bit spooky. I opened my right eye again and I could see both realities.

Of course I had to play with that. I shut my right eye over and over again, getting a good look at this snowy place. It was like a 3-D dream.

Was that what I should have done with the mystery dude? I wondered what I would have seen if I'd known to play the eye game.

It was almost—but not quite—enough for me to wish him back.

Meanwhile Granny kept knitting. Steadily. It—a blanket? a shawl?—spilled over her lap and piled around her feet like a snowdrift. It grew deeper and wider and it even glittered a little. That made me think of the diamonds that the sun picks out in the snow.

But it was April and there was no real snow left in Chicago. Just those flurries during the day.

The dream made no sense. I started to sit up, determined to talk to her, but she gave me that hard look again. It might not have stopped me, but she lifted one hand, dropping her knitting into her lap. The needles disappeared as if they'd fallen into deep snow.

She blew something off her palm toward me.

It looked like a stone, which made no sense. I caught it instinctively and closed my hand firmly around it—proof positive that this was a dream and not gym class.

An instant later, I was surrounded by swirling snowflakes. I couldn't see anything else—there had to be thousands of them, and they were huge. They landed on me and around me. I could have been inside one of those paperweights, the kind you shake to create a snowstorm.

I opened my hand to look at what I'd caught. It *was* a stone, maybe two inches across, irregularly shaped, and red. There was a circle on one side, etched into the surface, although the marks looked old. I wondered whether the circle was part of the natural shape of the stone.

When I turned the stone over, there was a symbol scratched into the other side. Like an *F*. Or a tree with two branches to the right. I ran my thumb over it: these cuts were ground deeply into the stone. Fresh and raw.

What did it mean?

I looked to Granny for more information, but she was gone, gone as surely as if she'd never been.

The snow was gone, too, and so was the tree.

No matter which eye I used to look around.

It was just my room, as much of a pit as ever.

The weirdest thing was not that I went right back to sleep, but that I woke up with the red stone still in my hand.

Was I gathering Wyvern accessories? Nothing happened when I looked through one eye—the view didn't change at all—but I had the stone.

I decided to pack it for boot camp.

Just in case Granny had given it to me for a reason.

Even better, when I did my routine bathroom check, there it was.

Yes! After I'd waited so long, it didn't seem to be real, but there was honest-to-goodness blood. Meagan's flaky visioning session was a success! I couldn't wait to tell her. I ran for my mom, who matter-of-factly pulled out supplies and set me up.

As if it were no big deal.

As if it weren't the beginning of *everything*. Boys. Bras. Dragon powers and destiny.

Not necessarily in that order.

"When do I get breasts?" I asked, cupping my hands where they should be. I was tired of looking like a tall twelve-year-old, with guys treating me as if I were a kid. A kid sister. I could imagine myself with torpedo boobs, Nick checking me out....

She was amused. "Maybe never."

"No, seriously."

"No, seriously."

"When do I get Wyvern powers?"

My mom shrugged and gave me a hug. "Maybe I'm not in that much of a hurry for you to grow up," she whispered into my hair, then kissed me.

Her eyes were all sparkly when she pulled away, as if she were going to cry.

But my mom pretty much never cries.

Even so, I gave her a hug back. “It’s okay, Mom. I promise I won’t get suspended again.”

She smiled, although she still looked a bit sad. “No matter how big you get or what you learn to do, I still get to worry about you. Deal?”

“Deal.”

I took a chance, since we were having this mushy chick moment of confidences. “Will you tell me what Wyvern things I used to be able to do?”

My mom glanced toward the living room, where my dad was already working on his computer, then looked back at me. I knew that she knew he could hear whatever she said.

“Not my responsibility,” she said lightly.

“What about the story of the Wyvern and Nick having a destiny together?” No one would ever tell me this one, although I’d heard snippets over the years from the adults before they caught me listening.

My mom shook her head. “Ditto. But I’ll make you another deal. If you still want to know when you get home from boot camp, I’ll tell you a story about a Wyvern named Sophie.”

So...the last Wyvern had been Sophie.

And my mom thought I would learn more at boot camp. I was excited enough to dance, but I’d take the insurance where I could get it.

“Deal.” We hugged again and I was glad she wasn’t mad at me anymore. “You tell the best stories, so maybe I’ll ask you anyway.”

She smiled then but her eyes stayed serious. “Be careful, Zoë. None of this is a gimme.”

I smiled at her, because she was just worrying about me again, exactly as she’d said she would.

Everything was starting!

I had to send Meagan a message. I might not be able to tell my best friend all of the truth, but sharing some of it was better than nothing. I retreated to my room before my mom could confiscate my messenger and render me incommunicado.

. . .

MEAGAN CAME by with my homework after lunch. My mom had decided to work at home because of yours truly getting suspended, and my dad was off in meetings for some big upcoming fireworks display. (That's what he does—coordinate big pyrotechnics shows, which is cool, but not as cool as being a dragon shape shifter. Call me biased.)

It was the last day before spring break and I truly couldn't believe that there was anything important for me to do for school.

Nothing more important than packing for boot camp, that was for sure. I couldn't decide what to wear for a week of Supergym with the guys.

I was glad to see Meagan. We sat on the stools at the kitchen counter and she spun on one, the way she always did. My mom was on the other side of the living room, focused on her computer screen, tapping on the keyboard.

Meagan had a killer bruise on her jaw, which tempered my excitement. She showed me the additional chunks of plastic and metal that the orthodontist had installed in her mouth the night before.

"Ow," I said with sympathy.

"And then some," she agreed.

"Frankenstein city." I felt bad that she'd taken such a hit. It just didn't seem fair.

She was trying to be upbeat, but I wasn't fooled. "So much for losing the hardware before senior prom."

"No!"

"Yes. He said I might have added a year to the treatment protocol with my *carelessness*." Meagan avoided my gaze, picking through my trig homework as if it were interesting. I knew she could have done it in two minutes, blindfolded, with one hand tied behind her back. It would take me a while longer. A lot longer.

She sighed. "No point arguing with my mom about contacts now."

The thing is that Meagan is pretty as well as smart. She's got it all going on—the braces and the glasses just obstruct the view. She's getting really curvy, too. If it had been anyone else getting those boobs, I would have been beyond jealous. As it was, I wanted to cheer for my best friend. She was going to be *hot* when the equipment came off, and we had schemed together over her making a big entrance at senior prom.

To lose that moment because of Suzanne was just wrong.

"But you weren't careless! Suzanne started it."

Meagan shrugged. "Doesn't matter much in the end, does it?" For the first time ever, I heard bitterness in Meagan's tone. "She didn't even get detention."

It was so unfair.

We spun on the stools in silence. I couldn't think of one thing to say to cheer Meagan up. She had her old glasses on, the ugly Coke bottles, and it was just sad.

"What did you say to Suzanne?" Meagan asked finally.

"What do you mean?"

"In the corner. You must have said something, even though I didn't hear it. She's telling everyone that you're a freak."

My heart skipped a beat. I could feel my mom glancing over from the computer. "Nothing I remember," I lied, then decided to check my sanity again. "Maybe she didn't want to lose, with that guy watching."

"What guy?"

"The one in the bleachers."

"There was no guy in the bleachers, Zoë. I would have noticed that. I would have *missed*."

I opened my mouth to say that she had missed, then shut it again. Meagan laughed, liking that she'd almost faked me out.

I liked a whole lot less that I'd just lied to my best friend. Again. But I couldn't tell Meagan about my dawning abilities. I couldn't break the Covenant a third time in just a day.

My messenger chimed suddenly. Mine is a combination phone and digital notepad. Like all the others, it gets text messages and e-mails. It's so painfully antique, though, that I can store only half a dozen books in its memory, and its outdated drawing features are enough to make me weep. And it's huge—almost as big as my hand and as thick as my finger. I try not to yearn for any of the fabulous fast-featured new models, and I pretty much fail. Meagan and I are the only two girls in school to still be toting such ancient hardware.

At least when we're alone together, I don't mind tugging mine out of my pocket.

"Who's that?" Meagan asked, which was fair. She was the one person in the world most likely to send me a message at any point in time, and she was sitting right beside me.

We're not *that* dorky.

I scanned the message, surprised and skeptical. So skeptical that I read it twice.

"What is it? Phone spam?" Meagan said.

"It's from Trevor Wilson."

"*The* Trevor Wilson?" Meagan nearly leaped across the counter. "As in Suzanne's Trevor?"

I nodded. This was one of the great mysteries of our time, that Suzanne would take up with Trevor Wilson. We had spent many nights trying to figure out this relationship. Meagan and I agreed that Trevor was hot, because he could play the sax so incredibly that it gave you shivers, but Suzanne was usually more for the football-captain type.

Meagan leaned closer. "So he wants to beat you up for scaring his girlfriend?"

I shook my head. "He wants me to go out with him."

"No!" Meagan grabbed my messenger and read the display, just as shocked as I was.

"It's a trick." She handed it back to me. It says a great deal for my social life and general level of popularity that neither of us could take this seriously, even for a moment. "He's trying to lull you into complacency so he can get even for Suzanne."

Only Meagan could say "lull you into complacency" and not sound like she was putting it on.

She was right. It had to be a joke.

Although it didn't do much for my ego that the conclusion was inevitable.

"Well, I'm not that stupid." I deleted the message.

"He should know that." Meagan spun on her chair. "But then again, he's the one who needs tutoring in math."

I stared at her. "No."

"Oh, yeah." She acted casual, but she was blushing. Big-time. I remembered that it was Meagan who had talked so much about Trevor's musical skill. Was it possible that we both had secrets? She couldn't even look me in the eye. "Order of operations completely blows his circuits."

"You *tutored* Trevor Wilson and you never told me? I thought we were friends!"

Meagan's face was so red, and she started to stammer a bit. "It was only...only the once, at the math clinic." She tried to shrug it off. "Not like I made a difference to his skill set. I'm sure he doesn't even remember me."

She was right. He'd pinged me, Meagan's best friend, instead of her. I'd never even talked to him. I certainly hadn't spent hours working through equations with him.

Ouch. I developed sudden and complete confusion over my homework. Needing to be smart always perks Meagan up.

It worked like a charm. We poked through the homework for a few minutes while she explained things to me. Being arty, you know, means that everyone is ready to believe I don't get much else. In this case, I was glad.

She complimented the dragon I'd drawn on her new notebook, and I felt like we had our own mutual admiration society. "What are you doing next week, anyway?" she asked, spinning on the chair. "Want to do our homework together?"

"I thought you were going to California."

Meagan shook her head. "Dad says I blew the budget."

More injustice. I knew Meagan was dying to go to San Francisco. She'd been talking about it since Christmas. The plan had been to check out Silicon Valley and the AI labs at Carnegie, as that was likely where Meagan would end up after high school.

I'd always thought it must be nice to have a destiny that had some chance of coming true. Me, I was okay at a lot of things, but not brilliant at any one subject. I got good grades but had to work for them. Nothing, but nothing, came easily—well, drawing did. Drawing dragons. I hadn't yet found a career option that fit that.

Even this dragon stuff, which Nick and the other *Pyr* guys made look so easy, wasn't effortless for me. They had just gotten it overnight, along with hair on their chests.

I'd tried the nail trick again this morning, with no luck. And I couldn't help feeling betrayed—shape shifting was *supposed* to be in my blood.

"The thing is," Meagan said, spinning her stool, "it was kind of my fault."

"What do you mean? They tripped you!"

Meagan grimaced. "Suzanne came to the math lab, you know. Last month."

This was news. "With Trevor?"

Meagan shook her head. "Alone." She traced a pattern on the counter and I knew she was going to tell me something important. "She acted like we could be friends, but she only wanted me to help her cheat."

"So you said no," I guessed.

Meagan nodded. "She was pretty mad." She pushed up her glasses. "I guess I had it coming."

"No!" I said. "No, you did the right thing...."

"Doesn't feel like it."

And there was nothing I could say to that.

Meagan sighed. "Want to hang out next week?"

"I can't. I'm going to Minnesota."

Her face fell even further. "I thought you were staying home."

"So did I. I found out last night."

"Minnesota? What for?"

I shrugged, pretending to be less excited than I was. "Friends of my parents." I left out the bit about their hunky son and our entwined destinies.

Meagan grimaced. "Let me guess. They have kids and you're all supposed to get along together."

"Got it in one." I stuck out my tongue as if the whole idea were hideous. We laughed and joked around then, but I felt bad. It just wasn't right. My best friend was seriously on the wrong end of every deal, *and* I'd lied to her.

More than once.

Was this the price of my dragon's return? That I lose my best friend? It felt like a catch, and one I hadn't anticipated. I felt trapped between what I had been and what I might become, without the advantages of either dragon or human.

That just made me more impatient for the future to happen.

For boot camp.

Bring it on.

4

I got a message really late, and to make it worse, my messenger chimed loudly. I had to jam it under my pillow to muffle its perky sound. House rules: no socializing after ten. But the message was from Nick, so there was no chance of my waiting until the morning. Had he heard? Was he as excited as me? I had to know.

My fingers shook as I—one more time—broke the rules.

As messages went, this one was disappointing. Nick hadn't written anything. Not one word. There was just an attachment.

It looked like a song file.

Bracing myself for some kind of joke—he'd sent me a version of "Happy Birthday" woofed by dogs just last year, which had been too lame to even be funny—I loaded it up and listened.

He must have heard. This was sexy music.

I didn't recognize the song. I was sure I'd never heard it before. It was instrumental, but haunting.

Romantic.

Wow. Things were looking up.

I put in my earbuds and listened to it again. It made me feel alive and alert in a different way, the way I'd felt in the showers at school. I could imagine slow dancing to this music, unaware of anyone but Nick, our bodies bumping together. It made me tingle.

Maybe it was some kind of *Pyr* music. I felt as if my dragon were uncoiling like a cobra, dangerous in the dark. That felt good, forbidden, a peek into the darkness ahead.

I listened to it thirty-nine times in a row.

I stopped only because I fell asleep.

If we were going to Minneapolis, odds were that we'd fly. And given the choice between commercial airlines and dragon power, Dragon Air is the only way to go. I love it when my dad flies us somewhere, when he shifts shape and carries my mom and me to our destination. There's something amazing about flying with a dragon and feeling the wind in your hair. I don't even care if it rains.

Theoretically, I should be able to fly myself. Of course, I'd need to be able to shift more than my thumbnail, and be able to do it by choice.

I'd work on that at boot camp.

In the meantime, I was seriously excited about having my dad fly me to Minneapolis, so excited that I was ready early.

But there was an airline ticket at my place at the breakfast table.

I couldn't even try to hide my disappointment. "I thought you were flying me."

My dad gave me a grim look. "How much did you pack?"

Okay, there were two bulging duffel bags by the door. I hadn't been able to whittle it down. I looked at the pile, knowing he was following my gaze.

"I don't do checked baggage." He snapped his newspaper. My dad is the only person left in the world who reads the news on paper. I'm sure of it. He says dragons are never in a hurry to change.

"But..."

"And you broke the Covenant," my mom added from the kitchen. My dad looked at me and I understood.

This was my punishment.

"I am hoping no one believes this Suzanne," my dad said, speaking with precision, the way he did when he was annoyed. His British accent gets stronger then.

"I could beguile her after break."

I got a look for that, then he returned to his paper. End of discussion.

I fingered the airline ticket as I ate. I didn't have to like the plan, even if I knew it wasn't unfair and that I wouldn't be able to negotiate my way out of it.

It was true that my dad always traveled with a black messenger bag slung over one shoulder, nothing more and nothing less. My mom, too, packed light. I guess she'd learned.

Maybe she'd been given airline tickets once, too.

But worse than not having the dragon flight—which completely would have started the trip off right—was the lost opportunity to interrogate my dad.

I felt a dire need for more information of the dragon variety. I quickly formulated plan B—I'd ask him questions on the way to the airport. Maybe I'd manage to get in two or three. They'd better be good ones.

But my dad got a call right then and left for work before I even finished eating.

My mom took me to the airport.

At least she didn't ding the car again.

I CHECKED in and got to the gate before they started to board. I tried a human strategy and sent a message to my dad, but after five minutes, it was clear he wasn't going to reply.

I could guess why. He was testing me. I took a deep breath and tried a dragon trick. I closed my eyes tightly and tried to send him a question in old-speak.

Over distance.

Graduate work in old-speak.

I'd never managed it before, but maybe things had changed. It couldn't hurt to try.

I thought about where my dad would be—at the warehouse, where they stored and rigged the fireworks. He'd be on his messenger, directing his foreman at the same time that he talked to the client, rummaging through a delivery. Super-multi-tasker, that's my dad.

I concentrated on the warehouse's precise location, how exactly I'd get there from the airport, and tried my best.

"*I have questions,*" I said, hoping it would work.

I sensed my father's surprise, but it didn't slow him down. I was pretty much stunned that I could feel his reaction.

"Then you'll have to find the answers." He was as curt in old-speak as he could be in real life.

He was busy.

"But..."

"Work it out, Zoë." His old-speak softened. *"That's part of the challenge. Everyone's different, so you'll have to find your own way."*

The *Pyr*, you know, could have used instruction manuals.

On the other hand, I was the only one who seemed to need one. Which said nothing good about my being a runaway success as a dragon. Was it possible that the talents I'd lost when I'd started to talk were gone forever? Had I blown the chance to become the Wyvern before I could even read the job description?

And what did that mean I would become instead?

I've always liked riddles and puzzles. When it seems as if a riddle has no solution, it pays to review the clues. I pulled out my messenger and began to type out what I did know, in the hope of finding a clue to what I didn't know.

I had some time to fill anyhow.

The first thing I wrote down was the most obvious.

> In the beginning, there was the fire, and the fire burned hot because it was cradled by the earth. The fire burned bright because it was nurtured by the air. The fire burned lower only when it was quenched by the water. And these were the four elements of divine design, of which all would be built and with which all would be destroyed. And the elements were placed at the cornerstones of the material world and it was good.
>
> But the elements were alone and undefended, incapable of communicating with one another, snared within the matter that was theirs to control.
>
> And so out of the endless void were created a race of guardians whose

appointed task was to protect and defend the integrity of the four sacred elements. They were given powers, the better to fulfill their responsibilities; they were given strength and cunning and longevity to safeguard the treasures surrendered to their stewardship. To them alone would the elements respond. These guardians were—and are—the *Pyr*.

That was the first thing I ever learned about dragons. My mom calls it a creation story. My dad made me memorize it when I was about four, and now I knew it as well as my own name.

It calmed me down to write it out again, reminded me of the good bits of being a dragon shape shifter.

But it gave me no answers.

Onward.

Five Things the *Pyr* Can Do in Dragon Form:

1. Breathe fire. (Duh.)
2. Breathe smoke. Dragonsmoke is a protective barrier that only other dragons can perceive. Any *Pyr* who crosses another *Pyr*'s dragonsmoke without permission gets burned. Literally.
3. Communicate in old-speak.
4. Beguile. Beguiling is a kind of hypnosis, which can be used to persuade humans of things—like, for example, that they haven't seen dragons flying through the air over Chicago.
5. Fly. I said it before, but it bears repeating. It's that cool.

Pyr power that I want the most badly: number five.

Duh.

So, out of five, I could do two. With varying levels of success. I had a ways to go this week to even score a B on any *Pyr* final exam.

But it got worse:

Five Things about the Wyvern:

1. She's the only female *Pyr* in existence. One Wyvern has to die for the next one to be conceived.
2. She can dispatch dreams, both to *Pyr* and to humans.

3. She can take other forms than dragon and girl, including salamander.
4. She's a prophetess, one who can see past, present, and future simultaneously.
5. She can travel instantly to other locations. This means that dragonsmoke, for example, is not a barrier to her. She just appears on the other side of it.

Number of these things I could do with any level of expertise: zero.

Okay, I was depressed enough. I saved my files and listened to Nick's music instead.

At least it made me feel better.

It was snowing in Minneapolis.

Not the way it does in Christmas movies, with harmless fluffy flakes. No, no, no. There was an honest-to-goodness blizzard going on. I could have left April behind in Chicago, and landed in January instead.

I hadn't thought Minneapolis was that far away.

The other passengers complained about the unseasonal weather, and I hoped I'd brought enough warm gear. We descended until I could see the airport, shrouded in white. The snowdrifts on the roof looked like giant marshmallows. There were snowplows driving up and down everywhere, their blue lights flashing.

The airplane landed with a thump, then skidded, tipping in a crosswind. Then we slid sideways. It was a crappy moment to be traveling alone, with no one's hand to hold.

Everyone cheered when the plane came to a halt. The pilot announced that we had been the last flight allowed to land, that they were closing the airport until the blizzard stopped.

The rough landing had shaken me up a bit. But now I was closer to Nick! And maybe he would have some answers for me about the whole dragon thing. Some tips. After all, he was in full control of his dragon.

My dad had gone through the change so long ago, he probably didn't even remember what it was like. Maybe it had been different in the olden days, when avenging knights had to be barbecued and damsels plucked from danger.

By the time I hefted both of my bags from the carousel, I had to consider the merit of packing more lightly. I was panting as I left the baggage claim area. Super-killer gym class had evidently started early.

Bonus that my aching shoulders were my own fault.

But it didn't matter. I was here and so was Nick and it was destiny time. The doors opened to the arrivals area and my heart began to thump. I scanned the crowd. I saw Donovan immediately, head and shoulders above the rest.

Sure enough, Nick was right beside his dad.

"Nick!" I shouted, and jumped up and down. This was a feat with two loaded duffel bags, but I was motivated. Nobody heard me, even with their keen *Pyr* hearing, which should have warned me.

But I refused to care. What would I say first? What would I do first? How much did he already know? I galloped toward Nick, the weight of my junk forgotten.

As I got closer, my heart squeezed so tightly that I could barely breathe. Nick must have grown another six inches taller since I'd seen him last, and he'd been working out. *Oh, yes.* His shoulders were really broad and there couldn't have been an ounce of fat on him. His hair brushed his collar and it was the same russet as his dad's—straight instead of wavy.

Yum.

He was facing the other way, surrounded by the others.

"Nick!" I yelled, and this time he glanced my way.

He smiled.

He nodded.

Then he turned away again.

What?

I was expecting at least a hug. Especially after he'd sent that music.

I rushed forward, unable to believe that anything could be more interesting than seeing me—especially as I didn't think there was anything more interesting than seeing him. I realized that I was last to arrive, and that even Rafferty was here.

Rafferty?

All the way from England?

But why? He didn't even have a son.

Maybe Rafferty was going to teach us something special. Rafferty could communicate with the earth, after all.

Then the group parted and I saw who held Nick's undivided attention.

Crap. My sucker heart ripped itself in half, then went splat on the tile floor.

Because Nick was talking to Isabelle.

Isabelle. Rafferty's adopted daughter.

Older than any of us.

Gorgeous.

Curvy.

She had a thick chestnut ponytail, which bounced as she walked. That should tell you everything you need to know. Gorgeous girls with ponytails are a painful amount of trouble.

Worst of all, she had a British accent.

The guys were already starting to drool.

And Nick was first in line.

As I stood there looking on, I thought my knees would give out. That would have made me look even more stupid than I did with my mouth hanging open in dismay. I shouldered my stuff, forced a smile, and joined the group.

Rafferty and his mate couldn't have kids, so Isabelle was adopted. Her presence explained his, but I couldn't figure out why she had come. Was she attending boot camp?

Please, Great Wyvern, make it not be so.

No one else had any issues, though. In fact, I was thinking the airport would have to call in an extra shift of janitors to mop up all the slobber from the three guys. They were interrupting one another, trying so hard to get Isabelle's attention that I barely recognized them.

Nick gave me a punch in the shoulder as a kind of greeting, which absolutely did not meet my expectations—especially not after he'd sent that song. (Which, yes, I had been listening to all day, and which, yes, had raised my expectations somewhat.) Liam gave me a hug—he's like that—and Garrett shook my hand. They were all taller than me, and I'm not exactly short.

I hauled my own bag to the car, while the guys fought (*fought!*) over the chance to carry Isabelle's pretty suitcases.

So much for my exciting vacation.

So much for my great extended bonding time with Nick.

Crap.

We all piled into Donovan's hybrid four-wheel-drive and Nick's electric sports car, and you can guess who sat where. Me, I won the backseat of the four-wheel-drive, Donovan driving and Rafferty in front.

Isabelle—queen of all she surveyed—was in the front seat of Nick's car, with the other guys piled in the back and leaning over the seats, desperate for her attention. Most of the baggage was with me.

Enough said.

My only consolation was that Nick would have to clean up the drool in his car.

It wasn't nearly good enough.

Just so you know.

Donovan and Rafferty talked in old-speak the whole way to the house.

Fascinating.

Not.

Donovan was telling Rafferty about a Mage sending him a ransom letter, and how easily he'd gotten rid of him. Rafferty was having a good laugh over the idea of Mages casting spells to ensnare the *Pyr*. Rafferty said he hadn't even caught scent of a Mage in two hundred years.

Yawn. For the lack of anything better to do, I added to my list of Known Facts. It occurred to me that although there wasn't a guidebook to the *Pyr* —much less to becoming one—I was kind of building my own.

A DIY dragon survival guide. How sad is that

Five Things about Mages:

1. They are humans who do magic, and first were noticed by *Pyr* during the Renaissance. Their magic must be pretty lame, though. I'd seen the *Pyr* Lorenzo do *his* magic, and that smoked anything else around. His stage show was awesome. And what he did offstage was even more incredible. Dragon magic rocks.

2. The *Pyr* have never lost a battle to the Mages.
3. None of the *Pyr* have seen a Mage in recent memory.
4. None of the *Pyr* are worried about the Mages.
5. The only reason they were even talking about this was that warriors of all kinds get bored in peacetime. With the *Slayers* defeated and eliminated, we dragons were fresh out of enemies, and the old guard were making up spooky ghosts. Now, that is sad.

Rafferty's ring glinted in the light as he talked. He'd worn that black-and-white ring for as long as I'd known him. My parents told me that, as a kid, I always went to Rafferty to touch his ring. When the light was right—as it was now—the ring looked as if it had a light deep inside it. It looked as if it were made of glass, black and white glass swirled together.

When there was a lull in their old-speak, I leaned forward and spoke out loud. "Rafferty? Can I ask you a question?"

"You just did." He smiled at me, teasing.

"When I was little, my dad said I could do some Wyvern stuff. Do you know what it was?"

Rafferty took a deep breath and frowned into the snow swirling against the windshield. One thing about Rafferty—he takes his time, even for a dragon. (Which is saying something.) "You used to send us dreams."

"Really?"

He turned to smile at me. "You gave me a vision, one that saved the day."

"Really?" I squeaked a bit. This was unbelievably cool.

Even though I'd lost that power.

"Why can't I do it anymore?"

Rafferty looked down and I thought he wouldn't answer me. "*Maybe the time isn't right*," he said in old-speak. "*There's a solar eclipse on Monday. See what happens then.*"

The motion of the sun was linked to my becoming a Wyvern? I couldn't believe it.

I thought Rafferty must be putting me on. He smiled, and I decided that if he was going to razz me—or not take this Wyvern stuff seriously—then there wasn't much more to say. I tucked in my earbuds and listened to Nick's music.

And that just put everything in perspective. Nick had sent me this provocative song. Even if he was putting on a good show of being polite to Isabelle, this song said it all.

I wasn't giving up on Nick and our entwined destiny yet.

After all, I hadn't had a chance to show him what I could do.

5

It was snowing like crazy, drifts piling up white against the windows, but I felt cozy once we were inside Donovan's house. And dinner was good. I didn't eat the barbecued ribs—no meat for me—but the guys ate as if they'd never see another meal again. Donovan's partner Alex made a joke about being glad they didn't all live at her house. Two dragon sons were enough, I guess. Nick's kid brother, Darcy, was staying with a friend for the night.

Isabelle also abstained from eating meat, explaining in her posh accent to Alex that she was vegetarian. Like me. I felt that she was trying to be friends, but I knew better.

The ponytail said it all.

We were crowded around the dining room table, more tightly squeezed in than the last time I'd been with the guys. They were all getting broader in the shoulders.

Garrett is the oldest of the guys—sixteen and the son of the *Pyr*'s blacksmith, Quinn. He looks like Quinn—black hair, blue eyes, and powerful shoulders—and he's quiet like his dad.

You could think of him as being like smoldering coals—they could burn slowly forever or flare up with the right impetus. A breath of wind. New fuel.

Whenever the guys arm wrestle, Garrett wins. Period. His shoulder muscles are something else and he earned them the hard way—hammering hot iron.

Nick is next-oldest, also sixteen. He's the classic, popular, captain-of-the-football-team, every-cheerleader's-dream kind of guy.

He's like a bonfire that everyone wants to gather around. Sociable. Attractive. Girls are drawn to him like, well, moths to the flame.

Including me.

And, apparently, Isabelle.

I'm next-oldest; then there's Liam. He's always been called Carrots because of his hair. He's about as freckled and wholesome as a farm kid can be, but he's easy to talk to. I like that he has no ability to lie. At all. It's quite sweet, really.

I'd compare Liam to a roaring blaze on the hearth. Comforting. Reliable. Predictable in a way. Liam is someone I'd want to have at my back in a dragon fight.

These three had done boot camp together for two years now.

I usually find it easy to be with the guys, probably because we've known one another so long. Like finding your fave jeans at the bottom of the drawer in the fall—you pull them on and they're still perfect. But even though we joked around like usual, I felt off.

Maybe this was PMS.

Except I wasn't pre-anything.

"You okay, Zoë?" Alex asked when I passed on dessert. "I thought chocolate cake was your favorite."

"It is, Alex. I'm sorry. I'm just tired."

"Rough flight?" Liam asked, bumping my arm in a companionable way. "Our plane was all over the fricking sky."

"You came on a plane, too?" Nick teased.

"Sure." Liam smiled at me. "Me and Zoë were keeping our cover, just like the Covenant says." See? Liam knows how to make me feel better.

"We also came by commercial carrier," Rafferty said smoothly, and got up. "I'll head out now, on my own."

"You sure, in this weather?" Donovan asked, and the two adult *Pyr* changed to old-speak They kept talking as we carried on with regular conversation. It's kind of protocol–when your elders switch to old-speak, you're supposed to pretend you can't hear. Like human parents spelling out words.

"I can see the rough flight put you off dinner," Nick said to Liam.

"Good thing, or we wouldn't have gotten anything," Garrett teased. "I flew in yesterday and am still starving." He accepted another piece of cake from Alex.

"By yourself?" I had to ask.

"Under my own steam," Garrett said with satisfaction.

I was impressed and probably didn't hide it well. It wasn't that far to Traverse City–at least not compared to Rafferty flying home to England–but still, he'd flown alone. Liam looked impressed, too.

"He's just showing off," Nick said, trying to make light of it.

"Or lobbying for extra points," Liam suggested.

"Too early for that," Alex said. Rafferty kissed Isabelle and waved to all of us. I got up to give him a hug and to thank him again. He winked at me, then strode out of the house. I wanted to see him shift shape and take flight, but he walked down the street until the flying snow obscured his figure.

I remembered the Covenant. He'd find somewhere deserted before he changed forms.

"Which reminds me." Donovan went into the living room and returned with a box, which he placed on the table. It was the perfect distraction. We all stared in shock and delight at it, every one of us knowing what it contained.

We were literate, after all.

"It's the boot camp grand prize," he added, although we'd all done that math.

No way.

"Awesome," Garrett breathed.

The box was for the newest messenger, the hottest piece of hardware available in the civilized world. It was smaller than any messenger ever made before and yet more powerful. Maybe three inches by three inches. It was supposed to be wafer-thin and supple, so you could just jam it into your pocket.

We all gaped at the pictures on the box, raging with simultaneous, overwhelming gadget lust.

"It's not supposed to ship until Christmas." Nick's awe was almost tangible.

Donovan smiled. "Alex has connections." He flicked a look at his partner, who smiled.

"You can text the moon with this," Garrett said, excitement in his voice. "It's got that much range."

"Chat simultaneously with twelve friends." Liam's eyes were round.

"Store forty-five million songs," Nick contributed. "And play them in stereo."

"Carry fifty thousand books," Isabelle added.

"And draw in forty million colors," I concluded. "Look. It's even the metallic anthracite version."

My fave color option.

We sighed as one, lost in complete admiration, then snatched for the box in unison. Nick—bigger and faster than any of us—got it and ripped off the lid. The protective foam that should have been cradling the eighth wonder of the world was...

Empty.

"Gone," Garrett whispered.

"Who stole it?" Nick demanded.

"Oops." Donovan's eyes glinted with humor.

Alex laughed. "Vanished." She snapped her fingers and chuckled. Their laughter told me everything I needed to know to solve that riddle.

"Hidden!" I leapt to my feet. I knew the first challenge and I knew who was going to win.

I love puzzles.

Donovan quickly summarized the clues. "It's somewhere in the house. Alex has pulled the drapes in case you need to shift. Whoever finds it and manages to bring it to me gets today's point. Whoever has the most points at the end of the week takes it home." He put out his left hand, palm up, and his eyes gleamed. "Go."

We lunged from the table.

• • •

WHERE WOULD Donovan hide the messenger? Their house was huge, which left tons of possibilities. Dragons tend to vacation together, so we all knew one another's houses really well, as well as our own. A person could search for a lifetime in Donovan's house and lair but not find every trinket in his hoard.

But Donovan didn't want us to find his hoard. He wouldn't want us to even see it.

No. The messenger was somewhere else.

Garrett and Liam raced toward the garage, which housed Donovan's motorcycle collection. Their thinking was probably that he'd hide it with his most precious treasures.

I thought otherwise.

But where?

Isabelle started to look between books on the shelf in the library. I thought that was too obvious, even though it would have easily slipped between two books and disappeared.

Nick streaked toward the basement stairs and I figured he knew something I didn't know. I went after him, heart aflutter.

Being in the dark with Nick could be a good enough door prize for me.

Was that why he headed down there? So I'd follow? So we could really talk? I dared to hope.

There were two staircases to Donovan's basement, because it was that big. Nick took the one closest to the kitchen, but I ran down the hall to the other one.

I opened the door just a crack, seeing instantly that the lights were off downstairs. This was promising. My mouth went dry and my pulse leapt.

I stepped onto the top step and closed the door behind myself, letting the darkness surround me.

That seductive music played in my thoughts, persuading me that Nick had a different agenda.

Destiny.

One kiss to start a future.

The prospect made me tingle.

Even with my keen *Pyr* senses, I couldn't hear or see anything. But I knew that Nick was down there. I could smell the cool dampness of the basement and feel the weight of the earth pressing against the walls. I thought I could hear the snow falling outside.

And I heard someone breathing.

Not too far away.

I inhaled and caught his clean scent. Yup. He was there.

Waiting for me.

It was almost too good to be true.

I eased down a step, moving in silence. I felt sharp and observant, aware of every detail. My *Pyr* senses were on full alert.

As I took another step and another, the cool air closed around me. I could smell the tile floor and plaster walls, the wooden shelves in the wine cellar, and the stones in the foundation.

And Nick.

He caught his breath. He was close. He was listening.

To me.

I shivered. He had to know it was me. His senses were probably even more developed than mine.

He was waiting for me to get closer.

He'd probably been listening to that music, too.

I swallowed, my heart leaping with anticipation. I moved down the last half dozen steps, wondering whether he could hear my heartbeat. Smell my excitement. Feel the hairs standing up on my nape. It's said that when the *Pyr* mate, their pulses synchronize. They breathe as one. The *Pyr* essentially becomes one with his destined human partner.

What would it be like when two *Pyr* paired off? Would it double the reaction?

Or square it?

My palms were damp just at my thinking about the possibilities.

I reached the bottom step and waited, one hand on the banister. Nick was close, closer than he had been, maybe four steps to my right. I could almost discern his silhouette, dark against the shadows, and I could see the gleam of his eyes.

Amber.

He began to shimmer blue, the sight electrifying me.

I could live with Nick being protective of me.

"*You won't beat me*," he taunted in old-speak. Hearing his low voice in my thoughts was unspeakably sexy. It made me shiver, but made me hot at the same time.

Then I realized what he'd said. Right. Theoretically, we were looking for the messenger.

Maybe his plan was that we'd wrestle for it.

I'd play along. I peered into the darkness and saw a glimmer of anthracite on the far side of the basement.

"*Dream on*," I retorted, and dashed forward.

Nick leapt for the messenger's shine, just slightly ahead of me. I hip-checked him by accident and he stumbled.

He was agile, though—he turned a somersault in midair and landed on his feet. I was impressed, but he didn't need to know that.

He really didn't need to know that I would have been sprawled across the floor.

I took advantage of the moment and snatched up the messenger. "Ha!" I shouted, victorious.

I felt rather than saw that brilliant shimmer of blue. Nick was shifting. I pivoted to run back toward the stairs but wasn't fast enough.

Brilliant orange light flashed through the basement as Nick breathed dragonfire. I had to figure that Donovan had planned for this kind of hazard in the house's construction.

Then Nick pounced.

Oh. Yes.

For one precious moment, Nick was wrapped around me, his strength against my back. A golden dragon held me in his grasp and there was nowhere else I wanted to be. This was exactly what I had wanted to happen.

Maybe I even swooned a little. I certainly stumbled and lost my balance. I fell to the floor, and Nick didn't exactly cradle my fall. When I hit, the wind was taken right out of my lungs. The messenger bounced out of my hand and danced across the tiles, sliding into the wine cellar. I didn't care.

Because Nick was still wrapped around me. On top of me. All muscled golden power. I felt dizzy with the prospect of a kiss.

Finally.

But there was no kiss. One second Nick was on top of me, warm hard scales against my back; the next he was gone.

He went after the messenger, his eyes gleaming amber.

So much for romance.

So much for *me*.

What?

He grabbed the messenger and held it up, triumphant. "Got it!"

"No!" This time the tide of lava inside me moved so fast that it took me off guard. I lunged after Nick and snatched at his ankle. The dragon's heat ripped through my body like nothing I'd felt before. It roared through me, raging, hungry, incredibly powerful.

But something was wrong. It felt mean and angry and not like me at all. Where was the blue shimmer that my dad had told me about? Where was my ability to control the shift? I had none and I knew it.

This wasn't right.

But there were two talons on my hand. I could see my third nail shimmering on the cusp of change and fought to contain the urge to shift.

Without a lot of success.

Holy shit.

House rules had nothing on this. My eyes widened in terror as the bloodlust seized me. How could anything in me make me want to hurt Nick?

I thought, oddly enough, about the guy who had turned up in my bedroom. What had he said?

Nick meanwhile spun to fight me, easily breathing a spout of fire that missed me completely.

Probably on purpose. He had his dragon in check.

Not mine. His dragonfire made me let go of his ankle, but that crimson tide welled higher and stronger within me. Nick backed away and beckoned to me, spoiling for a fight, as I fought against the force within me.

What if I lost?

Nick's old-speak slid into my thoughts. *"C'mon, Zoë. Shift already. Let's see what you've got."*

His dare only fed the fire, I can tell you. I panicked as I fought for supremacy. I don't know what gave me the edge—terror, maybe—but I finally felt the tide turn. I shoved and I pushed and I fought with every scrap of strength I had.

I was panting by the time I shoved the dragon back in the jar. I was shaking so hard that I didn't truly give a crap what color my dragon was. One thing was for sure: I never wanted to let the dragon loose again.

But if I didn't ever shift shape, could I manage to be the Wyvern?

Was it all or nothing?

THE LIGHTS CAME on and I found myself on the tile floor of the basement, shaking so hard I thought I might puke.

"What's the matter with you?" Nick asked, serious now. As if he were concerned. He was back in human form, and knelt beside me. Of course he had the messenger in his hand. "I thought you'd shift." He sounded disappointed.

"Joke's on you." I wasn't quite ready to talk about what had just happened.

"I thought we were finally going to wrestle." Nick looked mischievous.

"You could have shifted back to wrestle."

He grinned. "It's better dragon-style."

"You only want to wrestle with Isabelle."

"Jealous?" Nick was unrepentant. He bent to tickle me, just like he always did. Just like I was his baby sister. I wished he didn't know all my spots. "Is your dragon green, Zoë?"

I swung at him and missed, noting as I did that one nail was still a dragon talon. Nick saw it, too, and he mocked me as only a big brother can do.

I didn't want him to act like my brother.

"Come on, Zoë, let's wrestle for the messenger." Nick tossed it into the air, then caught it, waggling it in front of me. "Show me what you've got."

I stood up and folded my arms across my chest. It seemed like a good way to hold myself together. There was no way I was even going to think about shifting again.

Not without knowing more about what would happen.

"I don't want to hurt you."

He laughed, which was fair but insulting. "I'm not too worried," he teased, but I couldn't smile. He considered me for a moment, then shrugged. "Well, if you don't want to wrestle, let's score some more cake."

He turned to the stairs and I knew he'd take them three at a time. Much as I was looking forward to a view of his butt, some information of the dragon variety would be more useful.

"Hey, Nick."

He paused, glanced back.

I could only wish for his confidence. I hoped my question didn't sound stupid. "Your dragon...does it want you to do things you wouldn't do otherwise?"

"What do you mean?"

"Is it like you? Under your control?"

"Well, yeah."

"Is it mean?"

He chuckled again. "Not any more than I am."

I stared across the tiled floor. Was it different for girls? Or was there something wrong with my dragon? Was it a Wyvern issue or a failure?

When I didn't say anything more, Nick shook his head. "Zoë, this vegetarian thing is screwing with your head. The dragon is part of us, not something else inside us. It's not like we're possessed or anything." He shrugged, at ease in his own skin. I was wicked jealous of that. "We just have more abilities than most people."

Right.

Nick came back down the stairs, his voice softer. "Is that why you didn't shift? Because you're afraid of it?"

"No, no, of course not." I saw that he thought I was lying. I wasn't. I hadn't shifted because I wasn't sure I could shift.

Back.

And yeah, that did spook me.

Nick gave me a quick hug, too quick a hug. "You can do it, Zoë. We all did. Just go with it. Don't think about it too much."

"I didn't want to hurt you."

"Be serious. You think I can't win a fight with a girl?" He laughed as if I were a comedian or something. Okay, he was a foot taller than me and a lot more muscled, but still. "Don't stay awake nights worrying about that." He tried to tickle me again, but I didn't want to play.

Why had he sent me that song anyway?

Before I could ask, he strode to the stairs. “C’mon. I’ve got to give this to my dad, prove I won.”

I watched him go, and even the view of his butt didn’t help much. As romantic fantasies went, this one had really fallen short.

And I had a feeling it was my own fault.

Maybe I would have some chocolate cake.

6

We were leaving early in the morning for some rural property Donovan had rented, so after some cake, I made excuses to the group and bailed. I had to think. I was going to draw. Maybe work on my list of clues. Alex pointed me to the spare room.

When I saw the two single beds, I knew I'd get to share the spare room with Isabelle.

Yippee.

Maybe I could be in a coma by the time she came to bed.

I pulled out the red stone and checked it out. I played the eye game Granny had taught me and got a surprise again.

I saw a face within the circle on the one side of the stone. It was like catching a glimpse of a passing car, gone almost before I saw it. It was a guy's face, with dark hair and dark eyes. And a knowing smile.

I slammed the stone down onto the mattress, truly spooked. It was the guy who had been in my room, the one I'd seen at school and again on the bleachers. How did he get there?

Where had he gone?

What did he want? I took a deep breath and turned the stone over. It was just a rock now. I played the eye game over and over, trying to catch sight of him again.

No luck.

"Hey, Zoë." I jumped when Garrett spoke. He stood in the doorway with his hands shoved in his pockets, watching me peer at a rock as if it held the secrets of the universe. Nice to have witnesses when you lose your mind. He looked uncomfortable, as Garrett just about never does, almost as uncomfortable as I felt.

"I wondered if I could ask you something."

"Sure."

He glanced back to the kitchen, then to me again. "My dad said that the last Wyvern opened a conduit between himself and his dad. He learned the secrets of being the Smith from his father that way."

I didn't have to be a whiz kid to guess what Garrett wanted from me—or to recognize that I had absolutely no idea how I might deliver.

"So my dad says he can't teach me more, not until I master the connection with fire." His gaze was searching—interrogation blue—and I knew he'd see if I lied. "Can you help me?"

I stalled. "What's it like?"

"My dad can talk to the fire." Garrett raised his hands, molding invisible flames in the air. His awe was clear. "He can coax a fire to burn higher or lower, hotter or colder. He can bend the flames, extinguish them, direct them, light them."

I was surprised. "Quinn can light a fire out of nothing?"

Garrett nodded. "He refuses to tell me how to do it. He says I need to find the way myself."

Didn't that sound familiar?

"I figure I need the new Wyvern to make that connection for me." Garrett eyed me. "Would you?"

"I'm not sure..."

He stepped into the room, eyes bright, and sat on the bed beside me. "Zoë, I want to be the next Smith." His intensity made my mouth go dry. "I want to be able to heal our scales, so that none of us have to head out there without our armor intact. I have to nail this! This isn't a joke. I need your help."

His request made sense, except that I had no clue how to fulfill it. "Do you know what happens if we mess up?"

He shook his head, surprised by the notion. Here was another confident dragon to whom all dragon feats had come easily. I would have been irritated with the guys if they hadn't been my best pals in the world.

"Then we'd better be right the first time," I said with a confidence I didn't feel. "Planning, you know."

"Maybe we can try this week."

I forced a smile. "Give me a few days."

Garrett's eyes narrowed and I knew he'd heard something in my tone. "Do you have your powers yet?"

I ducked the question. "I just don't want to mess up. Wyvern stuff isn't exactly cut-and-dried. Let me think about it."

Garrett stared at me for a long moment, long enough that my cheeks started to heat. "Sleep well, then. Tomorrow will be killer."

"Right."

I fell back on the bed when he was gone, perching the stone on my chest. So all I had to do was figure out how to foster Garrett's missing connection with fire. Uh-huh. While I managed to figure out my own powers, both as *Pyr* and as Wyvern, and win the boot camp challenge on the side.

No pressure, Zoë. No pressure.

Sleep well. Ha.

I felt like a failure to the *n*th degree, so I sent Meagan a message. If nothing else, my having a crap vacation would make her feel better about her canceled vacation.

She didn't answer me, which fit the day's pattern perfectly.

I tried to sleep, but I couldn't stop the questions that kept running through my mind.

Why had Granny given me a rock?

Why had Nick sent me a love song?

Had I finally found some riddles I couldn't solve?

Impossible. I added to my list.

Five Traditional Roles Assumed by the *Pyr*:

1. *Leader*. He calls the shots. That's my dad.

2. *Apothecary*. He heals our wounds, mostly with herbal remedies. That's Sloane, who lives in California.

3. *Warrior.* He commands the four elements as weapons to be used in battle. That's Donovan, Nick's dad.
4. *Smith.* He uses a hammer and forge to fix our scales. A missing scale is a point of vulnerability for a dragon. That's Quinn, Garrett's dad.
5. *Wyvern.* Prophetess chick, who typically remains apart from dragon society—maybe because other dragons ask her for stuff she can't do. That would be yours truly.

Theoretically.

As I've said.

I WOKE UP IN DARKNESS. All I could hear was the sound of someone breathing.

And the tinkle of icy snow against the windows.

I still had the stone in my hand.

Isabelle was asleep in the other bed, her hair spilling over the pillow. She even looked pretty when she slept. She could have been an enchanted princess.

I was tempted to chuck the rock at her head.

Temptation from my badass dragon was exactly what I didn't need. I burrowed lower in my blankets, intending to go back to sleep. That was when I noticed that there was snow drifting across the carpet.

I sat up and stared, then realized it wasn't really there. The eye game revealed that it was only half there.

Like Granny in my room at home.

And the tree root.

And *him*.

Okay, so this was a dream. Good. I was better with screwy dreams than screwy reality, mostly because there were fewer witnesses. I opened my hand and looked at my stone. It had the same tree *F* on it, no matter which eye I used, but with my left eye, the tree *F* was red.

Dark red.

As if it were dipped in blood.

Nice. I caught my breath, then glanced at Isabelle. She looked ethereal, half there and half not.

What was my dream trying to tell me? There had to be a message here.

Like a puzzle.

I was on that like ketchup on fries.

I stared at Isabelle and shut my left eye. There was the Isabelle I knew and did not love, the perfect fairy princess lost in her enchanted sleep. I was *not* going to get Nick to come kiss her awake. (For all I knew, that was what *he* was dreaming about. Ugh.)

When I shut my right eye, she changed. She wasn't Isabelle at all. She was an entirely different woman. An adult. This woman was blond, very fair and petite. She looked fragile.

And her eyes were wide open. She was watching me, as if she'd expected me to look at her. She held my gaze without blinking, and soon she was outlined in that familiar blue shimmer.

Wait. I was the only girl dragon.

My mouth had time to fall open in shock before she shifted shape. A slender white-and-silver dragon filled the bedroom, its eyes filled with the same knowingness as those of the other woman. She bared her teeth—smiling at me? defying me to believe?—then shimmered again.

This time she became a white salamander, a small glittering lizard on the carpet.

The salamander flicked its tongue, then changed back to a dragon again.

By this point, I was gaping. A woman becoming a dragon? That could mean only one thing in the world of the *Pyr*, but my brain stalled on the inescapable conclusion.

This was supposed to be *my* trick.

Was it a vision of my future?

But I would never be blond in this lifetime, not without the aid of many nasty chemicals.

I shouldn't have been surprised that this dream dragon spoke in old-speak, but when she did, I nearly fell out of bed.

"*The present is where the past shakes hands with the future,*" she said, her voice melodious and deep. It resonated in my mind, the way my dad's old-speak does, merging with my thoughts. In a moment I wasn't sure whether she'd said the words, I'd thought them, or I'd dreamed them.

Except that she was still there.

Watching me.

She extended one dragon claw toward me. Her talons glimmered like they were made of stardust.

I reached out to shake her claw. Just before we made contact, I blinked.

And she was gone.

So was the snow.

No matter which eye I used, the room looked normal, Isabelle asleep in the other bed.

I threw myself back in my bed, worrying at the stone as I frowned at the ceiling. Okay, the only female *Pyr* was the Wyvern. I was (theoretically) the Wyvern. So who had this woman been?

The present is where the past shakes hands with the future.

I blinked. I, as the future Wyvern, had been visited by the dead (i.e., past) Wyvern.

That had been *Sophie.*

I sat up straight. Wow.

And I hadn't even thought to ask her any good questions. Would she come back? Would she mentor me? Could she tell me how to help Garrett manipulate fire? How could I find her again?

Figuring out the puzzle only gave me more questions.

Plus one biggie. I looked across the room, watching Isabelle sleep. What did Sophie have to do with Isabelle?

I didn't know.

I couldn't think of a single person who might tell me.

Except my dad.

And he was in Chicago.

Plus, odds were very long that he wouldn't have told me, even if he did know. *Figure it out,* he'd say.

Well, I would.

Somehow.

It's always about clothes, isn't it?

Never mind dragons having armor; people do, too. "Clothes make the man" is a saying my mom likes a lot, but even without being a man, I couldn't help giving serious consideration to wardrobe choices.

I woke up early, rummaged in my duffel bags, eyed Isabelle, and chose my outfit. I was in competition for Nick's attention; that much was clear. I had to show that I had the right stuff.

At the same time, I had to be ready for boot camp. Wildly romantic girly things would not be a good choice. Plus, I needed two zippered pockets to carry my stone and my messenger with me.

Ha. Two treasures. I already had a hoard.

I liked that.

I went with my charcoal skinny jeans and a cabled alpaca turtleneck my mom had knit for me in the same dark gray. Silver earrings with malachite, because my dad said they highlighted my eyes and I liked the swirly green of the stones. Black boots with low heels and thick soles that laced up the front.

It was a bit of an austere look, even for me, so I added a swoosh of green eyeliner, a heart-shaped black beauty mark on my right cheek, and a lace shawl in acid green. My mom had made that, too, on request, and it had iridescent copper beads in it. It was one of my fave things because I could wear it so many ways.

For the moment, I wrapped it over my shoulders and knotted it around my waist, making an impromptu cardigan. I had gloves in coppery fake leather, too. My usual array of silver rings, my messenger, and my rune stone in my pockets, and I was ready to go.

I knew I looked good. That had to count for something.

Queen Bee was still asleep. Double bonus.

The day was starting off right.

"Sleep well, Zoë?" Nick's mom asked when I turned up in the kitchen, looking for breakfast.

"Yes, thanks." I smiled. I like Alex—she's a scientist, which is really cool. Puzzle solving in a big way. She doesn't nag or hassle anyone, either. When Alex throws out advice, which isn't very often, I listen.

I thought she looked a bit tense, but I wasn't sure how to ask her about it.

And she probably wouldn't want me to ask.

“Yogurt and fruit, I’ll bet.” Alex put a bowl in front of me. There were fresh strawberries and peaches on top of the yogurt and it looked delicious.

Of course, I was starving.

“Local greenhouse,” she added, indicating the strawberries. “Picked when ripe, so they’re really good.”

“Thanks.” I felt spoiled.

“You might want to have some toast, too.” She was pulling a ton of food out of the fridge, but then, there were three teenage boys on their way. “Seeing as boot camp is on.”

“Isn’t there an official announcement or anything?”

Alex smiled, a fast and thin smile, gone almost before it appeared. “That test last night with the messenger was the opening ceremony.”

“Did I miss anything during the night?”

“Only Donovan setting his plans in motion.” She shook her head. “I’m not sure who has more fun.” She held two pieces of whole-wheat bread above the toaster and gave me a look.

I nodded. “Toast would be great, then, thanks. Is Donovan coming?”

She frowned and her lips tightened. “No, he’s gone.” She turned back to the counter, fast.

Was it that Alex didn’t like boot camp?

Or had she and Donovan had an argument?

“Hey, Zoë.” Liam was yawning and stretching in the kitchen doorway. “Leave some for me.”

“Hey, Carrots. Pull up a chair and tell me the rules.”

Liam grinned as he poured himself a massive bowl of cereal. “There are no rules. Donovan sets challenges left, right, and center, and we deal with them as best as we can.”

“What kind of challenges?”

“All kinds. Physical tests, riddles, teamwork.” He shrugged and dug in. “Changes every year,” he added, mumbling around a mouthful of cereal and milk. “Depends what he thinks we need to know. Last year the theme was fire. We had to focus on breathing dragonfire, fighting, and shifting fast.” He grinned, looking like a kid on Christmas morning. “It’s more fun than it should be.”

“Is there a clue?” Garrett tugged on his T-shirt as he came into the kitchen. He looked rumpled and sleepy, which made me wonder how late they'd all stayed up. Garrett is a morning person, not a party animal, which said a lot about Isabelle's allure. "Sometimes Donovan leaves us a hint."

"Sometimes not." Nick was already wearing a heavy fisherman's knit sweater and his jeans, ready to go. He looked good enough to eat.

"He did say we were going into the country," I said.

"Pick a direction," Liam muttered.

"Still thinking?" Garrett asked me quietly, and I nodded.

Alex handed me a plate with my toast. I acted cool, but my heart started to thump when Nick sat down beside me.

If Isabelle weren't coming along, things at boot camp could radically improve.

Starting now.

Nick's leg bumped against mine and I had a hard time catching my breath. I thought of that music he'd sent me and was filled with a yearning so strong it made my knees go weak. Good thing I was sitting down.

"You okay?" He leaned closer to look into my eyes. "I thought maybe you were sick last night."

"Just tired," I lied.

"Sore loser?" he teased, and I elbowed him.

"Haven't lost yet." We grinned at each other.

Nick bumped my arm and the contact had my heart thumping. "Good. We don't want to have to leave you behind."

"Or have to carry you," Garrett added.

"Ah, Zoë's so skinny that she'd be light," Liam said.

I gave him a look. "Thanks a lot, Carrots."

"Why are you here, anyway?" Liam asked. "Did you get your Wyvern powers?"

"That would be awesome," Nick said, and leaned closer. I could smell his soap and liked it a lot. "We could use someone with psychic powers at boot camp."

I stared into his eyes. It was entirely possible that this week could be saved. I had time to hope....

Then *she* came into the kitchen.

The guys pivoted as one, me and everything else forgotten.

So much for that.

7

"Psychic powers? That's my gift." Even early in the morning, Isabelle was all bright and perky and British. As a non–morning person, I found this offensive. "Is there room for me?"

The guys stumbled to their feet. "Take my chair," Liam offered.

"No, there's room here." Garrett moved over.

"I can stand," Nick insisted, and the warm bump of his leg against mine was gone before I could get used to it.

I realized a bit late that Liam was watching me closely. By the time I glanced at him, he decided to be fascinated with his cereal.

"Why, thank you." Isabelle smiled and slid into Nick's chair, smelling like spring flowers. She wore riding pants and caramel leather riding boots worn to a soft patina.

I felt boot lust, big-time. I love boots and shoes. Hers were gorgeous. Life-of-the-gentry, lady-of-the-manse, fantasy riding boots. Perfectly worn in.

Isabelle was wearing a white cotton shirt, but it was pleated and tucked to make her look like a curvy goddess, and her chestnut hair fell in shiny loose waves over her shoulders. She wore no discernible makeup, although maybe a bit of pink lip gloss. She was as wholesome as a shampoo commercial.

Actually, her look reminded me of a bunch of ads Meagan and I had torn out of vintage magazines for an art project, ads for some designer named Ralph Lauren. Everything in those ads was carefully composed and evocative of a British-country-life ideal. I loved them, but it was a bit disconcerting to find Isabelle channeling that vision.

And doing it so well.

She sat beside me and I could see down the front of that shirt to the white lace of her bra.

My camisole—which was really just an undershirt with aspirations—suddenly seemed impossibly juvenile.

Her bra almost certainly had underwires.

I took that as a warning. Nick was gaping at her like he'd been hit with a brick. I bit into my toast with ferocity. It was appropriate that I'd worn acid green—I felt as if there were a green monster on my shoulder.

Nick had never, ever looked at me like that.

"Seriously? You're psychic?" Nick asked Isabelle.

"But Zoë's supposed to be the Wyvern," Garrett argued.

I heard the implication. "I'm not psychic," I said into my toast, but no one cared.

Maybe my dream had meant that Isabelle was going to steal the whole role from me. Maybe I'd lost my destiny due to incompetence.

The guys started to pester Isabelle with questions about her powers, Isabelle laughing in all the right places.

I might as well have been invisible. Nick was completely fixated on Isabelle. I didn't doubt that he'd seen the lace on her bra, too. He smiled at her warmly and she smiled back. I could practically feel the little zing of sexual awareness between them.

Even Liam made kissy noises toward Nick and Isabelle. Garrett laughed. Nick was too besotted to even notice.

Ugh.

When I couldn't stand it anymore, I tried to remind everyone why we were here. "Shouldn't we talk about boot camp? What happens next?" I asked.

Liam looked at Isabelle. "I guess you're not here for that."

"Oh, but I am. I don't really get it, but Donovan insisted that I had to come along."

"Maybe it's because you're psychic," Nick suggested.

"But you're not *Pyr*," I argued, knowing as soon as I said it that I should have shut up.

"Zoë!" Nick hissed. "Don't be rude!"

"She's just jealous," Liam contributed.

Nick looked between Liam and me, and a blush started to creep up my neck.

"Don't be ridiculous," Isabelle said easily. *She* was defending me? "I'm not *Pyr*, so Zoë's absolutely right to wonder why I'm here." I realized at that moment that I could have liked her—if circumstances had been different.

If I hadn't known about pretty popular girls already. I reminded myself about Suzanne and Meagan, and kept my guard up.

Isabelle shrugged. "Rafferty said that my attendance wasn't optional. So here I am, goddess only knows why, and my internship canceled." She looked a bit annoyed.

"Internship?" I blinked, astounded that Isabelle could be less than thrilled to be at boot camp.

Her face lit up as she turned to me. "I met this amazing woman who reads tarot cards and casts astrological charts. Her interpretations are incredibly accurate. She says you just have to know how to look at the evidence. She was going to tutor me this month because she saw my psychic abilities. I already know how to cast charts, but can you imagine being able to see people's futures with clarity?"

"It would be pretty awesome," I had to admit.

"Can't you do it after you get home?" Garrett asked.

"No. She's leaving. It was now or never." Isabelle pushed her bowl of fruit away. "Never is what it will be." She forced a smile. "So I'm hoping I *am* here for a reason."

I started to feel bad for her then, at least until she smiled at Nick and he sat taller.

She leaned toward him, earnest and wide-eyed. "It's important, don't you think, to learn about destiny? The reason you were born?" She spread her hands. "If we know why we're here, we can make the choices to fulfill our fate...."

"Never thought about it," Nick said. "Hey, can you pass the peanut butter?"

Isabelle watched him for a moment, visibly disappointed.

What *was* her deal?

Nick was supposed to have some destiny thing with the Wyvern. That would be *me*.

"Maybe your being here is one of the riddles we need to solve," Liam suggested to her. "Maybe you're here for a different reason."

Isabelle granted him a thin smile, clearly unconvinced. "I wondered." She watched Nick covertly.

Kind of the way I did.

Nick ate breakfast, confident, hunky, and oblivious.

"Maybe you should all eat up," Alex said, just as there was a knock at the door.

The guy standing there made a mock salute when Alex opened the door. "Reporting for duty," he said, then swaggered into the kitchen.

I stared. I couldn't help it.

IT WAS possible that my previous experience hadn't prepared me for extremely hot guys. This guy had to be at least twenty, with long dark blond hair hanging over his shoulders. It was wavy and thick, the sort of hair I'd always wished for. His eyes were green, and he was tall, too, probably taller than me. He was dressed all in black and shook the snow off the shoulders of his leather jacket. He moved like an athlete. Or a dancer. All muscle and ease.

He had a tattoo on his arm, although I could glimpse only the end of it beneath the hem of his cuff. He had a dangerous smile, and held a black motorcycle helmet. He was slapping a pair of black gloves against his thigh.

He had long legs covered in tight jeans and leather chaps.

And a silver stud in his left ear.

A renegade.

An impatient one. He looked like the kind of person you'd meet downtown in a big city, maybe in the middle of the night, outside a bar—not someone who'd come knocking at the door of a nice suburban Minneapolis house in a snowstorm.

He kept looking at me, hard. I glanced behind myself, wondering what the deal was, and his smile flashed at that.

But he kept staring.

My mouth went dry.

My heart went thumpity-bump.

"Hey, Jared." Nick waved. "My cousin," he informed us.

Jared wasn't *Pyr*; I'd known that instantly. Dragon boys have a definite scent. His was yummy, but not dragon.

Human.

Other side of the family. Alex's side.

"Right on time, too," Jared added, as if he expected to be challenged.

"For once." Alex exuded disapproval. "What duty is that?"

"The one Donovan made me swear to complete." Jared flicked the door shut with his fingertips and grabbed a piece of toast. He gave Alex a wolfish smile, as if he knew he could get away with anything, and she tightened her lips.

He leaned against the counter, ate dry toast, and considered me. Thoroughly. "Not what I expected." He finished his toast in one great bite. "Not at all."

I was having a full-body blush, just so you know. It's one thing to find a guy incredibly hot, another for him to tell the world that you don't measure up to his expectations.

Whatever they might have been.

Although they probably involved underwire bras.

"Are you *Pyr*?" Isabelle smiled at Jared. Nick frowned, glancing between the two of them.

So, now *he* had some competition.

Jared laughed. He had a great laugh, a hearty, deep one, which surprised me. In fact, it made him look like a different person. I liked how his eyes twinkled when he laughed, but he still looked wicked.

"No. But that doesn't mean I can't get roped into Donovan's plans."

So, Mr. Urban Pirate knew something about the *Pyr*.

Interesting.

"You could say no," Garrett suggested.

"Not a chance. Not to Donovan." Jared slapped his gloves again and eyed me. "Let's go. I haven't got all day."

"What are you supposed to do?" Liam asked.

"Give someone named Zoë a ride." Jared pointed at me. My heart leapt to my throat, right on cue. "That must be you."

My face burned. "Wild guess?"

He wasn't daunted by my tone. If anything, his grin got wider. He had a dimple on the left side, a deep one.

"Well, Zoë is a girl's name." He indicated Isabelle, his gesture almost dismissive. "And she's not *Pyr*. I know I'm giving the Wyvern a ride, so that leaves you."

I nearly choked. How could this human guy know about my destined role? It was against the Covenant....

"Forget it," Alex protested.

"Donovan's orders." Jared watched me. There was a dare in his eyes and I understood that it was up to me.

He didn't think I had the nerve.

That made me decide instantly that I was going to do it.

I stood up. He *was* taller than me, but I refused to be daunted. "First you have to tell me something. You can't know anything about Wyverns. It's against the rules."

He shrugged, unapologetic. "Well, I do. Screw rules." He winked at me as Alex glared at him. Then he proved that he knew some Wyvern lore. "Send me a dream, Zoë. Or maybe you already have."

The guys hooted and Nick gave a wolf whistle. But Jared just smiled at me, smiled in a way that made me get even warmer and more flustered.

"On the other hand, you might be right. Maybe I don't know nearly enough about this particular Wyvern." His voice dropped low. "Yet."

I was blushing furiously and the guys were laughing. I felt awkward as the center of attention, and slightly confused that the one person on the planet convinced that I was the Wyvern was this hot guy.

"Well, I can't do all the stuff I should be able to do," I said quickly, wishing he'd just look away, wishing he'd give me a minute to catch my breath.

Wishing I were cooler than I was.

Jared leaned closer, dead sober. "Maybe you're just not trying hard enough, Zoë."

My mouth fell open in shock, and even the guys looked between us in surprise.

Jared, absolutely untroubled, offered me a helmet. "Come on; we'll be late."

I didn't take it. "A motorcycle? In this weather?" My mother would have a fit if she knew. "Nobody rides a motorcycle in a blizzard."

Jared was dismissive of such concern. "Blizzard's over. Streets are plowed." He smiled at me, that daredevil light in his eyes again. "Don't tell me you're scared? A dragon girl, scared of snow?"

I glared at him. "I'm not scared—not of you and not of motorcycles. Let's go. Where are we going anyway?"

Mr. Trouble grinned. "You'll see."

"Wait a minute." Alex stopped Jared and me. "Donovan really told you to do this?"

Jared nodded. "Gave me a schedule, too. Don't make me piss him off."

"He never mentioned it to me," Alex said.

"It could be the clue, Mom." Nick got to his feet. "After all, Dad sold Jared his bike, and he wouldn't trust the Ducati to just anyone."

Alex looked unconvinced.

"Come on, you guys; we'll follow Jared." Nick inhaled the rest of his breakfast.

"Good luck," Jared said, reckless and confident. "You'll be eating my dust in five."

You know, I described the other guys in terms of flames. Let's go with that. Jared was like darkfire. That's a special kind of fire known to the *Pyr*. It burns blue-green. It's erratic and unpredictable, flares up suddenly, and can burn you to a crisp.

But it's exciting, too.

That was Jared. Dangerous but impossible to resist. I sensed that the destination wasn't important to him. Getting there would be a heck of a ride. Surviving the journey was optional.

But I had a feeling the adventure would be worth it.

"I'll get my stuff," I said.

"No stuff," Jared insisted. "Unless it fits in your pockets."

"Let me at least lend Zoë a leather jacket," Alex said. "Otherwise she'll freeze."

Jared flashed that killer grin when Alex left the kitchen. "Maybe you'll just have to breathe a little dragonfire, Wyvern, to keep us both warm." He dropped his voice to a sexy whisper that made my heart stop—then race. “Or light my fire.” His eyes were dancing and they seemed to promise magic and unpredictability.

For the second time in minutes, I didn’t know what to say.

THE ONLY THINGS I took were the stone, my ID (at least my body would be identifiable in case of a fatal accident), my messenger (shoved in my pocket), and supplies for my period. The shawl was bunched around my neck, since most of it didn’t fit into the leather jacket, but I figured I’d need the insulation.

Even though I didn’t take long to put on Alex’s jacket and grab my boots, Jared was already waiting on me outside, stamping his feet.

The cold air slapped me hard as soon as I opened the door. I didn’t even want to breathe, in case my lungs froze into big icicles. The sky was such a bright, clear blue that it looked fake, like the skies Photoshopped into postcards. The snow was crunchy enough to squeak under my awesome black thick-tread boots. The roads were clear, just as he’d said.

Jared had his helmet on and the bike idling. It was still on the kickstand, making puffs of exhaust. I did like its throaty rumble. It looked pampered and polished.

Okay, so he took care of the bike.

That didn’t necessarily mean he’d take care of me.

He handed me the other helmet, and this time I took it. I tugged it on, but fumbled with the strap. I was juggling the stone in one gloved hand, which didn’t help, and couldn’t find the catch.

“Let me.” Jared leaned in close, really close, close enough that I could see all the shades of green in his eyes. His fingers were warm on my chin as he fastened the strap, and I got all shivery at his touch. I had to close my eyes as he checked it. “Okay?”

I nodded.

It was hard to say anything with my heart lunging around my chest as if it were trying to break free.

He tapped the helmet where it wrapped around his chin, and I heard his next words right in my ear. “Speaker okay?” His voice was strangely close, almost like old-speak but not quite.

It was intimate to hear his voice this way.

What kind of moron was I to find this guy attractive? He'd be in jail before I finished high school. Maybe he'd already been there. Alex didn't like him—that should have been good enough for me.

I nodded, but Jared arched one brow. "It's good."

"Good, I can hear you, too." He got back on the bike, swinging one long leg over the seat. He braced his boots on the ground, then offered me one hand.

Unexpected gallantry, but I liked it. I passed the stone to the other hand, then grabbed his hand to get on the bike behind him. His grip was strong.

Wow. It was a tight fit on the bike. My legs were wrapped right around his hips, and there was no way to wiggle away or leave a gap between us. I was glad to be a skinny chick. His shoulders were broad and he was quite a bit taller than me—he blocked a lot of my view.

On the other hand, he'd block the wind, as well. It'd be warmer than if I were in front. He showed me where to put my feet, and it was kind of surprising how careful he was. That built up my confidence about the prospects of my survival.

"What's that in your hand, anyway?"

"Just a stone." I hid it from view.

"It looks like a rune stone." He revved the bike and kicked off the stand.

"What's that?" I stole another peek at it.

"Kind of like tarot cards for Vikings. They carved symbols on small stones, then used them to tell the future."

Interesting. "How do you know that?"

He shrugged. "I know lots of things. Does it have a symbol on it?"

I opened my hand and showed him one side. "It looks like an *F*."

"That's a rune, all right. You'd have to look up the symbol and its meaning. I don't remember them."

"How many are there?"

"Don't you know?" He didn't seem to expect an answer, because he just continued talking. "The Elder Futhark, which is the oldest part of the rune alphabet, has twenty-four characters. There were more runes added in other places afterward. Where'd you get it?"

"Someone gave it to me."

"And you just carry it around without knowing what it is?" He scoffed. "Guess I'm right about you not trying."

"You don't know anything about me!"

"Just making conclusions from the available evidence. You're coasting, Zoë, and that's not going to cut it if you really want to be the Wyvern. In fact, it doesn't cut it for pretty much anything."

I bristled. "And I should take advice from you? What do you do, anyway?"

He laughed. I wished I could have seen his eyes. "I do what makes me happy. I call that success." He revved the bike. "Put the stone in your zippered pocket, pull down your visor, and let's go."

I did as he instructed, because it made sense. He closed his own visor and drove the bike slowly toward the road. His heels were still on the ground, as if he were walking it. The motor thrummed beneath me and it was kind of exciting. I'd never been on a motorcycle before, but it occurred to me that it might be like riding a dragon.

"Now hang on to me."

"I can hang on to the back."

"You can, but it's not as safe."

"But—"

He interrupted me with impatience. "Zoë, I promise not to bite, at least not today. That's supposed to be a dragon's tendency, anyway."

"You sound skeptical."

"I'm not the one who doubts that you're the Wyvern."

What was I supposed to say to that? I put my arms around his waist. He was hard, all muscle, and felt strong.

Male.

Something heated deep inside of me. I felt something new, something strange and quivery.

Something good.

But that was nothing compared to when he let the bike loose. I hung on for dear life as the bike rocketed down the street.

No, I clutched Jared, and yes, I screamed.

It seemed as if there were nothing but frosty air between us and disaster, and I knew that if we hit anything, we'd be smeared from Minneapolis to Santa Fe in the blink of an eye.

And Jared was loving it.

Oh.

My.

God.

8

"Zoë, you've got to let me breathe," Jared said a minute later. I guess he'd been giving me time to adjust, but was now moving on to plan B. "What are you going to do when we get on the highway?"

"Have heart failure."

"Some Wyvern! You should be bold!" He took a turn with more verve than I felt it deserved. I clenched my teeth, positive that he was trying to scare me.

He didn't need to know how well it was working.

Maybe he already did. My gloved fingers were digging into him in a big way. I tried to relax.

Talking would be good. A distraction.

I asked the first question that popped into my thoughts. "How do you know anything about the Wyvern, anyhow? How can you know anything about the *Pyr*? There's a Covenant...."

"Which forbids *Pyr* to willingly reveal themselves in both forms to humans without serious advance planning, and was established by your father, Erik Sorensson, leader of the *Pyr*, after the events of the Dragon's Tail." He sounded as if he were reading from a textbook, although his knowledge made my eyes widen. "And you are the new Wyvern, although you're only coming into your powers, because there's only one female *Pyr* at any given time, and you're the daughter of Erik, conceived during his firestorm, so you *must* be the Wyvern."

I was shocked. "You shouldn't know all this."

"I told you. I know lots of stuff." He passed a sedan, the bike engine roaring. "Call it a hobby."

"But the rules..."

"Fuck rules."

Right. "Did Donovan tell you about the *Pyr*?"

"No way. He'd have been breaking the Covenant."

"Then how did you find out?"

Jared hesitated a beat before he answered me. "There's this book called *The Habits and Habitats of Dragons: A Compleat Guide for* Slayers. I've read it through a bunch of times. I think I might have it memorized."

My heart was in my throat. I knew about this book. I'd heard about it from my dad. It was the only compilation of *Pyr* lore, and even though it was incomplete, my dad had been pretty annoyed when the only known copy had vanished years ago.

How could Jared even have seen this book?

He must have taken my silence for disbelief—which it was, in a way—and added more information. "It was written by a guy named Sigmund Guthrie. Nineteenth-century stuff."

"That book is lost," I said in a whisper.

"Not so lost as that. I have a copy."

Maybe the copy I knew about had been stolen.

I wondered whether I had my arms around the best suspect.

I tried to sound cool. "Where'd you get it?"

"I found a copy in a used bookstore, about ten years ago."

No, that couldn't be the same copy. The copy I'd heard about had been in the possession of Sara, Garrett's mom. She'd had it until five or six years ago, when it had disappeared from her bookshop. I was relieved.

Although Jared could have been lying about the timing.

Of course, it was a book. There had probably been more than one printed in the first place.

Who had the other copies? I'd never thought of that before.

Maybe I just wasn't trying as hard as I should be. I ground my teeth.

"It talks about everything. Firestorms, dragonsmoke, the Wyvern—"

I interrupted him. "But where is it?"

"Safe." Jared shut up so fast that I knew he wasn't going to tell me where it was.

"You could loan it to me."

"Why?"

"So I could read it."

"Don't you know what you are?" he asked, laughter in his voice.

"Not all the lore."

"Forget it. I'm not lending it to anyone."

"Don't you think it should be kept by the *Pyr*? We have a personal interest in its contents."

"Don't you think it should be kept by the person who bought it? That's the definition of personal property."

Okay, he wasn't going to give it up.

"So, that book is what made you interested in the *Pyr*?"

"Oh, no. I've been interested in dragons for a long time. Since I was a little kid, actually." He paused, as if debating what to tell me. His voice dropped lower. "Since I saw one for the first time."

"A dragon or a *Pyr*?"

"Guess." He took the ramp on to the highway, merged with the traffic, and accelerated beyond my worst fears.

I bit back a scream.

This thing could *move*.

I had to be squeezing the life out of him in my terror, but he didn't complain. My teeth were clenched so hard that I thought they might crack.

Then he said something that changed everything.

"I've always thought riding a bike must be like flying," he murmured, his deep voice as soft as a whisper. It sent shivers over my skin. "Or as close to flying as I'll ever get. What is it like to fly, Zoë?"

"I've never done it myself."

"Why not? You afraid of that, too?" I heard him *tut-tut*. "You're some kind of lame Wyvern; that's for sure."

And that made me angry. "Look, I can't shift shape, so I can't fly. It's that simple." It was easy to admit it when I couldn't see his eyes. I thought of how incredible it was to fly with my dad. Even as a passenger, it was wonderful.

I really wanted to be able to do it.

He was right. Riding the bike was similar. That helped me to ease up and enjoy it.

"You can't shift shape at all?"

"I did a bit. When I got mad." I heaved a sigh, not sure why I was telling him anything. Maybe it was because I thought I was going to die soon, when the bike skidded into a minivan and we were both crushed to oblivion under transport trucks.

"What made you mad?"

I was reluctant to tell him the story, as it would sound so high-school. Juvenile.

"Well?"

"These girls were picking on my friend."

I heard the smile in his voice. "You know that it's a defensive posture, right? Seems reasonable to me that you'd shift the first time to protect a friend."

I blinked. I hadn't seen it quite that way—just hoped for leniency, since I'd defended a human—but it made perfect sense. On the other hand, it was kind of annoying to have Jared be the one to explain my own nature to me.

"So why haven't you done it again?"

I leaned my forehead on his shoulder. "It scares me." I spoke quietly, but he heard me.

"What?"

"The dragon. I'm scared to let it loose."

"In case you can't get the genie back in the jar." He wasn't making fun of me, which was nice.

I nodded, then realized he couldn't see it. "Yeah, pretty much."

"Is that typical?"

"Nick doesn't know what I'm talking about."

"So what are you going to do about it?"

He was right. I needed a plan. It would be better if I could test-drive the shift first, gain a little confidence in my ability to control it before I went the whole way.

I reviewed the available clues.

"Is there anything in that book about controlling the shift?"

Jared shook his head. “No. I’m sure of it. Won’t the others tell you?”

“Nick says his is easy to control. No biggie.”

“Maybe it’s different for Wyverns.”

Maybe. I realized then that I did have one clue. Maybe there was a reason Granny had given me the rune stone.

“Is there a library on the way to wherever we’re going?”

“Why?”

“I could look up the meaning of the rune.”

“Didn’t you look it up already?”

I ground my teeth. “No. And I can’t exactly use my messenger here.”

Jared nodded slightly, clearly reviewing the route we were going to take. “Yeah. I think there is. I don’t think there’s time, though.”

“But I need to find out. It could be important.”

“I don’t want to let Donovan down.”

“I don’t want to let my friends down either. Boot camp is about tests.”

“Point taken.” Jared was silent for a moment, calculating; then he nodded. “I think I can make up the time.”

He was going to drive *faster*? I bit back a protest. He was trying to accommodate my request, right?

“Maybe if we stop at the library, we’ll give the guys a fighting chance to catch up.” I heard the laughter in his voice. “How about a trade?”

“What kind of trade?” No surprise that I was suspicious. Who knew what this guy would ask of me?

“Take me for a ride when you do learn to fly?”

His question made me smile. “That depends.”

“Depends on what?”

“Whether I survive this ride.”

Jared laughed then, that great laugh that made me want to laugh, too. “I think I can guarantee that,” he said, all breezy confidence one more time. “Come on, let’s move. I hate being late.” Then he leaned lower over the bike and I leaned with him.

It was easier this time to curve myself against him. I closed my eyes and dared to enjoy the feeling of speed and power.

Flying.

Donovan had entrusted me to Jared’s escort. That must mean that Mr. Urban Pirate had good intentions. And nothing bad had happened.

Yet.

Maybe I could even get that book for the *Pyr*.

WE'D BEEN GOING for less than two hours when Jared took an exit from the highway. He turned into a small town, one that he evidently knew, and headed downtown. He parked the bike and once again offered me his hand for balance as I got off.

I was stiff and cold, and it felt good to stretch. The town was pretty, a main street lined with old buildings and shops. A post office. A corner store. Town hall. A couple of restaurants and a coffee place. Snow all over everything, like a Christmas card.

We were standing at the bottom of a set of steps. At the top was a red sandstone building.

The public library.

He turned to march up the steps, swinging his helmet by the strap. It would be so easy to follow him, to play along, to do the research together.

But then, that was just what he expected, wasn't it?

I had a moment of doubt there, something prickling at the back of my thoughts. He had kind of set me up for this detour by chiding me for not doing any research. Anyone could have bet that a schoolgirl would want to go to a library, and he had chosen this particular library. I wasn't sure where I was, much less where he was taking me.

I should just stop right on the steps and use my messenger to get some answers.

But Jared was already on the move and I wanted to go with him.

Was it stupid to be so cooperative?

It was weird that Jared had found that book, when the *Pyr* had been looking for copies for so long. Humans shouldn't know much about our identities, even though they now know that we exist. Could there be another reason for his interest in me?

Did the *Pyr* have stalkers?

Fans? I had heard rumors of it happening before.

Donovan wouldn't have put my welfare at risk, would he?

No. My dad would have had his liver for that.

But what if Donovan was wrong about Jared?

My gut insisted I should trust Jared, but my mind was full of doubts.

On the other hand, if ever there had been someone who would know things he shouldn't know—maybe just for the principle of it—I already understood it would be Jared. Plus, what harm could come to me at a public library? I had asked him to modify his travel plan and he'd agreed.

That could, however, have been a trick to win my trust.

I might find out something other than what the rune meant.

I hate riddles with no clear solution. I had a feeling that Jared was just that—and it wouldn't change anytime soon.

He turned, realizing I wasn't immediately behind him. "Chickening out?" The glint in his eye had me moving.

"Maybe it's foresight."

He laughed, then opened the door for me. There was an appreciative gleam in his eye, one that flustered me even more. "Oh, I hope so."

It's so hard to be cool when you can't stop blushing.

The librarians were not pleased to see Jared saunter into their refuge. And it wasn't my imagination—he did saunter. He was perfectly polite but he moved in a loose-limbed way.

A suggestive way.

The sight made my mouth go dry.

"He's helping me with my homework," I said to one disgruntled librarian, and she sniffed.

"Careful what you learn," she muttered.

"Let's check the catalog." Jared was typing quickly on the keypad of the library's computer. If he was going to be a superstudent, then I could go one better. I memorized the call number of the most promising title, and headed into the stacks. He strode right behind me, and I glanced back to find him smiling slightly.

Okay, so maybe I wasn't hiding my awareness of him that well.

Or at all.

There were three books on runes. I grabbed two and he took the third. I chose a big table in full view of the circulation desk. He glanced between me and the librarian—who was practically swallowing her lips in disapproval—then put the helmets beside me. I was already deep into one book.

"It's called Fehu." I liked the sound of the word. It felt familiar in a way, and I said it again, softly.

He sat down beside me. Close. Really close. I pretended to be indifferent and pretty much failed. He wouldn't have had to be *Pyr* to hear my heart pounding.

"First rune of the first aett of the Elder Futhark." Jared bumped his shoulder against mine as he read.

He had to be deliberately messing with me, so I didn't respond. Like I hadn't noticed how close he was sitting. (I'd have noticed even if I'd been dead—and he knew it as well as I did.)

I kept reading. "What does that mean?"

"It's like they divided their alphabet into chunks. The Elder Futhark is one alphabet, maybe the oldest one."

"And the first aett is the first group of runes. Okay."

I turned back to the book.

"It means *cattle*!" I wrinkled my nose. "I don't even eat meat. Last thing I need is a cow."

"No." Jared tapped the book with an emphatic finger. "Wealth, which was cattle in ancient times." He dropped his voice to a pitch that gave me shivers. "Look beyond the metaphor, Zoë. We're talking symbols."

"Money and credit." I read further but still didn't understand why Granny had given me this stone.

"Don't skip the story," he chided.

"Okay." I read aloud in a muted voice. "'The symbol is associated with cattle and their life-giving powers. In the Norse creation myth, the primal cow, Audhumla, licked a block of salt until the first man emerged. That was Buri, father of humans.'"

"Beginnings." Jared leaned back in the chair, balancing it on its back two legs, folding his arms behind his head. I stared. You know you would have, too. His black T-shirt was tight enough to show his six-pack to advantage. "It means something is beginning." He lifted one brow, inviting...something.

How did a person manage to have such green eyes?

Could he see right through to my heart? My deepest secrets? My thoughts? I had a feeling he could, and as soon as I thought that, he smiled.

I looked away. I forced myself to think straight. (It was tougher than it should have been.)

Something *had* started after Granny gave me the rune stone. My period had turned up. Just the day before—which technically could have been the same day—I'd been able to make a partial shift into dragon form.

And then there was that guy.

I had an easier time believing that Granny and the rune stone had kick-started everything than that it had been Meagan's visioning session. Maybe she and I had just prodded the change.

Jared tipped forward, chair legs landing with a thump. He flipped through the second book, his arm against mine. His eyes gleamed as he pushed it toward me and tapped a single word.

Right after *beginnings*, this book listed *fire* as a meaning for my rune.

Our gazes locked. "In the beginning, there was the fire," Jared said quietly, and I caught my breath that he was voicing my thoughts. I knew the phrase well enough to finish the paragraph. It was typed into my file of clues on my messenger.

You already know that it's from the foundation myth of the *Pyr*.

JARED WAS WATCHING me as I rolled through this verse in my mind. "So, what powers do you have already, baby Wyvern?" he asked.

I shrugged and looked away, not really wanting to itemize my incompetence.

"Come on, you can tell me. I've got the book, remember." Jared leaned closer and counted off on his fingers, his expectation persuasive. "Communicating in old-speak?"

"I'm getting better."

"Shifting shape?"

"Not fully."

"Breathing fire?"

I shook my head.

"Dispatching dreams?"

I bit my lip and dared to meet his gaze. "I have them."

Jared was unimpressed. "Everyone does. Foresight?"

"That's my dad's power."

"No, the Wyvern sees past and present and future. If you can see the future, that's a kind of foresight, but the Wyvern gets the whole enchilada simultaneously."

I frowned, thinking about my dreams. I worried the rune stone in one hand. Had I invoked those dreams? Or invited them? It was a possibility. "Maybe. I'm not sure."

"I'll guess that taking alternate forms and spontaneous manifestation are part of the advanced class." He drummed his fingers on the table and I sensed that I'd disappointed him. It was not a good feeling. "Can you feel the earth? Take its mood?"

I shook my head.

"Control any of the elements?"

Nyet. I was feeling as suave as a toddler.

The fact that I had been more on my game as a toddler was pretty depressing.

Jared leaned even closer, his nose almost touching mine. "Well, here's the thing, Zoë. I think the problem is that you doubt that you're the Wyvern, and until you believe it yourself, you're not going to be able to do any of this."

I was insulted. "What do you know about it?"

"More than you do, from the sound of it."

I hated that his argument made so much sense, so I disagreed. "I don't think so!"

"Can you sense the location of the other *Pyr*?"

"No!"

"Be serious. You could at least try." His shoulder pressed against mine; I could feel his breath in my ear. "I *dare* you to try," he murmured. His eyes shone brightly, as brightly as a cat's, and I understood that he was pushing me.

In fact, that was his point.

I wanted to deck him. I wasn't a loser and I wasn't a sloth. What did he —a human!—know about the challenges I faced? He could never understand. I wanted to wipe that half smile off his mouth and eliminate that daring glint from his eyes.

There was only one way to do that.

I had to try.

9

"You're on." I shut my eyes before Jared could look triumphant.

I felt with all my senses for the *Pyr*. I was sure it wouldn't work, so wasn't surprised that I didn't feel a thing. "Satisfied? Or are you just trying to embarrass me?"

"I'm trying to get you to claim your legacy," he replied. "Nothing worth having comes for free, Zoë."

"Well, I tried!"

"But you need to believe."

"I believe."

"Bullshit."

I closed my eyes. I willed myself to believe. I was the Wyvern, the only female *Pyr*, our prophetess, the one born to lead us into the future with my innate powers.

I am the Wyvern.

I will shift shape and I will cast dreams and I will be everything that I am forecast to be.

I.

Am.

The.

Wyvern.

And I will claim my birthright, right here and now.

I felt a prickle of awareness then. A hum like the current on an electrical line. The sound a motor makes just before it starts to turn.

Jared's hand closed over mine. "Chase it," he whispered.

How did he know? I'd worry about that later.

I listened to the hum, and it developed into a vague sense that Nick and the others were behind us. I felt them on the same road we'd taken, saw the point where they were, then lost it.

Jared squeezed my hand, as if to encourage me.

"I felt them," I whispered. "I saw them! They're at that turn by the gas station four, maybe five exits back." I met Jared's gaze, unable to hide my astonishment.

"And now?"

I frowned, seeking that sense, and found nothing. "I lost them."

"Can you send them old-speak? Maybe you could pinpoint their location by the sound of their reply?" Jared leaned closer.

Great Wyvern, but he was hot. Having him so near made bits of me tingle that I hadn't even known I had. I had to nail this, but Jared was seriously distracting.

He started to slide his thumb across the back of my hand, rhythmic and sexy, until I couldn't think of one other thing but his touch.

"The book says something about ley lines," he murmured. "They used to be called dragonlines, and are lines of force that somehow encircle the Earth. The description is pretty vague, but maybe you can feel them."

It made enough sense that I wanted to try.

It couldn't have been all bad that I wanted to impress him, either. Actually, I realized that his caress—which he was doing only to mess with me—seemed to be awakening my senses. Or taking them to a sharper pitch.

I sensed that I could work with that. "Maybe I can try both together."

Jared nodded, anticipation lighting his eyes.

I'd check on my dad first. I closed my eyes and listened. Nothing beyond the library and the town pressed around us. I felt, stretching my mind out into the world, tentative, listening.

Suddenly I sensed a glimmer, like a gold line, one that flashed in the periphery of my vision. It hummed, just as it had before. I could see it vibrating, like a piano wire that had been struck.

It gleamed, then disappeared.

I looked but couldn't find it again.

"Stay calm." Jared's voice was low and soothing. His fingers slid up and down my forearm, and even through the leather jacket, he gave me tingles. "Agitation never helps this kind of stuff."

I took a deep breath, then tried Jared's other idea.

"*Dad?*" I asked in old-speak.

"*Very good,*" my dad replied immediately, his praise sliding into my mind as if he were sitting beside me and murmuring into my ear. I probably bounced a bit as I heard him.

I definitely gripped Jared's hand.

"Go for it," Jared murmured.

The thing is that I heard pride in Jared's words, a pride that echoed my own. That was exciting.

I stretched my thoughts again and found that place in my mind more readily. I realized I could sense my father's presence. It was at the terminus of a line of heat in my thoughts. I could see a ribbon of fire, one that hummed a little, one that led directly to my dad. A copper conduit. He was miles away, and even though I couldn't see him, I knew that he was in dragon form.

I could feel the wind beneath his wings and the sizzle of snow landing on his scales. I could hear the beat of his heart and could have dropped a finger onto a map to indicate his location.

He was on the roof of our loft in Chicago.

My dad was with me, too, though. His attention was upon me and his senses mingled with my thoughts, even though he was hundreds of miles away. I understood suddenly how he played super-dad, how he kept track of all the *Pyr*, regardless of where they were.

Wow.

"*Yes. But you should be able to do it better than me,*" my dad confided. "*Now you know how it feels. Reach for more. Stretch.*"

I did, and it was easy, now that I knew the trick. I found the guys more easily this time: Nick's car was some forty miles behind us. I could have been sitting on the top of the rearview mirror and could see the highway around them. I could hear them joking around, vying for Isabelle's attention, and thought the car was too warm.

Too much testosterone.

"You're doing it," Jared murmured, his hands locked over mine. His fingers were warm and strong, the way his thumb caressed my pinkie ring distracting me. My mouth went dry and I nearly lost the coppery glimmer.

Then I realized this ability could be used to tell me exactly what I wanted to know.

I stretched out and found Donovan. He was far ahead, waiting in a rustic cabin. It was a single room, no amenities. There was a fire burning on the hearth and a map spread on the table as he waited for us. The light of the fire painted the simple interior in shades of gold, making it look like a haven.

Could he hear me, too? Or could I speak at distance only with my dad? Was the blood link part of it?

"*Donovan?*" I asked in old-speak, daring to hope.

Donovan started. *"Zoë?"* He lifted his head and looked toward me, as if he sensed my being there. But I knew by the way his gaze danced over the room that he couldn't see me.

"*Did you really send Jared to pick me up?*" I asked.

Donovan smiled. *"Yes."*

"But can I trust him?"

He bent his attention on his map again. *"I sold him my old Ducati, Zoë. He'll do what I asked. No more and no less. Okay?"*

"Okay." I smiled then; I couldn't help it.

You can't lie in old-speak, you know. It comes right from the heart.

Donovan spun around all of a sudden, looking past me. I wondered what he saw. He frowned. He folded up the map quickly and stuffed it into his pocket. I saw him shimmer blue; then he strode out of the cabin into the snow, slamming the door behind himself.

What was going on?

Maybe it was cheating to check up on him this way. Maybe I wasn't supposed to peek on boot camp doings in advance.

I took a deep breath, followed the gleam in my thoughts, and sought Rafferty.

He was at our loft in Chicago, in the spare room. He started in his sleep when I followed the line of fire to him, but he looked straight at me. He sat up with care, as if he feared I would slip away.

Then he smiled and nodded approval. "*Hail, Wyvern*," he murmured, raising one hand in salute, and his ring reflected the light.

I had done it! I *was* the Wyvern!

My eyes flew open and the library looked strange—as if the world in my thoughts were more real than this one. I played the eye game, and Rafferty was still in front of me when I looked through my left eye. Then he faded from sight, the view from both eyes becoming the library.

I glanced down to find my hand locked within Jared's, and I was uncertain how long I had been hunting the *Pyr* in my thoughts. I was trembling a little.

I had done Wyvern stuff!

The librarian was watching from the circulation desk, her expression dour.

Jared squeezed my fingers. "That was old-speak, wasn't it? The book says that old-speak sounds like thunder to humans, and I heard thunder."

I nodded, sensing his excitement. "You were right. Once I could hear them, I could find them."

"Excellent!" His eyes gleamed as he leaned closer. "Score one for the new Wyvern."

His arm slipped around my shoulders, and I could feel his muscles even through the leather. I felt his heartbeat and my eyes widened as mine adjusted its beat to synchronize with his. The sensation made me dizzy, but it could just have been his proximity. Jared's gaze dropped to my lips, and his eyes were bright, a little wild. Daring. I was sure he was going to kiss me.

And you know, I thought it would be okay.

No, I thought it would be exciting, awesome, and totally the right thing to happen.

Celebratory.

That was why I was determined to kiss him back.

I'd show him that this Wyvern *was* bold.

It was time I surprised Jared, maybe shook *his* tree.

I leaned closer, saw him start to smile....

. . .

AND THE LIBRARIAN cleared her throat. Loudly. She was right behind us, peering down at us, her lips so tight they nearly disappeared.

"Did you find what you were looking for?" She reached between us for the books.

"Yes, thank you," I said.

"You'd better believe it," Jared agreed. The librarian gave him a full-octane glare.

When I looked down at the table again, my rune stone was gone. Jared was on his feet, heading to the door, and I could see something in his hand.

My rune stone.

"Hey! That's mine!"

"Not if you don't take care of it," he taunted. He tossed it into the air, caught it, and headed out the door. I grabbed the second helmet and bolted after him, almost knocking over the chair in my hurry to catch up.

I jumped down the stairs, running faster than I ever had before. Even so, Jared was already on the bike when I got down the steps, his helmet on and the engine running. I thought he would leave me behind, wherever the heck we were, and that made me livid.

"I thought you couldn't say no to Donovan? How does stealing my stuff and leaving me here mesh with that?"

Jared grinned and opened his hand. The rune stone was on his palm. "I'm just giving you some motivation. I told you I hate being late."

I snatched the stone from him, compulsively checking it over, ignoring his astonishment. I was shaken by the prospect of losing it, more shaken than I would have expected. It suddenly felt like the key to everything, and I'd nearly lost it.

Because I'd trusted him. I heard that song again, playing in my thoughts, the one Nick had sent me, and my doubts about Jared seemed to feed one another. My suspicion grew and I took a step away from him.

Jared watched me, his expression inscrutable. "Has anyone ever told you that you have trust issues?"

"I'm glad I didn't kiss you," I blurted. "Only a jerk would try to steal my rune stone." I shoved the stone into my pocket, feeling hostile and jangled.

Jared's smile faded. "You're welcome, Zoë," he said, frost dripping from his words. "I was happy to give you some suggestions on following ley lines so that you could get your powers without having to figure anything out yourself."

Then he flicked down his visor and turned on the bike.

That was all it took to eliminate my anger.

As soon as it faded, I could see that my reaction had been fear.

Fear that I nearly lost the stone.

Fear that this one promising sign was the only bit of Wyvern-ness I'd experienced so far, and might be all there would be.

But Jared had been the one to give me a hint, to help me get closer than I'd been yet.

I was the jerk.

I scuffed my toe in the snow. "I'm sorry, Jared. I really am. Thank you for helping me."

Jared ignored me.

But he waited, fingers tapping on the handles.

I put on my helmet and got on the bike. I hesitated a moment before putting my arms around him again. Jared held himself stiff this time, as if he didn't want to touch me, either.

"Like I said," he said softly, his words coming through the speaker to my ear, "your problem is that you expect everyone to believe in you, but you don't believe in yourself. Never mind that you're too proud to accept any help."

There was nothing I could say to that.

Then we were off, the roar of the bike filling any conversational gap. I felt like I'd just taken a final exam and failed it completely.

Smooth, Zoë, really smooth.

ANOTHER TWO HOURS of raw speed and wind left my fingers numb on Jared's chest. My enthusiasm for the motorcycle as winter transport was waning, exactly proportionate to the amount of ice in my hands. I was relieved when he left the highway. He turned south, taking a series of turns until all I could see on either side of the narrow road was bush.

And snow.

He slowed the bike and idled beside a driveway that I would have missed completely if it hadn't had a silver mailbox. It wasn't even shoveled.

A single set of tracks led down the drive, the tires having made deep grooves in the snow.

"Jeep." Jared opened his visor to eye the tracks. "Donovan's four-wheel-drive." He stayed on the bike, apparently indecisive.

"Too deep for the Ducati?" I opened my visor, too.

He shrugged. "I'm supposed to drop you off here anyway." I started to get off the bike, but he caught my knee with one hand. "I don't want to leave you here alone."

"Why not?"

"There is that." His smile turned rueful, and I was ashamed of my outburst all over again. He watched me, those bright eyes seeming not to miss a thing.

"I'm sorry...."

"Listen." Jared turned off the engine and there was only the sound of the wind. It was still overcast, still snowing, the wind rustling through the pines.

There was no other sound around us.

I shivered. I could hear the beat of Jared's heart, courtesy of my *Pyr* hearing, and the rate of his pulse confirmed that he wasn't thrilled with the situation. I fought against letting my own heartbeat match his, guessing that that wouldn't help me remain detached and logical. Had that been my mistake earlier?

Our breath made white clouds, and the cold air stung my cheeks. I thought of Granny and wondered whether I had moved from my world to hers.

The thing was that I really didn't want to be left alone in the middle of nowhere, either.

"It's not safe, Zoë. Not smart."

It was odd to hear Jared be so cautious. "I thought risk was your style."

"Maybe. But it's not yours."

"You could stay."

He smiled. "Uninvited, at boot camp? I think not. Besides, I've got a gig in Sioux Falls on Monday, and practice tonight. The guys took my gear down."

"What guys?"

"The other guys in the band."

"You have a band?" I sounded like a moron but couldn't help it. Why else would he have a gig? Duh.

He smiled. "Didn't you know?"

I shook my head. I wanted to ask what kind of music they played, the name of the band, lots of stuff, but didn't want to push my luck. Too often when I opened my mouth in Jared's presence, something stupid fell out. Maybe I should just shut up.

It was nice to have him be a bit worried about me.

That, in fact, made me want to prove to him that I was just as independent as he was. This was not a guy who would be interested in a clingy chick. (And yes, it was a long shot that he'd be interested in me anyway, but I didn't want to think that far ahead.)

"Then I shouldn't hold you up. Thanks for the ride. Hope the gig goes well." I handed him the extra helmet.

He fastened it on the back of the bike. "I still don't like this."

"But you said those are the treads from Donovan's truck," I argued, trying to stay in the spirit of boot camp and self-sufficiency and confident girls. "And the guys aren't far behind."

Jared shook his head. "You don't have any gear, Zoë, and you don't know the way. It would be irresponsible for me to leave you here alone." He gave me a quick glance. "Can you sense Donovan? Is he here?"

"I just saw him here, when I was tracking the *Pyr* at the library."

"I thought someone else would be here to meet you." I heard him make a little growl of frustration, which was really neat. "But I can't *not* do what Donovan asks of me."

His concern warmed me right to my toes. "Why not?"

"He's pretty much the only person in the world who trusts me." Jared tossed me a grin. "Who would want to mess with that?"

"But this has got to be one of the tests of boot camp. That's the point—to find out what we can do and maybe learn to do some new things." I had a feeling Jared could teach me some other things, some things that might have been fun to learn. "You were the one who said the Wyvern should be bold."

"That was different." He looked annoyed. "My gut tells me that this is a bad idea, and I have a policy of following my instincts."

"Even if Donovan made you promise otherwise?"

"Even if." He gave me a hot look, one that was filled with protectiveness.

Oh. I could have fallen right into his eyes and stayed there forever.

I'm supposed to be a smart kid, so I forced myself to look away from Jared, temptation, and things my mother thinks I'm too young to know. He was all about living in the moment.

I'd always wanted forever.

I was pretty sure his band had a posse of fan girls, gorgeous, sexy babes who would give him anything in exchange for five seconds of his attention.

Maybe five minutes.

They'd all have perfect boobs; you just know it.

IO

When I looked away from Jared, I noticed that the little red flag on the mailbox was up.

I opened it, intending to take Donovan his mail. I was making the walk anyway. But there were five envelopes in the mailbox, and none of them was addressed to Donovan.

Boot camp. Only the top one was addressed to me. The next three were for Garrett, Liam, and Nick. The last was for someone named Adrian.

I waved my envelope at Jared in excitement. “It’s a clue! And it’s for me.” I left the other messages as a test for the guys. Some of the snow had fallen off the top of the mailbox, and I hoped that I hadn’t left them a hint of what they should do.

It was possible that I just might survive boot camp.

“You decide, Zoë. You want me to leave?”

I nodded, even though I didn’t want him to go. Maybe this was another test. I would be bold. A Wyvern in the making. I would be confident in my powers and identity.

A real live dragon girl.

It was worth a shot.

“I’ll follow the tracks to the cabin. I can follow the ley lines if I get lost.”

I held up the envelope. "Besides, I've got to figure out the clue before I get there."

I heard something then, the engine of a car.

No, two cars.

"The others are almost here," I said. "See? All good."

"That's a relative term." Jared was surprisingly sour.

I didn't have time to ask him what he meant, because a four-wheel-drive I didn't recognize pulled onto the shoulder behind us. Jared eyed the driver with suspicion. I thought he even inhaled sharply, which was weird.

This guy was dark haired and he wore sunglasses. He was cute, in a big-brother kind of way, and maybe five years older than me.

Cute, but not hot.

Nice, maybe.

He was also *Pyr*.

I caught a whiff of something else, too, something unfamiliar. I couldn't place it.

"You must be Zoë." The guy got out of his vehicle, leaving it running. As soon as he spoke, my doubts evaporated. He had the most beautiful voice. I just wanted to listen to it all day.

And that scent was gone.

Maybe I'd imagined it.

"You must be Adrian," I guessed.

He grinned, his gaze dancing over me. His appreciation was clear. "I'm honored to meet the Wyvern." He made a little bow. "Is that foresight or just intelligence?"

Wow. He was flirting with *me*.

Things were looking up. That he was cute but not stupendously gorgeous made it easier to flirt back. That Jared was scowling at us didn't hurt, either.

"Puzzle solving," I said. "My best trick."

He took off his sunglasses and I had an overwhelming sense of what a normal, trustworthy *Pyr* he was. It was impossible not to like him.

"We'll probably all learn some new ones this week." Adrian spared a glance toward Jared.

"I know when I'm not welcome." Jared gave me a sizzling look. I knew he wanted me to come to his side, but I didn't move.

If Jared was trying to warn me about the perils of flirting with easy-going guys, that they were a lot less trouble than extremely hot guys who wanted more and more, then I considered myself warned. If he was jealous, that wasn't all bad either.

Jared started the bike, his gestures a little more savage than necessary. "Remember, Zoë: just as you're more than you seem to be, so is everyone else."

Before I could answer, he closed his visor, gunned the bike hard, and headed back toward the highway.

Without one backward glance.

I watched him go, feeling like I'd made a big mistake.

Another one.

I SWALLOWED my disappointment as the bike disappeared.

I'd probably never see Jared again. I wasn't going to think about the fact that I'd missed my chance for a kiss from him. I certainly didn't want to think about him surrounded by squealing fan girls, because I was pretty sure he wasn't going to think about me.

Adrian came to stand beside me. "Friend of yours? He seems a bit prickly."

"Part of his charm," I said. "Or maybe not."

Adrian laughed. "You want a ride? I'm not sure how far we'll get down this road before we have to walk, but it can't hurt to try the easy way first. You look cold."

"Freezing." I got into the four-wheel-drive, which was nice and warm. The seats were even heated, with fuzzy covers on them. I could have curled up like a cat and gone to sleep.

Adrian took one look at me and turned up the heat. "You're out of your mind to be on a bike in this weather."

"Donovan set it up. I had no choice."

"So, did Attitude Boy know something you needed to know, then?"

I was startled by the question, but Adrian was concentrating on turning into the driveway. The tires sank into the snow and he changed gears, taking it slow. He handed me his sunglasses, locking both hands on the wheel.

For some reason, I wanted to lie.

I went with it. "I don't know. Mostly I just got cold."

Adrian's gaze was fixed on the road. "I can believe it."

I wondered then, had Donovan known Jared would challenge me? Had the plan been that I'd learn about the ley lines?

Had Jared been *told* to challenge me?

Or did Donovan just know what kind of guy he was?

What had Donovan seen when he'd left the cabin?

"So, why haven't we met before?" I asked.

"My dad." Adrian rolled his eyes. "You probably know him, or know of him. Felix."

I knew no *Pyr* named Felix. I knew that with complete certainty, until Adrian continued talking in those deep masculine tones. I forgot about wondering who Felix was and leaned back to luxuriate in the rich sound of his voice.

It kind of reminded me of that music from Nick.

Maybe there was a different side of me waking up, along with my newfound Wyvern powers.

Adrian kept talking. "He's a cousin of Sloane's, but they had a big argument a long time ago and stopped speaking. Something to do with my mother, who was a bit, um, troubled."

"Troubled?" This story suddenly sounded familiar. I must have heard the story, but forgotten about it.

Until now.

Adrian winced. "Crazy, more like. Dragon-crazy."

"My dad's said some *Pyr* have firestorms with complete dragon fans."

"Well, my dad was the original. At first he thought it could work out." Adrian grimaced. "But it got nasty once she got pregnant. She even tried to disappear and hide me. My dad got fed up with the *Pyr* and their advice—he'd say their meddling—so he bailed on them."

"But he found you." I could understand that a *Pyr* wouldn't handle it very well if his mate fled with his son. They're really protective dads.

Adrian nodded.

"What happened to your mom?"

"She lost it completely." His expression was strained, and I knew that something awful had happened to his mom. I reached out and touched his hand.

He cleared his throat, his fingers brushing mine quickly. "It wasn't easy growing up without anyone knowing what I was, or having any friends who were *Pyr*." I could totally relate to that—even with *Pyr* friends and my dad, I found the secrecy tough. "But I finally talked my dad into breaking his silence, and he came to Donovan to ask about having me invited to boot camp." He forced a smile, obviously trying to be more upbeat. "I'm really looking forward to the chance to learn more."

"I wonder whether he had a hard time convincing Donovan."

Adrian laughed. "Do the *Pyr* ever kiss and make up without fireworks?"

I laughed at that, because he was right. We are stubborn, proud, and passionate. It was nice to talk to someone I hadn't known before, and to tell the truth, I felt a bit sorry for Adrian. It couldn't have been easy to grow up not only without the *Pyr*, but without his mom around.

Even if she was nuts.

I hugged myself, missing my own mom a bit.

Adrian and I didn't say anything for a while, him just driving and me holding his sunglasses. I could feel the weight of the rune stone in my pocket. I didn't want to draw his attention to it by pulling it out for a look.

It seemed heavier somehow.

Beginnings.

I thought of Jared and the way he seemed to know what I was thinking, and how he laughed and he needled me to try harder, and wished we had parted differently.

Because I wanted to see him again someday.

"You've got to be careful with humans, Zoë," Adrian said. "Some of them are just into the dragon thing so much that they don't care what they have to do to get close to us."

"Or what happens to us." I thought of his story.

"Watch out for that guy. Whoever he was. There's something about him that I don't trust."

"I doubt I'll ever see him again, anyway."

"That's probably for the best."

We didn't talk any more about Jared, because the tracks from Donovan's truck abruptly stopped. There was nothing but snow and forest all around us. He must have backed out. I could see where the road must be for about another twenty feet ahead of us.

Then nothing but a lot of snow.

"I'm hoping our future looks better than our present," Adrian joked, but he didn't wait for me to do any prophesying. He just got out of the truck to look around.

I liked that. I was a little more reluctant to leave the warmth of that seat, but I got out, too.

It seemed colder in the forest. The snow fell around us in fat flakes. The quiet was soothing in a way, but in another, it felt disorienting. I'm a city girl, used to the hum of traffic.

This was Granny's turf.

Maybe just as unpredictable and attractive as Jared.

A girl could get hurt. Either way. I shivered.

"I wish I had an idea where we're supposed to be going," Adrian said.

"There's a cabin."

He turned to me with interest. "Do you have any idea how far it is? Or in which direction?"

I could have told him about the ley lines, and about seeing Donovan in a cabin, but it would take longer to explain it than to do it again. And he was watching me in an expectant way.

I closed my eyes, letting my mind slide along the same paths it had taken in the library. I felt the sparky hum, like electrical current, the one that shone like a line of copper in my thoughts. I followed it, more quickly now that I trusted it.

I found the guys behind us almost immediately. They were close, close enough that they must be beside the mailbox.

Ahead of me, though, I sensed nothing.

I tried to follow the ley lines again, but I couldn't sense Donovan. I couldn't find him. I couldn't perceive him at all. Where had he gone? It was as if the current had gone dead.

Or been shut off.

I felt a bit of dread then.

No, maybe Donovan was hiding from me. A test. I'd tipped my hand too early.

I sought the others, just to confirm that. My father seemed more distant than he had, a dim shimmer in the distance. As if the wire were losing current.

At least he was there. I felt Rafferty, but my sense of him was fainter than before. I couldn't see him at all. There was just the slow vibration of his presence.

But I couldn't pinpoint his location.

Then the hum cut out.

Completely. I frowned and tried old-speak with my dad again, but that brought zero results. It was as if the older *Pyr* had melted out of the world.

Impossible!

I opened my eyes to find Adrian still intent upon me. "I'm sorry. I can't feel the cabin's location anymore."

"Maybe you're not supposed to." He touched my shoulder with one gloved hand, as if to encourage me.

It was nice to be with someone who cut me some slack, instead of criticizing all the time.

Then I guessed what was going on. The *Pyr* were deliberately hiding themselves from me. Donovan had seen me and ensured that I didn't have an unauthorized advantage. It was part of the boot camp test.

It was also reassuring that Adrian came to the same conclusion. I explained it to him and he nodded.

"Maybe finding the cabin is the first part of what we have to solve together. Donovan didn't want you to have an edge over the rest of us." He grinned. "Thank the Great Wyvern for that!"

I smiled at him. I heard Nick's car behind us, moving slowly. We both turned at the sound of the car revving more and more loudly.

"Nick must be stuck." He'd be embarrassed in front of Isabelle, especially as Liam and Garrett would razz him. I had to like that, and wished I'd been there to see it.

Adrian winked at me. "Which gives us a minute to solve this ourselves and be the winners of the day. Isn't that how it works?"

"The prize is the new messenger, the one that doesn't ship until the end of the year. Donovan showed us last night." I didn't have to pretend to be excited.

Adrian shared my enthusiasm. "Wow! Let's go look for the cabin now."

I wondered for a second why Adrian hadn't been at Donovan's house the night before, but then he shimmered, his broad shoulders outlined in vivid blue light. I was completely distracted by the prospect of his change. In the blink of an eye, he had shifted shape, becoming a powerful dragon.

In my fave colors.

It was funny because the dragon form didn't look quite right to me for a moment. He seemed to waver a bit, more like a reflection in an old mirror than anything real. An illusion, maybe.

Then I was distracted by the magnificence of his dragon power. Now, that was *wow*. Adrian was pewter and purple with silver accents. I stared. Maybe he had hot-guy potential after all.

Adrian watched me, probably expecting me to shift. I blushed, then gestured back toward the others as if I'd decided to wait on them.

He nodded once, so regal that he took my breath away. Then he leapt into the air, two beats of his powerful wings taking him over the canopy of trees. He soared into the snow-filled sky, a vision of majestic *Pyr* power. Just the sight made me ache with longing.

Jared was right about one thing: I really, really, *really* wanted to fly. I shoved my hands into my pockets and felt the crinkle of paper.

My envelope.

Maybe I could solve something, too.

THERE WAS a single sheet of paper inside the envelope, with one line of type on it.

It was a riddle.

Or maybe just part of one.

I slide before the sun, but make no shadow.

I stood and thought about it, the snow falling all around me, then shoved the note back into my pocket. It wasn't as if I couldn't memorize it.

What didn't make a shadow?

Hydrogen molecules. Thoughts. Fog. I needed another clue to narrow it down. Was that what the guys' messages included?

I realized that Adrian hadn't picked up his envelope.

I had no chance to tell him, because a second dragon ripped through the sky in pursuit of Adrian.

A gleaming gold one.

Breathing fire.

Nick.

Looking for a fight.

Oh, no.

"Behind you!" I called to Adrian. I had to warn him, even though I knew that Nick would hear me, too.

"*What are you doing?*" Nick demanded in old-speak. *"I'm defending you!"*

From what? Or who? I didn't need defending.

Although it was kind of nice that he even had the inclination.

Two more dragons flew overhead, ripping through the air like fighter jets. Garnet with gold—that was Garrett. A green as vivid as my malachite earrings, tipped in silver—that was Liam.

They were at Nick's back.

"Hey! Where is everyone?" a woman with a British accent shouted from behind me.

Isabelle.

I paused. She was obviously having trouble in the snow, but was safe. I had more important things to do than hold her hand, so I ran after the guys.

Or at least in the direction of the dragon fight. I could hear them colliding with each other overhead. Trees were getting trashed, and dragonfire was flashing orange over the leafless trees.

I wanted to see the action.

The road that had seemed obvious became less clear with every step. I slipped, finding myself up to my hips in snow. There were brambles beneath the snow, ones with nasty prickles.

I shoved my way through the snow, irritated that I couldn't just shift and fly above the trees. The forest seemed to break ahead of me, and I guessed I'd be able to see the fight from there. Vivid orange flames lit the sky as I hurried.

I was so anxious to see that I forgot to pay attention.

On the other hand, I got my wish to witness the action.

I tripped on a root buried under the snow and fell. Face-first. There was an instant when I was up to my eyes in snow, nothing but white; then I felt the snow give on one side.

It wasn't the end of the forest. It was a hill. A steep one.

I slid.

Down.

It was a toboggan ride without the toboggan. I snatched in every direction, finding nothing to grab, even as I tumbled down. I suddenly found myself on my back, staring up at a snowy sky. I was helpless to stop myself as I raced down the hill, spinning as I went.

Powerless to stop what was happening.

I SPIRALED to a halt a thousand years later, a blizzard's worth of snow piled under Alex's leather jacket.

"You okay?" Liam landed beside me with powerful grace. He extended a claw to help me up. His green-and-silver scales gleamed so brightly in the sunlight that I had to squint to look at him.

"We couldn't grab you sooner." Garrett landed on my other side. It said something for my upbringing that having a dragon on either side of me wasn't at all remarkable. Their scales were really sparkly in the sunshine, so I had to narrow my eyes.

I shook the snow out of the jacket as Liam exhaled a gentle flicker of dragonfire in my direction.

I admired his control. "Very nice. Thanks."

"Easy," Garrett warned him. "You don't want to melt the ice."

That was when I knew we weren't in a clearing—we were standing on a frozen lake. Liam nodded, and turned the furnace off.

"Why didn't you just shift?" Garrett demanded.

"You might have gotten hurt this way," Liam chided.

"I didn't think of it." I was irritated and self-conscious.

They exchanged glances, their surprise clear.

I didn't want to get into it. Not yet. I gestured to the two dragons continuing to fight overhead, and changed the subject. Nick was taunting Adrian while Adrian tried to reason with him. "Who's winning?"

"No one," Garrett said. "The other *Pyr* is pulling his punches."

Adrian was larger, more graceful, and he *was* pulling his punches. Nick looked like an amateur, fighting out of passion, not strategy. Nick snarled and slashed at him again, but his claws didn't connect.

"Hothead," Adrian chided.

Nick breathed dragonfire and lifted his talons.

"Who is he, anyway?" Liam asked.

"Adrian." I shared his story, and Garrett frowned.

"I don't remember that story."

"Me neither," Liam agreed. "I didn't think Sloane had any more cousins than Brandt."

"Maybe he's not who he says he is," Garrett suggested.

"He's *Pyr*," I argued, impatient that they were being difficult. "Obviously. And he knew where boot camp was."

Garrett spoke with care. "He could be *Slayer*."

"They're pretty much eradicated," Liam noted. They both tensed, as if they'd join the fight.

"But Donovan invited him to boot camp," I said.

Garrett frowned. "If Adrian told you that, you don't know that it's true."

"Wouldn't Donovan have mentioned that someone else would be here? Wouldn't Adrian have been at the house last night?" Liam asked. "Ouch," he added, when Nick took a hit and fell back.

Adrian might be losing patience, but he spoke to Nick with control. "I told you that I was invited by your father. I have as much right to be here as you do."

"And I say you're lying!"

"Donovan left Adrian an envelope, just like all of us," I shouted. Nick either ignored me or couldn't hear me–you can guess which seemed most likely to me. "That means Donovan *did* know he was coming."

"Left him an envelope? Where?" Garrett was surprised.

I pulled out my envelope. "Right where you'd think." They were so shocked that I knew they'd missed the mailbox. "It's a clue. You guys just failed the first test."

"Shit," Liam muttered.

Just then Nick launched himself at the pewter-and-purple dragon. He slashed, and Adrian flinched as one talon tore at the side of his face. Adrian pivoted with amazing speed, his eyes flashing even as red blood flowed over his scales.

I knew Nick was about to lose the fight, but Nick didn't see it coming. Adrian moved with lightning speed, hitting Nick hard. When Nick lost the rhythm of his flight, Adrian went after him, striking him twice more, then giving him a wallop with his tail. He didn't cut him; he didn't burn him—he just thumped him.

Guess that was what you learned when the only person you could practice fighting with was your dad.

Nick, meanwhile, was falling like a rock.

II

Nick landed hard on the frozen surface of the lake, cracks radiating from his point of impact. Adrian hovered overhead, the beat of his wings so slow that it seemed impossible for him to remain aloft.

"Fuck." Nick opened his eyes for a moment before he closed them again. He shifted shape, turning to his human form, winced, and exhaled in a long shudder. Garrett and Liam shifted shape to land by his side. The ice made ominous noises even with their lighter weight. I walked across the ice to join them.

"Nothing broken," Garrett said.

"But plenty of bruises." Liam grimaced.

"Looks like a lesson in manners to me," I said.

Nick glared at me. "I was defending you!"

"But I didn't need defending. You could have just asked."

Nick's lips set and I knew he wasn't convinced.

"Let's get him off the lake." Adrian swooped down and picked up Nick, who moaned.

"What about you?" I asked Adrian. "Are you okay?"

He gave me a look, appearing both touched by my concern and insulted that I could imagine the fight had hurt him. That was so *Pyr* that I almost laughed.

"I'll be fine, thanks." He lifted Nick high into the sky.

"He was looking for the cabin," I told the guys. "I'll bet he spotted it."

"Let's follow him, then," Garrett said. "Come on, Zoë; I'll give you a lift."

"Sweet talker," I teased. "You just want something in exchange." Garrett's grin widened; then he shifted shape. The glimmer of his garnet scales in the sun nearly blinded me again.

"Do you guys buff and wax your scales?" I joked. "They're so shiny."

"Protein," Garrett said. "Lots of protein is the secret to strong scales." I made a mental note to cross-check my own protein intake. I wanted to be serious eye candy in dragon form.

Whenever I managed to do it.

"I'll get those envelopes," Liam offered. "Where are they, Zoë? You can tell us, now that you've already won the round."

"In the mailbox by the road, of course." The guys groaned in unison that they'd missed something so obvious. I rubbed salt in that wound. "The little red flag was even up."

"Okay, now we feel stupid," Liam said.

That was nothing compared to how we all felt when a scream rang out. We turned as one to stare at the shore.

Isabelle.

We'd forgotten all about her.

And our mission as *Pyr* was to defend humans.

Oops.

Isabelle was okay. More or less. She'd wiped out trying to keep up, and had twisted her ankle. Those covet-worthy riding boots apparently had leather soles, which weren't so great in the snow.

I still loved them. I would have taken them from her in a heartbeat and saved them for city wear. The issue was that she had delicate, small princess feet.

Of course.

Garrett carried Isabelle to the cabin instead of me. I picked up the stuff she'd dropped—her purse and a small bag—feeling like staff following behind with milady's possessions. That wasn't entirely fair, but I reminded myself about popular girls as I walked.

You just couldn't trust them, not for a minute.

It wasn't smart.

I saw Liam fly overhead, all malachite and silver power, laden with duffel bags from the car. Presumably he also had the envelopes. Either way, he was carrying too much to scoop me up. I kept trudging through the snow.

I checked my messenger, thinking some commiseration with Meagan would be just the thing, and discovered that we were off the edge of the world.

Out of the range of any communications service.

Like the borders of old maps, where it said, "Here Be Dragons."

Ha, ha.

By the time I got to the cabin, there was smoke curling out of the chimney and I could smell food. I'd had time to think of Jared's almost-kiss—the one I hadn't received—which didn't exactly improve my spirits.

It would have been educational. An experience. A new sensation. That was the only reason I was curious.

Not because I had any expectations about something happening between us.

The cabin was rustic, just one room with a stone fireplace built into one wall. Exactly the way I'd seen it when I'd found Donovan. So that had worked, anyway. The fire was crackling on the hearth, a small stack of firewood beside it. There was an iron grille on a hinge that could be put over the fire.

It was simple, but that didn't usually bother me.

Nick was sitting on one of the four chairs that faced the fire, wincing as Isabelle wiped at his face. He was already developing a nice shiner. Adrian was beside the one counter that passed as a kitchen, taking inventory. Our gear was all piled in one corner, boots crowded near the door, and Garrett was surveying the firewood.

"So, how much food is there?" Garrett asked Adrian.

"A pot of vegetarian chili, some crisp bread, and oatmeal." Adrian dug in a cupboard that was under the counter. "About ten pounds of mixed onions, potatoes, and carrots. Raw."

"Great." Nick rolled his eyes. "How about some burgers?"

"No luck." Adrian shrugged. "We'll have to make do."

"Sounds like enough for a day," Liam said.

"Enough wood for one night," Garrett added. "If we're careful."

"Maybe we're supposed to be moving out by then." I really liked that possibility. "Maybe Donovan will come to get us."

"Nobody's going to come get us, Zoë. We're not little kids anymore." Nick slanted a smile at Isabelle that was anything but childish.

I refused to notice that she, too, looked unhappy with the cabin. We were not going to have anything in common.

"Maybe it's just not supposed to be an all-inclusive hotel," Adrian suggested.

"Maybe we're supposed to be self-sufficient," Liam agreed.

"We should look for Donovan's tracks," I said. "Maybe we can find him."

"If there were any tracks outside the cabin, they've been stomped over too many times now," Adrian said, and his reasoning made perfect sense. Donovan had been on the cusp of change—if he'd shifted and flown away, there would be no tracks. "I vote that we focus on getting through the night okay."

Garrett was leaning on the counter, watching Adrian, his arms folded across his chest. "And who was your dad again?" He was polite, but I heard his suspicion.

I bristled on Adrian's behalf, but he told the guys the same story he'd told me. It was a longer and more detailed version, but the gist was the same. I could almost feel the tension melting from the cabin as he spoke.

"So we're here and might as well make the best of it," Adrian said, so cheerful that I wanted to be part of the solution. "Who wants to cut firewood?"

Nick still watched Adrian with hostility. Maybe his wounded pride made him more antagonistic. "So you're taking charge now? Just like that?"

"No." Adrian spoke with care. "Just trying to figure out the plan. Got a problem with that?"

"Who asked you to?" Nick demanded, and Isabelle put a hand on his arm.

As if she were the one running his show.

"Take it easy, Nick," Garrett said.

"Take it easy? What's wrong with all of you?" Nick's voice rose. "We don't know this guy. We don't know anything about him, except what he says about himself. Why should we trust him?" Nick pushed to his feet. "Maybe he knows more than he's admitting."

"Like what?" Liam asked.

"Like where's my dad? He's always met us at boot camp."

A shadow filled the cabin, and it seemed much darker inside. More dangerous. I shivered, getting gooseflesh, as if someone were walking on my grave.

Adrian smiled. "I'm not answerable for your father. I don't know any more of his plan than you do."

"Still—" Nick started to argue.

"Still," I interrupted. "Adrian was expected, just like the rest of us."

"See?" Liam scooped the envelopes off the table and handed them around. Nick stared at his own envelope, some of his resistance dissolving when he saw that Adrian had one.

"There isn't one for me?" Isabelle asked.

Liam glanced at me, but I shook my head.

"Don't worry." Nick smiled at her. "We all know that *you* were invited." He sat down again and patted the arm of his chair. She sat down beside him.

No, she nestled against his shoulder.

I wanted to gag. Adrian rolled his eyes. I couldn't help but smile at him. Then I saw that there was still a bit of blood on his cheek.

"Are you okay? You should clean that up."

"It's nothing," he said. "It'll heal by morning. But thanks for asking, Zoë. It's good to know that someone's glad I'm here." There was something new in his eyes, something warm.

It wasn't reassuring at all to realize that I'd been right all along: that as soon as my period showed up, everything would change. First there had been that almost-kiss from Jared the Extremely Hot. And now Adrian was looking at me as if I were interesting.

That something I'd yearned for was finally happening didn't leave me any better prepared to deal with it.

I changed the subject. "So? What's in your envelopes? I've got one line, maybe from a riddle."

The guys went for the distraction like fruit flies after bruised bananas.

I did hear Adrian chuckle a little, though.

So maybe he wasn't so distracted.

And maybe I didn't mind that he came to sit right beside me.

I pretended not to notice that his leg bumped against mine. Instead, I pulled out my messenger and created a file for the clues, intending to compile them.

I made a few notes about riddles while I was there.

Five Things about Riddles:

1. They're designed to fake you into making the wrong conclusion. It's like sleight of hand with words—that's what Lorenzo says. For his stage magic, he gestures to his right to make you look right, when the action is happening on the left.
2. They're one of the oldest forms of stories or jokes. Older maybe than the *Pyr*.
3. Dragons are supposed to be good at solving riddles. Maybe it's because we're both ancient ideas.
4. They can be funny or rude or both.
5. You can't solve a riddle by thinking straight. You have to think sideways. Outside the box. A little bit twisted. In an unexpected or unconventional way.

Maybe that's why dragons are good at solving riddles.
Maybe my being a dragon is why I'm good at solving them.
Huh.

I was thinking about that as Liam handed out the envelopes. Was I looking in the wrong place for evidence of my Wyvern powers? Maybe.

"Okay, let's get to it." Garrett ripped his open.

"I'm starving." Nick got to his feet, grimacing as he limped toward the table. "Let's eat first."

"No way." Garrett tugged out his clue. "Boot camp is the first order of business. Zoë's already up a point for the day." He frowned at his note. Nick and Adrian tore their envelopes open as well. There was silence for a moment.

"'I touch everyone, but no one catches me.'" Nick shrugged.

"'I am a city vast, thick with people but no streets,'" Liam read, and I typed those two into my messenger.

"'I am a boundless buffet from which everyone eats but no one fills,'" added Garrett.

"'Valued by all, sold by none, I have no price,'" added Adrian.

"'I slide before the sun, but make no shadow.'" I contributed mine. I frowned at the five clues, thinking.

"Thought?" Garrett suggested.

"That doesn't touch anyone," Isabelle said.

"Smoke?" Liam offered.

"Who eats smoke?" Nick asked.

"Besides, it leaves a shadow," Adrian said.

Silence reigned. Then all of the guys looked at me.

"Well, Zoë?" Nick's manner was expectant.

I felt as if I should know the answer, but couldn't quite grasp the solution.

No pressure.

"I thought you were good with riddles," Nick teased. "Losing your touch?"

"You wish." That was more like our usual teasing. "I'll think of it. Maybe we just need some food."

The guys didn't argue with that. We heated the chili and dug in, and there was only the sound of happy consumption for a while. In no time, the pot was empty.

"What do you think the deal is with Donovan?" I asked. I was concerned, given how I'd seen him shimmer as he'd left.

Adrian nodded at the guys. "You've done boot camp before. What's your take?"

"Maybe we're in the wrong place," Isabelle said, and shuddered. "It's awful here."

"No, this is the right place," I said.

"How do you know?" Nick asked.

"I saw Donovan in this very cabin when I was sensing the other *Pyr* this morning." I let him make what he wanted of that. Isabelle's eyes widened.

"Where is he now?" Nick asked.

"I don't know. I can't find them anymore."

"They must be deliberately hiding," Adrian said, once again the voice of reason. "Donovan realized what Zoë could do and told the others to ensure she couldn't find them. Evens the playing field for all of us."

Garrett snorted and I felt their sudden displeasure. No, it was resentment. What could I say? I couldn't explain it any better than Adrian had.

The guys could cut me some slack.

"Maybe we're supposed to hunt my dad," Nick suggested after several moments. "Maybe we're supposed to stop for a meal, solve the riddle, and head out after him."

"Except Zoë isn't helping," Garrett noted.

"Anyone can solve the riddle!" I protested.

"But that's your thing." There was a new edge of hostility in Garrett's voice, one that surprised me. "We're each here for a reason, and using our skills makes us a better team. You could tell us where Donovan is, or you could solve the riddle."

He gave me a challenging look.

Trouble was, I couldn't do either.

And Garrett thought I was lying about it.

Why would he assume that I'd lie?

"Otherwise, why are you here?" he added softly. Our gazes locked and held, and it seemed that everyone else was watching. I was shocked that Garrett was turning against me. It surprised me so much that I wasn't ready to argue my own side.

How could he do that?

"Arguing won't solve anything," Adrian said finally, stepping between us. "It's not Zoë's fault. We have to work together."

"We should divide the area into quadrants, then fly out to find my dad, or whatever he's planned for us." Nick spoke with resolve.

Liam nodded. "At the very least, we'll familiarize ourselves with our surroundings."

"I think that's wrong," Adrian said, and Nick glared at him. He didn't flinch but just kept talking, and again, his words seemed to make everyone settle back into their chairs. "Who would defend Isabelle? Plus there's firewood for one night, used with care, so I think that means we're supposed to stay here tonight."

"Donovan does usually leave clear directions," Liam acknowledged. "Maybe there's another clue coming."

"Or maybe it's hidden here," Isabelle said.

"Maybe he's coming back," I suggested.

"We have the clue," Garrett insisted. "It's the riddle." His eyes snapped as he looked at me.

Adrian nodded, subtly taking charge. "Solving the riddle would give us more insight, but like Zoë said, some things can't be hurried. Let's work together to ensure that we're here and well in the morning."

"He could be right," Liam acknowledged.

"I think the first test is meant to be survival," Adrian said. "Can we survive on our own in the woods?"

"Of course we can," Nick scoffed. "That's a lame challenge."

"Maybe we *should* plan for the worst," Isabelle said. She wrapped her arms around herself. "Maybe we should get more supplies, show some initiative."

"Prove that we can do it," Garrett said. "Boot camp is a week long. Food for one night implies that we need to find the rest."

I didn't even think about the guys going hunting.

"There's got to be a town somewhere on this road." Adrian glanced out the window. "If we go now, we'll probably be back before dark."

"Hey, some of us could fly to a store," I suggested, but Adrian gave me a look.

"The Covenant," he said, and I blushed at the reminder. "How would you land outside a store in the middle of nowhere and shift to human form without anyone there noticing?"

I heard Nick catch his breath. "If you mean to drive, you're forgetting that my car's stuck." His tone was tight.

Adrian grinned. "How'd that happen?" he teased, as if they were old buddies. "Mine's not stuck."

Nick glowered.

Liam chuckled and ribbed Nick. "You'd think a Minnesota boy would know how to drive in the snow."

"Can't you push it out?" Isabelle asked Nick.

Garrett smiled. "Dragons don't need to work that hard."

"Even if Nick did wedge it into that snowbank pretty good," Liam teased. "Maybe he was just trying to impress you."

"Hey!" Nick's neck turned red.

But Isabelle turned to Adrian. "I have a bad feeling in this place. I don't think we should just sit here." She spoke with surprising urgency. "Let's take your car into town while the guys haul Nick's out of the snow."

Nick started to get to his feet. "I can drive to town."

"The light's already fading." Isabelle put on her coat again. "It'll be too late. You look for another clue and I'll go with Adrian."

Nick looked like someone had just kicked him in the gut.

"You stay put," Garrett said to Nick. "Liam and I will get your car out."

"You'll just have to owe us," Liam joked.

"Big-time," Garrett agreed.

"But..." Nick protested.

"Find the clue that's hidden here," I told him. "Or solve the riddle."

He looked grim. "I don't like this."

"No one does, but we need to work together. Zoë?" Adrian asked, jingling his keys. "You coming with us?" He smiled. I had been tempted to stay with Nick, but Adrian's smile changed everything.

I was rewarded by Adrian offering me the front seat.

Yup, Isabelle had to sit in the back.

12

We drove for what seemed like forever before we found a town. In reality, it was maybe forty minutes, but every inch of it was exactly the same. The road just went on and on and on through the trees, with no sign of life anywhere. If anyone else had been driving, I might have thought he'd avoided towns on purpose.

But then, we *were* off the edge of the world.

And Adrian was part of the team.

The town we did find was small, small enough for us to have missed if we blinked. There was a post office, a gas station, and a pizza parlor. The pizza place also advertised burgers, wings, and fried chicken. The post office was also a drugstore and grocery—and it was where you paid for gas, too.

Adrian pulled in to fill the gas tank while Isabelle and I set out to explore the possibilities.

Such as they were.

"Does this even count as a town?" I asked.

"I don't care." Isabelle took a deep breath and shoved her hands deep into her pockets. "I just had to get out of that cabin. It's horrible there."

I knew exactly what she meant, but pretended otherwise. The place had given me the creeps, too. "What do you mean?"

"No." She was emphatic. "Something really bad happened there. It has terrible energy. I wish we didn't have to go back." She shuddered as she opened the door to the post office and store. Bells rang on the door, and a woman looked up from behind the counter.

"Well, we have to go back," I said, putting half a dozen cans of soup into a basket. "It's not like there's a choice. It's boot camp."

But Isabelle wasn't behind me anymore.

I found her in the aisle that offered a small selection of alcohol. She grimaced, then grabbed a bottle of sparkling wine. "Beggars can't be choosers," she muttered.

"What are you doing?"

"Making sure I get some sleep in that place."

Before I could argue, the bells rang again. Adrian had come in to pay. He grinned when he saw what Isabelle had chosen. "You legal?"

"I thought you might buy it for me." She smiled. "For us." Her elbow dug into my side, warning me to agree with her. The notion of being on the same side as Isabelle was so surprising that I didn't manage to say anything. "Zoë likes bubbles, too."

She was just making a guess, but it did sound good.

After all, there were no adults around. Why shouldn't we get a bit wild? Plus, recent experience had shown me that bad behavior could be rewarded.

I was ready for another bonus.

I nodded, trying to look as if I drank sparkling wine all the time. "Sounds good to me."

"Well, you two can't drink alone." Adrian took a second bottle from the shelf. He also grabbed a case of beer and a bottle of bourbon. He winked at me, conspiratorially. "One sip will do you."

It would do me. I couldn't drink the hard stuff, but I didn't admit any more weaknesses. I was aware that I was the little high school girl hanging with the two über-cool college students. I tried to act like I belonged.

Adrian was looking better by the minute. I wished there were something I could do to be part of the cool club. Otherwise, I would just be the kid tagging along.

I couldn't instantly become five years older. I couldn't spontaneously develop great breasts. My best shot was looking like conquering my dragon powers.

ASAP.

I was sure we'd be carded at the register and Adrian wouldn't be able to buy stuff. I could beguile the clerk, I decided, and be part of Team Cool.

We took the soup and the booze, as well as some other groceries—cereal and milk and bread and hot dogs and buns. A massive jar of mustard because they didn't have small ones. Isabelle and I agreed to pass on the tofu hot dogs, which had an expiration date of the previous month. She took processed cheese slices instead and a couple bags of nuts.

The woman at the register didn't even check Adrian's ID. She was too busy watching some game show with the volume turned off.

So much for my contributing to the cause.

Adrian sniffed appreciatively as he balanced the beer on the back bumper of his car and unlocked the gate. "There is something about pizza and beer."

"It does smell good," Isabelle agreed.

I turned toward the pizza shop. "As opposed to raw carrots and onions."

"Cheese slices and soup." Isabelle grimaced.

There was one car parked out front of the pizza shop and I could see the fender of one parked around the back. As I watched, a delivery guy came out with one of those padded carriers and took off in the car that had been parked out front.

Adrian shook his head. "Bet they won't deliver to the cabin. It's off the edge of the known world."

I was startled that his words echoed my own thoughts. "Here be dragons," I muttered, and he chuckled.

Isabelle sighed. "I guess we'll have to have soup. At least it will be hot. A pizza would be stone-cold by the time we got back anyway."

"Too bad they don't lend out those padded carriers," Adrian joked, turning to get into the car.

I froze. I knew right then and there what I could do to impress Adrian. "Maybe they could be persuaded to give us one."

"You're not going to beguile them!" Adrian's eyes twinkled.

I bit my lip. "It would be wicked."

He laughed at my token argument. I did love the idea of our surprising the guys with hot pizza and beer.

"Wicked?" Adrian shook his head. "*Wicked* is bigger stakes than that, Zoë. It wouldn't even be *naughty*." He nodded, eyes gleaming. "Mischievous, maybe."

"It would be wrong." Isabelle folded her arms across her chest. "I forbid you to do it."

Adrian widened his eyes and looked at her. He let his pupils change, and I was awed by how smoothly—and how quickly—they became vertical slits. "You forbid her?" he repeated quietly, the dragon in his tone.

Isabelle took a step back. "It would be wrong and you know it. That's not what beguiling is for."

I smiled. "But isn't boot camp about mastering new abilities? Maybe I need the practice."

Adrian said nothing—he just handed me a couple of twenties. I could see the approval in his eyes, though.

Before Isabelle could give me a lecture, I headed for the pizza shop. I could practically taste the melted mozzarella.

On the way, I reviewed everything Lorenzo had taught me.

And crossed my fingers.

WHAT CAN I tell you about beguiling?

Beguiling is a special dragon power. Essentially it's a kind of hypnosis that works on humans. It's very handy—for example, in persuading humans that they haven't just seen a human transform into a dragon before their very eyes.

Tone of voice is critical to a successful beguiling. The dragon speaks low and slow, in a melodic tone, for best results. The human is fascinated and begins to repeat whatever the dragon says.

The other key to beguiling is the dragon lighting flames in his (or her) eyes. Humans are fascinated by fire and stare at those flames, which then makes them susceptible to believing whatever the dragon tells them.

Everything I know about beguiling I learned from Lorenzo, the dragon magician whose show in Las Vegas has run since the Ice Age. (Or maybe since the 1990s. Either way.) Lorenzo beguiles roughly five thousand people five nights a week, and twice on Sunday. Make that five thousand twenty-two—the ushers fall for it, too. Lorenzo is the best at beguiling—and a couple of summers ago, he took me as an apprentice.

The best thing about beguiling is that it's one dragon thing I can (usually) do pretty well.

It was almost too easy.

I ordered three jumbo pizzas—one meat-lover's special, one with double pepperoni, and one with my fave combo: black olives, green peppers, and feta cheese.

After I'd paid (I wasn't *that* mischievous), I leaned over the counter. I caught the guy's sleeve with my fingertips. He was maybe thirty, skinny, not unattractive. He could have used a shave. He looked at my hand, then into my eyes.

I smiled.

He blinked. Maybe girls didn't smile at him that often.

Or maybe I was coming into my Wyvern-ness.

I conjured the flame in my eyes, just the way I'd been taught. He frowned and looked more closely, fascinated by the flames, yet doubting what he saw. I widened my eyes and he stared.

I dropped my voice low, to that precise melodic pitch.

"I'd like them to take out," I said, starting with something easy.

"To take out," he echoed. "Sure."

"Even though I have to go far."

"Go far," he repeated, scowling slightly.

I was losing him. I tried for something he'd find easier to agree with. "I hate cold pizza."

He almost shuddered as he repeated my words. "I hate cold pizza."

Okay, we had a connection there. I turned up the flame, widening my eyes and letting him see more of the fire. He leaned across the counter, intrigued—or snared—and clutched my hand. I could feel his pulse, heard it skip, then accelerate.

I had him.

I needed to make it count.

"Cold pizza is gross."

"Gross," he agreed.

"Plus a waste of a masterpiece."

He almost smiled. "Waste of a masterpiece."

"I'll need an insulated carrier."

He nodded. "You'll need an insulated carrier."

"Just like the delivery guy uses."

"Just like the delivery guy uses."

"You could give me one."

"I could give you one." He said it just as easily as that.

I smiled.

He smiled.

"You'll forget you ever saw me," I added.

"I'll forget I ever saw you."

"And you won't remember anything about the carrier. It'll just be gone."

"Just be gone." He was twitching a bit, knowing on some level that he had to check the pizzas.

I let his sleeve go and hoped for the best. His sense of timing was right—the pizzas were done. I held my breath as he slid them out of the oven and put them into boxes.

They smelled like heaven, and my stomach growled in anticipation. That made him smile.

I halfway thought the beguiling wouldn't work or that I'd have to start over, but he pulled out a big padded green carrier from under the counter. As if he did it all the time. He loaded those three boxes into it, added a bunch of napkins and a menu, and sealed it shut.

"Hope it's hot when you get home," he said, pushing it across the counter with a smile. "I hate cold pizza."

I snatched it up and practically flew back to the car. I was so excited at what I'd done. Isabelle took one look, then got into the backseat of the car and slammed the door. Adrian grinned at me as if I were the most incredible chick in the world.

This was the good stuff.

We loaded up and headed back to the cabin, the car full of the smell of hot pizza, just as the first stars were coming out.

I couldn't wait to see what the guys said.

Maybe they'd even be glad I'd come to boot camp.

THE GUYS FELL on the pizzas like a pack of starving wolves. I guess hauling cars out of snowbanks is hungry work. The mood in the cabin was even worse than it had been, as if the solitude of the place were feeding dissent among us. I hated it. Isabelle retreated to one corner with a big glass of wine and a carrot. She refused to take even one slice of pizza.

"But it's good," Nick said.

"It's stolen goods," she retorted, taking a gulp of wine. Nick looked at me.

"Not true," I argued. "I paid for the pizza."

"If not the carrier," Adrian teased. The guys demanded to hear the story. Nick and Liam laughed that I'd done it.

"The Wyvern can beguile," Liam teased. He licked his finger, touched it to my shoulder, and made a hissing sound. "She's hot stuff."

"Isabelle's right." Garrett was stern. "That's not what beguiling is for."

"Then let's throw your pizza in the snow." I surprised myself with the challenge. "You can have yours cold."

Big surprise—Garrett didn't go for it.

He backed off, wariness in his eyes. Nick gave a low whistle, then winked at me. "Have another drink, Zoë. Things are getting interesting."

I knew he was daring me, so I did just that.

The thing is that I wasn't feeling so proud of my beguiling. It felt like a really juvenile trick I'd pulled and a waste of my powers. I wondered what Jared would think. I was pretty sure he'd agree with Isabelle.

The wine made me feel edgier than usual. Spoiling for a fight, which wasn't like me. When I closed my right eye, I could see little orange sparks inside the cabin, like static electricity. It seemed to be drawn to each of us, clustering around Garrett and Nick with particular strength.

So I was back to losing my mind again. It should have felt like familiar territory.

I poured myself another glass of wine.

I'd never been drunk before. I'd had a sip of wine once in a while, even a glass a couple of times. Meagan and I were too squeaky clean to get invited to parties where other kids got wasted.

All of a sudden I missed Meagan, and wished I were sharing the sparkling wine with her instead of Isabelle.

Isabelle came back for more wine, still disapproving. The guys were getting loud and boastful, the beer eliminating what few inhibitions they had in one another's company.

This time, Isabelle grabbed her coat and headed for the enclosed porch. It had to be freezing out there, which said something about her opinion of our company.

It wasn't ten minutes before Nick seized the bottle of sparkling wine and headed in pursuit.

"Hey!" I shouted. "Some of that's supposed to be for me."

But Nick didn't even look back.

"Private party," Liam said, with a roll of his eyes.

My disquietude grew as quickly as I got drunk. I was feeling woozy, but I didn't care. It dulled the edges of disappointment, if nothing else.

Adrian handed Liam another beer. Adrian poured himself a shot of bourbon, baring his teeth after he threw it back. "Hair of the dragon," he said with a grin.

"What's that stuff taste like, anyway?" Garrett asked around a slice of pizza.

"Liquid fire," Adrian said, and Garrett reached for a glass instantly. Seemed he'd do anything for any kind of fire. "You can try it, but take it easy."

In no time, Liam and Garrett were daring each other to drink shots faster and faster.

Meanwhile, the pizza was gone and the beer stock visibly diminished. Adrian was drinking more slowly, kind of savoring his bourbon. He seemed to be enjoying how much they liked his treat. I finished my glass of wine and went to get more, a little tipsy on my feet.

I opened the door to the porch, surprised by the silence. Had Nick and Isabelle gone for a walk in the snow? They couldn't be *that* drunk.

The bottle shone on the table in the moonlight, still a third full. I headed for it, stumbling as I went.

That was when I saw them. Two shadows entangled on the Adirondack chair, making little purrs of pleasure.

I stared.

It was Nick and Isabelle, making out like they'd invented it.

But Nick was supposed to have a destined future with the Wyvern. With *me*.

My only excuse is the alcohol. Otherwise, I would never have done what I did.

I grabbed the bottle of wine, put my thumb over the top, and shook it. Then I sprayed them down. "Time for a cold shower!" The wine was gone in a matter of seconds.

"Hey!" Nick roared.

Isabelle yelped. "My coat!"

"Zoë!" Nick leapt up, intent on defending his female of choice.

Against his female of not-choice.

I saw him shimmer on the cusp of change.

I saw his eyes shine amber.

I dropped the bottle and ran back into the cabin, slamming the door behind me. I knew I'd just pushed him too far.

Oops.

"Zoë wants to play games," Nick said. He'd lunged into the cabin and the guys had turned to stare at him. I'd made it to the far side of the cabin, putting a good bit of furniture between the porch door and myself. Isabelle came inside behind him, looking both wet and flushed.

Nick had a dangerous glint in his eye. "Maybe it's time to see what our Wyvern can do."

"Maybe not when you're drunk," I retorted.

Just FYI, I was feeling pretty sober right then and there. Terror will do that to you.

"In Donovan's absence, I'm setting the rules," Nick continued as if I hadn't spoken. He peeled off his watch, a piece of precision equipment that he'd scored the Christmas before, and handed it to Isabelle. "Whoever can shift the fastest wins the point for today."

"I'm in." Garrett pushed to his feet. Liam just blinked at the guys, the bourbon having hit him hard.

"We'd better take this outside," Adrian advised. "Not enough room in here for four dragons."

"Five," Nick corrected, glaring at me. "Assuming Zoë's not completely full of shit."

I eyed each of them in turn, seeing their doubt. I supposed it was time to come clean.

"I've never done a full shift yet," I admitted, even though it nearly killed me to do so. "Only partway."

"Like we're going to believe anything you tell us now," Garrett said with a snort. His attitude stung.

"I said I'd try," I said to Garrett.

He spread his hands. "I see no progress. Go ahead—change my mind." Then he marched out of the cabin, letting the door slam behind him.

"Maybe it's time you tried harder." Nick followed Garrett. En route, he pulled off his sweater and chucked it on the couch.

Isabelle trotted behind him like an obedient dog, his watch in her hand. "Can you show me how this works?"

He paused and smiled for her, all his antagonism gone. "Like this." He slid one arm around her to show her how to use the timer, so kind and thoughtful that I knew I'd been crazy to think there could ever be anything between us.

Destiny or not.

Only Liam and Adrian waited for me, concern in their gazes. "What's up with them?" Adrian asked, and I had no answer.

"You okay with this?" Liam was holding on to the table, quite unsteady on his feet.

"Doesn't matter much, does it?" I pretended to be indifferent, even though my heart was pounding.

What if I couldn't shift?

I really didn't want to try for the first time in front of everyone. Not when I was sloshed and they were wasted. Not when I'd been spooked by my dragon's anger the last time. That smelled like an accident about to happen.

I wanted to be completely on my game when I let myself shift.

That wasn't now.

So I knew what I'd do.

I *wouldn't* shift.

I'd steal Nick's clothes when he shifted, and hide them until he calmed down.

That could take a while, but I'd wait.

Dragons can do patience, you know?

So, here's the inside story on shifting shape. It's not instant. Anyone who has sharp powers of observation, like the *Pyr* do, can see this incremental change. You'll just have to trust me. The body changes shape, shifting from human to dragon form, in the blink of an eye.

But within that blink, two other things happen: The dragon pulls his scales over himself like a coat of mail. It's like reaching back for the hood on your sweatshirt, then hauling it over your head.

At the same time, he stashes the clothes he was wearing in human form. I've told you before about the hazards of not hiding clothes fast or having them stolen.

No surprise that this combo makes for some wild eye candy. Probably good that it happens so fast. This might be why witnessing the shift is rumored to make some humans lose their marbles.

It also takes practice to be smooth at this transition. No one nails it the first time, or even the hundredth time. Shifting itself, even as little as I've done, is overwhelming.

So this exercise is like folding your laundry and putting it away in the same moment that your house is being hit by a tornado.

The guys are *guys*. Folding clothes was not going to be in their skill sets. I knew they'd stink at this.

And I knew I could use that information to my advantage.

Maybe even to distract them from the deficiencies in my own skill set.

As plans went, I thought this one had definite promise.

By perfect coincidence, it also was the only plan I had.

13

I walked outside to the clearing beside the cabin. There could have been a million stars glinting overhead. The only sounds were the whisper of the wind in the trees and the crackling of the ice on the lake. The forest was dark on either side. It was cold enough to slap a person sober.

Almost.

I wrapped my arms around myself as I took my place in the impromptu circle the guys had made.

"Ladies first," Nick said, bowing toward me. His tone was mocking and so was his gesture. He never used to be such a jerk.

But then, I'd never interrupted one of his seductions before. I checked him out with my left eye, and those orange sparks were radiating around his head.

I wouldn't be the one to tell him he looked like a saint.

"Show me what I'm up against first."

His eyes flashed; then he gestured to Adrian.

"So now *you're* in charge," Adrian said. He sounded amused.

"Believe it." Nick was adversarial, his gaze darting between Adrian and me. If I hadn't known better, I'd have thought he was jealous. "You first."

Isabelle held her finger above one button on the watch, probably the one that made it work like a stopwatch. Actually, I thought Nick was just being inclusive because he was sweet on her. In reality, only we dragons could assess our relative speed with any accuracy.

"Go," she said.

Adrian shimmered vivid blue and shifted shape.

He was fast. I didn't catch one glimpse of his clothes.

He wavered again, just for a heartbeat, just long enough for me to remember that it had happened before. And that I had forgotten it. Then I forgot it all over again.

I remembered how gorgeous he was, all pewter and purple and silver colors, sleek muscled power right to the tip of his tail. The starlight gleamed on his scales, making him look like a precious treasure. It was enough to make a girl sigh with longing.

I couldn't stop myself.

Nick inhaled sharply.

Adrian settled back on his haunches, bared his teeth, and smiled at Nick with dragon confidence. I could feel the guys' agitation, even as I applauded and Adrian bowed to me.

He'd set a tough benchmark.

Nick pointed to Liam. Isabelle reset the watch, held up her hand, then said, "Go!"

Liam straightened and threw his hands toward the sky. He shimmered, but then faltered. The blue shimmer around his body sparked, faded, then burned brighter once more. When he shifted, he fumbled with his clothes.

He staggered even in dragon form.

Isabelle shook her head, saying what we all knew already. "Too slow."

Liam looked as if he had more pressing troubles, like his need to ditch the bourbon. He headed for the forest, not making anything near a straight line.

If you've never seen a dragon puke, trust me—you can do without the view.

Nick gestured to Garrett. They eyed each other, and I knew that neither of them wanted Adrian to win.

I kind of did.

Especially since they were both being such jerks.

Strange how Garrett had even more of those orange sparks clustered around his head than Nick. Maybe they were affecting his brain.

Isabelle gave Garrett a mark and he roared with fury, shifting so quickly that the blue of his shimmer nearly blinded me. It was as if he had been struck by lightning.

Or he had generated it.

Either way, the blue flash was so bright that I had no idea where he hid his clothes. He was suddenly in front of us, resplendent and gleaming in his dragon form. His garnet scales were gorgeous and rich in hue, the gold edges making him look like a real prize.

There was a challenge in his eyes, as well as a whole lot of pride when he looked at Isabelle.

"You're in first place," she told him. It was an unnecessary confirmation of an obvious truth, but maybe made her feel a part of it all.

Adrian offered one claw in congratulations. Gracious. I liked that. Garrett smiled as they shook.

Funny, but dragons always look hungry when they smile.

Nick eyed me, but I shook my head. "Lady's choice," I said when he might have argued. "After you."

Isabelle gave him a kiss on his cheek, then reset the timer. As soon as she gave him a mark, I was ready.

Nick spun as he began to shimmer, probably trying to do some flashy dance move. As if there were going to be extra points for style.

I didn't care. His choice meant that he lost track of me.

He spun. He shimmered.

Isabelle stared, transfixed.

I dashed behind her and was right beside Nick when he shifted. I saw his clothes blur as he tried to fold them away. I grabbed, tugging them out of his grip. I had his jeans and his T-shirt, and that was good enough.

I definitely had surprise on my side.

He roared as he finished his shift, then snatched at his clothing. His talons sliced through the air.

I was already out of range.

"Three wishes!" I shouted, and ran as if my life depended on it.

Chances were good that it did.

• • •

If you have ever run drunk through a snowy forest in the middle of the night, you might have an idea how dumb my choice was. I didn't have my coat, but there was no chance of my getting cold—I was sweating as I ran as fast as I could. I also had no real plan as to what to do with Nick's clothes, something I realized when he was breathing fire and flying right behind me.

A distinct lack of planning there.

My chances of outrunning him, at least so long as I was in human form, were minimal at best.

My chances of negotiating or even talking reason to him were about nil. He was furious.

I blamed the wine for messing me up.

He shouted, then breathed a plume of fire, scorching my butt and my best jeans.

"Hey!" I shouted.

"Thief!" he roared. "Come on, Zoë. Shift already! Let's square it up the old-fashioned way."

I realized then that he would hound me until I changed to dragon form.

Because he wanted to wrestle in front of Isabelle and impress her with his abilities. Which showed exactly zero concern for my fears.

I wasn't going to play.

I ducked under a branch and into a thickly grown section of the woods, turned hard, and headed back toward the clearing. I was practically crawling, brambles grabbing me from every side, the jeans and T-shirt tucked under my elbow. There was a gap in the trees ahead, and I ran more quickly, hoping to cross it unobserved.

Fat chance.

I was right in the middle when my boots sank into soft muck. It was swampy, which was why the trees didn't grow there. How could the muck not be frozen? It wasn't, though, probably because it was deep. I'd broken through the veneer of ice and was sinking fast.

Nick came peeling over the trees, all hot orange fury. He saw me, laughed, and dove like an arrow toward me. Garrett hung back, watching. He wasn't going to help me.

Oops.

I tried to run but the muck grabbed at my boots, pulling me in past my knees. I struggled but only sank deeper. I panicked.

I heard a whistle just then and looked up to see Adrian cutting through the air, sleek and strong.

He collided with Nick overhead. "You can't attack the Wyvern," he cried as he and Nick locked talons. They spun end over end through the sky, propelled by the force of their collision.

"Get lost. This is between Zoë and me." Nick took a swing at Adrian with his tail. Adrian grunted as the blow hit home. Neither of them was fighting as cleanly as they had earlier.

It looked like a grudge match. Garrett was watching, staying out of it.

For the moment.

I grabbed a tree branch and hauled myself closer to the other side of the muck. It was heavy work. Gym class cubed, not squared. Meagan would have laughed at that feeble math joke.

I was just thinking how much I would have appreciated some help when Liam's old-speak slipped into my thoughts.

"*Take my claw,*" he whispered, clearly trying to keep the others from overhearing. I knew it wouldn't work. They'd hear him.

Whether they'd do anything about it was debatable. Nick looked pretty busy.

Liam's silver talon shone in the starlight. I reached for his claw, taking a chance. He looked pale and tired, courtesy of the bourbon.

But he was powerful. He hauled me out of the muck with ease.

It was possible that it would have been easy for me in dragon form, too.

"Wait!" Just before I was clear of the swamp, I dropped Nick's clothes and kicked them down into the mud with my boot. I wasn't able to push them in all the way, but they were still a mess.

Then Liam took flight, soaring high above the trees. He dragged me into the sky, holding my hand, then caught me up against his side. It was awesome to fly, and I wanted to stretch out my arms to feel more of the wind.

This was what I wanted most of all.

I thought of Jared then, and wished I'd played our last moments together differently.

Would I get another chance? I hoped so.

"No!" Nick bellowed. I looked back to see him fling Adrian aside. He pursued us, hot on Liam's trail. He fired off a plume of dragonfire and I saw orange flames brilliant against the night. The fire was coming straight at me, which had to be an accident.

Liam spun to defend me, taking the fire's onslaught across his back.

I felt him stiffen in pain.

I smelled his scales burning.

And I heard the rhythm of his wings falter.

Just before we fell out of the sky.

Shit.

LIAM and I crashed into the top of a tree. Its branches were bare for the winter, but its wood was plenty hard enough. The collision knocked all the snow from its branches and the breath out of me.

Liam was out cold.

"You should have shifted to save him," Nick scolded when he arrived.

"You shouldn't have breathed dragonfire on him," I snapped.

"That was for you."

"Nice."

"You shouldn't have stolen my clothes."

"Arguing isn't going to solve anything." I ignored Nick and looked at Liam's wound. About a dozen of the scales on his back were burned and misshapen, some skin left bare by the damage. It looked pink.

Like a sunburn.

It made him vulnerable. My chest tightened and I felt awful at my role in this.

Now I really wanted to puke.

"He'll be all right," Adrian said, hovering beside us. "He'll sleep off the booze, then just need a scale repair."

"And who's going to do that?" Garrett asked quietly, his tone full of recrimination.

"This is *not* my fault," I said.

Neither Nick nor Garrett appeared to be convinced. So they were going to turn against me, one at a time, were they? First Garrett was angry with me and now Nick. Maybe it was a good thing that Liam was out cold.

At least Adrian wasn't giving me a hard time.

Maybe boot camp showed you who your real friends were.

"Is everyone all right?" Isabelle called. "Nick? Are you hurt?"

I turned my back on Nick and Garrett and talked to Adrian. "Can you carry Liam back to the cabin?"

I figured I'd walk by myself.

I wasn't much for the company of my so-called friends.

If I'd disliked the cabin before, I hated it then. You could have cut the air with a knife. We got Liam into his sleeping bag—he'd shifted to human form while Adrian had been carrying him and passed out again—then Garrett banked the fire.

I made one last trip to the outhouse, glanced down to the dock, then couldn't look away.

I stood there, snared by the sight.

Isabelle was on the dock, washing Nick's clothes. There was a hole in the ice, one that opened to a jagged bit of dark lake. A midnight star. Starlight was all around her, the sky a gazillion hues of indigo all around.

Then there was Nick. He hovered just above her, so beautifully golden that it made my heart ache. At her gesture, he breathed fire to dry his laundry with the heat of a flickering yellow flame.

Perfect. He was so light against the darkness. She could have been that princess, her hair lifting behind her, her face lit by the flames he breathed. My throat was tight and I knew I should look away.

But I couldn't. There was something magical about them together, something *right.*

I would have loved for it not to be so, but it was.

Isabelle laughed at him as he made the flames dance, then reached out to caress his scales. They both froze. I knew his eyes would be gleaming amber. I knew she would have given him anything, right then and right there.

My heart stopped when he took his clothes and landed on the dock, shifting back to human form so smoothly that I never saw the transition.

He was just Nick then, Nick in his T-shirt and jeans, Nick with his fabulous shoulders and amber eyes. I knew he was smiling at her, that one corner of his mouth would be higher than the other in a crooked smile that had always destroyed me.

But that smile was for Isabelle. Not for me.

They locked into one hummer of a kiss, one that seemed to go on and on forever. No chance of their getting cold.

I watched. And if I cried a little for what would never be mine, then that's between you and me. If I did, I did it silently.

Because sometimes even hot guys you've known all your life are out of your league.

When they finally parted, Isabelle framed Nick's face in her hands.

"Nicholas," she whispered. I could hear the one word even at a distance.

But no one ever called Nick by his full name.

Maybe it was a British thing.

Maybe I wasn't doing my mental health any favors by watching this.

I walked away, knowing that one day—maybe soon—I'd paint that scene. In full color. I usually drew my dragons individually, although they tended to look like the dragons I knew. Maybe it was time to push the limits and do a full scene. I smiled at the idea that maybe I wasn't trying hard enough.

Maybe I'd give the finished work to Nick and Isabelle.

Either way, I knew I'd never forget what I'd just witnessed.

THE WINE CHURNED in my gut, doing a tango with the pizza. I felt awful when I got back inside the cabin, awful in too many ways to count. The cabin seemed even smaller and darker than it had before, and I was getting a headache.

Adrian pushed the furniture toward the walls, and we laid out the sleeping bags in a row. I crawled into mine, then peeled off my jeans to sleep. I had my hoodie and underwear and heavy socks. It was a fashion statement, let me tell you, but it was warm.

I slipped my rune stone into the kangaroo pocket of my hoodie. I put in my earbuds, but stopped myself in time.

No. I was never again going to listen to the tune Nick had sent me. That dream was over.

. . .

I WASN'T surprised when I dreamed of snow.

In fact, I was relieved. I dreamed of snow blowing inside the cabin and melting before the fire. The others were all asleep. The doors and windows were still closed.

But the snow drifted in as if the wall closest to the lake were missing. I played the eye game, and there was no cabin when I looked with my left eye.

In fact, I was all alone when I peered through that eye.

I was back on the endless snow-covered plain, with one big honking tree close to me.

There was no sign of Granny.

Or her knitting.

That was a bit disconcerting.

The wind whistled through my hair and around my bare legs—yes, even in my dream, I was wearing the same thing I'd worn to bed. Let me tell you, it wasn't the most primo choice for a night in a blizzard.

So if Granny wasn't here, what was the point?

There was something red on the ground, something intermittently obscured by the blowing snow. I knelt down and cleared a space with my hands. I was actually standing on a ridge of red rock.

And it was carved all over with symbols. I pushed away snow as quickly as I could, but the wind made that impossible. I'd seen symbols like that before. I pulled out my rune stone.

It was the same red rock.

And there was blood running in the carvings, staining the marks dark red.

Just the way my rune stone had been the night before.

I could see the spine of rock extending a good distance in either direction before the shape of the land changed. Had my rune stone been chipped off this ridge?

If so, could I find the place where it belonged?

Was I supposed to put it back?

I looked up, startled to see that the huge tree was in full foliage, despite the season. Its leaves were vivid green and they rustled in the wind. I looked more closely and noticed something swinging from one of its boughs. I couldn't figure out what it was and couldn't get a better look without climbing the tree.

That seemed like a bad idea.

There was a hole by one of the tree's roots. That root wound down into the hole, so there must have been water at the bottom. When I leaned over it, I could see the stars reflected waaaaaaaaaay down there.

A well, then. Huh. I wondered whether it was frozen. Maybe the tree root kept the surface open.

There was something odd about the well, though. I had a sense of it as being dangerous.

Not water you'd want to drink.

Water that might give you more than you expected when you did drink from it. Yes. That was it.

I shivered and straightened, looking up into the tree. From here, the swinging weight was obviously a person.

Who had been hanged.

Ick. Although I knew I needed to try to help. It was a guy, but he was so still that I knew he was dead. I was too late. He swung, a noose around his neck, his body limp. He was naked and I saw he had a feather tattoo on his left biceps.

But instead of his right arm, there was a black-feathered wing.

At that moment, the wind blew through the branches and his body turned around in the flying snow. He spun and I could see his face. His skin was tanned darker than mine, his hair black. He was staring right at me, his eyes as dark as obsidian.

It was the guy from my room.

From school.

The guy whose face I'd seen in the stone.

I stared in shock.

And he blinked, as if surprised to see me there.

"*Unktehila*," he said, just like last time.

Then he reached for me.

Okay, I screamed.

I ran.

I fled into the snow, wanting only to get away from that tree and the corpse that wasn't one. It made no sense that someone could hang like that and still be alive, but I knew he was.

And I was scared shitless of him.

In the distance, there was a pinprick of light. It was orange and flickering, like a bonfire. Exactly what I needed. It couldn't be that far away if I could see it.

I headed straight for the fire.

The snow started to fall then, swirling around me in fat flakes, much as it had earlier that day near the cabin. The sky was filling with clouds, fast-moving clouds with pewter bellies that obscured the sky.

A sense of dread blossomed within me and grew like wildfire.

I kept my gaze fixed on the fire, starting to panic that I wasn't getting closer faster. I glanced back and the tree was gone, as if I'd left it a thousand miles behind.

I freaked.

I ran across the snow, racing toward the bonfire. It seemed to take forever to get to it, but I finally did. It was huge, the flames probably twenty feet high. An inferno. I stretched out my hands toward its heat, slipping in my rush to get closer.

And then it disappeared.

As surely as if someone had flicked a switch.

Worse, there was no sign of where it had been.

I was all alone, surrounded by white and cold.

14

I woke up with a gasp, my heart pounding and sweat running down my back. The guys were sleeping all around me, the fire down to glowing embers on the hearth. It was snowing again outside, but inside everything was normal.

Except that Isabelle was sitting up beside me, her eyes wide and her hands on her mouth. "His name is Kohana," she whispered.

No! We could *not* have shared a dream.

"I don't know what you're talking about," I said, flopping back down into my warm sleeping bag. I turned my back on her, facing Adrian, eyes open.

Isabelle exhaled shakily. She settled back into her sleeping bag. I could tell by the rate of her breathing that she was wide-awake.

One thing was for sure: this Wyvern gig could have used a manual. I wasn't going to think about the fact that Jared had the closest thing to one in his possession.

In fact, I wasn't going to think about him at all.

And I wasn't going to think about Garrett turning against me.

Or Nick being angry with me.

Or Liam getting hurt because of me.

I had a crick in my neck. My head was pounding and my tongue felt thick and icky. My stomach was still unhappy. I decided right then and there that I didn't like sparkling wine after all.

I knew I had to get out of that cabin. I'd suffocate if I stayed. The sky was turning pearly gray, but the cabin seemed filled with an oppressive darkness.

I couldn't stand it one moment longer.

I tugged my jeans into my sleeping bag to warm them up a bit, then pulled them on. I sorted my boots out of the pile by the door, grabbed Alex's leather jacket—which I was starting to hope I could keep for the duration—and headed to the outhouse.

It was snowing lightly. The sky looked as if the storm clouds were settling into place, intending to bury us alive in fresh snow.

Not that I was getting negative or anything.

I felt better, though, just getting out of there.

I pulled my rune stone from my pocket as I walked. It had changed again. The *F* tree looked more insubstantial than it had before. Like it was fading. I couldn't begin to imagine what that meant.

I was in the outhouse when I heard footsteps; then someone coughed. I was bundling back up when voices started to whisper.

Practically begging me to eavesdrop.

"She can't be holding out on us." Liam sounded cranky. "I don't know why you'd think that."

"I can't *not* think it. Nothing else makes sense." Garrett spoke in an undertone.

"Do you think anyone has any aspirin?"

"Never mind that. The Wyvern traditionally stayed away from the *Pyr*, didn't she?"

"So? You mean she'd deliberately hold out on us?"

"What else could she be doing?"

"But why?"

"To teach us that we can't rely upon her, maybe. I don't know! Wyverns are supposed to be mysterious, too."

"I don't know. Doesn't seem like Zoë."

"Then what's she doing here?" Garrett challenged. "She doesn't shift; she won't solve the riddle; if she has any foresight, she's not telling."

"Hey, maybe she's learning...."

"Maybe she's not playing for the team." Garrett's voice turned hard. "That's what I dreamed."

"What?"

"That she betrayed us all." Garrett was grim. "I had the same dream over and over again, like a warning. I mean, look at you. You took a hit for her and she did *nothing* to help you. She didn't even break your fall."

Liam sighed. "Okay. I thought it was weird that she didn't solve the riddle right away."

"Yeah," Garrett said. "I thought we were getting that riddle in the first place to make her part of the team."

"But she didn't figure it out."

"Either that or she didn't tell us the solution. Maybe she's keeping it secret to give herself an advantage."

"I don't know if that's fair. Zoë wouldn't do that."

"Isn't it? My dad said the last Wyvern helped him make the connection to fire, so I should ask Zoë for help."

"And?"

"She said she wasn't sure she could do it." Garrett snorted. "It was a lie. I could tell. Maybe she wasn't sure she *wanted* to do it."

"That's harsh, Garrett."

"No. Harsh is you getting injured and me not being able to repair your scales because I don't have the full power of the Smith."

"Maybe she doesn't know how to do what you want," Liam suggested.

"Come on! She's the Wyvern."

Liam's tone turned thoughtful. "Maybe she's here because she's *not* the Wyvern. Maybe Donovan is calling her bluff. Maybe that's her test."

"Well, that sucks. I don't think we should have to do without a Wyvern, not if her powers are meant to help us come into our own. I think we should *make* her help."

I'd heard plenty.

I kicked open the door of the latrine hard enough that it swung all the way back and banged on the outside wall.

Liam and Garrett nearly jumped out of their skins.

"Gee, why wouldn't I want to help you guys?" I demanded. "Seeing as you all have so much faith in me. Seeing as we're all such good *friends*? One day in the woods and you're turning against me, just like that." I snapped my fingers.

I didn't wait for an answer, just marched past them.

"Well, what are we supposed to think?" Garrett said, his tone hostile. "It's not like you've done anything to participate."

"I found the riddles!"

"But you didn't solve them."

Liam eyed me and spoke more quietly. "Are you holding out on us, Zoë?"

That was it. You can probably guess what happened next.

Yup. *That.*

The crimson tide raged through me, claiming me body and soul. It filled every vein, every crevice, every nerve in my body, heating it all to red-hot. It shorted my circuits and overwhelmed me completely

The dragon was loose, and I was completely lost in the maelstrom.

There was no blue shimmer. There was nothing I could control. There was nothing I could stop or start.

The change happened fast, ripping through me and changing my shape so quickly that it left me dizzy. One second I was indulging that flicker of anger; the next I was an enormous dragon. I didn't manage to hide my leather jacket in the heat of the moment and it fell to the snow.

My senses were even sharper than before, and when I turned to tell Garrett off, flames erupted from my mouth.

On the one hand, I felt awesome power and pride in what I could do. (I was finally *doing* it!) On the other hand, I was terrified.

And furious.

Uh-oh.

The guys didn't have a chance. I roared and leapt at them. I swiped at Garrett with one claw and caught him across the side of the face. Four long scratches marked his cheek and started to bleed. He fell back in the snow, his eyes wide with fear.

Of *me.*

He scrambled backward like a crab. He never even blinked, not wanting to risk losing sight of me. He shimmered on the cusp of change, but I breathed fire again.

"Easy, Zoë. I was just joking. Really." He was stammering, freaking out.

I'd never seen Garrett afraid before.

"Take it easy, Zoë," Liam added, hands held high in surrender. "Deep breath."

That was when I realized that I *was* a freak, just like Suzanne was telling everyone at school.

Because the dragon was running me.

No more. I'd rather hurt anything else before I injured my friends more than I already had. I turned away, threw myself at the forest. I had to get control of myself and figure out how to shift back.

Nobody tried to stop me.

Nobody begged me to stay.

You know, I couldn't blame them. I tried to feel for my dad, being in desperate need of some dragon advice, but he was still out of range.

Boot camp just kept getting better and better.

Not.

"Zoë!"

I ignored the shout. It was, after all, a woman's voice. One with a British accent. Three guesses who was hunting me, and the first two don't count.

I was perfectly happy sulking quietly on a rock far from everyone I knew. I was back in human form, having been able to shift once guilt replaced my anger. I didn't care if it was starting to snow. I didn't care if I was cold.

I was a bona fide freak.

As well as a failure, a disappointment, and a delusional chick.

Worse, I didn't know what to do about any of it.

Even though I didn't answer, Isabelle found me anyway. Maybe she *was* psychic.

She wore her white down-filled winter coat with fake fur around the hood, and her boots were slipping in the snow. She was carrying the leather jacket that Alex had lent to me. She came to a sliding halt before me, held out the jacket, and smiled.

Tentatively.

"We have to talk," she said, her breath making a white puff in the cold air.

"I don't think so." I started to turn away, but her next words stopped me.

"I don't believe you meant to hurt the guys."

I was both curious and skeptical. "Why not?"

She gestured vaguely with one hand and frowned. "Look, I don't know exactly why, but I feel that it's the truth." She smiled again. "I know it."

That didn't make me a whole lot less skeptical of her.

But curiosity was winning the day. Even if she was trying to trick me, I couldn't figure out why.

I told you that I like a puzzle.

I took the jacket and tugged it on. "What did you want to talk about?"

Isabelle glanced back toward the cabin, as if fearing she might be overheard. It wasn't exactly a long shot, given the superhearing of the *Pyr*. She lowered her voice and stepped closer. "Something weird is going on. Maybe you'll be able to figure it out with me."

"I'm listening. But you know, a whisper draws attention. Makes people want to eavesdrop."

She nodded, then looked around, uncertain.

I rummaged in my pocket, pulled out the notebook and pencil that I always have—in case I have a desperate need to draw—then handed both to her.

She smiled, her eyes lighting with a pleasure that made me feel like less of a loser. She grabbed the pencil, flipped open the book, and hesitated. I know she'd just found one of my dragon drawings, but I didn't want to talk about it.

I looked away.

If I'd had a newer messenger, I could have drawn on it and secured the file with bunches of passwords. It would have been private forever, or for as long as I'd wanted it to be. Paper has its limitations.

But I had bigger issues right now than a lack of gadgetry.

She considered me, then turned the page. She scribbled for a moment, then handed the notebook back to me.

I want to talk about dreams, she had written, which startled me. *Particularly the ones I have about you. And about Nick.*

Bingo. With three short sentences, Isabelle had my undivided attention.

WE WALKED IN THE SNOW, away from the cabin. We found a bunch of rocks on the side of a frozen river. Isabelle looked in every direction, brushed the snow from a big rock, then pulled a deck of cards from her pocket. She shuffled them and drew one, putting it faceup on the rock.

Then she stared at it, unblinking, as the snow fell steadily all around us. I stepped closer to have a look.

Curiosity doesn't kill the dragon.

Just so you know.

The card was bigger than the playing cards I knew, and I didn't recognize the illustration on it. The guy on the card looked like he was about to step off a cliff—and he seemed to be whistling. It said, *The Fool,* at the bottom and had a zero at the top.

Null and void. That pretty much summed up the current tone of my life.

"Fresh starts," Isabelle said with satisfaction. "I drew it right side up, which means an auspicious beginning. Taking a chance, maybe on faith, and making it work." She smiled at me. "Which means that telling you about this is exactly the right thing to do." Then she took the pad of paper, sat down on the rock, and started to write.

It might as well have been an essay. I sat down beside her, listening to the wind in the woods. I wondered about my ability to shift, how I could do it only when I was deeply pissed off, and fretted that I'd never get control of it. I worried about the discord between me and the guys, and wondered what I could do to fix it—especially since everything I did just made it worse.

I pulled out my rune stone and ran my thumb over the symbol etched into its surface.

That was about beginnings, too.

As I waited for her, I turned those clues around in my thoughts. When in doubt, solve a riddle, right? I pulled out my messenger and mulled over the clues.

Valued by all, sold by none, I have no price.
I slide before the sun, but make no shadow.
I touch everyone, but no one catches me.

The answer was something invisible, yet pervasive: something we all took for granted even though we needed it. Not smoke. Maybe thought.

Lust, maybe.

But I wasn't going there.

I am a boundless buffet from which everyone eats but no one fills.

Something apparently limitless. Self-propagating.

Lust could be like that, from what I'd heard.

I had a hard time believing that this boot camp's theme was lust. I rubbed my stone harder.

I am a city vast, thick with people but no streets.

I'd heard that one or something like it before.

Air. Of course! One of the four elements, perfect as a focus for boot camp. I straightened and looked around, amazed that I'd missed something so obvious.

I thought about going back to share my revelation with the guys, but wasn't so hot to do that. They might not want to talk to me at all.

I heard Jared's voice in my thoughts then.

A dragon girl, afraid?

Yeah, pretty much.

But maybe it was time to ditch that perspective.

"MAY I HOLD YOUR STONE?" Isabelle asked, startling me with the reminder of her presence.

"It's just a rock," I said gruffly, and shoved it back into my pocket. I felt rude, but she didn't seem offended. Instead she held out the notebook for me. I took it back and read what she'd written.

I dreamed of you Friday night in Minneapolis. We were together, you and I, and we were both large white birds. Swans, maybe. And we were flying together, not saying anything. It was easy to be together, as if we were old friends, as if we had no need to chatter about this and that. I felt a connection with you.

And I thought that was pretty strange, given that you and Nick obviously have had something going on in the past, yet it seems that he and I have some potential for the future. You probably don't want to hear this, but I've been dreaming of Nick all my life—and my dreams always come true.

Last night, I dreamed of being drawn to a bonfire. I was in some cold place and it was snowing. And as I walked to the bonfire to get warm, it suddenly disappeared. I was left in a blizzard to freeze. And I woke up, terrified, to see the same look on your face. Did you have the same dream? I think you did. Maybe you know what it means.

Do you know anything about the guy who was hanging from the rope?

Maybe you know why I want to call Nick Nikolas.

Maybe we need to work together to make our dreams—and our destinies—come true.

What do you think?

I read it twice and looked away before responding. I had not been in a hurry to become pals with Isabelle or help her make a permanent connection with Nick. And I still wasn't in a hurry to tell her any of my secrets, either.

She was waiting, though.

On impulse, I asked what I really didn't want to know. No point in having doubts. On the notepad, I wrote, *What do you dream about Nick?*

She smiled.

She blushed.

She looked away and knotted her hands together. It was interesting to see her so discomfited. With clumsy fingers, she rummaged through her deck of tarot cards and deliberately chose one, turning it so I could see it.

THE LOVERS.

Well, that pretty much said it all, didn't it?

15

"It's getting dark," I said, pushing to my feet. "And my butt's cold. We'd better head back."

"Wait," she said. Isabelle had chosen another card, but I hadn't noticed it in her hand.

The second card was DEATH.

I had a bad feeling of my own, then, as if I were going to be the cause of someone dying. I was doing a fairly crap job of playing for the team, and didn't see how to bring my dragon powers around quickly.

Isabelle watched me for a long moment. "There's a storm coming," she said finally, then put her cards away.

That wasn't half of it.

I strode back in the direction we'd come, not really waiting for her. It was funny, but the closer we got to the cabin, the more I resented Isabelle. Maybe she was turning the guys against me. Maybe she was stealing my dreams—or maybe she was psychic enough to get glimpses of them.

Lots of nasty thoughts seemed to breed in my mind without any help from me. They felt toxic and poisonous, but I couldn't get rid of them.

I didn't like having them in my head, but couldn't ditch them. It was like an ear worm, the chorus of a catchy song that you can't quite get out of your memory.

I spun to face Isabelle. I scribbled in the notebook while she got closer. She really was no good at walking in snow, and it wasn't just because of her boots. I handed her the notebook instead.

What do you know about the last Wyvern?

Isabelle shrugged, then took the pencil. *That there was one, and she died.* She met my gaze, apparently finished.

I was sure she was lying.

I would have snatched the notebook back, certain our time of girly bonding was over. Doomed, maybe.

"There's something else," Isabelle said. *It's Adrian*, she wrote. *I don't trust him....*

I didn't let her write any more. I guessed where this was going. She had to be jealous of his interest in me.

You can't have all the guys to yourself, I wrote, and she blinked in surprise. Then I shut the notebook and shoved it into my pocket again.

Isabelle watched me for a moment, then swore.

That made me blink.

"I hate this place," she said, surprisingly fierce. "It's wicked here; you have to feel it, too. It's making us fight with one another, and ruining everything."

"You weren't fighting with Nick last night." I had to say it but managed to stop myself there.

She frowned. "But we can connect emotionally only when we leave that cabin behind. It's like there's something in that place, something that disguises the truth. Or turns it bitter. Something evil."

I wanted to argue, but I knew she was right. I didn't dislike her nearly as much away from the cabin as within it. In the forest, that simmering resentment was diminished, and I could even see that we had some things in common.

I'd hated the cabin from the first as well.

And I'd never felt unappreciated by the guys before arriving at the cabin.

What was the deal with those orange sparks? I needed to look for them while I was sober, see if they were real.

"But how could it do that?" I asked her. "Why?"

"I don't know, but there's something powerful at work." She met my gaze again. "Nasty. I think someone's trying to turn us against one another."

A test of Donovan's? I had a hard time believing that.

I thought about the older *Pyr* disappearing from my Wyvern radar. Was it really their choice? Or my inability to track them?

Or was something wrong?

I shivered. Before I could formulate good questions, Isabelle tugged her zipper up higher and headed back to the cabin at a crisp pace. Maybe she thought I didn't believe her.

I followed her slowly, thinking things over.

And there was that song Nick had sent me. Why had he done that?

It was time to find out.

I HEARD the steady tap of a hammer before we could see the cabin. I knew exactly what the guys were doing and I hurried. I loved seeing a Smith at work.

There were two dragons outside the cabin. They looked especially magical in the falling snow, one malachite green and silver, the other garnet and gold.

Nick stood close by in human form. He wore heavy gloves and had a pair of tongs, and was heating Liam's damaged scales for Garrett to work upon. They must have been loose, and Garrett worked them free. Adrian, also in human form, watched. I wondered whether he'd ever seen a Smith before.

Garrett had obviously brought a small jeweler's forge with him, and he had a fire roaring within it. The flame burned a rich gold, lighting up the dragon scales and the faces of the other guys.

It looked like the repository of an ancient hoard. I smiled, my chest tight with a fierce love of what we are.

The snow swirled around the guys, piling on the roof of the log cabin. It landed on Liam and Garrett, adorning their wings and tails, and dusted the hair and shoulders of Adrian and Nick.

Another scene to paint. It was too perfect. I studied them all once more, greedy for every last detail that would make the painting more real.

Was this my destiny? To document my own kind? To create an illustrated record of what we are?

Maybe to create a manual for the next Wyvern.

Garrett was focused on his work, intent upon repairing a scale that must have come from Liam's back. The scale itself was all green whorls, outlined in a thin edge of silver. Nick heated it on the forge; then Garrett hammered it, working it gradually back into shape.

Liam lay in the snow, watching us approach with gleaming eyes. Isabelle continued to the cabin, hunched down in her fluffy coat, but I hesitated on the perimeter of the forest.

As much as I wanted to be part of this, I doubted my presence would be welcome.

Nick started at Isabelle's arrival and smiled in her direction. Soon she stood beside him, keeping her hands shoved in her pockets, watching. Warming herself by the forge, maybe. Adrian smiled at me and waved.

Garrett glanced up, perhaps sensing Adrian's interest, and his gaze locked with mine. I saw the four long wounds on his cheek, so much larger in his dragon form, and the wariness in his eyes.

I had done that. I had scarred his cheek and put the doubt in his eyes.

I saw the scorched scales on Liam's back: the three that had already been repaired and the four still waiting.

I was responsible for that, too.

I'd never failed any course in my life, but I was failing Wyvern 101.

Or maybe just Dragon 101.

"*Can you fix it?*" I asked Garrett in old-speak.

He shrugged and returned to his work.

I couldn't blame him.

The others remained silent. Watchful. I felt the mood of the cabin pressing against me, provoking my anger and resentment. I could have insisted that I'd been unfairly treated, that the guys should pay. I could have started a fight.

But I knew I had to move past whatever ominous power this place had. That was the test. I had to do something different to break its influence.

"*I solved the riddle,*" I continued in old-speak. Nick glanced up. Garrett's lips tightened. "*It's air.*"

No one said anything.

I dared to walk closer to the group and spoke aloud. "Air governs unions, ideas, negotiations. Thoughts and dreams. Reasoned discussion. Logic."

I saw Garrett flick a glance at me; then he breathed a slow and steady stream of fire upon the scale he held. The forge had heated it to the point that his dragonfire could just provide the last burst of heat. Quinn worked with a forge most of the time, too, relying solely on dragonfire only when there wasn't a choice. The scale glittered in Garrett's grasp, and I marveled at how adept he was. He had already learned so much from Quinn. I sensed his passion for his craft and understood his desire to be the best.

I had to figure out how to help him. That dark force whispered at me, picking at my doubts, but I forced myself not to listen to it.

These were my friends.

I knew that in my heart and had to hold fast to it.

Garrett turned the scale in his talons, heating it evenly, coaxing the hole to mend. I watched him fix three scales, working with steady patience even as the light got poor.

The clouds were getting darker and the snow was falling more thickly. Nick shifted shape and focused on keeping the embers glowing hot for Garrett. But the last increment of heat, the part that made the scale repair possible, had to come from the Smith.

The last scale was the worst one, and I knew that Garrett had been working up to it. It had a big hole right in the middle.

A hole that was too large to patch.

No matter how Garrett heated it and coaxed it, that hole kept opening again. If it wasn't fixed, Liam would have a spot that was vulnerable.

Unarmed.

I couldn't let that happen.

I knew that dragon scales could be healed with jewelry. Often a mate contributed a piece of her own treasure to help heal an injury sustained by her dragon of choice.

I pulled off my malachite-and-silver earrings and walked closer, offering them to Garrett on the flat of my hand. "You'll need these, I think."

Garrett faltered. He was that surprised by my gesture. He looked between the earrings and me, uncertain. "But only a mate can give a gift to mend the scales of a *Pyr*...."

"Liam can't wait that long. It could be years before he meets his destined mate and has his firestorm." I stretched my hand out.

"Centuries, even," Isabelle added.

"Doesn't a friend count, too?" I asked.

Garrett studied me in silence.

"Take them," Nick murmured.

"Thanks, Zoë," Liam said quietly.

Garrett accepted the earrings with care. I felt his talon brush my palm, and our gazes met for a second. He checked the earrings and I saw his relief. I smiled, knowing that he'd confirmed that the jewelry was pure silver. He was a craftsman, and picky about his materials.

I watched him heat one so the silver was fluid, and he worked it with dexterity. Each earring had one large oval stone and one small round one, He arranged them into a diamond, spreading the silver in between to make a badge. As it took shape, I saw his confidence grow that he could make the repair.

I wanted to help him.

When an adult *Pyr* has his scale repaired, with the help of his mate, they achieve a balance. We all have a link to two elements—fire is usually a gimme—and the circle of the four elements is completed with our partner's complementary affinities.

I wondered whether that was what made scale repair work.

Could we replicate that?

Even without Liam's having a mate?

I thought about our respective natures. Garrett's main connection had to be with fire, and he was already honing his affinity with it. He was passionate, seldom angry, but when he was angry he made it worth the trouble.

What about Nick? I thought of Nick as practical, powerful, stubborn, and strong. Confident in a different way. Rooted. One of his affinities must be with the earth.

And Liam was everybody's best friend. He was the one who understood before you even said anything, the one who could forgive and forget. Water had to be Liam's affinity.

What if mine was air? The Wyvern was associated with dreams and foresight, both governed by air. I drew and I solved riddles—more air, in the realms of imagination and intellect.

We had all four elements covered among us! Could we secure Liam's scale repair if we managed to pull together?

The idea excited me. I wanted to make it happen.

Meanwhile, Nick heated the scale. Garrett heated the other earring. He fused the earrings together into a kind of a medallion, one that looked like it had a silver rope around it.

A medallion that perfectly fit the hole. Liam bared his teeth as Garrett fused the pieces together. He worked both the back side and the front of the scale to secure it, making Liam's coat of armor complete again.

When he stepped back, nodding with satisfaction, it looked to me as if my earrings and the scale had become one. There was no clear line to show where one ended and the other began.

I liked that.

I liked it a lot.

"Fire," I said, gesturing to Garrett. He smiled in sudden understanding. The repair of an adult dragon's scale ended with this ritual acknowledgment of the elements, and I knew he got it. He proved that by breathing a short stream of flame upon Liam's mended scales.

"Earth," I said to Nick, and he braced his hands on Liam's shoulders.

"Water," I said to Liam, and he nodded in understanding.

"Here," Isabelle said, bending to lift a drop of moisture from Liam's cheek. She placed it carefully on the mended scales and it hissed.

"Air," I added, then bent to blow across the repaired scales.

"All for one and one for all," Nick concluded with satisfaction. There was a moment when we smiled at one another, when the darkness of the cabin's mood seemed to have disappeared.

Then Adrian cleared his throat. "What about me?" he asked lightly, and I was ashamed that I had forgotten him.

How could I have done that?

"Old joke," Liam said, lying to cover for me.

Adrian shrugged and smiled as if it didn't matter. But something had changed. We were edgy with one another again.

And I couldn't explain why.

. . .

Maybe it was the storm.

Isabelle had been right: there was a storm coming, and it was moving fast. I hadn't been paying attention while Garrett worked, but the truth was inescapable.

The snow was falling faster by the time Liam's scales were repaired, and the sky was the color of smoke, even though it was only midafternoon. The wind stirred, making the snow dance in spirals.

The air in the cabin was so charged it felt as if the whole thing would blow if someone dropped a match. Isabelle had nailed it in one. I was haunted by Jared's words, even as I watched whatever was at work in the cabin affect the guys.

You're coasting, Zoë, and that's not going to cut it if you really want to be the Wyvern. In fact, it doesn't cut it for pretty much anything.

Don't you hate when an extremely hot guy also proves to be right?

I had to solve the puzzle of the cabin's power over us. Whether I ever saw Jared again or not. I really wished I had his book to refer to. But I was determined to work through the clues I had, looking for loose ends. There were a lot of them.

"Why did you send me that song?" I asked Nick. "Where'd you get it in the first place?"

"What song?"

"The one you sent me when our dads decided I was coming to boot camp."

I know Nick well enough to know when he isn't putting me on. "I never sent you a song."

I pulled out my messenger and showed him the message. He was completely confused. "You're right. It looks like it's from me. But I never sent it."

"What kind of song?" Isabelle asked. I put it on audio and let it play. Agitation rippled through the cabin and Isabelle backed away. "Turn it off. It's awful!"

"It's kind of catchy," Adrian said.

"It's *wrong*!" Isabelle said, almost shouting. Nick went to her side, as if preparing to defend her, and the air crackled in the cabin.

Against what?

I had an idea then. I played the eye game as I turned on the music again.

With my left eye, I could see glimmers in the air. They seemed to emanate from my messenger, circle around the ceiling, then target the guys.

The brightest ones clustered around Garrett. There was a dimmer cloud around Nick, but Liam seemed to be able to repel them somehow. Adrian had none around him.

By playing this song, I'd brought this dissent into the cabin? This was my fault, too?

"Turn it off!" Isabelle cried, making a snatch for my messenger.

I did, even as I tried to work out what could be happening.

It was a puzzle, after all. I needed more information. I sat down at the table, shoved my messenger away, and pulled out my notebook. "What do you guys know about the last Wyvern? What have your parents told you?"

"Why?" Liam asked. I should have expected my first ally would be Liam. That affinity with water again.

"Because I don't know everything I'm supposed to be able to do. It would be nice to have a clue."

"Dead Wyverns don't give clues?" Adrian asked. It sounded like he was trying to lighten the mood by making a joke, but it fell flat.

"Erik didn't give you a hint?" Garrett asked.

"I think my dad is waiting to see what I figure out for myself. Or what the *Pyr* tell me. My mom said her name was Sophie."

"Sophie died," Liam said.

"She showed my dad how to connect with his legacy," Garrett said. "She was okay." The implication there was as clear as crystal, but again, I didn't bite. I thought that maybe if I didn't play along with the negativity in the cabin, it might be undermined.

It was worth a shot.

In fact, this might be a boot camp test, set up by Donovan. Maybe he had sent me the song, using Nick's account. He would have had easy access to it, after all.

If the theme was air, as the riddle indicated, spells and magic were governed by the element of air. Maybe—since he was the one worried about Mages—he was trying to teach us how to fight them.

If that was the case, there had to be a way to break this spell. I was growing excited, determined to pull the guys together on this challenge.

"But she wasn't *supposed* to engage with the world," I said, keeping my tone upbeat. Liam pulled up a chair beside me and I smiled at him in encouragement. "That's the thing. The Wyvern is supposed to remain aloof, kind of beyond it all. I wonder whether that's why she can see farther."

"Because she's above it all?" Isabelle suggested. She sat at the table, too. I felt the tension among all of us start to ease.

We were winning!

I shrugged. "Maybe. But Sophie, she got involved. And she died, I think young."

"It would be helpful for you to know what went wrong," Isabelle agreed.

"I'd like to avoid making the same mistake. If there was one."

"How did she get involved?" Nick took a couple of steps closer. With my left eye I could still see those orange sparks circling overhead, as if seeking a target.

Liam snapped his fingers. "I remember this! She and this *Pyr* were the ones who destroyed the Academy where the Elixir was forced into near-dead *Pyr*. Like my dad. The Wyvern and this *Pyr* sacrificed themselves to ensure that no more *Pyr* could be made into shadow dragons."

"But who was that *Pyr*?" I asked, seeking both information and cooperation. "Someone's uncle or brother?"

Nick frowned. "No. He was some kind of outsider." He sat down beside Isabelle.

"An outsider?" Adrian echoed.

"He was the first of the Dragon's Tooth Warriors," Garrett said, his tone more normal than it had been. "I remember that story now. He was different, hard to understand, my dad said. He'd been enchanted for a couple of thousand years, after all, and the world had changed. A lot."

"Like Drake?" Liam named the current commander of the Dragon's Tooth Warriors.

"Yes, but not like Drake." Garrett shrugged. "Maybe like Drake before he got used to the way the world had changed."

Now we were working together, and it felt good.

"But why did he sacrifice himself?" I asked. "I mean, I can see the Wyvern working for the universal good, but why him?"

"Because he knew she was right?" Liam suggested.

"Because she asked for his help?" Nick offered. "The Wyvern isn't supposed to be a fighter, after all. Maybe she wanted to go in with some muscle."

"That's still a big move," I said. "To commit to a mission that you won't survive."

"It must have been because he loved her," Isabelle said. We all turned to look at her. She smiled with confidence. "It's the only thing that makes sense."

In a way, it did.

And in a way, it didn't.

Which meant there was still a piece missing.

"I wonder whether she loved him." I stared into the fire, drumming my fingers on the arm of the chair. It wouldn't have been a very nice thing to trick a *Pyr* into going to his death. I couldn't imagine a Wyvern doing that.

Because I wouldn't do it.

If she loved the *Pyr*, why wouldn't she have wanted to be with him? Live with him, and get involved in the world in a more basic way?

If she didn't love him, it would have been an even more improbable thing for her to do, like killing an inappropriate suitor instead of just ditching him.

An inappropriate suitor.

I had it!

16

"You're right!" I said to Isabelle, unable to hide my excitement. "She loved him and he loved her."

"Sooooo?" Liam said, dragging out the question.

"But they couldn't be together." I was certain I'd solved the riddle. "That was why they chose to sacrifice themselves. They could make a difference to the world—and they couldn't have had a life together anyway."

"Is that supposed to make sense?" Nick asked.

"They were both *Pyr*."

"Okay," Liam said.

I could see that the guys weren't following my line of thinking. "Okay. Each of you will have a firestorm with a human woman."

"Right," Nick said.

"And the firestorm will result in the conception of another *Pyr*."

"We know all the basics, Zoë."

I ignored Garrett's tone. Adrian was hanging back, and I smiled at him. I was sure that if we all worked together, we could beat the spell. He folded his arms across his chest and stayed in the kitchen area, though.

I felt that sense of working together start to fracture, but I kept talking.

"But what about me? We don't mate with our own kind, which means that I must be going to have a firestorm with a *human* guy."

(I instantly thought of Jared, but let's just keep that between you and me, okay?)

"Maybe Wyverns don't even get to have firestorms," Nick said.

I ignored that troubling possibility.

"Even if they do, I still don't get it," Liam said.

There were suddenly more orange bits of lightning zipping around the ceiling, and the cabin started to darken. I talked faster. "Sophie was the Wyvern. The guy she died with was a *Pyr*. If they were in love, their love defied that one-human-one-dragon convention."

Oh. They all sat back in sudden understanding. And I got thwacked in the brain with a realization of my own—I could never be with Nick. Not in that way.

For exactly the same reason: we're both *Pyr*.

Duh.

"They couldn't be together," Isabelle said with excitement. "Ever. Unless they were dead—like Romeo and Juliet. I think you're right, Zoë."

"So they made a choice to do something together that would leave a legacy for the *Pyr* and the world." I held up my hands, happy with my solution and expecting applause.

I didn't get any.

In fact, only Isabelle and I were still on the same page. The guys were looking around, bored maybe with the notion of romantic love, seeming irritable again. I closed my right eye and the vivid orange light overhead nearly blinded me.

Okay, we hadn't beaten it yet, but we'd made some progress.

I needed a new plan. There were still lots of errant puzzle bits to fit into the big picture.

The not-dead guy in my dream, for example.

I hunkered down in front of the fire to doodle and think sideways about puzzles.

It was Adrian who eventually sat on the floor beside me. It was quite a bit later, and Isabelle was making soup for dinner. No one was talking much, the impatience rising with every passing hour. The cabin was cold, despite the blaze of the fire, and Garrett was rationing the wood.

Adrian's shoulder bumped my knee and I could have reached out to bury my fingers in his dark curls. "I'm sorry the guys are so tough on you," he said quietly. "You can't do everything, and you can't learn everything overnight. They forget that it took them years to hone their skills, such as they are. How long have you been at it?"

My heart glowed. "Two days."

"See? It's different for you. I wish they'd back off."

Okay, I liked the sound of that. It made me feel all warm and fuzzy. "Thanks."

"No problem." He smiled at me, and I smiled back for a long moment. My heart started to pound a little faster.

"You could be wrong about Sophie, you know," he murmured.

"How so?"

"Well, everyone likes a love story, but what if it was something else?"

"Like what?"

Adrian hesitated, so I slid out of the chair to sit beside him on the rug.

"Go on, tell me."

He gestured that he wanted to write something. I turned to a fresh page of my notebook.

What if she did something for herself, and this Pyr *guy just got caught in the crossfire?* He wrote more quickly. *Or what if she had a plan the* Pyr *didn't like and he was trying to stop her?*

My eyes were wide.

What could the Wyvern want to do that the *Pyr* wouldn't like? I'd never thought of the Wyvern acting against the *Pyr*. It was an astonishing idea. She might be evasive or inaccessible, but she didn't plot against the others.

Adrian's eyes were really dark as he watched me work through this; then he bent to scribble again. *What if she felt unappreciated, and acted for herself, not the team?*

That was a pretty compelling possibility.

I looked and saw that Adrian had more to say about this—and I wanted to know what he was thinking.

I took the notebook and pen. *We should talk.*

Adrian nodded. *Tomorrow.*

Then he tore the page off the notebook, crumpled it up, and tossed it into the fire. Was it my imagination that the flames devoured that piece of paper more greedily than I would have expected?

LATER THAT NIGHT, I dreamed of my dad.

I had to be dreaming, because I was back in the snowy otherworld, in the middle of a frozen lake that looked a lot like the one down below the cabin. My dad was sleeping on the ice. That was strange, but it seemed consistent with Granny's world.

I'd never seen him look so peaceful.

I moved closer and looked at him. I knelt down in front of him, and his eyelids didn't even flicker.

That was when I knew something was wrong.

My dad, remember, is a dragon. He never really sleeps. In fact, I'm not sure I've ever seen him out cold. His eyes are always open a little slit, and, if you look carefully, you can see the glitter of his eyes. He's always monitoring the situation, ready to respond.

Ready to fight.

Or defend the hoard.

Maybe *hibernating* is a better choice of word than *sleeping*. Or *dozing*.

But in my dream, he was dead to the world. He didn't notice me standing before him. No flicker. No response. I walked right up to him and he didn't respond. I waved my hand in front of his face, even snapped my fingers close to his nose.

"*Dad?*" I asked in old-speak. "*Dad?*"

He didn't move. Not one muscle.

I panicked. I reached out to grab his shoulder and shake him awake.

"*Dad!*"

As soon as I touched his shoulder, he rolled to his back. Limply. His head landed on the ice with a thump and his mouth fell open.

He still didn't wake up.

That was when I saw the blood that stained the ice. There was a dark red cloud of it, slowly spreading wider. In places it was darker, as if it had run down into the carvings.

Snakes and circles and lightning bolts.

Just like the carvings on the red rock.

I WOKE UP, heart pounding with terror. I sat straight up. I might have yelled.

It was cold in the cabin, and I could see brilliant sunshine outside the windows. The sky was scrubbed-clean blue—the storm had passed.

I closed my eyes and tried to feel my dad's presence, tried to find a current or a glimmer or some sense of his being out there in the world. And I couldn't find him.

At all.

After that dream, I was freaked.

I was terrified that something had happened to my dad.

Maybe to all of the *Pyr*.

Seeing blood in my dream hadn't exactly been reassuring.

What was I going to do?

What *could* I do?

I got up, tugged on my clothes, and left the others sleeping. My thoughts felt more clear outside, as if the wind had blown away my doubts and worries.

Where would I start to hunt Donovan? He had been in the cabin just before we arrived. He had prepared to shift into dragon form at the sight of something.

And he had vanished into thin air.

By choice? Or not? I was starting to think option B, but that didn't give me any clues.

Then I recalled that this lake looked a lot like the lake in my dream, the one where my dad had been, well, down. It beckoned to me.

I chose to trust my impulse.

IT WAS INCREDIBLY COLD, cold enough to freeze your lungs with one breath. The little hairs inside my nose felt like icicles, and even my gloves weren't enough to keep my fingertips from going numb. I had my shawl wrapped around my head, and my ears were cold before I even got to the shore.

The snow was deep, too. We must have gotten six feet of it the night before. Again, I considered how strange it was to have such a wintry April.

Had Donovan overlooked that variable in his planning? Was that what was wrong here?

No. It was more than that.

At least I'd been right about one thing: my dad had been on this very lake in my dream. At night instead of in the morning, but I recognized it as the same place. I slid out onto the surface—with the snow on top of the ice, my boots didn't get enough traction.

My dad had been far from shore, in the middle of the lake. So that was where I headed.

Away from the shore, the wind had blown the snow away from the ice. The ice was buffed smooth, like a mirror, very slippery underfoot. I made slow progress, and my fingers got colder, but I carried on. I heard the guys wake up. I heard them arguing and knew whatever spell was on the cabin was working its worst.

I ignored them, focusing on my own quest.

I walked for ages. I was so far away that I couldn't hear the guys anymore, even with my keen *Pyr* hearing. The sun rose over the line of trees, burning a path high into the bright blue sky. I thought about the ice melting beneath my feet, but knew it was too thick for that.

It creaked, though. That was spooky. It murmured on all sides, groaning and shifting beneath the sun's touch. I was far from the shore and all alone —if I went through the ice, I'd die before anyone even guessed I was in trouble.

Still, I kept going. The shape of the trees around the shore of the lake was almost right. I was nearly at the spot, although I didn't know what I expected to find there. Where was my dad? Why did I have this sense that I'd failed him?

And that it mattered big-time.

"Zoë!" someone yelled.

I heard the beat of dragon wings and spun to scan the sky. A dark gray dragon was flying straight toward me. I had a moment to hope—my dad is onyx-and-silver in dragon form—before I saw that the proportions were wrong. My dad was bigger, leaner, more powerful than this dragon. Older.

This dragon was shadowy and insubstantial, as my dad was not.

I squinted and looked again, but realized I'd been wrong.

But he was pewter and purple.

Adrian!

He'd wanted to talk. The middle of the lake was a good choice.

I waved.

He came closer and I felt a flicker of dread. I attributed it to the long shadow of whatever haunted that cabin. He shifted shape just as his feet touched down, an elegant transition that I longed to master.

"Are you okay? I was worried about you."

"Thanks. You wanted to talk about your idea."

Adrian nodded. "You know how I said that my dad has kept himself apart from the *Pyr*?" I nodded. "Well, that's not exactly true. He's been hanging out with different *Pyr*. Actually, it's a group of different shifters. They're committed to learning more about their powers and becoming more than what they already are." He held my gaze. "That's where I met Sophie."

I was shocked. "You *met* her? When?"

"She didn't die, Zoë."

I gaped at him.

"That's just what the *Pyr* say. The truth is that they didn't appreciate her any more than they appreciate you." Adrian winced. "And when she figured it out, she left them. She made a choice to follow her own path."

My father had lied to me? But Adrian kept talking, and the more he said, the more plausible it sounded.

"She's worried about you. She said she'd been trying to send you dreams, but wasn't sure it was working. So she asked my dad to send me here."

"Why?"

"To invite you to join her. She thinks that two Wyverns will be able to change the world."

"But that's what the Wyvern is supposed to do, along with the *Pyr*."

"Those days are past. That's what she said. The Wyvern can work with the *Pyr* only if she stays apart from them. If she gets involved, well, it doesn't work out."

"What does that mean?"

"She says they betrayed her, Zoë. Because she was different, they used her to get some academy destroyed. She didn't know. The *Pyr* she loved didn't know. The other *Pyr* lied to her. They set her up and he got killed. She only barely escaped, but she decided she'd never go back."

It sounded all too plausible.

But still, my dad couldn't have lied to me.

He wouldn't have. "So maybe they're not lying now. Maybe they really don't know she's alive."

"Come on, Zoë. Can't your father feel the presence of every single *Pyr* on the planet? He knows; he's just not telling you." Adrian cleared his throat. "Just the way he hasn't told you about the other *Pyr*, the ones who chose the other path. The ones who don't report to him."

I still couldn't wrap my mind around the idea of my dad being deceptive. He tells it like it is, whether you want to hear it or not. "But..."

"Your father has his own agenda, Zoë," Adrian insisted. "It's time for you to choose yours. Come with me and talk to Sophie, at least."

"Talk to her?" It seemed like a decent offer.

A very reasonable suggestion.

Then why did I not want to go?

"You can learn the truth from her." He smiled and put out his hand. "I'll take you to her. We'll be back before the guys even notice that we were gone." He shrugged. "Unless you decide that Wyverns should stick together."

I was torn in a way that shook me. I wanted to do as he suggested, wanted to put my hand in his with all my might. Yet a little voice deep inside me was screaming, *No, no,* no.

It reminded me of what humans said about beguiling, if and when it was explained to them.

It reminded me of what Lorenzo said once about beguiling—that you can only really beguile a human into believing something he or she already wants to believe.

Or doing something that he or she really wants to do.

And I didn't want to do this.

There were no flames in Adrian's eyes.

Still, his words were making me consider a choice that I normally wouldn't make. What was going on?

I felt a shadow pass over me and shivered.

I glanced around and everything looked normal.

Until I closed my right eye.

In Granny's world, part of the sun was obscured. It looked as if someone had taken a bite out of one side of it.

No, it was the shadow of the moon falling over the sun.

The solar eclipse Rafferty had mentioned. There are times when it's good to be an attentive student, and this was one of them. (Don't tell my mom I admitted that.) I also have a thing for eclipses, given that important firestorms of the adult *Pyr* are triggered by lunar eclipses.

Call me a romantic.

There was supposed to be a solar eclipse on Monday at about noon. It wouldn't be visible in Chicago or even in Minnesota—I'd done an assignment on it a couple of months before and remembered that—but with my freaky eye, I could have been standing right beneath it.

The strange thing was that the eclipse was creeping me out, making all the little hairs on the back of my neck stand up and quiver simultaneously. And I *like* eclipses. I knew it was just the shadow of the moon blocking the sun, just a trick of location and light, but it felt like a warning. Danger was approaching.

Something snapped into focus.

Something broke.

Something lost its hold over me. I suddenly knew that what Adrian was telling me was bullshit.

Sophie was dead.

My father hadn't lied to me.

There could only be one Wyvern, and if Sophie was alive, then I wasn't the Wyvern.

But I *was* the Wyvern, which meant she was dead.

Sophie was not with some other group of *Pyr*. There was no other group of *Pyr*, because my dad would have told me.

Someone must have lied to Adrian.

Fortunately, I could set him straight.

I turned back to Adrian and what I saw silenced anything I was going to say. In fact, my mouth fell open.

Holy frick.
What *was* he?

17

Right in front of me, Adrian flickered and shifted, rotating through a bewildering number of forms.

First he was a dragon, but a ghostly one. The edges of his dragon shape were blurry and he seemed insubstantial, even with my right eye. The eclipse's light was merciless. I saw that my fleeting impression each time he'd taken dragon form—that there was something wrong with his dragon form—had been right on the money. How had he made me ignore that? I had a second to wonder, then he shifted again.

With my left eye, he was a griffin.

Then he was a unicorn.

He was a basilisk.

He was all of those things and more, changing rapidly between forms. I knew that if I blinked I'd miss at least three. Those forms, though, were substantial. How were they different from him being a dragon?

And how could he take so many shapes?

The eclipse swept away even more. Not only did I recall those moments of doubt over Adrian looking wrong, but I suddenly remembered Adrian's scent when he'd first arrived. I recalled how I had been surprised by that initial whiff of it, back when he'd pulled up beside the driveway.

And I knew with complete conviction that he wasn't *Pyr*.

I wasn't sure what the hell he was.

How had he fooled us? The flickering of his forms continued, adding a whole suite more.

He was a snake.

He was a Medusa.

He was a manticore.

He was a Harpy.

I felt like I needed to sit down and put my head between my knees. There was something deeply wrong with this.

Wicked.

Unnatural. That might sound strange coming from someone who hangs with dragon shape shifters, but trust me—his rapid shape shifting was wrong.

"You can see me," Adrian said, his surprise clear. I knew then that it would have been smarter to have hidden my reaction from him, but it was too late.

I nodded. "Whatever you are."

A minotaur.

A boar.

A Sphinx.

A different man. An older one. Which was he really?

Was he *human*?

"Maybe that makes it easier." He spoke with a smooth confidence, but this time his words didn't reassure me. They sounded oily. Manipulative. Powerful and dark.

Like the mood in the cabin.

I suddenly had the solution to the riddle. I knew then what Adrian had done. He'd cast a spell over all of us; he could enchant with the power of his voice. That was how he'd made me believe that he was *Pyr*. I could see the same glimmers of light as I'd seen in the cabin.

But they were emanating from Adrian.

He was some kind of sorcerer.

And this was an offer he didn't intend for me to refuse. He'd used deception only because the truth wasn't so pretty. I continued to watch him as he changed shape.

A deer.

A serpent.

A phoenix.

A dragon again. Again the dragon form was less real than the others, more shadowy.

Why was it different?

"Can you stop it? Or just slow it down?" I asked. I couldn't look away, but watching him shift so quickly made me want to puke. My brain couldn't deal with it. (And yes, I thought of those humans losing their minds when they witnessed our shift.)

Adrian stopped.

He was in human form, looking just like the guy I'd met at the side of the highway. I remained suspicious. His edges wavered as he surveyed me, proof that I'd nailed it in one when I'd wondered whether he was actually any of these forms.

"Thanks." I took a deep breath and concentrated on looking at him with my right eye. He was less fluid that way. "What *are* you?"

Adrian smiled, and again I was not reassured. "The future."

"I guess I don't understand."

His words flowed gently, as soothing as the current of a lazy river. That was how he cast his spell: with his voice. I recognized it now. He'd persuaded us to stay put when we would have gone after Donovan with his suggestions. He'd convinced us about his credentials—which had to be a lie—with his story. He'd tempted us to get drunk and distracted us from what we'd known we should do.

With his words.

But now the river of his spell was one that rolled right past me, leaving me on the shore. Now I could see how dirty the water was. Thanks to the light of the eclipse, the illusion was completely shattered.

I looked at Adrian with my left eye. His form was dark and a bit twisted. It wasn't real. He wasn't real. Granny was showing me the truth. I felt like I'd gotten hit in the head with a rune stone.

Adrian had deceived me.

He'd lied to my friends.

He'd probably hurt Donovan.

I had a horrible feeling he knew what had happened to Rafferty and my dad—or that he'd been a part of something nasty. He was no friend, although he'd pretended to be one.

Remember, Zoë. Just as you're more than you seem to be, so is everyone else. I heard Jared's parting words. Forewarned in this case hadn't meant forearmed.

I had no time to feel dumb. I had to fix this.

I reached inside myself and I tried to summon the shimmer. I intended to ensure that Adrian paid the price. I meant to embrace my legacy and use it for good.

The problem was that I couldn't find the shimmer.

Had he done that to me, too?

Adrian continued, trying to persuade me. "I'm where Sophie went, Zoë. This is what we can become, shifters like you and me. We can rise beyond the limitations of our innate forms and become so much more."

He was excited enough that this might be the truth. I hid my disgust and pretended to be interested. What I was really doing was trying to figure out how to get out of this situation.

Preferably alive.

Here, shimmer, shimmer...

"Tell me more."

"All the *Pyr* are doomed, except those who choose this other path. Like Sophie did. That's why they cling to you and lie to you—they're afraid."

"That makes sense. The guys have been pretty tough." I wanted him to keep talking while I kept trying to coax the shimmer to show itself.

It was better than panicking.

"Why does the world need the *Pyr*?" he asked. "The traditional role of defeating *Slayers* is fulfilled."

"But there is the Earth to defend, and the elements to guard."

Adrian snorted. "A task we can do better when we have more skills. But don't just believe me—come with me. Let Sophie tell you about it." As he spoke, I felt his words slide into my thoughts, trying to enchant me into doing what he wanted.

The very fact that he felt the need to cast a spell meant that going with him wasn't such a great option. Problem was, I really didn't know what

Adrian could do. I fingered the rune stone in my pocket, figuring it was the only weapon I had if plan A didn't work.

Here, shimmer, shimmer...

"All you have to do is take my hand," Adrian said smoothly. He reached out toward me and smiled.

In that same moment, in Granny's world, the eclipse became complete. The shadow of the moon had slipped fully over the sun. Everything was dark, except the corona of fire of the obscured sun. It was like night, but reddish in a creepy way.

Something danced over my skin like quicksilver, and I shivered as I looked down. There a glinting light moved over me—a red glow changing to a blue shimmer.

Yes! The sight thrilled me.

I followed it and felt where it had been hiding in my mind.

As if the eclipse's light showed me the way.

I felt more confident. I felt the shimmer stir and dared to believe in myself. It was mine. I was running it. I was going to shift and stay in control.

And then I'd kick Adrian's butt.

Adrian stepped closer, taking my silence for submission. "Come and talk to Sophie about the better side."

"Oh, I don't think so," I said, shoving my hands into my pockets and offering Adrian a smile. "I think I'll just stay put. But thanks for the offer."

"Oh, no," Adrian said. He became darker then, and more ominous. His form swelled larger, large enough to make me nervous. "This isn't an invitation you can refuse."

"I just did."

Adrian roared and switched to his dark dragon form with lightning speed. He lunged toward me, snatching with those silver talons, his teeth bared. Even shadowy, they were scary. My heart skipped in terror.

I would be toast.

Unless I could pull this off.

I hauled hard on that shimmer.

And I felt it come on demand.

Woo-hoo!

. . .

THE BLUE SHIMMER that heralded the shift crashed through me like a tidal wave. It was different from the red current of anger, but every bit as powerful. It was cold and cleansing, similar to a wall of water that would flood everything in its path. It ripped through me, pushing down barriers, shoving everything aside except the essence of dragon.

It felt right.

It was a part of me, not some alien beast taking control of me.

I welcomed it. It didn't need much encouragement to claim every molecule of my body, seize me heart and soul, change everything it touched.

This was my destiny.

This was my power.

And it arrived with explosive force.

Right on time.

The shift happened in a heartbeat. One second, Adrian was closing in on me fast, and I was a scrawny teenage girl, looking like lunch. He could destroy me and there'd be no witnesses.

The next second I was soaring above the lake, massive wings unfurled behind me. I was beating the air with them, soaring higher, stunned by the weight and mass of myself.

I'd done it!

I'd shifted and I was still in charge.

For one instant, Adrian simply stared. I seized the moment and I had a look myself.

I was a dragon, all right, a long, slender white one. My scales had a glitter to them, as if I had been born of the ice itself, and there were long white feathers trailing from my shoulders and tail. My talons could have been made of glass.

Not just a dragon. I knew now about the color, now that I'd seen Sophie.

I am the Wyvern.

With my left eye, under the light of the eclipse, I looked fluorescent. I glowed like those stars my mom had stuck on my bedroom ceiling roughly a zillion years ago.

But I had no time to feel triumphant. Adrian snarled; he turned and dove toward me.

And I remembered that I had no idea how to fight.

Oops.

My time as the Wyvern might be very, very short.

I shouted in old-speak, calling to the guys to help, but having zero confidence that they would do so.

Who knew what spell Adrian had laid on them before he left the cabin? I was on my own.

Maybe this was my test. I raised my talons in the traditional fighting pose. I turned to face Adrian straight on, and resolved to do my best.

Even if it wasn't going to be nearly good enough.

Any doubts I might have had about Adrian's intent didn't last long. He fell on me with force, knocking me sideways through the air with a heavy body check. My wings faltered as I lost my flying rhythm. He took advantage of that to slash at my side, cutting across my gut with four of his sharp talons.

This wasn't just fun and games. He meant to kill me.

I yelled in pain as my blood dripped onto the ice far below us.

Adrian circled around for another hit. "It doesn't have to be this way, Zoë. You could just come along quietly."

"Then what?"

"Sophie's waiting."

"Sophie's dead!"

He shook his head sadly, shifting to a flying horse. "They lied to you, Zoë."

His shift came at exactly the right time to remind me of his deceptiveness. He'd say anything to get me to go with him.

Which meant I shouldn't.

"No. You're the one lying to me."

"Stubborn." Adrian lowered his head, shifting to dragon form again, and dove toward me, breathing dragonfire. His eyes glittered, visible through the flames, and he moved like nothing I'd ever seen before.

I needed a plan.

Fast.

I yelped and lost my rhythm as I tried to fly faster. It was track day all over again, hurdles crashing on every side. For lack of a better strategy, I decided to go with incompetence.

I pretended to faint in terror and let myself fall.

It was strange, dropping through the cold air. I kept my eyes open a slit and watched the ice get ever closer. I steeled my nerve, telling myself to keep my pulse slow, not to give myself away. It was nearly impossible.

I could only hope that he didn't have *Pyr* perceptiveness.

Adrian took the bait. He came after me, altering his trajectory. He was diving fast, really fast, and that improved my chances of success.

Could it work?

Five seconds to impact. Max. I watched the ice as I felt the heat of him drawing closer.

Three. I kept my body limp.

Two. I poised to flee.

One.

In the last instant, I came to life. I flapped my wings with all my might. I turned my course, heading straight up.

It wasn't pretty but I got the job done. I faltered—no gymnast here—then shot into the sky.

Adrian missed me, his talons slicing through the air just below my tail. I flew harder when I felt the current of air as he passed me.

Adrian was so surprised that he didn't have time to turn. He slammed into the ice, smashing his shoulder into it and making it crack.

That made him shift through a couple of forms again. He skidded across the surface of the lake, rolling to his back as he tried to stop his slide, swearing all the way. I didn't dare watch. I flew straight up, my heart thundering.

Could I get far enough away from him for it to matter? I doubted it.

Talk about a primer in dragon fighting.

With the ultimate stakes.

I glanced down to see a bull stamping on the ice, breathing red smoke. He had eyes that could have been made of fire. Then he bounded into the air, shifting to a dragon again.

He shot skyward like an arrow launched from a bow.

Shit.

Adrian accelerated with an agility I could only admire, and once again targeted me. Holy frick, but he was fast. I realized he'd been *really* holding back when he'd fought with Nick.

It wasn't encouraging that even Nick hadn't managed to best him.

And Adrian hadn't been trying to kill Nick.

I raced toward the sky with no hope of outrunning him and no backup plan. Flying farther and faster for as long as possible was the best I could do.

I didn't get far enough. Adrian grabbed me from behind and bit at the tendon of my wing in one shoulder. I looked down, saw how far I could fall, and panicked.

"Bad choice, Zoë," he said softly.

I had pretty much nothing to lose at this point. I spun in his grip, then locked my tail around his. He bucked against me and nearly pulled free.

But not quite. I slashed at him with my talons, caught him across the snout, and ripped the skin from the corner of his eye to the edge of his nostril. He bellowed in pain, then belted me.

I tumbled through the sky, rolling end over end and unable to stop myself. I hit the ice and skidded across the surface. My left eye gave me a vision of bodies floating beneath the ice.

Pyr corpses.

All the *Pyr* I knew.

I'd dreamed of my dad being hurt and hadn't been able to feel the presence of the older *Pyr*—because they were in danger, too.

And I'd been too stupid to trust the instincts I'd been born with.

That was going to change.

If I survived this fight.

Adrian soared after me, pursuing me without urgency. He knew he'd won and was gloating. He settled beside me on the ice, then poked me with a talon.

"Stubborn, aren't you?" he muttered. "Such a waste. You could have ensured that at least one of the *Pyr* survived. Oh, well, you'll live on in stories, just as you always have." He shifted to a lion and bent to rip open my guts.

He planned to eat me alive.

As if.

That he didn't care whether he deceived me or turned us against one another told me everything I needed to know about his moral code and so-called vision for the future. How dared he attack us? How dared he attack me? Anger tore through me.

And I let it.

No, I channeled it and put it to work.

Fury flooded my body, giving me incredible strength. I opened my mouth and the dragonfire spewed in a torrent. It was white-hot. Way beyond orange and yellow, this stuff was fierce. The hungry flames sizzled against his chest, setting his lion fur alight. Adrian hollered in pain.

Even better, he let go of me.

He ran and I pursued him. He shifted on the fly, slipping into alternate forms in rapid succession. I had the sense he was searching for a specific one, maybe one that came in a fireproof suit, but he didn't find it.

I singed feathers. I fried fur. I burned scales and I roasted skin. I blew fire high and I blew it low. I followed him across the ice, hearing it crack, leaving pools of water behind us, taking flight when he did. No matter what he did, I kept the furnace on.

Or his toes to the fire.

Either way.

He was the one who was toast.

18

In the same moment that the guys shouted and cleared the shore, flying high in their dragon forms, the sun slipped free of the moon's shadow in the alternate dreamworld. The red tinge disappeared from the light, no matter which eye I used, and everything returned to normal.

And after one ripple of his dragon form – it rippled the way the surface of a lake ripples in the wind - Adrian looked substantial and *Pyr* once more.

It was obviously an illusion, but how did he do it?

Could the guys even see that his form was unstable at first?

Adrian smiled at me. I took that as a bad sign.

"Help me!" he screamed to the guys. "She's gone crazy. She's trying to kill me!"

"He attacked me!" I shouted. The three guys hovered in flight, keeping their distance from me. They looked good in their dragon forms, sparkling like jewels in the sunshine. Adrian appealed to them, looking more pathetic than I could believe.

That stupid orange light was hanging around the guys, as if its sparks had followed them from the cabin. This was also a bad sign.

And it became more radiant with every word Adrian said.

"Right," Adrian said with disdain. "And why would I attack the Wyvern?" He shook his head, his voice turning to that persuasive, easy tone again. The orange light brightened with every word. "I tried to help. She was stranded out here on the ice. I thought something was wrong. I came to help her back to the cabin and she went crazy on me. She could have just said no!"

"Wait a minute," Liam began to argue, but I felt their hesitation. The orange light wound around them like snakes.

"He's lying. He tried to kill me out here—"

"Look!" Adrian interrupted and whimpered. "She *burned* me."

The guys halted to consider this—and their doubt was almost tangible. But I knew who had made Garrett dream of me betraying the *Pyr* and given him the idea that I was holding out on them. I knew who had turned the guys against me, and why the cabin felt so oppressively hostile.

And I knew his voice was the strongest weapon he had against us.

"He's not *Pyr*," I argued. "He's here to destroy us...."

"You were the one who let Liam get hurt," Nick said.

"And you were the one who stole Nick's clothes in the first place," Liam added.

"Don't you care about anything but yourself?" Garrett asked me.

I could see those invisible spell lines dancing all around them, weaving into a net that would trap them.

And it was all coming from Adrian.

"I don't think she does," Adrian said. "I just tried to help."

"No! It's a spell...."

"Right. Like the story that you don't know how to take dragon form." Nick shook his head. "Looks like you've nailed it pretty well."

"She can't even tell us the truth," Adrian said. "It's like we're her enemies, not her friends."

I saw their expressions harden and knew his charm was working.

"Yesterday was the first time...."

"Enough lies, Zoë," Garrett said.

"Yet you were thumping Adrian the first time you ever fought?" Nick challenged.

"When Nick couldn't touch him?" Garrett shook his head in disbelief. "We're not stupid, Zoë."

"Maybe we're better off without a Wyvern, if she isn't going to play on our team," Adrian said, his tone sly. "Maybe we shouldn't have anyone on the team we can't trust."

"But..." Liam said.

"Adrian is casting a spell," I argued. "He's turning us against one another."

"No. You're the one trying to turn us all against one another." Adrian said, so soft and persuasive. "Why?"

"I'm not the bad guy here!"

"All I did was try to bring her back to the cabin," Adrian said to the guys. "All I did was try to help her."

"You were trying to kill me!" I shouted. I saw the orange sparks get brighter, gathering more tightly around Garrett and Nick, and knew I was in deep trouble.

"Maybe we should just talk about it," Liam suggested.

"I think we've heard enough," Nick said, preparing to face off against me.

"*Now,*" Garrett commanded in old-speak.

"No! You liar!" I would have screamed a lot more at Adrian, but Garrett came after me in a frenzy. His talons were extended and he was closing in fast.

Garrett launched a torrent of dragonfire as he dove. His eyes gleamed with malice and I saw that the spell light was completely surrounding him.

Holding him in its thrall.

Making him want to hurt me.

And neither Nick nor Liam was going to stop him.

Holy shit.

I flew straight at Garrett, though. I snatched at his claws, wanting to get this part over with. (I told you about the perils of arm wrestling with Garrett.)

We locked talons in the traditional fighting pose, wrestling and thrashing furiously. I ripped free of Garrett's grip as quickly as possible, although I knew I'd be sore for a while. I went for his back, wrapping myself around his wings and upper arms. I wouldn't be able to hold him, but maybe he'd lose altitude.

He did.

I saw the light of the spell winding around us, binding us both. It made me dizzy, polluting my mind with Adrian's hatred.

It made Garrett seethe.

And gave him new strength. He spun suddenly and belted me. I managed to duck the worst of the blow. I snapped at him, livid at what the spell was making him do. Something in my eyes made him back away. I chased him, breathing fire and lashing my tail.

"We should help her," I heard Liam say.

"Let them work it out," Adrian said to him in that oily and persuasive tone. I sensed the guys struggling against this argument.

Before they accepted it.

The next thing I knew Garrett pivoted abruptly, launching a volley of blows that I was hard-pressed to block. He was all over me, and all I could do was duck and flinch. I definitely had made a mistake in not being more enthused about gym class.

Then Garrett caught me right on the temple. I spun in pain, trying even so to keep myself aloft. Before I hit the ice, he caught me from behind in a tight bear hug, one that I feared I'd never escape.

He started to squeeze the life out of me.

Then I felt him take a deep breath. He was going to turn his dragonfire on me.

Shit.

I squeezed my eyes shut and wished with all my heart that I were anywhere in the world other than where I was right then.

The incredible thing was that my wish came true.

I FELT DIFFERENT.

Different from when I was filled with the blue shimmer of shape shifting or even with red rage. I felt neutral—cool as a cucumber, my mom would say—and that was a relief. I still had four long, bleeding wounds on my abdomen and they hurt more than ever. As a bonus, I was nauseated and dizzy.

And freezing.

But I wasn't over the lake anymore. And I wasn't getting cooked by

Garrett's dragonfire. I was in the snow. It was cold. And judging by the size of the trees surrounding me, I wasn't a dragon anymore either.

Either that, or I'd ended up in some magical forest.

(Which wasn't out of the question.)

I also felt like I was really going to puke.

I kept my eyes closed until that wave of nausea passed, then had a look at myself. I was as white as milk. My skin was smooth, not scaled. I had webbed feet and an undeniable compulsion to flick my tongue.

I was a salamander.

Okay, I knew this was another form that the Wyvern could take, and while it was fab that I could do this too, it would have been much more helpful if I had any clue as to *how* I had done it.

Never mind how to change back to my own self.

Where in the world I had ended up would have been a useful detail, too.

I glanced around and realized that I wasn't in the forest exactly, but in the middle of a clearing. A long, narrow clearing. With two trenches worked into the snow, one of which I was sitting in. Yes, the snow was packed down into distinctive patterns. I wasn't used to seeing tire treads as wide as I was tall....

I did the math, just as a car appeared. It wasn't going that fast in the snow, but those tires looked as if they would squish me before I could get away.

I squeaked.

I leapt out of the trench o' death.

And I sank way down into the snow. It didn't matter how much I scrambled and struggled. My efforts just made me sink down, down, down. I'd never get out of here.

Well, maybe when the snow melted.

If I survived that long.

The car stopped right beside me. I could see the gleaming blue paint.

Nick's car was that color.

This was not good. Nick wanted to kill me because of Adrian's spell. I panicked. I fought to dig a tunnel through the snow. Maybe I could disappear—white on white—if I could just put some distance between us.

I didn't get far before someone snatched me up.

I squeaked and squirmed.

"Hi, Zoë."

Isabelle. It would be an understatement to say I was shocked. She knew it was me.

How?

Why?

How had she known where I was?

"I *knew* I'd find you up here," she said quietly. "I had a premonition, and I had to follow it. And here you are, but hurt!" She wrinkled her nose. "I bet you feel awful, too."

She didn't seem to be talking about my wounds. I tried to speak and was a bit surprised when it worked. "Why?"

"Rafferty says moving through space makes him feel terrible. Nauseous and dizzy. You need something to eat and to drink; plus you need that bleeding stopped."

"But the guys are trying to kill me!"

A fierce light dawned in her eyes. "They'll have to get past me first. Come on."

I decided I was going to have to like Isabelle, after all.

She got back into the car and held me in her lap. She unwrapped the end of a granola bar and I had a bite; then she dabbed at my wounds with a tissue. "They look like surface cuts."

"They hurt."

"I'll bet. There's a first-aid kit in the glove box." She put me on the passenger seat and eyed me. "You'll have to shift back to human form. I can't bandage a salamander."

That made sense.

If I could just do it.

"I won't look," she said. She put on her seat belt, then put the car into gear again. We started to roll slowly along the road, and I realized the cant was uphill.

She was leaving the cabin.

"I don't suppose you know how to drive," she said. "I mean, I do, but everything is backward. In this snow, it would be good to have a driver who wasn't distracted by the gearshift being on the wrong side."

I closed my eyes, looked for that sweet spot in my thoughts, and hoped like heck I could shift.

I did. It took a bit to take hold, long enough for me to despair; then it happened really fast.

In fact, I changed so fast that I didn't have time to think about position. As a salamander, I'd been lying on the seat—in human form I was in exactly the same pose, but my forehead banged on the door to the glove compartment and my legs were all folded up in a strange yoga posture.

"That was graceful," I muttered as I swung myself around.

"Well, you did it. That's good." Isabelle flashed me a smile. She pointed to the glove compartment and I got out the first-aid kit. I pulled up my shirt and wrapped some gauze over my cuts. They'd mostly stopped bleeding. Isabelle handed me the rest of the granola bar.

"You should drink some water, too." She gestured to her purse in the back and I found a new bottle of water there.

I did as she instructed and felt roughly 10,645 times better.

Give or take.

"I drew a card this morning," she said, frowning at the road. "THE HANGED MAN."

"Sounds optimistic."

She half laughed. "It's not good. I knew it was a sign that I should leave, somehow; then I could see the two of us leaving together. I had the strongest sense before I left the cabin that I'd find you on this road. Maybe that made me watch extra carefully, but when I saw a white salamander, I knew it had to be you."

"Not a lot of newts out in the snow."

She laughed for real then. "No. Especially not any that shimmer blue as they appear. I'd have missed you without that light. Feel better?"

"Yes, thanks. I'm glad you were here." I meant it, too. I smiled at her. "I'd have been a newtsicle otherwise."

She laughed at my joke, even though it was lame, and I found myself smiling even more. I liked her.

In fact, maybe I needed her help.

Because the sad fact was that I'd not listened to Isabelle, or paid attention to my dreams in which she featured, simply out of jealousy. (I tell you, Granny is one tough cookie—when she pulls aside the veil, she really goes for it. That solar eclipse had left me with buckets of revelations.) I had been petty and unfriendly. With my impatience to be Wyvern, I'd set something in motion that had worked against all of us.

And by my own logic—*Pyr* plus human equals mating—Nick was out-of-bounds to me anyhow. We could never be more than friends. Or at least, we could never be in a romantic relationship and have anything come of it.

That had been the last Wyvern's mistake, and it would have been really stupid for me to make the same one all over again.

I suddenly remembered one bit of my dream.

The present is where the past shakes hands with the future.

And I'd shaken hands with not just Sophie, but Isabelle, too. So we should be allies. I was good with that. I surrendered to Granny's wisdom and insight.

Like Jared said, I'd been the one doubting my powers.

I believed now. I'd shifted. I'd moved through space. I'd even taken shape as a salamander. I was stepping into my destiny. All I had to do was survive Adrian and break the spell he had over the guys.

Then figure out how to save our dads, whatever had happened to them.

No pressure, right?

Before I could ask for Isabelle's help with all of the above, I heard the low thrum of a motorcycle engine.

It was coming closer.

I don't know beans about motorcycles, but I would have bet you my Wyvern powers that it was a vintage Ducati.

Being ridden by an urban pirate.

Oh, yes.

My luck was turning. Big-time.

"Can we go any faster?" I was even leaning forward.

"Not without visiting the ditch."

I flung open the door of the car and jumped out into the snow.

"Where are you going? What's wrong?" I knew the moment that Isabelle heard the bike, too. "Oh!" she said, and coaxed the car to go a bit faster.

On foot, I was still faster than she was. And impatient, too. I wanted to see Jared, and I wanted to see him now.

If not sooner.

Isabelle kept driving behind me, but there could have been wings on my feet.

Suddenly, the bike engine stopped.

No! He couldn't leave!

I ran faster, determined to change his mind.

Then I heard the steady crunch of footsteps in the snow, along with the sound of a bike being rolled.

Closer.

Right. Jared had said there was too much snow for the bike. He wouldn't leave it behind on the road, but the obstacle wasn't going to stop him either.

What was not to love about that?

I raced around the curve in the road and skidded to a halt. It was Jared. And he was here. Against the odds.

He didn't just look dangerous and sexy.

He looked uncomfortable.

If his face hadn't lit at the sight of me, I would have been a lot more worried than I was. As it was, he glanced away and frowned, then pointed a finger at me. "Look. I couldn't just leave you here. Not with that guy."

Meanwhile, Isabelle stopped the car behind me and got out. Eavesdropping shamelessly. I was really starting to like her.

Jared continued, his tone defensive. (As if I would have issues with his presence. Right.) "He might look okay, but he's trouble, and he has bad intentions toward you—"

"She knows," Isabelle interrupted in that chirpy British way of hers.

Jared blinked. "Excuse me?"

I strode toward him as I explained. "He just tried to kill me, and now he's set the guys on me. Actually, that's what he's been doing all along. He's made a spell. He's not *Pyr*, even though he seems like it."

"Then what is he?" Isabelle asked.

"A Mage," Jared said with conviction. "They're spellcasters, intent on taking control of everything."

That made sense.

"He's been casting a spell since we got here," I said. "Turning the guys against me, keeping us here. He showed himself when I refused to go with him." I shuddered, feeling Jared watching me.

His lips tightened. "Never believe those guys." His tone was bitter. "They change the deal after they have you powerless." Then he studied me, as if trying to confirm that I was okay.

I liked that a lot.

So, of course, I blushed. And I had to change the subject. "How do you know about Mages?"

"They've been trying to recruit me for years." He frowned. "They recruit humans who have a natural ability to cast spells, take them as apprentices and train them. I knew what he was right away, but I'd promised Donovan that I'd leave you here."

I understood. "And you can't break a promise to Donovan."

"I tried to think it was part of Donovan's plan." Jared shook his head. "I tried to do what I'd promised. I went to Sioux City. But it drove me nuts. I called Donovan, but he didn't answer his phone. I finally drove back to Minneapolis, but Alex said there'd been no sign of him. That's when I got worried."

"My dad?"

"Alex called him, but your mom said he'd disappeared, too." He swallowed, as Isabelle and I exchanged worried glances. "They can't find any of the *Pyr*, which meant I had to get back here and find out what was going on."

I couldn't help thinking of all the blood in my dreams.

"You wanted to check on Zoë anyhow," Isabelle said, and Jared shot her a look. My heart skipped a beat at his expression. He had been worried about me.

"Got a problem with that?" Jared said, and Isabelle held up her hands in mock surrender. Then she winked at me. I blushed more and Jared pretended not to notice. He made a sound of frustration. "You can't call anybody in this place."

"We're off the map," I said. "Here be dragons and all that."

"Not funny, Zoë." Jared was stern. "The *Pyr* are in trouble."

"I know, but I can't find them either. At the library was the only time I was able to sense the other *Pyr*." I had a sudden realization. "No, I felt for them on this road, when I was with Adrian. And the connection was broken right then."

"By him." Jared grimaced. "I should never have left."

"His spell was meant to keep us all here," Isabelle said.

"And distracted." I was thinking about pizza and beer, about the way Adrian had turned the decision to staying put instead of seeking Donovan. We'd been duped.

I was afraid of what the price of that might be.

"Which means whatever has happened to the other *Pyr* required all of you to be out of the picture for a while." Jared was grim.

I felt more grim.

I heard dragon wings.

Shit.

"Here they come," I said, scanning the sky. I knew the two humans with me wouldn't hear the sound just yet. "They must have heard me."

"How are we going to break Adrian's spell before Zoë gets hurt?" Isabelle asked. She clutched my hand and I felt her fear.

"Hold the bike," Jared said with determination. "This is what I do."

Excuse me?

19

You know, I'd never considered myself to be a damsel in distress, much less one in need of a rescue—having a mom who calls herself a rabid feminist will do that for you. On the other hand, Jared's protectiveness was working for me in a big way.

It was sexy.

Plus, there had to be some reason why the Mages wanted to recruit him. I didn't know much about spells or spellcasting or whatever magic Adrian could do. But I'd seen its effects, and I knew enough to be worried.

Even though I knew that Adrian's spell wasn't a whole lot different from beguiling, what spooked me was that he had made two of my three best friends believe not just that they should hate my guts, but that they should try to kill me.

Whatever he was tossing out there, it was powerful stuff.

So, while I was scared crapless of dragons shredding me alive, I was afraid for Jared, too. He hadn't signed up for the Mages' advanced spell-casting program, which meant he might not know all the tricks he needed to win.

All of this ensured that the withdraw-with-smelling-salts-and-await-the-outcome option was out of the question.

Since I wanted to live with myself after this day.

"Hide," Isabelle suggested to me in an undertone. Jared was staring at the sky, preparing to do...something.

But hiding was the damsel choice, and I was a dragon.

I reached into my mind for the blue shimmer and gave it a poke. It was easier to find now that I knew where it lived. The shimmer danced over my flesh, much as I would imagine it felt to shower in minty mouthwash. I felt alive and tingly, as if I were stepping into my destiny.

And I was.

I summoned that cool blue tide and coaxed it to greater power. I held on to it better this time, keeping control a little bit longer, before it swept through me with a vengeance. The wave crashed through me and over me, inundating me with its power. I barely had time to fold my clothes away and hide them beneath my scales.

Isabelle and Jared, fortunately, weren't watching me. They were staring at the sky.

I stretched my wings and roared, excited to be getting the hang of this. I was a white dragon again and right on time.

Isabelle jumped as I launched into the sky, savoring the power in my wings. I caught a glimpse of Jared's proud smile, had an instant to enjoy it; then the guys came screaming over the tops of the trees, their scales gleaming in the sun. They moved at incredible speed, driven by fury and bloodlust.

Snared in a nasty spell.

One that had gotten meaner. With my left eye, I could see the radiance of it, and the places where it burned hotter.

Like before, it was brightest around Garrett, then around Nick. Like shooting sparks. Liam was fending it off somehow. We'd have to figure out how and why later. Adrian was sending out more magic threads, feeding the spell.

I flew higher, moving out in front of the two humans I'd go down defending. I saw Jared moving his hands, as if he were making a snowball. But there was nothing in his hands.

No, wait. With my left eye I could see a jumble of light in his hand. Purple and green lightning, dancing together, being bent into a sphere. And I could hear him humming, just barely.

And as he hummed, the light grew brighter. He was conjuring something, and he needed time.

Time I was going to give him.

The guys flew lower.

They extended their talons.

Four against one.

No pressure.

I took a deep breath and lifted my claws in the traditional fighting pose, as ready as I'd ever be. My heart was thundering in terror.

I hovered over Jared and Isabelle, shielding them. I couldn't rely on the guys to remember our mission to defend humans, not when they were under the influence of Adrian's spell.

Not when he'd made them forget so much else.

"Traitor!" Nick cried, and spiraled toward me. I noticed the gleam of his scales, the power of his flight, the angry glow in his eyes.

But that anger wasn't really Nick's. It was the result of Adrian's spell.

I breathed a stream of fire, challenging him. The plume of flame flicked brilliantly in the cold air and I saw Nick's surprise. He'd expected me to back off.

He could get ready for another surprise or two.

It's traditional to trade taunts, and he took the initiative.

"*You can't win,*" he taunted in old-speak. "*Surrender the fight now.*"

"*In your dreams,*" I retorted. "*You're just afraid you'll lose to a girl.*"

His eyes flashed like molten gold and he lunged at me.

Yikes.

"Wait!" Liam cried. "Isabelle's here!"

"I'm not going to hurt Isabelle," Nick snarled, just as he locked talons with me, some twenty feet over Jared's head.

Nick wasn't just joking around either—he hit me like a brick wall. The force of the collision sent us end over end. We locked all four claws, our tails lashing as we tumbled through the air. It was all teeth and talon and fire. I was fighting for my life.

"Don't hurt Zoë," Liam cried, launching himself at Nick. Garrett snarled and attacked Liam, the pair of them wrestling.

Jared kept humming that strange tune.

Just before we hit a tree, I ducked and pushed back against Nick's grip.

He stumbled in surprise and I seized the moment. I struck him with my tail and raged fire at him for his stupidity.

"I'm on your side, you moron!"

"As if!" He came after me again. We wrestled through the sky, biting and scratching and striking. It wasn't a pretty fight, and we were both getting a lot of minor injuries. I could hear grunts as Liam and Garrett fought, too.

This wasn't right!

"Adrian's cast a spell!" I shouted at them in old-speak. *"Don't listen to it!"*

Nick snarled. *"Adrian's the one on our side."*

"Idiot!" I thwacked Nick across the face with my tail and snapped at him. I didn't really want to hurt him. Nick backed away, but clearly didn't have the same urge to play nice—he was aiming to take me down.

He was also ready to play dirty. He drove his shoulder into those cuts on my stomach and I faltered in pain.

"Nick!" Isabelle shouted in dismay. "Don't hurt Zoë."

"It's her or us." Nick breathed fire, then shot after me again. I spun at the last minute to backhand him, anger giving me strength. I slammed him in the cojones with my tail at the same time that I punched him under the chin.

Then he was the one reeling in pain.

His eyes gleamed and I knew he'd make me pay for that. I blew a long torrent of dragonfire after him, proud of myself for its sheer quantity. I was hoping to keep him at a distance, knowing it was a long shot.

All the while, I heard Jared's humming, rising beneath my wings like a tangible force. When I glanced down at him, Adrian gasped.

"What are *you* doing here?" Adrian sounded surprised, maybe a bit worried. Nick fell on me heavily, wrapping himself around me in a wrestler's clinch. I couldn't look at Adrian. I was busy trying to breathe.

"You must have missed me," Jared said, his voice all melodic and soothing. I looked down to see him smiling with a strange serenity.

I caught a bit of his mood, though, as I listened to that humming. I felt calmer. I breathed more slowly. It was as if a cool breeze had blown in from the ocean, pushing away dark clouds and stale air. I felt invigorated. Clean.

And Nick's grip loosened enough for me to wriggle free. I quickly put some distance between us.

Liam and Garrett stopped fighting.

What was going on? All three guys were staring at Jared.

Hovering in the air, their leathery wings beating.

"I wanted to catch up, hear your news," Jared continued in that same singsong voice. "How is the Mage plan for world domination coming along? Still looking for recruits stupid enough to sign on?"

"What are you talking about?" Garrett looked between Adrian and Jared in confusion.

Whatever Jared was doing was working.

How could I help him?

"You know each other?" Nick sounded sleepy, as if he were awakening from a dream.

Or a nightmare.

"He's lying." The darkness grew with every word Adrian uttered. "We only met on the road the other day. He's trying to trick you. Don't be fooled!"

I guessed and closed my right eye. I could see the shadow of that dark spell roiling like thunderheads, pushing back against the clean wind, snapping with orange light. A battle was beginning—one for the hearts and minds of these three *Pyr*.

I could see the effect of Adrian's words upon the guys. I found his argument a little bit persuasive myself, even though I knew it wasn't true.

"What's a Mage?" Liam asked.

"A liar!" Isabelle shouted. "Someone who pretends to be a friend but isn't. Adrian's not *Pyr*, and it's his fault that everyone has been fighting. He enchanted us in that cabin."

"He was supposed to keep us busy while our dads were in danger." I noticed that all three guys started at that news.

"Don't be ridiculous. I'm trying to save you," Adrian said in that soothing tone. Shadows multiplied all around us, at least in my left-eye view. "You've been deceived. I was the one trying to fix things. I was trying to continue in the spirit of boot camp...."

The dark cloud grew with every word he uttered.

"I was following Donovan's rules for boot camp, learning new skills and helping others," Adrian continued. "I played for the team—unlike one of us."

With my left eye, I saw his words foster the doubts within the guys, turn their minds against what they knew to be the truth, and gather like a storm.

Not just any storm.

A storm with a precise target.

Yours truly.

"But which team?" Jared shouted. "You were keeping them busy while the Mages destroyed the *Pyr*!"

"No!" Adrian cried, insulted.

"Yes!" Jared roared. He gestured then, as if he were throwing a baseball. That ball of brilliant light flew into the air and exploded amid the guys.

I'm not sure they could see it, but even through the bright flames of dragonfire I could—with my left eye. In fact, I think it burned my retina. The released sparks of blue and green shot out in all directions, making Adrian cower.

Jared sang with vigor. It was the same tune he'd hummed, but now it had words. Words in another language, words that I didn't understand. It sounded old. Powerful.

And the words seemed to guide those waves of light. They moved in straight lines, changing direction at the command of Jared's song.

The Mages had wanted him because he was a spellcaster, too. It must come naturally, like being *Pyr*.

I was in awe of his abilities.

The battle had moved to new ground.

Jared's song was like the sun breaking through the clouds. I understood that it was shattering the hold of Adrian's spell, burning it away, maybe. The guys stared at the light he directed, the anger fading from their eyes.

"Get her! Get him!" Adrian cried, to no avail.

Maybe spellcasting *was* like beguiling. Maybe what a person wanted to believe took precedence, or let them choose which spell to heed.

When they had a choice.

I felt a wind again, a steady, cool wind that pushed back the clouds. With my left eye, I saw Jared's song in the air. I saw the sound morph into new beams of light, sine waves of light, sound waves that changed their frequency based on the rhythm of his song.

It was Jared's battle cry, a song launched into the air to attack, becoming more demanding with every bar. The geek in me adored the eye candy. Purple and green and electric blue.

Adrian retreated, proof that he could see or sense them, too.

Liam was closest to Jared, and a beam struck him right in the heart. He lost his flying rhythm for a second, like he had stuck his finger in an electrical socket. His shocked expression said it all.

Then Liam turned on Adrian, scowling at him. "Liar!" he cried, and breathed fire. "You tried to make us destroy our Wyvern!"

"Jared's trying to bewitch you! He's dividing you!" I heard desperation in Adrian's tone. He continued to create shadows and dark clouds. "Close your ears. Don't listen. You'll all be forced to act against your will."

His words weren't as compelling to Liam as they once had been. Even Adrian seemed smaller and more insubstantial than he had. And his dragon form was rippling, like a flag in the wind.

"He made you guys target Zoë," Isabelle said. "He tried to recruit her; then he wanted to kill her."

"It's part of a plan to eliminate the *Pyr*," I added.

"So he wanted us to do the dirty work for him." Liam breathed a stream of fire at Adrian, who yelped. "He wants to destroy our Wyvern."

"No," Garrett said. "It was Zoë who didn't support us."

"She's the one betraying us," Nick agreed.

"And she's still doing it!" Adrian shouted. "Can't you see that Zoë is fighting back in her own way? She can't even do it herself. She has to use a human sorcerer to persuade you. Doesn't that say it all?"

I worried that Adrian might convince them, but Jared's next beam of light struck Nick in the chest. Nick fell back, shocked, but I knew from the look on his face when he eyed Adrian that the spell over him had been shattered, too.

"Adrian is the one who got us drunk," Nick said, hostility in his tone.

"So you wouldn't leave the cabin," Isabelle agreed. "Adrian's the one who stopped you all every time you talked about trying to help the *Pyr*."

"No," Garrett insisted. "What's wrong with you guys?" He turned on me and I knew he was going to attack.

Again.

"You're still enchanted," Nick said, putting himself between Garrett and me. They began to wrestle, Nick trying to stop Garrett from coming after me. "Give it up!"

"We're going to lose this chance!" Garrett cried.

"That story about Adrian's father was all a lie." Liam was disgusted. "And we believed it."

"This is the lie!" Adrian insisted, mustering his spell and focusing on Garrett. Nick and Garrett fought hard, Garrett decking Nick. Nick fell back and I had a moment to be afraid.

When I looked into the burning anger in the eyes of the next Smith.

"Remove the traitor," Adrian hissed, and Garrett lunged for me.

Uh-oh.

Liam and Nick snatched at Garrett, but he was too fast and evaded them. There was no one between us. I lifted my talons, knowing I'd lose this battle but determined to go down fighting.

Jared kept singing, and a third beam hit Garrett when he was just a couple of yards away from me.

The tension rolled out of him as if his body were relieved to be freed from the spell. He fell toward the ground, limp like a rag doll.

"Wait! Don't be tricked!" Adrian cried. "Move now, while you can."

Garrett flapped his wings. He straightened, lifting his head proudly. He exhaled a puff of smoke and his scales glittered as he turned his gaze slowly....

On Adrian.

I saw Adrian swallow. I heard the leap of his pulse. And I saw the terror in his eyes.

"We already were tricked." Garrett's words were low and hot. "And now you will pay for what you have done." He pointed at Adrian and the three *Pyr* targeted the impostor. They lunged toward him even as he tried to flee.

Jared's spell was faster. The light beams raced ahead of the guys and struck Adrian like barbs. Or arrows. One after another after another fell on him and he couldn't flee. He was in that much pain, which worked for me.

I watched, enthralled, as Jared's song changed.

With the change in beat, Jared's light beams were transformed, too.

They became long, like ropes, or maybe serpents. I was sure I saw a forked tongue or two. They rippled through the air with a definite purpose. He raised his voice, and they convened on Adrian.

Adrian tried to sing and fend off the spell, but he clearly couldn't do both. The spell waves wound around Adrian, binding him from head to toe in a brilliant net of blue and green and purple. He shifted shapes in rapid succession, just as he had before me, and I felt the astonishment of Isabelle and the *Pyr*.

He was a bull, a mermaid, a unicorn, a monkey....

Jared sang louder and louder. I could see the sweat on his forehead, but he didn't give it up. His hands were clenched into fists, his voice strong and deep. Rich. The bonds of light kept getting tighter around Adrian, despite how he struggled. In moments, they were so close together that he had become a wriggling bundle of light.

Adrian roared in agony, or maybe in pain.

Jared stopped his song.

And Adrian fell to the ground.

The spell was complete. I couldn't see the light anymore, not with either eye. Adrian was rolling around on the ground, helpless. Well, he was swearing as he writhed.

I shifted shape, unfolding my clothes with greater dexterity than before. I was getting in the groove of this shape shifting stuff.

And it felt good to be just a skinny chick again.

Jared strode toward Adrian, every line of his body filled with purpose. He looked as if he were going to throttle his opponent.

Adrian glared at Jared. "I won't tell you anything."

Jared smiled, looking as hungry and unpredictable as a dragon. "We'll see."

Just as Jared reached for Adrian, a brilliant bolt of orange light fell out of the sky. It was like lightning, but the wrong color.

And it struck Adrian, flashing brilliantly as it slapped him across the face. He screamed.

When the light faded, Adrian was gone.

Jared stared at the sky, shook his head, then came to my side. He looked exhausted, as if he'd just performed a concert, his hair all wet at his temples. But those green eyes were locked on me, filled with a concern that made my belly do flip-flops.

"You okay?" he asked, his voice low.

"I'll be fine." I swallowed, his intensity making me nervous. "Did you send him away?"

Jared looked displeased. "No. Someone collected him."

"Probably to make sure he didn't talk."

He nodded and I knew he was irritated. Then he flicked a quick smile at me, his eyes warm. "Thanks for giving me cover, dragon girl."

I felt that blush again, but it was okay. "Thanks for breaking the spell." We stared at each other for a long moment, one that left me all tingly and warm.

I wanted to kiss him. Or I wanted him to kiss me.

But had he come back for me or the *Pyr*?

He was a major dragon fan, but I wanted him to be a Wyvern fan.

There was no good way to ask, not without sounding needy, and I wasn't going there. I gestured to the place Adrian had been. "What did you do there?"

"A binding spell, after the counterspell." He shoved a hand through his hair. "I've never done two back-to-back before." His quick conspiratorial smile made my heart leap one more time. "Guess I just needed the right motivation."

"Thanks."

"Least I could do, after screwing up."

"Did you recognize him the other day?"

Jared shook his head. "I don't know Adrian. But I did recognize what he was." He grimaced. "I should never have left, no matter what Donovan had said. I didn't want to mess with his plans for boot camp, but I should have trusted my instincts."

"Someone gave me that advice a while ago. It's good."

"Yeah. I guess it is." Jared grinned. Then he reached out and took my hand, giving my fingers a tight squeeze.

It felt really good.

Like coming home.

You know what I was thinking? *Pyr* plus human equals a good pairing. Could Jared, the hottest guy I'd ever known, really be the one for me?

I had to hope.

20

I squeezed Jared's hand, my throat all tight, and once again had nothing clever to say.

"We should take care of your wounds." Isabelle joined us, her hand clasped in Nick's. He'd already shifted shape and looked a lot less cocky than usual. I glanced at him and he averted his gaze, the back of his neck turning red.

"I'll heal," I said to Isabelle, as if I were a bold, confident chick who survived dragon fights all the time. No biggie. *Uh-huh*. "And we've got more important things to do."

"You okay?" Liam asked as he landed on my other side. He shifted quickly, concern in his eyes.

"All good, Carrots. Thanks for holding fast."

He grinned and squeezed my shoulder. "I didn't do anything on purpose."

"Maybe it's an affinity thing," I suggested.

"Hey, Zoë," Nick said. I was sure I'd never seen him shuffle his feet like that. "I'm really sorry."

"Too bad we didn't get to see you lose to a girl," I teased, and he shoved a hand through his hair, not smiling.

"I'm not sure it would have shaken out that way." He sighed. "You did come on hard, Zoë. Good job."

I returned his smile. "I'm just glad Jared got here before you served me up medium-rare."

"I made a big mistake...."

Isabelle squeezed Nick's hand. "You couldn't help it."

"But I was wrong. Zoë could have been really hurt."

There wasn't much anyone could say to that.

Garrett landed then and shifted shape with that grace I so envied. (Practice makes perfect, right?) Without missing a beat, he dropped to one knee in front of me, his head bowed. "Forgive me, Wyvern," he said, his voice thick.

And the others seemed to hold their breath. I felt like a queen, her court waiting as she judged a wrongdoer. I knew they'd support whatever I decided.

It was kind of weird to feel so influential.

But I was the Wyvern. I knew that.

I had to do this right.

The fact was that Garrett had doubted me. He had challenged me. He had burned me. He had broken the most basic rule in the *Pyr* book by trying to do me injury.

But he had been enchanted, as well, and it had been one powerful spell. I certainly couldn't have guaranteed that I would have acted any differently.

I had to forgive him.

Jared's lips tightened and I saw his nostrils flare as he glanced at me. He wasn't in agreement with me.

Again, I was startled that he knew what I was thinking before I said anything. How did he do that?

"You were under the influence of an evil spell," I said to Garrett, my confidence growing as I spoke. "I can't hold that against you, because you didn't choose it. I made mistakes, too." I held tightly to Jared's hand, liking that his grip was sure even though he disagreed with me. I felt like we could be a team. "I owe all of you an apology for not trying harder to master my powers."

The guys protested, Nick and Liam closing in for a group hug even as I tugged Garrett to his feet.

"You couldn't have known, Zoë," Nick said.

"I still think that I made the bigger mistake," Garrett said.

"It's not your fault, Zoë," Liam said.

"Friends?" Isabelle offered with a smile. I nodded and smiled back. It might have been a big, shiny, happy moment, but Jared cleared his throat.

"Actually, it *is* Zoë's fault, in a way."

"How so?" Nick bristled.

"A spellcaster has to find something to work with, a bit of resentment or anger or jealousy, in order to work a dark spell like this one." Jared shrugged, but he didn't let go of my hand. "You need a hook for your bait."

"So I let him in," I said, realizing the full import of my jealousy of Isabelle.

Jared nodded. "In more ways than one."

I had an idea then who had really sent me that song.

Jared didn't even listen to all of the song before he pulled my ear buds out of his ears with disgust. "It's a jealousy spell," he said. "A nasty one."

"I didn't send it to you," Nick insisted, but I knew that already.

"We have to trust one another from this point onward," Garrett said, and we all nodded. "Airing doubts is the only way they get resolved."

"Air!" Nick said. "Wasn't that supposed to be our lesson this year? That's communication."

"And spells," I said.

"Dreams," Jared noted, which made me think.

"But Donovan didn't set this up," Isabelle argued.

"I think all of the older *Pyr* are in trouble," I told them. "Adrian was supposed to keep us busy while they were captured. Then he was trying to draw me in, too."

"But what happened to Adrian?" Nick demanded.

"He's not working alone," Jared said. "Someone summoned him with a spell, someone a lot stronger than Adrian is."

That didn't bode well for us.

"Someone who didn't want us to learn anything from him." Garrett nodded. "How can we help our dads if we don't know where they are?"

Everyone turned to look at me.

I looked at Jared. "What do the Mages want?"

"To use the world as their plaything. To be rich and powerful, to do what they want without answering to anybody." Jared grimaced. "They don't care who they destroy, not on the way to getting more for themselves."

"That's why you didn't join them?" I had to ask.

He smiled. "Right. Not my style."

"What changed?" Nick asked. "We've been hearing all our lives that they're no real threat."

"Maybe they've added to their powers," Jared said.

"But how?" Liam asked.

I remembered all the forms Adrian had taken and guessed. "Shape shifters. It's got something to do with shape shifters."

"The guy we both saw in that dream had a wing where his arm should have been," Isabelle said. "I think you're right, Zoë. He was a shape shifter in trouble. He was looking for help from you."

Jared smiled at me. "And what do we know about the Wyvern and dreams?"

"I can't control them, not yet."

He gave me a look and didn't have to say anything.

It was time to try.

I reached into my pocket and pulled out the rune stone. That guy on the tree—Kohana—had something to do with the red ridge of rock. I ran through all the clues again, trying to find which piece of the puzzle I'd missed.

I found an unexpected one.

"Wait a minute," I said. "If Adrian basically crashed the party, why was there an envelope addressed to him?"

"Do you still have the envelopes?" Jared asked. "Because I'll bet that it *wasn't* addressed to him."

"His name was written in my dad's handwriting."

"No. It was probably a glamour." Jared headed toward his bike, giving my hand a tug so that I followed him.

I did.

Like we were together.

"A glamour?" Garrett echoed.

"It's a spell," Isabelle said. "One that makes a thing look like something it's not. Like fairies leaving coins at night, coins that turn out to be just leaves the next day."

I had a thought. "Is that how he managed to look like a dragon?"

Jared nodded. "It was another glamour. An illusion. Didn't you see how it wavered when he was under duress?"

I nodded. "He just couldn't do everything."

"Right," Jared agreed.

Isabelle pointed to the cabin. "Let's see if Jared is right about the envelopes, too." The others went with her, talking to one another with excitement. I liked that we had our familiar rhythm back.

I really liked that Jared was holding my hand. That he'd come back to help me. That he was a spellcaster and one who wanted to use his abilities for good. Our shoulders bumped as we walked. My heart was doing the skippity-bip and I could have danced on starlight. Which meant, of course, that I had nothing clever to say.

"I've got the book," Jared said, as if it were no big deal. "You might want to have a look at it before you try the dream thing."

That was it. I couldn't resist any longer. I leaned across the teeny space between us and I kissed his cheek.

Just like that.

And the world stopped.

We stared at each other, oblivious to anything or anyone else. How could he have such green eyes? I could have stared into them forever.

"Well," Jared murmured finally, his voice sexy-low and his smile crooked. "This Wyvern *is* bold, after all."

I was blushing down to my toenails. Rooted to the spot. Snared in his gaze.

Maybe he'd enchanted me.

If so, it was a spell I wasn't going to fight.

"Zoë!" Nick called from ahead, and I realized I was being a dolt. Jared probably thought I was some lovesick kid, making an idiot of myself over the first guy who was impressed by my so-called abilities. Pathetic. I turned away and would have bolted to the cabin.

But Jared didn't let me.

He gripped my fingers even more tightly, tugging me back toward him. He caught my neck in his hand and smiled down at me. "It looks good on you, Zoë," he murmured.

I loved how he said my name. His fingers were wrapped in my hair, the strength of his hand turning my knees to butter. I stared into his eyes and couldn't imagine anywhere I'd rather be.

"Me, neither," he whispered, startling me that he *could* read my thoughts.

Then he kissed me.

Oh.

MY FIRST KISS was definitely worth the wait.

"*Earth to Zoë,*" Nick said in old-speak, his words tinged with both impatience and amusement. I straightened and ended the kiss with my usual clumsy style. We bumped noses and I almost tripped myself stepping back.

Some things, apparently, would never change.

Jared didn't seem to mind. His gaze searched mine. "Thunder or old-speak?"

I liked that he knew some of the drill. "Old-speak. They're waiting on me."

"Maybe they should get used to it," he said with impatience. "There's only one Wyvern, and you can't be everywhere."

He was right. I could *choose* where I wanted to be. And I was a rare commodity.

It didn't feel so bad to be special, now that I could actually do some Wyvern feats.

Although there were other skills I wanted to work on, ones that had nothing to do with the *Pyr*. I longed to kiss Jared again, just to linger there and perfect my technique.

But there had been all that blood....

"We have to help the *Pyr* before it's too late," I said.

"Probably the responsible choice," Jared said, that twinkle in his eyes telling me that he might have decided otherwise.

"Come on; you're not so irresponsible as that." I had to tease him, just to check.

That dangerous grin flashed. "Gotta keep people guessing."

"You don't fool me. You came back to help me."

"Like I said, that's not all I came back for."

Jared reached into the saddlebag on the bike and pulled out a cloth-bound book. The red cover was faded, and the edges rubbed down. I couldn't even read the type embossed on the front cover, but my heart leapt all the same.

He opened it to the title page and handed it to me.

"'*The Habits and Habitats of Dragons: A Compleat Guide for* Slayers, by Sigmund Guthrie,'" I read aloud. I took the book with reverence. I held it in my hands. It had to hold all the secrets I yearned to know; I couldn't wait to start reading. "I wonder how he knew so much about us."

"Ask your dad," Jared said. I was confused but he didn't elaborate. He flipped through the pages, leaning close enough to make my heart flutter.

"Where did you get this again?"

"You don't want to know."

"Actually, I do. Because if you're not going to let it go, I'd like a copy of my own, and if you know a shop that stocks this title, I want to go there."

He smiled at me. "I lied about the shop."

"Then..."

"You don't want to know, Zoë."

"Wrong."

"I'll trade you—the story for that flight."

"You should just tell me anyhow."

He smiled, proof that he wasn't going to tell me. Not now, anyway. So I made an effort to concentrate on what was important.

Jared was *helping* me.

I looked through the book, taking advantage of the opportunity. The pages were yellowed on the outer edges, and worn soft. The margins were huge to my eyes, and the type was tiny. I saw that it was organized like an encyclopedia, with many short entries sorted in alphabetical order.

"Here. Read this." He turned to the entry entitled, "Dreams."

"I've got to push the bike. I don't want to leave it out here. Go ahead of me; I'll catch up." Jared smiled quickly, then turned his attention to the motorcycle. I watched him check it over—he didn't fool me about being irresponsible—then ease it off the stand and begin to push it.

He'd protect anything he cared about.

Could that include me?

I had to believe that mastering my Wyvern-ness could only help increase my appeal to a guy who was a fan of dragons.

This called for intensive study.

You could say I was motivated.

I walked beside Jared, reading as I went, a skill I'd mastered a long time before. (It worked brilliantly at home, in the loft, but I had been known to collide with a wall or two in other places. The forest had no walls, so I figured I was good to go.)

Dreams—Similar to visions, dreams are generally viewed as involuntary or "given." Visions, in contrast, occur while the individual in question is conscious, albeit in a more meditative state than is usually described as wakefulness. Visions can occur involuntarily, as well, but may be deliberately conjured.

The Wyvern is traditionally considered a source of dreams for the *Pyr* themselves, and associated with the ability to dispatch dreams to individuals. There are stories of the Wyvern sending a message to a *Pyr* or group of *Pyr*, warning of a future event that would be the result of current actions or advising of an unanticipated threat. Less commonly, there are tales of the Wyvern sending a *Pyr* a memory, generally not one of his own, in order to provide insight to his current circumstance.

As for the Wyvern herself, it is implied that she can direct her own dreams in order to see past, present, and future. It must be noted that the link between the Wyvern and the *Pyr* has traditionally been a loose one, so that such dreams were accepted by the *Pyr* as rare gifts of counsel, not to be ignored. On the majority of occasions, the Wyvern does not involve herself in earthly affairs, perhaps choosing to abide in dreams herself.

I closed the book and continued to walk, not really seeing what was in front me any more clearly than when I'd been reading. I pulled out the red stone and thought about the guy I had seen hanging from the tree. I shivered. He'd turned up first, my first clue. I knew he had some connection with the stone. He'd said something to me, something I couldn't remember, probably because I hadn't known what it meant.

But that gesture of reaching out one hand had said it all. He'd been appealing for my help. Had he been responding to Meagan's visioning session? Had we awakened him? If so, I had an obligation to him.

Plus, he'd had that feathered wing instead of an arm. He was a shifter, like us, even if he changed to a different creature from a dragon.

Isabelle was right.

I had to go find him again. I had to help him.

And I'd bet my rune stone he'd tell me what I needed to know in order to save the other *Pyr*. He was our best shot at saving our dads.

Whatever the Mages had done to them.

I paused to wait for Jared, turning the stone over in my hand as he parked the bike beside Nick's car. I could see that he was dissatisfied with this spot, probably because the bike would be exposed to the elements. I'd bet that bike was usually tucked into a nice warm and dry garage.

"Tough being reckless and irresponsible," I teased.

His eyes danced. "Best choice possible, I guess. It'll have to do." He considered me then. "You look like you have a plan."

"I do. Thanks for the book." I offered it to him, not sure whether it had been a gift or a loan. (You know which option I was hoping for.)

Jared smiled, took it, and tucked it under his arm. I had a moment to think that that must be that—that the kiss was no big deal to him, that he'd act as if we were just friends—then he took my hand in his again.

As if there were no doubt that was where my hand belonged. He'd taken off his gloves, and his grip was warm around my fingers. Strong. Protective, even.

I could live with his carrying the book.

THE GUYS WERE outraged when we got to the cabin. Before I could ask what was going on, Liam shoved a pile of envelopes at me.

"Look at that!" he said. "Jared was right."

They were the envelopes from the clues that had been left in the mailbox. There was one addressed to me, one to Nick, one to Garrett, and one to Liam.

The last one, though, was addressed to Isabelle. I frowned and flipped through them again. "Where's the one to Adrian?"

"There isn't one," Garrett said, his disgust clear. "The clues are all the same, though."

"But you all thought this one said 'Adrian'?" Jared took the envelope carefully and I saw him flinch when he first touched it. He examined it with care. "It *has* had a glamour on it."

He put it aside, his manner thoughtful. I thought he maybe didn't want to touch it any longer.

"What's bothering you?" I asked.

He was surprised that I'd guessed his reaction. "I didn't think he was that strong a Mage. After all, I beat him, and I haven't had any training."

"So?" Nick asked.

"So a glamour, especially one that holds for very long on an inanimate object, takes experience and power."

"Not like the illusion of him being a dragon?" I asked.

"It's easier to manage a glamour wrapped around your body," Jared said. "Like keeping your coat closed. He wasn't holding this most of the time. That's tough to do."

"Maybe he just let you win," Nick suggested.

"Maybe." Jared frowned and drummed his fingers on the table. "But I'm thinking about that lightning bolt that snatched him away."

"He has powerful backup," Liam said.

Jared nodded. "Who was also maybe the one who supplied the glamour on this envelope."

"Okay, how do you fight a Mage?" Nick turned to Jared.

Jared smiled. "You meet fire with fire. Counter each spell with another stronger one, ideally one that can turn the first one to your own favor. It's like a riddling contest, where each tries to anticipate and best the other."

I could tell that he liked that part of it, which meant a liking for puzzles was something we had in common.

"First of all, we need to know where to find the Mages, however many there are," Garrett said. "And to figure out what they want."

"Then we can fight them," Nick said.

"No," I argued quietly. "I need to find the answer in a dream."

Jared watched me, a slight smile playing over his lips. I could see that the guys were uncertain, although Isabelle was as sure as Jared.

"The guy in the dream," she said.

I nodded. "He asked for my help. I want to see if I can get back there. Maybe we can make a deal."

21

It was surprisingly easy to fall asleep, even with all of them hanging around and watching me. Sometimes just knowing that something can be done makes it easier to do it.

(I knew it wasn't a universal rule. Knowing that teenage girls grew breasts had so far done nothing to increase my cup size.)

Or maybe I was just exhausted.

I closed my eyes and relaxed. I breathed more slowly and made my heartbeat slower. It occurred to me that this must be like going into a trance to breathe dragonsmoke–something I'd yet to do because it's easier to learn to breathe dragonsmoke in dragon form. I let calm radiate through my body. I called to the dream and was surprised by how quickly it came to me.

I ran on instinct then, there being no Wyvern manual. I had the idea that maybe some of the deal was wired right in and didn't require instructions. It might just work.

Jared would say I chose to believe.

I directed the dream. I wanted to go back to the red rock and the tree. I wanted to return to the part-bird guy.

The dream took me, all expenses paid.

Careful what you wish for.

As soon as I saw the red rock under the snow, I freaked a bit. I was terrified of going to this place, since I'd been scared shitless there. Why did I keep seeing blood on that stone? My heart took off at a gallop, and the dream lost focus. Adrenaline worked against me for a few minutes, and I had to try again, calming myself and starting from the beginning once more

I felt Jared take my hand in his.

He'd sensed my unease.

His touch immediately made me feel better.

And you know, the contact also made it easier for me to stay calm. Maybe it was more than that. He was humming something softly, something that seemed to wind into my ears and push me toward that dreamy place.

Whatever he did, it worked. I saw the red rock through the snow beneath my feet. It was like a replay of the dream I'd had before. I was on the same spot, living the same dream one more time. I suspected that I had to do the same things to get to the same ending.

I bent and brushed the snow away, noting the carvings on the rock.

I compared my rune stone with what I was seeing. I felt as if I were reenacting a ritual, and that if I got any part wrong, the dream might veer off to destinations unknown.

One that didn't include Kohana.

I looked left and right, just as I had before, peering along the length of the red stone ridge as if I'd never been there before.

I noticed the well at the root of the tree, approached it, looked down. It was just as dark as before. Just as spooky.

I looked up, afraid he wouldn't be there.

He *was* there, swinging bonelessly.

Terror struck my heart cold, just as it had the first time.

I saw the feather tattoo on his shoulder, along with the black feathered wing where his right arm should be. I felt the wind gather and braced myself for his swinging body to turn toward me.

It did.

He looked into my eyes.

He lifted his hand.

He said it again: "*Unktehila.*" It was more obviously an appeal this time. Maybe I was listening better.

Instead of running, this time I nodded.

He watched me in silence. I climbed the tree until I was over him. It wasn't any easier than it would have been in real life—the tree's bark was smooth—but I had to cut him down.

I realized a bit late that I had no tools. Although...the rune stone was sharp on one side. I sawed through the rope with my stone, but progress was slow. I despaired that I would get the job done.

He looked up at me, which was a shock.

It was even more shocking that he was laughing at me.

"*Unktehila,*" he said again, then exhaled with his teeth bared.

I got it. *Unktehila* meant *Pyr*. I was a *dragon* and he knew it. He was reminding me that there were easier ways to get this job done.

Duh.

No wonder he was laughing at me.

I tried not to blush and failed completely. I heard him chuckle but ignored him.

I was busy. After all, I wasn't sure whether I was working with a time limit. I summoned the blue shimmer and let it push through my body, shifting my shape. It was so easy now, since I'd witnessed that eclipse.

Was that what I'd been waiting for?

I had no time to think about it. I caught up Kohana's weight and hovered beside the tree. I felt him check out my scales with his one hand, tentatively, which was odd.

Not feeling me up. Just curious.

Distracting me just when I didn't need to be distracted.

I focused the stream of dragonfire on the sturdy rope, ensuring that I didn't scorch the tree. Damaging this tree had to be a very bad move. I could sense it. It took a bit of concentration to keep the stream of fire thin. My personal blowtorch burned through the rope, which gave with a crackle and a flurry of sparks.

As if I were sharpening a knife.

It took more dragonfire to break the rope than I'd expected. The sparks that flew from the rope were that odd bright orange, too, brighter than fire usually was.

When the rope was frayed, Kohana pulled it loose with an impatient gesture. He flung it away, as if it were a poisonous viper.

And I understood. It had been bewitched. I'd broken the spell that had held him captive.

Wow!

I saw him smile; then he flung up his arms.

He shifted in a glorious halo of yellow light. It was like staring into the sun: radiant and warm.

He became a large bird, one covered in gleaming black feathers. He was far bigger than any bird I'd ever seen, but still much smaller than me in my dragon form.

But talk about fast. He shot into the sky, and I sensed he couldn't get away from this place soon enough. The night sky was thick with stars, more stars than I'd ever seen in my life. I marveled as I raced after him.

He left me completely in his dust.

Way above the ground, up where the air was thin, he waited for me. I was a bit out of breath when I reached his side.

He bowed his head, hovering in the air with slow, steady beats. His eyes were such a brilliant yellow that they could have been burning orbs. I saw something that looked like crooked spears in his talons.

"There is an old idea that once one being saves the life of another, their lives are forever entwined," he said. I didn't exactly hear his words like normal language. I kind of felt them, and understood instantly. It was like telepathy, but not invasive.

A variant of old-speak? Or something special for dreams?

His eyes blazed. "That rope was wound with a spell."

"By the Mages?"

He nodded, then flung one of the bolts in his talons toward the earth. It hit the ground with a flash, and was accompanied by a boom of thunder. "But even they could do it only in such a sacred place."

"In dreams?"

"We're in the dreaming, but the site is real." He indicated the red rock far below us. "It's where Mother Earth herself speaks of past, present, and future."

"So it's a good place." I wondered where exactly it was. I wondered whether I could get there in real life.

"It was. The Mages are using its natural power against those who would revere it."

I made a guess. "Is my dad trapped there, too?"

He nodded. "And the others. You can save them all. I wasn't sure before, but now I know that you can."

"Why?"

"Because you came back into the dreaming. You found the same spot in the same dream, and you changed the end of it. Your dream power is strong." Although his words were flattering, his tone wasn't very positive. I wondered why. "Of course, you won't be able to do the rest, not unless I help you."

I had a feeling that wasn't the number one item on his to-do list, despite the new bond between us.

Or maybe this was a test.

"I saw you at school. In my room and in the stone. Like you were stalking me."

He smiled a little. It was a disquieting expression, as if he were laughing at me. "You summoned me. Didn't you know?"

Of course I didn't. And I had just about nothing to lose in seeking more information. "Maybe you can help me out with the details a bit. What exactly are you?"

"I am a *Wakiya*." He spoke with pride. "You might call me a Thunderbird."

"You called me *Unktehila* before."

"It is what you are."

"I'm *Pyr*." I said this with new confidence.

He made a dismissive gesture.

"But how can you know my kind and I don't know yours?"

"Don't you know the story?" He spoke with disdain.

I shook my head. He didn't explain and I knew somehow that he wouldn't. Okay, on to plan B. "Well, can you tell me more about the Mages?"

He looked away, impassive. "They learned a feat in the jungles of the Amazon from other magicians. They learned that to eat the flesh of the last of a species is to gain the powers of that race."

I suddenly understood Adrian's shifting. "Those are the forms of all the shifters they've eliminated?"

He nodded. "They believe that when they finish the task, when they have eliminated and devoured the last of every kind of shifter, their powers will multiply by a thousand."

I guessed. "Thunderbirds and dragons are left."

"Also wolves and cats."

"But he became an eagle. There still are eagles."

He shrugged. "Some shifters are closely related to other species that do not shift. Eagles with no power to change are those that survive. The eagle shifters are gone." Before I could even formulate more questions, he continued. "We are but four species left of dozens."

That there had been so many kinds of shifters was news, but I hid my surprise. I knew the *Pyr* kept to themselves, but I'd always assumed it was just from humans. Now I knew better.

"Help me save the *Pyr* and I'll help defend the *Wakiya*."

He smiled at me, so enigmatic that I had no idea what he was thinking. I had a moment to feel doubt; then he pivoted.

And he was gone.

KOHANA FLEW TOWARD THE EARTH, a gleaming spear of obsidian. I raced after him, lacking his powerful grace. He dipped low over the big tree, zooming over it like a fighter pilot at an air show. As he did so, he threw two more of the spears from his talons.

Like the first, they fell as lightning bolts, striking the earth with force.

An orange lightning bolt of a Mage spell erupted from the rock face, targeting us, but Kohana spun away. I had no time to warn him before lighting flew from his eyes. It made a great illuminating flash, like heat lightning, as he glared at the orange bolt.

That orange spell was cooked to cinders before it got fifty feet off the ground. The cinders fell to the earth, like soot on the snow.

"That won't hold them for long," he muttered, spinning to rocket away. He flew low and fast over a snowy forest.

I wondered where the heck we were going, but it was taking all I had just to keep up with him.

Yet another indication that I really did need to try harder in gym class.

Otherwise, this dragon stuff was going to kill me. It was all high-octane action.

When I saw a highway snaking through the forest, with tractor-trailers on it, I realized that this dream place *did* exist in real life. It was part of our world. And Kohana was showing me how to find the red rock once I left the dream.

He was helping me!

I had a good look to orient myself. I could see towns scattered around, and a city far off to one side. Without a map, that wasn't a ton of help—except that the red rock was in the opposite direction.

Meanwhile Kohana dove toward a frozen lake, targeting a cabin. I raced after him, heart pounding as I tried to catch up. There was a blue electric car parked at the top of the hill outside that cabin, a motorcycle close beside it.

Hey! I knew where we were! I was going to shout to him, but everything went black.

I opened my eyes in the cabin, among my friends.

Just like that.

And there was a dark-haired guy leaning against the fireplace, his arms folded across his chest. He stood perfectly still in the shadows. He was barefoot and bare chested, wearing only jeans, and there was a feather tattoo on his left biceps. His eyes were dark and glinted with humor. He evidently enjoyed that the others didn't realize he was there.

"WELL?" Jared demanded, giving my fingers a squeeze. "What did you dream?"

"Did you learn anything?" Nick asked at almost the same time.

"Where are they?" Garrett asked.

"How can we free them?" Liam asked.

I didn't say anything, not right away. I was out of breath. Exhaustion apparently followed me between forms.

I looked across the room to draw their attention to the newcomer among us. "Kohana," I said quietly, and he inclined his head in silent acknowledgment.

Garrett yelped in surprise. Liam took a step back. The others gaped. I saw Jared's lips tighten. He dropped my hand as if it were nuclear waste and folded his arms across his chest.

Uh-oh.

"Are we sharing your dream?" Liam asked, looking between me and Kohana.

I almost laughed. I wasn't nearly that strong.

"No. This is Kohana," Isabelle said, as if it were perfectly obvious. "I've seen him before. Both Zoë and I dreamed of him. Simultaneously. In the tree." She eyed him. "Did you send that dream on purpose?"

He nodded. "I needed help. Zoë opened a conduit for me."

"He showed me the way home," I said. "He's a shifter, too. A Thunderbird."

"Here." Isabelle handed me a granola bar.

Kohana didn't appear to need the sugar hit. That could have made me feel like a serious amateur, but I was too bagged to care.

Besides, I *was* a serious amateur.

"I didn't know there were other shifters," Liam said.

Kohana smiled. "You thought we were just stories, maybe?"

Liam blushed.

"We need to save the older *Pyr*," I said. "They're in trouble. Kohana knows where and how we can free them."

"Not exactly," Kohana said to my surprise. "They're trapped at the red rock, and you should prepare yourself—they are injured." We exchanged concerned glances. "Also, I don't know what holds them there. It must be something specific to your kind."

"Something the Mages use against the *Pyr*?" Jared asked.

"But why?" Liam asked. "What did we ever do to them?"

"You exist." Kohana was grim.

I gave them a rundown of the Mage Plan for World Domination. Jared was quiet.

Kohana eyed him before he spoke. "Mages want to transcend the physical, but they need our abilities to do it. They take our strengths the crude way."

"They kill shifters," Isabelle guessed.

"They *eat* shifters," Kohana corrected, and we shuddered as one. "Right to the last shred and drop."

I swallowed, remembering how Adrian had become a lion in order to gnaw me to bits. I shivered and Jared took my hand again.

Wait a minute. Adrian had become a lion and a lion was a kind of cat.

Had Kohana lied to me about the four kinds of shifters left?

No. It had to have been a glamour, like his dragon form. Maybe I just hadn't noticed its instability because I wasn't a cat shifter.

"So they use tricks to lure us close enough that they can do it," Nick guessed.

Kohana nodded. "The red rock is a legendary place. My kind have always held it in reverence and treated it with dignity. We honor it for what it is and listen to its counsel."

"But the Mages twist the song of the Earth, subverting it to their own purposes." Jared's tone was thoughtful.

Kohana nodded. "They use it to fortify their spells, and to disguise them."

"And we don't expect to find any deceit in the Earth's songs, so they have an advantage over us," Garrett said. Kohana nodded agreement, his gaze lingering on Garrett. I wondered what he saw in our fledgling Smith, but there was no chance to ask.

"So we need to go to this red rock and save our dads." Nick nodded at Kohana. "Thanks for showing Zoë the way." Nick, being Nick, was ready to head out right away.

"It is not that simple," Kohana said.

There's always a catch, isn't there?

We all looked at Kohana. "You mean there are defensive spells?" Nick asked.

"You'll need a spellsinger, or you have no chance."

"We have one." I touched Jared's sleeve. "He already took down the Mage who was supposed to confine us."

Kohana looked skeptical. "There are many of them, and the spells are strong."

Jared straightened. "I'll give it a try."

Kohana's tone turned mocking. "I watched a spellsinger *die* giving it a try. Maybe you should have more of a plan."

"Like what?" Nick asked. "Do you have any suggestions to share?"

Kohana smiled. Evidently he had wanted to be asked. "They'll be in an uproar right now. They'll know that I escaped, but they won't be able to guess how. They'll assume I managed it on my own, that maybe they underestimated my powers. But the area will be swarming with them as they try to hunt me down."

Isabelle glanced up at the roof of the cabin.

Kohana must have noticed. "Yes, they might realize I've come here. Or they might have sensed Zoë's presence."

"Nice." Liam was grim.

"I don't believe that they will abandon their fresh prey just for me."

"Why not?" Garrett asked.

"They are too close to success."

This was not what any of us wanted to hear.

"I was an unexpected bonus for them. They aren't close to destroying my kind yet. But capturing all of you along with your fathers would put them very close to eliminating the *Pyr*."

If they had captured my dad and everyone who followed him, that would account for most of the *Pyr*. I didn't even want to think about losing them all.

"How do you know this?" Nick asked.

"It's what I overheard while I was hanging in the tree."

"But Zoë? They could follow her here," Isabelle said.

"No." Jared spoke with conviction before Kohana could reply. "They'll wait for her to come to them."

Once again he and Kohana stared at each other, the battle of wills between them growing stronger by the minute. What could Jared hear in Kohana's thoughts?

"For *us* to come to them," I corrected. "Our dads are the bait in the trap."

"When do we go, then?" Nick demanded, looking between us.

Kohana frowned. "Let's wait a few hours. Give them time to assume that I fled or that you're too afraid to attack."

"*Then* take them by surprise," Nick concluded.

"Get some sleep to ensure we're at our best," Liam said. "Can you tell us what we'll find at the red rock?"

Kohana dropped his gaze. "Little that's good. I believe that you will be in time to save most of them."

We couldn't even look at one another.

"This is a fight we can't afford to lose," Garrett said, then looked at me. "How far is it?"

"Not far. I think I could find it."

"I'll take you back there," Kohana said. "We'll go around and approach from the other side."

"Another surprise." Liam nodded.

"We can't leave Isabelle and Jared behind," Nick said. "I can carry Isabelle."

"I'll carry Jared," I offered, trying to be casual even though my heart was thumping. "I owe him a ride anyway."

He turned then, his warm smile giving me tingles that rivaled the blue shimmer. "Thanks, Zoë." He took my hand again and gave my fingers a tight squeeze.

I didn't complain.

But I did wish that I had the power to read minds. I would have given anything to know what Jared was thinking.

Of course, he smiled at me just as I had that thought.

22

As the others kept talking and scheming, their excitement growing, I pulled out my rune stone and worried it between my fingers, feeling Kohana's gaze drop to it. He watched me, but didn't say anything. Maybe he felt he'd said enough.

Somehow I had to defend the *Pyr* against every possibility of a bad ending. I'd gotten us into this, after all. And I was supposed to be able to see the past, the present, and the future all at once.

It really would have been a kick-ass ability to have in my arsenal.

How were the Mages keeping the *Pyr* captive?

How badly were the *Pyr* hurt? All that blood in my dreams didn't bode well.

If we were going to succeed in saving our dads, we had to know what it was that held them in the Mages' custody. We *Pyr* had weaknesses, of course, but I needed to know which of them the Mages had exploited.

What weakness did we all share? Those *Pyr* with partners had a vulnerability in their human counterpart—who could be taken hostage or injured or whatever—but that didn't feel right.

"Did you say you talked to Alex?" I asked Jared. "And my mom?"

He nodded. "Yeah, why?"

"And they're okay?"

"Worried but okay."

So that wasn't it. And we kids were all here, together.

No, it had to be something else.

I didn't know what it was, but I realized there was a way to find out. "Your book says that the Wyvern could summon and share memories," I said to Jared. He nodded agreement. "Does it say any more on that?"

"Why?"

"I need to share my dad's memory from Saturday. That's how I'll know what happened to him, and what's holding him hostage."

Jared got the book from his bag. "Have at it."

I accepted the book, then paused. If you really want something, you might as well ask for it, right?

"You could give me this book," I said, giving him my best attempt at a seductive smile.

He laughed. He glanced at the others, who were still chattering, then hunkered down beside me. "And surrender the one thing that might make me interesting to a dragon girl?" His eyes glinted as he shook his head; then his voice dropped low enough to make me shiver. "I'm not that easy to ditch, Zoë."

Oh.

"You just want that ride," I teased, making a joke because everything in me was fluttering.

"That's not all I want," he said, mysterious and intriguing all over again.

I might have asked him what he meant, but he straightened and started to glare at Kohana again, all the way across the room. I had the sense that he was standing guard over me.

A girl could get used to that sort of attention.

THE BOOK, of course, was vague about the mechanics of dreaming.

Actually it was vague about anything important. I wondered whether this Sigmund Guthrie guy had really known anything, or whether he'd been making it up.

"Maybe he was hiding the truth," Jared suggested, doing that thought-listening thing when I was least expecting it.

"What?"

"Like a smoke screen. Medieval herbalists did that. You have one active ingredient, but you hide it in plain sight, in lots of ingredients that don't matter. Ideally, they might gross someone out, too."

"Eye of newt and toe of frog," I said.

"Exactly. Find what you needed?"

"No, and you probably know it."

"The book's not an instruction manual."

"Clearly. I could use one."

Jared smiled crookedly at me. "So you'll just have to give it a try. Trust your instincts."

"No pressure," I muttered, and he laughed again.

He leaned close. "*I* believe you can do it, Zoë."

I squared my shoulders. "Okay. So do I."

I closed my eyes and tried to summon a memory.

Well, you can probably guess what happened. Can't you? In hindsight, it shouldn't have been a huge surprise. I was feeling really good, like I was completely nailing this Wyvern thing. I'd saved Kohana in the dreaming world. I'd shifted fully to dragon form. I'd fought against a Mage—not well, but it had been my first fight as a dragon and I hadn't died. I was never going to be great at anything resembling gym class. I'd changed to a salamander, too. I had Jared looking at me as if I were It—apparently I was also mastering the Girl with a Bit of Something Special.

I was feeling confident and brave, sure that this dreaming trick couldn't be that tough. I was tired, but, hey, I was the Wyvern!

I reached out for my father's memory of Saturday, stretching my mind into the direction it went when I dreamed.

And I choked.

Nada.

I tried again, stretched farther.

Zip.

I tried the eye game.

Nope.

I summoned the blue shimmer, and even it was elusive, giving me a bit of a run for my money. When I finally coaxed the shimmer closer, I had a heartbeat to feel triumphant that I'd done something right, then *ooomph*.

Nothing.

Like sticking a pin in a balloon. I had nothing to share, nothing to offer, no clue and no idea where to find one. Worse, I was completely beat. Those cuts on my stomach started to throb and even the rune stone felt heavy to me.

I might have been evading the others and their expectations, but either way, I decided to go to bed. I fell asleep immediately.

It was divine.

Dreamless.

Deep.

Heaven.

THE MEMORY SLAPPED me in the mind so hard I thought I might jolt awake and lose my hold on it.

I was on the roof of the loft in Chicago. I was listening to the distant hum of another *Pyr*, and smiling to myself that she was so clumsy in feeling my presence.

Right. I was an onyx-and-silver dragon deep in my *Pyr* heart, cool, composed, and worried about the kid.

I was in my dad's mind.

I didn't want to poke around too much there, certainly didn't want to learn things I'd rather not know about my parents—I mean, they must have had sex, right? At least once?—so I took a moment to get my bearings.

It looked like I was standing in a corridor, one lined with stainless steel filing cabinets. The floor was black, the walls were white and the ceiling glowed, as if it provided some kind of ambient light source. Was I really in my dad's memory? I checked out the label on one drawer and saw that it had a date.

I shouldn't have been surprised that he was so ruthlessly organized.

I moved down the corridor with purpose, checking labels until I found the drawer that didn't have a closing date. It started earlier this year. I took a breath, pulled open the drawer.

The memory sharpened, becoming so clear that it could have been my own recollection.

I felt my dad listen to everything around him. The hum of traffic. The chatter of kids in the park. The sound of my mother's hunt-and-peck typing. The breath of the wind. His senses were incredibly keen, and I knew he'd worked to achieve this.

That gave me a new goal.

I felt him explore the world around him, stretching his awareness beyond his immediate vicinity. I felt him sense the presence of each *Pyr* in succession, checking on them like the super-dad he is. I heard the murmur of old-speak from Donovan and from Rafferty, as familiar as my favorite homemade mac and cheese for supper.

I saw the blue shimmer on the edge of his talons, dancing there, just within reach.

And he was listening to me "feel" him for the first time.

I knew how he wanted to help me, understood that he knew that the best course was to let me master the trick myself. I felt his awareness of Monday's solar eclipse and the question in his mind as to whether it would influence my development.

Interesting. I'd never even anticipated that.

But important firestorms for the *Pyr* are triggered by lunar eclipses.

I'd worry about that later.

I supposed that for him this was like watching a kid learn to ride a bike. You might want to reach out and steady them, but it's better to let them wipe out a few times. They'll learn more from falling than from being saved from falling.

That wasn't my analogy.

It was my dad's. I heard him think it. It was how he kept himself from making it easy for me.

I heard our conversation and smiled to myself at the familiar sound of his old-speak. I heard him eavesdrop on my conversations with Donovan and Rafferty, heard him sigh and head back inside to bring my mom up–to-date.

And I heard the taunt.

It hurtled into his thoughts like a rock, one that shot orange sparks in every direction. It exploded into his mind like a bomb that he hadn't expected.

I felt him recoil.

I felt his anger at the intrusion.

And I sensed his outrage.

He was dared to save Quinn, the Smith, from certain death.

By a Mage, who had no right to do injury to a *Pyr* of any stature.

I didn't know how the Mage had hurt Quinn—the notion pretty much shook my world—but I felt how livid the very prospect made my father. He demanded proof and I saw the image spill into his mind. It was awful. There was so much blood. I felt his anger boil and his need for justice light.

I knew he'd go.

So did the Mage.

Quinn was the Smith, the one of our kind who can heal our scales and repair our armor. A Smith is an imperative member of the *Pyr* team, especially when we fight—my father would have said that Quinn was more important than he was himself. He'd risked everything for Quinn before. Saving Quinn was quite literally the offer my dad couldn't refuse.

And he didn't.

He shifted and shot into the sky, zero hesitation. He didn't even tell my mother where he was going, as if he feared the chance would be lost if he didn't act immediately. He didn't leave her undefended—the loft is always encircled with a powerful boundary mark of dragonsmoke—and I'm sure he didn't think he'd be long.

He was wrong.

I saw him lured.

I saw him tricked.

They stole his *scales*.

And left him trapped on a ridge of red rock dusted with snow. My dad knelt down beside Quinn, checking that he was still alive. I felt his despair and didn't know what he'd discovered.

He'd always relied upon himself and upon the *Pyr* of his generation. This rescue was up to us.

It was one hell of a coming-of-age challenge.

We had to win—there was no choice.

I WOKE UP SUDDENLY, my mouth dry and my palms damp with sweat. All I could see was my dad, despondent. The sight shook me to my core.

The Mages had taken his scales. That wasn't even supposed to be possible. It must have been a new enchantment they had devised, one that caught every *Pyr* off guard because it had never been a variable before.

I opened my eyes again and tried to force the vision away. The cabin was almost completely dark, the fire down to glowing coals.

Kohana glanced up at my movement, or maybe he heard my agitation. Jared was still sitting beside me, and he was wide-awake. He slipped one arm around my shoulders, maybe thinking I was cold. I was glad to lean against him for a moment, although there was work to do.

I can't give you a ride, I thought, looking into his eyes. *Not today.*

He tilted his head slightly, inviting me to explain.

I took his book and opened it to the entry on clothes. There was a brief explanation there of how we *Pyr* fold our clothes away when we shift shape, yada, yada, yada.

Jared scanned the entry quickly and shrugged. I understood that this was old news to him.

It's backward, I thought, and his gaze brightened. *At least now. It's our* scales *we have to hide. The Mages made a spell to twist this. They've got our dads' scales and it's keeping them captive. That's how they snared them.*

He reached into his jacket, but he didn't seem to find what he was looking for. He rummaged in mine—well, Alex's—and pulled out that pad and paper. *Where?* he wrote.

Right.

That was the kicker.

I only had half the answer. The *Pyr* dads were at the red rock—but where were their scales? There'd been no sign of them in my dream. The Mages must have hidden the scales in a separate location.

When you can't solve a riddle, you might as well ask for help.

How can we find out where they've hidden the scales? I thought, meeting Jared's gaze.

He gave me that reckless smile, grabbed my hand, and led me quietly out of the cabin. We moved with as much silence as possible, but I saw the glint of Kohana's eyes.

He slept like my dad, except that the shine of his eyes was yellow.

Molten gold.

Once out in the snow, Jared scanned the sky. The stars were still out, but the sky was turning a lighter blue in the east. He walked up to where the bike and car were parked, then turned me to face him.

I didn't tell him that the guys would still be able to hear him.

"There was a place in Adrian's mind when I was fighting him. I don't know where it is, but I can tell you what it looks like."

"Can you show it to me?" I asked. "That might be good enough."

My reasoning was that if I could travel through space and manifest in other locations as Wyvern, then I should be able to direct where I went. If I knew what a place looked like or had a strong enough sense of where it was, maybe that was good enough.

Jared nodded. He framed my face in his hands and looked into my eyes. His fingers were warm. "I've never given anyone my thoughts before. But if you think it can work, it's worth a try."

"What do I need to do?"

"Relax. Don't blink. Just stare into my eyes and don't blink. I'll try to do all the work."

"Wait!" I opened Nick's car and dug in the bag that Isabelle had left behind. Just as I'd suspected, there were three granola bars. I shoved them into my pockets, then went back to Jared.

He looked confused but didn't ask. Instead, he put his hands on my face again and he opened his eyes wide. He began to hum and I noticed how long his eyelashes were. I looked at all the shades of green in his eyes, then looked straight into the darkness of his pupil. His chant grew a little louder, surrounding me with a sense of safety.

I felt something nudge against my thoughts, something that was not mine. Instinctively, I slammed a door.

But wait. Jared was trying to give me the key.

I needed his help.

I had shared my dad's memory. I could do this.

I had to trust him completely.

I looked deeply into Jared's eyes and let that mental door swing open. I surrendered to whatever he wanted to share with me, and, all of a sudden, it was there.

Someone else's thought in my own mind.

No, it was one of Adrian's memories.

This time, I didn't see the organizational system of choice. I was flung right into the recollection itself.

I was standing alone in a cinder-block room. A basement. It could have been anywhere. It was damp and chilly, maybe because the floor was dirt. Cold, too. The window was barred and the door was steel. Probably locked. I couldn't hear anything or anyone above me.

As if the house or building above this cellar were empty.

But on the floor were piles of dragon scales. They were like suits of armor, more like chain mail, discarded in heaps.

It was a hoard of priceless treasure. I knew which belonged to whom by its color, by the talisman secured into the coat of scales by the mate of that *Pyr*. I recognized them all. Every single one.

The sight of them, dropped on the floor, shook me to my marrow. It was so wrong.

My dad's scales were onyx and silver; Donovan's were lapis lazuli and gold; Quinn's were sapphire and steel; Delaney's—they had Liam's dad, Delaney, too?—were copper and emerald; Rafferty's were opal and gold. Thorolf's were moonstone and silver, and they were there, too.

I felt sick at the sight. All of these *Pyr*, captured. Helpless. Reliant upon us.

No pressure.

I could guess how it had happened, though. Somehow the Mages had gotten Quinn and all the other *Pyr* had tried to save him. They'd each been trapped.

Because the Mages had known our weakness, and had twisted it in a way that none of us would expect.

It was their first step in destroying us all.

Like I was going to stand back and let that happen.

I KNEW Jared could read my thoughts, so I didn't waste time with explanations. I beckoned to the blue shimmer. I let it dance over my skin, flood through my veins, fill my body with its elusive starlight. I let it build and play; I coaxed it and made it stronger.

All the while, I studied details of the room Jared showed me, refining my sense of that place.

And my will to appear in that place.

The tide grew to a tsunami. The shimmer grew blindingly bright. I roared as I let it claim me.

I heard Jared swear.

But he was way behind me. I was hurtling through space. My stomach rolled as everything spun all around me. I was sure I'd retch this time and thought maybe I should have eaten for strength before getting the memory.

Then the whirlwind stopped as quickly as it had begun. The blue shimmer faded.

I opened my eyes.

There was a dirt floor beneath my hands.

And a sapphire-and-steel coat of dragon scales right beside me. There was a lot of dried blood on the scales and under them, and it looked almost like rust. I wasn't going to think about that. I heard boots running as someone approached. I grabbed those scales right beside me. They rattled, making too much noise.

I wanted to take more than one set, but it was impossible. They were too large, too heavy for me to carry more than one at a time.

I wouldn't even think about making six trips.

Not yet.

Keys jingled outside the steel door. I could hear two guys arguing. Shit! I couldn't be discovered before I even started!

Maybe, somehow, they already knew I was there.

Terror made me falter. I fought against my panic, knowing I had to be calm to summon the shimmer.

Otherwise I would be caught there.

Trapped like the other *Pyr*.

I clutched the scales close, exhaled shakily, and forced myself to get calm. I called to the shimmer, and wished with all my heart to be at the red rock.

A key turned in the lock.

Okay, I prayed.

To every deity I'd ever heard of.

One of them must have listened.

23

I kept my eyes squeezed shut, even when I felt snow under my hands. There was rock under the snow, and I was sure I could feel a curved shape cut into the rock face.

I exhaled in relief.

I had time to think that Jared would be impressed; then someone moaned close by me.

I opened my eyes cautiously. I was back on the red rock. Snow was swirling on all sides, obscuring everything beyond the rock itself. It was like being inside a tornado—or what I'd expect it to be like inside a tornado: dead calm, with that riotous storm just yards away.

The bizarre thing was that the rock was oblong in shape, the crest of a ridge. This particular tornado followed the shape of the rock, making an oval swirl.

Completely unnatural.

Quinn was right beside me—he was the one who had moaned. He looked more like a ghost than the robust Quinn I knew so well. There was a slick shadow beneath his body, a dark one that made me fear for him.

Then familiar old-speak rolled into my thoughts.

"*Fair enough,*" Quinn murmured, and I just about dissolved in relief. I moved closer to him, reached for his hand, and put it on the scales. I felt his hand tremble; then the scales vanished, hidden from view in an instant.

Quinn fell back, even the glimmer between his lids gone. I thought he'd maybe passed out from the effort. I hunkered close to him. He looked exhausted.

At least the scales were back in the custody of their rightful owner. I didn't need to know where Quinn had secreted them, just that he had them.

I would have answered him in old-speak, but he opened his eyes and I caught a flash of warning there. He'd probably guessed what I intended to do.

He shook his head minutely—which seemed to exhaust him—and I understood.

The Mages could hear old-speak.

Got it.

Just for the reconnaissance value—and because I needed to catch my breath—I played the eye game. Sure enough, the view through my left eye was different. That wall of swirling snow was filled with a network of orange flashes of light.

I didn't dare move and attract attention. I peered up and down the length of the rock and saw the *Pyr* I knew and loved in various poses.

There was Thorolf, shadowboxing, his disgust with his situation clear. There was a makeshift bandage on his thigh, and I liked that he hadn't gone down without a fight. Knowing Thorolf, he was working off his anger over getting caught. Probably healthier for everyone.

There was Delaney, drumming his fingers on the rock.

There was Donovan, murmuring to himself. Actually, I figured he was murmuring to the elements he controlled as Warrior, but his frustrated expression said it all—they weren't listening to him here. His gaze flicked to me and away, repeatedly, and I heard the rate of his breathing change.

Donovan wouldn't give me away.

There was Rafferty, lounging on the stone, utterly still except for the glint of his eyes. He seemed to be an outcropping of the rock itself, and about as flexible.

And there was my dad, on his feet, hands on his hips, glaring into the vivid maelstrom. He was deeply pissed off. I smiled at the sight of him. He might be trapped but he was okay.

They were all trapped, and saving them was up to me.

I had work to do. If Jared thought I wasn't trying, he'd soon learn differently. I was ready to push myself as far as necessary.

I reached into my pocket for a granola bar and scarfed down half of it fast enough that my mom would have told me to chew slowly. I scooped some snow into my mouth—closest available alternative to a drink of water—and reviewed the situation. Quinn had passed out or fallen asleep beside me.

I wanted to go back to that room, even though I knew there were Mage types there. I could picture the room. I could smell it. I wanted to get my dad's scales next. I recalled the layout of the room, and the position of the onyx-and-silver scales.

To avoid detection, I should arrive as a salamander.

Yes.

And I should manifest *under* the scales. I reviewed the room again, focused my intent, then touched Quinn's hand with my fingertips. His pulse was weak but still there. I had to hurry. I met Donovan's gaze and nodded slightly. He pretended not to see me. I called to my shimmer and felt it tingle over my flesh.

Then the feel of Quinn's hand was gone.

No. *I* was gone.

"I TOLD YOU, there's one suit of scales missing," a guy complained. It was Adrian. "You fucked up."

I smelled the musty aroma of a basement. I felt soil under my feet. I trembled from head to toe and closed my eyes against the tide of nausea. Salamanders don't have pockets, which meant my granola bars were inaccessible at this time.

Live and learn.

"I didn't do anything," another complained. There was something familiar about his voice, too. I couldn't quite place it. "The door's been locked all along."

"You can say what you want," Adrian argued. "I gave you one stupid job and you blew it."

I was busy keeping my salamander self from being mashed under the weight of the suit of scales on top of me. It was dark under there, so I couldn't confirm that I'd manifested under the right ones.

But really, I had to move them all eventually.

One down; five to go.

So long as the Mages didn't capture more *Pyr* while I was trying to save these. There was still Niall and Sloane and Brandt.... No. I wouldn't make that long list of possibilities just yet.

No pressure.

"It was your watch and your responsibility, and it'll be your butt for losing the scales," Adrian continued, his tone menacing. "If this is some kind of joke, you'd better put them back."

"I told you, I don't know what happened to them. The door was locked!" Why did I recognize his voice? I didn't know any Mages or Mage minions. But I couldn't deny that there was something familiar about it.

So, what should I do? Wait for them to leave? The blue shimmer would give me away—if they saw it (and as Mages, they'd have to notice it), the big mystery of the disappearing scales would be solved. Waiting seemed like the best idea, and it would give me time to recover.

As much as I *could* recover with my heart racing in terror.

"Then what happened to it? You can count, can't you?" I heard the chink of scales being kicked on the other side of the room. "One." Another kick of scales, this one closer to me. "Two."

Crap. Would I be revealed when they kicked the scales?

Or just mashed to oblivion?

My question was answered one second later. I heard a set of scales being picked up and dropped. "Three. And no extras underneath this set."

"I told you. I don't know what happened to them."

"Bullshit." Adrian was hostile. "You're hiding them, or studying them, or doing something to undermine this effort. You've never really been committed to becoming a Mage, have you?"

"I have! I am!"

"Tell me where they are."

"I don't know!"

A set of scales hit the far wall with a clatter, then slid to the floor.

"Four!" Adrian shouted. "And just one more. That makes *five*, not six." I heard the scales above me rattle as he grabbed for them. I saw his fingers sliding between the scales. I knew I didn't have a lot of time.

Unfortunately, I wasn't entirely positive that I could take them with me, not in my salamander form.

I could save myself. Maybe.

I wrapped my salamander tail around the scales, hung on tight, and wished as hard as I could. I called to the shimmer, telling it to get a move on.

"What the heck is that?" the second guy cried.

And I knew suddenly why I recognized his voice.

It was Trevor Wilson.

Yes, *the* Trevor Wilson. Suzanne's boyfriend. The guy who had asked me out, against all logic and expectation.

Because he was an apprentice Mage.

The shock nearly made me screw up.

But not quite.

Clearly, there is a Great Wyvern and she loves me.

So far.

I SKIDDED across the red rock face, spreading snow in every direction. It was somewhat less than an elegant entrance, and I skinned my newt cheek as well. The good news was that the scales had made it with me.

The bad news was that I didn't have my dad's scales, after all.

These were lapis lazuli and gold. I had one glimpse of them before they were gone, hidden from sight.

"*Nice*," Donovan murmured in old-speak.

I was disappointed, though. I was doing my best, but things were not working out as planned. Not exactly. I mean, Quinn had his scales but was unconscious. Someone—probably multiple someones—would have to carry him to safety. This would seriously impact the *Pyr*'s ability to fight.

How many Mages were there to fight? How much time did I have before the guys attacked? How much did I have to do alone?

What if I failed?

Donovan leaned back, bracing himself on his hands, one of which was tented over my salamander form.

My dad moved in a flash, sitting down beside Donovan. He scooped me up in one smooth move and dropped me into the pocket of his shirt. I was right against his chest, and I could hear the sound of his heart beneath my scratched cheek. He cupped his hand over the pocket, holding me close. I heard that his pulse was racing, which I knew wasn't typical for him. He was worried sick.

I cried a little, overwhelmed. His thumb stroked my back, reassuring me. "*Stronger than you know,*" he said, and I shuddered, the tremor moving through me from nose to tail.

"*Absolutely,*" Donovan agreed, covering for his comment. I remembered Quinn's warning that the Mages could hear old-speak. *"That spell is more powerful than any I've ever seen."*

Could I do this four more times? Successfully? I had serious doubts.

What had happened in the room after Adrian and Trevor saw my shimmer?

Would they move the scales away? Or lock them up somewhere else? Maybe with a stronger spell protecting them? I didn't feel in primo shape, and there were plenty of challenges on my plate already. I knew I was shaking in my dad's pocket, and he had to have felt it, too.

This was hard.

What would Jared have told me to do? To believe in myself, definitely. To trust my instincts. To put it all on the line and hold nothing back.

Okay. I was good to go.

"*Rafferty,*" my dad said softly, as if noticing that *Pyr* had moved.

"*This is hard on him,*" Donovan said, covering again by pretending my dad meant something different.

But my dad was telling me to bring Rafferty's scales next. I wanted to argue with him; then I remembered something.

Isabelle knew that a *Pyr* needed sugar and water after traveling through space, because Rafferty could do it, too. He was the only one of the *Pyr* who had mastered that feat.

So he could help me.

It was a good idea, one that gave me new hope. Rafferty would probably be able to carry two sets of scales. He was really powerful. Which meant just two more trips for me, not four.

I thought I could do that.

I sure as heck was going to try.

Besides, I wanted to know whether I was right about Trevor Wilson. It seemed beyond belief that he could be a Mage apprentice. I had to know for sure.

I called that shimmer and got it in gear.

THE TWO GUYS were still in the basement room when I manifested there again. The air was crackling with tension as they argued and blamed each other. Fortunately, I'd nailed the salamander bit.

Unfortunately, I didn't manifest under any scales.

No one seemed to notice when I scurried under the closest set.

My dad's.

Rafferty's were a good six feet away.

Crap!

Decision time.

"I told you," Adrian insisted. "I saw a blue light. Go ahead and show me that you've learned *something*. What does a blue light mean?"

"I don't know," the other guy said. He really did sound like Trevor Wilson. I crept to the edge of the pile of scales. "There are no spells that make blue light. Even the lowest initiate knows that."

"And you're lower than that, I guess. I'd give you a zero on that answer. Give me your explanation, then," Adrian said. "Where's the fifth set of scales, smart-ass?"

"Maybe you're hiding it. Maybe you're trying to make me look bad." The other guy snorted. "Or make yourself look good. That's a hobby of yours, isn't it?"

I crept out a little farther, my heart racing.

But I still couldn't see him clearly. I was going to have to go out into the open.

On the other hand, that was also the only way to get to Rafferty's scales.

Nothing ventured, nothing gained, right?

I took a breath and scooted across the floor. I rubbernecked on the way, then saw I'd miscalculated the distance. I accelerated, heart pounding, and slid beneath the opal-and-gold pile of scales.

It *was* Trevor.

"What was that?" Adrian demanded.

"I didn't see anything."

"I'll tell you what shimmers blue," Adrian said, his voice low. "The *Pyr* when they shift shape."

Crap.

Trevor fell silent, then started to stammer. "B-b-but they're huge. I mean, we'd notice a dragon in here."

"Not if he was in a different form," Adrian said. "Or *she* was."

Make that: *Shit.*

My heart was as loud as a brass band in my ears.

"Shouldn't we get one of the elders?" Trevor said. "Shouldn't we get help?"

"And lose the credit for trapping her?" Adrian asked, his tone oily again. "I don't think so."

He started to hum and when the sound gave me gooseflesh I knew I had big trouble. He was making another spell.

Which meant I had just about nothing left to lose.

I seized the scales and called that fricking shimmer. With my left eye, I could see a net of orange sparks forming, encircling the pile of scales. I fought my panic and tried to concentrate on the slowly building shimmer of blue light.

In fact, I told it to move its glittery butt.

In the meantime, I thought I'd give Trevor a surprise.

I shifted to my human shape right in front of him. "Boo!"

He just about jumped out of his skin.

Okay, I enjoyed his astonishment.

Adrian cried out in shock, so surprised he forgot to hum. The orange sparks thinned.

"Bye!" I shouted, then mustered the shimmer and got the hell out of there.

Okay, that had been fun.

24

I was back on the red rock, arriving in an inglorious splat that would have smashed a salamander to nothing. I barely had time to gasp before the scales were gone, snatched up and secured by Rafferty.

"*My thanks*," he said, his old-speak a reassuring rumble. "*You should eat.*"

I remembered the granola bars in my pocket and inhaled another one. It was pretty smashed up—hey, just like me—but wow, did it ever help.

By the time my dad came to my side, I wasn't nearly so ready to heave. He caught me close in a tight hug. I leaned against him for a long moment, taking strength from him.

Then he pulled back, looking into my face. His eyes were all glittery, halfway to dragon, the way they got when he was really intense about something.

"So long as you try your best, you will never, ever disappoint me," he said. "Understand?"

I nodded and fought the urge to cry.

"I am so proud of you today."

Would Jared be proud of me, too? If this wasn't trying, I didn't know what the heck was.

"No matter what happens," Rafferty added, "you have exceeded all expectations, Zoë."

That was when I realized that they'd both spoken aloud. And they weren't trying to hide me. What had changed?

The captive *Pyr* were all on their feet, looking skyward. Quinn was leaning heavily on Donovan. My dad moved to support him on the other side. Otherwise, they were all as still as stones.

I stared into the swirling wall of snow, but it looked exactly the same.

Until I closed my right eye. Then I could see the orange network of light dimming. There were even a couple of places where it looked as though it were being torn to shreds. Soon holes would appear in the fabric it had woven to enclose the *Pyr*.

I wondered why, and then I knew.

I heard Jared singing.

Yes! The rescue party had arrived.

My dad and Rafferty were smiling. Rafferty offered me his hand, the hand with his black-and-white ring. I realized then that he never took it off—which meant that in dragon form, it somehow changed size to fit his talon.

"Shall we go?" he asked.

I looked at the ring. I looked at Rafferty. I smiled at my dad. I wished I could have seen Jared, but I had to content myself with the sound of his spellsong.

And the promise of seeing him later.

When we were triumphant.

I put my hand in Rafferty's. I saw the way he called to his shimmer, so elegant and restrained, and tried to call mine the same way.

With mixed results.

The ring on Rafferty's hand began to spin around his finger. I stared at it, watching the black and white colors blur into each other.

"*You direct,*" he said, his old-speak resonant and reassuring. *"I'll follow."*

"Deal." I imagined the room, saw the last three piles of scales. I could taste success and the near completion of the mission. I felt the confidence of having someone at my back. I heard Jared's song become louder and felt the fabric of the spell start to tear. The *Pyr* shouted all around us, and Donovan shifted shape to fight.

Just as the young *Pyr* started to come through the veil of sorcery to help. With most of the older *Pyr* in human form, Nick and Garrett and Liam had to take the brunt of the battle. It seemed as if there were Mages everywhere, and I feared for our side.

"*Be safe*," my father said, his kiss brushing against my temple.

I had no time to say good-bye, because the shimmer claimed me, rolling through me with staggering force.

"Pyr," Rafferty advised in old-speak, in the same moment that the shimmer built to a crescendo.

I knew what he was going to do.

We were going to arrive in style.

Dragon style.

Rafferty's grip was tight on my hand.

Then his claw held fast to mine.

The ring spun so fast that it was a blur of black and white. It rubbed against my talon, sparks flying from it as we left the red rock.

A heartbeat later, we exploded into that basement room. I'd done it! I'd led us both there.

I staggered a bit, even more shaken by the transition this time. Rafferty was like a rock, one I could cling to.

One that was breathing fire.

Sure enough, we weren't alone. Through the fiery flames of dragonfire that Rafferty exhaled, I could see Adrian and Trevor, as well as three older men.

They were chanting something in unison.

Spellcasting.

I followed Rafferty's cue and conjured up some fire of my own. The air was thick with orange bolts and raging dragonfire. There wasn't enough space in that room for the seven of us, especially with the flames and smoke. The Mages had backed into corners, and I guessed the three I'd never seen before were elders–they all appeared to be older than Adrian and Trevor. Also, each of them claimed a corner of his own. Adrian and Trevor were stuck in one corner together.

Maybe they thought we'd shift to smaller forms for lack of space, but

Rafferty didn't give them an inch of room. He and I were back-to-back, breathing fire, standing guard over our precious hoard.

Three sets of dragon scales.

I breathed fire at Trevor and Adrian, enjoying how Adrian flinched. When I closed one eye, I could see that his spell wasn't coming together well, probably because of the pressure. I set his shirt on fire, just to mess with his game a bit more.

Then I turned my dragonfire on the elder on my side.

Maybe he needed to work on his tan. I exhaled slow and hot and even, roasting him so that he closed his eyes and turned away. He kept singing, though, his spell gathering form before him. It was a blob at first. Then it lengthened into a cylinder. It became brighter and brighter, then took on an inner light of brilliant orange.

I knew that color.

Suddenly it shredded itself, expanding abruptly into a net. He hurled it at me and I ducked it, slamming Rafferty down, too. The spell went right over the two of us and hit the far wall.

It slid down to the ground, its light extinguishing as it fell.

Dead.

I looked back and the Mage was gone.

There was a snake on the floor. I stepped on it, hard, and ground my heel down into the floor. I'm not such a skinny chick in dragon form. There was major mass on top of that snake.

His scream was very satisfying.

Trevor watched, his eyes widening in terror. I saw him lose control of his spell, heard him swear, and realized that Adrian was having some trouble with his spells, too. I guess having his shirt on fire distracted him. Poor boy. They weren't dangerous for the moment.

Meanwhile, Rafferty began to chant, humming the slow chorus I'd heard from him many times before. It was more guttural. Older. Less tuneful than the Mages' singing.

It felt honest to me. As old as stone. As strong as iron.

I felt a shudder roll through the floor, actually far beneath the floor.

Rafferty was summoning an earthquake.

Which worked for me. I felt my confidence increase with another *Pyr* at my side. I was already becoming strong enough to play on the team.

I caught a glimpse of movement and spun. A second Mage lifted his hands to toss a similar spell net at Rafferty. I had to have his back! I raged fire at the Mage, sending a scorching torrent of flames in his direction. It should have cooked him dead, but he shifted shape.

Next I saw the beetle on the floor.

I spit at it, miring it in dragon spittle.

The Mage changed to a snake, but he was easy to snatch up that way. He shifted to a bird in my grasp, but I pulled out a fistful of his feathers. He became a minotaur, but I had him by the horns. I slammed his body into the cinder-block wall, helping it to crumble.

He became a butterfly and flitted away before I could snatch him.

How many kinds of shape shifters had there been, once upon a time? Now just the partner species, the ones who couldn't shift, survived.

Thanks to the Mages.

Kohana said there were four varieties of shape shifters left. Just four.

I wasn't going to let that drop down to three, not so long as I could do anything about it.

The other Mage continued to sing, weaving a luminous barrier all around us. It was only halfway up the walls, glowing with that brilliant orange.

But the floor heaved and rippled as the earth answered Rafferty's song.

The walls cracked.

The ceiling fell, chunks of plaster and wood falling over our shoulders. It was a good moment to be in dragon form. I wondered whether this was what Godzilla felt like in those cheesy old movies.

The Mage wasn't so lucky. He stopped singing when a piece of concrete hit him in the skull. I saw his blood under the rubble, and couldn't feel a lot of regret.

The walls trembled one last time; then the building that was above the basement room started to collapse into rubble. Rafferty and I pushed aside the debris and freed ourselves from the ruins. There was more dust than I would have believed possible, but Rafferty reared up and spread his wings high. He sang with force and power, such force and power that it seemed he was one with the heaving earth.

It was certainly keeping time to his beat.

Trevor and Adrian climbed out of the wreckage and ran. I could have gone after Adrian, taken some justice out of his hide, but I had more important work to do.

Rafferty stopped singing, holding one long last note. Then he nodded at me.

It was time. I grabbed my dad's scales in my claws and Rafferty seized the other two sets. He had Thorolf's moonstone scales and Delaney's copper-and-emerald ones.

"We can fly back," he said. "Although I can move through space, it exhausts me to do it more than once."

I could relate to that. In fact, I was relieved not to have to do the manifestation tango again.

We were so out of there!

We had already launched ourselves into the air, triumphant with our victory, when I saw that there was a barrier forming around us.

A network of brilliant orange mesh.

"*Trap!*" I shouted in old-speak, and Rafferty shot skyward. He couldn't see the spell, but maybe he could sense it.

Or maybe he believed me.

Either way, we both flew straight up as hard and as fast as we could. That must have been why neither one of us saw the lightning bolt.

The brilliant yellow came right out of nowhere.

It struck Rafferty in the chest.

He was flung backward by the force of its impact.

And knocked unconscious. He dropped the two sets of scales and fell earthward. The orange mesh spell wall continued to climb high on either side, already curving in to close the top.

I could guess that there'd be no escape once it sealed itself.

I looked down at Rafferty, then at the scales in my grasp, then at the ever-diminishing hole overhead. I had to choose between helping Rafferty and keeping hold of my dad's scales.

With no confidence I could get out of this myself.

I had time to panic before I heard Kohana's laugh.

That was when I remembered who could throw lightning bolts. Yellow ones.

We'd been tricked.

. . .

THE RED TIDE of rage rolled through me with savage power. It practically sparked from the tips of my claws. It gave me new power and strength unlike anything I'd ever felt before.

I'd helped Kohana. Even if his ploy had been a setup, I'd gone back to help him in good faith. He'd used my own nature against me.

And that was just evil.

I understood that Jared had sensed deceit in Kohana, that that was why he'd been so hostile. I knew Jared couldn't have seen the whole truth of it, because he would have warned me, but he'd sensed trouble.

I spun and saw Kohana. It wasn't a coincidence that I had to go back toward the ground to attack him, that retaliation would lead me deeper into the realm of the spell.

I didn't care.

"*Rafferty!*" I screamed in old-speak. To my relief, he stirred. He didn't manage it in time to keep from hitting the earth, but he didn't slam into it as hard as he might have. He managed to land on his feet, stumbling a bit, but still an improvement.

I could see that he was shaken. I swooped down toward him, dropping my dad's scales into his custody. I hovered beside him, simmering with anger.

"I'll be fine," he said, and coughed. He smiled. "Just not as young as I once was."

"He's mine," I said, eyeing the laughing Kohana. "He lied to me."

Rafferty considered the other shape shifter, then pulled that black-and-white ring from his talon. He pushed it onto mine. "You can do it, Zoë."

"Do what, exactly?"

Rafferty smiled. He settled atop his hoard of scales, giving them a pat. "Do what needs to be done. You *are* the Wyvern. Never doubt it."

He was sounding like Jared.

Okay. What needed to be done was that Kohana needed to be thumped.

And I'd won the job.

It was me and my inner dragon, kicking ass and taking names. Guess who had moved to the top of my Incinerate Next list?

I launched myself toward Kohana, letting that crimson rage fuel the blue shimmer. It was a strange feeling, like flying on the leading edge of a tornado. A dangerous balance. A precarious one. A single false move and I could be fried.

No, Kohana was the goose who'd get cooked.

"Why?" I shouted after him.

"You or us," he retorted. "Not much of a choice."

I was incredulous. "You made a deal with the Mages?"

Kohana's sneer was my only answer.

"But they want to eliminate all shifters. You had to know they'd betray you next."

"More time is always better than less time." And with that, he flung a lightning bolt at me.

I dodged it easily. I flew right past him, breathing dragonfire. I singed maybe the tip of one feather, but he moved quickly, dodging my assault. I snatched at him and missed. He was nimble, that was for sure.

He turned and I followed him.

He twisted and I went after him.

He flew in tight circles, but I was right on his butt, snatching for a piece of him and breathing fire.

Never mind gym class—this was contortionist class.

But I had motivation like never before.

His eyes flashed and heat lightning struck all around us, lighting the ground with blinding intensity. The spell shield sparked and glowed, seeming to respond to the lightning. He threw lightning bolts, never seeming to run out. I scratched him. I bit at him. I tossed in a little dragonsmoke, but he seemed unaffected. We wound an erratic pattern across the confined chunk of sky.

As soon as I got my chance, I seized him and flung him into the spell wall.

He went right through it.

He screamed and came back through it, his eyes blazing as he targeted me. I ducked; he missed; I zipped back and caught the end of his tail. One ebony feather tugged loose and he spun to cast a lightning bolt at me.

It caught me in the hip, burning, but I didn't let go. "Why?" I shouted at him again.

"*Wakiya* and *Unktehila* fought aeons ago, and we won this land for our kind." He threw another lightning bolt. It missed me. "You were supposed to stay in *your* lands."

"Where's that, exactly?"

"Over the water. Europe." His eyes flashed. "Your kind abandoned our treaty." He spun faster, twisting like a cyclone. Maybe he hoped I'd get dizzy and let go, but I was too angry for that.

"Or forgot it. We lost a ton of lore in the Middle Ages."

His disdain was clear. "No one with any dignity forgets the history of their kind."

"And that makes us disposable?"

"Better your kind than mine." His eyes gleamed. "Besides, you opened the door. You summoned me. Don't blame me for answering your call."

It wasn't my fault. He'd twisted things around, betrayed us, and used my inexperience against me. It wouldn't happen again.

At least we understood each other. We spun around and around and around, faster and faster, black and white swirling together so that the colors were no longer distinct from each other.

A swirl of black and white.

I had a vision suddenly, a vision of a black dragon and a white one locked in an endless circle. I saw them spinning faster and faster and faster beneath a pulsing red light.

In time to Rafferty's song to the earth.

They disappeared, coalescing into a spiral that looked like liquid glass.

And when they were gone, a ring rolled across the stone floor. The vision faded abruptly.

That had been the ring that was now on my talon.

I knew it with complete conviction.

This ring was the product of a white dragon and a black dragon sacrificing themselves. In a flash, I guessed whom they had been.

Sophie and her *Pyr* lover.

And I had them right in my hand.

"*Wyvern!*" I roared in old-speak. *"Help me, Sophie!"*

25

Sophie was there in a flash, as if she'd been waiting for me to invite her.

I recognized her from my dream.

But Sophie was transparent, not truly there. Fair and finely boned and truly beautiful, she had the most expressive eyes. A gentle demeanor. Maybe it was her ghost.

More important, there was a *Pyr* with her, as dark as she was pale. He was no more substantial than she.

"Never to be bound by sorcery again!" he roared, and slashed at Kohana.

Kohana didn't see the blow coming. Was I the only one who could see Sophie and her lover?

Kohana could feel them, that was for sure, because the *Pyr* beat the crap out of the *Wakiya*.

He was one mean fighting machine.

When he cast Kohana toward the earth, unconscious and bleeding, the *Pyr* spit after his falling body with disgust. "Liar," he said, making the word sound ominous. "Vermin. Oath breaker."

He turned to look at me, dark eyes glittering, and I had a moment of uncertainty. What did he want? What would he do? He hovered before me like an avenging angel with something to prove.

Sophie smiled at him with affection, which was encouraging.

"Wyvern present," he said, inclining his head formally. "I am Nikolas of Thebes, and I stand pledged to your service forever."

"Um. Thanks."

"You have loosed us to do your bidding. What else is your desire?"

So I had a magic genie in my ring. Bonus. Did I get three wishes or more? I decided to prioritize, just in case. "Can you break the spell so Rafferty and I can go free?"

Nikolas smiled. It was a slightly condescending smile, if you must know. Very dragonlike. "Of our kind, only the Wyvern can cast a spell," he said, then smiled at Sophie. His heart was in his eyes. I wanted a guy to look at me like that one day—and yes, I had a specific guy in mind. "Only her spell endures forever."

He offered his claw to Sophie.

Romeo and Juliet. Just like Isabelle had said.

Sophie met my gaze, then lifted a single talon, making a cutting gesture.

I blinked, not understanding. But she was done with giving me clues, if that's what she had been doing. She turned away and flew to Nikolas's side. They were crazy in love with each other, these two ghosts. I'd have to be stupid to miss it. I wondered whether they were real at all, or some kind of vision.

I could see them only with my left eye. And even then, they were kind of hazy.

But he had thumped Kohana.

The pair started to spiral slowly before me, then spun faster and faster. They turned so that she held his tail in her mouth and he had hers in his. It was just like my vision. They spun in a circle that moved so fast, it seemed to cast sparks in every direction.

Red sparks.

They rose higher and higher in the sky, as if they would spin their way up to the stars. That circle spun furiously, faster and faster, so they were a brilliant blur.

And then there was just a ring falling through the sky toward me. I snatched it out of the air and shoved it back onto my talon. Funny, I didn't remember taking it off.

It glinted for a moment, seemingly filled with starlight, then looked like glass again. Just as it always had.

I looked down at Rafferty, who was watching me. He didn't look surprised, just interested. He probably couldn't play the eye game.

I looked at the ring with new appreciation. Sophie and Nikolas. They had sacrificed their lives for the good of the *Pyr* and the world. Maybe they had helped me because I'd been ready to make the same sacrifice.

Maybe I'd just gotten lucky.

I wanted to see Jared again, to tell him what I'd seen and to compare notes. I wanted to tell him about Sophie and Nikolas, because I was sure that wasn't in his book. It was a little addendum we could add to his collection of dragon lore.

And then...who knew?

His spellsong was so close. Tempting.

But I was trapped in this fiery spell prison.

That was when I realized that my talon—the one adorned with the ring—had a long, sharp edge.

Like a knife.

I guessed what Sophie had meant.

I had exactly nothing to lose.

I FLEW to the top of the spell wall, reasoning that it might be weaker where it had been joined at the top. I took a deep breath, then shoved my talon into its glittering mesh.

I heard my nail pop through the barrier.

And the orange glitter dimmed around the hole I'd made. Encouraged, I slid my nail down, slicing the barrier formed by the spell. It cut like a knife through butter.

I let out a hoot of joy and cut faster, flying down toward Rafferty with incredible speed. I watched the light of the spell die, like an electrical grid going dark, on either side of the cut. It shredded beneath my nail more and more readily, tearing like rotten cloth.

I cut it all the way down to the ground, then flew in a little flourish.

Rafferty was grinning at me. There's something about a dragon grin. It just makes you want to laugh out loud.

He tossed me my dad's scales, grabbed the other two sets, and we soared upward through that gap. There were stars on every side of us, glittering and magical, and I felt like I had conquered the world.

I knew exactly how I wanted to celebrate.

I owed a certain somebody a flight.

We heard Jared's song and saw the flash of dragonfire in the distance. The dads who had their scales were fighting alongside the young *Pyr*, battling Mages, even as they wrought new spells to replace the ones Jared destroyed. The dads on the red rock fought in human form, smashing Mages who became snakes, pummeling those who could be grabbed, and generally doing what damage they could. The guys defended Quinn, who was down on the rock again.

I had a bad feeling about that.

"*The Wyvern returns triumphant!*" Rafferty roared, first in old-speak, then aloud. It seemed that the Earth herself took up his victorious cry.

As soon as the Mages heard that, they scattered.

Nick and the guys chased a few of them into the distance as we landed on the red rock. The last coats of scales disappeared in record time, secreted away by their rightful owners.

Thorolf spit after the Mages, his frustration clear. Then he bumped fists with Nick and Liam in congratulations for what they'd achieved. "Couldn't have done it without you."

"Guess you taught us something after all," Nick countered, and Thorolf grinned. The guys were looking pretty proud of themselves as the older *Pyr* congratulated them.

I shifted back to human form, immediately spotting Jared. He was kneeling beside Quinn with my dad, both of them focused on the fallen Smith.

Quinn wasn't the only one of the older *Pyr* who was wounded, but he was the only one who wasn't moving. He hadn't left the red rock, although he had managed to shift shape. Maybe the transformation had exhausted him. He was sprawled across the red rock as a massive sapphire-and-steel dragon, barely breathing.

Uh-oh.

We weren't out of the woods yet.

GARRETT KNELT BESIDE HIS DAD, his fingertips hovering over his injury. The scales on Quinn's back were blackened and shriveled, looking more like burned paper than burned armor. Even if he had been conscious, Quinn couldn't have reached the injury to repair it.

"He was cycling between forms before," Liam said.

"A sign of serious injury," Jared said.

Jared got to his feet and glanced at me. He was on the other side of the group, and I wished he'd been beside me. He looked exhausted, too—he was pale and there were shadows under his eyes. Our gazes held for a long moment, but there was nothing to celebrate yet.

"Is Quinn going to die?" Nick demanded, voicing the fear we all felt.

There was no old-speak, but we all knew the answer. As one, we turned to look at Garrett.

I saw that Garrett already understood that he'd have to fix his father's scales.

And that he was terrified.

"It's like a dragonsmoke wound," Donovan said, which didn't sound promising.

"But made with a spell," Jared said, sounding disgusted. "They've figured out how to replicate *Pyr* weaknesses."

A shudder ran through our entire group. The Mages weren't just alive and well and making trouble for us—they were really good at it. While the *Pyr* had been thinking everything was quiet, they'd been learning and refining new skills.

Now the Smith, our healer, had to be healed by a younger apprentice, one who had not learned all the necessary skills yet.

And there was no one who could help him out.

Or was there? I remembered Garrett's request. I tried to think of how I could fulfill it. Jared's head snapped up and he stared at me, new hope in his eyes.

Could I do it?

Jared held my gaze and nodded.

Meanwhile, my dad put his hand on Garrett's shoulder. "Your father used to cleanse a dragonsmoke wound with fire."

"Did it work?" Nick asked.

My dad shrugged, his features drawn with concern.

I'm sure I wasn't the only one who noticed that he had referred to Quinn in the past tense. I closed my right eye to look at him, and could see a slow spiral rising from his body. It looked like a waft of smoke, silvery and almost insubstantial.

A silvery cord that stretched into the sky. I stared upward but couldn't see where it went.

I could guess.

"There's a connection between him and the Mages," I said.

"It was how *Slayers* used to steal our life force, back before we eliminated them," Rafferty said. "That link has to be broken if Quinn's going to survive."

"Burn it!" Liam said. "Tell us where it is, Zoë."

"No," Jared said. "That won't work."

He knew more about spells than the rest of us, and I trusted him.

Rafferty flicked a look at him. "Never worked with dragonsmoke, either."

I put my hand on Garrett's shoulder. My heart stopped cold when I met his gaze. He was terrified, but no more than I was. His dad's survival depended upon his making a repair quickly and correctly.

With fire.

I wasn't sure I could give Garrett the connection he needed, but we had to try.

For Quinn's sake.

"Let's go for it," I said, and he didn't argue.

Garrett and I bent over Quinn's body, both in dragon form. The other *Pyr* surrounded us in a circle, and we were beneath an umbrella of brilliant flames. The snow was melting away from the red rock in the heat, but I could only watch Garrett. He fussed over his lack of a forge, and frowned as he examined the wound. He lifted the damaged scales with care, blanching at the dark, festering cut.

I knew it was the worst injury he'd ever seen, and understood that he desperately wanted his dad's advice.

He'd said that Sophie had opened a connection to past Smiths for his dad. Well, she'd just helped us once. Maybe she'd help me again.

"*Sophie*," I murmured in old-speak, the single word sounding like an incantation. I turned the ring on my talon and murmured her name over and over again, a plea for her to listen.

Garrett closed his eyes and mustered his dragonfire. I saw him build it in his chest, coaxing it to burn higher, doing the best he could with what he knew. When his eyes opened, they were blazing, lit by an inner fire. And when the flames erupted from his mouth, they were so vivid a yellow that I couldn't look straight at them.

He bent over his dad, turning his dragonfire on the wound. The silver cord thickened then and seemed to burrow deeper beneath Quinn's skin, as if it understood that he meant to destroy it. Quinn shuddered and gasped and looked even more frail.

"No!" Delaney cried.

Garrett shook, but still he breathed his fire. I could see him fighting for control, wishing for more strength. I could see his knowledge that his power wasn't enough. The wound seemed to boil, some black stuff bubbling out of it.

I spun the ring on my talon, feeling when it took its own momentum. "*Sophie!*" I entreated, then tried old-speak. I felt my tears rise as Quinn shuddered again, as Garrett took a breath, as I feared Sophie had shared all the favors she would.

Or could.

I felt a hand on my shoulder and assumed it was my dad.

In the beginning, there was the fire, Sophie whispered in my ear. I knew this passage as well as I knew my name.

I looked up at her, not understanding, and shook my head. This was no time for reciting old verses.

Sophie was beside me, as ethereal and beautiful as ever. I realized that no one else had noticed her—or could see her. She smiled. *The union of the four elements creates a power that can overcome anything.* I looked into her eyes, her enormous pupils defying belief. I saw the guys and thought it was a reflection; then the pieces of the puzzle snapped into place.

"We have to do this together!" I shouted. "Nick, you're earth. And Liam, you're water. I'm air. Garrett is fire. Come on!"

They came and we made a circle around Quinn's fallen form, holding claws so that we made an unbroken ring. As soon as Nick took my left claw and the circle was complete, I felt a shiver run through me. I saw Quinn's body quiver, as well.

"Breathe fire on the wound," I instructed them, running on instinct. "Bring your element to bear." Then I leaned toward Garrett, opening my thoughts to whatever Sophie had to offer.

I felt a dizzying rush in my mind. I was surrounded by stars, or falling snowflakes, something brilliant and glittery that swirled around us. Sophie's claw was light on my back, anchoring me in the onslaught.

I held Garrett's gaze, and I saw him gasp. I saw him nod and swallow back a tear. "Oui, Grandpère," he murmured in old-speak. I'd forgotten that Quinn's family was French. "Oui. Je comprends maintenant." He swallowed. "Merci mille fois."

And when he turned his dragonfire upon Quinn's wound, it burned white and hot and was filled with sparkles. The silvery conduit sizzled, spewing orange sparks, then abruptly snapped. Black venom boiled out of the wound. Quinn's skin lost its pale hue, and the sapphire and steel scales began to regain their proper shape.

I watched in awe, marveling at what he could do.

Lock the portal, Sophie murmured in my thoughts, and I paid attention as she secured that door in my mind. There was my connection to the wisdom of the ages, but I sensed it was something that should be sampled in moderation.

We stood as one, all breathing fire simultaneously, as Quinn grew more substantial again. He was taking power from his son's dragonfire, recovering before our very eyes. His scales brightened and shone. I saw his claws flex and there was power in his grip once more. I felt the older *Pyr* draw closer, felt my dad's hand on my shoulder. I couldn't even look at Jared, I was so excited by what he would say.

He couldn't accuse me of not trying, not anymore.

Maybe we could share a celebratory kiss.

When Quinn sighed with relief, I knew it was going to be okay. He rolled over, and we stopped the onslaught of dragonfire.

He shifted shape and smiled crookedly at Garrett, who was still pale and shaking. His gaze was bright and assessing as he surveyed his son.

"Fair enough. We have a new Smith," he said, his voice the low rumble we all knew so well. "His apprenticeship is complete." Quinn stood and hugged Garrett tightly, while all the *Pyr* cheered.

Then I looked for Jared. I had lots of ideas of how we could celebrate—another kiss, or maybe that ride I owed him—but I heard the revving of a motorcycle engine.

Fading into the distance.

Which pretty much said it all.

I am the Wyvern. I'm not some clingy chick. So I wasn't going to hang around pining for some biker rock-star rebel who couldn't even be bothered to say good-bye to me. I had become what I was destined to be—or at least I'd made some big steps in that direction.

I had better things to do than whine.

This was cool. This was a triumph. And if Jared was too proud or stuck-up to enjoy the moment with us, well, that was his loss.

No. I didn't really believe it either. But it sounded good.

I was hugged by most of the *Pyr*, kissed by a few, had my hand shaken so many times that I thought my arm might fall off. I could feel how proud my dad was, especially when he put his arm across my shoulders and tugged me closer.

"You must be exhausted," he said, while the *Pyr* continued to talk.

"Pretty much. But I have a question."

"Ask away."

"What happened to the last Wyvern, to Sophie and Nikolas?"

My dad looked down at me. "You know their names?"

"I saw their ghosts." I gestured, and I noticed how his gaze locked on the black-and-white ring. "They helped us. He said that the *Pyr* should never be enchanted again."

"Nikolas was one of Drake's Dragon's Tooth Warriors. They were cursed for thousands of years, until first Nikolas was freed and then the rest." My father frowned. "And Nikolas loved Sophie as soon as he saw her. He adored her."

"Sounds like that was a problem."

"It is forbidden for us to mate with our own kind."

"Mates are always women."

"Human," my father corrected. "And I can only assume that it will be so with you."

"You're not sure?"

"I've never known a Wyvern well, Zoë. They have been elusive creatures, in my time."

"Do we even get firestorms?"

He shrugged.

Great. I was getting used to the less information package. "But what about Sophie and Nikolas?"

"They loved each other. I don't know exactly what happened between them—"

"But you can guess."

My father chose his words with care. "Something happened that persuaded Sophie that they couldn't be together, after all. It wasn't that she didn't care for him."

"You think they did it."

My father inclined his head, too diplomatic to speculate on anyone else's sexual relations. "Whatever happened, I believe she lost her Wyvern powers over her choice."

Wait a minute....

He continued, not waiting at all. "And so she chose the greater good. They destroyed the Academy together, dying for a good cause."

But she lost her powers with her virginity. This sounded like a very bad deal to me. Was it because she lost her virginity at all, or because she lost it to the wrong guy? I was pretty interested in the nitpickity details. I was already fond of my powers, such as they were, but not excited by the prospect of lifelong celibacy just to ensure that I kept them.

It seemed unfair to have to choose one option or the other without getting to try both first.

It seemed unreasonable not to know absolutely for sure, in advance.

Jared, though, was human. Theoretically that shouldn't be an issue....

Have you noticed that there's not a really good way to ask your dad about sex? It would take me a while to formulate *that* question.

My dad and I left the red rock to walk through the prairie that surrounded it. I could hear the snow melting, a little trickle of water coming from all sides, and the snow didn't seem as deep. The sky was perfectly clear above us—it was a brilliant, clear midday blue.

I was thinking about my dream when my vision of Sophie morphed into Isabelle. "Can I ask you something else?"

My dad smiled.

"This is going to sound weird, but do you think people can be reincarnated?"

I thought he would laugh. Instead he turned and looked back at the group of *Pyr* still on the rock, his expression thoughtful. "Sophie and Nikolas died during my firestorm with your mother."

I knew that was why they'd assumed I was a Wyvern when I'd been born a girl, so I didn't interrupt him.

I was glad I didn't, because his next words surprised me.

"Donovan had a bond with Nikolas, as Nikolas had been freed from enchantment during his firestorm. Alex was pregnant with Donovan's child when Sophie and Nikolas died, and when that son was born, Donovan was struck by how much the boy reminded him of Nikolas." My father met my gaze. "That's why they named him Nick. It wasn't just to honor a lost comrade. Donovan believed that Nick *was* Nikolas reborn."

"But why?"

"A romantic would say that he'd come back to find his Sophie."

I looked at the celebrating group and spotted Isabelle with Nick.

The present is where the future shakes hands with the past.

And I knew then why she and Sophie had merged into each other in my dream. I knew why Rafferty had ended up adopting a human daughter, and I knew that I had the power to help the former Wyvern win her heart's desire in this life.

And maybe get a good friend in the bargain. I smiled at Isabelle and she smiled back at me.

I still wanted her boots. Just so you know.

"Should we fly home?" My dad bumped my shoulder with his. "Your mom will be worried sick."

I nodded and my dad shifted in a brilliant shimmer of blue, a jubilant shimmer. He was magnificent. Then he gestured to me and I shifted right after him, loving the feel of that change racing through my body. We leapt into the sky together and flew straight toward the sun. There was no one to fight.

Just Dragon Air, under my own speed.

And it was every bit as fabulous as I'd always expected it to be.

Even if I couldn't share it with my human of choice.

Five Things I Will Tell Meagan about My Spring Break:

1. I met an extremely hot guy who is a musician, and I found his band's music online.
2. I've listened to the eleven songs available for download on their site 943 times already.
3. I have in my possession the newest, shiniest, most fabulous messenger ever, even though it doesn't ship to the rest of the world until Christmas. It incidentally has amazing sound and lets me take those eleven songs everywhere I go. I can hear Jared as clearly as if he were singing just for me. He's not and I know it. But still.
4. I stole an insulated pizza carrier to keep our pizza hot, the closest thing to breaking the law I've ever done. I took it back later to make sure the guy didn't get fired over it. My life of crime is officially over.
5. I had my first kiss and it was with an extremely hot guy. Who has a band. And a vintage Ducati motorcycle. And the greenest eyes I've ever seen.

WINGING IT

THE DRAGON DIARIES BOOK TWO

Zoë Sorensson yearns to come into her powers as the only female dragon shifter. But being part of two worlds is more complicated than she expected. It's bad enough that she's the target of the Mages' plan to eliminate all shifters—she also has to hide her true nature from her best friend Meagan, a human. For her sixteenth birthday, all Zoë wants is one normal day, including a tattoo and a chance to see hot rocker Jared.

Instead, the *Pyr* throw her a birthday party but ban Meagan from attendance, putting Zoë in a tight spot. Things get even worse when Zoë is invited to the popular kids' Halloween party and Meagan's left out. Zoë knows the party is a trap laid by the host, an apprentice Mage. When Meagan gets a last-minute invite, Zoë must save the day—and her best friend—without revealing her fire-breathing secrets...

I

October 24, 2024

The black envelope fell out of my locker when I unlocked the door before lunch.

I distrusted that envelope on sight.

Not because it was black. Not because it looked like an invitation. Not because I couldn't think of anyone who would invite me anywhere.

Because it was the first weird thing to happen in six months.

I watched it fall, reluctant to touch it.

Why would someone shove an envelope into my locker instead of just talking to me? I couldn't think of one good reason.

I'm not *that* scary.

And if I am, courtesy of my ability to shift into a dragon at will, no one at school knows it. I'm all about managing information these days. I'd been cut slack as a newbie for letting humans see me shift shape—twice—when my Wyvern powers had made their debut in April, but it wouldn't happen again.

My dad, leader of the *Pyr*, had made that perfectly clear.

The envelope landed right side up, my name printed on the front in sparkly gold ink. Not a case of mistaken identity, then. I glanced up and down the corridor but no one was paying any attention to me, just like usual.

The envelope looked more like an invitation the longer I studied it. I lifted it with the toe of my boot, still skeptical. It didn't look thick enough to hold a practical joke.

Suspicious, me? You bet. And with good reason. In April, we younger dragon shifters had discovered that our old enemy the Mages had concocted an evil plan—to eliminate all shifters, one species at a time. We'd found out because they'd targeted us *Pyr*, invading the boot camp held for teenage dragons in Minnesota. The apprentice Mage Adrian had turned us against each other with his nasty magic spells, keeping us busy while the superior Mages tricked and trapped the older *Pyr*. The Mages must have been thinking they could take us dragons down easily, but my friends Liam and Nick and Garrett and I had (ultimately) saved the day.

With—it must be said—the help of two humans in the know.

Jared and Isabelle.

All humans know dragons exist, of course—that's why there are so many stories about us—and many humans know about the *Pyr*, dragon shape shifters on a quest to save Earth. The Covenant was designed by my father for our protection, to keep our identities as secret as possible. We have pledged to use the utmost discretion in shifting—to make sure that very few humans know any *Pyr* in both dragon and human form, yada yada yada.

The thing was, the *Pyr* hadn't known until last spring that there still were other kinds of shifters in the world. Call us isolationist. Kohana—the Thunderbird shifter who'd tried to sell us to the Mages to save his own kind—had told me that there were four varieties of shape shifters left. Wolves, jaguars, dragons, and Thunderbirds. The Mages, he'd told me, had eliminated all the rest and claimed their shapes.

Like a right of conquest: exterminate a species, snag its second skin.

I still have no idea whether this is true, or whether he'd left out some important detail(s). He has an unfortunate tendency to manipulate information. I do know that the Mages somehow get a power boost once they've exterminated an entire race of shifters, and they also become able to assume their forms.

Without having been exterminated ourselves—and thus having no actual data from the experience—details are fuzzy.

The adult *Pyr* had been predictably, well, adult about the whole crisis—after we'd saved them from certain death. My dad had negotiated a treaty with the Mages. They all thought that was that.

Please. I didn't buy it. The *Pyr* were still in the hot seat, so to speak, at least as far as I could see. Just because we'd foiled the Mages once didn't persuade me that they had abandoned their scheme.

That they had been completely quiet since April just made me more suspicious. (In contrast, it made my dad sure that he was right, plus persuaded a whole bunch of other *Pyr,* who'd had their doubts that he was right, too.) But laying low was exactly the kind of thing Mages would do to make us believe they were reconciled to keeping the treaty.

Never mind that Trevor Wilson, the hot guy in my school who played the sax like he was making love to it, was one of them. He was an apprentice Mage, although I didn't exactly know their education process, much less how close to graduation he was. I'd been watching him so carefully this fall that my best friend, Meagan, was convinced that I had a crush on him.

That couldn't be further from the truth.

It also complicated things because *she* had a crush on him.

Not that anything was simple between me and Meagan these days. She has a best friend's radar for knowing when she isn't being told the whole truth—and I can't confide in her, thanks to the restrictions of the Covenant.

As if that wasn't enough, I hadn't heard a thing from the hot motorcycle-riding rebel rocker Jared—yes, the guy who had melted my synapses with one kiss. Last summer I'd finally worked up my nerve to contact him, and he'd sent me only a short reply.

Two sentences, then silence.

Even after that kiss.

I told myself I didn't care, that my only interest in him was that he had the one copy of the only book about the *Pyr* that I knew existed. I needed to talk to him for the sake of the *Pyr.*

Even I knew that was a lie.

The thing is, Jared has the ability to read minds, as well as being a spellsinger who had once been recruited by the Mages because of his innate musical abilities. He'd turned down the Mages, and I had to wonder whether he'd read my thoughts, not liked the view, and decided to turn me down, too.

So, back to the envelope. I was cautiously picking it up just as Meagan appeared beside me. Her timing was perfect.

Perfectly awful, that is.

"What's that?"

"I don't know."

She tilted her head to read the front. "Then maybe you should open it and find out. It looks like an invitation."

Which just reminded me of another issue I wanted to avoid with Meagan. My birthday was coming up in two weeks, my sixteenth, and my dad wanted to invite all of the *Pyr*. That meant my human friends—specifically, my very best friend, Meagan—couldn't be invited, in case she saw something she shouldn't.

I was really starting to hate the Covenant.

I hadn't yet figured out how I'd tell Meagan about the party she wasn't invited to attend.

I ripped open the envelope, avoiding the inevitable.

"It *is* an invitation," Meagan said, reading over my shoulder. "To Trevor Wilson's Halloween party!" She was amazed and impressed. "Lucky you. It's like a dream come true."

Uh, no. In fact, there was a shiver of dread running down my spine. Trevor's party was the last place I'd be on October 31. It'd be thick with Mages of all experience levels. Nuh-uh. The invitation had to be a trick, or a trap, and I wasn't going to walk right into it—like the heroine in a scary movie who goes down to the basement by herself to check out the strange noise, despite the creepy organ music.

I read the invitation again and had a feeling Trevor wasn't going to take no for an answer without a fight. Funny that I'd been itching all summer for something to happen but now that it *was* happening, I wanted it to stop.

Meagan poked me with one finger. "You must have known!"

"I didn't."

"Oh, come on. You've been talking to him, haven't you? He doesn't invite just anybody."

"No, I haven't talked to him at all. You're the one who tutors him in math."

Meagan opened her own locker with obvious optimism.

No envelope fell out.

She rummaged a little, then gave me a look. "I thought we were friends. Forever." Her voice was quiet and I knew she was hurt.

And I'd done the hurting. Inadvertently, but still. "We are."

"So, why don't you tell me what's going on?"

"There's nothing going on that you don't know about."

Have I mentioned that I'm the world's worst liar? Well, I am and Meagan has my number. One of the hazards of having known someone most of your life.

She leaned in really close and said something completely uncharacteristic. "Bullshit."

I blinked.

"Something happened on spring break, and you've been holding out on me ever since. You never even told me what you said to scare Suzanne so much in the locker room, when she picked on me. That was right before you went to Minnesota. Something's changed. Don't think I don't know it."

Something *had* changed. I had changed. In coming to Meagan's defense, I'd started to shift shape for the first time. My eye and my nail had been the only things that changed, but Suzanne had seen both and freaked.

The only good thing was that it was so weird no one believed her.

Meagan took a deep breath and I saw a shimmer of tears on her lashes. Her next words were tight. "If you don't want to be friends anymore, maybe because you suddenly know all kinds of cool people, then at least have the guts to say so."

"That's not true!"

Her lips tightened. "Okay, then. Promise me that you've told me everything."

Trust the math queen to put me in a logical corner. "Well, I haven't and you know it, but that's because I can't, not because I don't want to."

"Why can't you?"

"Because I promised not to tell anyone."

"Promised who?"

I fidgeted. There was no way to make this better. "I can't tell you that."

"Sounds like the same excuse to me." She folded her arms across her chest and leaned against the lockers beside mine. "You think I didn't notice that you haven't mentioned your birthday party?"

Here it came. "My dad wants me to have a family party."

"For your sixteenth? I don't believe it. Your dad isn't a jerk."

"Well, he's determined this time."

"Your mom would never put up with it. If he wanted you to have a family party, she'd let you have another one with your friends." Meagan was on a roll and it wasn't one that made me look good. My mom and I had talked about a friends party. Problem was that most of my friends were also dragon shifters. Except Meagan. Which kind of brought us back to the same place of my dad worrying about what she might see. "You know what I think? I think you're having a party and you're just not inviting me."

She stared at me, daring me to correct her.

And I couldn't hold her gaze.

Because she was right.

"Nice, Zoë," she said, her tone more bitter than I'd ever heard it. Meagan is not a bitch—that I've made her sound this way said more about me than about her. "Really nice. Here's hoping that your new friends are more worth keeping than your old ones." She closed her locker and started to walk away.

"But, Meagan, it's not like that...."

She paused to look back at me. "You can tell me anytime how it is," she said. "But I know already that you won't."

I looked down at the stupid invitation, wishing I'd never gotten it. As much as I liked my new *Pyr* powers, it really sucked to have to keep everything secret from my best friend.

"Have fun at Trevor's party," Meagan added. "And don't worry about me. I've got a new friend of my own."

She slung her pack over one shoulder and marched down the hall, and I knew I couldn't change her mind. I watched as she stopped beside the locker of the new girl, the one who had switched to our school earlier that year.

The one I really didn't like, although I couldn't have said why.

Jessica has dark hair and dark eyes. She's slim and pretty and quiet. She's another math whiz, so she and Meagan bonded in the land where calculating derivatives is as easy as pie. (Pi, maybe. As in recalling the first hundred digits of. So not my territory. Never mind citizenship: I don't even have a visitor's visa to that place.) The thing is, I should have liked Jessica; there was no reason why I shouldn't.

But she gave me the creeps.

Big time.

I was pretty sure it wasn't just jealousy. I just had this sense that she was hiding something. As someone who has a pretty hefty secret myself, I think I know something about keeping secrets. It wasn't because she wore really baggy clothes—like she'd raided her brother's closet—or even that she kept a baseball hat jammed on her head all the time.

Maybe my Wyvern sense was tingling. There's only one female dragon shifter at a time, and she's the Wyvern. *I'm* the Wyvern. And the Wyvern is supposed to have mystical powers. The ability to see the future. The power to give prophecies. Lots of seriously cool stuff.

So far I couldn't do any of it.

But Jessica creeped me out.

And I didn't know why.

Maybe it *was* a Wyvern thing.

I watched as Jessica smiled at Meagan now and hugged her, then looked over Meagan's shoulder at me. She held my gaze for a minute, like she was daring me, then looked away. A sly smile stole over her lips.

That smile sent a shudder right down my spine.

And gave me the worst feeling I've ever had in my life.

Then it was gone.

Precognition?

Jealousy?

Overactive imagination? You choose. I have no idea.

Jessica and Meagan walked toward the cafeteria, their heads bent together as they talked. I noticed the new guy at school, Derek Black, leaning against the lockers, watching me. He looked after Jessica and Meagan, then back at me, and shrugged.

I was embarrassed to have been caught staring at them—like a pathetic loser, not invited to have lunch with two math whizzes. Which I was, but still. I was used to not being noticed by anyone at school. I felt myself blush

—no surprise there. A smile tugged at the corner of Derek's mouth and I turned to my locker, apparently fascinated by its contents.

I had the sense that the slightest encouragement from me would have brought him right to my side, but I wasn't in the mood to look for new friends. I had enough issues with my current ones. I kicked my locker shut, jammed the invitation into my backpack, and headed out to the bleachers to eat my lunch.

Alone.

I had no idea how to fix things with Meagan, and no one to ask. An older sibling, even one who found me annoying and tedious, could have been helpful. At least he or she would have dealt with the Covenant's restrictions in the past.

But I have no brothers or sisters. My mom is human. My dad is a dragon shifter, but he's hundreds of years old. I doubt he even remembers being a teenager—I doubt he remembers being a frisky young dragon of three centuries. The guys, who are roughly my contemporaries and also dragon shifters—Liam, Garrett, and Nick—always tell me I worry too much about it.

They are not much help.

I WAS SITTING on the bleachers, debating the merits of asking one of the guys for help anyway, when Derek came out of the school.

No, that's not how it was. I was alone one minute, and the next, he was there.

Just as if he'd been sitting at the other end of the bleachers all along.

I didn't hear him coming, not at all. That might not seem like much of a big deal, but I *should* have heard him. No matter how quiet he was. We dragons have sharp senses, sharper than human senses, but I didn't hear him come outside. I'm not used to having people sneak up on me—because it never happens.

Was I losing the *Pyr* powers that I had?

Or had I just been really really lost in my thoughts?

I thought for a minute that Derek had followed me, but he didn't glance my way. His back was toward me as he unpacked his lunch. Courtesy of my extra-keen vision, I could check it out. His lunch looked a lot like mine—

homemade sandwich, piece of fruit, granola bar. Except he had two sandwiches, and he'd bought a carton of milk.

I studied him as he ate, pretending not to. He was a bit stocky, solidly built but not fat. Dark hair, and he wore dark clothes. I'd guess that he was an inch or two taller than me, and I'm the tall skinny type. Not sure because I'd never been that close to him. He was the kind of quiet guy people overlooked. He slid in and out of English class like a shadow and never said much. Even when he got called on, his answers were always short and gruff. He could have used a haircut—I'd noticed before that his hair hung over his eyes. It made him look a little wild. Or just scruffy.

He seemed to spend a lot of time alone, which made me wonder whether we had something in common. The fact that we were the only two outside having lunch on a snowy day just reinforced that sense. In a few hours, the bleachers would be crowded for the big football game against Central, but I liked it better quiet. It was snowing lightly, a bit cold for a picnic, but a little frigid solitude suited my mood.

Which was bleak, in case you weren't sure.

I decided not to send messages to the guys. I wasn't ready to be told that I was being a dope. They're good friends, but they're *guys*. I would have loved to talk to Meagan.

But she was with Jessica.

Which brought me right back to square one.

I could have used a confidence boost, the kind I get from shifting shape, but Derek was too close. He would notice the sudden appearance of a dragon in the bleachers and he'd guess that the dragon and I were one and the same. (He didn't seem to be stupid.) That was Covenant-breaking territory again. I shoved my hands into my pockets and tried to content myself with shifting my thumbnail to a talon instead.

It was no substitute.

I didn't eat my granola bar, even though it was chocolate-dipped. That tells you everything you need to know about the state of the world in Zoë terms.

Like I said, it was nearly my sixteenth birthday. There were three things I wanted for the big day:

1. A grudge match against Kohana, the Thunderbird shifter who'd lied to me, plus worked with the Mages to nearly wipe me and the rest of the *Pyr* off the map
2. A tattoo
3. A chance to see Jared again, if only to find out that I was never going to see him again.

Of the above, I had a remote chance of achieving only #3. Even with it being my birthday. I knew what my dad thought about me fighting anyone, and I knew what my mom thought of tattoos. But they both knew Jared, and they knew I knew him. And his band was playing a concert right in town, on Saturday (thus not a school night) at a co-op club downtown that didn't serve alcohol.

The way I saw it, Jared had chosen the venue because he *expected* me to come.

Or he was daring me.

He's like that. Irreverent. Challenging.

Hot.

Whether it was to deliver the flight on Dragon Air that I owed him, to snag another kiss—just to verify that the first one had, in fact, been amazing and of the bone-melting variety—or to barter for another peek at the book he had on my kind, didn't really matter.

I wanted to go.

I *needed* to go.

Which meant that I needed to persuade my mom that going was a good idea. And do it without beguiling her. Beguiling is kind of like hypnosis and it's a dragon trick I mastered pretty early. We conjure flames in our eyes; the humans look closer; we make suggestions. That's beguiling. As you might expect, it works best when it's a suggestion the person already wants to take—which meant that beguiling my mom wasn't a good plan on a whole bunch of fronts. She'd likely catch me—she's not stupid, either—and then I'd be toast.

Better to go with plain old begging.

Negotiating.

Shameless groveling.

Even being a dragon girl didn't make me think that sneaking out to go to the concert without parental approval would end well.

So, I *had* to convince my mom.

I was running out of time—it was Thursday and the concert was Saturday. This had to be the day.

I figured I was due for *something* to go right.

DURING ART CLASS I sent a message to Nick, asking his advice about Meagan (and nearly had my fabulous shiny new messenger confiscated in the process. My mom says kids used to have cell phones, which were plenty good enough, that they didn't need messengers with all their apps and computing powers, right in their hands all the time. Wrong. Mine is my umbilical cord to the world). He told me—predictably—that I was making too big of a deal about it.

TALK TO HER.
HANG OUT WITH HER.
JUST DON'T TALK ABOUT THAT.
YOU CAN BE FRIENDS AND STILL HAVE ONE SECRET.

Right.

Meagan was at her locker when I got out of science class at the end of the day. She was alone, which had to be a good sign for making up, and tugging on her coat.

I decided to make a valiant effort.

"Hi," I said as I unlocked my locker. She glanced up but didn't say anything. Then she started to rummage in her locker.

At least she hadn't left.

"Going to the game?" I asked, even though I could guess the answer.

She shook her head. "I've got two hours of piano practice to finish before dinner." She shoved a couple of books into her bag and zipped it up.

She didn't ask me if I was going, which would have been a nice opening, but I'd make my own.

"So, I was thinking, maybe I could have lunch with you and Jessica one day. Maybe tomorrow. You know, so I could get to know her a bit."

Meagan looked at me. She tended to be very serious, but even if she hadn't been, her glasses made her look that way.

I smiled. "I don't want to fight with you," I said, feeling that it was impossibly lame. "Maybe we can hang out."

Meagan sighed. She glanced down the hall, then back at me. She looked me right in the eye. "Will you tell me what's going on when you can?"

"I'd tell you everything right this minute if I could."

She smiled a little then, a bit of a sad smile, but anything she might have said was cut short.

By guess who.

"Meagan!" Jessica shouted. "You'll never believe what I got on that math test! Woo-HOOO!"

Meagan turned toward her new friend, and I stared at my boots. They squealed together about Jessica's perfect score—how either of them could be surprised by that was a mystery—and I felt completely excluded from the discussion. Forgotten.

"Going to the game?" a guy asked, from my other side.

I nearly jumped out of my skin.

It was Derek. How long had he been there? I was surprised that he'd done that silent approach thing again, but there was no disputing it—I hadn't heard him.

I looked him up and down. He *was* just a bit taller than me. He was watching me closely. His eyes were a very pale blue, almost icy, and he didn't seem to blink much.

That made me feel awkward, too. I got interested in my books.

Dropped three.

He reached for them when I reached for them and our hands brushed. I pulled mine back like I'd been burned. He picked up my books and handed them to me. If I'd been blushing before, I had to be as red as a beet then.

"Sorry," he said. "Didn't mean to surprise you." He shrugged and hefted his bag of gear. "Just thought I'd ask."

"You're on the team?" The fact that he had a bag of football gear made that a stupid question, but it was too late to pretend I hadn't said it.

He glanced at the bag, then back at me, and almost smiled. "So?"

I liked that he didn't make a big deal of my stupid question. Or about me being awkward and flustered. He was still giving me a shy smile, like he would wait all week for me to answer. I was a bit disconcerted by how steadily he watched me.

"Um, I'm not sure." I turned to Meagan as if I would ask her, but she had already moved down the hall, hauling her backpack onto her shoulders and laughing with Jessica. They hugged and then Jessica headed for the far doors. Meagan turned toward the bathroom, her coat swinging open and her gloves in her hands.

In that moment, I saw my nemesis, Suzanne, and her followers coming down the corridor toward us. They were already in their cheerleader uniforms, the four of them cutting a path through the kids in the hallway like they were royalty. Suzanne was—naturally—in the lead. She swung her hips hard as she walked, making the pleats of her little skirt flip up. Every guy in the vicinity was watching her thighs. Probably salivating. Suzanne knew it—and she loved it. She had buckets of confidence and seemed to expect to be the center of attention.

All the time.

I swear she was taking inventory of who was looking.

But her smile dimmed when she saw Meagan. She watched Meagan go into the bathroom—oblivious—and her expression turned mean. She waved off her minions and strolled in after Meagan.

I had a really bad feeling about that.

"Good luck in the game, then," I said brightly to Derek, remembering a bit late that he was still there, waiting. I smiled at him, grabbed my stuff, slammed my locker, and headed down the hall.

"Thanks." His single word seemed to follow me.

Like old-speak, almost.

That caught my attention. Old-speak is dragon stuff, speech uttered at a lower frequency than humans can hear. It slides into your thoughts, mingles with them, starts to seem like your own idea.

But only dragons can do it (yes, some better than others) and Derek wasn't *Pyr*.

By the time I looked back, Derek was striding toward the guys' locker room.

As if he'd forgotten me, too.

At that moment, though, I had bigger mysteries to solve than guys and their presto-chango interest.

Meagan. No coincidence that the first time I'd made even a partial shift to dragon form had been in defense of Meagan.

When Suzanne had picked a fight in gym.

I wasn't going to let Suzanne bully my friend again.

I opened the door to the bathroom silently, freezing when I overheard Suzanne's words.

"Listen, Jameson." There was menace in Suzanne's tone, a menace I would have heard even if I hadn't had sensitive hearing. The sound of it made me shiver. "We're going to come to an understanding right here and right now."

"B-b-but I—I—I—," Meagan stammered, the way she always does when she's nervous. I closed the bathroom door quietly behind myself. I turned the dead bolt—silently—so no one else could join us, then stood completely still as I listened.

Lucky for me the bathroom was designed to provide some privacy. There was a short wall opposite the door, one that hid the stalls from the hallway even when the door was open. I lurked in that space, invisible to Meagan and to Suzanne, too.

And I eavesdropped.

I could almost hear Meagan sweat.

"I need to pass this trig test or they're going to cancel my extracurricular activities," Suzanne whispered.

"Th-th-that's too bad."

"It would be, if it happened, but nobody takes cheerleading away from me." I heard Suzanne take a step. "So, you're going to help me."

"Are you c-c-coming to the math lab for t-t-tutoring?"

Suzanne laughed. "No. You already sit in front of me in math. Tomorrow, during the test, you're going to pass me the answers."

"I can't do that!" Meagan was too horrified even to stammer.

"Can't you?" Suzanne's voice was low and silky. Trouble. "Maybe I haven't made myself clear. This isn't optional."

"I t-t-told you last year, I wouldn't help you ch-ch-cheat." Now there were shuffling footsteps—Meagan retreating.

"Maybe I can change your mind."

"N-n-no..." I heard Meagan gasp, then something smash.

That was followed by a muffled thump and a moan.

Something heavy fell to the floor.

I peeked around the wall to see Meagan doubled over and Suzanne aiming another punch at her gut. Meagan's bag was on the ground where she'd dropped it. Her glasses were shattered against the far wall, where Suzanne had thrown them.

So Meagan couldn't see the blow coming.

Suzanne had always been a contender on my Incinerate Now list, but with this move she zoomed right to the number one slot.

I wasn't going to stand aside and let my friend get thumped for doing the right thing.

It was dragon time.

I summoned the shimmer, let it rip through my body, and shifted shape with a dull roar.

I'VE GOT to tell you that it feels amazing to shift shape. It's kind of spooky at first, because the sensation is so powerful. Your instinct is to try to control it, to manage the transition, but that's not really possible. You have to go with it.

You have to abandon control and trust your body.

Maybe it's like surfing. You have to get on the wave the right way, but then you just ride and ride and ride. Over time, the getting-on-the-wave bit becomes instinctive and you just look forward to the ride.

It's exhilarating stuff.

It was no different this time, even in a plain old taupe and white high school bathroom. The change ripped through me with lightning speed, surging through my veins and filling me with ferocious power. One minute, I was zitty Zoë of the virtually nonexistent breasts, and the next, I was an enormous white dragon, my talons stretching for Suzanne before she had any clue what was happening.

She took one look at me and screamed. I did enjoy that. She fell back against the metal wall of the cubicles, shrieking. She apparently didn't dare look away from me—she slid her hands along the edges of the cubicles, feeling her way as she put distance between us.

I heard her cronies—Trish and Anna probably—bang on the door. "Suzanne! You okay? Let us in!"

Suzanne couldn't even answer them, she was so shocked. Her mouth was opening and closing, but just a little whimper was coming out.

She crossed herself then, which made me laugh.

I breathed fire as I laughed, which made her turn even more pale. I did ensure that the plume of flame roared right over her head. I wanted to scare her, not hurt her. Not really—mostly because I didn't want to deal with repercussions. I slashed in her general direction with one claw. I sent a playful little plume of flame to burn her skirt and she screamed again.

She stumbled over her own feet in her anxiety to get away. She grabbed the door to the next stall, and it swung open suddenly beneath her weight. She lost her balance, shouted, and fell.

She landed sprawling on the toilet, then covered her face with her hands. She looked so graceless that I nearly laughed out loud.

I took a step closer and smiled, letting her see all my sharp dragon teeth. She peeked through her fingers and trembled.

"Don't hurt me!" she whispered.

I reared back, showing off my full dragon-scaled magnificence. I gripped the walls of the cubicles and gave them a mighty shake, ripping them loose from their moorings.

I was just warming up, but Suzanne fainted.

Her eyes rolled back in her head and she slumped against the wall. Her elbow hit the lever and the toilet flushed, getting her cute little skirt wet.

"Suzanne! Are you all right?" Trish shouted, as the banging on the door grew louder.

I had one minute to think I had done something right, and then I glanced toward Meagan. She'd retrieved her glasses and was peering through the broken lenses at me.

I knew that look.

I called it her Einstein look.

She got it when she was figuring something out, connecting the dots, finding the key to the universe. My heart clenched, because Meagan is pretty much the smartest sixteen-year-old I've ever met.

"Open this door, right this minute!" someone shouted sternly. It sounded like the principal. I heard the jingle of keys.

Meagan turned to the door, panic in her expression. The Einstein look was gone so fast that I wondered whether I'd imagined it. "I'm c-c-coming," she said, sparing one last look at me.

I had to get out of there ASAP—and without Meagan seeing more than she had.

No pressure.

I raged fire at the ceiling, a great orange plume of crackling fire. I heard the paint blister and crack. Meagan covered her eyes against the brightness of the flames, which was all I needed. I conjured the image of exactly where I wanted to be and willed myself to be there.

And when I opened my eyes, I was on the roof of the building where my family's loft took up most of the top floor.

In salamander form.

My heart thundering.

I took a shaky breath, crawled into the shadows by the air-conditioning units to give myself cover, then shifted to my human form.

As usual, it felt good to just be a skinny chick again.

And it felt awesome to have frightened Suzanne.

She'd deserved no less.

Being a dragon shifter completely rocks.

Just in case I haven't mentioned it.

I grinned as I rummaged in my pocket for that granola bar. I needed a sugar hit before I could figure out whether I had technically broken the Covenant again or not.

The Covenant is a creed all we dragon shifters have to swear. Essentially we are forbidden from revealing ourselves in both human and dragon form to humans, and when some human does know us in both forms, my dad—as leader of the *Pyr*—adds that person's name to his list.

Those people-in-the-know are not always trusted, and he makes decisions on a case-bv-case basis, but this theoretically creates a Go To list in case one of us gets targeted or stalked. My dad remembers our kind being hunted almost to extinction in the Middle Ages. He likes us staying under the radar, so to speak.

He'd let it go when I partly shifted the previous spring, mostly because he was glad I was finally starting to shift and also because it had been only a partial shift seen by one person. Also, the punishment was tough stuff—exile, for as long as my dad decreed, to his location of choice. Corralled by his dragonsmoke, which is invisible but burns if crossed by a *Pyr* without permission.

That would be the exiled dragon.

As I snacked—and it snowed—and I thought about it, I was pretty sure I was in the clear on this incident, too. Neither Suzanne nor Meagan had seen me enter the bathroom. Neither of them had seen me before I shifted shape, so technically they'd seen me only in dragon form. Even if they suspected that there was a dragon shifter among them, they didn't know that Zoë Sorensson had become that dragon.

I could have believed all of that, if Meagan hadn't given me that look.

Had she really guessed the truth? I wasn't sure.

I was confident that I could argue the technicalities with my dad. I halfway believed I could win. I was pretty sure he wouldn't exile me for another comparatively small transgression. And I wasn't afraid of Suzanne or what she might tell her friends.

I was most worried about Meagan.

The standard solution for inadvertently revealing oneself as a dragon shape shifter is to beguile the human in question. But it seemed like a complete betrayal of my friendship with Meagan to beguile her. I didn't want to do it unless it was absolutely necessary.

I also wasn't sure it would work.

Because I knew Meagan and I knew that look. If she was convinced she'd seen a dragon, a whole pack of beguiling *Pyr* wouldn't persuade her otherwise.

I guessed she wouldn't tell the principal what she'd seen. After all, the school administration might think she was delusional. No, she'd come up with some story about Suzanne falling, and let Suzanne be the one to sound delusional.

And in the meantime, having shifted in defense of a human made me feel much more optimistic about the chances of convincing my mom to let me go to the concert. There's just something about becoming a dragon that makes me feel invincible.

Omnipotent.

In charge of my universe.
It is the good stuff.

2

I should have guessed that my High Queen of the Universe moment couldn't last. I got all the way to the door to our loft before I sensed trouble.

Big trouble.

As soon as I unlocked the door and walked into the apartment, I got slammed with glacial temps. The next ice age had begun.

The mood between my parents in recent months had made home feel as cozy as a meat locker at times, but the tension between them hadn't escalated—until now. I had no idea what they'd been fighting about and didn't really want to know. Now I stopped on the threshold, scared to take a breath, much less step inside.

Would it be smarter to make a dash for my room?

Or should I just bail and come home again in an hour?

My mom came raging out of the master bedroom with a suitcase before I could decide. The suitcase wasn't what initially surprised me—not even the way it was only half-closed, with clothes hanging out the edges.

It was her tears. My mother was *crying*. Not pretty crying, either, like the kind you see in movies. Nope, she was gulping and grimacing, and the tears were running down her face and dripping off her chin.

She froze when she saw me, like she'd been caught in the act of doing something horrible, and stared at me.

A suitcase? How could that be good?

My dad emerged from the kitchen and stood behind her, looking shaken. "Eileen," he said quietly, but she ignored him.

I might not have the Wyvern's powers of foresight (yet), but I had a pretty good idea of what was about to happen.

And it sucked.

It sucked so badly that I couldn't really believe it.

My parents couldn't be splitting up.

Could they?

But I knew the truth as soon as I thought it, knew it with that absolute certainty that makes me think maybe I do have a bit of Wyvern stuff going on. It made me want to puke and at the same time turned me numb. It made me want to cry or scream—or just freeze this moment in time and make it stop. My mom watched me, then bit her lip.

"I'm sorry, Zoë," she whispered. She caught me in a tight and abrupt hug. I thought she might break my ribs, but I didn't dare pull away. My father watched with narrowed eyes but didn't move.

"I'm not abandoning you." My mom's voice was thick when she spoke and I could feel her shaking. "But I have to leave for a bit, Zoë. I'm sorry. I have to go away and catch my breath and try to remember why I love your father so very much."

Sometimes being right completely sucks.

Life as I knew it was ending—and I couldn't fix it, even though I was a dragon shifter. Those particular superpowers didn't come with the *Pyr* package.

My mom pulled back and caught my face in her hands, smiling at me before she kissed the tip of my nose. She used to do that when I was a kid. I had the most enormous lump in my throat and couldn't make a sound.

"You could come with me," she said, hope in her tone. "You could come with me and forget all this dragon stuff."

I looked at my dad, but he seemed to have been turned to stone. Just his eyes glittered. Was *that* what had set them off? For years my mom had been cool with our dragon-shifting abilities.

Or was it *my* shifting abilities that were the problem?

Why else would she ask me to forget the dragon stuff?

I spoke with care, feeling like I was on thin ice. "How can I forget what I am?"

My mom closed her eyes and took a deep breath. "Goddess, you even sound like him." Then she wiped her tears and picked up her suitcase, purposeful once again. "Well, that's that, then," she said with a finality that was terrifying.

Terrifying enough that I had to say something. I wanted some reassurance that she'd be back and so I said the first thing that came to mind. "Will you be back by my birthday?"

She looked at me, a thousand shadows in her eyes, and I was afraid of her answer. "I don't know." Before I could freak that my mom was leaving for good and my dad was just standing back, watching her go, my mom dug into the pocket of her sweater. "Just in case, Rafferty asked me to give you this for your birthday."

"Rafferty!" It's not often that my dad is surprised, but I could see that he was shocked. And really, it would have made more sense for his oldest friend to have entrusted him with a gift for me. Rafferty is another of the *Pyr*. He and my dad have been pals for centuries.

My mom's tone was challenging as she turned to glare at my dad. "Maybe Rafferty didn't think you'd let it go."

My dad frowned. My mom turned her back on him again, put down her suitcase, then held out a small fabric bag. I took it from her, not knowing what else to do.

There was something heavy inside it.

Something round.

"You might as well open it now," my mom said, shrugging into her coat and slamming things into her purse.

My dad exuded disapproval at that, because he's pretty big on his integrity. What could Rafferty have sent that might have tempted my dad to keep it? I opened the ties, and dumped the contents into my hand.

It was a ring.

No, it was *the* ring. My dad evidently saw it because he caught his breath sharply. No wonder.

For as long as I can remember, Rafferty has worn this ring. It's black and white, like black glass and white glass swirled together. It's not just an ordinary ring, though; it changes to fit his finger or his talon. It shifts with him, always the perfect size. I love it and he knows it, but I was astounded that he would let it go.

Ever. To anyone. It's part of Rafferty.

In fact, I felt like I had a piece of him in my hand. Did he really intend to *give* it to me? Forever?

He'd loaned it to me the previous spring in our battle against the Mages, and something weird had happened. I'd been able to call on the previous Wyvern and had gotten a clue from her to help save the *Pyr*. Afterward, the ring had looked the same as always, and every time I'd asked Rafferty or my dad about it, neither of them would answer.

So what had changed? Why was Rafferty giving me the ring now? Did he know anything about the party invitation, and how I thought the Mages were up to something?

If he disagreed with my dad about the threat posed by the Mages—and the power of the treaty—it would make sense that he'd asked my mom to give me the ring.

Unfortunately, there was no note. I would have bet everything that Rafferty wouldn't answer any question I sent.

No, he'd play that "figure it out" game that my dad also loves, the one that drives me bananas.

I was going to ask anyway. Just because.

I looked at my mom.

"He just said to make sure you got it. That's all I know." She hefted her bag.

"Eileen," my dad said, his tone low, "don't go."

"I can't stay and watch. Not anymore."

"But..."

She pivoted then, as ferocious as any dragon. "But *nothing*, Erik. Listen—I've stood by and watched you choose the *Pyr* over your marriage, time and time again. I've recognized that this was your role and your responsibility." My mom lifted her chin and glared at him. My dad even flinched a bit, which is saying something. "But I can't stand by and let you choose the *Pyr* over the welfare of your own daughter."

This was about *me*.

How could my new powers ruin everything?

"You're pushing her too hard," my mom continued. "You can't let her just be a kid, or come to things in her own time."

"But—" My dad did try to argue his side, but my mom cut him off. She was a lot more angry than he was.

"But *nothing*. How many nights did you take her out late to practice flying and shifting? How much time does she have left to spend with her friends? Human friends? Have you even noticed that Meagan isn't here very often anymore? That girl used to practically live here."

"Mom, that's something else...."

"Is it?" My mom glared at me and I couldn't argue the point. It was about my dragon powers in a way, because I couldn't tell Meagan about them.

"But I want to learn about my powers...." I argued.

"Of course you do. But it shouldn't be the *only* thing you do." My mom turned back to my dad. "I can't take it anymore. And if this is the only way to show you that I'm serious, then I'm going to do it, no matter how much it hurts. I'll live without you, if I have to." My mom sighed and tears shimmered in her eyes again. She ran her finger down my cheek. "I'll call you. Every day. I promise."

I nodded, my own tears blurring my vision. My mom was leaving.

"Where are you going?" my dad asked, low and hot.

My mom paused in the corridor outside our loft, but didn't look back. She spoke very softly and looked at her boots. "You told me once that you could find me anywhere, anytime, that if I was afraid, you'd come to me before I could even scream." She glanced over her shoulder and I saw her swallow. "Is that still true, Erik?"

My dad cleared his throat. He shoved a hand through his hair and looked as if he'd like to argue in his own defense.

If he could just think of what to say.

My mom didn't wait for him to find the words. "Fine." She spun and marched out the door. I heard her on her messenger as she strode down the corridor, calling a cab.

The loft seemed to echo with her absence, and she wasn't even out of the building yet. I felt cold and uncertain, and pretty sure I was going to be sick.

The worst possible scenario was really happening.

My parents were splitting up.

As if that wasn't bad enough, it was all because of me. I shut the door when my dad didn't move and leaned back against it, staring at him. I didn't know this script. I didn't want to know it.

He stared at the floor.

"Where will she go?" I asked. Saying something had to be better than bursting into tears.

"Her sister's, maybe. I don't know." My dad fixed me with a look. "Don't imagine for one minute that I won't find out." He raised a finger and shook it at me. "Don't imagine for one second that I don't love your mother with all my heart and soul."

That declaration came a bit too late, to my thinking.

"Really? You're the only one who could have made her stay, but you didn't even try," I said, hearing my own anger. "Maybe she's right. Maybe you don't give a shit."

I shouldn't have said it, but once I had, I didn't regret the words, not one bit. Our gazes locked for a moment and the air seemed to crackle between us. I saw my dad's nostrils flare.

"I felt you shift today," he said tightly. "Were there humans present?"

"They didn't really see..."

"Grounded!" he bellowed, jabbing his finger through the air at me. My dad almost never shouts, but he was roaring now. "You are grounded for breaking the Covenant!"

"You didn't even let me explain!"

"Nothing you can say can exonerate you." He pointed at me and his hand was shaking. "This time, you *will* be punished. The rules also apply to you. I made a mistake in being lenient last time." He turned to walk away but I shouted after him.

"You can't exile me, not without a hearing!"

My dad spun and his eyes flashed. "Can't I?" He murmured something low and deep, something even I didn't quite hear. I didn't realize right away what he was doing, not until the hair prickled on the back of my neck.

Then I knew. He was changing the permissions on his dragonsmoke.

Our home is encircled by my father's dragonsmoke, which is both a territory mark and a protective barrier. Humans cross it easily, but a dragon can cross the dragonsmoke of another dragon only with explicit permission.

Exiled dragons were surrounded and trapped by my dad's dragonsmoke.

Guess who was getting locked in.

I pivoted, hauled open the door to the corridor, but his dragonsmoke shimmered before me like a wall of glass. I plunged my hand into it, not really believing that he would barricade me in the apartment.

The touch burned.

I pulled back with lightning speed.

I swore, whirled to face him, and slammed the door. I don't think I've ever been so furious in my life. We glared at each other, both livid, both shimmering blue around our perimeters, hovering on the cusp of change. The air crackled between us.

We'd never come this close to an actual dragon battle before, but I recognized that my dad wasn't in the mood to back down. My hand wasn't really hurt, but I'd felt the singe of the dragonsmoke and knew that if I tried to cross it, I'd be fried alive.

"Fine." I marched to my room, slamming the door hard, so hard that two drawings fell off my bulletin board.

I dropped all my stuff and threw myself across the bed, letting myself cry. My mom was gone! My dad didn't care.

Would she ever come back?

I felt sick that she might not. When would I see her again?

I turned Rafferty's ring in my hands, not daring to put it on. I didn't even know all of its powers, but I knew better than to mess with it.

I wasn't, after all, having the luckiest day of my life.

"Zoë?" Even in old-speak, I could hear the wariness in my dad's tone.

"I have homework," I snarled back in kind. *"Leave me alone."*

And he did.

No doubt about it, this was going to be the worst birthday ever.

THERE ARE good things that have changed since my dragon powers turned up last spring. And there are some seriously less than great things, too. To call my transformation a mixed blessing would be an understatement.

I keep track of my dragon observations, primarily because of one exchange I'd had with Jared this past summer. I'd sent him a message when I couldn't stand it any longer, offering to take him for a dragon flight in exchange for his lending me his copy of the only known book on the *Pyr*.

He'd written back immediately, which had made me crazy with hope. At least until I'd read the message:

YOU ALREADY OWE ME A RIDE, DRAGON GIRL.
IF YOU NEED A *PYR* MANUAL, WHY DON'T YOU WRITE YOUR OWN?

And that had been it.

Two sentences sum total from him since April.

He hadn't replied to any other messages. There'd been, um, a few from me.

I tried not to find this too depressing.

On the other hand, in May he had released a new song on his band's site called "Snow Princess," which I dared to imagine was about me. It was haunting and evocative and romantic as could be.

I've only listened to it twelve hundred and sixty-two times, according to the last displayed count on my messenger. It's a bit compulsive about tracking those kinds of things. Me, I would have just said I'd listened to it a lot.

Mixed messages seemed to be Jared's specialty. Leave it to me to fall for a guy who is mysterious and keeps his distance. I seem to specialize in long shots.

It *was* Jared's style to push me and to dare me. It was also his tendency to be right about dragon stuff. Not to belabor the point, but he has read the book, which gives him an edge over me.

And the fact is that I'm the only female dragon shifter, known among us *Pyr* as the Wyvern. Theoretically, this should give me a bonus pack of powers—but there being only one Wyvern at a time was seriously hampering my ability to even find out what those powers were supposed to be. The past Wyvern hadn't exactly left her diary to me.

But Jared was right in that sooner or later I'm going to die—sooner if the Mages get their way—because we dragons are just long-lived, not immortal. If all worked as it should, there would be another Wyvern born then. And she wouldn't have any more of a clue than I did as to how the whole Wyvern role and responsibility worked. I could do a service to the future of my kind by creating a guidebook.

I'd started documenting what I did know, compiling lists on my messenger. Before that message from Jared, I'd already begun a number of digital illustrations, inspired by boot camp, and I had a lot of lists on the go as well. Now I had a big honking file, called...

Ready?

On Becoming the Wyvern.

Not too snappy, but it got the job done.

Here's an excerpt for your entertainment:

Good Things About Developing Dragon Shifter Powers

1. I can shift shape. I have the dragon shift completely nailed. I've also mastered the shift to the salamander form said to be unique to the Wyvern.
2. I can spontaneously manifest in other locations, if my blood sugar is high enough and there are no serious distractions. This gives me another item of success on the list of things I know the Wyvern can do. It's progress.
3. I can fly. This rocks. Totally. It's the only physical feat I've ever wanted to do, and so—no surprise—it's the one that's got me working out. All dragons can do it, not just the Wyvern, but that doesn't make flying any less amazing.
4. I've developed an interest in astronomy. It stands to reason that since my Wyvern powers were set in motion by a total solar eclipse, I should learn more. I didn't expect to find it so fascinating. It is a bizarre twist of fate (and a shock to Mr. MacPherson, our science teacher) that I'm becoming a bit of a science enthusiast. Go ahead—ask me about astral dust.
5. As a result of #3, I am no longer a complete write-off in gym. I still can't catch a projectile or aim one at anything with accuracy, but I'm less likely to trip over my own feet when I run. So, I'm not quite such a liability on, say, a baseball team. Volleyball and basketball are still disaster areas, but again, it's progress.
6. As a result of my breach of the Covenant last spring when I

flashed some dragon goodness at Suzanne, the über-bitch has not come near me since April. Complete bonus.
7. As a result of #1, the dragons I draw are better. I can check dragon anatomy with a mirror if there's room to shift. My dragons are more fierce and more lifelike, very much in demand as notebook embellishments at school. It's strange to be popular in any way for any reason, but I'm getting over it. Kind of.
8. I have breasts. They're small, too small to bounce even, but at least there's some dimensionality there—and some justification for lingerie.

Again, I'll take even incremental progress if it's all that's on the menu.

Things That Completely Suck About Dragon Shifter Powers
1. The Covenant means that I can't tell humans about dragon business. This includes Meagan. This means I end up having to lie to her to protect the privacy of the dragon shifters.
2. My mom is right about lies—they're like cockroaches; there's no such thing as just one. The domino effect is alive and well in my life of lies, and I hate it. Because Meagan would still be my best friend if I didn't have to lie to her all the time.
3. The one human guy I know who knows the truth about my shifting talent is apparently no longer speaking to me. Or has forgotten about me. Or something equally ego-bolstering. I can't ask Meagan for advice on Jared because I can't tell her the whole story, because of #1.
4. I still have no real clue about how to fully develop my Wyvern powers, or even what they all are. There is no manual or other record. It's completely unfair that my friend, Isabelle, who is practically family, was the last Wyvern in a past life, but doesn't remember any of it. This is really annoying. No. It bites.
5. The only possible reference book—less than ideal because it's so damn enigmatic, but at least it's *something*—is in the possession of Mr. Elusive, referenced in #3 above.
6. There was another solar eclipse on October 2, but nothing seems to have changed. I expected it to have *some* impact on my powers.

7. The next total solar eclipse happens August 12, 2026. Almost two years! With the Mages hunting shifters, I might be dead by then.

So, if nothing else, the next Wyvern would have some reference materials, courtesy of *moi*.

I CAME out of my room later, but only because I was starving. My dad was in the kitchen, measuring out pasta. There was butter and Parmesan on the table and a green salad. He didn't turn around when I arrived, just added another serving of pasta. The water boiled and he dumped it in, stirring. The timing was perfect, as if he'd anticipated my arrival.

But then, he does have the gift of foresight.

"I have had two firestorms," he said quietly.

I blinked in astonishment. He was confiding in me about his relationship with my mom. This was a first.

Then I blinked again at what he'd said. The firestorm is the mark of a dragon shifter meeting his destined mate and the opportunity for that dragon to conceive an heir. It's a once in a lifetime—even a long lifetime—opportunity. "I thought we only get one."

"That's what we're told, but I had two."

Before I could ask about the other woman in his life, he continued. "They were both with your mother, although the first was in a previous life for her."

I waited. I didn't dare say anything in case my dad stopped the story.

He stirred the pasta, staring into the steam. "I thought that I was lucky to have a second chance, but your mother is right. There are things I have not done differently."

He fell silent for longer this time, so I prompted him. "How so?"

"I have not found a way to live more fully in the human world, as well as in our own. I have also failed to find the balance in raising children, between too much control and not enough."

Children. My eyes widened at that. "Children? As in more than me?"

He nodded. "There was a son."

"I have a brother?" I was stunned that no one had ever mentioned this.

My brother would be a dragon, which meant he would have lived for centuries and I could hit him up for advice...

"You *had* a brother. Sigmund is dead." My father sighed. "But not before he turned *Slayer* and wrote a book documenting the ways to destroy the *Pyr*."

My mouth went dry. A *Slayer*? *Slayers* were extinct now, but they'd existed when I was born. *Slayers* were *Pyr* gone bad. They were selfish and evil and...

My brother became one? It's always a choice. Why would he choose to go bad?

What else didn't I know?

Wait—if my brother had written a book. I could guess which one. I named the book that Jared had, the only book on our kind that was known to exist. "*The Habits and Habitats of Dragons: A Compleat Guide for* Slayers, by Sigmund Guthrie."

My father nodded again, sadly.

There was another one of those huge silences, just the ticking of the timer filling the kitchen.

I had to know. "What happened to Sigmund?"

"He died, during my second firestorm with your mother." My dad paused again. "I used to see him sometimes, walking among the dead." The timer rang and he moved to drain the pasta. Relieved to have an excuse to abandon the subject, maybe.

My dad is not big on confidences and confessions. I could see how hard it was for him to tell me this much, and I appreciated that he was trying.

Although it sure wouldn't have hurt for him to have told me this sooner. Didn't I have a right to know?

He was just bringing the plates to the table when my messenger rang. Of course, I had it on me—it's like another part of me. My link to the universe.

It was my mom, calling from the airport to say that she was going to my aunt's place in England and giving me her schedule. She didn't ask about my dad, and he didn't ask to talk to her.

She sounded awful, as if she was still crying. I know my dad strained to hear her side of our phone conversation, his hunger for the sound of her voice more than clear in his expression. He tried to hide it from me but failed.

We ate in silence after she hung up, until I suddenly put down my fork. I couldn't stand it anymore.

I was going to take a page from Jared's rulebook and push a little. I was, after all, a dragon girl.

"I was going to ask Mom tonight whether I could go to a concert on Saturday."

He didn't glance up. "Don't forget you're grounded."

"You could hear me out."

He flicked me a look. A wary look. "And what concert is this?"

On the upside, he was giving me a chance. On the downside, he was using "and" questions. With my mom, "and" questions are a bad sign. She asks them when she's already made up her mind to say no—"and" questions show that we're just going through the motions of making her look unbiased before she does say no.

I decided to hope that my dad didn't play the same way. "Jared's band is playing downtown. You remember Jared."

"And where is this?"

"At a co-op place downtown that doesn't serve booze..."

"No."

Come to think of it, a few more "and" questions to argue my case might have been good.

I stared at my dad in dismay. His face was set, which meant his mind was made up. I tried again. "But you've met Jared. I thought you thought he was okay. He helped us beat the Mages—"

He interrupted me with a fierce look. "And how old is he?"

"I don't know. Twenty. Twenty-one maybe." Independent, exciting, rebellious, hot, and a great kisser. I knew these would not be attributes of Jared's that would change my dad's mind. "Donovan trusts him," I threw out the name of one of my dad's *Pyr* pals.

"But you are not even sixteen. No."

I was outraged. If Jared didn't think I was a little girl, why did my dad have to? "What difference does that make?"

My dad put down his fork so he could really glare at me. "Five years' disparity at your age makes all the difference in the world."

"I don't think—"

"But I do. And I say that you will not go to this concert."

"I think Mom would have let me—"

"She's not here. And you weren't grounded before she left. She would have declined you now, and I forbid you to go."

Forbid me? How medieval was that? "It's just a concert, and you know that he's a spellsinger. It's because of Jared and his abilities that the Mages' spells were broken last April! He helped to save you all—"

My dad interrupted me flatly. "Zoë, a young man of twenty-one has a vastly different agenda than a sixteen-year-old girl. You are idealistic. You are thinking of love and romance. Jared is thinking of *now*, he is thinking of sex, and he almost certainly does not have your welfare at the forefront of his thoughts, whether he is a spellsinger or not." He picked up his fork and resumed eating.

I stumbled to my feet. "How can you say that about him? You make him sound like a predator. You don't even know him!"

"I remember being that age," my dad said grimly. "And Jared's trouble-making reputation does precede him."

"This is so unfair. He said that no one trusted him, but I thought Donovan would have defended him to you."

"I assure you that if you were Donovan's daughter, you would also be forbidden from attending this concert."

"You're not being fair...."

He looked at me. "And how many times have you had contact with Jared since last April? How many messages has he sent you?"

"One."

"And I will guess that it was in reply to one from you."

I blushed, but my dad kept talking.

"And what effort has he made to see you while he's in town for this concert? Has he invited you? Has he contacted you?"

"No." I folded my arms across my chest. "But he's playing at a club where I could go. It's like an invitation—"

"But it is not one. If he wanted to see you, he would have ensured that he did. He could have come here and met your parents and asked you to go with him. His failure to do any of those things tells me all I need to know about a romantic future with this young man."

"So, it wouldn't hurt for me to go and find out for sure."

He gave me a cold look. There was a lot of dragon in that look. I should have flinched, but I looked right back. He spoke very softly. "I guarantee you that if you go, Jared will recall that you are attractive and he will try to make the most of the opportunity you present. Now sit down and finish your dinner."

I would not.

"What if he's my destiny?"

"Is that what you truly believe?"

I fidgeted. "I can't see the future just yet."

"I can."

"You could be wrong."

"Then we shall address the matter at that point in time."

We? No way!

I noticed the blue shimmer that surrounded us and realized that my father and I were both on the cusp of change, facing off in the kitchen, a situation that could go up in flames. That made twice in almost as many hours.

And I didn't care.

"Is the firestorm a lie?" I demanded. "Is that why you've had two of them and screwed them both up? I thought a firestorm was supposed to be about destiny and forever! Because if it's a lie, then you should tell us all now, all us young dragons. You should give us the facts, not the fantasy. You should give us the chance not to fuck up our lives by trying to make your stories come true."

He stared at me. I stared back. I'd never talked to my dad like that, let alone used the f-bomb in his presence.

I felt my face turn red.

But I didn't look away.

Then I spun and took my plate to the sink, still a goody girl deep in my heart. It was a bit late to make an effort to stay out of trouble, but there you go. I dumped the pasta in the trash and rinsed the plate, my hands shaking all the while.

My dad was still staring at me.

The way a predator eyes lunch.

He was mad, but holding back.

Well, that made two of us. How could he not stop my mom from leaving? How could he think such crappy things about Jared? How could he ground me and lock me in with dragonsmoke without hearing my side of the story? I retreated to my room, knowing that he was the most unfair person on the planet.

I heard him toss his pasta after mine, right before I slammed my door.

But he didn't come after me, or make an appeal in old-speak.

Maybe he didn't care about either me or my mom.

I HAD HIDDEN my new ring in a secret corner of my desk drawer, where I stash all the best stuff. It was beside the red rune stone that Granny had given me in the spring, with a little gap between them.

Just so you're straight on this, I don't actually have a living grandmother. Never have. Granny is this old woman I dream about sometimes. And last spring, she threw this round, flat rock at me. I'm not sure what it's for, but it seems like it must be important. It has a rune carved on one side, one that means "beginnings," so maybe that's why she gave it to me then.

Like I said, details on the Wyvern deal are sketchy.

For some reason, I thought the stone and the ring shouldn't touch each other and I decided to go with my gut on that. I dug the ring out twice that evening and turned it in the light, wondering why Rafferty had sent it to me.

And yes, worrying about the ring being a portent of pending Mage hostility.

Then I worried about my mom, and about my parents maybe never getting it together, about my never getting to see Jared again, and just generally fretted about the entire foundation of my universe.

Which seemed to suddenly be on pretty shaky ground.

I did send Rafferty a message, asking him about the ring.

There certainly wasn't an instant reply.

Or any reply.

Receipt acknowledged. That's it. It had been delivered.

I tried to work on an illustration I had started of two of my dragon friends. I was trying to depict Garrett fixing one of Liam's scales with his dragonfire, but I screwed it up and had to revert to the previously saved version. The only good thing was that I was working digitally.

I really wanted to call Meagan, even though I couldn't tell her all of what was bothering me. I pulled out my messenger, fingered it for a minute, then took a chance.

YOU THERE?

She answered immediately. But then, she always did her homework with her messenger on the desk beside her.

Z! YOU WON'T BELIEVE WHAT HAPPENED TODAY!

I smiled, reassured by her quick reply, then typed my own.

NEITHER WILL YOU. MY MOM WALKED OUT.
MAYBE FOR GOOD.

My messenger rang instantly on its voice setting. It was Meagan.

Like I said, she's the best friend in the world.

I GAVE her the squeaky-clean Covenant-approved version of what had happened—because I knew that my dad would be able to hear anything I said to Meagan, even if I whispered, thanks to that super-keen *Pyr* hearing. (And I could hear him breathing dragonsmoke, weaving it more thickly around the apartment. He was going to be a hard-ass about the Covenant this time, my rotten luck.) Basically, I told Meagan that I'd come home to find my mom walking out the door, that they'd been fighting, and that I wasn't sure when she'd be back.

All true.

Just not all of the truth.

We speculated on possibilities for a while, whether they would reconcile, but then I couldn't stand it any longer.

"You said something happened today," I asked, keeping my tone level. I knew what had happened in the bathroom, but I wasn't supposed to know. I was cool.

Until she answered me.

"It did!" Meagan said with excitement. "You'll never believe this, but you know those dragon shifter guys we see on television sometimes?"

"Yeah?" I sat up, a bit worried.

"One of them goes to our school!" Meagan crowed, unaware that my mouth had fallen open. "And he defended me against Suzanne. *Me!*" Her voice dropped to an excited whisper. "Who do you think it is? Peter Morris? Mike Gallagher? You know, it could be Tony Amario. I've always thought he was a bit mysterious."

It was good that she was on a roll. I couldn't think of a thing to say, but Meagan had plenty of guesses as to who the previously unsuspected *Pyr* student might be.

She didn't know—or hadn't realized—that there could be a girl dragon in her vicinity.

At least not so far.

You might have thought that that was plenty of action for one day in the life of a Wyvern, but one more thing happened that day.

When I fell asleep, Granny came back.

With a friend.

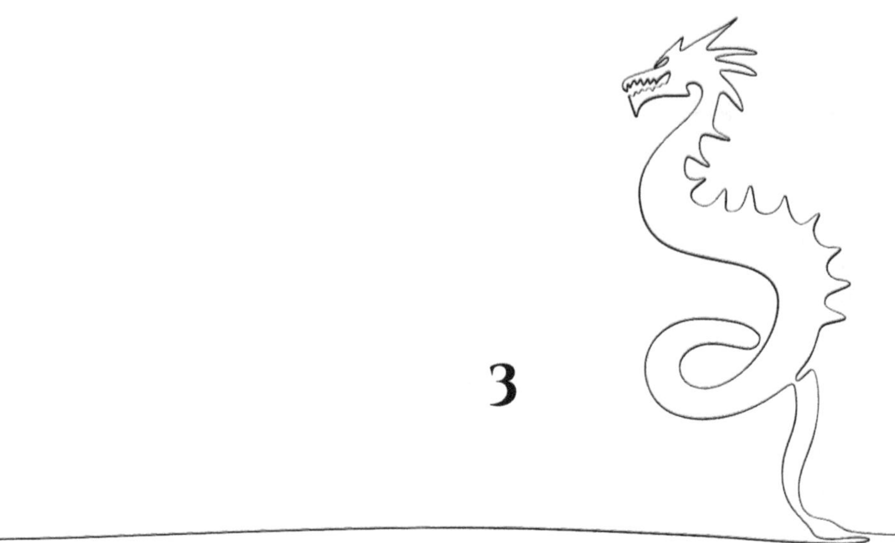

3

I woke up in the middle of the night, shivering in my bed. I rolled over to pull up the covers and saw snow in my room.

But only when I looked with my left eye. When I opened only my right eye, my bedroom looked perfectly normal. If I closed that eye and looked just with the left again, I was out on the tundra, the walls of my room dissolved, a big tree right where the door should be.

I knew the eye game well. I'd learned to play it when my Wyvern powers first appeared. That had been the first time I'd dreamed of Granny, when she'd given me the rune stone. She'd also showed me how the eye game worked. It was kind of reassuring to have it make a second appearance—I'd been a bit disappointed by its absence all summer long.

Even better, Granny herself was back. I felt like waving hello. She still looked like Mrs. Claus, and she was still knitting with silent efficiency. Just like before, she could have been knitting a snowdrift.

But this time, she had company.

There was another woman beside her—at least, I think it was a woman. She was wearing a cape, with a hood, one that wrapped her completely in silvery gray. Her hood was filled with shadows, as if she didn't even have a head, but I could see her eyes gleaming in the darkness. She had a weird-looking gizmo in her hands, like a top that she constantly kept spinning.

She moved so quickly that her hands were just a blur. I watched her, fascinated by the rhythm and eventually realized that she was making thread.

Like knitting wool. Yes! There was a loose stream of white over her shoulder, soft as a cloud, and she was feeding it into the spinning top, pulling it into long, twisted thread.

That must be a drop spindle. I'd heard my mom talk about them before and was pretty sure she even had one.

And sure enough, the spun wool that came from the bottom of the top, all sleek and slender and tight, seemed to be feeding the knitting that Granny was doing.

Would the sheep turn up next? I wondered.

"I am Urd," said the new arrival, startling me with her words. Granny had never spoken to me. She'd just chucked a rune stone at my head. I wasn't expecting audio. "You already know my sister, Verdandi."

I opened my mouth, intending to ask questions, but Urd suddenly held up one finger. It was creepy, that finger, like a skeleton's finger. I was kind of glad not to be seeing her face just then.

I did as I was told and kept silent.

"'Verdandi' means 'what is.' 'Urd' means 'what was.'" Then she pointed that finger at the ground, down to the root of the tree where there was a dark hole. I'd peered into the hole before. It was like a well, a dark hole that stretched down farther than I could see, with a shimmer of water's reflection at the bottom.

It gave me the heebie-jeebies, that well. Granny knit faster, as if she were troubled, and her gaze was locked on me. Her lips were tight with concern, the way my mom's get when she's fighting against her urge to argue with my dad.

Hmm. Guess she'd gotten over that.

Urd put down her spindle and did a little sleight of hand, reaching into the air and closing her fist on something that wasn't there. I blinked and then she opened her palm to show me what she held.

Rafferty's ring.

No, *my* ring.

"Hey!" I leapt from my bed to grab the ring from her. She waited until I almost had it, then closed her fist and flung the ring down the well.

I fell to the ground beside the well, too slow to snatch the ring out of the air. I could see it glinting as it fell, a red glow emanating from it. Then it splashed into that water way down at the bottom.

And disappeared.

I caught a whiff of shadows and rot. Whatever was down there, it could stay put as far as I was concerned. The ring, I was ready to concede, was lost. Even in a dream, I didn't see any reason to dive into a pit that I wouldn't be able to escape.

But Urd had other ideas. She moved fast. When I would have stood up again, I found her bony hand was on my shoulder. She was strong, stronger that anyone would expect, and she shoved me toward the well. I stumbled, because she caught me by surprise.

I fought and struggled, but Urd pushed me steadily closer. I twisted to fight her grip. She had fingers of steel, and she was winning.

No, she had fingers of bone. Skeleton hands.

I panicked when I saw that. I thrashed. I caught her hood with one hand and pulled, desperate for a grip on anything.

I heard it tear and looked up when I heard her laugh.

Holy frick! Her head was a bare skull.

One with eyes that burned like twin flames. She opened her mouth to laugh at me, and it looked like she had a snake for a tongue. She released me and I fell over my own feet in my hurry to get away from that face.

But she tripped me.

And I fell into the darkness of the well.

Down and down and down. Urd's laughter echoed all around me as I fell. There was an inky shimmer, like black water, but it was a long way down.

This was not good.

I WOKE UP, my heart hammering and my fingers knotted in the sheets. There was sweat running down my back.

There was no snow.

There was no tree and there was no dark well.

There was no sign of Granny, or her nasty sister.

But that black envelope from Trevor was perched on the carpet beside my stack of books. I was sure I hadn't left it there. I had the irrational thought that it was spying on me—although with Mages, that might not be very irrational at all.

I wasn't entirely sure of everything they could do. And the one guy who did know more had declined to fill me in.

Never mind that recent events meant it was unlikely I'd be able to hit Jared up for advice, live and in person, at his concert. Looked like I'd be solving my Mage-related issues myself, thanks.

I leapt from the bed, snatched up the envelope, and ripped it to shreds. Then I flung it out the window, watching the pieces flutter toward the pavement far below. That stupid dragonsmoke singed my fingers when my hand passed through it just for a second. There was an unwelcome reminder that my dad meant business.

Only when the pieces had all disappeared from sight and nothing else had happened did I shut the window and lock it securely. I rummaged in the drawer with the secret corner in a panic. To my relief, the ring was right where I'd hidden it.

My ring.

I locked my hand around it, still freaked, then opened my hand to look at it. Had it changed?

It had. It seemed to glitter a little in the light, as if the white part was full of snow crystals and the black part was full of stars.

What kind of magic did this ring possess, anyhow?

How could I find out?

I shuddered at the prospect and got into bed, sitting with my back against the wall and my knees pulled up to my chest. I had the ring trapped in my right fist, my left hand locked around the right. There was no way I was going to sleep again soon, not with Urd lurking in dreamland, on the lookout for me.

I checked with both eyes, but my room looked normal even with the eye game. I sat vigil, armed only with a ring, unconvinced of my safety. I had a feeling that Granny and her weird sister could change things on me without notice.

I could have called my dad. He might even have believed me. But I wasn't exactly feeling confident about his inclination to defend me or even see my point of view.

Call it a learned response.

The thing about being scared crapless by strange old women in the night is that it helps put things in perspective. There had to be something I could do to improve the odds of my not having a completely miserable birthday.

There had to be a plan I could make.

I like riddles and I had a great big clue, right in my hand.

Who would know about the ring? I wasn't going to ask my dad because I knew what he'd say. "Figure it out." Thanks very much. Rafferty had already proved to be unhelpful.

Then the answer hit me.

Of course. I could ask Isabelle.

Rafferty's adopted daughter.

Who was attending college right in Chicago.

Perfect.

THE NEXT MORNING my dad was standing in the kitchen, waiting for me. This was unusual enough to make me wary.

Especially after what I'd said to him the night before.

I had a definite sense that I would be called on the carpet for challenging him.

Was he going to escort me through his dragonsmoke? Or did he intend to leave me holed up here for the duration? Or would my exile be elsewhere? I both wanted to know and dreaded hearing his decision.

That there was a small black satchel at his feet just added to my uncertainty. It was bigger than his briefcase or laptop bag. He had his leather jacket on and his boots, and looked ready to walk out the door.

Was he leaving, too?

As much as I wanted to be an adult right this minute, this change was happening a bit fast—and in entirely the wrong way.

Maybe I should be careful what I wished for.

"You'll need to pack a bag," he said curtly. His British accent was stronger than usual, which was never good. "You'll be staying at Meagan's. Her mother knows that you're grounded, although there will, of course, be no dragonsmoke barrier there."

I opened the fridge, as if there were no urgency. I wasn't in a real hurry to make anything easy for him. I was sure he was going to tell me that he had to make a business trip to secure a pyrotechnics contract in another city. That's what he does—big pyrotechnics displays timed to music. It is cool, but I resented his ability to carry on as if nothing had happened, as if my mom's departure meant nothing at all. I was prepared to argue that I was nearly sixteen and could take care of myself. It seemed that someone should have asked me before making plans for my immediate future.

Wasn't this the same thing he'd done with my mom? Just decided and let her deal with the consequences?

Bottom line—if getting rid of me would be convenient to his career, I wasn't inclined to be convenient.

I considered a tub of yogurt, as if it held all the world's secrets. "For how long?"

"I don't know." He exuded impatience.

I put the plain yogurt back and picked up a flavored yogurt instead. Hmm. Peach. "I didn't hear you call anybody."

"Meagan's mother and I e-mailed last night."

"Why do I have to go anywhere? I thought this loft would be my prison."

My dad fixed a look on me, one that was so intent I shivered. I braced myself for a reckoning.

But he surprised me.

"Because I am going to follow your mother, and try my utmost to change her mind about remaining in this partnership." I had a moment to be shocked and delighted before he continued. "You cannot stay here alone because you are a minor. That is the law."

"Human law." I had to say it.

"Human law." His lips tightened at the concession. "Which in this case and in the very short term trumps *Pyr* law. Don't imagine I'll forget your transgression."

Right. Mr. Responsibility was back. Maybe he'd never left. Did he really care about my mom? Or did he just feel responsible for pursuing her? "How long will you be gone?"

He winced. "However long it takes." He glanced at his watch. "You have five minutes. I have a flight to catch."

A commercial carrier? What about Dragon Air? "You're not flying yourself?"

His eyes, if anything, glittered more coldly. "Your mother wishes to live like a normal human. Therefore, I will arrive to plead my case like a normal human. I have made arrangements for your care like a normal human. I suspect these are but the first of many concessions I will make in the near future."

I had the urge to tell him he should have made concessions sooner, but I bit back that piece of advice. It should have been good enough for me that he was going after her.

Funny, but it wasn't. I wanted him to show more emotion for once, to be visibly upset. Maybe to cry. Instead, it felt as if he was going to collect a forgotten umbrella from the Lost and Found.

"Four minutes," he said, biting off the words.

I was halfway out of the kitchen when I remembered who I was talking to. My dad. The dragon who hid his emotions—and his vulnerabilities—better than any six poker faces put together.

I turned back to watch him rinse his coffee mug. His expression was grim and as I looked more closely, I saw an unfamiliar tension in him. He was trying to hide his reaction and unable to do so. That meant he was really upset. I wondered whether he'd slept at all. And he had nearly lost it the night before. I guessed that he blamed himself even more than I blamed him.

In a strange way, that made me feel better.

"Do you think you can convince her?" I asked quietly.

I didn't miss his grimace, even though it was quickly gone. "I am not sure." It was maybe the first time I'd ever heard him speak without conviction. That made my stomach queasy. "But I guarantee you that I will do my best to persuade her."

"I think you can be pretty persuasive."

He smiled then, a humorless expression that lasted less than a heartbeat. "And I think your mother is a woman who knows her own mind." He frowned and spoke softly. "I shall try, Zoë. It's the only thing that I can promise."

When he looked up, there was a shadow in his eyes, a doubt I never thought I'd glimpse in my dad. I'd always believed he was in charge of the whole universe, that he could do anything or achieve anything. He could do a lot, even more than most dads.

But he wasn't sure he could convince my mom to stay with him.

And that was ripping his guts out, doing more damage than the most ferocious dragon attack.

I crossed the room and gave him an impulsive hug, shocked by how tightly he hugged me back. We stood there for a long moment, clutching each other and I heard his breath catch.

My invincible dad was scared crapless.

He really did care.

"I'll be ready in five," I said to him when I pulled back, realizing belatedly that I sounded a lot like my mom when she has a To Do list. "Could you pack me a couple of granola bars and an apple? I'll eat on the way."

My inclination to play as part of the team was cut short, but quick. My dad drummed his fingers on the counter as I was leaving the room. I had a fleeting sense that he was going to say something I wouldn't like.

And he did.

"You should also be aware that I have decided to modify the Covenant in your case, given the circumstances."

I froze on the threshold of the kitchen to look back. "What?"

He gave me one of those glittering looks. "You are forbidden to shift to dragon form without prior approval from me."

I looked away in a futile effort to control my temper. The very idea that anyone could know when they would need to shift, in advance, in time to ask permission, was so stupid that only a parent could have come up with it.

This was about his lack of confidence in my abilities.

Or some need for control.

And I chafed at the restriction. "I can't shift without your permission?" I asked, making him say it again.

"No." He glared at me. "And I'm not giving it."

It was pretty easy to guess that the other older *Pyr* would back the choice of my dad, who is their leader, after all. "But you're leaving. What about self-defense?"

"You'll have no cause to defend yourself."

I flung out my hands. "What about the Mages and their plan to eliminate shifters?"

"We have a treaty with them. It's resolved." He ground out the words, convinced of the power of diplomacy. His eyes narrowed. "Did you not shift yesterday, in front of Meagan?"

"Well, yeah, but Suzanne had punched her—"

"But you could not have dealt with this threat in human form?"

I was at a loss there. I could have, but it wouldn't have been nearly as cool.

"You have shown that your judgment is not sound. We will discuss this more upon my return. Until then, you will not shift."

"But—"

"I do not want to exile my own daughter, but I will do it if you insist on my making an example of you."

"What if we're attacked?"

"You will not be. Two minutes."

I didn't share his confidence at all, but he was unshakable. His decision was completely unfair and unreasonable—but there is no *Pyr* court of appeals. I know I must have looked mutinous when I stared at him, but he stared right back.

Dragon-stared.

"One minute," he reminded me curtly.

One more time I retreated and slammed the door of my room.

I hurled clothes into a backpack, mad enough that there must have been steam coming out of my ears. This wasn't about me, or even about the Covenant. This was all about my dad keeping up appearances for his *Pyr* buddies. Maybe it was about my brother turning *Slayer*. Either way, it had nothing to do with me being safe.

That was when I knew what I would do. I wouldn't shift. I'd follow my dad's stupid rule to show that I was trustworthy.

But I would also prove him wrong, about one thing at least.

And Isabelle would help me.

MEAGAN'S MOM met us at school and stored my bag in their car. She tried to offer a bit of sensitive encouragement to my dad, but he was brusque with her. I took this as a sign of his own doubts and felt kind of bad for him.

"You can do it, Dad," I murmured in old-speak after he turned away, and saw him jerk in response. Then he shot me a vivid glance, got in the car and was gone.

I shoved my hands into my pockets and found the ring. I felt superstitious about putting it on without knowing everything it could do, and trusted my instinct. I wasn't going to leave it anywhere, either, though. I would just keep it close, and touch it sometimes.

"I'm sorry about your mom." Meagan bumped her shoulder against mine, the way we used to. "It's good he's going after her."

"Yeah." I sighed. "I'm glad about that."

"Fingers crossed," Meagan said and flashed me a smile. Her smile really did flash—she had a mouthful of metal. "Hey, you know, we could try one of my mom's visioning sessions after school and see if we can help your dad. We could get my mom to help—"

"I have to go somewhere after school," I said, thinking about the weight of the ring in my pocket. I'd have to persuade Mrs. Jameson to let me meet Isabelle somehow.

"That's okay. We'll go take care of that first, then do the visioning session. After dinner, if we have to." Meagan was trying to accommodate me, which said a lot either about how nice she is or about how long we've been pals. "Where do you have to go?"

She obviously thought I had a dentist's appointment or something. I felt my gut knot, because there was no avoiding what I had to say. I couldn't exactly ask Isabelle about the ring with Meagan present. It was pure dragon biz. "Um...I have to visit someone. Alone."

I just wanted to stop her before she planned everything, but I handled it badly. She tensed and I knew I'd hurt her feelings.

Again.

"I see." Her tone said it all. "And I suppose that if you're still staying with us on Halloween, you'll go to Trevor's party alone, too?"

"I told you I'm not going to his party—"

"Don't lie to me, Zoë!" Meagan snapped. "It's bad enough that you won't tell me things."

"But I swear I *can't* tell you...."

"No, you *won't* tell me." She grabbed the door and hauled it open. "I suppose it's better to find out who your real friends are."

It would have been great if I'd thought of the perfect reply, but instead I just stood there with my mouth hanging open.

And you know what happened next.

"Meagan!" Jessica called and waved from down the hall. "Did you solve the bonus questions from math?"

Meagan grinned. "Even better! I have the coolest thing to tell you. You'll never guess what I saw yesterday."

And they were gone, speculating on the identity of the dragon kid in our school, leaving me behind—me, who could have told them the real story, IF it hadn't been for the stupid Covenant. Even if there was a marginal chance of my not getting exiled, it depended upon my playing by my dad's rules in the short term. Just the scorch of that dragonsmoke had been enough to convince me that he was serious about reinforcing the rules.

Even on me.

Derek appeared in my peripheral vision when I was opening my locker.

"Fight?" he asked. I didn't have to ask what he meant. I knew he must have been watching our exchange.

"Kind of." I shrugged, as if it would blow over. "How was the game?"

"Central won." He didn't sound surprised.

I wasn't either.

We ran out of conversation at that point. I got my books for the morning classes, sure that he'd leave.

He didn't.

He cleared his throat. For the first time I'd ever noticed, Derek looked uncomfortable. He almost shuffled his feet. That made me curious as to what he wanted to say. "So, they say you draw."

Now I was the one watching him intently. "Some. Yeah."

Those eyes were icy blue, his gaze fixed on me. "Dragons."

I swallowed, feeling like I was under a microscope. "Usually." I felt myself blushing. "Call it a weakness."

"I don't." I wasn't sure what he meant by that, but he was digging in his bag. He offered a new notebook to me, as if he thought I'd refuse to take it. "Draw me one?"

Kids asked me to do this all the time, to embellish one of their notebooks with a dragon. For some reason, Derek's request felt different, maybe just because he was different.

Intense. That was the word for him.

Like the weight of the world was hanging on my decision.

Or maybe I was making too much of it.

I tried to shake off my sense of foreboding. "Sure," I said, as if it was no big deal.

It wasn't.

At least it shouldn't have been.

"Gotta get in line early," he said, to my surprise. "Haven't you heard?" He was studying me again. "Everyone's talking about the dragon who spooked Suzanne." He jerked his head toward the bathroom, scene of the crime, which was closed off.

"Oh, I did hear something," I said, trying to sound disinterested.

"I thought you'd be all over that story, since it stars a dragon."

I blushed. Again. "I like them better in fiction."

"Really?" He couldn't have sounded more skeptical.

I changed the subject. "So, any preferences? Flying? Perching?"

"Kicking butt." He spoke with resolve. "I want to see a dragon kicking some bully's ass."

My mouth went dry. I had those prickles on the back of my neck again.

There couldn't be any way that Derek knew my secret.

Could there?

He looked one more time into my eyes, hard, as if he was trying to tell me something. I couldn't think what it might be. I couldn't think of a thing to say.

Not one thing.

Derek smiled a little, that secret smile he seemed to keep especially for me, then turned and walked away. I stared after him, wondering.

Was Derek intense because he *liked* me? It was an astonishing possibility. I'd never had a guy like me at school before. In fact, I had so far shown a talent for liking guys who didn't like me back. Or ran hot and cold about liking me back.

But Derek seemed to be interested. And he kept coming to talk to me. I didn't think it was just about a dragon drawing. He also didn't run hot and cold. He was consistent. I got my books out for class, pondering the possibilities. Just because it was strange and unusual for a guy to like me didn't mean it was impossible.

Right?

Derek was right about one thing—the school was buzzing with the story and speculation was running wild. Some people thought the whole thing was a hoax, a story made up by Suzanne and spread by her friends to make her look special. But many people shared Meagan's conviction that one of the guys at school must be a dragon shifter. Who was the dragon hidden among us? People really wanted to know—and in the absence of any real information, they were prepared to make something up that sounded plausible.

It would have been funny if I hadn't been so terrified of being found out.

Suzanne was absent. I'd been right—Meagan had told the principal that she didn't see anything, just Suzanne freaking out. Apparently, Suzanne had talked a lot about dragons attacking her and the principal had concluded that she was tripping on something. Her parents had refused to let her have a blood test or to have her seen by a doctor, so she'd been suspended for the day.

Her groupies seemed a bit shaken by their idol's tumble from grace, and I overheard Trish defending Suzanne a couple of times. She even talked about identifying the dragon kid and "taking him down," which was pretty funny.

I wanted to see her try.

I just kept my head down—even if I found Derek watching me at every turn. You'd think I could have gotten control of my crazy blushing, but no luck. I spent the day as red as a lobster, hugging my secret close and avoiding conversation.

In other words, like usual, but more red.

On the upside, Meagan was Ms. Popularity, everyone wanting to hear the story from her side. That she deviated from her official version, telling Jessica and others about the dragon, just made her a bigger hit. Trish and

Anna were watching Meagan from a distance—like circling piranhas—but apparently didn't dare get close to her.

Or maybe they were waiting for the Queen Bee to make a plan.

IN MATH CLASS, Trish was busy on her messenger, probably researching the *Pyr* for Suzanne. Everyone around me had dragon fever, and everyone was on the dragon's side. And that was when I realized three things:

1. I could instantly and immediately become the most popular girl in school, if I just revealed my secret. I could feel the tide of support for the dragon. I could become cool overnight. This was such a novel concept that it threw me a bit, enough that it took me until the end of class to remember my dad's last instruction: no shifting without authorization.
2. That made me wonder whether my dad, with his gift of foresight, had glimpsed the temptation in my future. Who wouldn't want to be cool? Who wouldn't want to be popular? All I'd have to do is shift shape in front of witnesses.
3. And finally: courtesy of all the drama in my life, I'd completely forgotten about the English essay I had to hand in right after lunch. "The Depiction of Weather as a Character in *Jane Eyre, Rebecca*, and *Persuasion*." Crap. Crappity crap crap. I hadn't even finished reading the last book and time was a-wasting.

So much for lunch with Meagan and Jessica.

I SPENT lunch in the library, madly reading and scribbling, barely managing to pull together an essay that was somewhat coherent in time.

On the way to English class, I joined the group of people gathered outside the closed bathroom that had been the scene of the crime. I had a peek around the temporary barrier—easy since there were worker dudes who had moved it aside in their assessment of the damage—and smiled to myself at the diameter of the peeling scorch mark on the ceiling.

"They're trying to say that she was smoking something," Stacey said, with a roll of her eyes.

"It'd be a helluva toke to burn that much," Mike replied.

"I think we would have smelled it before it wrecked the ceiling," Tanya added, and they all laughed.

When I got to English class, Derek was already there, watching me from his fave seat at the back. I stumbled right on cue. He didn't miss one bit of it and I was glad to take my seat and turn my back to him.

The day couldn't end soon enough.

Gym was my last class and predictably painful, even with Suzanne absent. Volleyball. Ugh. Whenever I hit the ball—which was infrequent—it went straight into the net.

Eventually, the last bell rang. Meagan was ignoring me, probably because I hadn't showed at lunch.

I was late already, so I just headed out, reasoning that I'd patch things up with her later. I'd also have to think of a story to tell Mrs. Jameson. Maybe a dentist appointment. I'd sent Isabelle a message and she'd agreed to meet me at a coffee shop at four. I'd met her at the same place a couple of other times. I had to take the bus and the L to get there, but I was used to that.

I like meeting up with Isabelle. In a way, she's everything I want to be. In another, she's *been* everything I want to be. It's odd, hanging with someone who had your job before but doesn't remember doing it.

Last spring, I discovered that she's the previous Wyvern reincarnated. This would be incredibly useful, if she remembered all of the Wyvern goodness she once must have known and could thus help me get a grip on my slippery new powers.

Of course, it doesn't work that way. Nothing about this Wyvern gig is easy. She doesn't remember anything about a past life and is pretty much taking my word on the whole reincarnation thing.

Why am I so sure of who Isabelle was? Granny showed me. One thing I have learned is that what goes down in my dreams, especially when Granny is on the scene, proves to be real. Every time.

Maybe that's a Wyvern trick.

Memory or not, there was no telling what Isabelle had inadvertently learned about the ring while growing up in Rafferty's house. I still had hopes for more information.

Usually Isabelle's in England—where Rafferty and his partner, Melissa, live—taking courses on tarot cards and auras while being effortlessly gorgeous. She's older than me, but doesn't get snotty about it. This year, Isabelle had decided to enroll in some exchange program and study in Chicago. I'm pretty sure she did this to be close to Nick and I had to wonder how well that was working.

I got on the bus, reminding myself that my mom never minded if I went downtown to meet Isabelle before dinner. (Well, if I wasn't grounded. Details.) I felt as if I was (sort of) following house rules, even in the absence of parents and home.

For whatever that was worth.

In fact, the likelihood of having either again, or having things return to any kind of normalcy, seemed pretty low. I was afraid my dad had decided to compromise too late for it to matter.

Which made me wonder why I even cared about house rules.

And helped me to rationalize what I intended to do.

Sure, I'd never asked my mom about the concert and my dad had said I couldn't go, but they'd both left town. I was the only one in Chicago who knew I wasn't supposed to go. Even if Meagan's mom knew I was supposed to be grounded, it didn't seem as if she was too hot about enforcing it. Maybe she thought it unimportant compared to my parents' splitting up. Maybe she was giving me a break.

I'd run with it, either way.

If I could get to Jared's concert, prove that I was right about him, and maybe get a peek at the book or even learn the Mages' revised plan, that would justify defying my dad. Right? It might also score me at least one item from my birthday wish list.

I wasn't going to be irresponsible, though, or get myself into an unsafe situation. I'm not stupid. The co-op where Jared's band was going to play was in a crummy neighborhood and not the place to be alone at night. I needed someone to go with me—a partner in crime, as it were.

Which brought me to Isabelle.

. . .

Isabelle was already sipping a big foamy coffee when I arrived. She was perched at a table for two by the window and if I didn't like her so much, I could have been green with envy that she could look so good and make it seem so easy.

Make no mistake—Isabelle is *gorgeous*. Even though I know it, I'm astounded every time I see her again.

The weather had turned crummy. It was windy and starting to snow, the kind of snow that falls in big flakes and then melts on contact with anything. I was wet and chilled after my walk from the L. I shivered and kept my fave shawl wrapped around my neck like a big cowl when I sat down.

They were playing hokey Halloween music, those novelty tunes which just about made me barf. There were jack-o'-lantern posters on the walls and everything in the place was black and orange. They had posters up for a pumpkin spice coffee special and the staff were dressed up—one wore a witch hat and a green wig, while the other wore a zombie costume.

Isabelle was wearing a thick burgundy sweater with a wide cowl neck that showed her throat. She has that flawless skin that British girls tend to have, all creamy silk. I doubt she's ever had a zit. She's feminine and mysterious, and confident too. Like I said, Isabelle's everything I want to be. Her chestnut hair was loose and wavy over her shoulders—no bad-hair days for her. With her jeans tucked into her high boots and her pale pink lip gloss, she looked like a lingerie model.

Or every guy's winter fantasy.

That she has a scrumptious British accent would have sealed the deal for pretty much anyone. Most of the guys in the coffee shop were checking her out, probably imagining that I was her baby sister.

The plain one.

Isabelle had also bought a big foamy drink for me, which she pushed toward me. I'm not much for coffee, but was cold enough to drink it. I thanked her and wrapped my hands around the warm cup, realizing as I raised it to my lips that it was actually hot chocolate.

Yummy. I smiled at her in appreciation.

"Heard from Jared?" she asked, right when I was taking a sip.

I choked.

Figuratively and literally.

4

Trust Isabelle to cut right to the chase. Here was my opening, if sooner than expected. "He has a concert here on Saturday, at this club...."

"I know. Knightshade." She watched me carefully, and she knew I had ducked her question. "Did you message him?"

"Once. Last summer."

She looked a bit annoyed. "Didn't he answer you? Didn't he get in touch about this weekend?"

"Yes and no." I put down the cup. "He sent me a short answer last summer."

"Blowing you off," Isabelle muttered into her coffee. "Guys!"

"I think he's busy." I tried not to think about Jared being amused by high school girls who send him messages just because they've kissed him once. "And, you know, that's fine."

Isabelle's eyes gleamed. "Is it?"

"The thing is, I need to talk to him about that book on the *Pyr* he has. I need to look at it again. Reference, you know."

Isabelle started to smile. "Uh-huh," she said and I blushed.

"So I wondered whether you would take me to the concert Saturday."

It wasn't smooth, but maybe it would get the job done.

I probably looked as hopeful as a puppy.

Isabelle's smile widened. "Just to talk about the book, of course."

I blushed even more. "Look, I'm trying not to be pathetic about it. You could help."

"Try harder," Isabelle said teasingly.

I had to be red enough to glow in the dark. She reached across the table and squeezed my hand. "I wish he'd gotten in touch with you, Zoë. I thought you two had some magic."

"Me, too."

Isabelle sighed. She looked out into the falling snow. "Why is it that guys just don't get it?"

I was surprised by her despondency. "How's Nick?"

Isabelle grimaced. "Oh, he tells me he has a girlfriend."

"You."

Isabelle shook her head. "Teresa, I think is her name." She widened her eyes slightly and sipped her coffee.

I was appalled. "No way! You two are made for each other."

"Nick seems to think that love, romance, and sex are all the same thing." She shook her head and looked unhappy. I couldn't help hearing my dad's warning about Jared. He couldn't be right about guys, could he?

Isabelle sighed again. "I think maybe he's just not ready."

Nick is hot and fun and the life of the party, the jock everyone wants to be —or be with. I could see him having tons of friends and going to lots of parties.

But a girlfriend who wasn't Isabelle?

The idea bummed me out even more than the reality of my parents' trashed relationship.

I took a big swig of hot chocolate and it burned all the way down. "Maybe he'll appreciate you more after he's been with someone else."

"Maybe." Isabelle didn't look as if she believed that. She pulled out her tarot cards and began to shuffle them absently.

I love her tarot cards. They're huge, each card more than twice the size of a normal playing card. And the illustrations are beautiful. Isabelle seems to always pull a card that has meaning for the situation at hand, and I love watching her do what she does.

Maybe because she always tries to explain it to me.

Maybe because it fascinates and mystifies me. How could pieces of cardboard—even ones with great illustrations—give a glimpse of what the future will be? If there's a portal or a dimension or a sense that allows a person to peer into the future, shouldn't I be aware of it? The Wyvern is supposed to be able to see past, present, and future simultaneously, but I had no such prophetic abilities.

Maybe I was hoping that it was contagious.

Because Isabelle certainly had that power.

Or maybe it was in the cards themselves.

She glanced up at me without drawing a card and smiled. "So, what else is new, other than the fact that guys are jerks? Maybe that's not even new."

It was likely to be the best intro I'd get.

"Well, I wanted to talk to you about this ring." I dug it out of my pocket, then placed it on the table between us. Isabelle caught her breath at the sight of it. "My mom said Rafferty sent it to me for my birthday. I'm wondering why he would give it to me."

Isabelle eyed the ring but didn't touch it.

"He loaned it to you last spring."

"Well, yeah."

"And something happened."

I nodded. "It turned into the ghosts of Sophie and Nikolas."

"The last Wyvern and her lover."

"And they helped me defeat the Mages, as well as get Rafferty and me free of their spell trap."

"And then?"

"They spun back into the ring." I picked it up, turned it in the light. It didn't have any of that starlight inside it anymore. Strange. "Like Aladdin's lamp, but more portable."

"Do you get more than three wishes?"

"I don't know." We both looked at the ring. It appeared to be just a piece of glass, reflecting the twinkle lights hung in the windows. It was hard to believe at this moment that it had any power at all.

"Maybe Rafferty thinks you awakened something in it," Isabelle said. "Like now it's rightfully yours."

"Then he would have just given it to me in the spring, I think." I shook my head. "I think it's something else. I thought you might know."

Isabelle shook her head. "You could ask him."

"I did."

"Let me guess—he told you to work it out for yourself."

I nodded agreement. "He didn't answer at all."

Isabelle smiled. "Maybe he doesn't even know the answer."

She studied me for a long moment, then took a deep breath. "Let's see what the cards can tell us." She shuffled the deck of tarot cards as I watched. She drew a card and snapped it flat on the table beside the ring.

THE FALLING TOWER.

I don't know much about the meanings of the cards, but this picture—of a castle being struck by lightning and tumbling to pieces—seemed somewhat less than optimistic.

IF I WAS WARY, Isabelle was spooked.

Her hand shook as she set the rest of the tarot deck down on the table. She stared unblinkingly at the card, which wasn't a particularly encouraging sign either. I waited, thinking that maybe she was meditating on it or something. With Isabelle, you can never be sure.

Finally I couldn't stand it anymore. "So, what does it mean?"

"Maybe Rafferty thinks he won't need the ring much longer," she said, her voice uneven. "Not in this life."

Now *I* was horrified. I hadn't even thought of it as a legacy. "Wait a minute. You can't mean that he's sick."

Isabelle folded her arms around herself and sat back. "He's not exactly young, even for a *Pyr*."

And Rafferty had had his firestorm, which is supposed to start the aging process in dragon dudes.

He couldn't be dying, though. "No, I don't believe it. It has to mean something else." I didn't want to think about a world without Rafferty.

Isabelle visibly braced herself to pick up the cards again. "Have you noticed that I always draw from the higher arcana when we're together?"

"Should I know what you're talking about?"

Isabelle turned the deck over and spread the cards across the table.

"There are seventy-four cards in the tarot deck. Four suits of thirteen, similar to regular playing cards, which are called the lower arcana. In addition, there are twenty-two allegorical cards, called the higher arcana."

"You sound like a professor."

"*Fortune-telling Through the Ages: Tools and Techniques* is one of the courses I'm taking this semester." Isabelle leaned forward. "The thing is that the higher arcana are powerful cards. They usually turn up when a message is important. Like a warning, or a huge life change. But every single time I draw a card in your presence, it's a higher-arcana card."

I shivered despite myself. "So...?"

"So the cards are responding to your energy."

I leaned forward, intrigued. Could I learn to use the cards? Was this where I would discover the Wyvern's traditional ability to predict the future? "What does this one mean?"

Isabelle grimaced. "Big changes. Dramatic and violent ones. Like electrical storms."

"Or ideas?" I suggested. "A bolt out of the blue?"

She considered that. "Maybe. More likely someone gets hit by lightning. Destruction."

Nice.

"You think Rafferty is ensuring that the ring has a new custodian?"

"Because he senses danger to himself." Isabelle finished my sentence so neatly that I knew she'd been thinking exactly the same thing.

Great. I'd just given Isabelle something to worry about.

She took a gulp of coffee, then shoved the card back into the deck, shuffling it with practiced ease. Then she offered me the deck. "Go ahead. Try it."

I hesitated. "Don't you believe they're your cards and attuned to your energy, and that anyone else touching them messes that up?" I remembered her saying as much before, whenever people had asked to touch the cards.

"They're already responding to you. Let's see how much."

I took them with some reluctance. The deck was heavier than I'd expected and the cards were so big that they were hard to handle. "What do I do?"

"Shuffle them. Think of a question. Then when it feels right, pick a card, and turn it up on the table."

Call me weak, but I thought about Jared. I wondered how a guy could kiss a girl like that and then just forget that she existed. I thought about him insisting he couldn't give me the book because he wasn't going to risk losing the interest of a dragon girl. I wondered whether there was any chance I might see him this weekend—either to get the book or to get another kiss—and I yearned.

Then I chose a card and put it on the table with care.

The Hermit.

I was starting to think I didn't need a manual to understand these cards.

"It's right side up," Isabelle said.

"What does that mean?"

"You consider the orientation from the reader's perspective. Right side up means the card has its usual meaning. If it's reversed, or upside down, then the meaning is the opposite."

"So, the flip side would be the Party Girl."

Isabelle smiled fleetingly. "Something like that. The Hermit means a quest for information and knowledge. It indicates you going on a journey in search of the truth."

"Alone," I added, as this seemed to be key.

"Usually alone." Isabelle shrugged. "Although anyone can be alone in a crowd, too."

"Lost in their own world." I couldn't argue that the card had nailed my current status. I was certainly flying solo, whether I was seeking knowledge or not. Maybe it meant that I should put this moment of isolation to work, use it as an opportunity to investigate...what, exactly?

Isabelle glanced at her watch, then picked up her cards. She tapped them on the table so the stack was neat, then slipped them into a silk bag with a drawstring. She tucked them into her purse with care. "So, what's the deal with the concert?"

It was a typical Isabelle change of subject, a rough transition that made sense to her but left me a bit dizzy. “I want to go. I was going to ask my mom, but she’s gone.”

“Gone?”

I gave her the condensed version of events Chez Sorensson, but she didn’t look either surprised or concerned. I decided to take that as a sign of confidence in a happy ending. “And the thing is that his band is playing at this club that isn’t licensed. It’s right here in town and it won’t be a problem for minors to attend. And the concert’s on Saturday night.” I sat back and voiced my secret thought. “I think he’s daring me to show up.”

Isabelle considered this. “He does like to push you.”

A Wyvern should be bold. That’s what he’d said to me.

“I don’t want to be a fangirl. I just want to know.” I saved all the stuff my dad had said about young men just wanting sex, given that the generalization seemed to apply to Nick.

“Don’t we all?” Isabelle murmured. “All right, we have to go. How else will we know if the cards are really attuned to your energy?” It was a typical Isabelle rationalization, in that it wasn’t particularly rational at all. That made it hard to argue with her.

She pulled out a notepad. Isabelle and her paper books. She’s a real throwback. “Give me the address and phone number of Meagan’s house,” she said. “I’ll pick you up there.”

“Really?”

“Happy birthday. Early.”

I was simultaneously elated and terrified. I wasn’t sure I could stand it if Jared turned me down, right to my face.

On the other hand, I wouldn’t be able to live with myself if I let this opportunity slip away.

I told her the address, then confided one other potential obstacle. “I don’t know if Meagan’s mom will let me go to a concert.” I told her the bit about my being grounded and why.

Isabelle tapped her pen on her notepad. “You could beguile her.”

“Right! You’re the one that says beguiling shouldn’t be used for personal gain.”

“Don’t be ridiculous. This is about kismet and destiny, and following your quest in becoming the Wyvern. This is about self-determination! It’s not selfish at all to ensure that you embrace your fate.”

Only Isabelle can talk like that and not sound insane.

"Still. I'm not going to beguile Meagan's mom. It would be taking advantage."

Isabelle shrugged. "Suit yourself. We'll find another way. I'll pick you up at seven."

"But what about Meagan?"

"Meagan can come, too. My treat."

Wow. Maybe there *was* a magic genie in the ring. I thanked Isabelle, gave her a hug, then shoved the ring back into my pocket. I finished my chocolate on the way back to Meagan's place, unable to deny that the world was looking better.

Because I was going to see Jared this weekend.

It was sad to be so easily affected by the prospect of just seeing a guy, but I refused to think of myself as pathetic.

At least in this particular instance.

I was a dragon girl, on a mission.

A bold Wyvern.

One thing was for sure—I desperately needed a sexy bra before Saturday night.

STAYING at someone else's place is a bit odd. I wasn't sure whether I could just walk into Meagan's town house or not. I was living there, technically, but only for the short term—or so I hoped. Uncertain, I went with the conservative choice.

I rang the bell.

"Done with your real friends?" Meagan asked when she opened the door. I knew she wasn't being mean. She was hurt, because I had hurt her, and it was coming out of her pores. I wished I knew how to fix it.

I tried.

"I had to go see Isabelle." I chattered as we went to her room and felt her relax as I explained. "I think I've told you about her. She's like a cousin, but not exactly. Her dad and my dad are old friends."

Older friends than any human could have guessed. I was thinking that my dad and Rafferty had been hanging out for four or five hundred years, give or take.

Meagan's eyes flickered with interest. "The Isabelle in England?"

"That's her, but she's studying here for a year. Some kind of cultural transfer program."

"What's she studying?"

"I'm not sure." I realized that I wasn't. "She wanted me to meet her for a hot chocolate today, so I did. I thought maybe something was wrong. She sounded a bit upset."

Meagan immediately looked concerned. "That's why you wanted to meet her alone. Is she lonely, being so far away from home?"

This was the Meagan I knew best. Thoughtful and sensitive.

Was this why she'd befriended Jessica? Because Jessica had been alone, and maybe a bit lonely? That made me feel less jealous of how well they had hit it off.

"Maybe. She seemed glad to see me." I glanced at her. "I would have asked you but I wasn't sure what was up. Besides, I thought you'd be busy with Jessica."

Meagan blushed.

Lightning, interestingly, did not strike me dead.

Even though I'd lied to Meagan again. She could *not* have come to meet Isabelle, since we'd been talking about dragon business.

It was unnatural for me to get away with bad behavior. Even marginally naughty behavior.

Unless...

Was I moving into another upgrade zone for my Wyvern powers? Had the eclipse earlier this month had some effect after all? It seemed to be bringing me a decent string of luck—Meagan seemed willing to be my friend again and Isabelle was going to take us to Jared's concert.

"You didn't have lunch with us today," Meagan pointed out.

"No. I had to do the English homework I'd forgotten."

It was true, but Meagan wasn't buying it.

"Why don't you like Jessica?" she asked as if I was just making an excuse. "You hardly know her."

I shrugged. "She hasn't made much effort to get to know me, either. And it just feels like she's hiding something."

"Well, she is." Meagan smiled at my surprise. "Jessica's not her real name. She just hates her name."

I was intrigued. "Which is?"

"Josephina Maria." Meagan frowned. "Her parents came from Argentina. She's an only child and they're super ambitious for her. They moved here for her and left everybody they knew. Her dad's a doctor, but he's driving a taxi because he has to get recertified to practice here. They really, really want her to get into an Ivy League college."

"Oh." No pressure on Jessica, then. I felt a twinge of sympathy for her.

Meagan gave me a look. "I thought you might have a lot in common with her. Your parents push you pretty hard."

I had to think about that. Maybe there was more to Jessica than met the eye. "Okay, I was wrong. Maybe we should have lunch together Monday. I'll get my homework done this time. Really."

"My mom won't let you forget it."

"Wait. I have a better idea. Maybe we should all go shopping together."

Meagan smiled, obviously happy with the idea, then her face fell. "Jessica's parents won't let her. She has to study all day every Saturday."

I did like the idea of being just with Meagan. "Will you shop with me?"

"Absolutely. Let's go to those vintage shops you like." We planned a bit, then Meagan gave me a nudge. "I'd like to meet Isabelle sometime, too. Doesn't she read tarot cards?"

"She does. She had them today."

She bit her lip and sighed.

I seized the moment. "She wants to go to this concert tomorrow night. This guy we know is in a band and they have a gig downtown."

"What guy?"

"He's a cousin of Nick's...."

"The son of your parents' friends in Minneapolis," Meagan concluded, nodding as she remembered. "The one you got stuck hanging out with during spring break."

I felt a twinge of conscience then. I'd lied to Meagan in the spring about Nick being so hot, just so she wouldn't feel bad.

"Isabelle said you could come, too, but that we need to ask your parents."

"To a concert?" Meagan's face lit. "My dad will be good with that." I remembered a bit late that Meagan's dad is a concert pianist. That's why she takes piano classes. "Would your mom have let you go?"

In the absence of information, I went with optimism. If no one else was going to insist on my being grounded, I wasn't going to argue. "Sure. She likes Isabelle and is always saying how responsible she is." I smiled. "It's my birthday present from Isabelle."

"Then we'll ask." Meagan looked so determined that I had a feeling her parents had no chance. "And, hey, we have to figure out who the dragon guy is. Jessica thinks it's Derek."

"Derek?"

Meagan laughed at my reaction. "Don't you think he's kind of mysterious? He could have a secret like that. Jessica thinks his eyes are creepy."

"They are a really light blue...."

"I knew you'd noticed!" She started to sing. "*Derek and Zoë, sitting in a tree...*"

"What are you talking about?"

"Oh, come on. He watches you as much as you watch Trevor. If you weren't always looking for Trevor, you would have noticed." Meagan made a kissing sound and I swatted her playfully.

"It's not Trevor who interests me."

"Who then? You're blushing like crazy."

"You'll see. Tomorrow night." And that was all I'd tell her.

Until I knew how Jared would respond to seeing me there.

Meagan's mom *did* remember that I was supposed to be grounded and was all for saying no to the concert plan. Meagan's dad argued in favor of musical education and was ready to let us go. Meagan insisted that it wasn't fair to punish me for my parents' having problems. I tried just to eat my dinner and look like a good girl while Meagan's parents discussed it.

So, my dad had said I was grounded but not why. Of course, it would have been a breach of the Covenant to explain the details.

I had to like that the Covenant cut both ways.

As a complete bonus, my mom did call me on Saturday morning, just like she'd promised. She didn't have a whole lot to say, except that she was staying at my aunt's and checking that I had the number. She didn't mention my dad and neither did I. It was a short call, but made me feel less like everything was falling apart.

The Falling Tower. Hmm.

Meagan's parents let us go shopping on Saturday, which I took as a good sign. They were still waffling about the concert at dinner on Saturday night. I got the impression that they liked to debate issues endlessly, but didn't intervene.

I just hoped.

In the end, it was Isabelle who made the sale. She turned up looking even more perfect than usual. Her hair was pulled back into a ponytail and she wore a teal tweed jacket with her jeans. She was wearing glasses, even though I'd never seen her with glasses before.

Meagan's parents were sold with one look. How could it be bad for us to accompany such a respectable young adult anywhere?

The sucker punch was Isabelle's apparent delight that Meagan's mom is a visioning counselor. Isabelle launched into this discussion of a lab experiment in one of her university courses, which was investigating the ability of people to psychically create their own realities.

Meagan's mom was completely entranced.

Who says that only dragons can beguile humans? Some humans do pretty well at enchanting each other.

We were out the door and running for the bus in record time.

Heading toward Jared.

My stomach turned somersaults all the way. What if he didn't talk to me? What if he *did* talk to me? What if he kissed me again? I didn't know what to expect and just couldn't stand it.

"What kind of concert is it?" Meagan huffed after we'd piled onto the bus. "Classical? Chamber music?"

Isabelle laughed as she shoved her glasses into her purse. She pulled out a little case and balanced it on her lap, popping in her contacts as the bus rocked down the street. Meagan watched with awe, even though her own glasses were fogged. Isabelle shook out her hair, doing that model thing again. Meagan's eyes went round. "A rock concert, of course."

"You didn't tell my parents that."

Isabelle smiled. "I know. Sometimes we fairy godmothers have to manage information."

Meagan looked between the two of us in confusion. "What do you mean?"

Isabelle leaned close to whisper. “Zoë has a crush on this guy who sings in the band. They’re playing a concert in town tonight, so I decided to take her.”

“So we can be pathetic needy fangirls,” I added.

“An early birthday present,” Isabelle said. She nudged Meagan. “And I thought she should bring a friend.”

Meagan glanced my way.

“And only my best friend would do,” I added.

“Moral support,” Isabelle concluded.

Meagan teared up and had to clean her glasses. I hugged her and we had a warm fuzzy moment. It’s so easy to get along when you don’t have to lie to your friends.

Then Meagan snapped her fingers. “Wait a minute. Is this the guy whose music you’re always listening to on your messenger?” She gasped and grabbed my arm when I nodded. “The guy who *kissed* you on spring break? Is *that* the guy you’re crazy for?”

I blushed from head to toe, which they both enjoyed far more than I did.

“Now I know why you had to get that new bra,” Meagan teased, and my face got even hotter.

“And that purple shirt,” Isabelle added. “Where’d you get a shirt that cool?”

“I think you gave it to me,” I admitted and she laughed.

She leaned against Meagan. “I have such good taste, don’t I?”

“It looks great on Zoë,” Meagan agreed. “Makes her look both slim and curvy.”

“He won’t be able to resist her,” Isabelle said.

I was so mortified that I wanted to sink into the bus floor. Given the slush and muck on it, that was saying something.

They laughed together at me, enjoying my discomfort, and then Meagan demanded that I do her eyeliner for her. She likes the way I do mine. More importantly, she can’t apply eye makeup with her glasses on, and can’t see to apply it without them. She took off her glasses and I took advantage of a red light. Two flicks of the wrist and it was perfect.

“You should get contacts,” Isabelle said. “You have such great eyes.”

“And a mouthful of steel.” Meagan did her shark smile.

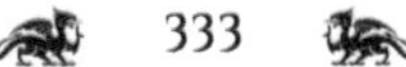

"Gives the rest of us a chance," I said and she smiled for real.

She put her glasses back on, then borrowed Isabelle's mirror to check out the eyeliner. "I am so getting contacts as soon as my braces come off. I don't care what my mom says. I'll figure out a way to buy them myself." She then demanded an earbud to listen to Jared's music. "What's your favorite song?"

"'Snow Goddess.' Here." I gave her one and put the other in my ear. I did not present my theory that this song was about me, even though it had appeared for download on the band's site only after Jared and I had met—and we had met in an unseasonable snowstorm.

Kind of like the one that was starting now.

Hmm.

More importantly, Meagan and I were both listening to the same song at the same time as the bus rocked toward downtown.

Like we were best friends again.

It was sweet.

Knightshade, the club, looked smaller than I'd expected. In fact, it looked kind of like a restaurant, but with dark drapes over the windows and lots of people standing outside.

There was a steady thud of bass carrying through the open door past the bouncer, and there was a line forming along the sidewalk. I think the city's entire allocation of black leather, shiny zippers, and facial studs had been claimed by the people who were already waiting there.

Never mind the tattoos. The bouncer was wearing only a tight black T-shirt despite the weather, the better to show off his muscles and the seriously fabulous koi tattoo that wound down his left arm. One look and I had a major case of tattoo lust.

My fascination with tattoos had started the previous spring when, yes, I'd seen the end of one on the back of Jared's left hand. It had protruded from the cuff of his leather jacket, although I hadn't actually seen all of it.

I'd seen the tip of a newt's nose and one little webbed foot.

I liked it a lot. And I'd done a ton of research since—easier than it would be for most people, because the partner of one of the *Pyr* is a tattoo artist. I'd nearly driven Rox crazy with my questions about tattoos and tattoo art, about design constraints and hygiene and everything else tattoo-related. I was sure that one of my own dragons would make a perfect tattoo.

His head would come over my left shoulder, eyes looking front, one wing spreading across my shoulder blades, the other down my arm, and his tail twirling around my upper arm to the elbow.

This was the one I wanted for my birthday.

Rox had endorsed the design—and she should know, being a fab tattoo artist herself—but she refused to put it on my skin. Being sixteen meant needing parental approval, and my mom wasn't giving it. Rox knew my mom, so there was no way around it. I didn't have the balls to go to another tattoo artist, because I *had* done my research.

But I had the drawing safely saved on my messenger, ready for the day I could have it transferred to my skin.

Like Meagan and her contacts, I was going to find a way to make it happen.

Somehow.

The bouncer was huge and he was casting a fierce eye over the line. He looked inclined to be picky. I was pretty sure he wouldn't let Meagan and me in, we being minors and all, despite there being no alcohol in the place. He would turn us away just because we wouldn't look good enough for the crowd he was building to suit himself.

But Isabelle turned a bright smile on him and he visibly melted. That was before she opened her mouth and her accent turned him to a puddle of acquiescence. Then she stretched up and whispered in the guy's ear. I thought he would fall to his knees in delight.

Maybe swoon.

"Wow," Meagan murmured and pushed up her glasses. I could almost sense her taking notes.

"I so want to be Isabelle when I grow up," I said under my breath.

"Absolutely," Meagan agreed.

Isabelle turned then, smiled and beckoned to us. The bouncer unclipped the red velvet rope that held the line at bay and gestured us in. Those in the line—most of whom were older, better-dressed, more stylish, and better-looking than me—watched hungrily.

"How'd you do that?" I whispered to Isabelle.

"I said we knew the band. It's true."

Both of us were crowding behind Isabelle, trying to look cool and blowing it. "We know Jared," I pointed out.

Isabelle laughed. "I've read the album notes, and done a little research. Fairy godmothers need to do their prep. We'll meet the others now."

It was dark and smoky inside. Everything was painted either black or deep purple, except the floor, which was black-and-white checkerboard. There was no furniture, just people standing in clusters.

Jared had chosen this place so I could come to hear him play—or to see him. Either way. I shivered with anticipation.

Isabelle scanned the dark interior, then pointed to the back, where the kitchen should have been. Instead there was a stage and a glittering curtain. "Backstage would be there."

She headed off at a purposeful clip, cutting her way through the crowd easily. Meagan followed, mimicking her new idol. I considered the irony of my having worried about Jared being my dragon stalker, particularly when I appeared to be stalking him, then pushed that thought out of my mind.

I'd keep our conversation focused and friendly. I needed a reference guide, and he had the closest thing to one.

This was about the book.

After all, if he'd wanted to see me before this, he would have made it happen. My dad and Isabelle were right about that. Jared was a get-stuff-done kind of a guy.

I decided to try for cool, elusive, and mysterious. I'd never manage indifferent, but this was a step in the right direction. Besides, mysterious seemed like the right attitude for a Wyvern, and I knew he was a dragon fan.

That plan went right out the proverbial window as soon as I saw him. He was wearing jeans and a T-shirt so tight that it could have been painted on. Every muscle was delineated, and he had a bunch of them. He was bent over his guitar, listening as he tuned it, completely lost in his task. He looked tons older than me, than all the guys at school, and I heard my dad's words all over again.

Like a warning.

One that I had no interest in heeding.

It's impossible to be cool, elusive, or even mysterious when your heart is racing. Just so you know.

"Wow," Meagan murmured. "Forget Derek."

And I had to agree.

I could see the entire tattoo on Jared's left forearm, too. It was a good one. Rox would have admired it.

It was a newt or a salamander, head on the back of his wrist and tail wound around his arm right above the elbow. It was looking up, as if surprised at its newty business. It had a red forked tongue that stretched down to his middle finger, which I knew hadn't been part of it before. The newt seemed to move as he plucked the strings of the guitar, as if it were possessed of a life beyond ink and skin.

Was it a Wyvern salamander? I dared to hope.

I had just enough time to realize I had no smooth intro before Jared suddenly glanced up. His eyes lit—those eyes are greener than any deity should allow—and he smiled at me.

My heart stopped.

Then galloped.

I was a goner, and we were still twenty feet apart.

5

Jared's gaze flicked to Meagan and back to me, and I sensed that he was choosing his words. "Zoë! Awesome. And Isabelle, too."

Isabelle stepped toward him, perky as only she can be, and gave him kisses on each cheek.

"So Euro," Meagan sighed, her desire to be Isabelle visibly doubling again.

I could relate to that.

I wasn't entirely sure what to do, and couldn't bring myself to do the cheek kiss as casually as Isabelle. I stuck out my hand. "Hi."

Jared took my hand, tugging me closer to kiss my cheek. "Glad you're here, dragon girl," he murmured when his lips were right against my ear. His words were so quiet that only I could have heard them and they gave me palpitations.

"This is my friend, Meagan," I said and she blushed.

"Nice to meet you," Jared said with an easy smile.

I was a mess. He still had my hand and I was still standing close to him. I could hear his pulse, courtesy of my sharp hearing, and it had accelerated.

Like he was glad to see me.

And mine was doing that spooky dragon thing of matching its pace to his. Believe me when I tell you that's a dizzying sensation. I managed to stand there, blushing like crazy, but clever conversation was completely out of the current range of my abilities.

Fortunately, Meagan was not impaired in that regard.

"I've h-h-heard some of your band's music," she said. "Do you write your own s-s-songs?"

Jared indicated a tall woman with orange hair and yellow leather pants. "Angie usually writes the ones she sings and I write the ones I do. A couple of our songs are collaborations between us."

Meagan nodded and bit her lip, thinking. "So, you're the one who l-l-likes minor keys so much."

Jared looked at her then, really looked at her. I knew he was surprised. "Yeah. They're kind of ethereal." He smiled that crooked smile, the one that drove me crazy, and his gaze flicked to me. He winked and the bottom fell out of my world for a moment. I held on to his hand a bit more tightly. "I like a bit of mystery, maybe a dreamy quality."

I said nothing, trying to maintain my mysterious air.

Actually, I was trying to find some equilibrium again. Just being in Jared's vicinity made it difficult to remember to breathe.

Meagan nodded with excitement, then pushed her glasses up her nose. "I like the way you transitioned from the minor key for the chorus in 'Snow Goddess.'" She wasn't stammering anymore, and I liked that Jared made her feel comfortable.

They talked about music and keys and timing for a couple of minutes, the two of them clearly finding some common ground. It might as well have been Greek to me. I had no idea what they were talking about. I just liked the song.

Isabelle, meanwhile, went to talk to the drummer, a tall skinny guy with dreadlocks who had been openly checking her out.

"Sorry!" Meagan said abruptly, glancing at me and blushing again. "It's just really interesting to talk to someone about the structure of music."

"You don't have to apologize," I said and bumped her arm. She smiled again. "Meagan plays piano," I told Jared, then glanced at her. "But I didn't know you were so into composition."

"It's math. I love math." She smiled sunnily, then elbowed me in a very unsubtle way. "Hey, I'm going to talk to Isabelle and the drummer."

"Rick," Jared said.

"He has those new syntho drums, doesn't he?" Meagan's eyes were shining and she was nearly salivating at the prospect of checking out new gadgets.

Jared nodded. "And the traditional percussion, too. He says the syntho drums don't replicate all of the sounds."

"Oh, but they should," Meagan said, frowning as she pushed her glasses up again. "The sine waves were perfectly matched by the engineers behind the project. It was a really interesting initiative and—" She glanced between us, flushed and smiled again, then excused herself.

"She's nice," Jared said, watching Meagan.

"My best friend."

"Cute," he said, surprising me. I thought I was the only one who saw beyond Meagan's glasses and braces. He winked at me, appreciation in his gaze as he glanced over me.

Okay, I was having heart failure again.

I tried to look mysterious and was pretty sure I failed. Instead, I watched Meagan.

It was better than losing myself in the green of Jared's eyes.

Rick seemed a bit condescending when Meagan first spoke to him, as if he was entertaining a fangirl, but within seconds, Meagan's technical questions brought out his enthusiasm. He started to show her the syntho drums and tapped out a couple of beats so she could compare the sound. She was riveted.

"They'll be buddies before the night is through," Jared said with a smile. "Unless Rick talks her ear off about the specs."

"Meagan will love it."

He slanted a long look at me, one that was simmering hot and ten thousand shades of green. His voice dropped low, to that pitch that makes me shiver. "I missed you, dragon girl."

My knees went weak right on cue. I couldn't even look at him.

And maybe because I wasn't looking at him, I thought more clearly. If he'd missed me, then why hadn't I heard from him? His words simultaneously made me feel special and fed my own doubts.

"Funny I never heard from you, then," I said, trying to keep my tone light.

It didn't work. I sounded desperate.

He gave me a steady look, like a warning. "I don't answer to anyone."

That didn't sound promising. I pulled my hand out of his and folded my arms across my chest, needing to keep a bit of distance until I had things straight. "You left before we could talk last spring."

"Places to go," he said, turning his attention to his guitar as if he didn't care that I'd pulled my hand away. He was doing it again, leading me on, then becoming evasive.

Because I'd expected some contact from him?

Well, that wasn't unreasonable, was it? My frustration grew—because I knew I hadn't expected much, because I wanted him to be everything wonderful I believed him to be, and because I really really really didn't want my dad to be right.

I needed to know for sure, no matter how much reality bit. "And you blew me off when I sent you that message in the summer."

"No, I told you the truth."

This wasn't going at all as I'd hoped. I'd secretly dreamed of a happy reunion—or at least another kiss. Right now, his guitar seemed to be more interesting than me.

I hugged myself a little tighter. "I owe you a ride. I thought that was what you wanted." Great. Now I sounded hurt.

Well, I was, but still.

Maybe that was why he didn't answer me, just kept tuning the guitar.

Okay, I'm not stupid. "Have a good show," I said and started to turn away.

Jared froze in the act of plucking a chord, then laid his hand flat across the strings. I glanced back at him, ever (pathetically) hopeful. He put the guitar down, then looked up at me, the intensity of his expression taking my breath away "Okay. Here's the deal. I have had it explained to me by a certain individual that I need to stay in my place." He arched a brow, inviting me to figure out what he meant.

"What place?"

"Away. From you."

"Who?"

His gaze flickered and I knew. There was only one person whose advice he took.

"Donovan," I guessed and Jared frowned. Donovan was Nick's dad,

Jared's uncle, and the *Pyr* who had sold Jared that vintage Ducati motorcycle. "But why?"

"Well, he has a good point." Jared folded his arms across his chest but leaned closer to me. Our arms brushed against each other as his gaze bored into mine. My mouth went dry and my heart did a cartwheel or two. My doubts faded big time. "You're not on the same timeline as I am, Zoë."

It was disgusting that he would make the same argument as my dad.

"A couple of years doesn't make that much difference," I protested. "I mean, it's a lot now, but eventually..."

"And that's just the thing." His voice dropped impossibly lower, so I was feeling it as much as I was hearing it. "You're going to live for centuries, Zoë, maybe even more than that. It's part of the dragon plan. Me, I'm in for maybe eighty years."

"But..."

He reached out and touched my cheek with one fingertip. I quivered, the touch of his finger making me feel hot and unsettled. "The thing is, it doesn't matter how fascinated I am by you or how good I think it could be between us. I've read the book." He slid that fingertip down to my chin. My knees were dissolving. I could barely listen to what he was saying, especially with my heart pounding so loud. "You're going to have a firestorm with some guy, and it's going to be your duty to your kind to follow the heat of that firestorm."

I parted my lips, but he touched his fingertip to them. Oh. Was there ever a better way to silence anyone? I could feel the callus on one side from him playing guitar. He watched his finger's progress, his gaze heating exactly the way my blood did.

I wanted to protest. I wanted to argue with him, to defend the cause of true love and the power of choice, but I sensed that he was right.

Because the firestorms I'd witnessed had been overwhelmingly powerful forces, a tide of heat and desire that shorted the mental circuits of a *Pyr*. The firestorm heated to greater intensity the longer it was denied, and never sputtered until it was satisfied. None of the dragon dudes I knew had managed to step away, even if they had been dead set against satisfying the firestorm.

I didn't know what I could say that wouldn't be untrue or at best unreasonably optimistic. My chest was tight.

There was no air left in that club.

We stood there, his gaze boring into mine and my heart leaping all over my chest, and then he looked away, his expression grim. And when he did, something changed. The connection between us was severed, cut as cleanly as if it had never been. Or a door was closed. His interest in me was nonexistent.

I think he practically forgot I was standing there.

I felt forty-five thousand kinds of stupid. Even if I really wanted to have something with Jared, that wasn't enough to ensure that he wanted something with me.

If he had really been interested, he would have contacted me. He wouldn't have been able to *not* contact me. He wouldn't have been able to leave me standing here, wanting something—anything—from him.

Maybe it was time I stopped liking guys who didn't like me.

"Too bad I wasted a birthday present," I said, turning away. There was no reason to prolong my humiliation. "See you around."

"Your birthday? When's that?" he asked, to my surprise.

I glanced back, wary. "Soon." I sighed. "I only wanted three things."

His eyes glinted. "What else?"

That he'd guessed seeing him was one was mortifying, but I answered him anyway. "A grudge match with Kohana."

"Forget it." His protective determination made me smile. I was the dragon, after all.

And what difference did it make to him anyway?

"What else?" he demanded.

"A tattoo."

His surprise was clear. "No way."

"A dragon, here." I gestured to my left shoulder, my tone nearly daring him to question me. "On my back and upper arm. Watching out for me."

"Got an artist in mind?"

"Me. I drew it. I love it."

He watched me carefully. "But...?"

"My mom says no ink before I'm legal."

He smiled, as if he had a secret, and turned back to his guitar. You can believe I wanted to know what he was thinking. You can believe I knew he wouldn't share.

I'd had enough. I turned away again. "Have a good show," I said, but my heart wasn't in it. I felt the weight of his gaze on my back, and my feet dragged. I like to think Jared might have called me back—once a relentless optimist, always one—but Angie in the tight pants clapped her hands abruptly.

"Let's get it together, people!" she said as she strode past. "We need to put some money in the jar."

Jared tugged the guitar strap over his shoulders. He looked even more like a renegade with that electric guitar slung low over his hips than he did riding his Ducati. He saw me looking and after a long moment, he blew me a kiss. My heart leapt, which just made me feel even more stupid.

Then he was gone, striding to the stage.

I needed some air.

THE FIRST CHORDS OF "SNOW GODDESS" rang out as I got to the door of the club. It was an anthem, a love song, a call to fight for justice and love. It made my blood simmer and my heart thump.

Just like Jared did. With the touch of one fingertip, he'd left me jangled, my lips burning. I wondered whether he was confusing me on purpose.

How could he blow me off, then play that song? He could read people's thoughts. He knew what I was thinking. He knew what I wanted.

And he'd deliberately done the opposite.

I made the mistake of glancing toward the stage. Then I couldn't take my eyes off him as he played and sang. He was really enjoying himself, totally into it, and I understood that making music was what he'd been born to do. I listened to him, savoring how his voice seemed to resonate in the deepest part of my heart. I felt the power of his song enthrall the audience.

It certainly enchanted me.

I'd seen Mage spells before and I'd known that the Mages had wanted to recruit Jared once upon a time. I'd assumed it was because of some raw talent he had, and on this night I saw that it was true.

I shoved my hands into my pockets and found the ring. I pulled it out, saw that it was twinkling again, and on impulse, shoved it onto my finger.

It was mine now. Why shouldn't I wear it? To tell the truth, I wasn't in the mood to think about repercussions from anything.

Suddenly, the scene before me changed. I could see the vibrations of Jared's songs spiral into the air. They weren't orange and binding like Mage spells. They weren't yellow bolts of lightning like the weapons Kohana and the Thunderbirds threw.

They were spirals, bouncing and frolicking through the air. Plus there were little explosions in between the dancing spirals, like sunbursts. They were all different colors of light, as joyous as a rainbow. They reminded me of confetti and streamers, the kind that people throw from the deck of a ship in old movies as the ship pulls out from the dock.

As the spell light emanated from Jared's throat and his guitar, it was cast over the crowd. It infected the mood in the club. Instead of being pressed together to listen, or just marking the beat, people started to dance. The pulse of the music slipped into our veins and took us all to the same rocking place. Most people weren't drunk. We were just lost in the joy of the music.

It was wonderful.

I wondered whether that was how he mixed me up and turned me inside out. I wondered whether he was casting a spell on me. I couldn't see that any of his spells targeted me, though. They were dancing around the crowd, cajoling people into dancing along. The crowd swayed, a few people sang, and the mood became festive.

Because of Jared's spell.

At that point I remembered I'd intended to ask him about the book.

A bit late.

Had he steered the conversation deliberately, setting me off balance so I didn't ask for the book? I didn't want to think about it, but once I had the thought, it stuck. Was Jared manipulating me?

I needed to think, and do it away from Jared's spell. I told Meagan I'd be back, and waited for her nod. I strode across the club, shoved the door open, and stepped into the night.

The thing was, I had a hard time believing that anything anybody said to Jared would stop him from doing whatever he wanted to do. He said he didn't answer to anybody. Even Donovan couldn't have that power over him. Donovan's argument was just a convenient excuse for blowing me off.

But why? What else didn't I know?

IN THE END, I can only blame my complete fixation on the problem of Jared for the fact that I missed the obvious. I should have been paying attention. I should have been using the keen *Pyr* senses I'd been born with instead of trying to figure out Jared Madison.

That's how Kohana surprised me. I wasn't looking for trouble, and so it —or he—found me.

Maybe he even guessed that I would be under Jared's spell.

Maybe he was counting on it.

I was surprised when I stepped outside the club. The cold air was bracing, but I'd expected that. What I hadn't anticipated was that there would be no one on the street.

I mean, not one living soul.

It was really cold, the sky inky black and the windows on every side dark. The only motion was a fistful of dry leaves blowing down the gutter. The pulse of music behind me sounded as if it was coming from another world.

It had been snowing when we arrived, but there was no snow now. Where had it gone?

I looked harder. I could have stepped into a cemetery, or a dead zone, which made no sense. It wasn't that late, and although the club wasn't in a fabulous area of town, there had been some other businesses in the vicinity.

Now every shop window was boarded up. Not as if businesses were closed for the night—as if they were closed for the duration.

Abandoned.

But we'd been in the club for only an hour.

The hair stood up on the back of my neck. What was going on? I looked down at my hand and guessed.

I tugged the ring off and the street looked as I had expected it to. Quiet, but not deserted. Pretty much as it had been when we'd arrived. Snow falling thickly all around. I couldn't see the spells from Jared, but I could hear the music.

I shoved the ring over my knuckle again. Instantly, the desolate scene appeared.

This was way better than the eye game.

But it must be happening for a reason.

I was reassured to see the happy confetti of sound generated by Jared traveling out into the night. It was brilliant against the shadows.

But I also noticed now that orange spears of light were emerging. I recognized them as Mage binding spells. They were spilling out of sewers and manholes, from basement windows and vents, spreading into the night like a net. There were zillions of them, more with every passing second, and I had the sense that they were breeding. They trussed up the confetti spells and tossed them into the gutter. They would imprison anyone trapped within them. I'd watched them do that in the spring.

But now they were coming for me.

Suddenly, a raven cried far overhead. At least I thought it was a raven until I saw Kohana leap from the roof of the building across the street and spread his arms wide. I knew it couldn't be anyone else but him. My *Pyr* sense of smell gave me that clue.

He shifted shape in midair, becoming a dark Thunderbird. I'd seen him in this form before and I knew he was fast. He gave a cry as he targeted me, his claws outspread and his eyes gleaming.

"I knew you would come to him," Kohana cried. "I knew when I heard his music that you'd be here."

It wasn't a crazy assumption. Kohana had seen us together at boot camp.

I pivoted and tugged on the door of the club, but it had locked.

I looked up and saw Kohana closing in fast. He didn't want to chat. I pulled at the door again in desperation, then pounded on it. The music ensured that no one heard me.

I was tempted to defy my dad's edict, but he'd know I shifted and then he'd know where I was, and then there would be hell to pay on a number of levels. Exile wasn't a tempting possibility for my future. There was nowhere to run and nowhere to hide, so I made a quick decision.

I closed my eyes, summoned every scrap of Wyvern within me, and wished with all my heart to be someplace else.

Someplace safe.

I was immediately engulfed in the blue shimmer I knew so well, its light skimming over my skin like an electrical tide. I closed my eyes tightly against its brilliance just as I heard Kohana shout.

He didn't sound happy, which I took as a good sign.

IT WAS DARK. Fuzzy. A bit stuffy.

I could hear the music, but it was muffled. I was hyperventilating but not shredded.

I'd take good news as it came.

I smelled a chocolate bar and felt a lipstick under one foot. The scent of a familiar perfume gave me an idea of where I was, but it wasn't until I felt the case for her contacts that I knew my precise location.

In Isabelle's purse.

Which meant that I'd changed to salamander form en route.

This spontaneous manifestation stuff still had a whiff of the random about it. When I forgot to concentrate or was tired, odd things happened. I mostly went where I wanted and became what I wanted to be, but every once in a while, stuff happened.

Like ending up in salamander form in Isabelle's purse.

Really, if I was going to be in salamander form anywhere, I would have voted for being in Jared's pocket. Although, given that he was onstage and being watched by several hundred people, that probably wouldn't have been very discreet.

"Where did Zoë go?" Isabelle shouted at Meagan.

"She said she'd be back in a minute. I thought she'd gone to the bathroom."

Isabelle swore with an earthiness that made me blink. It does sound better with her accent, but I recognized that she was worried about me.

Which meant I had to get out of her purse, and do it without freaking anybody out.

There was really only one place to go.

I gnawed on her chocolate bar, which was a British Mars bar. They are so much better than anything we get here that I can hardly believe it. I took a beat to deeply appreciate Isabelle's tendency to carry such things, then summoned the shimmer again.

It was both easier and harder the second time. The shimmer tends to be more biddable the more I call it, but the shift does kick my butt. Which is a long way of saying that I manifested off balance in human form, then fell into a whole bunch of gear backstage and created an avalanche.

It must have made quite a noise, because when I opened my eyes, Rick and Angie were glaring at me and the music had stopped. Behind the band, I could see members of the audience who'd followed them. Jared winked and offered me his hand, and I was glad to accept his help. Isabelle was behind them, looking both exasperated and relieved. Meagan was swiveling her head between the club and the backstage area, clearly trying to calculate how I had managed to get backstage without her seeing me.

"Do us a favor, Jared," Angie said, her tone impatient. "Keep your girls away from the gear. The insurance doesn't cover whatever they break."

"I'll take care of it," Jared said, his hand tightening over mine for a second. It felt good to have someone know that I wasn't just being a pain, that I hadn't had a lot of choice. And how sad was it that this teeny bit of attention from him fed my relentless optimism all over again?

The thing was that once again, I had the fleeting—and tempting—sense that Jared and I could make a good team.

Then I was on my feet and Jared gave my fingers a last squeeze, then was gone.

As if he barely knew me.

Business as usual. This was a guy who could seriously deal in mixed messages. I wasn't sure what to think and I was starting to believe he wanted it that way.

"I hope she's worth it," Angie muttered as they walked back to the stage. "We'd better do another short set, to keep the crowd happy."

Isabelle took one look at me and saw a whole lot more than I probably should have let her see. "Let's head home," she said, all bustling responsibility. "It's getting a bit late and I don't want Meagan's mom to be worried."

She looked pretty concerned herself, her gaze lingering on me, but I was too bagged to care. When the three of us stepped out into the night, the street looked just as it should, and there was no sign of Kohana. I couldn't see those Mage spells coming out of the sewer grates, either, not even with my ring on.

They must have spun the spells to coincide with Jared's music. Were there Mages in the crowd all night? Were they using him? I wanted to go back and talk to him, maybe find out what he knew—relentless optimism is tough to beat down—but Isabelle hooked her hand through my arm and tugged me toward the L.

I did, though, have time to confirm that the door didn't even lock behind us. Weird. Why had it been locked when I was alone outside? Had that been because of a spell? Spun by who? Jared? The Mages? Or Kohana?

Isabelle frowned at me. Her eyes narrowed and then she reached into her purse. She was visibly surprised that the Mars bar had been opened and part of it eaten.

It wasn't as if she had mice in her purse.

Just an uninvited salamander once in a while.

I smiled, shrugged, and saw her understand.

She slipped her other hand through the crook of Meagan's arm. "So, what did you think?" she asked brightly, handing the chocolate bar surreptitiously to me as she set off for the main street at a brisk pace. The snow was up to our ankles and Meagan kicked some happily as we walked down the street.

Meagan was excited. She talked about the music and the band and Jared, and more about musical composition again, giving me plenty of time to make the chocolate disappear. No chance of her noticing that I was off my game. I practically inhaled the chocolate bar, throwing it back as fast as a hungry dog.

It was exactly what I needed to feel human again.

Even if I did glance back as we turned the corner, seeking the silhouette of a guy or a bird on a roof.

I didn't see Kohana.

But that didn't mean he wasn't there.

6

What is it about Mages? I had to wonder about the pervasiveness of their spells. I had them on the brain after the events of the evening, but the weird thing was that Meagan did, too.

Was it a coincidence that she talked about Trevor Wilson?

Or was something more sinister at work?

I was crashed on the twin bed in her room and the lights were out. It was late and we should have been asleep, but Meagan was still wound up after the concert. I was fine with her chatting, just kind of dozing as she talked about the music and the band and the syntho drums and, wow, that Jared.

I pretty much agreed with the wow part.

I kept thinking about the protective flash of his eyes when I'd told him about wanting a grudge match with Kohana and the wild roller-coaster feeling of our hearts matching their pace. Never mind Kohana's assertion that he knew I'd be with Jared.

Was Jared trying to protect me by staying away from me?

You know I liked that idea.

A lot.

When Meagan took a deep breath, I suspected she was going to say something I wouldn't like, but she still surprised me. "I'll bet Trevor knows Jared's music."

"What?" I was wide-awake at the mention of the apprentice Mage's name. "Why would you think that?"

"Because he's so into music. Haven't you seen how he plays the sax? He closes his eyes and moves with the music. Just like Jared with his guitar. Trevor told me he's always in trouble in marching band for losing his place in line."

I rolled over to look at her. Even in the shadows, I could see her eyes shining. In fact, she was nearly radiating. "He told you that? When?"

"Well, he's failing trig again. I'm still tutoring him. On Tuesdays and Thursdays." She acted as if it was no big deal, but now she was blushing. Then she grimaced. "I really don't understand why he doesn't see the link between music and math. I've been studying it a lot, because I thought it might help him."

Meagan—good sweet generous Meagan—was trying to help a guy who was part of a team bent on world domination. And I couldn't think of any good way to warn her away from him. "Doesn't sound like he appreciates your help," I said, keeping my tone neutral.

She sighed. "No. He invited you to his party, not me."

"I'm not going."

"He asked you out last spring, too. Is it really true that nothing happened?"

"Nothing happened. I didn't go." I took a breath. "I'm not going on Halloween, either."

"You don't have to do that for me."

"I don't like him."

"Really?" She rolled over to face me. "He's so hot, Zoë. And so talented. He's not like the other guys whose parents have tons of money. You can tell by the way he plays the sax. He's *sensitive*."

I did not snort.

"How can you not like him? Is it because of Jared?"

"No. I didn't like him before. Maybe because he was dating Suzanne." I looked at her. "I mean, that says something, don't you think?"

"Lots of guys just see that she's pretty."

"On the outside."

She mused on that. "But she's probably different to Trevor."

"Maybe I don't like him because he's not very nice to you."

"What do you mean?"

"He should have asked you to his party, especially if you're tutoring him that much."

There was a beat of silence and I could see her blinking at the ceiling. When she spoke, her voice was very soft. "Do you think he thinks I'm just useful?"

"I think he's just not a very nice person," I said, my tone fierce. "You deserve better."

She turned to study me, probably noticing my tone. "You really don't like him, do you? All he did was ask you to his party."

That wasn't all Trevor had done, but I couldn't tell her the truth. That was getting old fast. "I can't explain it," I said, which was pretty much true. "He just gives me the creeps."

"Huh." Meagan turned her back again. I could practically hear her thinking. "You usually have really good instincts about people. I'd just like to know what he's thinking, though."

"I'm not sure my instincts are good about Jared," I admitted. I could do it only because it was dark and I was tired and we were alone.

"He is so hot, though," Meagan said with a sigh. A moment later she sighed again. "Guys are so hard to understand."

I almost laughed—our thoughts were so similar. "I know *exactly* what you mean."

I heard her fall asleep then, and listened to the sound of her breathing for a while. I could hear the snow falling outside, and was thinking about the similarities to the previous spring. Even though I was exhausted, I didn't really want to fall asleep.

I had a feeling Urd was waiting for me in dreamland.

I kept the ring on my finger, just in case.

URD APPARENTLY HAD other social obligations. She was a no-show.

I slept hard and dreamlessly. When I woke up, I could hear Meagan doing her piano practice. I smelled fresh coffee and heard her parents discussing the news in the kitchen. Nobody seemed to expect to see me soon, so I pulled out my messenger and did my tabulation of issues outstanding and associated clues.

I needed to figure out, in no particular order:

1. Why had Kohana attacked me this time?
2. How could I change his plan, whatever it was?
3. What was the Mages' scheme for Halloween?
4. What should—or could—I do about Jared?

Each and every item on this list was a pressing concern. Cumulatively, they were almost paralyzing.

I wasn't even sure where to begin.

The simple fact was that I needed backup. When you need support with dragon details, there's only one group of confidants who will do—other dragons.

As disappointed as Isabelle was with Nick, he was still my buddy. He was a hundred and seventy pounds of almost pure testosterone, and I could count on him.

I took my file *On Becoming the Wyvern* and sent it to Nick, along with a note that it should be opened if I died.

Kind of a last will and testament.

Or an insurance plan.

Then I sent it to Liam and to Garrett, along with the same message.

All three replied instantly, in characteristic fashion, their responses making my messenger chime three times in rapid succession.

Garrett, who had an affinity with fire, replied with quick heat:

WTF?

Nick, who had a connection to the earth, needed the facts:

WHAT'S GOING ON, Z? WHAT'S HAPPENED?

And Liam, whose affinity was with water, showed his usual empathy:

Z! R U OK?

I loved these guys. I realized that all over again when I read their messages. In fact, it made me tear up a bit. They were the real dragons at my back. And I hadn't been keeping them in the loop, the way I should have done.

So I typed a message, copying it to all of them:

We need to talk. Kohana showed up last night and wanted to fight.

They understood the urgency of the situation immediately. We agreed to do a joint call in half an hour. Then Nick replied:

You've got to set it up, Z. Since you're the only one with the flash new messenger.

I smiled. It still bugged him that I'd won the big prize at boot camp in April, but I wasn't above rubbing it in. I typed back:

You're right. It'll probably take me half an hour to persuade it to link to your antiques.

Not true. It would link almost instantly, but I could just about hear them groan simultaneously.

I had time to dress, eat, and conjure an excuse.

I needed a walk, I decided. Meagan's folks would be good with that on a Sunday morning, and it would be the perfect way to score a little privacy.

"We need to talk," There was a park opposite the Jamesons' town house, a pretty little park that everyone seemed to just walk past and admire. Ideal for my purposes. I swept a bench clear of snow with my gloved hand and had the guys connected in no time.

"First, tell us exactly what happened," Nick said.

I did. I didn't leave out one thing—not the invitation, not my mom and dad, not the incident with Suzanne, not my dad's reaction, not the attack by Kohana.

Oh, I did leave out the fact that Isabelle was disappointed that Nick had a girlfriend. I was saving that for later, when I could talk to Nick privately.

There was a beat of silence when I was done and then they all talked at once.

"What about this Halloween party?" Nick said. "Sounds like a trap to me."

"I'm not going."

"Why do you think Trevor invited you?" Garrett asked. "What could they have planned?"

"You really shouldn't have revealed yourself at school," Liam chided then. "Now that your dad has forbidden you to shift, you're not going to be able to protect yourself. What if you hadn't been able to get away last night?"

"At least I'm not exiled."

"Yet," Liam added.

"We need to know more about Kohana to understand *his* plan," Nick said.

"No, we need to know more about Mages and their plan," Garrett argued. "Then we'll be able to guess his, and we can make a plan ourselves."

I love a good riddle and I like solving these kinds of problems. So I took charge of making the list. On my messenger, I could do that as well as talk to them. "All right. We've got a bunch of questions here and not a lot of time. Let's divide it up, then talk after we each track down a chunk."

"Good plan," Nick said.

"We need to find out about the other shifters. Kohana said that there were only four kinds left, and that the Mages meant to eliminate all of us."

"Your dad made a treaty with the Mages," Liam said.

"But they'll never stand by it," Nick said. "Zoë's right in that." We'd been through our skepticism before.

"The thing is that we have to be careful not to be the ones to breach the terms of the treaty first," Liam said. There was some discussion, and Liam agreed to hunt down the exact text of the treaty.

"It's fair to assume that Kohana intends to betray the *Pyr* into being next," Garrett said with heat. "Why else would he go after Zoë?"

"But why would he play on their side?" Nick asked.

"He thought before that the Mages would cut the Thunderbirds some slack in exchange for turning in another kind of shifter," I said. "Maybe they've even promised to do that."

"But they won't keep that promise, either," Nick said.

I love how linear Nick is. It's right-and-wrong, either-or, black-or-white for him on every issue. He's a total straight arrow.

"You're right," Garrett agreed. "But the key to figuring out a way around that lies in understanding the Thunderbirds. What's their objective?"

"Survival?" Nick suggested.

"What else?" I asked.

"Maybe we're just the Mages' next target and that put us on the Thunderbirds' map," Liam said.

"No," I said. "I think it's about that treaty Kohana mentioned last time, the one he said we *Pyr* broke centuries ago. He thinks we're lower than pond scum."

"But what was the deal?" Nick asked. "How'd we break it?"

"And can we fix it?" Liam asked.

We didn't know.

"We only have Kohana's word that there ever was a big fight between our species and a deal," I noted. "But he keeps saying the *Unktehila* are oathbreakers who forget our own history."

"It's not much of a recommendation," Nick conceded. "If he's right."

"We can't exactly fix it if we don't know what the problem was," Liam said.

"I'm on it," Garrett said. "My mom has an amazing collection of New Age references at the bookstore. I'll have to sift through a lot of garbage, but I might be able to find something useful."

"Good. Thanks." I consulted my list. "Keep an eye out for these other shifters, too. We know there's us and there's the Thunderbirds. Kohana had said that the other two kinds were wolves and jaguars."

"We need better info about them, too," Garrett said. "Find out where they live, who their leaders are, whether they've already been fighting Mages."

"And we need to contact them," I added. "Maybe the way to beat the Mages is to work together."

"Kohana isn't giving that idea much support," Garrett noted.

"Well, we've got to find Kohana," Nick said. "Before he finds Zoë again. I'll see if I can sniff him out—or more of his kind."

"And I'm coming to Chicago," Liam said. "It won't take me long to find the treaty terms, and you can't be alone right now, Zoë. You might need someone able to shift to guard your back."

The guys agreed heartily on that, and I was relieved that Liam was coming. "What will you tell your parents?"

"I'll think of something," Liam said, which said something about his determination. He's an even worse liar than me. "Maybe I'll just tell them the truth."

I smiled at that.

"You don't think the Mages prompted Eileen and Erik's fight, do you?" Garrett asked. "I mean, we know that they can turn people's thoughts in different directions."

"And it would be a good way to ensure that Zoë is undefended." Liam sounded thoughtful.

We fell silent for a moment, and I knew I wasn't the only one worried about it.

Then Garrett sighed. "Okay, I've got to say it, Zoë, even though you're not going to like it."

"Go ahead." I didn't know what to expect.

"What about Jared? I know you like him, but the Mages did try to sign him up, didn't they?"

My heart clenched. "He declined, though. He told me."

"Do you really think the Mages take no for an answer that easily?" Garrett asked quietly. "I'm not saying he's lying to you, but I am wondering how anyone gets away from those guys."

There was a slither of uneasiness between us. I was pretty sure we were all remembering how Adrian's spell the previous spring had made us act against our own will.

"I trust him!" My protest sounded a bit shrill, even to myself.

"Maybe I'm wrong, but if we're checking out the angles, I think that's one to consider." Garrett tried to be conciliatory. "Maybe you can get the story from him, since he's in town."

"Don't get all prickly, Zoë," Nick said.

"No, your concern is fair. I see that. I'll go talk to him." My heart skipped and leapt at just the prospect of seeing Jared again.

How sad was that?

"Maybe someone should go there with you," Liam said. "Wait for me to get there before you go after him. Just in case."

"You've got to take care of yourself, Zoë," Garrett said. "You're our Wyvern."

"And we've got to work together, like we did last time," Nick said. "Let's all get to Chicago as soon as we can."

"Careful what you tell your parents," I said. "My dad is sure I'm wrong about the Mages. My only chance of avoiding exile is to prove that we're right."

"Without shifting," Liam said and I could practically see them all roll their eyes.

"If they don't trust the Wyvern, then we don't need to confide in them," Nick said. "Let's prove Zoë right and then tell them the deal."

Truth be told, I was relieved at their plan. Besides, I might be able to talk some sense into Nick about this girlfriend thing once he was here. My messenger chimed and I saw that I'd missed a call from my mom, but that it was receiving a message from her. I liked that she was doing what she'd promised. I would read it as soon as we were done.

"Do you think you can get the book from Jared?" Liam asked. "That might tell us something about Mages and other shifters."

I was skeptical that it would, doubly skeptical that he'd let it go. "I'll try, but he's told me that he's not giving it up."

"There has to be someplace else we can get some answers," Nick said. "I don't like waiting on chance."

That was when I knew. The answer was in the dark, at the bottom of the well. Urd might not be a looker, but she'd pushed me down there for my own good.

Just the way her sister, Verdandi, had given me the rune stone last spring, knowing I would need it.

For something.

Trusting them and my dreams was key.

I knew what I had to do. I didn't like it, but I knew there was no other choice.

I needed to go back into that dream and go down the well.

By choice.

It was a Wyvern thing.

MEAGAN WAS FINISHING her piano practice when I got back to the town house. We hung out as I read the message from my mom. My mom was doing all right, or at least she wanted me to believe as much. She still hadn't mentioned my dad.

Meagan and I tried to decide if that was important to the ultimate resolution, but we were interrupted when she got a call on her messenger. I grimaced as she crowed to Jessica about completing her math homework first. She told her about the concert in glowing terms, and I couldn't help but notice how easily they talked.

Like I wasn't even there.

Then Meagan chatted to Jessica about potential *Pyr* candidates among the guys at school. Apparently they agreed about Derek having a dark secret—it was in his eyes. I never saw anything much in his eyes, but no one was asking me.

I went to the fridge, feeling a bit forgotten.

"Your mom called," Meagan's mom said as she came into the kitchen with a magazine. She pulled out a stool and sat down.

"My mom called you?" I nearly hit my head on the freezer door, I straightened so fast.

"She wanted to make sure you were staying out of trouble."

I smiled, mentally adjusting my halo. "Pretty much."

Meagan's mom smiled. "That's what I told her, that there was nothing to worry about."

She started to read her magazine again and I was turning away, but then I stopped. "Mrs. Jameson?"

"Mm-hmm?"

"How did she sound?"

Meagan's mom glanced up. "What do you mean?"

I shrugged. "You know. Happy? Sad?"

Wildly in love?

Ready to return home?

In the act of filing for divorce?

I didn't say any of those things, but Meagan's mom smiled a little, as if she'd heard them. "She sounded"—she flipped a page of the magazine absently, as if searching for the right word, then smiled at me—"cautiously optimistic."

I decided to take that as progress.

"Good. Thanks."

Meagan was walking through the intricacies of a math proof with Jessica. I figured I'd better do some of my own homework. I drained my juice, rinsed the glass, then headed for Meagan's room to get the backpack I'd left there.

"I'll do a visioning for your mother tonight, Zoë," Meagan's mom called after me. "Just a gesture of goodwill."

I stopped, then glanced back. My mom rolls her eyes whenever Meagan or her mom talks about her mom being a vision counselor. I wasn't so sure. I'd been a bit spooked that Kohana had shown up the first time after Meagan had done a visioning session for me in the spring, and I wasn't quite so skeptical anymore. Who knew what Mrs. Jameson could conjure up? "That's very nice of you. Thanks."

Her lips tightened, as if she'd heard my uncertainty and was a bit offended by it. "You know, Zoë, the future doesn't have to happen by accident or by chance. And the thing is, if a woman can't imagine a future with a man, then nothing he says or does can persuade her to be with him. She needs to be able to *see* that future in order for it to be a possibility at all."

I stared at her for a long moment, then swallowed. "That makes sense." I headed to Meagan's room, my thoughts churning.

Mrs. Jameson had given me an idea.

Sending visions was supposed to be part of the Wyvern's arsenal. I'd forgotten that, maybe because I hadn't shown much promise in that department just yet. But somehow I had to send a vision to my mom before it was too late.

If it wasn't already too late.

First things first—a visit to Urd.

. . .

I crashed early, unable to concentrate on my homework. Meagan had hers done already and was easy to convince about going to bed early. She'd been power-yawning all day after our late night out.

Her parents, I'm sure, thought we were being responsible.

I was jumpy as I settled into bed, terrified of what I might see. Was Urd Death in disguise? The skull head certainly wasn't a reassuring detail. Did that mean I would die if I went back down that well? Could I even get there from Meagan's room? What would happen when I hit the bottom of the well?

It was hard to imagine that it would be anything good.

We said our good nights and I heard Meagan fall asleep almost right away. I could smell her toothpaste—she used a lot, making sure her teeth were superclean around her braces—and fabric softener from the sheets.

I took a deep breath, hoped for the best, and closed my eyes.

I'm not sure how much time had passed before I shivered. I reached for an extra blanket instinctively, then knew.

I opened my left eye to find snow drifting over the bed.

Holy frick.

It was happening again.

This dream could recur forty million times and it would still freak me out each and every time.

I rolled over, terrified. Granny was knitting snowdrifts busily, her sister motionless beside her. Like an angel of death. Not much of an angel, really. A skeleton of death.

With a drop spindle that whirled and whirled, spinning yarn.

I tried to keep calm and walk through the dream exactly the same way as I had before. Urd silenced me with a finger; she introduced herself and her sister; she conjured my ring out of the air.

I shouted and lunged for her, just as I had before.

She threw the ring down the well and we struggled. I knew when the fabric would tear and I would see her face, but still the sight shocked me. Then she flung me down the well, just as she had the last time, and I was falling to the eerie echo of her laughter.

So far so good. (Relatively speaking.)

I swallowed and braced myself for a disgusting and painful landing.

But no. The air changed. There was suddenly a powerful updraft, one that didn't stink. It slowed my descent, as if I was a feather. I landed on my feet, as easily as that.

And the inky water that had pooled at the bottom of the well? It was a black mirror of ice. I stood on it, astonished, and saw the white orb of Urd's face reflected in it from far above.

Like a moon shining down the well.

Until she smiled and I saw the green flick of her snake-tongue.

I jerked and looked up, way up, but she moved away. I heard something metal clang into place, like a manhole cover, just as I was plunged into complete darkness.

The prospect of finding my ring seemed a bit slim.

The mirror of ice cracked beneath my feet then and I felt cold water lap against my bare feet. Which way should I run? Where would it be safe? Could I run without falling through the ice?

Just then, just when I thought things couldn't get worse, I heard the sound of a match being struck.

I spun to face the flickering light. A guy held the match aloft while it sputtered, the light touching his face. He looked like one of my mom's grad students, a little bit scruffy, maybe thirty years old. Sandy hair. The kind of person you'd walk right past without a second look.

He smiled and waved with his other hand. "Hey, sis," he said and then he swore as the match sputtered. I saw the glowing tip as he tossed the match in the water and heard it sizzle on impact.

Sis?

Holy shit. Urd had tossed me into the land of the dead.

SIGMUND LIT ANOTHER MATCH, but this time, he used it to light a candle. "You're going to want to get off that ice," he said. "No telling how deep the well water is, and there's nobody can save you if you go under."

"Right." I could see that the ground was dry near him. Approaching my dead brother who had turned *Slayer* wasn't an appealing option for my longevity, but I didn't have a lot of choices.

And I was already in the realm of the dead.

I had nothing left to lose.

I slid across the ice and it cracked behind me in long, jagged lines, revealing a fathomless darkness. The well seemed to be stone, the walls uneven and gray. The space was about fifteen feet across. Round. So, Sigmund was standing on a kind of lip at one side, maybe one formed naturally.

"Some well," I said when I was safely on dry ground. "Big."

Or maybe we were really small.

You can't be too sure when you're dreaming.

"High volume in certain seasons," Sigmund said. "It's fed by all sorts of strange rivers." He gave me a look. "You seriously don't want to know."

He didn't look dead. Not really. A bit faded around the edges. Less vital than real live people. But if you didn't look twice, you might not notice it. "You're Sigmund, right? My brother from my dad's first firestorm."

"*Our* father." He stuck out his hand. "Sigmund Guthrie."

I shook his hand. He didn't feel dead, either. At least his hand didn't feel the way I expected dead people's hands to feel. His skin felt kind of papery, not, you know, like rotten meat. "Zoë Sorensson. How come you have a different last name?"

"Long story. How's this for the short version? When I was born, I was Sigmund Sorensson."

Ah, a name change. I would guess because my dad—*our* dad—had ticked him off. It wasn't much of a stretch for my imagination, given my recent interactions with that dragon. I folded my arms across my chest. There was no wind here, but it was still cold. Damp. "So, is this the land of the dead? I'd think it would be more crowded."

Sigmund smiled. "Technically, it's not, but you can get there from here."

"Excuse me?"

"The well is fed by several rivers, like I said, so when the tide is right, it's like an ancient sewer system down here. You can get from here to there, if you really want to go, but I have to tell you, there's not much to recommend it in the way of sights. Lousy company, too. Morose." He seemed to find this funny.

"Good to know. Thanks." I looked around, reminded myself that I had very little to lose. "So, does anyone ever get out of here?"

"Sure. The sisters send down the bucket every day. They have to water the tree, you know. Just hop in and they'll haul you up."

I was skeptical that Urd would do me any kind of favor like that, but I couldn't see the point in arguing.

"You came down here without knowing you could get back out?" I nodded and he whistled. "Braver than you look."

"Actually, I didn't have a lot of choice. I was chucked in the well." I remembered something else. "You didn't happen to see a ring fall down here, did you?"

"This one?" He held up the ring, smiling at my obvious relief. I reached for it, but he tossed it in the air, keeping it out of my grasp. I was terrified that he'd drop it and it would fall into that black water.

"Hey, give it to me!"

"Why should I?"

"Because it's mine!"

"Go ahead and make me."

I snatched and he moved it away once again. Then he laughed, his eyes twinkling. "Guess that's what brothers and sisters are supposed to do, isn't it? Had to try it out, just once." He offered me the ring.

I smiled and reached for it again. "Did you like being an only child?"

"No." He did his sleight of hand with the ring just before I could snag it and I was annoyed. Just like a little sister is supposed to be. "You?"

"No, but I'm starting to see its appeal."

He laughed easily. I kind of liked him.

"Catch," Sigmund said and tossed the ring toward me. It was an easy toss, but I stretched too far. (Told you about me and projectiles.) I grabbed the ring out of the air, then my foot slipped off the lip of the stone. Sigmund grabbed me and pulled me back, his hand firm around my elbow.

I leaned against the stone wall, my heart pounding, the ring clutched in my hand. "Thanks." I shoved the ring on to my finger.

The view didn't change. Interesting.

"No problem. Big brothers are supposed to look out for their sisters." He grinned wickedly. "As well as pester them and stuff frogs into their beds. Sorry, I've got to cram everything in together. We've got a lot of time to make up."

I laughed at that. "I can't even make fun of your girlfriends. Not without knowing them a little."

"Oh, that's too bad." He waggled his eyebrows in mock dismay, making me laugh again.

We were close together then and I saw that he was a bit taller than me. He didn't look that much like me, yet I could see some similarity around the eyes. I wondered how much else we had in common.

I had to ask. "Did you really turn *Slayer*?"

"Yup." He slanted me a glance. "Take it from me: bad choice."

"But why?"

Sigmund exhaled slowly. "Let's just say it was part of the whole name change and teenage rebellion thing."

I seriously felt that I had a lot in common with my brother then. We stood in silence for a moment, and I wondered whether he was waiting for me to ask the questions. I did. "Did you really write that book?"

He grimaced. "Yes. Bad choice. There was only ever a single copy of it, but it made plenty of trouble just the same."

I turned to look straight at him. "One copy? Are you sure?"

"Well, yes. I created it, page by page, bound it myself." He shrugged. "A work of art, from my own hands. Not that I'm being cocky or anything, but it was good work. Lasted over a century, too."

"Someone could have copied it."

He shook his head. "I had it for years in my possession. Locked away securely. No one could have copied it without my knowing. When I couldn't keep close watch on it, I ensured that it went to Sara's aunt's bookstore."

"Garrett's mom, Sara?"

He nodded.

"Someone could have copied it there."

"No. The Mages put a glamour on it so no one could see it who shouldn't." He winced. "They were involved by then, unfortunately."

"And who did see it? Someone must have, ultimately."

"It was Erik, of course. *Dad*." Sigmund smiled. "It's his foresight that gives him an edge. And maybe the connection to me. He might have smelled my scent on it." He shrugged. "Either way, he spotted it. He handed it to Sara and then she saw it, too. She kept it locked up for years after that." He shrugged. "Until it was stolen."

Stolen.

That was the copy of the book I knew about, the one that had been lost from Sara's shop. Although no one had ever said "stolen" in my presence, just "lost." And I hadn't known that bit about the glamour.

Either way, there was a puzzle here. "But there must be two copies."

"Why?"

"Because my friend Jared has a copy and he found it before Sara's was stolen."

"Found?" Sigmund's eyes danced with mischief. "Maybe someone's lying to you, little sister." Before I could argue with that, he pursed his lips and blew out the candle.

I reached for him in the darkness, but my hand closed on empty air. "Sigmund? *Sigmund!*" My own cry echoed in the well, but there was no other sound.

He was gone. I was abandoned in the dark in silence.

Except there was the sound of metal scraping, followed by the faint creak of a chain. I looked up to see a bucket swinging as it was lowered down the well and the white orb of a grinning skull face above it.

At least Sigmund had told me how to get out.

Although I wasn't that hot to see Urd up close and personal again, given the choice, I'd take the bucket lift. It had to be better than trying to find my way through an ancient sewer system in the dark—much less waiting for the tides to be right.

Because now I really had to find Jared and ask him some questions. Maybe just one question. Was he lying to me about the book? I really didn't want to believe it, but whatever he told me about the book would help me decide what to do about him.

With him.

Remembering that he could read my thoughts but I couldn't read his, did exactly nothing to build my confidence.

I grabbed the bucket when it swung by, climbing up to the handle as it sloshed into the dark water. Sure enough, it was steadily hauled upward, the chain creaking as Urd's face became more clear overhead. I held on tight and hoped for the best.

It seemed a long shot.

And about halfway up the well, the entire scene disappeared.

I was almost afraid to look.

But I opened my eyes to find myself back in Meagan's room. No matter which eye I used, everything looked normal.

And it was three fifteen.

I fell back on the pillows, planning my strategy. As I stretched out, my foot touched something cold and wet. Yuck! I flung back the covers, struggling to keep from screaming.

And a leopard frog hopped out of my bed to the floor. I swear it winked at me before it hopped under Meagan's bed. I fell to the floor and peered after it, but I saw only dust bunnies on the hardwood there.

The frog was gone.

As if it had never been.

Brothers.

7

Monday morning seemed to be filled with complications. I knew I needed to ask Jared about the book, as well as about the Mages, but Liam had wanted me to wait for him to arrive in Chicago before I did anything. When was he going to get here? We weren't that close to Ohio. I'd checked the site for Jared's band and saw that they had a gig in Des Moines Tuesday night.

So I didn't have much time. They might even be gone already.

I wasn't inclined to wait on Liam but was a bit nervous about acting alone. Had Kohana followed me to Jared on Saturday night? Or had he followed the sound of Jared's spellsinging? Would Kohana still be there, waiting on me to show? I decided he must have better things to do. Jared probably wouldn't be spellsinging when I found him this time, so there'd be no music to draw Kohana's attention, wherever he was.

My mom called when Meagan and I were walking to school. Another short and sweet call—she sounded more cheerful, which could have meant anything—and I filled Meagan in on the details afterward. The call reminded me of my plan to send my mom a vision—somehow—and try to turn the tide.

No pressure.

I had so much on my mind that I wasn't exactly a source of sparkling conversation.

As usual, Jessica was waiting at the school doors. She and Meagan called to each other and hugged like long-lost sisters, then scurried off to compare notes on homework and guys with secrets.

Derek was, as usual, loitering against the lockers, watching me and being ignored by everyone else. I hadn't finished his drawing, so I just smiled and pulled out my messenger again, needing to do something other than talk to him. I was self-conscious, given Meagan's theory about him having a crush on me, and thinking that I really had crap judgment when it came to guys.

Proof of that was that I sent Jared a message, trying not to look desperate while I waited for his reply. On the upside, it came quickly. On the downside, he blew me off.

Again.

I don't know why I was surprised. He said he couldn't meet me later. He and the other band members were packing up their gear to head out after lunch.

Then I realized that Jared was assuming that I would be in school until close to four.

I had a sudden uncharacteristic urge to cut class.

IN THE END, I didn't have to skip. English was canceled at the last minute because Miss Ross got sick abruptly—the school nurse was muttering about flu, but Trish was already spreading rumors that Miss Ross might be pregnant. Nice—and we were given a free period. I had lunch right after English on Mondays, which left just enough time to get downtown and back. If I was lucky. (It also, yet again, foiled my plan to get on Meagan's good side and have lunch with Jessica. Given the choice, I thought seeing Jared was more important. You probably saw that coming.) I fled the school like a bat out of hell and raced to the bus stop.

There was a bus idling there. I was sorely tempted to spontaneously manifest downtown—thereby saving lots of time and two bus fares—but it was broad daylight.

And I could hear someone loping along behind me.

"Hey!" Derek bellowed when the bus driver put the bus in gear. He was so loud that I nearly stumbled.

But the bus driver must have heard him. He stopped the bus and opened the door.

I halted, panting by the door, and glanced back.

Derek was catching his breath, too, and his eyes were gleaming. He gestured for me to go first and I did.

I wasn't enormously surprised when he dropped into a seat near mine. "Going downtown?" I asked.

He nodded once, then averted his gaze.

That was okay, I didn't feel like talking, either. It was snowing again, just light flurries that swirled around the bus. There were half a dozen riders on the bus, mostly older people. I fiddled with my ring as we rode.

I couldn't help stealing glances at Derek. He *was* kind of cute. It was true that he wasn't in Jared's league, but apparently Jared was out of mine.

I didn't mind how serious Derek was. I liked that he was tall. I liked that he was focused. I had the sense that he would do whatever he said he would do, that he'd be totally straight with everyone and would not—just for example—mess with someone's mind for inexplicable reasons or personal entertainment. Derek would be in or out, with you or against you.

Like Nick. The first guy I'd liked who hadn't liked me.

I was thinking I needed to review my romantic strategies.

That gave me something to do on the bus.

I liked Derek's eyes, too. That pale blue was really something.

Derek got on the L with me, too, but didn't sit beside me. I found myself intrigued by him and his silence, maybe because he offered a different puzzle, one that wasn't so key to my survival. An idle mind game. I could do with a few more of those.

Derek nodded once at me when he got off the L, two stops before my intended destination, and I felt curiously relieved.

He hadn't been following me, then.

Maybe Meagan was wrong.

The street outside the club was busier than it had been at night and even though I kept myself on guard, I felt pretty safe. I couldn't sense any other *Pyr* and didn't catch one glimpse of Kohana.

Everything seemed perfectly normal.

Which worked for me.

There was music emanating from the club. Loud music. And it was a bit erratic, as if the band was rehearsing. I had to pound on the door to get anyone to answer and then Rick hauled the door open.

His annoyance changed quickly to a grin. "Hey, Jared. Last chance!" He disappeared into the darkness of the interior, leaving the door standing open.

Jared was wearing a dark T-shirt and jeans, and my gaze fell to that salamander tattoo. He smiled when he noticed me looking, then gave me a stern look. His eyes kept twinkling. He leaned in the doorway, looking like trouble. "You're not skipping school, are you, dragon girl?" He pretended to be horrified. "I thought you were one to follow the rules."

"Maybe you're a bad influence."

He laughed, then studied me. "Seriously."

"We got a free period, and I have lunch right after. I'm taking advantage of the opportunity."

"To get into trouble?" His eyes glinted, as if he had definite ideas of what kind of trouble I could get into.

I had to look away.

"I need to ask you a couple of questions." It shouldn't have surprised me that his good mood vanished. He looked wary, but didn't say anything. I took a deep breath. "I want to know about the Mages."

Jared evaded my gaze. "I'm not sure there's much I can tell you." His tone was neutral.

Too neutral.

I chose to trust my instincts and pushed him.

That had been his advice, after all.

"I *need* to know about them. Self-defense."

Jared scuffed his boot and gazed down at it, considering something. Calculating. What didn't he want to tell me? Garrett's suspicions swirled into my thoughts and took hold.

"And the book," I added. "I need to know the truth about the book."

He glanced up in surprise. "What about it?"

"How you got it. *When* you got it."

Jared looked at me hard then and I could see that he wasn't really surprised by my question. He also didn't look inclined to tell me more. He was studying me closely.

I remembered that he could read my thoughts, a little bit too late to hide them. I saw his lips tighten and remembered that I had no secrets from him.

Although he could have plenty from me. I disliked the fact that I was even thinking about the advantage of building firewalls between us—never mind that the only way I would be able to check on my own success in doing so would be by seeing him again.

Which seemed unlikely at best.

Jared turned away when I thought that, and made to close the door. "You don't trust me."

I put my hand on the door to stop it. "I do trust you. I'm just wondering whether that's very smart."

"I told you...."

"I'm not asking for you to check in with me all the time, like I've got you on some kind of leash," I said, interrupting him. "I'm starting to think that counting on you is a long shot. I'd just like to know how long the odds are."

"Against what?"

"Against *anything*." I'd said more than I'd meant to say, but it was done, lying between us like a roadblock.

Jared took a breath and pursed his lips.

"So, you're just like everyone else after all," he said softly. "I thought dragons were extra perceptive. I thought a dragon girl would see the truth."

"Not fair," I said, my anger rising. "Why does trusting you mean that I can't ask you any questions? Why can't I ask you where you got the book, since everyone is telling me that there's only one? I'm not saying that you're lying to me. I'm saying that people have questions and I can't defend you without some answers. I'm saying I want to trust you, but you have to give me *something* to base that trust on."

"You're all shimmery." His gaze danced over me.

"Well, what do you expect?" I flung out my hands. "I saw the Mage spells Saturday night, and they were feeding off your music. Your songs were helping them build their power. I want to know why."

"You saw what?" he said, his face pale.

There was no doubt that I'd shocked him.

But I was still angry. "I told you. You know what I want to know. You can tell me or not. It's not like you owe me anything, as you've made clear."

I turned to walk away. I hated arguing with him. I hated that he was hiding things from me. And I hated that his decision to do that was destroying my trust in him.

Did everything I believed in have to turn out to be a lie?

All in the same week?

I GOT ONLY about fifty feet before Jared fell into step beside me. He was still shrugging into his black leather biker jacket, but he threw me an irreverent look. "Probably would have attracted too much attention if I'd asked you to keep me warm," he murmured, a mischievous glint in his eyes.

"Don't go there. Not now." I was angry, but I couldn't keep myself from blushing, which only seemed to amuse him.

"Okay, I'll answer three questions," he said, indicating the alley that ran behind the club.

"Why only three?"

His smile flashed. "Careful, dragon girl, that's one." He sobered and grabbed my hand. "Come this way."

Like an idiot, I couldn't say no or hold my ground or even stop my stupid heart from galloping. I should have been frightened by the power this guy had over me—but in this moment, it irritated me. "Have I told you lately that you can be really annoying?"

Jared laughed. "Trust me, Zoë, I don't have an exclusive on that." My heart stopped and raced at that. He seldom called me by my name. That he did made me hope that something would change.

That he was going to make a concession, just for me.

He tugged me toward the alley then, his grip so warm and strong on my fingers that I couldn't say a thing. He led me around the back of the building that housed the club.

He pulled down the ladder on a rickety metal fire escape. I halfway thought it would break as soon as it had any weight on it. He locked his fingers together to give me a boost. I swung onto the bottom rung, glad I'd been working out as hard this summer as I had. The metal ladder shook but held.

After I started to climb, Jared jumped and caught the bottom rung with his hands, swinging up behind me. It got colder as we ascended, the snow swirling all around us.

Eventually we were on a broad, flat roof. There was a water tower in the middle and nothing else.

But snow and sky and distant buildings.

I took a steadying breath. The building was maybe six stories high, a good distance away from the cluster of tall office buildings and taller than its immediate neighbors. The wind off the lake was chilly and I could see that the water was choppy. The snowstorm would get worse soon.

I turned to face Jared, only to find that he had been watching me. "I don't think we'll be overheard here," he said, zipping up his leather jacket against the wind. His hair was being tossed around. "Go for it." He held up his thumb, demanding my first question.

I decided to start small. "Why did the Mages' spells come out of the sewer grates on Saturday night?"

"When?" If nothing else, I had his complete attention.

"During the concert." I was ready to have a nice calm conversation, but the tone was already turning.

Jared frowned. "You couldn't have seen that from inside the club. The windows are blacked out."

"Well, no. It was when I left."

Jared leaned closer, his eyes snapping. "What?"

"I went outside. Alone."

"Why did you do that? Why would you leave alone?"

"Why *wouldn't* I do it? You weren't exactly being friendly. I had to think."

"Outside, alone, in a crappy part of town." His disgust was clear.

"Not quite alone. Kohana attacked me."

"What?" He stared at me, obviously unhappy with what I was telling him. Then he shoved one hand through his hair. "Holy shit, Zoë, that was stupid. You could have been killed."

His concern might have been gratifying if he hadn't been so sure that I'd lose a fight. "Thank you very much."

"I've seen you fight."

"Not lately." I folded my arms across my chest and glared at him. Our gazes locked and held, a definite sizzle in the air between us. "I refuse to be a damsel in distress."

He almost smiled, then shook his head. "You shouldn't have gone outside alone."

"And you shouldn't have been singing spells. Isn't that what drew the Mages closer? Weren't they using your music as fuel for their spells?"

He eyed me, wary again. "I'm not sure. What exactly did you see?"

"I can see spells. They're like beams of light. I saw the ones that you and your band were making and I saw Mage spells coming out of the sewer grates and manhole covers and basement windows. As if they were responding to the sound of your songs. They were wrapping around them."

"Absorbing them and feeding on the energy." Jared paced, his agitation clear. "You probably think I was making them stronger on purpose."

I blinked. That possibility had never occurred to me.

He saw that, too. I knew it because some of the tension slid out of his shoulders.

"Why did they try to recruit you, anyway?"

He winced. "And the implied question would be how did I decline the privilege."

"You said you took a pass on their offer."

"But you only have my word on that, don't you?" He spun to face me. "And what exactly is that worth, Zoë?"

"I'm trying to trust you."

"But should you?" His tone was challenging. I didn't like it. "Isn't it the point of a Mage spell to make someone believe something that isn't true? Maybe I've enchanted you, to persuade you to trust me against your own instincts. Maybe I'm deliberately drawing you into danger. Isn't that what you think?"

"No. It's what some of the guys think, but I trust you. That's why I'm asking questions. You need to tell me what's really going on."

His smile was more of a grimace. "What if I told you that I got the book by stealing it from Sara's shop? That ripping off the book was my initiation test from the Mages, the challenge they gave me to prove myself?" He stepped closer and raised one finger, holding my gaze with defiance. "What if I told you that I realized then that their plan was to recruit me, both because of my innate talent and because of my connection with the *Pyr*?"

"Because Donovan is your uncle?"

He nodded once and his voice softened. "What if I told you that they wanted me to be the bait to snare and destroy you?"

I held my ground, fighting to hold on to my instinctive trust of him. In reality, everything was spinning around me, spinning like a maelstrom of falling snow. Jared had stolen the book? Jared had been courted by the Mages to trap me?

I took a deep breath. "Then I would know why you declined."

"How do you know that, Zoë?" he demanded with heat. "How can you be sure?"

"You helped me. Last spring. You broke Adrian's spell and helped us save the older *Pyr*—"

He interrupted me. "That could have been a trick to gain your confidence," he argued, his voice rough.

"Or it could have been the truth."

He stared at me then, and I held his gaze, letting him look into my thoughts. Because the truth was that I did trust him, and I knew in my gut that if the details seemed to condemn him, it was just because I didn't have all of the facts.

I wanted to believe in him.

I wanted him to be everything that I believed him to be.

And maybe if I believed in Jared the way no one else did, maybe if I trusted him the way no one else did, maybe that could help him be the person I thought he could be.

The guy I yearned for.

I stared right back, unblinking, and I let him look.

Finally Jared sighed and closed his eyes, relief rippling through him. "I knew you were different," he murmured.

I'd thought he might touch me, but he turned away. He walked the perimeter of the roof. He scanned the sky, thinking, his fingertips drumming on his leg.

I gave him time to decide.

It seemed like I'd passed the test, after all.

"Okay, here's the deal." Jared spoke quickly when he came back to face me. "Mages work with an inherent ability. Only a few people are born with the particular kind of musical talent that the Mages can twist to their own use. You can't learn spellsinging. You either enchant with your song or your music or you don't. They sense those people, or maybe they hear their amateur spells. Either way, they target them and try to recruit them. More Mages mean more power."

"Because volume is part of the power?"

"Sure. If I can make your sternum vibrate with my spellsong, it's going to be a lot harder for you to ignore both me and it."

So, it was similar to beguiling.

"But not all musicians are spellsingers."

Jared shook his head. "No. Not even close. I know a lot of musicians and I've asked a lot of questions. Most of them don't know anything about Mages or spellsinging."

"But some..."

"Do." He finished my sentence and held my gaze. "Those are the ones who lie when asked about it. Those are the ones who might be Mages already. I just keep my distance from them." He shoved a hand through his hair. "You're sure their spells were absorbing mine?"

"Gobbling them up."

"And getting brighter afterward?"

I thought about it, then nodded. "Yeah. They were feeding on your strength."

"And what did you feel?"

"A pull. Like being tugged toward a vortex."

"Which was?"

"Underground."

"Fuck." He marched to the other side of the roof, almost vibrating with tension. He shoved his fists into his pockets and stared at the lake, the wind lifting his hair. I'd never seen him so troubled.

I followed him and put a hand on his shoulder. "Tell me."

"Don't you see, dragon girl?" He spoke through his teeth, then turned to face me. "I always wondered why they took no for an answer. I always wondered why they just let me walk away. I just figured they didn't want me very badly." He shrugged. "I mean, nobody else ever did. Why should Mages be different?"

I slid my hand down his sleeve, but he shrugged off its weight.

"But they didn't let me go," he said, almost snarling the words. "They let me think I was getting away, but they're still using me to get to you."

"You don't know that...."

"Yes, I do. Every time you're close to me, they show up. Now when I sing, they're stealing my energy to make themselves stronger." He swallowed. "To give themselves the power to destroy you. The plan is carrying on, and I'm complicit, even though I didn't know it."

"No..." But I was thinking of what Kohana had said.

He pivoted, maybe sensing that I'd stiffened. "What?" His gaze searched mine when I didn't immediately answer.

"Kohana said that when he heard your song, he knew I'd be in the vicinity. That's how he found me."

Jared winced, swore and turned away. "They're doing it, even without my cooperation," he murmured and my heart felt like a lead weight in my chest.

There was silence between us. I heard a bird cry. I felt the wind grow more harsh. I heard a dog growl on the street below. I felt the cold of winter chill me right to my marrow.

I reached out and touched his sleeve, knowing he needed something from me, acting on impulse. When he glanced my way, I couldn't look away from the vibrant green of his eyes, from his need.

"I trust you." I filled my mind with that thought, letting him see my conviction. I felt him shake a little; then he touched my cheek with his fingertip again. I felt him come closer and closed my eyes, not wanting him to read my thoughts at this moment.

Maybe he had to see my eyes. I wasn't sure, but he always looked deeply into my eyes before he understood my thoughts.

I couldn't bear for him to see that I needed so much right now.

I was surprised when he touched me. His hands landed on my shoulders, his fingers curling around them. I felt his breath and then his lips brushed mine. That barest touch filled me with yearning and made me shiver. My heart was thundering, doing that crazy thing of matching its beat to his. Our noses were almost touching, his hands framing my face and I didn't want to step away from him.

Ever.

"I'm not going to let them win," he said with quiet force. I opened my eyes to meet the conviction in his gaze. "I'm not going to be a part of that."

"What can you do?"

"Only one thing—leave." He smiled, but it was bitter. "They're not going to follow me to you. Not again, dragon girl."

"But...."

"So long as there are Mages hunting you, I won't risk it."

As much as I hated his conclusion, I feared he was right.

But I couldn't let him go just yet.

I leaned against his chest, touched my lips to his pulse at his throat. He kissed my forehead and pushed his fingers into my hair. "I'm sorry, Zoë. You trusted me and you shouldn't have. Turns out everybody else knew better."

I had a lump in my throat the size of Illinois.

He tipped my chin up and studied me for a long moment, then forced a smile. "Be good, dragon girl," he said, then turned and strode away without looking back. There was defeat in the line of his shoulders and a good chunk of it in my heart. The snow danced around him, white against black, and then he disappeared over the lip of the roof.

He still didn't look back.

And I was alone, the snow falling thickly around me.

I DON'T KNOW LONG I'd been standing there when I heard a van start. An old one. I heard doors slamming and heavy things being moved. Rick's and Angie's voices carried from the alley behind the club as they packed up, and I strained my ears for the sound of Jared's voice.

No luck.

I guess he wasn't taking any chances on inadvertently loosing a spell or two in my vicinity.

The van drove off, its tires leaving grooves in the snow on the street. I moved to the lip of the roof to watch, certain that he was driving out of my life.

Instead I saw a lone figure in black, one bag slung over his shoulder, standing at the curb, watching the van as it traveled down the road.

His band was leaving, without him.

Then he turned and started to walk in the opposite direction.

Alone.

As if he needed to think.

As if this wasn't any easier for him than it was for me.

I watched him go, wishing it could be different. I felt cheated, as if something I'd never really possessed—never mind had time to appreciate—had been stolen. But I was the Wyvern. If the future was going to be different, I was going to have to be the one to change it.

First up would be thwarting the Mages' plan. They considered me and my kind to be prey.

Well, that just meant that I was going to have to turn the tables on them. Treaty or truce would never be good enough. We would have to eliminate the Mages, one by one, in order to live safely again.

If I could lead the *Pyr* to victory, I could see Jared again. It was a heck of an incentive.

Even if I had no clue how to manage the deed.

Before I could think further than that, everything went to hell.

THE BIRD'S second cry startled me. It was closer, closer than it had been.

And I realized a bit late that I recognized that cry. I'd guessed wrong: Kohana had been waiting on me. Heart pounding, I spun to look for him.

He was swooping down toward me, talons extended. His eyes blazed yellow, a sure sign that this was no ordinary bird. He was larger than most birds, too. He held a brilliant yellow thunderbolt in one claw.

I'd seen his arsenal before. Those thunderbolts exploded on contact, burning everything in proximity. Like lightning strikes.

Here was my chance to finish him forever.

Screw my dad's new rule, the Covenant, and the risk of exile.

I roared and called to the power deep within me. The change rolled through me with breathless speed and I leapt into the air at the same time.

I felt my wings beat, lifting me higher. I saw the fire I exhaled at Kohana.

I saw his surprise, and I took advantage of it. I lunged toward him, struck him hard, and knocked him toward the earth. He was still fast and still slippery, but I was much, much stronger than I had been.

Plus I was mad. He'd lied to me. He'd targeted me. He'd tried to eliminate my friends. He'd allied with the Mages in an attempt to save his own kind, but he was stupid to trust them.

And he was part of the reason I was losing Jared.

I decked him and the rhythm of his flight faltered. I was right behind him, breathing fire on his tail, as he retreated. He spiraled into the snow-filled sky, but I snatched at him when he slowed to turn and pulled a fistful of ebony feathers out of his skin.

He screamed, but I let them fall, wanting more.

I snatched him and tightened my claws around him as he struggled. I had to be three times his size. He squirmed and fought, but I didn't let him go. My talons were long and white and sharp, and they drew blood where they pricked him. He fought against me and I squeezed, remembering his deception.

And the price we had nearly paid.

"You lied to me," I charged.

"No better than you deserve, *Unktehila*." He sneered. "Oathbreaker."

I held him captive. "Tell me more about this supposed treaty."

"Don't you know your own history?" he demanded.

"Maybe you're making it up."

"The Mages demanded a shifter." Kohana writhed in my grip. "It was me or you."

"So you would turn us in to save the Thunderbirds?"

"My first loyalty is to my own."

"Right!" Now I scoffed. "Only a moron would believe anything the Mages promised."

His eyes shone. "No one says they know all of the truth."

"Where do I find the wolf and jaguar shifters, if they really exist?"

"Open your eyes, *Unktehila*." He was mocking once again, and I tightened my grip.

Before I could ask more, pain flashed in his eyes and I was stupid enough to ease my grip just as he struggled violently. He wiggled free and I snatched after him. He danced beyond my reach, laughing, then spun and flung one of his thunderbolts. I winced and ducked, but was surprised to realize that he hadn't aimed it at me.

He laughed and flew away with astonishing speed. I followed the trajectory of the thunderbolt and my heart stopped cold.

Jared's hands were fisted in his pockets and his head was down as he continued to march away.

And Kohana's thunderbolt was headed straight at him.

I knew Jared couldn't see it, that even if he turned, he wouldn't be able to perceive it until it exploded against his skin.

It would kill him.

No! I forgot Kohana and his mocking laughter, pivoted, and dove toward Jared. I wasn't at all sure I could get to him in time, but I had to try. I flew harder than I ever had, pushing myself beyond what I knew I could do.

I drew alongside the thunderbolt maybe two hundred feet above Jared. I couldn't stop it. I couldn't reach him in time to push him aside. So, I did the only thing possible.

I threw myself into the thunderbolt's path.

I closed my eyes against the bright yellow flash of light and bared my teeth at the burning pain. I felt it shoot through me like a jolt of electricity, and I felt myself shifting forms involuntarily.

A sign of distress in dragon physiology.

Usually impending death.

I had time to realize I was falling, to know that I had zero regrets, and then everything went black.

Say good night, Zoë.

It was the nausea that woke me up.

My stomach was roiling and I hurt in places I hadn't even known I had. My back was blazing with pain, and I could feel concrete beneath my chin. The snow was freezing cold where it landed on me, but in a way, it felt good against my burning skin.

I opened my eyes. My hand was white and webbed, so I knew I had unconsciously shifted into salamander form.

I had a definite sense that I wasn't alone and looked around without moving. The street was completely deserted, doors closed and windows black.

But there was a wolf, sitting right in front of me.

Watching me.

The wolf was shaggy, his fur a thousand shades of gray and silver. His eyes were icy blue, shining with a disconcerting intelligence. He didn't blink. Major teeth, which made me wonder whether newts made a nice light snack.

Did I look tasty? Like a bite or two of barbecue?

In self-defense, I closed my eyes, summoned my will, and shifted to human form again. Then I was sitting with my back against the brick wall, my hands braced on either side of me. Ow ow ow.

The wolf didn't move, or even blink.

Was it possible to think of a wolf being unsurprised?

I glanced around and didn't recognize the street at all. How far was I from the club? There was no sign of Jared or of Kohana. How long had I been out? I winced and stretched. And how badly damaged was my back?

Suddenly there was a shimmer of pale blue light, which spooked me into getting up. I knew that light and shouldn't have been surprised when the wolf disappeared.

A heartbeat later Derek was squatting before me. Eyes the same shade of pale blue. Same intent stare. Same scent.

I belatedly did a little bit of math.

Open your eyes, Unktehila.

Okay, I felt stupid.

"You okay?" he asked. I realized that his voice was always low and deep, rough like a growl.

Duh.

"More or less." I moved my fingers and toes, scanned myself. My back hurt like hell, but I couldn't exactly see it. "You followed me."

He nodded, glanced away, looked back to hold my gaze again.

"Why?"

"I thought you might need help." He shrugged. "I was right."

"But you got off two stops before me."

"You were suspicious. Worried. I didn't want to throw your game."

"How'd you know all that?"

He touched the side of his nose.

Right. Wolves had keen senses of smell, too.

"I couldn't smell that you were a shifter."

He smiled. "You probably can't smell emotion, either, or sense the future before it happens."

"Can you?"

He nodded, but before I could get jealous, he shrugged. "I have a feeling when something big is going to go down, but I only see about two minutes ahead of the moment." He stared at me again and I realized that was the longest sentence I'd ever heard him utter. "Sometimes it's too late to matter."

"I wouldn't have expected anyone to stop the thunderbolt," I said.

"You did." He stood then, and brushed off his jeans. "And that guy? He has no idea of what you did for him." He spat into the snow, his disdain clear. When he looked at me again, his eyes seemed colder.

I froze at his words. "What do you mean?"

"He had his earbuds on. He didn't hear anything. He didn't turn around until I'd scooped you up."

"You what?"

"Someone could have stepped on you. You had to get out of there. The guy might have been curious, but I growled and he backed off."

Jared didn't know I'd followed him. He didn't know I'd taken that hit for him. I was disappointed by that bit of news.

"Where did he go?"

Derek shrugged. "Who cares?"

"Maybe I do."

"Maybe you shouldn't." His eyes flashed. "He *left* you."

"There's a situation. He's doing his best...."

Derek waved off my explanation, fixing me with a steady look. "Don't you know that dogs see in black and white?" Then he looked down the street, his eyes narrowed. "Who's going to tend your back?"

"No one."

He shook his head. "Wrong. You need help. It's bad."

It did hurt. And he had seen it. For a moment I couldn't think of anyone who I could let see the wound, but then it came to me.

Isabelle. "I know someone at the college."

He arched a brow. "Science labs?"

I smiled. "Arts student."

He pointed. "We can catch the L over there."

I had no chance to ask if he was going to keep me company. Apparently I now had a guard wolf.

It wasn't such a bad thing. Derek set a good pace, striding effortlessly down the street as I tried to keep up. He scanned our surroundings constantly, his gaze sliding from side to side, and I could see him inhaling with care.

Taking the scent of everything.

I was a bit short of breath, so it took me a minute to ask what I wanted to know. "Couldn't you follow his scent?"

He turned to face me, his expression chilling me. There was a challenge in those pale eyes. "Couldn't you?"

I could, but I wouldn't. "But you knew I'd been with him."

"And he left. Problem solved."

Problem? "Why don't you like Jared? You don't even know him."

Derek shrugged. "He's human. He's half-Mage. Neither is a great credential in my world."

"He turned down the Mages...."

"Technicality." Black and white, just like he'd said earlier. Derek held the door to the station for me, and met my gaze once more. "And he led you straight into a trap."

"He didn't do it on purpose!"

His gaze slid away. "I'm just glad I was there to help."

We rode the L in silence, as if we were complete strangers.

But Derek was never more than half a dozen steps away. Guarding me. Truth be told, I appreciated it. I wasn't at my best, and it was nice to have someone to rely upon.

Then I had a troubling thought. Was Derek, like Kohana, going to betray me to the Mages to save his own kind?

He inhaled sharply and glared at me across the car. I guessed that he'd caught a whiff of my suspicion. "Mages are liars," he said with low heat. "Only idiots trust liars."

With that, he turned to stare out the window again.

The real question was whether I could trust a wolf.

. . .

I CALLED Isabelle from the train and she agreed to meet me at her dorm room. Derek disappeared once we stepped onto the campus, but I knew he wasn't far away. I could smell wolf, even though I couldn't see him.

Isabelle was outraged and appalled by the story of the attack, but she also had some ointment for burns. I figured she would have packed it instinctively, having grown up in a *Pyr* household, and I was glad to have been right. It was some herbal stuff, cool and soothing, and I felt better within minutes.

I also scored another chocolate bar. I didn't care if she gave it to me out of pity. It was delicious.

She gave me strict instructions not to get the injury wet, and insisted I come back the next day for another lathering since I couldn't reach the spot. I promised to do so, and headed back to the L.

There was no sign of Derek. The train pulled in and I picked a seat. I wondered whether he'd abandoned me.

But he stepped into the car just before the doors closed, and sat down facing the other direction.

Ever vigilant.

We got back to school in time for the last class of the day, arriving separately.

And you know, it didn't break my heart to have missed gym.

8

I came out of a particularly excruciating history class—excruciating mainly because my back hurt and my thoughts were spinning and I got called on four times to answer questions I hadn't even heard, based on a reading I hadn't even done—to find Liam leaning against my locker, watching the other students go by.

I was really glad to see him.

The girls were all checking him out and he seemed to be amused by their reactions. Every time I see Liam, he's taller and broader. His hair has darkened to an auburn that makes it unreasonable to call him "Carrots" anymore.

I still do.

I remember him having a face full of freckles and orange hair, and that counts.

"Carrots! How'd you find my locker?"

He inhaled pointedly and I understood. We dragons don't just smell the presence of our kind. With time and familiarity, we can recognize the scents of those dragons we know.

Apparently, though, we had nothing on wolf shifters.

"Gotta take that gym bag home," I joked and gave him a hug.

He watched me intently, even though he leaned casually against the lockers. "You okay?"

"Spooked," I answered him in old-speak. *"I went to see Jared today."*

His eyes glittered and I knew he was going to chew me out. Before he could do that or I could explain, someone cleared her throat.

"Um, excuse me, p-p-please."

The locker Liam was leaning against was Meagan's.

She was beet red when he apologized and moved out of the way, so flustered that I was afraid the stutters would overtake the words. "Meagan, this is Liam. Liam, my best friend, Meagan."

"Nice to meet you." Liam gave her a smile as wide and honest as a thousand acres of prairie. Meagan blinked. Her mouth opened and closed. She reached for her lock and dropped all of her books.

I squatted down beside her to help pick them up.

She flicked me a resentful look, as if I'd been holding out on her. "How come you suddenly know all these hot guys?" she whispered.

I blushed because I knew Liam would hear whatever we said. "Liam's not hot," I said, as if he was my kid brother. "I grew up with him."

"Where? When? I grew up with you!"

"He's the son of a friend of my dad's."

Meagan glanced up, then looked at me again, then nodded. "Okay." She straightened up, with her books piled against her chest, and smiled at Liam. "Nice to m-m-meet you, too. Do you live in Chicago?"

Liam was all easy charm. "No. Ohio. We have a dairy farm."

His manner reassured Meagan a bit. "Are you visiting for long?"

"No, I just came to hang out with Zoë since her folks are away." He nudged me. "Hey, Zoë, maybe we should go see that movie you were talking about."

A movie. The last thing I wanted to do was go to a movie. I was sore enough that I wanted to go to bed.

And maybe never leave it again.

"You can bring me up to speed," Liam said, in old-speak. It was as much a threat as a promise.

"That's a great idea," I said out loud. "Way better than homework."

He turned to Meagan, flashing that easy smile. "You want to come, too, Meagan?"

I think she nearly had a heart attack.

For once, even math homework didn't have much appeal for Meagan. She shoved all her books in her backpack, blushed when Liam insisted on carrying it for her, and came to the movie with us.

I don't even know what it was about. I spent the whole ninety minutes briefing Liam in old-speak. And getting shit in old-speak for taking unnecessary chances. I felt better just talking about the encounter with Kohana, and we decided that he would walk us back to Meagan's, then keep watch over the Jamesons' town house.

I really like the idea of a dragon on the roof, on guard. We were going to breathe some dragonsmoke together later, mostly because it was a relaxation exercise.

We left the movie theater to find the snow a foot deep in the streets.

I wondered what had happened to Derek. Was he in the vicinity, but just out of sight? Or had he done all he was going to do? I did like the idea that he might not be smelling trouble in my immediate future and so could leave me to my own resources.

Maybe I'd been wrong to be suspicious of his motives.

Maybe I'd offended him. I felt guilty about that, as well as a bit flustered. Had I made sure Derek was cured of liking me? Had he liked me just because he had a plan like Kohana's? Or did he like me just because I was a shifter and we had something in common?

All the possibilities made my head spin.

Plus I probably should have talked to him about our making an alliance with the wolf shifters. Did they really call themselves werewolves?

It made my palms sweat just thinking about hunting Derek down the next day and asking him questions. Maybe he would smell my intent and make the first move.

I could hope.

"It's so weird," Meagan said. "This theater isn't anywhere near the L, but all I could hear was rumbling trains throughout the movie."

"Me, too," I said, deliberately avoiding Liam's gaze. One look and I knew I'd laugh. "They ought to do something about that."

I heard his snort of laughter, and then he was making snowballs. He shoved one down the back of my jacket and the fight was on.

. . .

"You are such a liar," Meagan said, hours later when we were crashed in her room and I thought she was asleep.

"What?" I nearly sat straight up in bed.

She threw a pillow at me. "You are such a liar. You said Liam isn't hot."

I closed my eyes in relief. "Is he? I don't know. I've known him too long, maybe."

Meagan made a snort of skepticism. "I don't care how long you've known him—you'd have to be blind not to see he's hot." Then she laughed again. "Maybe you're the one who needs glasses, Zoë. Want to borrow mine?"

We laughed together and I had a minute to think that everything was back to usual.

She rolled over to face me and I had a heartbeat to brace myself against whatever she was going to say. "Hey, I meant to tell you. Jessica found this site today, about the *Pyr*."

My throat got tight. "The what?"

Oh, I am such a lousy liar.

"The dragon guys! I told you there has to be one at our school."

"Oh, right."

"Why aren't you interested in this? You draw dragons all the time."

"I dunno. Maybe they make more sense to me as fiction."

Right. Liar, liar, pants on fire.

"As if," Meagan scoffed. "Real is ten zillion times better."

I didn't say anything to that.

"So, listen, this site says that the *Pyr* have these powers."

I looked around the room, wishing I knew where this was going. "What kind of powers?"

"One's called beguiling. They kind of hypnotize people by creating flames in their eyes. People stare at the flames and the dragon guy makes suggestions and they end up agreeing. How cool is that?"

The only possible solution was to sound skeptical. I tried. "Flames in their eyes? Really?"

"I think it would be awesome to see that dragon guy again. I wouldn't mind at all if he beguiled me."

"I think it sounds silly." My tone was cranky and gruff, sour enough to spoil Meagan's mood.

Smooth move, Zoë. Lie to her and piss her off. That's the way to treat a friend.

I heard Meagan typing in the darkness once she stopped talking to me, so I tugged out my messenger as well. Garrett had sent a message that he'd found some information and would call me in the morning to tell me about it. Nick was outraged that Kohana had attacked me. Both of them were very, very quiet about Jared.

"Huh," Meagan said suddenly. "Jessica thinks you were holding out on me, too."

"What?" That surprised me.

"She says you must have been trying to keep Liam to yourself."

I'd had enough of Jessica. "No way. Liam is just this guy I grew up with—"

"Zoë," Meagan said, interrupting me firmly. "I'm not fooled. Whether Jessica's right about this or not, you've been lying to me since spring break."

Caught. If I could have thought of a good comeback, I would have argued my own side. As it was, I was totally out of my daily allotment of lies. I just shut up.

Meagan sniffed with displeasure after a moment—sounding a lot like my mom—then rolled over so her back was toward me. She wasn't asleep. I could still see the glow of her messenger and hear the sound of her typing.

I knew who she was messaging.

Jessica. Jessica. It was always about Jessica. Jessica was right and I was wrong, and there was nothing I could say to change that.

Why did Jessica give me the creeps? I'd assumed I was just jealous of the attention Meagan was giving her. But maybe it was something else.

Or maybe thinking it was something else was a pathetic cover for jealousy.

There was only one way to find out more.

I told myself that I might like Jessica better if I just talked to her for once. It sounded like something my mom would say. I wasn't convinced, but I'd give it a try.

Because, you know, I didn't have anything else to do.

. . .

We were back to our awkward pattern again the next morning, much to my regret. Meagan and I walked to school in comparative silence. Actually, we kind of trudged along. It was painful, especially when I thought of how easy it used to be between us.

And I couldn't think of a good way to fix it.

Just how much trouble was I already in for shifting to fight Kohana? It was easier to dismiss the prospect of exile when I was angry and acting in the heat of the moment. Walking along with Meagan, I could only remember the burn of dragonsmoke on my hand and shiver. I'd gotten injured, too. There was negative reinforcement.

How was I going to negotiate a treaty with the wolves? I hadn't any clue how to go about it.

It was galling to admit that my dad might know something.

Jessica waved from the doorway to the school. Waiting, as usual.

"What about those trig problems?" she asked, all aglow with the thrill of solving them.

"The third one was tricky," Meagan said. "Because of the wording."

"Right. You had to look for the arctangent."

"You guys want to sit together at lunch?" I asked.

They both looked at me as if I'd just dropped in from Mars.

"On Tuesdays, we go to the library instead," Jessica informed me. "C'mon, Meagan."

"Didn't know the library was off-limits," I said. "I'll keep that in mind."

I hauled open the door to the school. Meagan hesitated for a minute, but then she stayed with Jessica.

So I knew where I stood.

I opened my locker a bit more savagely than was strictly necessary and threw my books in. I heard a step beside me and glanced up, surprised to find Trevor there.

Smiling.

Like a starving man checking out lunch.

I smiled back.

Like lunch that bites all the way down.

He was as neatly turned out as ever. I swear someone ironed his jeans.

He was pretty good-looking, if a bit stiff. As I surveyed him, I had to admit what an oddity he was. He could have been a jock, but he was a music fiend. He could have been a geek, but there was the way he played the sax.

But that was Mage stuff. He was enchanting everyone who listened.

His parents were totally loaded, which didn't hurt. He had this vintage MG in British racing green that he drove to school every day and they lived in one of those huge houses on Riverside Drive.

If he hadn't squealed into the parking lot with that car every day, I don't think someone like Suzanne would even have noticed him. Much.

Someone like Meagan would, though. If anything, Trevor seemed a bit too squeaky-clean to me to be real.

But then, I knew his secret.

And he knew mine.

Maybe he played it squeaky-clean because he really was sneaky. Maybe it was an act. And only the music—or the spell he cast with it—was real.

I had a vague sense of Derek's presence, somewhere in the hall. I liked knowing he was looking out for me.

"Get my invitation?" Trevor asked.

"Yes, thanks. What a surprise." I rummaged in my locker for my sketchbook and pencil box. Tuesday morning was the bright spot of my life—art class.

"You didn't get back to me about it."

"I didn't see an RSVP on it."

He smiled. "Just wanted to have an idea of numbers."

I shut my locker. "Sorry I can't make it."

"Busy?"

I shrugged and smiled. "Just one of those things. But thanks anyway."

To my dismay, he fell into step beside me. "Maybe you could just stop by for a while."

"I don't think so." I tried to be polite. "Maybe another time." After hell froze over and the planets dropped out of their orbits, the sun splashed down in the Pacific Ocean, etc.

He chuckled and I glanced up to find that his smile had broadened. "Or maybe I just have to find a way to change your mind."

Before I could ask, Trevor winked and turned away, leaving me looking after him. I felt threatened, that was for sure, although I couldn't imagine what he might do.

I didn't want to imagine what he might do.

I caught movement from the corner of my eye and saw Derek's back as he strode down the hall in the opposite direction. Meagan was standing back by the door with Jessica, her gaze locked on me. She looked hurt. I might have said something to her, but before I could think of what that might be, she pivoted and headed to class with Jessica.

Perfect. I could just guess what Jessica was telling her. That I was keeping Liam to myself while I did Trevor on the side.

A perfect start to another perfect day.

I HEADED FOR ART CLASS, glum. That had to be a first.

"You okay?" Derek asked. I jumped, shocked to find him behind me. I hadn't heard him coming at all. In fact, I'd thought he was going the other way.

"Sure. Thanks. How about you?"

His gaze searched mine, as if he wasn't going to take my word on it. "You're angry." I watched his nostrils flare. "Hurt."

I had to cede to a sense of smell that sharp. I smiled. "You have any human friends?"

His lips twisted and he glanced down the hall, as if scanning for likely candidates. Knowing he wouldn't find one. Resigned to it. "It's impossible." His gaze slid back to mine. "Better to run solo, or stick with those who understand."

He put a slight emphasis on this last word, and held my gaze for an unblinking moment. I couldn't read his expression. He was just watchful. Intent.

Okay, so he liked me because we were both shifters.

He almost smiled when I thought that and I knew I'd nailed it in one.

Now or never.

"I want to talk to you...." I started to say, but he straightened and stepped back.

"Call for you," he said, right before my messenger chimed.

I looked between it and him, and must have looked surprised.

He smiled. "Told you."

"Two minutes warning."

He shrugged. "Sometimes three." Then he sauntered away.

Oh, I wanted some of that. It wasn't much foresight, but it was more than I had. As Wyvern, I was supposed to have buckets of foresight, but thus far I had none.

Zero.

Nada.

And if ever there had been a moment when I'd have liked a peek at the future, this was it.

I answered my messenger and it was Garrett. I asked him to hang on for a second.

"That must be useful," I called after Derek.

"Good or bad, it just is." He shrugged. "Like Jessica."

Well, that was fair enough. I watched him head off to class. He moved with an athletic grace, his steady, long stride looking effortless even as he covered a lot of distance. I had the sense he could walk like that for days. He kept to the side of the corridor, evading the gaze and the notice of most of the students.

Like a moving shadow.

Or a wolf in the night. Solitary and purposeful.

I gave myself a shake and remembered Garrett. "Hey, sorry."

"Got a date?" he teased and I smiled. We weren't on video, though, so he didn't know it.

"I'll tell you in a minute. What did you find?"

"There's a book in my mom's store about Native American legends and stories. You know how your mom always says that myths and stories have their roots in a truth?"

"Right."

"Well, here's one that you'll find interesting. There are legends in many Native American tribes about Thunderbirds. They're supposed to be strong and fast, supernatural birds. The idea is that they cause storms by the beating of their wings, they can throw thunderbolts, and they cause lightning by the flash of their eyes. In some tribes, they control rainfall. The Lakota call them *Wakiya*."

"Okay." I started to walk to class, remembering that Kohana had called himself that. The description certainly was consistent with his powers.

Garrett continued, excitement in his voice. "But here's the thing—in some Pacific Northwest tribes, thunderbirds are believed to be shape shifters. They open their beaks and pull them back like a hood, then shed their feathers like a coat. They married humans ages ago, so there are families who pass this ability through the generations."

"Like us." I stopped in the hall, focused on Garrett's voice.

"Just like us." I could hear that Garrett had one more morsel to share. "In fact, the Sioux tell a story that the Thunderbirds fought and defeated a race of reptiles centuries ago. Guess what the reptiles were called?"

"Unktehila."

"Bingo. We must have made a treaty based on territory—they said we were defeated because we retreated to our own turf."

"Europe," I said. "And we forgot the deal over time because so many of us were killed."

"And ultimately we came back to North America," Garrett concluded. "That's Kohana's beef with the *Pyr*."

"And why he calls us oathbreakers."

So, the Thunderbirds were allying with the Mages to enforce the terms of an old treaty, intending to drive us *Pyr* out of North America and off the map if necessary. And the Mages found that useful. I guessed that Kohana and other Thunderbirds had a trick up their sleeves for the Mages, and wondered what it was.

Did Mages have a weakness?

How could I persuade Kohana and the Thunderbirds to fight *with* us, instead of against us?

"It says these families tend to live on the northern end of Vancouver Island," Garrett concluded. "That they stick to themselves and are very secretive."

"Sounds like the Covenant to me."

"Sure does. Maybe we have more in common than any of us realize."

That gave me an idea. "Can you have another look in your mom's books?"

"I think I've been through everything, Zoë...." Garrett started to argue.

"I need you to look for something different." I dropped my voice to a whisper. "Werewolves." If I was going to negotiate a treaty with Derek and his kind, more knowledge would be better.

Garrett didn't say anything for a minute. Then he spoke softly. "You found one."

"Right under my nose." The bell rang. "I've got to go."

"I'll look," Garrett said.

"Good. Thanks. Later." And I ran.

ART CLASS WAS A RELIEF, although I wasn't exactly as focused as usual. My still life in charcoal was less than my best effort and it showed. Mr. Hughes wasn't fooled. He didn't say anything, but his lips tightened before he returned to his desk.

He made a bunch of notes and I tried not to be so egotistical as to assume that they must be about me.

I was thinking about everything BUT school, it seemed.

Math class was next and right before lunch. I slid through the back door of the classroom and took my usual seat at the rear. I wished I could be invisible in this class, as I was falling behind on the work. I pulled out the homework that I hadn't completed and hoped we wouldn't have to turn it in. Meagan and Jessica were sitting together at the front, whispering. They never got in trouble for that—after all, they were the class stars.

"Bitch," Suzanne said, dumping her books one desk over from me. She always sat beside Trish in math class. I tried to avoid attracting their attention, as a rule.

"Bitch yourself," Trish said, making a joke, but Suzanne didn't laugh.

She threw herself into her chair instead. Her ponytail was less than perfect, a few loose tendrils hanging from one side, and her eyes were red. She folded her arms across her chest and glared at the front of the class.

Trish looked around, then leaned closer to her sidekick. I didn't even have to strain my hearing to eavesdrop. "Who?" she whispered, just as Mrs. Dawson strode into the room.

"Jessica." Suzanne said her name in a low hiss of fury. "Didn't you hear? Trevor just dumped me for that slut."

I was shocked. Suzanne and Trevor had been going out forever. More or less.

This made no sense. What was really going on?

"Get out," Trish said, outraged on Suzanne's behalf.

Suzanne grimaced. “That’s pretty much what he said.” And she settled in to look daggers at Jessica.

Was it love?

Or did it have something to do with me? I had a bad feeling then, remembering Trevor’s threat. But if he thought that his dating Jessica would change my mind about attending his party, he had another think coming. They were welcome to each other.

I recalled Derek’s comment about Jessica and wondered whether he knew anything else about her. Maybe he just didn’t like her either. I had to finish that drawing for him—it would give me the perfect reason to start a conversation with him.

“Take out your homework assignment, please,” Mrs. Dawson said. “I’ll be marking them today instead of giving a pop quiz. Put your name on the top right corner to ensure that you get credit. Meagan, would you collect everyone’s homework, please?”

It figured that it’d be collected on the one day I didn’t get it done. I winced and wished my luck would change.

“You didn’t even finish your math homework last night, did you?” Meagan asked when I got to my locker after English. I knew she’d noticed. Big clue: my hand-in sheet was almost completely blank.

Meagan was already packing books for her lunch break in the library. Looked like lunch was going to last through Friday.

“No.” It seemed best to stick with simple answers. After all, I couldn’t exactly tell her what had interfered with my concentration.

“You’re going to need tutoring if you don’t watch out.”

Being tutored by Meagan along with Trevor didn’t exactly sound like a dream come true to me.

Did Meagan know about Jessica and Trevor already?

Should I warn her, or let Jessica do her own dirty work?

An evil part of me thought that this might be what ended Jessica and Meagan’s new friendship, given how much Meagan liked Trevor.

I should have guessed I’d be totally wrong about that.

Or at least anticipated that a math whiz like Jessica would have planned for every eventuality.

"Are you ready, Meagan?" Jessica asked. I fought to hide my dislike. Even the sound of her voice grated on me, although I didn't know why.

"Almost. I just need one more book." Meagan was rummaging in her locker.

I glanced up, thinking I might try to make nice, but instead my mouth fell open in surprise. Trevor was with Jessica, his arm slung around her shoulders. She was smiling, as if she had a good joke to tell, holding one finger to her lips as she watched Meagan. This was not going to be a happy surprise. Trevor smiled, looking even more predatory than he had earlier.

What was he up to?

"Hi," I said, and dumped all my books in my locker. I needed to get away from school, even for just an hour. I grabbed Derek's notebook and my fave pencil set, shoving them into my backpack.

"Got your costume ready for Saturday?" Trevor asked and Meagan hit her head on the metal shelf in her locker. She straightened up and pushed her glasses up her nose, blinking at him in astonishment.

"You know Trevor, don't you?" Jessica said to Meagan. "He said you tutored him."

Meagan began to blush, red heat rising up her throat, and I felt bad for her. I knew that Jessica was living her fantasy. "Sure," she said, sounding squeaky. She looked at his arm and Jessica's smile and swallowed. "I didn't know you did."

"We met at the math lab, the one you missed." Jessica smiled and I wondered whether she knew she was twisting the knife in the wound. Meagan had missed that lab to go to the movie with Liam and me. Jessica smiled up at Trevor. "He couldn't figure out his homework and we just hit it off."

"Thank goodness for Jessica," Trevor said. "I aced my test this morning. First time ever."

They beamed at each other, the perfect smitten couple, and I ached for Meagan. I reached out to touch her shoulder, aware that Trevor was watching my gesture.

His eyes shone in a way that gave me the creeps.

"Oh, by the way, Meagan," Trevor said, smiling broadly. "Jessica wanted me to invite you to my Halloween party Saturday night. It's late notice, but I hope you can come."

His gaze flicked to me, triumphant.

Okay, so he had invited Meagan. I still didn't see how this would compel me to attend. Our gazes locked for a second. Why did he think this would change my mind?

Meagan meanwhile glanced up at the prospect, her expression ecstatic. "Thanks." She smiled and took a step away from me. "That would be fun. Thanks!"

"I thought we could all study together at lunch today," Jessica said. She nudged Trevor. "He still needs help with math. Maybe between the two of us, we can whip his skills into shape for midterms."

"Okay. Sure. That sounds great." Meagan zipped up her backpack and almost tripped over her feet in her haste to follow them.

The way Trevor smirked at me, glancing back over his shoulder, didn't make me feel any better.

I sensed someone else watching and glanced around. Derek was leaning in the far corner of the hallway, arms folded across his chest. Before I could say anything, he headed for the exit, slipped out the door, and was gone.

"Want to grab a tofu burger?" Liam asked in old-speak. I couldn't see him but he must be in the vicinity. He'd been bragging in the summer about getting better with casting his old-speak over a larger area.

I smiled and leaned my forehead against my locker in relief. Trust Liam to know that I needed a friend.

And some fuel.

That having lunch with a dragon shifter would be a return to routine said a great deal about my life.

"MAYBE BEING a wildcard makes you a magnet for shifters," Liam said, speaking around a mouthful of his second super burger special. "Isn't that what Kohana called you last spring?" I nodded. "Because if there are four kinds of shifters left, two have found you already. Maybe the third one isn't far behind."

"Jaguars," I said. "The last kind was supposed to be jaguars, according to Kohana." I'd cut my tofu burger in half and still hadn't finished the first half. I was too busy trying to find a solution to our problems to eat.

"It might be true. Lions are big cats, and Adrian became a lion when he shifted on the lake. Maybe the Mages have been taking cat shifters out in smaller groups."

"Or maybe Kohana lied."

Liam was already checking out the second half of my burger. "These things aren't very filling, are they? I could eat a dozen of them."

"What if some of the cat shifters have been eliminated, but not all?" I suggested. "Lions but not jaguars?"

Liam shrugged. "It could happen. Maybe there are other kinds left, too."

"Just not lions."

Liam grimaced. "Or maybe Kohana just lied. Maybe all the cat shifters are already gone and it's just us and the wolves." He was watching that last half of my tofu burger as if it was the source of the universe's secrets.

"You want this?"

"You're not hungry?"

I shook my head, then watched the rest of my lunch disappear. "How do we fight back against the Mages even if we do make an alliance?"

"Maybe we could find another spellsinger," Liam suggested.

"Yeah, but we could end up recruiting someone who would just betray us."

Liam dropped his gaze and ate, clearly not wanting to say anything about Jared.

My messenger chimed and I tugged it out. "It's Garrett," I said to Liam, then answered. I knew Liam would be able to hear Garrett even across the table, with his *Pyr* hearing.

"I've found something weird," Garrett said. "This book just jumped off the shelves at the bookstore, like it was looking for me."

"Okay, that's weird."

Liam rolled his eyes in agreement with that but otherwise kept eating.

"No," Garrett insisted. "The weird thing is that it's not in the inventory. My mom says she's never seen it before, and she knows every book in the place."

The hair stood up on the back of my neck. With another used-bookstore owner, I'd have my doubts, but Sara was incredibly organized. I leaned over the table, making sure Liam didn't miss a syllable. The restaurant was a bit busy. "Okay, I'll bite. What is it?"

"It's in Latin. I had to use a translator utility to even figure out the title. It's called *The Treatise of the Shadowmakers*. I think it's a book of spells."

"What kind of spells?" Liam asked.

"Well, the last section of the book is called 'Metamorphosis.'"

Liam and I looked at each other. "It could be a Mage book," I suggested..

Garrett sighed. "Is it really their book? Or was it planted, to trick us? Like a diversion. I'm skeptical, especially the way it turned up."

"We have to read it," I said.

"First I have to scan the whole thing and run it through that Latin utility," Garrett said. "Then we have to figure out what it actually means. Even what I've looked at so far isn't exactly crystal clear. You okay there for a couple of days? It'll be easier for me to do the grunt work here."

"Liam's here," I said.

"Nick's coming," Liam added.

"And it seems that I have a wolf at my back."

"You never told me about that," Garrett said and I told him then.

"Seems like too big of a coincidence for Derek just to happen to be at your school," Garrett said when I was done. Liam nodded agreement.

"I know. I'm going to ask him. Crap!" I remembered the drawing I needed to do and dug in my bag, hastily clearing the table. "He asked me to do a drawing for him. I figured I'd ask him some questions when I give it to him." I set to work as Liam claimed my messenger and gave Garrett the play-by-play.

"Let's ask Isabelle if she knows anything," Garrett suggested.

I nodded. "We'll wait for Nick." We could throw them together, force them to spend some time with each other. Then Nick would have to see the truth. It could be a subtle but effective strategy.

"Sounds like a plan," Liam said.

"I'd better get to it," Garrett said. "It's a long book."

"Nice messenger," Liam said, teasing me when the call was over. "Sure you need it?"

"Of course I do!" He made me jump for it, laughing that he could so easily hold it out of my reach.

When I'd snagged it again, Liam gathered up our trash and gave me a look. "Don't you have class?"

I did, and I was late. I grabbed my stuff and ran.

I SLID into English class a good ten minutes late. My hopes of passing under the radar were completely trashed within seconds.

Because I was handed a summons to the guidance counselor's office and dismissed.

Seems I was ten minutes late for an appointment I hadn't even known I had.

I've never been much for guidance counselors. They mean well and all, but there's not very much I can talk to them about. What are my life plans? Becoming the prophetess of the dragon shifters. How do I intend to earn a living? No worries—over centuries, any wage can add up, plus my dad is pretty good about sharing from his hoard. Do I want to have a family, and if so, do I intend to keep working? Well, yes, I'll breed when I have a firestorm and continue to be a Wyvern on the side.

It all sounds a bit delusional, doesn't it? And I have no plans to be locked away forever because I believe myself to be a dragon shape shifter. No goals to be like Jack Nicholson in *One Flew Over the Cuckoo's Nest*, getting my brain zapped at regular intervals.

Because the truth is that even though the *Pyr* have been revealed, and even though most humans are aware that there are dragon shape shifters in the world, no one imagines for one second that they know one or could meet one live.

Except Meagan, and that's new.

And my own fault.

So I mutter and murmur and the good people in the counselor's office write concerned little notes to the effect that I am devoid of ambition. That couldn't be further from the truth, but I have to let it go.

My parents think it's funny, which doesn't exactly make the guidance counselor happy.

On this particular day, I was less than thrilled with the meddling. I had things to do, and information to ferret out, and plans to make. How was I going to find Derek if I didn't follow him out of English class?

The prospect of another pointless hour spent with earnest, caring counselors was enough to make me want to let loose and incinerate the offices. Just for the sake of expediency. Then they'd have to believe me.

Of course, some fool might shoot me in the heat of the moment (ha), so I thought it better to keep my cool (ha ha).

My assigned counselor is Muriel O'Reilly. She's way too young to have a name like Muriel, but there you go. She's organized and her office is all soothing yellow and she smiles far too much.

Muriel smiled when I knocked on her office door.

"Hello, Ms. O'Reilly. I got a slip to come down."

"Hello, Zoë. Please call me Muriel." Muriel always wants to be called Muriel. (If my name was Muriel, I'd want to be called Bob.)

It is good, though, to have some constants in the world.

She gestured to the hot seat in her office and got up to shut the door behind me. Okay, so this was serious business.

I sat and waited for the bomb.

She sat back down behind her desk, folded her hands together, and regarded me with solemn compassion. "So, what seems to be the problem, Zoë?"

I do like that Muriel cuts to the chase.

Unfortunately, I wasn't clear on which particular problem was the issue in this place at this time.

Feigning ignorance is a good tool.

"What problem?"

Muriel opened the file. "You've been missing classes, and disappeared for the better part of the afternoon yesterday. Apparently, you haven't been completing your homework assignments and your grades are slipping. You were inattentive in art class, which is very uncharacteristic." She closed the folder and studied me, exuding earnest care. "This might be little cause for concern in another student, but we like to know our students individually. You've always been a good student, Zoë, and have no record of missing classes. Is there a problem?"

"No," I lied. "Everything's fine."

"Problems with other girls?"

"No." I tried a smile.

"Boys?"

"No." Mages, Thunderbirds, werewolves, and rebel rockers, but that was different.

"There's no need to be defensive. I'm here to help you." Muriel smiled. "To be your friend."

I smiled back. It was a better choice than laughing out loud. "There's no problem," I insisted. "I'll try to do better. In fact, I'm missing English class right now. Can I go?"

Muriel frowned. "Zoë, I had hoped that you and I could resolve this."

"Nothing to resolve," I said, trying to look enthused. "I'll just go back to English class...." I stood up.

Muriel didn't. "I don't want to call your parents about this. I know that your mother in particular dislikes whenever there are academic issues."

"My mom's away," I said before I thought it through.

Muriel checked my file. "Away?"

"She, um, well, she left. And my dad went after her, to talk."

Muriel completely failed to hide her astonishment. She began to take notes at lightning speed. "Then who is staying with you? You don't have siblings and you are a minor...."

"My dad arranged for me to stay with Meagan and the Jamesons while he's gone. So, it's all taken care of." I smiled.

Muriel put down her pen and sighed. She fixed me with a look of such concern that I almost squirmed. "I'm very sorry to hear about your parents and their marital difficulties, Zoë. Would you like to attend our course for students whose families are being damaged by divorce?"

I grabbed my bag. "No, I'm good, thanks. I don't think my family's going to be damaged by divorce." I smiled. "My dad, he can be pretty persuasive, and I'm sure..."

But I wasn't sure.

And Muriel knew it.

I really didn't want to think about it.

I ran out of words and we stared at each other for a moment. Then I slung my bag onto my shoulder. For once, the earnest compassion got to me. I felt my tears rising, but I blinked them away.

"Maybe later," she said softly. "Thank you for telling me about this, Zoë. If you don't mind, I'd like to chat with Mrs. Jameson about our concerns."

"Sure. Whatever. English!" And I was gone.

Muriel meant well, but she didn't know the half of it.

And I wasn't going to be the one to tell her. The Covenant, you know.

Which just meant I was going to have to cram in some extra schoolwork to avoid suspicion.

In my spare time.

Such as it was.

No pressure.

9

There was no way I was going back to English class. I wasn't interested in hearing about the weather as a character or in learning what I hadn't thought about including in my essay. I certainly didn't want to see that grade.

Instead I went to the library and did what I do best. I worked on that drawing for Derek and thought about what I needed to ask him.

It was shaping up to be a pretty good drawing. The dragon filled the cover of his book. It was rearing back, its tail coiled behind and beneath it, its wings stretching off the edges of the page. It had a fearsome number of teeth and was breathing fire, its claws raised to strike and its eyes flashing.

I'd sketched the pose in pencil, and now was filling it in with marker. First the outline in black, then all the detail of the scales. This dragon had a bit of an Asian look to it, so I'd put the traditional pearl in one claw. On impulse, I drew continents on the pearl, making it into the planet Earth. Kind of an inside *Pyr* joke, seeing as how we're supposed to be the defenders of Earth. This dragon was kicking butt in defense of his hoard. I did some Asian clouds behind him, the kind you see in tattoos.

I was trying to decide whether I should go with color or leave it a black line drawing when I felt someone beside me.

Derek.

Of course.

"Cool," he said and sat down beside me.

I knew he was watching me, but didn't look up. "Color or just like this?" It was his book—he could decide.

He leaned closer, his elbow pressing against mine. I could feel how warm he was, smell his skin. It was an awful lot like the moment I'd had in that other library with Jared in the spring—complete with the librarian watching us like a hawk.

I even felt something fluttery in my stomach. Not as strong as it was with Jared, but it was there.

Awareness.

And just the way I did when I was with Jared, I forgot whatever I was going to say next.

Derek glanced up at me then, those pale blue eyes seeming to pierce right through me. "What color would it be?"

I couldn't quite catch my breath. "Whatever you want."

The corner of his mouth lifted a little, not quite a smile. "What do you want? It's your drawing."

I looked away from his intensity, studying the drawing. "I guess I'd make him shades of purple, with some charcoal. It would contrast with the orange flames."

"Him?"

I looked at him again. "Sure. All dragons are guys."

"What about dragon shifters?"

"Most of them are guys."

"But not all." Derek reached for the drawing, turning it to examine it more closely. "I want you to color it like a girl dragon." And he pushed it back at me, a dare in his eyes.

"Which is?" I wasn't sure whether he'd seen me as a dragon or just as a salamander.

"White." He spoke with conviction and I knew he'd seen. "A thousand shades of white, from mist to snow to starlight."

It was strangely poetic for Derek the gruff. I looked at him, and was surprised to see the back of his neck turn red.

As if he were embarrassed.

Huh.

I leaned forward, bracing myself on my elbows and whispered. "Is there a reason you came to this school this year?"

His gaze flicked at me, then away, then back. "You."

Now I was blushing, but I didn't look away. "Why?"

He eyed the librarian, then pulled another notebook from his backpack. He wrote, then turned the page toward me.

> *There is a prophecy among my kind, that when the stars stand still in the sky, all shifters will be hunted. The only way to survive will be to form a larger pack, one that includes other kinds of shifters. The key to that union's success is our accepting the dragon unique to her kind as our pack leader. I came to make that union.*

He spun the book and pushed it toward me, staring across the library while I read what he'd written.

I came to make that union.

Those words left me uncertain, self-conscious, jittery. My Wyvern sense made me feel that his interest was about more than a treaty negotiation. How exactly did wolves seal their alliances?

The way he watched me made me pretty sure I could guess the answer and it left me flustered.

"Why you?" I asked quietly.

He smiled a little. "Not everyone believes in prophecies."

So, there was doubt among the werewolves, but Derek believed. Whether he'd been assigned to be an emissary or had chosen the role, he was here to make the union work. And I could guess that a big part of that would be my proving myself worthy of being pack leader.

From what I knew about wolves, males took precedence, particularly males in their prime.

No wonder there was skepticism in the pack about me, a young girl dragon.

I took a breath, then tapped the first sentence, the part about stars standing still. Derek tugged out his messenger, typed in a search term, then offered it to me.

It was a site about the Great Lunar Standstill. A great lunar standstill, it turned out, was a momentous astrological event.

And we were in the middle of one.

I skimmed the details and learned:

1. A great lunar standstill occurs roughly every nineteen years.
2. There's a theory that ancient peoples were totally into tracking great lunar standstills and that monuments like the Standing Stones of Callanish were built to showcase great lunar standstills. Astrologers warn to expect great upheavals, transformation and change during such events.

There was a bunch more, but it made my eyes glaze over, even with my newfound love of astronomy. When I finished reading, the notebook with Derek's handwritten message was gone, presumably tucked back into his bag. I gave him his messenger and our fingers brushed. I was pretty sure it wasn't an accident. I swallowed, and he watched me closely, his eyes gleaming pale.

"So, how do we make this happen? How do we convince..."

Derek shook his head and frowned to silence me, flicking another look at the librarian. Then he leaned close, his gaze fixed on me. "You lead. You triumph. You win them over. And until they believe, I'll defend you." His lips set. "Count on it."

Okay, I had to prove myself worthy of leading a pack of wolves.

No pressure.

"Dragon's done," I said, pushing his notebook toward him.

Derek pushed it back. "You didn't sign it."

"I never do."

"You should start. You have to claim ownership of what you do."

"Mark territory, you mean," I said, thinking of wolves.

He smiled then, really smiled. It illuminated his face, making him look a lot less secretive. More approachable.

He nodded.

I signed.

"Thanks, Zoë," he said quietly. "I mean what I said."

I didn't doubt that for a minute. I watched as he tucked the notebook into the bag from the store, then inserted it in his pack with care.

"Aren't you going to use it?"

He gave me a hot look. "It's too special for that."

And then he was gone, leaving me with lots to think about.

MEAGAN and I were walking home from school Wednesday, and I was still thinking about Derek. If it was up to me to figure out how to lead an attack on the Mages, I needed to have a foolproof plan. I didn't want to put my friends in unnecessary danger.

Actually, Liam and Meagan were walking together, talking, and I was trailing behind. Liam had turned up at our lockers and was talking to Meagan about movies. They had dissenting opinions about the latest hot boy star. Predictably, Meagan was cutting the star a lot of slack and Liam wasn't.

Unpredictably, disagreeing with Liam was having a miraculous effect on Meagan's stutter. She was so busy mustering her arguments that she forgot to be nervous.

I liked that a lot. I had visions of us becoming close again, now that Jessica was busy with Trevor.

Maybe the apprentice Mage had done me a favor.

As if.

Nick suddenly pulled up beside us in his little electric-blue compact car. "Hey, Zoë!" he shouted, as if surprised to see me. I knew Liam had probably told him where we were, or he homed in on our respective scents. "How are you?"

"What are you doing here?" I cried, as if surprised as well. (Maybe we overdid it a bit.) He parked the car and climbed out, all long-limbed and athletic. I felt Meagan's mouth fall open once more.

"Hey, Liam." Nick smiled at Meagan. "Hi, I'm Nick."

She blinked, pushed up her glasses, and looked between the guys and me.

"I've known Nick forever," I said.

"I'll bet he's the s-s-son of a friend of your father's," Meagan guessed.

"How'd she know that?" Nick asked.

"Meagan's brilliant," I said. "Everyone knows it."

"Nice to meet you." Nick shook her hand. "Any friend of Zoë's is a friend of mine." He was a bit too cheerful, if you ask me, but Meagan blushed scarlet at his attention.

"My dad needs hotter friends," Meagan muttered under her breath and I tried not to laugh. Liam looked away to hide his smile. Nick was fighting his own smile, his eyes dancing.

"What are you doing here?" I asked again.

He looked embarrassed. "I thought I'd come down to see Isabelle."

"You know Isabelle, too?" Meagan asked. Nick nodded.

This was my opportunity to give him a hard time. "What does your girlfriend think of that?" Nick looked mortified. "He dumped Isabelle," I told Meagan and she regarded Nick with horror.

"Maybe he needs glasses," Liam said, teasing.

Nick turned red. He looked away. He shuffled his feet. "Teresa and I are just kind of seeing each other, sometimes. It's no big deal. It's just, you know, just..."

"Sex," Liam supplied. He managed to look innocent while he did it, too.

Nick glared at him.

Meagan choked, outraged on behalf of her idol.

That was when I guessed who else Donovan had been advising.

His son, Nick.

Nick turned to Meagan. "I figured I'd come and talk to Isabelle, try to straighten things out. Maybe we can just be friends."

"I don't know why you'd want to date anyone other than Isabelle," Meagan said and Nick blushed even redder.

The thing was, I didn't think he knew either.

I DIDN'T HAVE a ton of spare time in the evenings for the rest of the week. As much as I would have liked to hang out with Liam and Nick, Meagan's mom had other ideas. She was taking her custodianship of me really seriously so I was guessing that Muriel had called. I got parked at the dining room table to do my homework under surveillance, every night from six thirty to ten.

And she took my messenger until I was done.

Meagan, of course, was finished with everything by eight. She stayed with me and read, and was helpful when I needed it.

In our respective beds at night, we argued about Trevor and Jessica. Meagan thought it was a sign of Trevor's sensitivity that he had seen the finer qualities of Jessica, even though she wasn't flashy like Suzanne. She refused to condemn Jessica for getting the bonus prize that she had wanted herself.

Maybe she thought that one day, if Jessica and Trevor didn't work out, Trevor would notice her. She certainly accepted every invitation from Jessica to include her in their plans.

I had deep dark feelings about all of this, but I couldn't say much without sounding like more of a bitch than Suzanne.

After that topic was exhausted every night, we argued about her Halloween costume. Meagan was determined to be Mozart, even though that was the least likely costume to get her noticed by any guy alive. She thought it would make Trevor aware of the interest in music they had in common. I thought she should go with something more sexy. Meagan was sure she was right, though, and had a long silver wig, a brocade jacket from a vintage store, breeches, and buckled shoes. And a conductor's wand.

Her glasses at least didn't look out of place. And who knew—maybe she and some other hot guy with musical skill would hit it off.

Maybe there was a guy like Trevor out there for her who wasn't an evil apprentice Mage.

I had to hope.

I had no costume, as I was determined I wasn't going anywhere.

Despite Meagan's entreaties.

Her messenger wasn't chiming very often, a sure sign that Jessica had found something more interesting to do. I was angry that she was treating Meagan so shabbily, but I wasn't sure what I could do about it. Meagan kept cutting her new friend slack, which made me even more mad. The guys kept me posted on their investigative progress, which was fairly minimal.

I had the definite impression that they were having more fun than me.

Derek was circling, not approaching unless I beckoned to him. All I needed was a foolproof plan to save the world.

Sadly, I hadn't refined that one yet.

I got one stern message from my dad, informing me that we would talk when he got home. I knew what he wanted to talk about, and that message made me hope he'd stay in England for a while.

Maybe for good. A "talk" with a pissed-off dragon is never a good time.

I heard from my mom every morning. She never said anything about the incident with the counselor, but someone must have told her something because she was more intent on asking questions. I'd put my nickel on Mrs. Jameson. It was good to hear my mom's voice, even though I couldn't read one thing in her tone and she wouldn't talk about my dad.

In bed, when Meagan was asleep, I tried to send visions to the *Pyr*, with no idea whether I was successful or not. The guys never mentioned having any dreams or receiving anything from me, but it was better than dozing off and meeting Urd.

By Friday, I was beat. I took one look at my English homework that night and thought I'd put my head down on the table and sleep.

Dostoyevsky. What joy was this? I'd be in a coma before I finished the first chapter.

Meagan finished early yet again, probably to starred reviews, and went to the piano to do her practice. She had her classes on Saturday morning for that, and I dared to imagine that I might have some free time.

She worked a scale, warming up. The Jamesons had a grand piano in their living room. In fact, it filled the living room with its glossy blackness. An imposing instrument. The sheer size of it made Meagan look petite and her hands seem small.

It was pretty much the only thing in the living room. This made a kind of sense for the piano to reign supreme, as Meagan's dad was a concert pianist himself—she came by that talent honestly. And the piano got a lot of use. They'd had an enthusiastic discussion on Sunday morning about keys and timing and all the stuff she'd pulled out of Rick about the syntho drums.

I sighed and cracked open my required reading. It was even more boring than expected. I read the first page five times, Meagan's aria tickling at the edge of my thoughts. The music was pretty. And it made me concentrate better, as if Meagan was sending me her scholarly vibes.

I read four pages before I made the connection.

Then I pulled my new ring out of my pocket and pushed it onto my finger.

The living and dining room were filled with dancing beams of light. They were joyous, not like the confetti that Jared had sung but more like ripples and waves of light. They reminded me of mirrored streamers, and they swirled around the room like a joyous whirlwind. They were all shades of red and purple and blue.

Meagan glanced up at me and smiled, playing a little trill with her right hand. She looked so happy and at ease. I understood then that her destiny wasn't with brainiacs and math geniuses.

It was with musicians.

Because the ribbons of light told me that Meagan was a spellsinger.

Crap.

I was suddenly very afraid that the Mages knew it, too. This put a whole new spin on things.

Was Meagan their real target, instead of me?

What could I do? I'd never manage to persuade her not to go to Trevor's Halloween party, not without explaining everything to her. I was in enough trouble with my dad that I didn't want to rush into breaking the Covenant again. I couldn't even beguile her, because she knew the deal and would realize just who—and what—I was.

I had to admire that Trevor had accomplished his goal. He had ensured that I would be at his party. Despite my reservations, I had to go to protect Meagan.

From whatever the Mages were planning.

Of course, Liam and Nick didn't see it that way.

We had an argument in old-speak Friday night. I was in Meagan's room and supposedly drawing, but they were a big distraction. They would have gone on and on, but I finally just ended it.

Meagan had already gotten up to look out the window. "So weird that there's thunder in a snowstorm," she said.

She turned to look at me, and I shrugged.

"Maybe it's an airplane flying low," I suggested and she looked out the window again. I wouldn't have put it past her to figure it out, though—Meagan is smart and she was already looking for *Pyr*, armed with data about us. She had that Einstein look, which was trouble.

I had to end the old-speak.

And that meant inflicting a decision on the guys.

"I've got the ring," I said, interrupting Nick. *"It cut the spells before and it'll do it again. We won't be trapped."*

"It's too risky," Liam argued, ready to go at it again.

"It's more risky for Meagan if we're not there."

"I vote we stay away," Nick said. *"You have no idea what they're planning..."*

"But we have to defend our Wyvern," Liam said.

"Suit yourselves either way," I said, knowing exactly how they'd take that challenge. *"I'm going. Maybe it'll be my chance to persuade the wolves to join us."*

They mumbled and grumbled a bit, but agreed that we'd all go. We set a time to meet and the old-speak fell silent.

I wondered when Derek would turn up but wasn't sure how to find out. School was over for the weekend and I didn't know where he lived.

Would he just sense it?

How sharp was his sense of smell?

Could I find him with mine?

I watched Meagan at the window until she turned away. "Either way, the thunder seems to have stopped," she said, getting back into bed.

"Maybe I'll come to the party after all," I said as casually as I could manage it.

Her face lit. "Really?"

"I need a costume, though."

"Why don't you come to my piano lesson tomorrow, and then we'll go shopping from there?"

"Great idea," I agreed, knowing it would give me the perfect cover to guard her.

And maybe I could find Derek.

I SHOULD HAVE KNOWN the harmony between Meagan and me couldn't last.

We were in my fave vintage shop, One More Time. Normally, I could spend everything I had within moments of crossing the threshold, but on this day, I just couldn't focus. I hadn't found anything for my costume, because that particular concern didn't have my attention. Compared to everything else that was going on, shopping for the perfect Halloween costume seemed ridiculously frivolous.

I'm not good at keeping up appearances.

Mostly I was trying to figure out how to warn Meagan without breaking the Covenant again.

So, I was fingering this crimson feather boa, trying to imagine something really simple that wouldn't look (quite) like I didn't care, when Meagan got a call.

From the look on her face, I knew it was Jessica.

"Sure," she said. "That's great. Seven's no problem. See you then." She ended the call and flashed me the stainless smile. Her eyes were sparkling in a way that didn't make me feel good. "Guess what? I'm going to get a ride in Trevor's MG!"

I dropped the boa. "What?"

"Trevor and Jessica are picking me up. They have to come early, because he wants to be home before everyone arrives." She hummed a bit, poking at things as she practically skipped through the store. "Isn't it nice of them to think of me?"

"No!" I was right behind her, close enough to see how startled she was by my reply. "I mean, why don't you just get a ride with me and the guys, like we planned? I thought you wanted to see Liam again." I tried not to sound panicky. "Nick is coming at eight. That'll give you more time to get ready."

"Oh, but I want to ride in Trevor's car. It's so cool."

"But Jessica is dating him. Won't you feel out of place?"

"I don't think so." Meagan pivoted to face me over a rack of kerchiefs. "After all, she's being really nice about it. She knows how much I like him, and she's not trying to be mean."

"How can you tell? Sounds to me like she's rubbing your nose in it."

"No, you're wrong." Meagan was emphatic. "You just don't know her like I do."

There wasn't much I could say to that. I was freaking, though, at what might happen to Meagan before I got to the party. I had zero data about the Mages' plans but I do have an active imagination. I didn't want her to be alone with Trevor—or Trevor and Jessica—for a whole hour. I flicked through the kerchiefs and seized a purple one, not really seeing it. "Let's go."

Meagan was skeptical. "That's your costume?"

"And this." I plucked a white plastic cowboy hat from a shelf. There was a plastic gun beside it in a cheap toy holster, lucky for me. "This too." Jeans, boots, a skinny shirt, and I'd be ready for the shoot-out at the OK Corral.

"I think you could try harder," Meagan said.

"I think Jessica could be nicer to you." I went to the cash register, wondering what I could do to change her mind.

Short of telling her the whole truth.

"We had a long talk about it. It's not her fault. She likes him, too." Meagan leaned against the counter beside me, checking out the bangles. They had a couple of sweet Bakelite ones, but I barely saw them. "She said when she tutored him, it just felt like magic between them." Meagan turned a smile on me. "Isn't it romantic?"

I couldn't believe it.

"So, explain this to me. You're Jessica's friend so you want her to be happy."

"Right."

"I'm your friend so I want you to be happy."

"Okay."

"Why doesn't Jessica have this concern, if she's your friend?"

Meagan's eyes flashed. "You're still jealous of her."

"I think you deserve better friends!"

"Oh, like ones who don't confide in me?"

So, we were back to that. Meagan left the shop and I ran after her, jamming my acquisitions into my backpack. The hat had to go on my head. Nice bonus to look like an idiot while I was trying to be persuasive. "Meagan, we need to talk about this."

She stopped in the street so abruptly that I nearly ran into her. "Go ahead," she said, a daring glint in her eyes. "Tell me what happened last spring."

I was tempted.

I was *really* tempted.

But my back was hurting like hell after taking that thunderbolt and I could still recall the sting of the dragonsmoke on my hand. If I told everything to Meagan, when she wasn't specifically in danger, it'd be exile city for me.

I dropped my gaze.

Meagan sniffed and walked away. I trailed behind her feeling like ninety-seven thousand kinds of loser.

It wasn't an easy choice.

It also wasn't one I didn't question over and over again for the rest of the day.

In fact, I sent my dad a message, asking for permission to break the Covenant because I feared Meagan was in danger. I didn't say what danger, because I knew he wouldn't believe anything I said about the Mages, and I also didn't want him reminding Mrs. Jameson that I shouldn't be allowed to go to a Halloween party at all.

This did undermine my argument.

The lack of those details was probably why he immediately declined my request.

But then, providing those details wouldn't have done me any favors, either.

I was getting tired of no-win situations.

Meagan and I returned to her house in silence. I mostly was thinking about how nice it would be to catch a break once in a while.

Before the party would have been good.

The doorbell rang promptly at seven and Meagan practically flew to the door in her excitement. I was right behind her.

She'd made a change from her Mozart idea, maybe because I'd finally gotten through to her. She was dressed as Rapunzel, an idea of her mother's, with long hair made of yellow yarn coiled around one arm. She and her mom had argued about her glasses ruining the costume and the immediate necessity of contacts, but Meagan had lost.

We were both sure who was at the door, but we were both wrong.

It was Derek.

Dressed as he usually was for school.

"Hey," he said, nodded at both of us and shoved his hands in his pockets. He looked uncomfortable.

I was ridiculously glad to see him and it probably showed. Meagan was looking between us (Einstein all the way) and started to smile when Derek didn't say anything more. I didn't say anything either, because everything I wanted to tell him couldn't be shared in front of Meagan.

"You two probably have lots to talk about," Meagan said, flashing a smile. "I'll just go back inside."

Before she could do that, we heard the roar of a car engine. The MG peeled around the corner, going way too fast, and squealed to a halt in front of the house. The top was up, but Jessica was waving out the window and calling Meagan's name.

Trevor honked the horn.

I wanted to shout, but Derek gave me a look and shook his head. I decided to trust his view of the future.

Meagan scooped up her miles of yarn hair, and ran to the sidewalk. Jessica got out of the front seat and they hugged. My eyes nearly fell out of my head. Jessica was wearing a superhero costume, all form-fitting spandex that could have been painted on. She was far more curvy than I'd ever imagined. She turned so I could see her face and my mouth fell open in shock. She had ditched her baseball cap. And she did have one whopper of a secret—she was so gorgeous that she could have been a pinup girl.

Was this Trevor's influence?

Then Meagan piled into the backseat and all my fears returned with force.

"Hey, Zoë!" Trevor shouted. "If you're ready, why don't you come, too?"

"No," Derek said, fast and low.

"Not quite ready, thanks," I shouted. "I'll see you later."

I heard Meagan say something to Jessica about me and Derek and hoped wolves didn't have as sharp hearing as dragons do. Jessica giggled and Trevor squealed the tires as he pulled away.

"You're sure?" I asked Derek.

He inhaled deeply. "There's nothing good ahead, but it's still brewing. I don't think anything bad will happen before you get to the party."

"But she's a spellsinger and doesn't know it."

He looked at me in shock. I realized I'd never surprised him before. "So that's it."

"What?"

"A scent I didn't know." He nodded and I watched him add that information to his knowledge. "Okay. That makes sense."

"Are you still sure she's okay?"

Derek shot me a look. There was just a glimmer of doubt in his eyes, and only for a second, but I saw it.

"The guys are coming soon to pick me up. I'll be okay."

He stepped back then. "See you there," he murmured and disappeared into the shadows. I saw the blue shimmer of light only because I was watching closely.

I had to watch even more closely to see the silhouette of a wolf slipping through the darkness, heading toward Riverside Drive.

Almost a whole hour to wait.

It was going to kill me.

ALMOST EXACTLY AN HOUR LATER, Nick parked down the street from Trevor's house.

We could hear the music clearly, even a block away. There was the sound of laughter as well, and, courtesy of my ring, I could see those Mage spells spinning in the air over the house. A spiral of orange Mage spell light surrounded the house, as if it stood at the center of a vortex.

Or a hurricane.

"I'll bet his parents are gone," Nick said. "It sounds like a good party."

"That's because they're spellcasting already, just as we thought."

"Shit," said Liam.

"Look, just so you know, there's something different about this spell," I said. "It's not a net, like last time, that's closing around the perimeter. It's more like a vortex. It seems to be drawing in, kind of the way water goes down a drain."

"Shit again," Liam said, eyeing the house. "I don't like that they're learning new tricks."

"Or maybe trying out different ones," I said.

"I think it sounds like a great party," Nick said and reached for the door handle. "We might have fun."

I grabbed his arm in sudden understanding. "You're *supposed* to think it sounds like a great party. You're supposed to want to go in. It's a lure."

"The spell's already working on you," Liam said. I wasn't the only one remembering that Nick had been susceptible to Adrian's spell in April.

"A trap," Nick said with a nod, his gaze locked on the house. I could almost feel him fighting the spell.

Liam leaned forward, his tone urgent. "Remember that they can make you think whatever they want. That's what they did before, Nick. We've got to listen to Zoë."

"Right," Nick said, but he couldn't seem to look away from the house.

This was not good. And we hadn't even entered the house yet. "Maybe you should wait for us," I suggested. "Hang with the car in case we need to make a quick getaway."

"Are you kidding?" His confident grin flashed. "I'm not going to miss a great party."

Liam and I exchanged a look as Nick got out of the car with purpose.

"I'll stick with him," Liam said. "You have other things to worry about."

"Right."

We looked funny gathering on the sidewalk in our costumes. Nick was dressed as a football player, his shoulder pads so huge that I had barely fit in the car beside him. Liam had made a Viking costume for himself out of some furry fabric. He had a blond wig and fake beard, an axe and big mukluks. I was a gunslinger.

I reached for Nick, but he was already striding toward the house, his cleats tapping on the sidewalk. Liam swore and went after him.

Just what I needed—someone else to guard.

The orange spell net swirled with greater speed as I watched. The sight made me dizzy, a carousel of throbbing light that almost obscured the house. I thought I might puke. I took off the ring and shoved it into my pocket, unable to deal with the eye candy and think straight at the same time. I had let Meagan go in there, with a bunch of Mages and who knew what else.

They knew that she was a spellsinger, and one way or the other, they intended to recruit her.

They'd have to get past me first.

. . .

A SHADOW SEPARATED itself from the landscaping as I marched down the sidewalk. I glanced sideways to find a wolf loping beside me, his head down and his ears folded back.

"Derek?" I asked and the wolf glanced me a look that was filled with disdain.

Right. Who else could it have been? He didn't have to talk for me to understand what he meant.

"Liam, Nick, this is Derek." It was a bit strange to be making introductions to a wolf, but the situation demanded it. Derek regarded them steadily, as if assessing their power.

"You told us about him," Liam said.

"Hey, Derek," Nick said and reached to scratch his ears.

Derek backed away, lifting his lip to display a large sharp fang.

"He's a wolf, not a poodle," I said and thought his eyes glinted with humor.

"Right," Nick said. "Glad to have you with us either way."

"In which form are you going in?" I asked Derek.

Again, I got the unblinking stare.

"Going with the element of surprise. Okay." I considered our costumes and made a choice. "You'd better stay with Liam, since you two look as if you might belong together."

"You can help me remind Nick not to listen," Liam said to Derek.

"No leash?" Nick teased and got a growl from Derek for that.

"Wolves don't wear leashes and collars," Liam said. "They need their autonomy."

Derek matched his pace to Liam then, and I knew they'd get along just fine.

"Well, you'd better tell them he's your dog and just looks like a wolf," Nick said and Liam nodded.

"I'll beguile to get him in, if I have to," Liam said. "We're going to need him."

Jessica seemed to be waiting just inside the house for us. She watched us come closer, that coy smile playing over her lips. She checked out Nick and her smile broadened.

He grinned right back at her. "Who's that? The cute girl with Meagan?"

Before I could answer, Jessica looked straight at me. I could see the glint of her eyes in the darkness as they narrowed.

Then she bared her teeth and hissed at me.

I put on the ring again and nearly fell over in shock. When I looked at her with my enhanced vision, it was clear that she was a jaguar, tawny, spotted, and powerful. With the same long-lashed amber eyes as she had in human form.

Shifter type number four, present and accounted for.

Open your eyes, Unktehila.

How could I have missed this? I felt more stupid than I ever had in my life—which was saying something. Derek had even warned me. There *were* jaguar shifters and evidently at least one of them went to our school.

Was that why Trevor was dating her?

What else hadn't I noticed?

Meanwhile, Jessica's tail lashed the way a cat's does when it's playing with a mouse. I saw her dig her claws into Meagan's shoulder.

And push her deeper into Trevor's house.

Was she helping the Mages?

Then she beckoned to Nick.

He moved at light speed, apparently forgetting all about us.

"Wait!" I cried, but he was already heading up the steps. He disappeared into the house, surrounded immediately by the golden spell light of the Mages. He was laughing, making friends with his usual easy charm, shaking hands with Jessica.

"What's wrong?" Liam said, but I just ran for the door.

Derek snarled and bounded after me. There was no time to consider our options or make a better plan. Nick and Meagan were in there already, so we had to follow.

I couldn't help thinking that this was exactly what the Mages had hoped would happen. And we hadn't been able to do anything about it.

"Zoë!" Trevor cried at the door as if I were the homecoming queen. I wondered just how drunk he would need to be to actually be so glad to see me. Obviously he was just gleeful that his plan was coming together so well.

The music poured into the street, pulsing with energy. The orange spell light was so bright that I had to keep my eyes narrowed. I didn't dare take off the ring, though. I needed all the information I could get.

Of course, I would never let Trevor know what I could see. Dumb ol' dragon, that was me.

"I can only stop in for a few minutes," I said with a smile. "We're just on our way to a party at the college."

Trevor's eyes glittered. "No problem. Come on in." His gaze fell on Derek and I wondered how much he knew. "Is your dog trained?" he asked Liam.

"Absolutely," Liam said. He buried his fingers in the scruff of Derek's neck, as if they were old allies. "I can count on him anywhere."

Trevor looked from one to the other for a moment, then smiled as he stepped back. I guessed that if he knew what—if not who—Derek was, then he hadn't counted on his presence tonight. That smile, though, made me wonder. Was he glad to have more hunted shifters present?

I was afraid that we weren't just contributing to the success of the Mage plan for the evening, but unwittingly improving upon it.

We had to lift our collective game.

I recognized a bunch of people from school, although the costumes made it tricky. Cleopatra was there, a caveman, a Martian, at least four vampires, Julius Caesar, the president, Cinderella (she was wearing one clear shoe, which was the clue), an Amazon tribesman with a bone through his nose, Dorothy in her gingham dress and ruby slippers, a zombie, and a mummy with bandages unraveling all over the carpet.

Worse, the room was thick with Mages. Thanks to my ring, I could see them, their forms flickering. They slipped from form to form in rapid succession, their edges blurring with the transformations. I'm not sure whether they do it on purpose, or whether I was seeing their truth. Either way, the cycling between forms—minotaur, unicorn, snake, eagle, centaur, griffin, etc., etc., etc.—was a shocking display of all the shape shifter species they'd eliminated. As before, it blew me away to see how many kinds of shifters there had once been. I wondered whether every kind of creature had once had a partner species: one kind shifted and one kind didn't. The Mages were cleaning up the shifter varieties, leaving just the unshifters.

And themselves, with all shifting powers.

The sight was a telling reminder of their plans for us.

The orange spell light wound all around them, a glowing ribbon that bound everyone more closely together. When I could stand to look at it, I could see its path—it led straight to the basement. I could hear people laughing down there and I truly didn't want to go down those stairs. I took off the ring for a moment to give myself a break from the visuals, and shoved it into my pocket.

There was also a lot of smoke in the house. Pot, incense, and cigarettes. The combination was overwhelming. I saw a couple of bottles of Jim Beam making the rounds and some huge jugs of cheap wine. There was a lot of giggling and a good number of fondling couples. Someone pinched my butt as I moved through the crowd, looking for Meagan.

There was no sign of her, which worried me.

How could she have already disappeared?

I headed toward the kitchen, as if looking for a drink. Artificial stimulus was the last thing I needed. Meagan was there, much to my relief. She was standing against the counter, looking a bit lost. She was explaining her costume to someone, with enough exasperation that I knew it wasn't the first time she'd been asked.

Jessica was beside her, in her superhero costume.

Standing guard, was my first impression.

Claws sharp.

Anyone else I knew would have been self-conscious—okay, except maybe Suzanne—but Jessica was working that costume. Guys were clustered around her, salivating. It seemed that the bookworm had shed her chrysalis, thanks to Trevor's attention.

Just like a twisted fairy tale.

Suzanne sulked by the fridge. I almost hadn't recognized her, because of her dark wig. She was yet another vampire, a line of blood painted down her chin, with plastic fangs and tons of eyeliner. She looked fit to kill when Trevor charged into the kitchen and flung his arm around Jessica. Jessica purred and ran one long-nailed finger down his chest and then they kissed with enthusiasm. The guys hooted and Jessica smiled as she nestled against his side.

As content as a cat in the sun.

She was in her element, no doubt about that.

"Bitch," Suzanne muttered and tossed back half of her glass of tomato juice. I was surprised by the wit of that, and wondered whether I'd underestimated her. I'd bet it had a little bonus in it—her eyes already looked glassy.

Then she looked at me and her eyes narrowed. "Freak. Don't think I don't get it, Sorensson."

"I don't know what you're talking about."

Suzanne laughed without humor. She pointed a finger at me. "No one calls me crazy, understand?"

"I never called you crazy."

"But other people did, and it was because of you. I might not have proof of what I saw, but you can count on me getting it." She sipped her juice with satisfaction, malice shining in her eyes. "Then we'll see who the real loser is."

It said something that I had bigger problems than Suzanne feeling vindictive. I smiled and made some innocuous comment about her being drunk early, then ignored her.

Meagan glanced at me and smiled. Her eyes lit at the sight of Liam. Derek was right at my knees, Liam behind, and Nick ahead of me, and it felt good to be among friends.

I accepted a Coke that I didn't want and gave it a careful sniff before I sipped it. It seemed to be okay, but I didn't plan to drink it anyway. I leaned against the counter near the back door, as if totally at ease, and pushed my ring onto my finger again.

The vivid orange spell slapped me in the retina. It was brighter than any I'd ever seen, swirling and spinning with a manic energy. It spiraled down the stairs to the basement in an accelerating tunnel of power. I could feel its allure and see its effect upon even the humans who were present.

Liam went over to talk to Meagan. She was obviously relieved to find someone she knew—never mind that he was a hot guy—and they started to dissect (again) the movie we'd seen together the other night.

Derek growled a little and I knew he was displeased that we weren't sticking together. He went to Liam, though, and sat in front of him. His pale gaze was restless, and he snarled at anyone who touched him.

Nick bumped my shoulder with his, then took a swig of his beer. *"Down there?"* he asked in old-speak. I knew he couldn't see the spell, so I looked at him in surprise. He grinned crookedly. *"I really* really *want to go down there."*

So, he was feeling the effects. He knew it, but his thoughts were still muddled. I nodded agreement, not wanting to say anything aloud or in old-speak. I saw the spell swirling around Nick with greater intensity. Had he drawn it closer because of his old-speak? I remembered that the Mages could hear old-speak and I quietly freaked.

I had no chance to warn Nick because he moved away from me, the orange light surrounding him with its glow. He gravitated toward the basement stairs. I exchanged a look with Liam and saw Derek's eyes narrow. I pretended to sip my Coke, as if everything was peachy, although I had a feeling everything was sliding into the crapper.

Good thing I was faking because Adrian walked into the kitchen just then.

If I'd been drinking for real, I would have choked.

IO

Adrian was the Mage who had pretended to be a dragon the previous spring and had cast a spell at boot camp that had turned the guys against me. Adrian had disappeared in the ensuing battle and we figured he'd been recalled to Mage headquarters—wherever that was. Since then, there'd been no sign of him.

I'd known that I hadn't seen the last of him.

But now I pretended not to know it was him.

Because he was in disguise. Beneath his construction worker costume—complete with hard hat, lunch box, and men at work sign—he was wearing a glamour that made him look sixteen, short and blond. He watched me with care as he entered the room, but I pretended to be interested in my drink.

Like I hadn't even noticed him.

My ring showed me the truth. Adrian flickered between forms on the periphery of my vision, his presence enough to make me queasy. I caught a glimpse of the human disguise he'd worn at boot camp—the easygoing college pal, the helpful guy with dark hair and dark eyes—as he shifted between forms. I had no idea whether the college pal was his real form or not, but it seemed to be one he liked. It made frequent appearances in his playlist.

Did Mages don glamours to fake out non-Mages? I wondered. The answer was not lurking at the bottom of my Coke. Suzanne sidled over to him and made a joke about his costume. She could see only his glamour.

Uh-huh. Even with the glamour, he wasn't exactly the hottest guy at the party. He smiled back at her and that was good enough for Suzanne. Maybe she *was* drunk. They sidled up close to each other, even though he kept checking me out.

Had he been planning to hit on me? I never thought I'd feel any gratitude toward Suzanne, but in that moment, she might just have been my favorite person in the universe for saving me some trouble.

The spell spun more wildly in Adrian's proximity, another golden thread weaving into its gilded spiral. It was moving faster and getting brighter all around us. Sparks danced from the Mages in attendance.

I felt the hair rise on the back of my neck as the clock struck nine. A visible frisson of energy crackled through the house. The party quickly got louder. The temperature rose. The beat of the music became more insistent.

Nick got even closer to the basement stairs.

Shit.

The spell targeted him, swirling around his head like a swarm of fireflies. I could see him fighting it.

And I knew that he was losing.

"Hey, Nick," Liam said. "Come tell Meagan about your car."

Nick shuddered from head to toe, then grinned. It was a shaky grin, far from his usual smile, but I was proud of him for trying. I was thinking we should snatch Meagan and bail.

But then the Mages would just regroup. I wanted to know what they were up to.

"Great idea," Nick said. He visibly gritted his teeth to head toward them, defying the allure of the spell. I could see that his temples were dark with sweat, but he moved toward Meagan.

Just when I thought we were out of the proverbial woods, Trevor laughed. "Hey, I've got a great idea! Let's jam!"

"Excellent," Jessica said. "I'm ready to sing."

They headed for the stairs, arms wrapped around each other.

"Meagan plays piano, you know," Jessica said to Trevor.

"Really?" He smiled at Meagan and she blushed, right on cue. "That's great. I have an electronic keyboard, but I'm not good at it. Will you come jam with us?"

Meagan's face lit up.

There was no way she'd refuse.

And there was no way she could play in a houseful of Mages without them realizing that she was a spellsinger.

I saw from Trevor's expression that he, at least, knew what she could do.

"Hey, but I wanted to talk to you," I said to Meagan. I had no excuse, not even something feeble.

"We can do that later," she said predictably, and followed Trevor. "Do you have your sax here?"

"Not the one I play at school. My dad bought me an amazing antique one. You should hear the sound of it."

"I can't wait."

Liam went after Meagan, his expression concerned. "I've never heard you play," he said to her and she smiled at him.

Derek snarled and went after Liam.

Nick looked at me, swallowed, and followed Liam.

Shit. The worst-case scenario was happening and there was nothing I could do about it.

I followed them all, my guts churning with dread.

"I love jazz," Suzanne purred at Adrian.

"Me, too." I saw Adrian smile, then heard him on the stairs behind me. If I'd hesitated, I'm sure he would have pushed me.

Shit shit shit. Without knowing what was going to happen, I couldn't make a plan of what to do to stop it. I heard the door at the top of the stairs slam and click behind us. I pivoted in surprise and Adrian smiled.

"Nothing like a little privacy," he said and Suzanne giggled.

Trevor played a trio of notes on his sax below us, warming up. I leapt down the last steps in time to see Meagan familiarizing herself with the controls of the keyboard.

She played a score, the same one she always used to warm up, and I could see that she loosed a shower of spellsinger lights. Trevor smiled encouragement. Adrian practically rubbed his hands together with glee.

Jessica smiled to herself and other Mages drew closer, easing toward Meagan from the perimeter of the room.

My mouth went dry

Then I saw the spell lock shut, trapping us in a maelstrom of orange light.

This was so not good.

I PRETENDED to be oblivious to the spell and its power, even though anyone with a speck of perception would have noticed that my heart was pounding in terror. No one could have heard my pulse, though, because they started to play.

And it was loud. I couldn't believe the amount of equipment down there. It would have made any member of Jared's band salivate, and showed a remarkable investment. I guessed then that Trevor's parents were Mages, too. I knew I'd never again look on anyone with any musical talent without wondering about their spellsinging abilities.

The ring was the only thing that let me see whether they were making spells. The color and behavior of the musical spells was the only clue as to whether the musician in question had joined the Mage team or not.

There were syntho drums and electric guitars, two bass guitars, the keyboard, a trombone, a trumpet, and Trevor's sax. There were amps like crazy, the collective sound making the beams of the house reverberate in time.

They were all warming up, creating a cacophony. The swirl of spell light was dizzying, contributing to the whole in a crazy swirl of gold. I couldn't discern any pattern or rhythm to it—it seemed that the spells spun more wildly because they were confined. To make the visual feast even worse, the Mages who played were flickering between forms as they did so. It was as if they weren't even real.

Nick stood on one side of me and swore under his breath. Liam was on my other side, his fingers buried in the scruff of Derek's fur. Derek had his ears folded back, as if offended by the sound.

Or its volume.

I wished I knew what he could see coming in the next two minutes.

"Wow," Liam said, obviously well aware that the Mages would hear us.

"And then some," Nick agreed, squaring his shoulders. They both looked at me.

"Wait for it," I said softly and then I smiled. Adrian was hovering near me, watching. I was determined to keep surprise on my side. "I'm sure they'll sound great once they warm up."

Trevor held up one hand and they fell silent. "Let's start with something classic," he said. "Everyone know 'Begin the Beguine'?" One of the Mages on guitar played a riff, Meagan joined in on the first bar, and they hit it.

They did sound good.

Or maybe their collective spell was persuasive like that. The spell light created a cohesion then, spinning like a spiral in a thousand shades of yellow and gold. I was reminded of hot caramel spirals drizzled over desserts. When they cooled they were hard, brittle and sparkly, perfect swirls of sweetness.

That's what the Mage spell started to look like. Meagan's spellsinging bounced around within the confines of the Mage spell as she played on, oblivious to what they were doing. Her music was blue and purple, in marked contrast to the Mage colors.

But confined by their spell.

Caged.

And their spell targeted hers, and sucked hers dry.

I fought the urge to shiver.

That was nothing compared to when Jessica began to sing. I was shocked. I'd never heard her sing. She had a gorgeous voice. Molten and rich and deep. Far more sophisticated than I would have expected from a teenage math whiz.

And she sang scat. She sang nonsense, ad-libbing a tune that riffed on the music. I didn't know what it was called then, but Meagan told me later. I thought, actually, that it was pretty cool that she could do that on the fly.

Jessica, it appeared, had bunches of secrets.

Her scat singing sent out an array of little bubbles, all different sizes and shaded from copper to burgundy. Trevor leaned in close beside her, getting into the music. She matched rhythm with him, the two of them jamming so perfectly it was obvious that they'd done it before. Meagan's fingers faltered as she watched with awe. The other band members kept the beat, letting Trevor and Jessica improvise with each other.

The temperature in the basement rose even further. It got hot, like the air was simmering. Pulsing. There was something exciting about the beat, a driving rhythm that made me keenly aware of my own skin. Someone turned on a strobe, which was timed perfectly to the beat. I looked at the way that light cut through the spell light, and swallowed in dread.

The Mage spell looked sharp. Like golden knives in the darkness.

And it was moving.

No, it was closing, a trap tightening on its prey.

But to my astonishment, its target was Jessica.

Jessica sang, her head tipped back and her eyes closed. She was lost in the music, unaware of the danger she was in. The strobe light flashed. The spell closed in around her like a gilded cage.

Should I warn her?

Or was that what they expected me to do?

Trevor finished their improv and played a little flourish on his sax, bridging back to the chorus. Meagan was watching, her fingers still as she looked around.

I knew she sensed that something was wrong.

Because Jessica opened her eyes then. She almost smiled, and I saw her take a breath, as if she was going to join in on the chorus.

But the Mage spell snapped right around her. She was enclosed in a net of golden light, light that buzzed all around her. She visibly panicked that she was trapped, and began to struggle, but to no avail. Her shadow stretched across the floor, surprisingly dark.

Derek snarled and would have taken a step forward, but Liam held him back with a touch and he reluctantly sat down. His ears were up and his fur was bristling.

Was she really in danger, or was this a trick? I couldn't tell.

The Mages sang louder.

And they stepped closer, forming a circle around Jessica. She thrashed in the golden mesh, but it continued to tighten. The next moment she was struggling on the floor, more like a fish in a net than a girl. I assumed everyone else would think she was having some kind of convulsion. The Mages barricaded her from the others, blocking their view. I was surprised that no one tried to move closer, but then I noticed that all the other kids were staring, unblinking. They weren't moving at all. Not even breathing. It was as if they'd been frozen in time. Or struck to stone.

Enchanted.

There was a shimmer of blue and Jessica shifted, becoming a golden jaguar right before everyone's eyes.

It looked like an involuntary shift and I knew what that meant. She *was* in real trouble.

Adrian bent toward her and she hissed, then slashed at him with her claws. He laughed as the mesh kept her contained.

And then he took a bite out of her shadow.

She screamed, and it was the yowl of a great cat.

The Mages swarmed her, clustering closer as each bit at her shadow. I was horrified to see that the attack was diminishing her strength. It was even more creepy that all the kids who weren't shifters or apprentice Mages were completely frozen. Only Meagan was still moving, and I had to guess that was because of her spellsinging abilities.

Even though they were undeveloped.

"You can't do this!" Nick shouted.

"You're hurting her!" Meagan screamed and threw a tambourine at them. It bounced off the back of the Mage closest to her, who turned to face her. I could see the darkness of Jessica's shadow running down their chins, like chocolate sauce.

"Stop!" Liam roared. He bounded forward and shifted shape in mid-leap. He shimmered that pale blue, then became a massive dragon. Liam in dragon form is the vivid green of malachite, his scales and talons tipped with silver. He ripped open the back of a Mage with his talons before the guy even saw him coming.

"That's it," Nick said. "We're in." He shifted shape as well and defended his buddy's back as the Mages turned on Liam. Nick was so bright in color that it was like looking into the sun. He breathed a stream of fire and about ten Mage costumes went up in flames.

Derek let out a howl and jumped into the fray. I saw him bite the ass of a Mage, and am pretty sure he ripped out a chunk of flesh. He immediately went for another chomp.

A couple of Mages screamed. The music faltered as dragons trashed the place. The Mages lost their rhythm under attack. Some turned to fight dragons and the wolf directly. Others flickered through their forms in agitation. Still others continued to consume Jessica, gobbling bites of shadow and looking over their shoulders as if fearing they'd be interrupted at their feast. She was shifting from human to jaguar and back again, moaning. I knew that wasn't good, but I had to choose my priorities.

I went for Meagan.

Trevor appeared beside her when I was halfway across the floor. I shifted shape, livid that he would try to get between me and my friend.

There was no choice.

I was already in deep with my dad.

Meagan gasped in shock when I became a white dragon, spitting sparks in every direction, but Trevor smiled.

"Don't worry, Meagan. I'll defend you." He spoke in that low, soothing tone, the same one Adrian had used on the guys at boot camp. Meagan touched his shoulder, looking at him with a kind of adoration.

Shit.

I spun the ring on my talon, wishing with all my heart for the help of the last Wyvern, who had appeared once before when I was in serious trouble.

Nothing happened. The ring didn't illuminate. There was no red pulse and no answer from wherever it was that the former Wyvern currently resided.

The guys were thrashing Mages on every side, but that didn't change the fact that we were trapped. It was up to me to get all of us out through the barrier of the Mage spell.

And I had to do it alone.

No pressure.

First things first.

I leapt toward Meagan and Trevor, talons bared. Trevor immediately sent up a barrage of spells, singing with low power. They were weak enough—few enough, new enough—that I shredded through their web and managed to scatter some of them. I exhaled a torrent of dragonfire before he could reinforce them. The spell light blackened and fell dead on the carpet, turning to ash underfoot.

Trevor paled and backed away. There was nothing between us and he was too freaked to make more spells.

I didn't intend to give him a chance to make more.

I headed right after him, breathing fire all the way. He stumbled over some wires and bumped into Meagan, who looked less impressed with him than she had.

I felt a presence behind me, smelled that it was Adrian but pretended to be oblivious. I leapt closer to Trevor as if closing in on my kill, felt Adrian raise his hands, then bailed pronto.

I manifested as a salamander on Meagan's shoulder, counting on her fascination with reptiles and knowledge of the *Pyr* to keep her from screaming. She did jump a bit.

"Wyvern?" she whispered, doing the math right on cue.

It's a bonus to have a genius friend.

"Just stick with me, and I'll get you out of here," I said.

She barely nodded, her gaze fixed on Adrian.

He was looking around, his eyes narrowed with suspicion. He started to kick over equipment, looking for me, and Trevor joined the effort. There were still half a dozen Mages singing, and I could have done without the sound.

Plus less volume and/or less music could only help our cause. If nothing else, the spell wouldn't be fed so easily. "Can you unplug the amps?" I asked Meagan.

She nodded again, then eased toward the wall. I hadn't even noticed the fuse box there—Meagan was going for the big kill.

I had to like that.

Trevor and Adrian were still looking for me. They started to argue about who had fucked up.

Time for another surprise.

"Here I go," I said to Meagan, just so she wouldn't be too startled.

She touched my back, encouraging me. I gathered my strength and disappeared, then spontaneously manifested again, right between Adrian and Trevor, a huge white dragon where there was no space for one.

"Looking for me?" I asked as I grabbed them each by the back of the neck. I slammed their heads together as hard as I could.

When I'm in dragon form, that's pretty hard.

They both went down, out cold. A trickle of blood ran from Adrian's nose, which worked for me.

At the same moment, Meagan hit the master switch and the basement went dark. The amps were silenced and even though a few Mages were still singing, I could see by the way the swirl of light dimmed that the spell had taken a hit.

I could see Jessica's limp form on the floor, her shadow in tatters and her body motionless, the golden swirl of spell light illuminating her. In an ideal universe, I would be able to save her, too, but I wasn't even sure it was possible. I had to protect my own kind first.

Just for the record, I wasn't positive that was possible, either.

Time was of the essence.

I shifted back to human form, grabbed Meagan's hand, and raced for the stairs. She should never have been involved in the battle between the shifters—I had to get her out of there. The basement was lit by flame and the occasional spurt of dragonfire. Liam swung his tail to clear a path for us, and Nick decked a couple of Mages. When they were staggering, he ignited their costumes with dragonfire, then laughed as they jumped around, trying to extinguish the flames. Derek stood guard at the bottom of the stairs, his pale eyes filled with menace and his teeth showing. A Mage dared to reach for him, but he snapped, nearly taking off the guy's fingers.

Meagan hesitated at that, but I tugged her toward him. "He's with us," I said and she came with me, even though I knew she wasn't convinced. In a flash of blue, Liam and Nick returned to their human forms, taking up positions behind Meagan.

To her credit, her eyes widened but she didn't say anything.

There was still the problem of the spell that kept us locked in the basement, though, and I wasn't sure how we were going to get through it. It seemed to be congealing at the top of the stairs, like a cork in a bottle. It wove into itself at frantic speed, creating another golden mesh barrier. I had no doubt that it would fold around us if we got close enough—or touched it—just as the other spell had enmeshed Jessica.

There were no windows in the basement—probably by design—and no other way out. We were on the stairs, Meagan and me and Liam and Nick, with Derek snarling at our rear.

I had to use everything I had.

I shifted shape, taking dragon form with a vengeance.

I tried to cut the spell with my talon, just as I had the previous spring.

No luck. My nail bounced off it, not even making a scratch.

That was when the Mages started to sing again.

Their chorus would have made the hair stand up on the back of my neck in human form. As it was, my scales prickled. I glanced back to find them standing at the bottom of the stairs, arranged like a chorus. They were bruised and battered and looked pissed off.

They were singing with passion.

Fortifying the spell.

I was pretty sure they had a taste for more shadows.

"Now what?" Meagan asked in a tiny voice, but I didn't have an answer.

I SHOULD HAVE GUESSED what was happening when I saw the flames that were already burning in the basement begin to flicker in unison.

They moved together, like candles directed by the same wind.

But there was no wind in the basement.

And there was no wind anywhere that could make them burn brighter simultaneously. There was no wind on the planet that could coax all flames to get bigger at once. The flames grew. The fire became more yellow and more hot, gradually turning to huge white flames.

I wondered for an instant whether this was the Mages' work, but I couldn't believe they'd be that interested in ensuring their own incineration. The way they themselves started to look around with alarm supported that conclusion. There was perspiration on more than one face and terror in more than one expression.

Then who? Or what?

I gasped in sudden understanding. Who else had an affinity with fire? Who else could make the element of fire do his bidding? Help had arrived.

"Garrett!" Nick shouted.

"Who?" Meagan asked, just as a massive garnet and gold dragon ripped the basement door off its hinges and flung it aside. He took out part of the ceiling too. Godzilla come to take our side. I heard Meagan gasp and might have gasped myself.

Garrett was magnificent.

The Mages' song faltered big time.

The firelight danced off the golden scales of his chest, lovingly caressing the metallic strength of each one. The Mage spell began to wink out, the mesh thinning as Garrett worked his power. I heard the Mages gather their strength behind me, and I knew we had to take advantage of the spell's weakness before they rebuilt it. I slashed my talon at the spell, and a bit of it broke beneath my touch. Whether it was because of my ring or because it would have shattered anyway was irrelevant.

I shoved Meagan through the gap. Garrett caught her against his chest and continued to roar. The hole wasn't big enough for us to go out in dragon form. But I wanted the strength of my dragon to get us out of there.

The guys were still in human form, still right behind me. I reached back, grabbed Liam and shoved him through the gap. He barely fit, but I was glad to see him safely on the kitchen floor.

When I reached back again, Nick was ready to argue with me. "You go next," he protested, but I snarled at him and flung him through the space.

"Point taken," he said when he landed in a sprawl beside Liam.

The Mages' song broke out with sudden intensity and I saw the gap getting smaller. These spell lines were different. They looked like wire or rebar, and even though Garrett kept trying, he didn't seem able to weaken their spell again.

It really sucked that they were fast learners.

Or maybe they just knew more about the rules than we did.

"Quick!" I said to Derek. He bounded up the stairs toward the hole. It was closing fast, spiraling in with force. There wouldn't be time for both of us to get through.

"Zoë!" Nick and Liam shouted, probably sensing that there was a problem. They raced back to the top of the stairs and reached for me.

But as Derek dashed past me, I shifted shape to my salamander form. I fell on his back and hung on as well as I was able to in his long silver fur.

Just so you know—salamanders don't have a particularly good grip. It's those soft toes.

Derek jumped through the closing hole in the nick of time, yelping when the spell light singed his back paw. Then the spell clanged shut behind us.

It sounded like a big brass gong.

One that would have sealed our collective fate.

But we were all in the kitchen, surrounded by vamps and tramps and costumed kids from school. They were still enchanted, just like the ones in the basement, staring into space like zombies. Frozen in time.

"Let's get the hell out of here," Garrett said. He made it to the bay window in the kitchen in one step, Meagan in his grip, and kicked out the glass. He soared into the sky and I was glad to see her finally safe.

Derek jumped through the broken window behind him. I shouted as I started to slip. I was seriously in need of some sugar and didn't think I could shift again.

"There!" Nick said, pointing to me.

Liam snatched me out of the wolf's fur just before I fell to the ground, then shifted in midstride himself. He ascended into the night with a mighty beat of his wings, Nick in dragon form right behind him. The three *Pyr* flew in formation, ascending ever higher, and I watched Derek trot into the protective shadows.

"What about the other kids?" I asked, as the golden Mage spell fell into chunks and extinguished itself. I heard shouting then, the enchantment over the other kids evidently failing. To my relief, some kids came out of the house and started to yell for help.

They guys hovered and we watched until the fire trucks were arriving at Trevor's house. It took only moments. Pretty much everyone had spilled out on the lawn and they were chattering with excitement as the firemen turned their big hoses on the house. The hiss of flames being extinguished was louder than it should have been.

Once everything looked to have ended well, I shivered, exhausted and feeling vulnerable. There had been evil in that basement and only after we were safely away did I realize how close a call we'd had. My grip on consciousness was slipping and I decided not to fight it.

There'd been enough fighting already.

"Where to?" Garrett asked in old-speak. *"We have to talk."*

"Isabelle," I managed to whisper.

And then the world went black.

I AWAKENED IN HUMAN FORM, crashed on the bed in Isabelle's dorm room. Liam and Nick were sitting on the floor, Meagan was spinning in Isabelle's desk chair, and Garrett was leaning against the door, with his arms folded across his chest.

There was definitely some tension in the air. I noticed that Isabelle was ignoring Nick and Nick was checking his messenger with unnecessary concentration. The back of his neck was red. Liam was glancing between the two of them expectantly.

Garrett rolled his eyes and seemed impatient.

Meagan was stealing glances at Garrett and was a flustered shade of pink. I had a feeling she wasn't going to be dreaming about Trevor anymore.

"Eat this," Isabelle said as soon as my eyes opened, handing me a chocolate-coated granola bar.

Meagan smiled at me, which was an encouraging sign. "So I guess this is what you weren't supposed to tell me." There was laughter in her tone.

I smiled. "Pretty much."

She slanted a glance at Garrett and her blush deepened. "Another one of your dad's friend's sons?"

I nodded, too busy chewing to say much more. I swallowed. "I'm sorry. We're not supposed to reveal ourselves in both forms to any humans."

"But you defended me from Suzanne."

"And I'm already in big trouble for that." I grimaced. "I'm sorry. I wanted to tell you." We looked at each other and maybe we would have hugged if we'd been alone. Then I did the introductions. "Meagan, Garrett. Garrett, Meagan."

Garrett smiled and shook Meagan's hand, his fingers almost engulfing hers. He'd bulked up even more over the summer. Meagan visibly swallowed, then gave me a look. She dropped her voice to a whisper and leaned toward me. "Can my dad be friends with your dad?"

I grinned, knowing I had to warn her. "They can hear you. We have sharper senses than humans."

She blushed even more crimson then. Garrett smiled a little but pretended not to notice.

I took the last bite of the granola bar, feeling my body respond quickly to the food.

Predictably, Meagan was making all the connections while I was recovering. "And that's why Suzanne calls you a freak?"

I nodded.

She grinned at me. "I knew you were lying when you said you didn't believe in the *Pyr*. I just didn't guess this was why." She glanced around the room, obviously awed that she now knew not just one but four dragon shifters.

Her gaze lingered on Garrett a little bit longer.

"You would have figured it out."

Meagan pushed up her glasses and considered me. "So, now that I know some, do I get to know the rest? Or do I only get half of the story?"

"We can't," Nick said in old-speak.

"We have to," I argued in kind. *"She's got innate spellsinging talent."*

"And I bet we need her help," Liam added.

Garrett inhaled sharply and spoke for the rest, his tone authoritative. *"Tell her."*

Meagan glanced around herself. "Old-speak," she said. "I read about old-speak on that Web site. That's what it was when I thought I heard thunder, wasn't it?"

I smiled and nodded. "See? Another day or so and you would have had it all."

"They can talk to each other at a really low frequency," Isabelle said. "We humans hear it as thunder."

"Then you're not a dragon either?"

"Just raised by one." Isabelle offered the others some of her chocolate stash. Meagan took one.

She looked around. "What were you saying to each other just now?"

Isabelle smiled. "Something they don't want us to hear, probably."

"We were deciding whether to tell you the whole deal," Liam said to Meagan.

"Zoë says yes, and we agree," Garrett added and Meagan blushed again.

"Because you have a power that Mages can use. They're trying to recruit you," I said. "You have to know it all."

Meagan's eyes widened.

Isabelle cleared her throat, maybe giving Meagan a minute to absorb that. "Even though I've had the rundown of events, I don't understand how Garrett broke the spell."

"Or why you couldn't," Liam said to me.

"Or why you were even here," Nick said to Garrett.

"I figured out the book and came to tell you about it," Garrett said. "Zoë wasn't at home or at Meagan's place, so I followed your scents and realized pretty quickly that you were in trouble."

"Lucky for us," Liam said. "What about the spell?" he asked me.

"The ring didn't work this time. And my nail didn't cut the spell mesh the way it did before."

"Shit," Nick said. "Do you think they've changed their spell?"

"Time to tell us what you found in that book," I said to Garrett and he nodded.

"It's strange and you're not going to like it much." Garrett pulled out his messenger and tapped up the file. "I should probably share the scanned file with someone for safekeeping. I don't want them to guess that we have it, though."

"Send it to my desktop," Isabelle said. "I'm not *Pyr* and they're less likely to target me."

I wasn't sure of that and I could see that Garrett had his doubts as well. "Send it to Meagan, too," I suggested and she gave him her messenger address, stammering a little.

I liked that he pretended not to notice.

He sent the file and Meagan started to read it on her messenger even as he talked about it.

"Like I told you earlier, the original is really old. It looks handwritten and the book has ancient binding. I hid it in my mom's bookstore, because we might need it again."

"It was in Latin?" Liam asked, pulling up the file on Isabelle's desktop. She had a big screen and we all looked at the text. It made no sense to me.

Garrett nodded. "Once I scanned the pages and digitized the text, I ran it through a utility that translated it to English. It was pretty slow and there are breaks where letters weren't legible."

"And probably other places where it's just enigmatic," Meagan said.

"Right," Garrett agreed. "The text seems to be a handbook or guide for apprentice Mages."

"Lots of music theory," Meagan said, nodding as she scanned through it. She paused and frowned. "They find minor keys particularly powerful."

I remembered what she'd said about Jared's music and sat up to contribute what I knew. "The humans who can become Mages have an innate musical talent. They call those people spellsingers. Their musical gift allows them to evoke a strong emotional response from other humans, in essence to enchant with their song or their music. If they never met a Mage, they would just be good performers with this gift."

"But the Mages pervert this natural inclination and use it to gain power over other people," Garrett said. "And more is better. So they specifically listen for people with this talent and try to recruit them."

"Apprentice Mages, like Trevor," Liam said.

"And Adrian," I said.

"Whatever happened to him?' Nick asked.

"He was there tonight, wearing a glamour. Didn't you see that blond kid dressed as a construction worker?"

The guys were shocked. "*That* was Adrian?" Liam asked.

"Live and in person."

"So, there are Mages and apprentice Mages," Meagan said, returning to the story. "But what's the point?"

Garrett gestured to the displayed text. "The point is to bring back the master Mages. The master Mages pushed their powers to the limit and lost their physical forms. So the plan is to build a big enough group of Mages to create enough spellpower to make it possible for the master Mages to manifest again."

I nodded. "So they get power for their spells by eliminating shifters and assuming our forms—"

"Which the master Mages can then utilize," Garrett added.

"—plus recruiting spellsingers to increase the power of their spells."

"But what about Jessica?" Meagan asked." What were they doing to her tonight?"

“I’m not exactly sure.” Garrett looked grim. “But the master Mages are called ShadowEaters.”

II

There was an outbreak of questions at that, but Garrett answered one from Meagan first.

"How?" she asked when there was a lull.

He smiled at her, and I wondered whether something was starting between them.

"The book lays out a development plan for apprentice Mages. It starts with the question of identifying spellsingers, then has lessons on building spellsinging power, and the casting of spells for deliberate results. There's a lot of talk about shadows and darkness and death that doesn't make a lot of sense to me."

"Might be a code," Meagan said. "That was a common way to hide arcane knowledge in books. Zoë and I can probably crack it."

"I never thought of that," Garrett said. "That'd be great."

"If we have time," Nick said.

"The first section ends with something called the Invocation of Midnight. It seems to be a ceremony that allows the Mages to become ShadowEaters. It's like a graduation ceremony, but there are lots of warnings about not doing it too soon."

"When's too soon?" Liam asked.

“I’ll guess it’s when you can’t shift back to your human form,” I said and Garrett nodded.

“That seems to be what happened to this last bunch. They did it too early, before there was enough spellsinging power for there to be a return trip.”

“A successful ceremony requires the NightBlade.” Meagan mused, scrolling through the text.

“What’s that?” Liam looked from Meagan to Garrett.

“It doesn’t say,” Garrett answered. “At least not clearly. But you need it for the ceremony at the end of the next section, the Invocation of the Eclipse.”

“Why?” Nick asked.

“Because in that one you make a sacrifice with the NightBlade.”

We shuddered in unison.

“Is that what we saw?” I asked. “Is that what they were doing to Jessica?”

“I don’t think so,” Garrett said. “Or maybe it was just practice. Because the Invocation of the Eclipse has to happen on the night of a full moon.”

Isabelle got up and checked her calendar. “That’s not until November 15, more than two weeks away.”

The day before my birthday. Coincidence?

“But why Jessica?” Meagan asked. “What did she ever do to them?”

There was a beat of silence. “Did any of you see her shift forms?”

“She looked like a cat at the end,” Liam said.

“A jaguar,” I corrected. “They wanted her because she’s a shifter.”

“Wait a minute,” Meagan said. “You lost me on the curve there.”

“The Mages are targeting different kinds of shifters,” I said. “The idea being that once they’ve eliminated all of us, they’ll control our forms.”

“And the ShadowEaters can use them,” Meagan said with a nod.

“Last spring this Kohana guy, who is a Thunderbird shifter, told Zoë that there were only four kinds of shifters left,” Liam said.

“Right before he lied to Zoë and tried to make it three,” Nick said.

“Because he’s helping the Mages, maybe hoping to get some amnesty for Thunderbirds,” Garrett said.

“Thunderbirds, dragons,” Meagan counted on her fingers, then looked around.

"Jaguars and wolves," Liam supplied.

"You had a wolf with you," she said to Liam. "Is he one?"

Liam nodded. "You know him from school."

She glanced at me.

"Derek," I said and her eyes widened.

"Is that why he likes you? Because he knows what you are?"

"He *likes* you?" Nick teased and I blushed right on cue.

"What about Jared?" Isabelle asked.

"I don't know," I said to Meagan, trying to ignore them. "But he did know what I am, right from the start."

"He seems to turn up at the right times," Liam said. "Should you trust him so much?"

"He says he can see several minutes into the future," I told them. "A very short range of foresight. And he can smell even things that we can't discern, like emotions."

"Wow," Nick said. "That's cool."

"It would be better if we knew more about his allegiances," Garrett said.

"He says he's like an emissary from the wolves," I said. "They have a prophecy that they have to make a union with other shifters and follow the dragon, but some aren't big on having a girl as pack leader."

"That's his story," Nick said. "How do we know it's true?"

Nobody knew the answer to that.

"So how come you're all at the same school?" Meagan asked.

Isabelle cleared her throat. "Maybe the Mages are targeting the new generation."

"And Jessica? What do you know about her and the jaguars?" Nick asked.

"Nothing. I had no idea that she was a jaguar shifter, not until last night," I admitted. "I think maybe Derek knew." I thought for a minute. "That might explain Trevor's interest in her."

"But what happened to her?" Meagan asked.

There was a beat of silence and then I said it. "I think she might be dead."

We fidgeted then, all of us uncomfortable with the prospect.

"But what if she isn't?" Meagan asked. "What if they're planning to do this big ceremony on the full moon and sacrifice her then? How can we find her? Could we save her?"

Garrett grimaced. "It could be like stepping into a trap."

"But Meagan's right—we can't just abandon her," Nick said.

"*If* she's still alive," Liam said. "We need to know for sure before we take that risk."

"Can you ask your cards?" I asked Isabelle.

Isabelle shuffled for a long time. I wasn't sure whether she was trying to focus or was avoiding the question. Then she handed the deck to Meagan. "You were closest to her. Will you shuffle?"

"Sure." I could tell that Meagan was thrilled.

"You need to focus on Jessica. Think about your question."

"Is she dead or alive?" Meagan said, nodding with resolve. She closed her eyes and shuffled the cards for a few minutes, then handed them back to Isabelle.

Isabelle cut the deck and turned up the card.

The Devil.

"What does that mean?" Garrett asked, leaning forward.

"Nothing good, I'll guess," Liam said.

"She's in hell?" Meagan asked.

Isabelle shook her head. "The Devil is a card that denotes slavery or entrapment. It can mean that someone is a slave to physical pleasure, for example, or that they're literally beholden to someone else. The person is trapped, either by choice or by circumstance."

"So, she's their captive, somewhere," I said.

"But why?" Nick asked. "What's the point?"

"Maybe she's bait," Garrett said. "Maybe they think that holding her will draw other shifters."

"Or the rest of the jaguars," Liam suggested.

Nick frowned. "I wonder whether Jessica is their equivalent of the Wyvern."

"Their wildcard," Isabelle said with a nod.

"Kohana told me last spring that there's a wildcard in every kind," I said. "One who can do more than most. And he implied that he and I are the wildcards in our respective kinds. If Derek is acting as an emissary, maybe that's how he got the job."

"Maybe you wildcards are the ones who have to make the treaty Derek talked about," Liam suggested.

I shivered again then, not wanting to experience whatever they had done—or were doing—to Jessica.

"That's it," Isabelle said with a nod. "They've cast a spell to draw you together so they can eliminate all the wildcards at once."

"Because if they eliminate the wildcards, there's no chance of that union happening," I said with excitement.

"Which means the Mages will win," Nick added.

"Which would also explain Jessica and Derek being at your school," Liam said.

"Kohana, too." Garrett said.

"So, are we going to help Jessica?" Meagan asked, looking around the group. We nodded as one, staring at the card.

"We have to," Liam said.

"We can't leave another shifter trapped like that," Nick said.

"But the real question," Garrett said, "is how we *can* help her."

No one had the answer to that.

WE AGREED that we needed to take some time to rest and keep thinking. Garrett and Nick escorted us back to Meagan's house and Liam remained behind to watch over Isabelle, just in case.

I probably wasn't the only one who noticed how Nick and Isabelle were pointedly ignoring each other, and that he didn't volunteer to defend her. I couldn't see the point in starting a discussion with him just yet, though. Plus I knew that anything I said to him aloud or in old-speak would be overheard by Garrett. I knew the guys were too bagged to carry me, so I shifted to dragon form myself for the sake of expediency.

We didn't talk much. I just flew beside Nick over the city, noting how the guys stayed on either side of me. Protective. I liked that. Meagan was clearly thrilled to have another ride from Garrett and her eyes were shining when we set down in the park across from the house.

We agreed to meet back there first thing in the morning. The guys took off quickly, their scales looking gilded in the streetlights, and Meagan sighed.

Then she flicked me a look and smiled. She touched her ear, a question in her expression and I nodded agreement. She was right—they'd be able to hear anything she said. She fluttered her fingers against her heart and I grinned.

Sometimes words just get in the way.

"So, you're the dragon who defended me," she said as we walked through the snow to her house. "Twice."

"What are friends for?" I joked and she grinned at me.

"I liked the idea of it being a guy dragon."

"Well, what about Garrett? He defended you."

Meagan blushed as red as a beet and pulled out her messenger. I could see that she was scrolling through the text Garrett had shared. "We need to beat the Mages, but we have to crack the code on this mumbo jumbo to find out more."

"Two weeks to the full moon doesn't give us much time," I said. "Still, we have to try." I walked beside her for a minute, choosing my words. "Look, you have to be really careful."

"Me? Why?"

"Because you've got spellsinging abilities and the Mages know it. I'm afraid they're going to try to recruit you...."

"Don't worry about me, Zoë."

"I am worried about you. They don't take no for an answer and you could get hurt."

She stopped with one hand on the door and looked at me. "How do you know that?"

"Because they tried to recruit Jared, and he tried to decline, but they've been using him anyway." I thought about his conviction—and Kohana's assertion—that they would use him to get to me, and I feared they'd do the same with Meagan.

"Then give me his number," she said easily. "I'll ask him for advice."

"But..."

"Zoë, I can take care of it. You've got to figure out how to make this union work, save the shifters and defeat the Mages."

Right.

"If I can convince them to follow me," I had to say. "And if I had a plan."

"But think about it. If your powers as Wyvern mean that you could foil the Mages' plan single-handedly, that would be a good reason for the wolves to have a prophecy about following you."

She was right.

But how could I persuade the other shifters to work with us? Derek's wolves needed me to do some big wolf thing to prove I could be a good pack leader. Jessica had been captured by the Mages and we dragons hadn't managed to save her. And Kohana seemed determined to surrender any of us in order to defend the Thunderbirds. If I could bring him—the most reluctant ally—into the union, maybe the others would follow.

But how?

A little bit too late, I realized I'd lost a negotiating tool when I'd had it right in my claws.

I should never have relinquished the feathers I'd tugged out of Kohana's tail during our last fight. It's dangerous for a shifter to lose the cloak of his alternate form. We have to keep track of both to be able to shift between forms. We dragons have to keep track of both our clothes and our scales. It must be the same for Kohana—he'd need his clothes and his feathers. There are tons of stories about people stealing the seal skins of selkies or the pelts of werewolves and holding the shifter in thrall. Those stories are based in truth.

I'd had some of Kohana's feathers. That could have given me some power over him, or at least an edge for negotiation, but I hadn't thought of it at the time. It seemed unlikely that I'd be able to find those particular feathers again. I could only assume Kohana would have gathered them up if it could be done.

I wondered if I could get my hands on more.

And if so, could I use them to get him and the Thunderbirds on our side?

It was long after Meagan had run out of superlatives to describe Garrett's dragon form—never mind his human one—and I was still staring at the ceiling of her room. I could hear the slow rhythm of her breathing, the quiet impact of snowflakes outside, the resonant hiss of two dragons on the roof, breathing dragonsmoke.

I closed my eyes, and missed my dad—well, actually, I missed our night flights over the city. I didn't much miss getting chewed out or barricaded within a ring of dragonsmoke. We never talked much when we flew, except for his occasional tips on technique, uttered in old-speak. And even as frustrated as I was with him, a night flight would have been good. I was restless.

Fortunately, there were other dragons in my proximity.

And I had just about nothing left to lose in terms of my dad's approval. He was already livid with me—or would be, once he figured out the full range of my disobedience. At this point, I had to save the day, somehow, in order to survive the reckoning that was coming.

Even then, the odds against me were long.

Right now, I needed the ego boost of being a dragon.

I slipped out of bed and pulled on my jeans and sweater. I crept out of Meagan's bedroom without disturbing her. The dead bolt on the front door made a slight snick when I unlocked it and I froze in the foyer, certain that I'd be caught, but no one stirred.

I could hear Meagan and both of her parents breathing at the slow rate of sleep.

Once outside the door, I raced around the house to the dark shadows of the back garden. I bounded into the air and shifted shape, loving the power of my body. I soared to the roof easily, and Garrett smiled at the sight of me.

"Wondered how long it would take you," he said in old-speak.

"Anyone want to fly with me?"

They exchanged glances and then Nick straightened. He spread his golden wings wide, stretching. *"I'm up for it."*

"I'll stay here," Garrett said.

I leapt off the roof, hearing the swoosh of Nick's wings behind me. I beat my wings hard, racing him a little, heading straight for the stratosphere. It felt so good that any repercussions of the parental variety would be worth it. The falling snow swirled around us, as if we were dancing with it. I saw the gleam of golden scales to my right as Nick came up beside me.

He grinned as he soared past. "You're not that fast."

"Faster than you think!" I pushed harder and caught up to him. "Losing your edge, Nick?"

"Not yet." He hooted and flew even faster.

"You just don't want to lose to a girl!" I taunted, sailing past him one more time.

He laughed and came raging up behind me. He caught my tail to hold me back, and I spun around to cuff him playfully. We wrestled, rolling through the air, our scales shining like jewels in the night.

Once upon a time, physical intimacy like this with Nick would have stopped my heart cold. Now he was like a big brother—another one—just a guy I could tease and harass and whose company I could enjoy. We cavorted through the air, each giving the other a talon as necessary to keep the game going.

I saw the glint of mischief in his eye just before he spiraled down into the city. He looked like a feathered golden spear, but one that turned corners with grace. I knew he was up to trouble, and was curious to see what he had in mind. I raced behind him, then laughed when I saw where he was going.

He buzzed the webcam of the local television station, flashing dragon teeth for the camera. Then he lifted his tail, like he was mooning it, even without pants. I laughed, wondering what anyone watching would make of that display.

I knew what the dads would make of it.

We spun together, showing off, then raced for the clouds, claw in claw. We pushed ourselves to go higher and faster, streaming through the night until we were panting for breath.

We landed on the top of the Willis Tower, beside the antennae, and surveyed the city in triumph.

"It's cool, isn't it?" Nick said with satisfaction.

I was still out of breath. "What is?"

"Being a dragon. Being powerful. Being able to breathe fire." He gestured with one claw at the twinkling city, dusted with snow. It didn't even look real from here. "Being able to fly."

His words reminded me of the ride that I owed Jared, the one I might never be able to deliver, and that flattened my mood. "Good and bad," I said.

He considered me, probably noticing my change of tone. "What's bad about it?"

"I still can't do everything I'm supposed to be able to do."

"But you can do a lot more than before." Nick shrugged with his usual confidence. "And we had enough ammo to finish those Mages tonight. Tell me that wasn't exciting."

"I don't think they're finished."

"So we live to fight another day." He grinned at me. "Our dads fought *Slayers* for centuries before they defeated them. Consider it part of the adventure. Imagine how good it will feel when we totally finish them." He bumped shoulders with me. "Come on, Zoë. What's really eating you? Is it that Jared isn't around? Where'd he go, anyway?"

I chose between reasons, because there was something I wanted to know. "Your dad warned him that I might not ultimately have a firestorm with him and so he bailed." Only half of the story, but Nick looked away, frowning. I knew I'd struck a nerve. "I'm thinking that it sucks that we don't get to choose who we fall in love with—or even if we do fall in love, we can't act on it until we know about the firestorm. The choice is made for us."

"Worked out all right for our parents."

"Aside from mine splitting up," I had to note. Nick eyed me and I saw his wariness. "I don't know. Maybe they will. Maybe they won't. The fact that they're thinking about it isn't much of an endorsement, though, is it?"

"They'll work it out," he insisted. "They did before. They love each other, don't they? Isn't that what counts?"

I thought of the things my mom had said about my dad always choosing the *Pyr* over her and I wasn't sure that love was enough.

"But what if the firestorm doesn't work out?" I asked.

"What?" Nick was incredulous. "It has to. That's the way it works."

It was my turn to stare at the city. I didn't think it was that simple. I heaved a sigh. "What if the old plan for us doesn't work anymore?"

Nick swallowed and spoke with force. "You make it work."

"How so?"

"You make more *Pyr*. You do what you can. You try to do what's right." He said this last word with even more emphasis and glared stubbornly over the city. It was all black and white to him.

I had to say it. "Do you really think you're doing the right thing by staying away from Isabelle?"

Nick avoided my gaze. "It might be." He turned to look at me before I could argue. "The firestorm is right," he said with force and I wondered who he was trying to convince. "And I will follow it. I won't make promises I might not be able to keep."

"But she thinks that you're meant to be together."

Nick looked down. He tapped his nails on the lip of the roof, thinking. "I hope she's right," he admitted so quietly that I had to strain to hear him.

Then he looked at me, his gaze tormented. "But what if she's wrong? What if we're just attracted to each other? What if it's just sex?"

I didn't know what to say to that.

Nick's voice dropped low. "If my firestorm is with someone else, I have a duty to my kind. We all do. And I'll have a duty to my son, whenever I have one."

"Your dad reminded you of this."

Nick looked away. "It would be easy to be with Isabelle, Zoë, but in the end, it might be wrong. It would hurt her more if I had to turn away from her later."

"So you're turning away now."

He dropped his head. "Sometimes you're crazy enough about someone to protect them even from yourself." And this time, when he met my gaze, his was clear with conviction.

I felt better for having Nick explain himself to me. He wasn't being a jerk, like Isabelle thought. He was being thoughtful. Considerate.

"They say patience is a virtue," I said, smiling at him. "But I think waiting bites."

Nick laughed and made a mock bite in my direction. I snapped back at him, and we leapt into the air simultaneously. We swung our tails and played at fighting again. Then Nick pointed back down to our neighborhood. "Race you to the roof!"

"Last one there is *Slayer* bait!" I retorted, using an old taunt from our childhood. We flung ourselves through the sky.

Nick was ahead of me, all golden strength.

"Look! It's Isabelle!" I cried and he halted to look.

"Where?"

"Not here, fool." I raced past him, laughing as he roared behind me. He caught my tail and spun me around. We fell onto the roof of the town house in a tangle of talons and scales, laughing all the while.

I shoved a fistful of snow into his face. He breathed fire at me in mock fury and I swung around to swat him. He caught my wing and we wrestled on the roof. I couldn't get a good hit in because we were laughing too hard.

"Nice quiet return," Garrett noted. *"I bet no one will notice."*

"Anything happen while we were gone?" Nick asked, brushing himself off and taking a serious tone.

Garrett shrugged. *"Just that."*

I realized suddenly that there were a lot of cats meowing. They were making that yowl that tomcats make at night, but it sounded like there were a lot more of them than was typical. I hadn't even noticed any tomcats around Meagan's house before.

"There must be hundreds of them," Garrett said. I looked at him in surprise. *"It started about an hour ago. And keeps getting louder."*

We stood up and looked as the cries became steadily louder. I could see the silhouettes of dozens of cats in the street. Maybe hundreds. They were all different colors—soot gray with white socks, black with white tuxedo bibs, ginger and tortoiseshell and whiter than snow. They walked with the delicate precision of cats, silent but purposeful. They clung to the shadows, as if they didn't want to be seen, but the gleam of their eyes gave them away.

Like gemstones shining in the dark.

They also were moving in the same direction, as if they gravitated toward some unknown destination. I wondered—were they all shifters? Or were cats in general drawn to a cat shifter's distress? What were they going to do? Where were they going?

"They're gathering," Nick said.

But why?

Then I noticed that something else had changed. I could see the orange swirl of Mage spell, bright again, winding out of the sewer grates with greater potency than before.

They were up to something, spinning their web and making it stronger. Were they feeding on Jessica's strength? What was the deal with the cats?

Were they drawn to Jessica's distress? Or were they leading the way for us? Was she still alive, then?

I saw a black cat hesitate on the lip of a sewer opening. It looked around, then stared straight at me. It held my gaze for a long moment, then turned and slipped through the grate, as sinuous as a snake.

Gone as surely as if it had never been.

I felt a shadow pass over me, and it chilled me to the bone.

"What is it?" Nick asked and I told them what I could see.

No one liked that news.

Garrett looked grim. *"We should sleep while we can."*

I wondered, though, whether I would ever sleep again, with my thoughts spinning so fast.

Like a Mage spell.

I watched the orange light, tugging down into the world beneath the city. I thought about the cats, maybe answering some summons we couldn't discern.

That was when I knew exactly what we had to do next. We had to go down into the sewers, just like those cats, and confront the Mages in their den.

Wherever it turned out to be.

I DIDN'T TELL the others my plan until the morning, when we all met up in the park. I'd spent the night trying to think of alternatives, but hadn't come up with a single one.

Predictably, there was dissent. The guys weren't big on risk, especially with so many unknown variables. Meagan was instantly ready to go and help her buddy.

We decided to vote.

Meagan voted first, in favor of the quest, then spent time busily researching the Chicago underground on her messenger. She was so proud of herself for finding maps that I didn't have the heart to tell her that we wouldn't need them.

I'd just follow the spell light.

Nick was sure the light I'd seen was a lure to draw us into a trap. Garrett pointed out that we weren't sure of Jessica's motives. Had she been targeted by the Mages and trapped? Or was she complicit with them, like Kohana? Liam wondered whether Jessica's capture was just an illusion, meant to draw us closer. Meagan was insulted by that idea, but before they could argue, Isabelle drew another card.

She'd been quietly shuffling the whole time. She brushed aside the snow on the park bench, then snapped the card onto the painted wood.

THE CHARIOT.

"Always the court cards when Zoë is around," she murmured with a smile. We waited expectantly. "THE CHARIOT indicates a conflict being resolved. Someone intervening in a situation."

"Like a rescue?" Liam said and Isabelle nodded.

"It has a military sense, like a planned campaign being executed."

"Successfully?" Garrett asked.

Isabelle nodded again. "It indicates preparation and planning, so check your plan and coordinate it. But yes, the card is right side up, which means triumph."

"Upside down for Zoë," Derek said softly.

I jumped to find him behind me, in his quiet human form. The guys looked startled—they hadn't heard him approach, either.

But he was right. Isabelle could have placed it on the other side of the bench, but she'd put it between us. I stared at the card as the guys reviewed events of the night before and planned their assault.

Was I crazy to let that detail bother me? What did the card mean when it was reversed? Failure? A temporary victory? Either possibility spooked me.

But it didn't much matter. The guys were on board. Derek and Meagan and Isabelle were in. We didn't have to tally the vote to know that we were going underground.

It had been my idea in the first place, so I couldn't bail.

OUR THINKING WAS that the Mages would be tired after their festivities of the night before. They'd be expecting us to take time to regroup. We would strike early and fast, before we were anticipated, and maybe have surprise on our side.

It was all a rationalization, but we convinced each other of its merit.

Meagan located access points to the underground on her map and we tried them in succession. The first manhole we tested was locked down or stuck. The second was on a street that bustled with traffic, probably because it was close to a big church.

The third was on a quiet side street. It also seemed to be locked, but Nick was impatient. He shifted shape quickly and hauled it open in his dragon form. Garrett went first into the hole, Meagan right behind him. Liam and Isabelle followed, then Derek, then me. Nick shifted back to his human form while we were slipping into the wet darkness, then pulled the manhole cover over the opening again.

Sealing us in darkness.

There was a ladder fixed to the side of the shaft and we descended in silence. Every sound echoed and was magnified, and we seemed to understand as one the need for quiet.

I could hear water running.

I could smell sewage—although I didn't need *Pyr* powers of perception for that.

And, thanks to my new ring, I could see the dizzy orange swirl of Mage spell light. It emanated clearly from one direction. It danced in spirals, tugging deeper into the system. I pointed and the others followed me, letting me lead the way.

The guys arrayed themselves behind me, Isabelle between Garrett and Liam, Meagan between Liam and Nick. There was a faint shimmer around the guys, as they were agitated enough to be on the cusp of change.

It said something for my state of mind that the sudden brilliant shimmer of light blue to my right reassured me. It reassured me even more when a silver gray wolf matched my stride, his pale eyes shining with wariness. I buried my fingers in the silken fur at Derek's neck and felt the tension in him.

It was the kind of place where a person could do with a pet predator.

12

I don't know how long we walked, never mind how far. The spell light was swirling ahead of me, leading me on a golden path that seemed to take us deeper and deeper into the underground. There was water in the bottom of the tunnel, but we walked to the left and the right of it, keeping our feet mostly dry.

It got colder. It got darker beyond the spell light. It was impossible to guess the amount of time that had passed. There were boarded-up passageways and blocked tunnels, but the spell cut a steady course through the darkness.

Like a thousand threads, twining together into a thicker rope.

Or a spiderweb, drawing its victims into a place of no return.

It was strange because I had this sense of dread, yet at the same time, the radiant spell had a soothing effect. Maybe it lulled me into complacency. It was pretty. It had a pleasant glow. It made me feel serene and outside of any tension.

Maybe the spiderweb analogy was a good one. Don't spiders drug their victims so they struggle less?

Either way, we drifted along the path that was laid for us, lulled into believing that we'd made our choice and now had to follow it to the end.

There wasn't a lot of conversation.

We weren't alone either. Derek kept looking over his shoulder and snarling into the shadows behind us. I finally looked back to see, and realized that not only did the spell light dim noticeably right behind us—like it was gathering us close—but there was a procession of cats heading in the same direction.

The cats from the street. They walked a little higher up the sides of the tunnel to keep their feet dry. They trailed behind us, as if trying to avoid the full power of the spell light. They also seemed to be enchanted by it. I saw one sitting in a side tunnel, batting at a swirl of gold as if it were a butterfly.

Then the cat rubbed against it, its expression euphoric.

A moment later it joined the procession.

What was going on with these cats? Were they another variety of cat shifter? Were they drawn to the plight of a jaguar shifter? I know cats tend to be mysterious, but this was extraordinary.

Another cat mewled at Isabelle from a side tunnel. He was a big handsome cat with presence to spare, sitting like a statue. He looked almost leonine, with a mane of long fur framing his face, his coat striped in coal black and gold. He had a white bib and white socks, and golden eyes. He purred with loud approval when Isabelle scooped him up into her arms.

"He must weigh thirty pounds," she said with surprise, hefting him higher.

"Then leave him behind," Nick suggested in an undertone. "You don't need the extra responsibility." I saw that he was nervous, too, his gaze darting back and forth. Even though he couldn't see the spells, he must be feeling their effect.

And trying to fight them.

Isabelle's eyes flashed and she hugged the cat more tightly. "Not a chance. That's not what I do." She and Nick glared at each other for a charged moment, and then Nick turned away.

"We've got to make sure we keep Zoë's back," Nick said to Garrett. "Not like the last time."

Garrett nodded, strain in his features. "It gets to you, doesn't it?"

"What's it like for you guys?" I asked.

"Like an earworm, a song you can't get out of your mind," Garrett said. "A pulsing, insistent one."

"A violent one," Nick agreed, wiping sweat from his brow. "Feeding doubt."

"Just don't give it anything to root in," Liam said. "Remember that we're a team and we're not going to split ranks."

"*Pyr* forever," Garrett said grimly and the guys nodded as one.

"One for all and all for one," I teased in old-speak, but they didn't smile.

They just crowded a little closer.

I saw Isabelle's expression soften as she watched Nick, but I had bigger responsibilities at the moment than fixing their relationship.

"What do you see it doing, anyway?" Nick asked me.

"Getting brighter. We're arriving somewhere."

"Can't get there soon enough," Garrett said. "This pulsing in my head is going to drive me crazy."

"That's the point," Liam said. "Fight it!"

"So we'll be all worn-out by the time we really need to fight," Nick muttered. "Fucking brilliant strategy."

Meagan hummed something that sounded familiar.

"Mozart's Eine Kleine Nachtmusik," Isabelle said.

"Also known as Serenade no. 13 in G Major," Meagan answered and continued to hum. I'm not sure whether it kept spells at bay or not, but we all tried to join in. It's a memorable piece of music, though not easy to hum.

We walked a bit faster.

The cat settled against Isabelle, his gaze flicking between Derek and me, that luxuriant tail lashing at the air. I must have looked at him too long, because he bared his teeth to hiss at me.

Fine. I wasn't in the mood to make friends anyway.

The tunnels were getting bigger in diameter. I couldn't even sense how high this one stretched overhead. It had to be four or five times my height. The concrete radiated a chill that went right through my bones.

The swirling spell light was getting brighter.

Just when I thought I couldn't stand the tension much longer, we turned a corner and the tunnel widened even more. Daylight was visible far ahead, as if the tunnel dumped out. There was a frenzy of Mage spell light crisscrossing that opening, almost blinding me with its intensity.

"Uh-oh," I said and Derek snarled.

“Let’s get out of here!” Nick said. The guys pushed past me and ran for the opening. They couldn’t see the spell light.

It was a lure, one that would trap them!

“Look out!” I shouted and raced after them. Derek galloped beside me. Even the cats hurried.

“No!” I shouted. “Stop! It’s a trap! There’s a spell over the opening, like a net!”

They ignored me. The girls did, too.

I ran faster, and kept shouting.

Suddenly Derek halted and turned back. He growled. I saw the hair stand up on the back of his shoulders, and his ears flattened against his head. He was staring back the way we had come. I looked back and strained my ears.

Water. I could hear water.

A *lot* of water.

The others heard it, too.

That made them stop and glance back. Once they looked away from the opening and that network of spell light, they seemed to recover themselves and comprehend what I had said.

“Zoë?” Nick said, his voice strained. “What do we do?”

There was a splash as a wall of water collided with that last corner. It frothed and the wave of it swelled; then it gushed toward us like an ocean wave.

No—like a tsunami.

It filled at least a third of the tunnel’s height and it was headed straight for us.

“Fuck!” Nick shouted.

“Holy shit!” Garrett cried and grabbed for Meagan. “Link hands!”

We grabbed hands as we ran away from the water. At least we’d keep track of each other in the deluge.

“Wait. We’ll be washed right into the spell trap!” I shouted. “Like fish in a net.”

“That can’t be good,” Liam muttered. The cat arched his back and lashed his tail, spitting. Isabelle held him more tightly.

“What do we do, Zoë?” Garrett demanded. “Drown or get trapped by Mages?”

There were no good choices and the water was surging closer. I had the scruff of Derek's neck in one hand and Meagan's hand clutched in my other. There was a cat winding around her ankles, a soot-colored one with white socks, and she snatched it up. She held it tightly against her chest, her eyes wide with fear.

But there was one thing we *could* do.

"Shift!" I shouted to the guys and let the shimmer rock through my body.

In a heartbeat, I was in dragon form and took flight in the tunnel. I snatched up both Derek and Meagan as I went, lifting them above the sudden flood. Meagan's fingers dug into me in panic, the water lapping at her feet. The herd of cats howled and yelped as they were washed away in the torrent.

The guys had followed my lead immediately and shifted, the pale blue light of the change illuminating the tunnel. Garrett had snatched up Isabelle. Liam hovered in the middle, watching the water with concentration. It churned beneath us, racing for the opening, murky and dark.

Fortunately, the tunnel was big enough for us to hover above the water.

So far.

Nick reached over and took Meagan from me. "Why didn't we think of that right away?" he asked with irritation. "Why do they have to screw with our heads like this?"

"Because they can," Garrett said.

The water gurgled and sloshed around that corner and it was clear that there was more coming. "Time for Plan B," Nick said, looking at me. We flew a little higher, crowding against the top of the tunnel. I hit my wings on the concrete with every beat, but it was better than drowning.

Soon more water surged around that bend.

And it flowed faster.

We were either going to drown or be Mage bait.

I had to do something.

I turned the ring on my talon and whispered in old-speak. *"Help me, Sophie. Help us, please."*

My mouth went dry. Would Sophie help me again? Or was her assistance a one-time offer? We could use all the help we could get. If there were still a pair of ghostly genies trapped in the ring, they might know what to do.

I saw the ring pulse with red.

I felt it spin of its own accord. My heart skipped in anticipation and I dared to hope.

Then the light went out. The ring turned cold. It stopped turning on my talon.

Sophie had declined to respond.

Shit.

I looked at the raging water and heard the guys' panic. The water seemed to be moving even faster.

I caught my breath as another wave crashed around the corner, nearly filling the tunnel to the top. It headed straight for us. The guys crowded higher against the top of the tunnel.

And a black bird soared around the corner in the last sliver of space. He had blazing yellow eyes and carried a lightning bolt in each claw. He flew straight toward me, his purpose clear as he sped up.

This was the chance I'd been hoping for.

Derek barked.

I roared with dragonfire, daring Kohana.

Kohana took the dare. He threw a lightning bolt at me and kept coming. I dodged it and it collided with the spell trap in a flurry of sparks. He screamed at me, the infuriated screech of a raven. He was close, almost close enough to snatch, when Derek suddenly lunged at him, teeth bared. The move ripped him free of my grasp, but his teeth closed on Kohana's wing.

Kohana lost the rhythm of his flight and dipped low with the weight of the wolf. He screamed again and glared at Derek, loosing a flash of heat lightning from his eyes.

I saw the jolt hit Derek and smelled burning fur. He lost his grip on Kohana with a whimper and splashed into the water that swirled beneath us. He was washed away in a heartbeat, swept into the spell trap before my very eyes.

Isabelle screamed. The water surged higher and engulfed our lower bodies. Meagan hummed even more loudly. The guys shouted in fear and anger.

But I snatched at Kohana with both front claws. I wanted his feathers. I wanted his shape-shifting coat. I wanted to have some power over him. Some feathers came free as he struggled, and I didn't drop them.

I wasn't going to let those feathers go. "Give me the whole coat," I muttered. "Then we can make a deal."

I felt him panic.

I braced myself for his reaction.

He took off like a shot for the wall of Mage spell, dragging me behind him.

"Zoë!" Garrett shouted. "No!"

I knew Kohana was trying to frighten me into letting go. I knew he was worried, which meant I was right about there being power in his feathers. That weakness *was* the same for all shifters. I held fast, even tightening my grip.

Just before we collided with the spell net, everything disappeared in a blinding flash of blue light.

I OPENED my eyes cautiously when the wind stilled. I was in human form, with those black feathers in my right hand, sprawled across a huge red rock.

One with petroglyphs carved in it.

I recognized this rock. I'd visited it in the spring, when the elder *Pyr* had been trapped on it by Mage spells. It was somewhere in Minnesota.

How the hell did I get here?

A massive black bird crouched beside me to offer one wing tip. He looked a bit the worse for wear.

He also looked angry.

I remembered that the red rock was a sacred place for the Thunderbirds. Kohana had told me that the earth's songs were strong there.

I wasn't taking any help from him.

I glanced pointedly at his wing, then got up by myself. Our gazes locked and held, as I brandished the feathers in front of him.

His eyes turned more vivid yellow, almost snapping with hostility. It was a reasonable approximation of the way I often felt about him. "Okay," Kohana said. "Let's make a deal."

I smiled. "Not yet. When you only get one wish, you've got to make it count."

He snatched at me with his claw, but I pivoted and called to the shimmer. I knew exactly where I wanted to be and it wasn't with a Thunderbird intent on sacrificing me to the Mages. I didn't think Kohana could travel through time and space like me, although I knew he could travel in dreams with ease.

This would be like a test. The shimmer consumed me, illuminated me, danced through my veins. I envisioned my destination, looked him in the eye one last time and smiled.

Then I was out of there.

"Zoë!" Kohana roared, but he didn't follow me.

Which meant he couldn't.

Either his own abilities or the feathers in my hand made sure of it.

I wasn't overly concerned with the technicalities.

I WAS SHAKING when I opened my eyes again. I had hopes in terms of my destination, but like I said before, this spontaneous manifestation feat has a bit of unpredictability to it.

Then I breathed a sigh of relief. I knew the inside of this purse, even when it was soaking wet. I scored another chunk of Isabelle's chocolate stash—I had to love that she'd restocked—as I eavesdropped on the situation beyond the zipper of the bag.

"We must have been in the Deep Tunnel system," Meagan said and I heard her tapping on her messenger. "Stupid old thing. It never links right once it gets wet."

"What's that?" Isabelle asked and I knew she didn't mean the messenger. I could hear the purring of a cat really close. I guessed it was the one she'd picked up in the tunnel.

"The Deep Tunnel system was built to move floodwater and storm water out of the city," Meagan said. "Huge engineering project. The idea was to move the water quickly to reservoirs and old quarries, where it could be slowly released into the lake and river. There! It's working again."

"Do you have any idea where we are?" Isabelle shivered so violently that I even felt it in her purse.

"Well, there aren't that many options, and they're mostly all in the suburbs. Good! I got a satellite connection. And"—Meagan tapped busily—"our location. Ta da!"

"Not too far to the subway," Isabelle mused and I guessed she was checking out a map. "Let's get moving before we freeze into icicles. Maybe we'll find the guys."

Oh, no. Meagan and Isabelle were alone? At that news, the bottom dropped out of my stomach.

"I don't think so," Meagan said.

The purse swung as Isabelle started to move.

"What do you mean?"

"We didn't get away because we were brilliant," Meagan said. "We got away because we're human. They just didn't want us."

Isabelle caught her breath. "But they wanted Zoë and the guys."

"And probably Derek, too." Meagan sounded determined. "We have to figure out what we can do to help."

"We have to figure out how we can get dry before we get sick," Isabelle said and I could hear her teeth chattering. "It looks like we're off the edge of the world."

"No, we're not. Maybe there's a coffee shop or something once we get to the street."

"Coffee. Don't give me fantasies that might not have a chance of being fulfilled." Isabelle sighed. "One of those is enough."

Before she could get too depressed, I left the purse and appeared beside them in human form.

"Zoë!" Meagan shouted and caught me in a tight hug. The soot-colored cat, caught between us and just as wet as Meagan, was a bit less glad to see me. It meowed with outrage, then leapt out of Meagan's arms.

It shook itself, then glowered at us both.

"Zoë!" Isabelle echoed and hugged me from the other side. The big cat she'd picked up also jumped to freedom. The two cats sat elegantly on their haunches in the gravel. They looked disdainful for a moment, then began to groom their paws.

As if nothing had happened at all.

I wished they could tell us the deal with all those cats, but no luck.

It did look as if we'd fallen off the edge of the world. We were on the shore of a reservoir that must have been made from a quarry. A gravel "beach" stretched around its perimeter and the water was gray in the winter light. I could see the dark circle of a pipe on the other side of the lake, one that would spew into the pond.

"Is that where we were?" I asked and Meagan nodded. She wrapped her arms around herself, shivering. Both Isabelle and Meagan were soaking wet and it was snowing slightly.

There was no sign of the guys or Derek.

The rest of the herd of cats was gone, too.

"How'd you get away?" Meagan asked and I showed them the ebony feathers I'd torn out of Kohana's hide.

"He wanted to make a deal to get them back."

"I hope you said no." Isabelle scoffed. "He'd just lie to you again, take what he wanted, and betray you all over again."

"I know. That's why I'm here, with the feathers. I'll wait to make him an offer he can't refuse."

"Which is?" Isabelle asked.

"I'm not sure yet."

"Can't hurt to have something to negotiate with," Meagan said, "but I don't really understand why they're important."

"Any chance of a little dragonfire?" Isabelle asked me, shivering. "I'll tell Meagan about the feathers while we get dry."

"I'll trade you for the rest of that chocolate bar in your purse."

She blinked with surprise, then opened her bag, staring at the chocolate bar that had one end gnawed off.

I grinned. "I thought you'd brought it for me."

Isabelle laughed and handed me the rest of it. As usual, the sugar hit helped enormously. I flung out my arms, shifted, then treated them both to the full furnace while Isabelle talked. Even the cats came closer, evidently getting over their distrust of me for the sake of the heat. Once everyone was dry and we headed toward civilization, the cats trailed behind us.

But then, there wasn't a Mage spell to draw them in any specific direction anymore. The sky was devoid of orange spell light. We could have just happened to be walking beside a quarry reservoir as a blizzard began.

Did that mean the Mages were satisfied with what they had?

Or that they were just busy, doing to Liam and Garrett and Nick and Derek whatever they had done to Jessica? The idea made me sick.

What did they do to shifters? I wasn't entirely sure I wanted to know, but I guessed that was the key to saving the guys.

How could we find out?

"Does your having his feathers mean Kohana can't shift at all?" Meagan asked.

"I don't know. I only have some of them. If I had the full coat, that would be the case. Maybe his power is just compromised."

"Well, there's got to be something going in our favor," Isabelle said. "Let's get out of here. I need that coffee now."

We found one coffee shop that was open and huddled in a corner as we sipped hot beverages of choice. It was warm enough in there for the windows to steam up. I put Kohana's black feathers in the middle of the table, between us. There were three of them, each more than a foot long, and they gleamed with dark highlights.

I thought I'd had more than that, maybe because they were each so wide. The quills on each feather were as wide as the whole length of my hand, at least six inches across. It was hard to hold even three.

I was amused to see the two cats take up position immediately outside the window, as if they were standing sentinel over Meagan and Isabelle. They sat with their backs pressed against the glass, surveying the street and flicking their tails in the air.

Then they cleaned their paws some more.

We talked the situation through, backward and forward. I had a slew of notes on my messenger, so many that it was hard to make sense of them.

"Do you think the guys are okay?" Meagan asked for the hundredth time.

"What do you think they'll do to them?" Isabelle asked, clutching her second extra-large cup of coffee.

"I don't know," I admitted, tapping away on my messenger. Sophie wasn't answering me. The guys were captured. I could tell my dad and the older *Pyr*, using old-speak or more mundane methods, but I wasn't at all sure they'd believe me.

Or that they could solve the problem. They might just get trapped, like they had the last time. Or they might get all agitated about exile over the breach of the Covenant and my breaking my dad's new rule. I felt that it was up to me to fix this first.

I wished I had the stupid book on the *Pyr* that Jared had, even though it hadn't been enormously helpful any of the other times I'd had a peek in it. I also wished that I could have asked Jared for more insider Mage information.

No luck.

I wished we had cracked the code of that Mage book.

This was one big puzzle, one that I had to solve myself.

The truth was there was no such guarantee, but I refused to take the easy path and believe that everyone was out to get me, much less that we were all doomed.

Saving Derek would have to get me some points with the wolves. And I had to think that the jaguars would be similarly relieved to have Jessica safe.

A rescue mission, then.

Based on zero data. Where were the Mages holed up? In what state were their captives? How could they be freed? We needed information and I had no idea where to get it.

Meagan finished her cocoa. "What do we do, Zoë?"

I surveyed my checklists of Wyvern abilities assumed and yet to be conquered—okay, out of a certain level of desperation—and that was when I knew something I'd left off the list.

The previous spring, I'd navigated my way through my father's memories to find his location. I'd followed the conduit that led to him and walked in his memories.

I wondered whether I could do the same to Trevor and learn what that apprentice Mage knew. There wasn't a conduit to him like the coppery lines I saw to each of the *Pyr*, but maybe I could follow the spell light to Trevor and slip into his mind. If I found the right memory, I could discover where the NightBlade was and what they had planned for the captive shape shifters.

It would be risky, but it had to be quicker than breaking the Mage book's code.

And we didn't have a whole lot of time.

"WHAT CAN GO WRONG?" Meagan asked. We were holed up in Isabelle's room that Sunday afternoon, partly because it was snowing like crazy outside. By the time we'd come out of the coffee shop, the blizzard had gotten serious and the dorm was the closest haven. The storm had provided the perfect excuse not to go back to Meagan's place, although Meagan's mom had pinged her about six times since she'd told her where we would be.

Neither Isabelle nor Meagan liked my plan, but neither of them could think of a better one, either. The cats had come with us—I'm not sure we could have left them behind at this point—and sat on opposite ends of Isabelle's windowsill, staring into the flying snow.

Meagan studied me with concern. "How will we know if something does go wrong?"

"And what can we do to help if it does?" Isabelle asked.

"I don't know." I smiled at them, trying to soften my words. "I'm guessing you won't be able to tell, and you won't be able to do much, but I really don't know."

Isabelle grimaced. "Could you get stuck there?"

"I haven't gotten stuck yet."

"You haven't poked around in someone else's memories yet," Meagan noted.

"Actually, I have. I did it with my dad. Last spring, when they were in trouble. I visited his memories to find out where he and the other *Pyr* were."

"So you could save him," Meagan said. "I think he'd be more likely to cut you some slack than Trevor if he caught you in his mind. After all, you want to steal his memories."

She was right. Deciding to poke around in someone else's memories without authorization was a lot like breaking into their house.

Still, I couldn't see another way to find out more.

"Would you actually be stealing them?" Isabelle asked, suddenly thoughtful. "Or would you just share them? Kind of like breaking into an office and reading the files but leaving them there?"

It was an interesting idea. "I'm not sure," I admitted, feeling as if the whole thing was very elusive. "This Wyvern thing isn't very well documented."

"Well, it wouldn't be all bad if you made him forget something. If you could." Meagan considered me and shrugged. "Just throwing that out there."

"Maybe you could mess with his memory so he messed up whatever they plan to do to the guys," Isabelle suggested.

It sounded unlikely to me, but I was determined to remain positive. I was terrified enough as it was. "I'll see what I can do."

"What about us?" Isabelle asked.

I remembered Jared helping me before with this kind of deliberate dreaming, but he knew his powers as a spellsinger. Meagan was uninitiated and might inadvertently make trouble for me.

I smiled at them. "Just watch the door. Hum something in a major key."

"Something easier," Isabelle said.

Meagan frowned. "The Hallelujah chorus of Handel's *Messiah* is in D Major."

"Excellent," Isabelle said. "We sang that in choir at Christmas."

I left them to it. How did anyone pass undetected in another person's mind? I didn't know. I slid my ring onto my finger so I could see any spells coming. I held Kohana's feathers in one hand, just in case I had to negotiate anything. He'd turned up when I did dream stuff in the spring. Maybe this would be similar.

Meagan and Isabelle watched me but didn't say anything. I could almost taste their worry.

But there was nothing I could say to reassure them.

I closed my eyes and breathed deeply, trying to lull myself to sleep. My heart was thumping, though, a sure sign of my trepidation.

How would I find Trevor's memories?

How would I know when I got there?

What was I really looking for?

How would I know when I found it?

I pushed these questions around and around in my thoughts, heard my breathing slow and my pulse calm. I relaxed and entered the same meditative state we use for breathing dragonsmoke. I recalled how I had found my dad's memories by feeling for the other *Pyr*. I'd seen a network of sparkling copper lines then, and followed the right one to him. I'm not sure what told me which one, but I knew it when I saw it.

You have to believe I was hoping for a similar conviction this time. I did not want to end up in the wrong Mage's memories.

So, I thought about Mages and their spells. I thought about Trevor's MG and his parents' house and all that musical gear. I thought about how they must live and looked in my mind for the orange spell light.

I saw it flickering and pulsing almost immediately. I followed it cautiously, drifting behind it but not coming too close. It swirled out of the sky toward a neighborhood and I saw that it was leading me to Riverside Drive. The spell light spiraled toward Trevor's parents' house, where we had been the night before. Snow fell thickly all around, piling on the roof and the walkway. The house didn't look very damaged, much to my surprise, and I couldn't smell any sign of fire.

It was surrounded by golden light, though.

I guessed that the Mages could cast a kind of enchantment on humans, too. Maybe it was an illusion. Maybe what had happened to us had seemed like an illusion to everyone else. I'd have to find out later.

One spell thread was thicker and brighter, so on impulse, I chose to follow that one. As I got closer to the house, I heard a saxophone playing. The spell thread I was following resonated with the music of the sax, undulating through the air.

Like a summons.

I steeled myself for trouble, turning the ring on my finger. Then I latched on to the spell line, swung myself onto its rippling width, and slid down the line into the house.

It led into a bedroom. I had a glimpse of Trevor with his antique sax, his eyes closed as he played, and his hair mussed. Then I slid into the mouth of the sax, and through the instrument. I braced myself for biological information I didn't need, expecting to be dumped into his mouth.

Instead, I found myself in a forest.

One filled with the silence of falling snow.

I was surrounded by dead and blackened trees, a forest with no perimeter. It just went on and on and on, essentially the same in all directions.

Was this Trevor's memory? Or some other dimension?

How could I move through it without leaving any tracks?

I stood there, knee-deep in snow, and considered my options.

There didn't seem to be many.

MEMORIES ARE strange places to visit. I guess everyone organizes his or her mind differently. I'm not even sure that people see their memories the same way that intruders like me do.

My dad's memories had been ruthlessly organized. Maybe he'd had time to get all that together, seeing as he's centuries old. It had appeared to me like a long corridor with a black stone floor and a white ceiling. There'd been no discernible light source—the ceiling just appeared luminescent.

Each wall had been lined with stainless-steel filing cabinets, one after the other after the other. I'd been pretty intimidated by this, until I'd noticed that each drawer was dated.

And they were in order.

I shouldn't have been surprised.

After that it had been easy. Find the right drawer, open it, be deluged by my dad's memory. Piece of cake.

To tell the truth, I'd expected something similar from Trevor's memory. The dead forest threw me off my game, making me wonder if I'd taken a wrong turn and ended up in Granny's snowy sphere instead. I had a good look at the tree closest to me, the one I could check out without making any more tracks.

Something glimmered at the base of it, halfway obscured by the snow. I brushed the snowflakes away carefully and saw that it was a gold plaque, screwed to the tree.

And engraved on the plaque were the words December 2010.

A month's worth of memories? In this tree? How? I tipped my head back to look up at its bare branches, so dark against the gray sky.

My heart stopped cold. There was a large black bird sitting in the boughs overhead.

Watching me.

It had yellow eyes, that bird, which told me who it was.

"More to you than meets the eye," Kohana said, and it sounded like admiration in his voice.

"I said, no deal."

"And I'm making a gesture of goodwill."

"Right." I didn't believe it for one minute. If Kohana was here, then I was history.

Or soon would be.

I pivoted and would have run, but I didn't manage to take one step. Kohana swooped down and grasped me by the shoulders of my jacket. I squirmed, biting back my yell of protest, but he took flight.

"At least you can shut up when someone does you a favor," he muttered. "Scream and we'll both be finished."

"Why would you be helping me? To trick me into trusting you again?"

"Messing with Mages, especially if it doesn't look as if I'm the one responsible, is always a good thing as far as I'm concerned."

"You're just trying to get me killed."

"If you'd taken one step, you would have managed it yourself. They don't take kindly to intruders." He made a sound that could have been a laugh. "Maybe they know we're here even now."

They?

Kohana flew over the forest, which truly did look as if it extended to the horizon in every direction.

Did he really imagine I was going to trust him?

Before I could think of asking, he hovered over a tree.

"Do your salamander thing," he ordered.

Then he dropped me.

We weren't very high above the trees. There was a hole in the trunk of a tree, one that could be seen only from the top. As I fell straight toward it, I realized his intent. I shifted shape, even as the branches of the tree touched my feet.

I barely managed the change in time. I lost some skin sliding into the hole, had time to wince, and then Trevor's memory engulfed me.

Kohana had dumped me into the memory of the night Trevor had joined the Mages.

13

We were somewhere out in the country. It was hard to tell exactly, because the air was so thick with Mage spells. The scene was almost lost in blindingly bright gold, a swirling network of spell light on every side. I could see individual spells of every shade of yellow and gold, tangling together to create an impenetrable mesh.

If I peered through the spell light, though, I could see a gathering of people, singing in a field. Well, a field with statues in it. Where were we? It was night, although the sky was clear and the moon was full. That moon cast its silvery light over the chorus of singers.

No, it wasn't exactly a field. It was a cemetery! A big one. But I could see the lights of streets and buildings beyond its dark perimeter. Gravestones glowed in the moonlight, more than a few showy memorials among them.

I saw a crusading knight carved of white stone, leaning on his shield as if he were watching the festivities.

The people who were singing—they must have been Mages—stood in concentric circles. Those in the two inner circles faced the center and the people in the last one faced outward. Sentries, maybe.

I hoped they wouldn't be able to see me.

I darted forward in salamander form, having a good bit of distance to cover but not wanting to risk a larger form. They'd probably notice a dragon.

On the other hand, I might not be discernible. I wasn't part of the memory, after all.

I stayed as a salamander, just in case. I did wish I might have been a darker color than white, as the moonlight had to be making me look like a silver flash. I paused to catch my breath at the base of a statue that had been enclosed in a glass box, presumably to protect it.

It depicted a little girl, holding a parasol and smiling slightly.

Did she wink at me?

Or was I just losing my mind?

I darted closer to the singers, keeping to the shadows. Most of the Mages had their eyes closed, which worked for me. I scooted past the outer circle, slipping between two participants, just as the chorus rose to a crescendo.

I saw the Mages on either side of me respond to the song, beginning to flicker between forms in that way that made me nauseous. I kept my head down and passed through the next circle, slipping between the ankles of another singer.

He started to stamp his foot right when I was between his feet, which made me race forward.

The occupants of the inner circle were seated, hands folded in their laps. They seemed to be kids and when I saw a younger version of Trevor, I guessed that they were apprentices. They had front-row seats for whatever the action was going to be.

There was a figure in the very center of the circle, bound with spell light just as Jessica had been. She wasn't moving. I switched between my alternate visions of the scene and discerned that she was still breathing.

And that she had a fishy tail.

A mermaid.

A shape shifter.

An older woman stood in the middle of the circle, beside the mermaid. She watched the moon as the song grew louder. Then she nodded and reached into her sleeves. I was sure they were flowing and empty, but she pulled a dark weapon from the folds of fabric.

The Mages gasped in appreciation.

The woman smiled.

The moonlight slipped over the weapon in a strange liquid way, making it look like it was coated in quicksilver.

I had a bad feeling about this.

"Behold the NightBlade," the woman sang as she held the blade high. The chorus echoed her words, singing them so that they reverberated. "Gift of the ShadowEaters. Carved of a meteorite. Possessed of the power to liberate shadows."

She waved the blade as she sang this. I assumed she was making symbols in the air, but I couldn't figure out what they were. The spell light was so vivid and the light emanating from the blade was blindingly bright.

"We invoke the ShadowEaters," she sang. "And invite them to our feast. Come, come among us, exalted ones. Come and partake of our offering."

The mermaid began to struggle, panicking maybe, shifting between human and half-fish form in agitation. The apprentices smiled, more than one leaning forward in anticipation.

The beat of the song changed and the words changed into a language I didn't know. The spell light began to pulse with insistence. The woman bent, murmuring in that same language, repeating a sentence over and over again. She took that blade and cut closely around the mermaid's body.

The mermaid thrashed. The mermaid fought. The mermaid screamed.

Then she was completely still.

The woman straightened, holding a dark form in one hand, the blade in the other. The mermaid's shadow dripped over the woman's fingers, limp.

Liberated.

"Last of her kind," she roared. "An offering worthy of our exalted ones. Come, feast with us, O blessed ones."

And they did. Silver forms materialized between the Mages, seeming to emerge from thin air. Or shadows. They were indistinct forms, faintly human but difficult to discern. I felt as if I could see them better out of the corner of my eye.

But they were real. They had a strange, powerful presence. As soon as they arrived, I felt astonished.

And terrified. There was something enormous and dark about them, and the threat they posed wasn't just smoke and mirrors.

The Mages and apprentices stared in awe at the forms flitting between them, appearing and disappearing. Many of them forgot to sing. The woman with the knife exalted and laughed as they all spun gleefully around the shadow that she offered.

It got visibly smaller.

ShadowEaters.

And then, abruptly, they disappeared.

The woman was obviously disappointed, and I wondered what she had hoped for.

Then she raised her hands, still holding one piece of the mermaid's shadow in her hand. "And so we are blessed to share in the feast, to revel in the power, to know that the divine ones still show us their favor." She tore the shadow into pieces and handed it to the other Mages and apprentice Mages.

She consumed the piece of shadow she held with glee.

I looked around to see the other participants eating as well. Some nibbled, some devoured, some threw it back with gusto while others savored the treat. There was no singing, just the frantic orange spin of spell light.

And the sound of chewing.

"And so we are driven to give flesh to those who have gone before," the woman cried. "And so we again will offer the shadow of the last of a shifter kind to the ShadowEaters, until they have consumed enough to walk among us once again."

This was the surge of power they would get by eliminating all shifters.

The woman raised her hands again. A shout rose from the Mages in the circle, the ones flickering between forms. Suddenly, in unison, they all shifted to the form of mer-people. I was surrounded by mermaids and mermen, by glittering glistening scales and luxuriant hair.

Laughing in their triumph.

Meanwhile, the mermaid whose shadow had been taken was dissolving. She turned into a fine mist, one that appeared to be a ghostly version of the mermaid in life.

The woman smiled coldly.

Then she deliberately blew on the mermaid. The form of the mermaid wavered, recovered, and then all of those gathered blew in its direction in unison.

The mermaid was dispersed.

Her body was completely gone.

I had just watched one more species of shifter pass into the realm of myth and fantasy.

That was when I knew for sure that I was going to puke.

THE GOOD NEWS was that I managed to spontaneously manifest back in Isabelle's dorm room.

The bad news was that I did puke, and on arrival.

It's not the most elegant way to make an entrance.

Fortunately, Isabelle thinks fast about all matters connected with spontaneous manifestation. She caught it all in the plastic wastebasket that was parked under her desk. She pushed me into her desk chair and I sat there with my feet braced against the floor and my head between my knees. The last thing I wanted that chair to do was spin.

"That bad?" Isabelle asked and I nodded. I couldn't shake the image of that mermaid being devoured and destroyed. I closed my eyes more tightly, as if that would make the sight go away.

Instead I saw a figure in a hooded cloak, its facial features hidden in the shadows of the cowl.

The last thing I needed was a visit from Urd and her laughing skull face. I opened my eyes and gulped down the glass of water that Meagan offered.

"You done?" Isabelle asked, holding up the wastebasket, and I nodded again. She left with that prize and I heard the water running in the bathroom.

"Chocolate?" Meagan asked, offering some of Isabelle's hoard. "Isabelle always gives you food."

I told you she was brilliant.

By the time Isabelle came back into the room, I'd pulled it together a bit.

"It helps with the change," I told Meagan. "My blood sugar seems to take a big hit." I wasn't sure my stomach was trustworthy, but the chocolate tasted good. I chewed slowly and willed my horror to subside. "Thanks."

Meagan gave me an expectant look. "So tell us."

"It's gross."

"We can take it," Isabelle said. Both cats turned, as if they, too, wanted to know.

I told them what I'd seen. I didn't leave out anything. When I was done, I wasn't any less upset than I'd been at the time.

Meagan grimaced. "That's what they're going to do to Jessica."

I stared at the wrapper of the chocolate bar, knowing she was right. "And they'll be one step closer to helping the ShadowEaters manifest," I said grimly.

"Two, if Derek is like the wolves' Wyvern," Isabelle said.

"Three if they get Zoë and the guys, too," Meagan concluded.

It wasn't the most upbeat possibility imaginable. "But we have to try to save them. We can't just stay away," I said and the other two nodded agreement.

"Did you recognize the woman who was leading them?" Isabelle asked.

I shook my head.

"Any of them?" she insisted.

I shook my head again. "Just Trevor."

Isabelle absently patted the striped cat, which had come to sit in her lap. "What about the memory forest?"

"Just a dead forest that went on forever."

The gray cat seemed to consider its options, then came to Meagan. I saw her wince as it kneaded her lap with its paws and knew it had its claws. It settled into a ball quickly, watching me as she scratched its ears.

"How many trees were there?" Meagan asked.

"I don't know. Thousands." I smiled. "I didn't count them."

Meagan didn't smile back. She chewed her lip and rubbed the cat. "If each month is a tree, how could Trevor's memory be such a big forest?"

She was right.

Kohana had said *they*.

She took my silence as skepticism. "Seriously. He's seventeen or so. That means he's lived seventeen times twelve months. Two hundred and four trees, give or take six or so. Were there more trees than that?"

"Lots more."

Isabelle looked between us. "So, either he's not what he seems to be—as old as he seems to be—or it's not just his memory."

"Well, he doesn't wear a glamour, like Adrian. I'd be able to see through that with the ring."

"There could be another way for them to disguise their identity," Isabelle said.

"But Trevor's an apprentice. It doesn't make sense that he'd know more tricks than Adrian."

Meagan stroked the cat's head, thinking. "If he is the age he appears to be, then what are all the other trees?" She glanced up at me. "Maybe they have a kind of hive memory. Shared real estate and shared memories."

"That's creepy." But it made sense.

"What else did you notice?" Isabelle asked.

"It was a full moon in the vision," I said.

"That's when the book says the ceremony has to be held," Meagan said.

"November 15," Isabelle reminded us. "The night before your birthday."

Meagan drummed her fingers on the mattress and I wondered what she was thinking. "Could you tell where the ceremony was held?"

"They might not meet in the same place every time," I had to note. "It was a cemetery, though."

"That could help. Were there any distinctive gravestones?"

"A knight. Like a crusader. And a little girl in a glass box."

"We've got to be able to research that," Isabelle said. "Draw it for me and I'll see if I can find it online."

"It'd be better to find out where the guys are being held," I said. I was drawing as I spoke, Meagan watching over my shoulder. "And spring them early, if we can."

"Maybe we should each work on something different," Meagan said, her tone purposeful. "Isabelle can look for the gravestones. I'll take another run at breaking the code on that Mage book."

"What about me?"

Meagan grinned. "You'd better get your homework done so you don't get called into the counselor's office again. You don't have time to take the families-of-divorce course." Her messenger chimed and the gray cat leapt out of her lap in indignation.

Her dad.

Coming to pick us up.

. . .

THE STRANGE THING wasn't that Jessica and Derek weren't at school on Monday.

The strange thing was that only Meagan and I noticed.

When Jessica wasn't at the front door, waiting for Meagan, we exchanged a look and headed for our lockers, not at all short of apprehension. Of course, we'd guessed she wouldn't be there, but it was that relentless optimism at work again.

The halls were filled with a golden orange glow that illuminated every corner.

"Can you see anything?" Meagan asked in an undertone.

I nodded. "What do you feel?"

"There's this awful music that's trying to slide into my head."

"Block it out as best you can. Hum something else."

She started to hum the Hallelujah chorus from Handel's *Messiah* again, gritting her teeth as she forced out every note. The light had to be a spell, one that acted like a glamour. One that made it seem as if Jessica and Derek had never even existed.

It had spread throughout the whole school, so we all had to walk through spell soup.

My messenger pinged. It was Isabelle. "Weird," she said when I answered the call. "I just called Sara, pretending to be looking for a textbook for one of my classes."

"Is Garrett there?" I asked, hope in my voice even though I was pretty sure I knew the answer. Meagan turned to watch me.

"No," Isabelle said. "Which is what I expected. What I didn't expect was that Sara isn't worried. In fact, it took her a minute to remember that Garrett *should* be there."

"Sara is not a crap mom."

"No, she's not." Isabelle paused, then whispered, "It was like she didn't even remember him for a minute."

That gave me a very bad feeling.

Meagan leaned closer to listen in as Isabelle continued. "Then she gave me some story about him staying at a friend's place, which didn't even sound plausible when she said it."

"So, their spells reach that far," Meagan mused.

"I'm going to call Delaney and Ginger to ask about Liam," Isabelle said. "Then Donovan and Alex. But I'm pretty sure all of the parents will have a similar story."

"And no one else even notices," I told her. "Being captured means you cease to exist." I shivered when I said that, thinking of that mermaid. I'd never felt so powerless in my life.

"Why do we remember, then?" Isabelle asked.

"Well, I'm a wildcard. Megan is a spellsinger."

"And they want Isabelle to remember," Meagan said grimly.

I nodded. "Because it's not over." I looked at her. "Maybe they think you'll want to join the winning side."

"Not a chance." Meagan straightened and scanned the corridor, looking grim and purposeful. "There has to be something we can do."

"Maybe you can find out more," Isabelle said. "And I'll check on the guys. Talk to you at lunch."

"Right."

First, I had to confirm our impressions. Suzanne was striding toward us, her blond ponytail swinging. She would have walked right past us, as usual, but she looked to be in a much better mood than she had been the week before, so I dared to speak to her.

"Have you seen Jessica?" I asked her.

"Who?" She looked to be genuinely puzzled. Then she rolled her eyes as if I'd been putting her on. "Don't pretend you know people I don't, freak," she muttered, and tossed her ponytail.

"What about that fire Saturday night?" Meagan said.

Suzanne looked at her with disdain. "Just because some loser set his costume on fire with a cigarette didn't mean the fire department had to come." She tossed her hair again. "It was probably a neighbor, trying to get Trevor in trouble."

Meagan and I exchanged a glance. The entire basement had been an inferno when we'd escaped.

But then, the house had been fine when I'd invaded Trevor's memory on Sunday.

I was starting to think that Mage spells were even more powerful and spooky than I'd believed.

Meanwhile, Suzanne went straight to Trevor. He put his arm around her shoulders and she kissed him, acting as if they had never broken up. I had to assume that the other kids hadn't noticed anything on Saturday night. When they'd been frozen, maybe it had been like time stood still for them.

Meagan and I went to our lockers in silence. Trish's locker is on the other side of Meagan's. Usually she ignores both of us, and that remained consistent.

Meagan gave me a questioning look and I nodded.

"Hi, Trish," she said brightly. "Didn't Suzanne and Trevor break up last week?"

Trish looked at her in surprise.

"Are you kidding?" she asked, with all the disdain she reserved for Meagan. Actually, she saved a good chunk of it for me, too. "They'll never break up. Their love is *forever*." Trish sneered. "Not that he'd notice you, even if they did."

Trish marched off to join Suzanne and Trevor.

Was Trevor smirking at us?

"This is so weird," Meagan murmured to me.

"Just play along. We'll talk about it after school."

She nodded and tightened her lips. Then she hummed a little more loudly.

"Hey, Meagan!" Trevor called and we both looked back to find him strolling behind us with Suzanne. "Great piano work Saturday night."

"I had no idea you could play like that," Suzanne added.

At least somebody remembered something.

Although I could have done without the Mages remembering Meagan's gift. I hovered close to her, not knowing what to expect from him. He looked as if he was really enjoying himself. His eyes were all sparkly. Jubilant. As if victory was within his grasp.

There was nothing to like about that.

"Um, th-th-thanks." Meagan pushed her glasses up her nose and clutched her books to her chest.

Trevor came to lean against Trish's locker. His smile was so friendly that I completely distrusted it. "You want to join our jazz improv group? We meet after class on Mondays and Thursdays, and we could use a piano player."

As if that was going to happen. I started to turn away, positive that Meagan would decline.

"Sure," she said and I spun back to stare at her in shock. She nodded firmly, her stutter completely banished. "That would be great."

Trevor's smile looked hungry to me. "See you there, then."

"Absolutely."

The first bell rang. Trevor and Suzanne turned away, talking quietly together as they headed to class. Meagan and I walked in the opposite direction. I had a major case of the creeps. "Are you nuts?" I whispered.

"Someone has to find out more," Meagan murmured. "I'm the most obvious choice, so I volunteered."

"No way. It's stupid."

She stopped and glared at me. "It's not stupid. It's brilliant. I'm going undercover."

"Don't you see? Their spell is getting to you, too, making you think things you wouldn't think otherwise."

"Bullshit. I know what I'm doing."

"But..."

"You're the one who said we should play along. How else are we going to find out where the others are? How else are we going to figure out how to save them?"

I shook my head. "It's too risky."

Meagan waved that aside. "If you want me to calculate the probability of success, I'll work it out for you."

"That's encouraging."

"But you have to know that if we do nothing, our chances of success are much lower."

"And you can tell me how much."

Meagan smiled.

I made one last appeal. "I'm good with risk. I just don't like you taking the risk." I sighed, because she wasn't persuaded. "I don't think this is a good idea at all. Let's think of something else."

"I don't think there's a better one." Meagan got that stubborn look, the one that told me she'd never change her mind. "I'm going in."

. . .

I'D ALWAYS THOUGHT that if I could just break the Covenant and tell Meagan the truth about my abilities, we'd be best friends again like we used to be. I'd always thought there'd be nothing left to argue about and we could be a team.

But it wasn't working out that way. Instead, we were fighting all over again.

We argued more about her decision to join the improv jazz group over tofu burgers at my fave restaurant. It was a relief to escape the pervasive power of the golden Mage spell that was filling the corridors at school. I'd thought it might help us think more clearly.

It hadn't done one thing to change Meagan's mind.

"The problem really is that you don't trust me," she said.

"No, the problem really is that you don't know what you're up against."

"What are you afraid of?" she demanded.

"Other than everybody dying or disappearing?" I eyed her and she nodded. "Okay. Mage spells can change your thinking. They can make you believe things that you know aren't true. Only a more advanced spellsinger can defeat them."

"And I'm not trained yet." She nodded thoughtfully, surveying the restaurant. "Okay, that's fair. Give me Jared's number."

I sat back in shock. "I don't think he'll help."

Meagan smiled. "Want to make a bet on that?"

"He bailed on me. He left...."

"Sure, but I'd be the one contacting him." Meagan made a flourish in the air with her fry. "And I'd be doing it to save you. Trust me—he'll help." She ate that fry with great satisfaction.

Was she right?

Couldn't hurt to try.

Would it be good enough?

Just pulling up his address made my pathetic heart go flippity-flop. I was even blushing when I forwarded it to Meagan. Derek was nice. Kinda cute. Maybe he was even safe—well, given that he was a wolf shifter—but Jared...

I had a feeling that no one was ever going to turn me inside out the way Jared did.

I just wasn't sure that was a good thing.

Meagan typed away, composing an entreaty to Jared. I desperately wanted to see it, but tried to be nonchalant. "You haven't eaten anything," she said without looking up.

"I'm not hungry."

"You'll need your strength to shift, if you have to." She pushed my tofu burger, still in its wrapping, toward me and sounded stern. "Eat."

"Promise me that you'll be careful."

She smiled. "This is going to be awesome. You'll see." She leaned closer. "All you have to do is trust me."

I couldn't say anything to that.

"Promise," Meagan insisted.

"Okay. I promise. But you have to ask me if you have any doubts. You can't take any more risks and..."

"Pinkie swear," she said, interrupting me. She held up her pinkie finger the way we used to promise things to each other in elementary school.

The sight made me smile. A little.

I pinkie swore. There was nothing more I could do.

I DIDN'T KNOW what to do with myself after school. As hard as I tried to persuade her, Meagan had insisted it would compromise her cover if I came to the jazz session. That drove me a bit nuts, as I was worried about what might happen to her. She was sure that nothing would happen in front of everyone. I reminded her that a lot had happened Saturday night in front of everyone, and she reminded me that almost everyone had been enchanted. I didn't see why that same spell couldn't be cast again.

We went round and round, each certain that she was right. She was determined to do this and since I couldn't stop her, I played by her rules.

For now.

I did seriously consider the merit of spying on her in my salamander form, but I had promised to trust her. It was a bit early to bail on a pinkie swear.

I tried to be responsible and do my homework.

In the end, I was too restless to make much progress and it felt strange to go to her house without her.

So, I went to my house.

My rationale was that it was time to check on the place, pick up the mail, water the plants, etc., etc. The truth was that I wanted to be alone, and I wanted to be alone someplace familiar. Someplace safe. It's never a bad thing to slide inside the protective barrier of your dad's dragonsmoke.

I closed my eyes when I unlocked the door to our loft and felt the glittery caress of his dragonsmoke. It was piled high and thick around the perimeter of the apartment, woven all around it like a protective cocoon. Stepping through the chill of my dad's dragonsmoke—breathed slowly and deliberately to defend his territory from invaders—made me shiver.

Then it made me want to cry.

Because I could already feel that the barrier was degenerating. Dragonsmoke erodes over time, gradually dispersing. My father's barrier had been a fortress wall, but in his absence, it was thinning. Not enough for anything to be at risk, but I could feel the difference and that made me keenly aware of his absence.

And the reason for his absence.

Would my parents come back?

Together?

The loft felt lonely and empty. Cold. The decor has always been a bit austere, but on this day, it felt impersonal. Vacant.

I locked the door behind myself and went through all the rooms, checking the locks on the windows. There was a smell in the kitchen and I realized that no one had remembered to take the trash out on that last day. Clearly, icky trash hadn't been at the forefront of my mom's thoughts when she'd walked out. It was out of character, though, because she always had a departure checklist. This time, she'd been too upset to follow it.

Or too determined to leave to care.

I did the dutiful thing. I took out the trash and emptied the dishwasher, cleaning up the kitchen in the hope that she would come back and wouldn't be disgusted when she did so. I got proactive with the contents of the fridge, too. I sorted the mail, leaving it on appropriate desks, as if everything would return to routine just because I wanted it to. And then I ran out of jobs to do.

That was when it occurred to me to visit my dad's hoard.

A dragon's hoard is a personal treasury of items of both monetary and emotional value—deeply personal and vigorously defended. I think sometimes that the secrets are more valuable than the gold.

My dad's hoard was housed in a windowless room with only one entry. It was located roughly in the middle of the loft—by design, not accident—nestled between the kitchen and the walk-in closet adjacent to the master bathroom. The master bath wrapped around the other side of the room that held the hoard, and if you hadn't been thinking about space, you might not have realized that an entire room was secreted there. You had to slide the clothes down one bar in the closet to even see the door, which was painted the same color as the closet walls. The hoard door was locked, too.

That was enough to keep human intruders away. My dad also had defenses against dragons. His dragonsmoke was almost impenetrable around the door of the hoard—when I pushed his shirts aside, I could see its frosty glitter. Unlike the dragonsmoke that surrounded the loft itself, this barrier permitted no one to cross other than my dad.

I had never been invited into his hoard. I had seen specific items that had been removed for me to view them elsewhere in the loft. I'd always wanted to know what else was in there. I'd never had the opportunity to find out—though it hadn't been for lack of trying. The dragonsmoke barrier had kept me out, even in my dad's absence.

But now I could spontaneously manifest elsewhere.

I should be able to bypass the barrier.

My dad would never know that I had crossed his dragonsmoke barrier. He'd never feel it burn me for daring to go where I shouldn't. He'd never feel it break. I would simply go around it.

I would prove that he couldn't exile me in the traditional way.

And I would finally know what else was in his hoard.

If that wasn't incentive, I didn't know what was.

14

It was ridiculously easy. One minute I was standing in the closet, gathering my nerve. The next, the whole world was sparkling with blue light.

I opened my eyes to find myself in a darkened room. I could smell that it was sealed against the world, and against the light that outlined a door I saw the glitter of dragonsmoke.

"Well done," someone said.

My heart leapt and I spun in terror. There was a radiance on the far side of the hoard, one that illuminated very little. I took a cautious step closer, mustering the cusp of change.

"You're learning fast, Sis," Sigmund said, a smile in his voice. "I love that you don't mind breaking the rules."

My dad had said that he saw Sigmund sometimes in his visions, so I had to check. "You aren't going to tell on me, are you?" I moved closer to the ghost of my big brother. He was leaning over something, cradling it in his hands. I couldn't tell whether the faint light was coming from it or him.

"Erik probably knows." Sigmund shrugged. "All that foresight. Maybe he guessed that you would come in here. I did." He smiled at me. "Or at least I hoped you'd have the nerve to do it."

I looked around, my eyes having adjusted to the darkness. There were the expected piles of coins and jewelry and shiny trinkets. The gold gleamed warmly, even with such faint light, but I saw that there was a lot of silver, too. Buckets of gems. I bent and grabbed a fistful, letting them run between my fingers like dried beans.

"It's incredible," I said.

"Just like the stories say." Sigmund sounded bored. "Over centuries, you can collect a lot of stuff. Erik was always big on financial security."

I glanced up. "What was in your hoard?"

He smiled. "Books." His tone turned rapturous. "Books with leather bindings and embossed covers. Books filled with secrets, inscribed by hand or letterpress on vellum or parchment. Engravings and drawings and symbols and knowledge. Books. I loved them as I never loved anything else."

"What happened to your hoard?"

His lips thinned and he turned away. "I destroyed it." I saw him swallow. "I burned it all, so no one else could ever have it."

I wondered how many things had been written in those books that might have been helpful to me. "Anything about Wyverns in those books?"

His eyes gleamed in the darkness. "You'll never know now, will you?"

That made me mad. "You could have left it as a legacy. You could have helped me out a bit here."

Sigmund frowned and tapped his fingers for a minute. He wouldn't look at me. "What you want is over here, you know."

I wasn't sure whether he had told me that because he felt guilty, or whether it had been his plan in the first place. I went to his side. "How'd you get in here, anyway?"

He gave me a look filled with pity. "I'm dead. I can go wherever I want. Usually no one sees me, though."

"You always turn up when I'm in the dark, and nearly give me a heart attack."

"Always been fond of dark corners," he said. When he smiled, he looked so mischievous that it was hard to be grumpy at him. "And deep shadows." He wiggled his eyebrows, then pointed down to the shelf in front of him.

I couldn't figure out what it was at first. "It's broken," I guessed finally.

Sigmund picked up the bigger piece of stone and turned it for me. It was dark stone, really dark, and when he held the pieces, I could see that it had once been a polished sphere. But it was broken now, and the fact that the pieces were carefully preserved in my dad's hoard told me that it had been important.

Whatever it had been.

"The Dragon's Egg," Sigmund supplied. "It used to show the location of a firestorm." He spun one piece, but it was lopsided. "The story of how it was found is lost."

I would have bet that my brother knew how it was found, but he averted his gaze, a sure sign that he wasn't telling.

"What about the story of how it got broken? Is it in your book?" I asked.

He shook his head. "Happened after publication."

"But you know."

"Once upon a time, a *Slayer* captured both the Wyvern and the Dragon's Egg. The *Pyr* Nikolas was given the choice of saving just one."

I looked at the broken stone. "He chose the Wyvern."

Sigmund sobered. "He loved the Wyvern. He would have done anything for her. But it is forbidden for any of our kind to be intimate with the Wyvern." He grimaced. "It's similar to the human edict against sleeping with one's sister." He arched a brow.

I ignored his expectant expression. "Why?"

"Maybe if you go back far enough, we dragons are truly all brethren."

"Is that why she died?"

Sigmund shook his head. "It's why she lost her powers." He snapped his fingers. "Presto! All gone."

"What?" She lost her powers because she had sex? *Once?* I was going to live for hundreds of years, but to keep my powers I'd have to be a virgin forever? "But I'm just *getting* my powers!"

"Then you'd better follow the rules, Sis."

"What rules? There's no rulebook or guide."

Sigmund scoffed. "Don't play games. You know instinctively what most of them are." Then he looked pointedly around the room to the door.

That was a telling reminder. "Right. You couldn't have mentioned this need for me to follow the rules before I entered the forbidden territory of Dad's hoard."

He grinned and I figured he was teasing me. "So, did you break an important one? Guess you'll find out when you try to leave. Think your powers have gone away already?"

I folded my arms across my chest. "You are not helping."

"We could both be dead in here. How fun would that be?"

"Not helping."

"Of course, you might not waste away to nothing and die before Erik gets back. You might be alive." Sigmund winked. "Until he killed you."

"Hello, could we stay on topic, please?" I indicated the Dragon's Egg. He didn't have to know that he had me seriously worried.

He patted it. "Erik could also use this like a scrying glass, see the future before it happened."

Sigmund was too smug and I guessed he was hiding something from me. "Don't tell me you can see the future, too?"

"All the dead can." He smiled. "We just don't care anymore."

"Do you care about anything?"

Sigmund straightened and looked straight at me. "I wouldn't be here otherwise, kiddo. Think about it."

I did.

Then he beckoned to me, inviting questions.

I had lots. "What happened to Sophie?"

"You have the answer on your finger."

I looked down. I'd seen a white dragon and a black one come out of the ring the previous spring. I knew they were Sophie and Nikolas. Being trapped in a ring with your beloved didn't sound to me like an ideal fate.

I would have asked another question, but when I looked up again, Sigmund was gone, one piece of the Dragon's Egg rocking slightly from his touch.

Scrying, huh.

Maybe it was time to give that a try.

I STEPPED CLOSER to the chunks of the Dragon's Egg. It would have been bigger than a basketball when all one piece—now five pieces lay on velvet in my dad's hoard.

I picked up one—not the biggest, as it was half the orb—and turned it over so that the smooth outside was facing me. I could see the reflection of myself in it, distorted the same way a fish-eye lens would distort it.

I made a face at myself and my reflection made it back.

Much uglier, though.

Then I got serious. I stared into the surface of the stone. It was very black, so dark that it was easy to think that the surface wasn't hard. It made me think of looking into a deep shadow, one that goes to depths beyond expectation.

I looked more deeply. I thought about Wyverns past and my almost complete lack of data about their history. I thought about needing to solve riddles without having very many clues.

And it suddenly seemed as if the piece of the orb I held was full of stars. It could have been a chunk of night sky in my hands. I stared more deeply and one star brightened.

It shot across the piece of stone—or deep inside it—like a falling star.

It flashed.

Then all the stars that had been in the stone disappeared.

I didn't have time to be disappointed. A verse popped into my head. I heard the words as clearly as if someone had read it to me, but it was in my own voice.

As if I was reading a verse to myself, even though I'd never heard this one.

I put down the piece of stone, tugged out my messenger, and tapped in the verse before I forgot it.

Wyverns past of snowy white
Gather to initiate
The newest member of their kind;
Always with hope that this one unbinds
Past errors and misjudgments
That condemn each Wyvern to lament
That love can never touch her life
Without instead a sacrifice.
Each new Wyvern may hold the key
To change the Wyverns' destiny.

Then I read it again. Twice.

What did it mean?

Could I be the one holding the key?

Suddenly I realized that the doorbell was ringing.

The time to find out whether I'd lost my powers or not was right now. I held my breath and called to the shimmer that let me move through space. It didn't answer right away, as if it just wanted to make me sweat.

I did.

My mouth went dry.

The doorbell rang again.

I shouted in my mind for the shimmer, wishing with all my heart to be on the other side of the door to the hoard and the dragonsmoke barrier. I squeezed my eyes shut, hoped hard, and...presto.

It worked.

THE DOORBELL RANG a third time as I fell into the closet, making a whole pile of my mom's shoes cascade to the floor.

I zipped out of my parents' suite and ran to the front door. There was a delivery guy already turning to leave.

"Oh, there is someone home," he said, then came back to the door.

"Sorry. I was, um, busy."

He eyed me, obviously tabulating possibilities, then decided it wasn't his business. Maybe I was mastering my dad's glare. "I've got a package for Zoë Sorensson."

"That's me." I saw the scribbled dates of failed deliveries noted on the label; then he turned for me to sign for the box. It had been sent overnight from Pennsylvania.

I don't even know anybody in Pennsylvania.

"I came twice last week. The ones that require a signature are a pain in the neck." He looked at my signature. "Have you got any identification? Can't be too careful."

I got my wallet and he had a look at my student card. Then he waved and shouldered his bag. "Have a good day," he said, heading for the elevator.

I shut the door and leaned against it, the package in my hands. It had no return address, really, just a post office box. It was flat and rectangular, not light but not heavy, either. I leaned closer and gave it a sniff. Then my eyes widened in surprise.

Jared.

I smelled *Jared.*

I ripped the box open then, making a mess of the kitchen one more time. I suppose I shouldn't have been surprised by its contents.

But I was. I stood there, staring at it in shock.

It was a book.

An old book I'd held in my hands a couple of times before.

The Habits and Habitats of Dragons: A Compleat Guide for Slayers, by Sigmund Guthrie.

There was no note, but really, the fact that Jared had sent me the book said it all. He didn't want me to contact him anymore. He didn't want to see me again.

He was bailing on this dragon girl.

Forever.

If you don't think that was the most depressing news I'd heard all day, you can think again. And if I was feeling a bit sorry for myself and my previously undiscovered talent for making everyone disappear from my life, at least there was no one to see it.

"Did you know?" I called to no one in particular.

I'm pretty sure I heard Sigmund chuckle in reply. But he didn't give me any more answers, and he didn't appear to advise me.

Brothers.

Well, I had the only reference book in existence on the *Pyr*. Might as well use it.

I MEANT to start reading my brother's book from page one, but when I opened the cover, the book fell open to a later page.

There was a bookmark.

With a note.

And it was from Jared.

YES!

It wasn't a long note or an especially romantic one. It wasn't even signed. But I knew it was from him because it was short and to the point, as well as challenging. That was Jared all over.

WHERE'S YOUR BERYL, DRAGON GIRL?

The bookmark was in the page with the appropriate entry.

Beryl—a gem or token of power, typically given from one *Pyr* to another. In the ancient history of the *Pyr*, there are far more references to beryls and their use, although even then, the vast majority of *Pyr* would never have any personal experience of a beryl. Like so many rare items, a beryl is frequently believed to be a myth.

According to *Pyr* lore, a beryl can seal an agreement. There is some implication that beryls carry power, although the references are vague as to how those powers are assumed by the recipient.

The one common element in stories involving beryls is the strong association between beryls and Wyverns. There has been some speculation that there is only one beryl, which takes different shapes at different times under the command of the one Wyvern, and that this token is passed as a legacy from each Wyvern to her successor. As each Wyvern must die before her successor can be conceived, it is unclear how this transaction might occur, or whether this tale—like so many others associated with the Wyvern—is simply fabrication.

I read it twice. Where *was* my beryl? I looked down at the ring on my hand, the one Rafferty had given to me.

Was it my beryl?

How was I supposed to shake any power from it?

There was a puzzle and I had to solve it.

Sooner would be better.

BY THURSDAY, I was convinced that this was going to be the worst two weeks of my life.

Unless things got infinitely more miserable on the Friday before my birthday.

I was worried sick about Meagan, because that goofy golden spell light was everywhere. It circled her like a flock of Day-Glo fireflies. I couldn't even look at her without feeling like freaking out.

We were arguing like crazy.

We were also making zero progress on finding where the others were being held captive.

And Trevor was loving it.

After Monday's session, Meagan had nothing but suspicions. Trevor had made just enough suggestive comments to lure her into coming back. And he had asked her to attend some ceremony on the night of the full moon with him.

She thought this was progress. I thought it was terrifying.

Meagan was confident that she could resist their spells and that she could get more information. I wished I shared her confidence. I had to believe that no matter how much—or how ferociously—she hummed, no matter how completely brilliant she was, the spell would eventually get to her.

I halfway thought it already had. She talked nonstop about Trevor and how amazing he was.

Would I be able to count on my best friend when everything went down? Or would she—against her will—be just drawing my kind into a final fatal trap?

I wasn't sleeping much, which was okay, because I wasn't hot to meet up with Urd and her skull face anytime soon. Take my word for it—the prospect of actual death makes it tougher to confront figurative and/or symbolic death in an unemotional way.

On Thursday when Meagan went to jazz practice with Trevor, I went back to her house feeling useless and futile and edgy. Homework was exactly what I wanted to do. Uh-huh. My messenger sounded just as I was settling in and I seized the excuse.

It was a message from my mom.

She said my dad would be home for my birthday. She didn't say more than that, but I understood the implication.

She wasn't coming back for it.

That was pretty much the last straw. Did I have to lose every single person I cared about? Jared had bailed on me, probably forever. The guys were trapped by Mages. Derek was trapped, too. My mom was staying in England.

If this kept up, my dad would have a fatal accident on the way home, Meagan would be sucked up and destroyed by the Mages, Isabelle would trek off to some ashram to find her inner fortune-teller, the other *Pyr* would be trashed by the Mages, Derek and Jessica would have their shadows eaten, and I would be completely alone.

I heard Meagan's mom come home and shout hello. I yelled back at her that I was studying, an activity that she adored. I knew she wouldn't interrupt me.

Except to maybe come and confiscate my messenger.

Then I remembered what she'd said about my mom needing to be able to envision a future with my dad to even want to be with him.

I couldn't see the future, much less conjure up some illusion of it for my mom. I had no idea what happened in the dark corners of their relationship and really did not want to know.

But I wanted her to come home.

And that meant I needed her to want to be with him.

Maybe the answer was in the past. There must have been some reason why she loved him in the first place. There must have been something good. She'd known what he was right from the start, but that hadn't mattered seventeen years ago. Maybe I could find her memory, if she was with my dad.

I closed my eyes and put my hands flat on the desk. I looked for the coppery conduits that led to each of the living *Pyr* and I found the one that was my dad's. I checked every line I could see, but there weren't any that led to the guys. They were in some lost zone, where I couldn't reach them.

I went back to the line that led to my dad and followed it, hoping against hope that this strategy would work. I was startled to find myself in his thoughts, that room of stainless-steel drawers stretching into the distance behind me. It was like I wandered out of that room, to go look out the windows.

I was where he was.

I saw what he saw.

I recognized Trafalgar Square. I'd been to England enough times with my parents, to visit my aunt.

It was snowing in England, too.

More importantly, a woman in a black cape, a woman with long red-gold hair and a decisive stride, was walking away.

And my dad wasn't pursuing her. He just watched her go.

I sensed his bleak mood and felt his yearning. I knew he believed there was nothing more he could say. I understood that he was convinced that he had failed.

I took a chance and leapt from his thoughts to my mom. I wasn't sure it would work. It was an intuitive choice, a jump I made without thinking too much about it. I wasn't sure I could slip into her thoughts, but I sure was going to try.

I prayed.

I hoped.

I leapt.

And I found myself in a kitchen filled with happy, colorful clutter. There was a sealer jar of knitting needles and baskets of wool, the colors spilling to the floor. A pile of books toppled on the counter, several cracked open in front. A kettle was whistling, being ignored even though it was boiling.

One entire wall of the room was a bulletin board. I moved closer to look. It was covered in photographs, postcards, scribbled notes, letters, and greeting cards.

I saw the snapshot of a dark-haired baby nestled in a familiar afghan—the one that was still on the end of my bed—and smiled.

I'd found my mom's memory.

I poked around, stirring a few things that seemed evocative of when she'd met my dad, and then I hoped for the best.

And got the heck out of there before I learned too much.

MEAGAN WAS jubilant when she got home from jazz.

She sat and bubbled and enthused, exuding confidence and Mage news.

I could only watch the sparkles in her eyes.

They were gold.

Mage light.

They were getting to her and she didn't even know it.

She'd been late getting home. She bounced in, that golden light having invaded her eyes and its lilt infecting her voice. Trevor had driven her home. Trevor had confided in her. The next Friday was going to be Trevor's initiation to the next level of Mage apprenticeship.

Trevor had kissed her.

This was not good.

And there were eight whole days until the ceremony. Two more jazz band practices. A seemingly infinite stretch of time for the Mage spells to wind into Meagan's thoughts and undermine everything.

We argued again, and she told me that I was wrong.

She was lost, or close enough to it.

It was time for me to make that deal with Kohana.

I DIDN'T WANT to meet Kohana in the dreaming, because I wasn't entirely sure what was possible there. Never mind that he was more adept with whatever was going on in that alternate reality.

Nope. I would meet him in plain old Chicago. I had his feathers and I knew he didn't like that. I had to believe that he was waiting for an opportunity to begin our discussion again.

I gave it to him.

I had three feathers. I needed to let him see that I had them, but I didn't want to lose my grip on them. On impulse, I shook out my ponytail, found some dark thread and bound one feather into the hair hanging on either side of my face. They flipped around a bit, catching the wind in a different way than my hair usually did.

He'd notice that.

He'd probably guess it was a lure, but I figured he'd take the bait.

The third feather I hid. Insurance. Even you don't need to know where it was.

Then I pulled on my leather coat and went walking, my hands shoved in my pockets and my hair blowing around.

I hadn't even gone a block before I felt his presence. His yellow gaze seemed to burn into my back. I kept walking, pretending I didn't know or didn't care that he was there.

By the second block he was following me, covertly. He darted from roof to roof, staying just out of sight, but I was aware of his hungry gaze.

I deliberately turned into the park, heading for the center where the trees would offer perches to Thunderbirds.

And he came, like a projectile out of the night.

"You said you didn't want to make a deal," Kohana said by way of introduction. He was in a nearby tree, eyes glowing as he looked down at me. We were alone in the park, just the way I wanted it. I felt in control of the exchange—a rare enough thing with Kohana that it made me a bit dizzy.

"Maybe I changed my mind." I twirled one feather. "I'd like some information."

"In exchange?"

I nodded and brushed the snow off the bench there. I sat down, seemingly at ease, and waited.

He looked around. He hopped to another branch. He looked at me, then scanned the perimeter of the park. He clearly suspected a trick. I did my dragon thing and didn't move one muscle. I could have waited through eternity for him to make up his mind. I breathed long and slow and deep, watching him without blinking.

I knew what he would do.

Although I smiled when he did it.

He landed in front of me, a black bird as tall as I am. His eyes blazed vivid yellow, and he fidgeted with the thunderbolts in his claw. "An answer for a feather," he offered.

"Only real answers count," I said. "No games."

I sensed his impatience. He looked away, then back at me again. "No tricks."

I untied the one feather from my hair, then held it between us. "Why does being a wildcard make me Mage prey?"

He didn't like the question. "That's complicated."

"It's one question." I spun the feather. "Answer it or not." I'd snagged some matches from Meagan's mom's array of candles and now I pulled them out. I lit one, scratching it on the bottom of the box, and held the flame toward the black feather.

Kohana caught his breath, then spoke quickly. "A wildcard is a one-off, a rogue variant in a species. A wildcard has extra powers. There's only one in every kind at any time, or there might not be one at all."

He stopped and I held the flame closer to the feather again.

"All right. All right. There is a story that there will come a day when special children are born to each kind of shifter. These children will have powers previously unknown outside of legend and they will change the world. They can change it either way, for better or for worse, but the change will be irrevocable."

I threw the match into the snow and it hissed as the flame went out.

"Answer your question?"

"Not really." I lit another match.

"Those children are the wildcards. You're one and I'm one, and Jessica and that wolf guy."

"Derek."

"Whatever. Four species of shifters left, four wildcards to bring it all home—or screw it up, from the Mages' perspective." He shrugged, his eyes glinting. "You should be able to work out the rest."

I let the firelight dance over the quills of the feather, thinking. "What kind of extra powers?"

He frowned. "Depends on your kind. There's never been an *Unktehila* in the dreaming, for example."

I arched a brow at that.

"Never," he insisted. "*We* keep track of our history."

I had to wonder what other kinds of bonus powers I could get. And what they could be used for.

What were his extra powers?

I thought I might know. "You told me that we would need a spellsinger to fight the Mages. But you're fighting the Mages and you're alone. Where's your spellsinger?"

If ever a bird could smile, he did.

Then he lunged for me. He cast his thunderbolts in all directions, setting off explosions of light all around the bench. Then he snatched one feather out of my grasp and grabbed at the one still in my hair.

"Hey!"

"Don't break your terms, *Unktehila*."

"That's only one answer!" I shifted shape as quickly as I could, intending to fight him for custody of one feather, but he ripped hard.

"I count two!" he replied.

My hair tore and broke, right when I was in the middle of the blue shimmer of change. He had the feather — and a chunk of my hair.

Before I could seize his traitorous little butt, Kohana the Thunderbird was soaring into the cloudy sky.

I let him go.

For now.

15

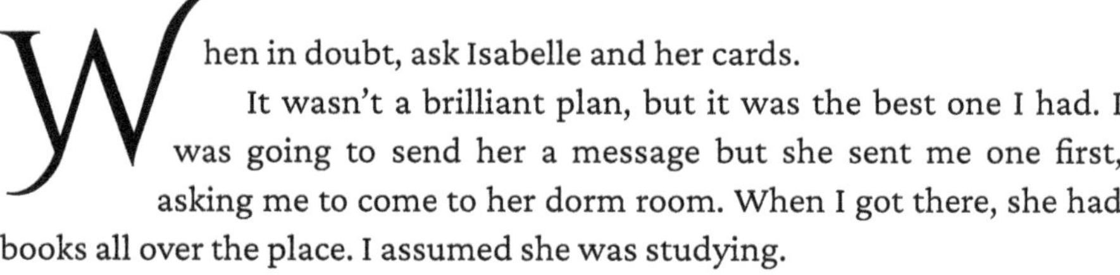

When in doubt, ask Isabelle and her cards.

It wasn't a brilliant plan, but it was the best one I had. I was going to send her a message but she sent me one first, asking me to come to her dorm room. When I got there, she had books all over the place. I assumed she was studying.

Books. Told you she was a throwback.

She insisted on checking the burn on my back again. She slathered on some more cream, even though she said it was nearly healed. I knew that—I could feel that it was better.

"Do you think the guys are okay?" she asked, her question echoing my own worries.

"I don't know. I don't like not knowing." I tugged my shirt back on. "Theoretically, they're just being held captive until the ceremony—"

"Bound by spells, maybe."

"—but I hate not being sure." I dropped onto her chair. "I'm not a fan of the fact that I don't know what to do to save them on that night either. On one hand, it seems to be ages away. On the other, I don't feel like we have nearly enough time to prepare." I pulled out my messenger. "I got this prophecy. Does it make any sense to you?"

Wyverns past of snowy white
Gather to initiate
The newest member of their kind;
Always with hope that this one unbinds
Past errors and misjudgments
That condemn each Wyvern to lament
That love can never touch her life
Without instead a sacrifice.
Each new Wyvern may hold the key
To change the Wyverns' destiny.

Isabelle made me read it twice. I was hoping, you know, that it might tweak some kind of Wyvern memory for her.

"So there's an initiation test for you, based on your making a sacrifice."

"I hate how vague this stuff is."

Isabelle smiled. "Well, maybe I can help. I found something last night. In fact, I can't believe I didn't look at this before." She handed me a couple of books, her excitement obvious. "See? There was a lunar eclipse last spring and then the solar eclipse two weeks later."

It had happened in April. "That's when we were at boot camp."

She went on for a few minutes about nodes of the moon and astrological signs, then must have seen that I was glazing over. "Point being that astrologically it was time for a new beginning." She pointed her finger at me. "The cue for the new Wyvern to take center stage."

"And the Great Lunar Standstill Derek mentioned?"

"Just started. We'll be at the midpoint in January, and it will end in the spring." Isabelle tapped her messenger. "Right when there's another solar eclipse, at the end of March." She looked at me. "Three solar eclipses over a year, and a lunar standstill. What if Wyvern powers are linked to solar eclipses?"

It made a lot of sense. "And the initiation?"

"There's always a test before the new kid gets the keys to the kingdom. Do you know how to invoke the past Wyverns?"

"No."

"What you should sacrifice?"

I shook my head. There were too many questions and no answers. "Am I right in thinking that I have to solve this to save the guys and Jessica?"

Isabelle looked worried. Then she reached up and snagged her tarot deck. The cat watched from the windowsill with interest. "Pick a card before you go," she said, shoving the deck at me.

I picked and turned it over.

THE MOON.

Right side up.

"Intuition and tides," Isabelle said with delight. "Mysteries of the feminine variety."

"A Wyvern card!" I said with excitement and we laughed together.

"I should give this deck to you. It responds so well to your presence."

"No, it's yours. I'll get another one."

"Take a copy of the translation on that book about the Mages," she suggested. "Maybe something will leap out at you if you let your intuition guide you."

Couldn't hurt. I loaded the file onto my messenger and turned to leave.

"Hey, wait!" Isabelle called when I was at the door. "Can you take the cat?"

"Excuse me?"

He regarded me with slitted eyes.

"I can't have a cat in the dorm."

"But he's been here."

She grimaced. "Well, now they know. They say he has to go, but I don't want to take him to the pound or toss him out."

"You have noticed that he hates me."

"Oh, don't be silly. He's just a big teddy bear." Isabelle crossed the room and scooped up the cat. When she carried him toward me, I saw him put out his claws. "You'll get along just fine."

"I don't think so," I said at the same time that Puss spat and slashed at me with one claw.

"Naughty, naughty," Isabelle chided him, kissing the back of his head. He began to purr as she talked to him, still keeping a wary eye on me. "You'll get used to each other. But you have to let me come and visit him."

I really didn't want the cat. "But..."

She held out the cat. “He can’t stay here, Zoë. They’re going to take him to the pound tonight if I don’t find him a home. Please?”

The cat glared at me.

There were tears in Isabelle’s eyes.

What could I say?

At least he’d retracted his claws.

I took the cat, stunned by the weight of him. I swear, he made himself heavier, just on principle. I don’t think either one of us was particularly thrilled about the situation.

But neither one of us could say no to Isabelle, either.

“I forgot to tell you!” Isabelle said, leaning around the doorframe of her room. It must be said that I looked back with some trepidation. She smiled. “I found the cemetery. It’s called Graceland and it’s at the north end of the city.”

Bonus!

I LOOKED for Mage spells all the way back to the Jamesons’, but there wasn’t a single one to be seen. I didn’t even see any cats. The city was quiet enough to completely creep me out.

I thought about going to that cemetery, just to check it out, but I didn’t want to tip my hand. The Mages might be watching it already. Instead, I found a map of it online and tried to memorize the layout.

Then I made a list of the clues I had in matters Wyvern. I needed all the data I could get to ensure that we could save our friends.

Mrs. Jameson thought I was hot for my homework when I got back to their place, but I was doing some more research online. I hadn’t forgotten that Urd had introduced herself and her sister to me—I just hadn’t thought it was important.

Now I realized that Granny never gave me anything that wasn’t important.

Even a clue.

The cat shot away from me as soon as he had the chance, leaping to a windowsill in the living room. The other cat, the one Meagan had picked up, sat on the piano and ignored us both.

Urd and Verdandi, it turned out, were two of the three Wyrd sisters who guard the well at the foot of Yggdrasil, the world tree. Urd spins, Verdandi weaves (or knits), and their third sister, Skuld, has the scissors to snip the thread. They're supposed to weave the fate of everyone.

Even better, just as Urd had told me, her name meant "what was." Verdandi meant "what is" and Skuld meant "what will be."

Past, present, and future.

The three realms that the Wyvern was supposed to be able to see simultaneously.

Three solar eclipses.

And a test of initiation that involved me fixing an error of the past.

I was starting to see a pattern. Urd, mistress of matters past, was in my dreams because my initiation test would be soon. I'd guess it would be concurrent with that eclipse.

And I had to nail it to save the others.

All I had to do was figure out what the Wyvern's error was, how to fix it, and how to invoke the Wyverns past in the first place. All while ensuring that my best friend wasn't sucked into the maw of the Mages, saving three of my dragon buddies, a wolf shifter, and a jaguar shifter, and getting my parents back together again.

No pressure.

On Sunday afternoon, Meagan was doing her piano practice while I worked on my endless homework at the dining room table. Truth be told, I wasn't making much progress.

Because the spell light coming out of her piano was gold.

Spiraling.

Making me shiver.

"I think you should stop going to those jazz practices," I said when she finished a piece and sorted through her sheet music for the next one to practice.

She gave me a look. "I don't agree. I'm finding out lots of stuff."

"Like what? Do you know where they are?"

Meagan shook her head and worked a scale with one hand. "Not yet. But I know they're okay."

The little trill of orange spell light that danced into the air made my tone more sharp than would have been ideal. “How okay is it to be captive?”

Meagan stopped and glared at me. ‘Don’t you trust me? Don’t you think I know what I’m doing?”

“I don’t think you understand how dangerous they are. You’re sitting here, spinning Mage spells. I can see them!”

“Well, of course I am.” Her tone was dismissive. ‘I have to practice, otherwise they’ll know I’m a spy.”

“Maybe they know it already. You and I have been friends forever.”

“But I’ve had a crush on Trevor forever, too. He knows that, that’s for sure.”

“Look. I could beguile you. It might help you to defend yourself.”

She gave me a scornful look. “I can defend myself without your help.” She pounded out a dark melody with force. “And if you think I’m going to just stop trying to learn more when I could help Garrett, you really don’t know anything about me.”

I leaned on the piano, desperate to make her listen. “Meagan, I can see the spell light all around you. You’re not just making it. You’re attracting it.”

She smiled with a confidence I didn’t share. “All the better to fool them into trusting me.” She held up her hand, her finger and thumb an increment apart. “I’m this close to learning the location of their hideaway.”

“They’re messing with you.”

“You’re not the only one who knows anything, Zoë.” Her lips set. “Derek and Liam and Nick and Jessica and Garrett are okay. For now. Trevor promised me that.”

Was it true? Did I dare to believe it?

Had Trevor lied to Meagan?

I watched the golden spell light dance around her head as she played, swirling like a swarm of fireflies, and I had to wonder.

Was it Meagan who was lying to me?

How far had she been tugged into the Mages’ plan?

Was that why she wouldn’t listen to me?

If so, how could I save her?

My dad came back on Sunday afternoon.

I sensed his return even before he called Meagan's mom to say I should come home.

I packed up my stuff with mixed feelings. Had my mom come, too? I thought not. How could my dad have failed to change her mind? Didn't he care? Didn't he want her to come back? What was I going to say to him?

I was worried about leaving Meagan alone. I might have stayed a few days, choosing my friend over my dad. I lingered in the living room to say good-bye, but she ignored me. In fact, she seemed to be so busy with her piano practice that she didn't even care that I was leaving.

I trudged home, uncertain what to expect. On the way there, I sent Jared a message, asking—no, begging—for his help with Meagan.

I got a single line reply:

SHE KNOWS WHAT SHE'S DOING.

Perfect.

Whatever I had expected to find at home, it wasn't what I found. Mr. Super-Neat had dropped his bag in the middle of the floor and left it there. That was more characteristic of me. He sat on the couch, still wearing his jacket and boots, staring into space.

I'd never seen him look so despondent.

Defeated.

Lost.

I slammed the door behind myself, just to make sure he heard it, and he jumped a little. He forced a ghost of a smile to his lips. It faded so quickly that if I'd blinked, I would have missed it. "I'll go shopping tomorrow," he said, his voice flat. "Why don't you order pizza tonight?"

Would my real dad please stand up?

The cat had slipped through the door before I slammed it and now sauntered into the loft. He sniffed my dad's bags, then headed for the kitchen. I figured he must be hungry and gave him some water, as well as a bowl of the food Mrs. Jameson had given me. She'd bought it for Meagan's new cat—now named Mozart—and had given me a care package of it.

The cat didn't eat the food.

My dad didn't eat the pizza.

The cat took up a vantage point on the far side of the loft and watched my dad.

My dad stared into space.

I even loaded up an old movie that night, the one with Sean Connery providing the voice of the dragon. He hates that movie. Just hearing the title of it mentioned gets him all fired up (ha) and launches him into his Dragons 101 lecture.

On this night, he just stared at the screen, indifferent.

Which said it all.

I went to bed.

I'm not sure he noticed I'd left.

The cat trotted behind me with purpose, then leapt to my windowsill to stare at the night.

"You're going to need a name," I said to him and he gave me a look, as if I had no business choosing a name for his regal fabulousness.

His choice.

The short version of the story is that Meagan and I argued big time on Monday.

I said (again) that she should bail on jazz practice.

She declined.

I said that she shouldn't let Trevor drive her home.

She declined.

I insisted on being allowed to accompany her to jazz.

She declined, saying I would blow her cover.

I intended to do it anyway, but I got another note from Muriel the guidance counselor.

Yup, I was enrolled in the program for kids of families damaged by divorce.

Go ahead. Guess when the classes were.

You got it. Mondays and Thursdays, right after school. Attendance not optional.

I couldn't have planned it better if I'd been a Mage.

. . .

On Friday night, I dressed for war.

I chose my favorite black jeans and my black lace-up boots with the heavy soles. My purple hoodie zipped right up to my chin and barely squished under the black leather jacket I'd permanently borrowed from Nick's mom, Alex. I had the ring on my finger and I shoved my rune stone into my pocket. I tucked the last feather of Kohana's into the pocket inside the left front of the jacket, pulled on a pair of acid green gloves, and was ready to go.

My dad didn't seem to notice my departure. He was still in the living room, breathing smoke, his eyes like embers in the dark.

"Going to Isabelle's!" I shouted without looking back.

I raced down the corridor and swung down the stairs of the building, erupting into the night. I could feel the glow of the rising moon and jammed my hands into my pockets as I headed for the cemetery.

To my astonishment, Fish Breath was right behind me, power-trotting through the snow. Maybe he'd heard me say I was going to see Isabelle.

I thought it was a bad idea for the cat to accompany me. He weighed a ton and I had a long walk ahead of me. The last thing I wanted was to need to carry him.

And Isabelle would flay me alive if I lost him.

Furball believed otherwise. We had a dispute in the street, during which I tried to persuade him to go home and he took a swipe at me with those claws of his when I tried to make him. I gave it up and kept walking. He trotted behind me, keeping up and only periodically complaining with a meow or two.

I decided I would not worry about it if he got lost on the way.

I knew it was a lie. I was getting used to His Majesty, watching over me as I slept and flicking his tail at me with attitude in the morning. He sat on the kitchen counter and yowled when he thought it was time to eat, which happened about twice a day.

He had, to his credit, even made my dad smile.

Looked like we were going to Graceland together.

That's an old song, isn't it?

The city was quiet.

Too quiet.

It gave me a sense of foreboding—assuming that I wasn't carrying that along all by myself. This was it, the big test.

And I still didn't have the answers or know what to do.

No pressure.

I shouldn't have been surprised that it started to snow again, much less that it would snow harder with every passing minute. The flakes were as big as my fist by the time I met Isabelle at the subway station.

The cat yowled and wound around her ankles, proprietary and obviously glad to see her. And no wonder—she picked up Ol' Lard Butt right away. We didn't talk much as we walked to the cemetery, although I was pretty sure we were both thinking about Meagan. Could we haul her back from the dark side?

Although the snow had been plowed on the city streets, we sank up to our knees in the white stuff as soon as we entered the cemetery. It was quiet there, and might have been peaceful if I hadn't been fretting about Mages.

We hadn't gone far before I noticed the wolf. It stood on the far side of a gravestone, as still as the shadows, watching us with those unblinking pale eyes.

"Derek?" I whispered, not daring to hope.

His Royal Fabulousness hissed.

I saw, though, that the wolf had one blue eye and one that was gray. So, it wasn't Derek—just one of his kind. Okay. I was encouraged that another wolf shifter had turned up. Would this one follow my lead? Be on my side? Or was he with the holdouts who didn't want to follow a dragon girl?

The wolf turned away, slipping into the darkness just the way Derek did. I wasn't quite ready for him to disappear. It seemed like I should be able to make some argument in my own favor. I leapt after him, sinking past my knees in the snow.

Then I saw that there were dozens of wolves in the shadows. Like the cats in the sewers, they were all heading toward a point of convergence. The moon touched their fur with silver, making them look both precious and ethereal.

Relentless hunters.

I remembered Derek's comment about dogs seeing in black and white.

They would decide whether to follow me based on my performance. Deeds over words. I was sure of it. The wolves turned as one and looked toward the far end of the cemetery.

I followed the direction of their gazes and saw the sickening swirl of spell light.

Beckoning.

The wolves were moving toward its vortex with purpose.

Could they see it? Smell it? Or were they just drawn to it?

"That way?" Isabelle guessed and I nodded. "Creepy enough place to eliminate species." She shuddered as we turned our steps in that direction. The wolves kept apart from us, several regularly casting glances our way.

I had the feeling that I was being watched. Not just by occasional wolves, either. I looked around and noticed a monument in front of me. It was a large square block of stone, which wasn't very interesting. The figure standing before it, though, made my heart stop cold.

It was a hooded figure, its face hidden by the shadows of the hood.

It could have been Urd, except the cloak wasn't black. It had the patina of verdigris.

I had the feeling it was the one watching me, like a guardian.

An angel of death, maybe.

But I couldn't see its eyes. I needed to see its eyes. I wanted to know who was watching me, friend or foe.

I swallowed and walked closer to it, seeing the spindle that had fallen in the snow only when I nearly stepped on it. I reached for the spindle, uncertain whether it was real or not. My fingers closed on cold wood. The eyes within the hood glinted.

Relief swept through me. Better the devil you know.

"Hey, Urd, want to come along?" I asked and handed her the spindle.

Isabelle had stopped to watch me. She probably thought I was nuts. I heard her swear for the first time ever when the figure's arm moved. Skeletal fingers reached out to grasp the spindle as I heard the creak of Urd's bones. She turned it in her hands, checking it. Then it and her hands disappeared beneath the hem of her sleeves.

She abruptly stepped down from the monument. I continued and she followed us, her cloak leaving a trail in the snow. Isabelle's eyes were round and she looked straight ahead, holding tightly to the cat. He stared over her shoulder, watching Urd with obvious suspicion.

Urd began to murmur as we walked. It was a spooky sound, one that made the hair stand up on the back of my neck. I halfway didn't want to know what she was doing. I couldn't see any spell light, but I could feel energy in the air.

A few moments later, I saw one monument from my trip to Trevor's memory. It was the crusading knight, shield planted on the ground, gaze fixed heroically on the horizon. This presumably was where daring deeds were being done. Urd strode to the side of the gravestone, still murmuring. As I watched, she made a gesture, like blowing a kiss to the knight.

He turned his head to look at her.

He lifted his visor.

He gripped his sword more resolutely.

Then he hefted his shield and marched behind us.

I stared. He was stone. He was a carving. But Urd's kiss had him moving like a man of flesh and blood.

Albeit one that was about nine feet tall.

When the monument of the little girl stepped out of her glass box to walk behind the knight, I guessed the pattern. I pivoted to stare over the cemetery, seeing the array of shadows following us. Urd had awakened the stones, turning stones to people instead of the other way around.

The exact opposite of the Mage spell cast at Trevor's party.

"I thought this place couldn't get more creepy," Isabelle murmured, but I was relieved.

We weren't going in alone. We were going in with an animated army of rock.

Couldn't hurt.

THERE WAS no question of our destination. The beat of the spell was insistent. Even if I hadn't been able to see the spell light, I would have felt its allure. It wound into my thoughts and urged me closer, drawing me to certain destruction.

Isabelle was caught in it, too, this time. We didn't have to confer at all about our path. We just trudged along. I didn't doubt that she was trying to keep it from completely claiming her thoughts, just like I was. It was really strong. I fought despair. Futility. A relentless sense of being doomed.

As we walked, the snow stopped falling. I felt the breath of wind and looked up to see the clouds being swept away. They were thinning fast, patches of starlight becoming visible.

We halted when we saw the triple circle of Mages. It was just like my dream. Two circles facing outward and one facing inward. In the middle, I could see Trevor, Meagan at his side, a frenzy of golden light swirling around her. She stared at Trevor with apparent adoration. The guys were there, too, and I was so relieved to see they were still alive that my knees nearly gave out.

They struggled against their spell bonds, snared in human form.

Jessica was there also, although she seemed to be more tired.

Or resigned to her fate.

Derek seemed watchful, caught in a haze of spells and snarling. What did he see two minutes into our collective future?

His Regalness leapt from Isabelle's arms and strode through the snow toward the circle with verve, his tail waving like a banner. Isabelle might have gone after him but I stopped her with a gesture.

The cat Meagan had saved, the gray one she'd named Mozart, was sitting on a stone closer to the circle. His tail lashed as he watched the scene avidly. Fish Breath leapt to sit beside him. They exchanged quick glances, then simultaneously began to clean their paws.

I wasn't fooled. They weren't that disinterested. They would have stayed warm and cozy at home if they didn't care.

I looked to either side and saw that the shadows were alive everywhere. I could barely discern the silhouettes of wolves all around us. Mostly I saw the pale glitter of their eyes.

And incredibly, mingled between them and gathered in smaller groups, there were dozens of cats. Maybe they were survivors from the sewer adventure. Maybe they were other ones.

But they weren't all house cats. I saw black panthers with golden eyes. I saw sleek and spotted jaguars. There were golden cougars with massive teeth watching from the trees. I understood that they were all shifters, all cat shifters, and that was why they'd come. Adrian had shifted to a lion, but lions must be the only cat shifters that the Mages had exterminated.

And Kohana had lied to me about it. Big surprise.

We were all here.

And we were all focused on the Mage circle.

The woman I'd seen in Trevor's memory stepped forward and there was a quickening in the air. Urd exhaled in a hiss behind me. The woman raised her hands just as the last of the clouds cleared and the light of the full moon shone on the circle.

She raised her hands and started to sing.

The ceremony began.

"Behold the NightBlade," the woman sang and held the dark blade high. I didn't like the look of it any more than I had in Trevor's memory. The chorus echoed her words, singing them so that they reverberated. "Gift of the ShadowEaters. Carved of a meteorite. Possessed of the power to liberate shadows."

Just as before, she waved the blade, making symbols in the air. Isabelle caught her breath, so she must have recognized them. The spell light was a vivid frenzy and the light emanating from the blade pounded into my brain. I thought my head might explode from the light show.

"We invoke the ShadowEaters," she sang. "And invite them to our feast. Come, come among us, exalted ones. Come and partake of our offering."

I was sure she would reach for Jessica or one of the guys. I was desperate to think of a way to stop her.

But she turned to Trevor.

He grabbed Meagan's shoulders from behind. I saw her horror. She struggled, but his grip was tight and the spells were wrapping around her as well.

"The ShadowEaters demand a sacrifice for your initiation," sang the woman to Trevor. The light was getting sparkly and I could see those shadowy shapes taking form between the Mages.

"And so it is offered, in good faith," sang Trevor, pushing Meagan forward.

Hey! It wasn't supposed to be this way!

Meagan fought and bit against Trevor's grip. The guys struggled with new force against their bonds, as if they wanted to help her. Even Jessica was writhing in the snow. The wolves slipped closer to the circle and the cats watched unblinkingly, their claws bared.

"The ShadowEaters demand a spellsinger as admission to the inner sanctum," the woman sang, her hands high in the air.

"And so I have snared one. Behold, your humble servant who does only your will." Trevor pushed Meagan forward so that she stumbled. He fell to his knees and pulled her down to hers.

"Blood and shadow," sang the woman as she grabbed Meagan's hair and pulled her head back. "We shall all eat well at this feast." She lifted the NightBlade, its edge gleaming with evil.

She wasn't going to cut Meagan's shadow.

She was going to cut her throat.

"No!" Isabelle screamed. She lunged forward through the snow.

And we were revealed.

"Don't touch her!" I cried and raced toward Meagan. Urd hissed and slid behind me, beckoning her army with a bony finger.

The Mages were astonished. The woman looked up in surprise, frozen with the blade an inch from Meagan's throat.

"No!" Trevor roared and pushed his way through the circle to fight me. I shifted shape en route and leapt into the fray in dragon form. It felt good to breathe fire and set a lot of Mage robes alight.

I heard the wolves growl and then they were in, too, biting and snapping. Cats slipped between Mages, slashing and snarling. Figures that had been stone just an hour before beat on Mages, making up for all the time they'd been trapped in rock.

The guys shifted shape, taking their dragon forms, but they were still helpless and bound in Mage light. Jessica became a snarling jaguar, but she, too, was still trapped.

The woman who led the Mages started to work what was obviously a familiar spell. They all joined in, adding their voices to the chorus even as they fought. They weren't going to sacrifice my friend to make Trevor more powerful.

Sacrifice.

The prophecy! I was kicking butt, my thoughts spinning, when I suddenly knew how to get the knowledge and power out of the beryl.

I had to surrender something.

I had to give up the beryl in order to get the rest of my powers. It was elegant, so perfectly logical that I knew it had to be right.

And Urd—Urd had come here to help me. They were like my fairy godmothers, the Wyrd sisters, and they were on my side.

Which explained the stone army.

I SMASHED TWO MAGES' heads together, then beckoned to the crusading knight. He came to me, then fell on one knee, his sword and shield outstretched.

I was running on instinct, but then, that's what Wyverns are supposed to do. I shifted back to human form to get this done.

Before I could think about it too much, I took off my ring and pushed it onto the sword instead, jamming it down the stone blade as far as it would go. I pulled the rune stone out of my pocket, focusing on the circle inscribed on one side. That clue had been there all along, looking me right in the eye, but I'd missed it.

And then I smashed the black-and-white glass ring and the rune stone together, shattering the ring against the knight's stone shield.

It broke into a thousand shards and made a sound like crashing glass. The sound stopped the fight, as if a movie had been frozen in mid-scene.

It was just like the party at Trevor's, except I was the only one who could move.

I saw ghosts rise from the debris of the ring to float above us all. Suddenly I was surrounded by the ghosts of all Wyverns past. There had to be a hundred of them, all in their shadowy dragon form. They were all white, all glittering like ice. They were ethereal and magical, a long line of female dragons of which I was the newest member.

Urd made a noise of approval. Yup, the past was her territory.

It looked like the snow had started again, falling thickly all around us. On closer examination, though, I saw that it was really an avalanche of feathers, white ghostly feathers shed by the Wyverns. They moved, I stared in wonder, Urd nodded.

This was it. My big test.

The Wyverns flew in a circle, making a blur of white and silver that surrounded me. The circle moved faster and faster. I heard their names like whispers on the wind, each echoing in my thoughts, then immediately disappearing. I felt like I was standing in a cloud.

And then I had it. Traditionally, the Wyvern retreated to the clouds and the mists. They avoided life and its entanglements. I didn't do very well with that worldview. I liked to be in the thick of things.

That was what had to be done differently to change the future.

In the same moment, I saw the flash of one Wyvern's eyes.

They flashed with fear.

On impulse, I leapt. I slipped into that Wyvern's memory. Her memory was like a fog bank, all half-glimpsed images and mysterious shapes. Then the mists parted and I saw her observing a Mage ritual. I tasted her dislike of them. I felt her horror when she witnessed the first sacrifice they made. Her revulsion flooded through me, her reaction the same as mine had been in seeing the mermaid lost.

That sacrifice had been a griffin, a ferocious shifter that screamed and bit until it breathed its last. Its death had not been easy and the Mages had not made a clean job of it.

I felt the Wyvern's horror, her sense that she should intervene.

But I felt her hesitation as well.

She chose to turn away rather than to expel this wickedness.

It was easier to retreat, to decide that what happened in the world was beyond her influence. I knew what had happened next. Unobstructed, the Mages had continued to recruit and slaughter, to grow in power and control.

Because my forebear had chosen to avert her gaze instead of make a difference.

I understood the prophecy with aching clarity. I knew the role I had been born to play. I knew what I had to do to change the role of the Wyvern forever. The fact that I couldn't sit back and watch the view was the good bit, the part of me that could make the difference. That's why it was my job to lead the fight.

I had to make this right.

Now.

It was time to trash the Mages and do what should have been done way back when that griffin had died. The Wyverns fluttered all around me, their eyes bright even as they trembled with fear. If sacrifices were on the menu, I had a bunch of possibilities.

I wasn't afraid.

Or if I was, I wouldn't show it.

I stepped forward and whistled to the Mages, setting the scene in motion one more time. Chaos and fighting surrounded me on all sides.

"I think I've got something you need," I shouted, and held Kohana's black feather aloft. "Want to trade?"

THE MAGES FELL SILENT.

They turned as one to stare at me.

Their spell light flickered orange, as if it too was uncertain how to proceed. The light was agitated, sparking as if calculating new variables.

Then the leader strode toward me, one hand outstretched for the feather and the other holding the NightBlade high. The moonlight glinted off that dark blade.

I stood my ground.

Even though I had guessed what would happen, I was still shocked by how fast he moved. Kohana streaked out of the sky, screaming outrage. He threw thunderbolts into the assembly of Mages, and the earth boomed with their impact. Lightning flashed from his eyes, crackling across the night sky.

He tackled the woman and she screamed as she fell. I saw that he had ripped out her eyes with his claws, then left her writhing in anguish and bleeding in the snow.

Then he leapt for me.

I shifted shape with a roar. Then I seized Kohana and willed myself into the dreaming. He yelped but I didn't let go. With the ring gone, I had to use the view of my left eye again to orient myself. I found the spell light in the dreaming and latched on to it.

I raced down the conduit of spell light, even as Kohana struggled against my grip. He was swearing and spitting and biting, but I didn't care.

We emerged suddenly in the wasteland of the Mages' collective memory.

"Stupid..." Kohana began, but I ignored him.

Instead, I breathed dragonfire at the forest. The trees closest to me erupted with brilliant orange flame, their dry wood crackling as it burned.

"What the fuck..." he murmured, but I breathed fire in the other direction. I still had a death grip on him, but he wasn't fighting me anymore. The fire danced high on both sides of us, orange and hot, as the smoke rose from the burning forest.

"You could help," I said and cast him aside. "Don't just stare."

He was visibly astounded. "They'll lose their recollection. Of everything."

For once, I could give him a look of disdain. "That would be the point."

Kohana turned to look at the burning forest. "Brilliant. It's fucking brilliant, unless..."

I had no time to chat. I didn't know what they might be able to do to retaliate, and time was of the essence.

They still had Meagan and Jessica and Derek and the guys in their grasp.

I flew low over the forest, spewing fire in every direction. The forest was soon aglow with a thousand flames, a raging inferno of light and heat.

To my relief, Kohana quickly decided to join forces with me. He swooped in to throw thunderbolts and heat lightning, his efforts spreading the fire beyond my reach. We flew back and forth, working together, relentless in destroying the hive memory of the Mages.

Far away, I could hear them screaming in anguish.

It worked for me.

And when Kohana and I met over the blaze of destruction we had created, he smiled at me. There was something a whole lot like admiration gleaming in his dark eyes as he surveyed me.

"Not bad, *Unktehila*," he said quietly. "Not bad at all."

"We need to work together," I said. "All of us, in union against the Mages. It's the only way we'll win."

He didn't say anything, just gave me that inscrutable stare.

And extended his claw.

Was it a trick? Or was he sincere?

Tick-tock. We had to get back.

I chose to trust him.

For the moment.

I placed his last feather in his claw.

He laughed and produced the NightBlade from the cluster of thunderbolts in one claw. He flourished it, swishing it through the air.

"You got it!" I cried.

"It's mine to destroy," he said, then shot into the sky. He ascended in a spiral of ebony feathers, seeming to fly straight at the sun. He was faster than ever. I could never catch him.

And really, I didn't want to.

I went back to save the others.

16

I closed my eyes and abandoned the destroyed hive mind of the Mages. I willed myself back to the fight in the cemetery and opened my eyes to find a kick-ass fight in progress.

I leapt right into the middle of it, with a roar.

The Mages were at a serious disadvantage. The older Mages—and probably the ones who had been initiated longer—had collapsed on the ground. They writhed wordlessly in the snow, their gazes blank. I could only assume that they had no memory other than what had been in the memory hive. The woman who had led them was only twitching where she had fallen, great bleeding holes where her eyes had been.

Their loss had trashed the ranks of the Mages. I could see Adrian, casting spell light with furious intensity, and Trevor, singing his heart out to cast spells, along with about a dozen other young Mages and Mage apprentices. Their spells cavorted in the air, all golden light, gathering power before they attacked.

The cemetery was full of wolves, all of them leaping and snapping and biting at the surviving Mages. I'd never seen such a furious pack of dogs, and I guessed the Mages hadn't either. Then there were the cats, slashing and spitting and ripping the guts out of anyone they could reach. And there was Urd, gesturing to her stone army, guiding them through the fray as they pounded and smashed fragile human bones.

Some Mages broke rank and ran away, only to be pursued and taken down. Others targeted their opponents with bright spells. There was a lot of blood in the snow, and a lot of fallen bodies. Any ethereal ShadowEater forms had been dispelled, but I doubted that they were completely destroyed.

The amazing thing was Meagan. I could see that she must have talked to Jared. She was standing with her feet braced against the snow, singing defiantly back at Trevor. Her spellsong had purpose as it hadn't before, and it gathered into a ball of furious light in front of her. Sparks flew from that sphere, flattening anyone who was hit.

She was a natural.

I was shocked to hear her singing Jared's song "Snow Goddess." Spell light in a thousand hues of blue and purple emanated from her, forming a barrier between her and the Mages.

I saw then that she stood over Garrett, who was still struggling against his binding spell. He was wriggling and fighting the tight cords of golden spell light, murmuring to himself. Sparks from Meagan's sphere fell on him and I saw one line of spell snap, then sizzle as it burned.

The ends of the broken spell light danced toward each other, like a pair of snakes that would join anew. Garrett glared at them, all fiery intensity, and they burned back several inches. It was enough that they couldn't touch again.

Yet.

I guessed that the spell had been fashioned to repair itself if any of it broke. Meagan saw what he had done and changed her tune, making a whole flurry of her spell sparks fall on the spells that bound him. There was sweat on Garrett's brow, but he laughed as more of the binding broke and he burned it back.

I roared and flew straight to Meagan in dragon form. I helped Garrett free himself, watching Meagan's back as she tossed spells into the crowd of Mages.

"Thanks," he said, then leapt into the air, shifting en route. He lunged past Meagan and attacked Trevor, his dragonfire vivid against the darkness.

I'd never seen anyone shoot such a huge plume of flame, and I stared in awe. He was glorious, his garnet and gold scales flashing in the night.

Meagan stopped singing for a moment, her face flushed as she caught her breath. She swallowed, her gaze fixed on Garrett, then smiled when Trevor fled across the cemetery, with Garrett's flames right at his heels to encourage him.

I gave Meagan a thumbs-up, although I'm not sure she noticed. She was focused on singing with all her might.

The other guys, though, were still securely trapped. Derek and Jessica were still trussed up as well, and now apparently caught in human form.

Isabelle, to my relief, was okay; she had a buff guy defending her on either side. One looked like a football player, a seriously large guy. The other was more slim. There was something about the way the first guy beckoned to an approaching Mage, as if daring him to rumble, that reminded me of Fish Breath.

And I understood exactly why we'd been adopted.

Garrett returned to defend Meagan, so I leapt toward Nick and breathed dragonfire at the spell bonds that held him captive. Nick roared as he shifted shape and joined the fight. Then I turned my dragonfire on Liam's bonds.

Nick decked Trevor, silencing his song for a moment. Liam leapt over my shoulder as he shifted shape, too. I barely saw the blur of a malachite dragon rip past me. He seized Adrian by the throat, that Mage having come up behind me. Liam held Adrian as the Mage shifted shapes in rapid succession, breathing dragonfire until he was singed in every shape.

I cut Derek free next. Derek shifted shape in a glimmer of pale blue light, then growled. His pale eyes glinted and then he leapt for the woman who had led the ceremony. She was still prostrate in the snow, but evidently he was taking no chances.

He ripped out her throat with one savage gesture.

I understood his point. She would never again eliminate another species of shifter.

He looked at me, blood on his jowls, as if to acknowledge my help. Then he joined the other wolves, disappearing into their midst.

Far above me, I saw the Wyverns gather in a circle and dared to hope that I had fulfilled the prophecy. A heartbeat later, I saw an orange center, surrounded by the black-and-white circle that looked a lot like Rafferty's ring, then a halo of white that was Wyverns past. I thought I saw the silhouettes of two dragons in the black-and-white part, but it moved so quickly that I couldn't be sure. The circle spun faster and faster, but I couldn't look away.

In fact, we all watched, uncertain what to expect.

Then it exploded in a brilliant blaze of light.

And the circle was gone. There were embers falling in the snow all around, black chunks of ash that sizzled as they hit the snow and then disappeared.

I caught my breath when I saw the ghostly apparition of Sophie high above me. She flickered between human form and dragon form, breathtakingly beautiful either way. *"Thank you, Wyvern new,"* she said in old-speak, then blew me a kiss.

She dissolved then, disappearing from sight like fog being dispersed by the wind. Had I seen the dark shadow of another dragon fly in the mist with her? Were she and Nikolas together forever? I hoped so.

I didn't even jump when Urd put her bony hand on my shoulder and squeezed. "Wyvern made and curse broken," she said with satisfaction.

That was when I knew: I'd passed my initiation test.

THE MOON SLID behind a cloud and the Mages—at least those who had survived—dispersed, running into the night. We let them go. We could tally up later who had survived and hunt them down—as Nick had said before, ridding the world of Mages was going to be a lot like our dads' mission to eliminate *Slayers*. It was going to take some time. And we'd made major progress.

The guys landed beside me, shifting shape when their feet touched the ground. They were giddy with triumph, ready to celebrate our success. We had a kind of group hug going, with Meagan and Isabelle and the guys and me.

But we weren't alone, we dragons and our human friends. The night air crackled with the blue shimmer of shape shifters reverting to human form. Derek shook hands with the guys and introduced some of his wolf friends. None of them had much to say, but they nodded and shook hands a lot.

Wolves mostly became guys, I noticed, while the cats mostly became girls.

Except Fish Breath, who still hovered beside Isabelle, along with Meagan's adopted cat. Isabelle thanked both cat-guys, and both acted as if they were disinterested in what was being said. I could see by the gleam of their eyes, though, that they were pleased.

And they'd continue to stand guard. I guessed that it was similar to my saving Kohana and him feeling that he owed me a debt. Isabelle and Meagan had saved the cats.

Jessica led the cats to us, falling on her knees in the snow. She looked up at me. "I didn't want to hurt you, but Trevor didn't give me much of a choice."

"Us or you?" I guessed.

She nodded, her tears falling.

"You had to swear your loyalty, I'll bet," Meagan said. "After they took the lion shifters."

Jessica nodded again as the burly guy who had defended Isabelle came to her side.

"If we didn't obey," Fish Breath added, "they would have taken the next of our kind."

"They've done it before," Jessica said. "We defied them once, and they eliminated the tiger shifters in retaliation."

"But it doesn't matter now," Fish Breath said, his tone fierce. His hand landed on Jessica's shoulder. "They broke their word by capturing you. All bets are off."

She blinked back her tears as she rose to her feet, and he hugged her tightly. He rubbed the back of her neck as she cried out the rest of her fear and my gaze locked with his.

I had a feeling that Jessica and I were going to get along a lot better in the future, since the secrets between us had been revealed.

And the cat shifters were going to be able to tell us a lot more about the Mages. As slaves, they would have seen a lot. Between us, we would find weaknesses we could exploit to defeat them forever.

"Kohana says he's going to destroy the NightBlade," I told them. "He took it."

Fish Breath shook his head. He was a pretty good looking guy. "He won't be able to do it. It's a ploy. They'll turn its power against him—you'll see."

"Just like they lied to me," Jessica said.

"Then we have to save the Thunderbirds and destroy that knife somehow, too." I paused to think. "Maybe that will persuade them to join us." I saw Derek hovering at the edge of the group. "I mean, join our union," I said to him, deliberately using his words, and I thought he smiled a bit.

Fish Breath shrugged. "Maybe. Maybe not."

"You have a name?" I asked him.

He smiled and put out one big hand. "Kincaid. Most people call me King."

"King works for me." I shook his hand and my fingers disappeared in his warm grip.

"Never been much for dragons, but you're changing my mind."

I smiled, knowing that he'd noticed that I wasn't much for cats. "Right back at you." We grinned at each other.

"We're all in this together," Derek said. "Thanks to Zoë."

Everyone nodded agreement and then Derek tipped his head back and let out a howl. It sent shivers down my spine, even more so when the other wolf-guys took up the call.

We had a lot to learn about each other, but I was optimistic that we could do it, and that we could work together to completely defeat the Mages. We were three-quarters of the way to making the union that would save all of us shifters.

There had to be a way to trash that NightBlade. It was just another riddle, waiting to be solved.

I saw that Garrett had taken Meagan's hand and that they had slipped away from the group a little bit. He bent to talk to her, his expression tender. She pushed up her glasses and smiled at him, almost radiant with pleasure.

"Privacy time," Derek murmured as Garrett bent lower and I looked away.

I smiled.

Then I saw Derek smiling and I blushed.

"Good job, Zoë," Liam said, giving me a quick hug.

"Happy birthday, Wyvern," Nick said, punching my shoulder lightly. "Nothing like kicking a little butt to mark the big day."

"But it's not..." I began to protest.

Nick tapped his watch. "Five past twelve. You're officially sixteen."

They all hooted and congratulated me.

Then we had the best snowball fight of all time, racing out of the cemetery toward the lights of the city as we lobbed snow at each other. We were all laughing and stumbling over ourselves, loud and having a lot of fun.

I'm sure there were dozens of scandalized humans calling the cops on us, disruptive teenagers that we were.

I stopped on the perimeter of the cemetery to look back. Urd wasn't following me anymore and there was a hooded statue in front of that block of stone again. It didn't have a drop spindle.

The monuments were all just as they had been. Motionless.

I wasn't sure whether the mess of fallen Mages would be there in the morning or not. I didn't much care. They could weave spell light to defend their own secrets. Ours were secure.

The wolves and the cats had taken their own, to celebrate their lives and mourn their losses, which was just as it should be.

"Time to go home," Liam said to me, and I nodded.

"You, uh, want a ride?" Nick said to Isabelle, shuffling his feet a bit in the snow. She looked at him, her expression a mix of caution and hope, but he smiled at her. "Truce?"

Isabelle thought about it for one heartbeat. "Okay."

Garrett turned to Meagan. "One last ride before we meet again?" he offered with a smile, and Meagan lit up.

"Just you and me," I said to Liam, giving him a nudge.

"And one big cat," Liam said. King shimmered and shifted, standing regally on the sidewalk as he awaited his chauffeur. "Come on, King. I'll give you a lift."

I GOT HOME exhausted but triumphant.

I wondered whether my dad would even notice my return.

It was late, later than I should have been out, so I climbed the stairs to our loft quietly. I didn't want to use the elevator, because it made a ton of noise, especially to dragon ears. When I got to the hallway that led to our door, I even took off my boots and carried them.

I punched my code into the keypad of the dead bolt, hating all the little beeps and whirs. In the daytime you could barely hear the lock.

At night it provided an avalanche of sound.

The hinges even creaked on the fricking door when it opened.

And that was when I knew there was something different.

A trio of candles burned low, perched in their holders on the coffee table. There was an empty bottle of wine and a pair of glasses there, as well as a pile of luggage just inside the door. A witchy pair of black boots with spike heels and pointed toes looked as if they'd been kicked aside.

I recognized those boots.

I also recognized the sweater that had been flung over the back of the couch. I recognized the scent of a familiar feminine perfume.

And the door to my parents' room was securely closed.

I smiled as I flicked the exterior door shut behind me. My mom wasn't just home.

She intended to stay.

I hooted as I bounded into my own room, and shouted with joy. I didn't care whether they heard me or not. It was ten past two when I crashed.

I'd gotten the best birthday gift of all.

And it hadn't even made my list of top three.

THAT NIGHT, I dreamed of Urd and Verdandi.

It shouldn't have surprised me.

I felt chilled in the night, and rolled over. It was good to be back in my own bed and my own room. I sighed and opened my eyes, then blinked.

The tree was back, growing out of the floor and through the opposite wall. Verdandi was knitting and Urd was spinning her spindle. They sat on either side of that dark pit of a well, the snow falling lightly all around them. The stars were out overhead, which made no sense, but there it was.

As I watched, Urd put her drop spindle carefully aside. She took the bucket I'd ridden before, the one with a rope around the handle, and lowered it into the well. She let a lot of rope go before the bucket splashed far below.

She glanced up then and I thought I saw her smile inside the shadows of her hood. Tough to tell if someone's smiling or grimacing when she has a skull face. Then she drew the bucket up with her bony hands. When it cleared the top of the well and Urd bent to grab the handle, Verdandi put her knitting aside. She straightened her glasses, then got to her feet. There was a ladle tucked beneath her stool, and it shone as if it was made of sterling silver.

Maybe it was made of moonlight.

She dipped it into the bucket and withdrew a sparkling scoop of water. She poured it carefully over the root of the tree, taking care to dampen all the bark.

She repeated the gesture over and over again, watering all of the tree root that she could reach. When necessary, Urd sent the bucket back down the well for more water. They worked steadily and methodically.

I dozed as I watched Verdandi ladle the water again and again and again. Finally satisfied, she tucked her ladle away and Urd stowed the bucket beside her stool. The pair sat down and began to work again, never having exchanged a word. The spindle spun and dipped, wool gathering on its stem. Verdandi pursed her lips as she knit, the product of her efforts spreading over her lap like a snowdrift.

Just before my eyes shut again, I saw it. A fresh green leaf appeared on one branch of the winter-deadened tree. Urd and Verdandi paused in their work to watch it unfurl. It opened with ridiculous speed, becoming a lushly green and shiny leaf about as big as the palm of my hand.

A second bud erupted farther down the same branch.

The sisters exchanged a glance and then Verdandi began to hum a little. Her needles flashed again and the drop spindle spun. But I saw her wink at me, quickly, just before I closed my eyes.

I smiled as I slipped into sleep. I knew the new growth was because of me.

There was a new Wyvern in town and the sisters liked that just fine.

YES! I woke up ready for the most awesome birthday party of all time. I lingered in bed, enjoying my sense of anticipation. I could smell coffee brewing and heard my mom humming in the kitchen. My dad was on the phone, making last-minute arrangements for something. I felt the *Pyr* coming closer, all of them gathering for my big day. That coppery conduit was all a-sizzle.

This was the good stuff.

I wasn't expecting the doorbell to ring, not so early. But it did, and my mom came to get me. "For you," she said, as if she'd never been gone. "Imagine."

I gave her a tight hug—because she had been gone—tugged on some clothes and ran for the door. I was sure it was Meagan, come to dissect events of the night before, or one of the *Pyr* guys.

But it was Derek.

And he looked awkward.

He cleared his throat when I appeared and didn't seem to know what to say. That my mom was standing there, obviously listening, probably didn't help. Even my dad did a crap job of pretending not to care.

"I, um, wanted to wish you happy birthday," he said. "Before you, um, got busy."

My parents exchanged a look and finally decided they had something to do in the kitchen.

"Thanks." I shoved my hands in my pockets, feeling as awkward as he looked. "I was going to send you a message this morning, and Jessica, too. It's kind of a *Pyr* party, but it'd be great if you could come, too."

"Thanks. I'll do that."

We stood there, neither of us looking at each other, until he cleared his throat again. "Look, about last night..."

"What about it?" I thought we might have forgotten something, something keyed to the other shifters, maybe insulted them. I looked at him to find that unblinking stare fixed upon me.

"You were amazing," Derek said. He smiled that crooked half smile. "I told you I always wanted to see a dragon kicking butt."

I blushed then, right to my toes.

To my astonishment, when I could manage to look back at him, he was holding out a box with a bow on it. He couldn't look me in the eye. "For you," he said gruffly. "No big deal. It's just something I thought you'd like."

I was even more astonished. I took the box and shook it a bit—force of habit.

"Open it," he said, sounding more like his usual self.

"You already know what comes next," I accused him, and he grinned.

I opened the box. There was a silver necklace in it, a necklace with a charm. It looked like a woman's hand. I glanced up at him in confusion.

"The hand of Fatima," he said. "It's supposed to avert the Evil Eye."

"Maybe even against Mage spells."

"Can't hurt."

I put it on then, using the mirror in the hall to fasten the clasp. The charm fell into the hollow of my collarbone. Derek took a look and nodded approval. "I noticed you like silver, too."

I do. I love silver. I never thought guys paid attention to stuff like that. He was watching me again, his hands shoved in his pockets, his eyes gleaming. I had a tingly feeling, one that made my skin feel all hot and me a bit dizzy.

I wasn't sure what came next, but I knew he was waiting for something.

"Well, I should go," he said finally. "See you later."

We confirmed the time for the party and he turned for the door. As much as I might fantasize about Jared, it looked like he was gone from my life. But Derek—Derek liked me just fine.

And I liked him, more all the time. Maybe I was finally getting it right.

Maybe I could like guys who liked me for a change.

"Wait." Before I could change my mind, I stepped after Derek. He glanced back, the twinkle in his eyes telling me that he wasn't going to be surprised by anything I did.

And that was okay.

I kissed him, right on the mouth. It was sweet and lingering, an entirely different kind of kiss than I'd had with Jared. Our lips clung a bit and I bumped his nose with mine when I stepped back.

But his eyes shone.

And my heart was pounding.

It was matching its pace to his, making me feel breathless and dizzy and just fine.

"Later," Derek whispered, and then he slipped out the door and was gone.

I leaned back against the door, trying to catch my breath.

Then I knew I had to call Meagan.

. . .

THE *PYR* CAME ROLLING in throughout the day, and my friends joined us for dinner, too. Derek and Jessica came, and Isabelle and Meagan, after I'd explained to the *Pyr* that these friends were among the trusted humans who knew my secret.

My dad had made it clear that I was in deep trouble and that we would talk about my punishment the next day, yada yada yada. But he'd already added Meagan to his list of humans in the know, and had had a conversation with her, probably about confidentiality. I think she reassured him about her trustworthiness more than I ever could have.

I might not have the gift of foresight—yet—but I had a feeling that he was going to cut me some slack one more time. The Mages, by capturing the guys, had saved me from exile.

And I was the new Wyvern.

Maybe all those victories were what made the celebration of my birthday so completely amazing. We had the most awesome Thai food for dinner—my mom was on a serious cooking spree—and then the best birthday surprise of all was revealed.

My dad had planned a pyrotechnics display just for me. We went up on the roof to watch it over the lake and my mouth fell open in shock when he turned on the music.

The fireworks were synchronized to a song he'd noticed me listening to eighty-seven thousand times.

"Snow Goddess."

It was perfect. Meagan grabbed my hand and squeezed my fingers tightly as we stood there in rapture.

Perfect.

MEAGAN STAYED OVER THAT NIGHT.

We were hanging out in my room after everyone else had gone, reviewing the events of the night before—well, actually, Meagan was talking about Garrett's deeds of the night before and how hot he was and how relieved she was that he was okay—when my messenger chimed. It was Rox, the tattoo artist and partner of dragon dude Niall. I assumed she'd called with birthday wishes.

"Hey, Rox."

Then I had a wild thought. Was Rox going to offer to do my tattoo, against my mom's objections? My heart took off at a gallop, fueled by crazy hope.

"Hi, Zoë. Happy birthday. Sorry we weren't there for your big day."

"That's okay. Thanks for the good wishes."

"Well, it's more than that. I need to ask you something." Rox sounded distracted, and I could hear music in the background. There were other people talking, so I assumed she was at her tattoo shop. It was open half the night, so it made sense that she was still there.

Working.

Meagan gave me a look, but I sat up, hoping that I knew what she wanted to ask. I sure knew the answer. "What's up?"

"Well, this guy came in tonight," Rox said. I could tell by her tone that there were others around her, and guessed that she would say only half of what she meant. Maybe the guy in question was standing right there. "And he wants a dragon tattoo." She paused, although I wasn't sure why.

"You do good ones. I like Thorolf's a lot."

That was, in fact, why I'd hoped Rox would do my tattoo.

"Yeah, well, that's the thing. He doesn't want one of mine. He insists that he wants one *you've* drawn."

"Me?"

"He says that you have one drawn out to go on and over your left shoulder and that he wants it. And he wants me to start on it tonight, because it's your birthday." Rox lowered her voice. "I know that's true and you know that's true, but how the hell does this guy know that?"

There was only one way any guy could know all of this.

In fact, there was only one guy who did.

I heard her slide her hand over the mouthpiece. "Do you have a stalker, Zoë?"

"Kind of, but it's okay."

"What?"

"I'm pretty sure I know who it is."

"Well, that's one thing," Rox said, sounding firm. "But just because he's seen your work doesn't mean he can just have it. You've put a lot of effort into that drawing and it's *yours*. People think they can just snag stuff because they want it, but artists need to have their rights defended...."

I interrupted her rant, my heart fluttering. "Is he there?"

"You really think you know him?"

"If it's who I think it is, I'm good with this."

"Really?"

"Yeah. The guy I'm thinking of is a...a friend."

There was the understatement of the century. Meagan had her "This is good and you'd better tell me now" expression, but I held up one hand.

"Okay. Hang on."

There was a hum of activity, and the sound of Rox's heels on the linoleum floor. I've been in that shop a bunch of times. I could close my eyes and imagine myself there, see it and smell it. I heard Niall's voice faintly, then those of their twin sons. Rox was putting them to work early.

Then someone picked up the phone. I caught my breath and made a wild and crazy birthday wish.

It came true.

"Hey, dragon girl."

Jared.

I felt like I'd been hit with a brick.

And I was just about as coherent as a brick.

There were roughly forty-seven million things I wanted to say to him, but I'd been struck mute.

"Hey, Jared," I managed to say. Meagan gasped and mimed a victory shout, both fists in the air.

"Look, I, uh, thought about what you said," he said, sounding less certain of himself than I could believe possible. "And you know, even though I don't answer to anybody, I could call you once in a while."

"But you let Rox do the dirty work tonight."

He laughed under his breath, and then his words came, really low. "Wasn't sure you'd talk to me, dragon girl."

I was gripping the messenger so tightly I thought it might crack. Of all the thousands of things I wanted to say to him, I chose an easy one. One that didn't sound entirely pathetic, or like my knees had dissolved beneath me. "Thanks for the book."

"You're welcome. It needed to be where it belonged." He cleared his throat. "I always meant for you to have it."

I closed my eyes, hearing the resonance of truth in his voice. I knew Jared was a long shot, but it seemed like there were at least possibilities.

Maybe he just needed somebody to believe in him.

I wasn't nearly sure that would be enough, but I was willing to try.

"You get your beryl?" he asked softly.

"Turned out I had it all along," I said. "I just didn't know it."

"Everything work out okay?"

I heard his worry and smiled. "We kicked ass."

He laughed.

I thought about offering that ride again.

"Look, I need a dragon at my back," Jared said quietly, then continued before I could volunteer. "One who can't get hurt. What do you say to letting me carry a part of you on my skin?"

It was—as I should have expected from Jared—a perfect solution. The ideal birthday gift. I liked the idea of my dragon taking ink and claiming skin. While it was frustrating that it couldn't be on my shoulder—at least not anytime soon—I really liked the idea of my work being on his.

I cleared my throat. "First you've got to tell me about your salamander."

He chuckled a little, the sound making me shiver in a good way. I felt, in fact, tingly and filled with anticipation.

"It's not a salamander," Jared said. "It's a Wyvern. Rox has some ideas about shading it to look white. She already gave it green eyes, just so you know."

I shivered with delight. He already had a part of me on his skin. Or a representation of me.

My heart was thudding because there was only one possible answer to his question. "I'll send her the drawing now. I already have it digital anyway. Are you going to be in New York for a while?"

"Long enough, but don't look for me, dragon girl." He was stern.

Protective.

"But..."

"You don't know everything they can do. Don't underestimate them. We can't risk it yet."

I liked him talking about us as if we were already a team. I had a compromise solution of my own. "So, maybe I'll send you a dream instead."

"I'd like that, dragon girl." I heard the smile in his words. I felt warm right to my toes.

And Rox could send me pictures of my dragon on Jared's naked back, to dream on. Uh-huh.

He cleared his throat and I knew he was going to tease me about something. I could close my eyes and imagine the sparkling green of his eyes, that glint of mischief and his troublemaking smile. His voice dropped deliciously low. "Especially since you still owe me a ride."

"Absolutely," I agreed. "All I have to do is finish off the Mages first."

"Go get 'em, Zoë."

Fortunately, I had a pretty good idea how we finally were going to eliminate the Mages. It would coincide perfectly with boot camp, another solar eclipse, the end of the Great Lunar Standstill of 2025, and me taking hold of the future as Wyvern du jour.

Stay tuned.

BLAZING THE TRAIL

THE DRAGON DIARIES BOOK THREE

It's almost Valentine's Day, and Zoë Sorensson's love life is heating up. Cute, loyal, and understanding, wolf shifter Derek is pretty much the perfect guy. He likes Zoë, and he knows what it's like to have to keep a secret. Yet, Zoë can't help but wish it was rebel rocker Jared asking her to the Valentine's dance instead. But Jared's too busy playing hot and cold with her heart, calling Zoë his dragon girl one minute and then taking special interest in her best friend the next.

Zoë is just about ready to breathe fire, especially once she uncovers a new threat that targets her friends. Although Zoë thought the Mages were defeated, they're back and have invoked an old spell to give them new power—they plan to eliminate all shape shifters on the night of the big dance. Now, Zoë must lead an alliance of young shifters to battle the Mages and figure out exactly what—and who—she wants, before it all goes up in smoke...

I

February 11, 2025

It was Tuesday, the day that stretches so long that you start to think the weekend will never, ever come—and I was actually hoping the weekend would never arrive. I'd avoided my locker all day, but when the last bell rang, I ran out of excuses.

For one thing, it was snowing like crazy outside. Two, I needed my coat. Therefore, I had to go to my locker before I could go home.

And Derek would pounce on me, and Meagan would be there with Jessica, listening to the whole thing, and the day would end even worse than a normal Tuesday.

I dragged my feet down the corridor, trying to delay the inevitable. Suzanne sailed past me with her cronies and snarled her favorite greeting —that would be "Freak!"—and they all laughed their mean girls' laugh. My dread was enough that I didn't even care about Ms. Popularity.

You would think that my outlook would be more positive. A bunch of great things had happened in the fall—some due to the efforts of yours truly—and it had been quiet in the realm of dragon shape shifters ever since. We'd kicked the proverbial butts of the Mages—that fun group of humans who were bent on wiping all shifters from the face of the earth—

by destroying their hive memory; we'd formed alliances with the wolf shifters and the cat shifters against the Mages; and I'd been given the blessing of the previous Wyverns as the new Wyvern. Kohana, a Thunderbird shifter, had stolen the powerful NightBlade from the Mages, thereby rendering them pretty much impotent, and we had a plan to help him destroy it on the next solar eclipse, coming to a sky near you in April. All we had to do was wait for the time to be right to completely consolidate our victory—forever.

My best friend Meagan had discovered that she had spellsinger powers and was learning to use them. I'd also had the most awesome sixteenth-birthday party ever at the end of all that drama. Plus I'd gotten my driver's license—a quest that my father insisted had cut at least a century off his life span—and had done so without fulfilling my dad's expectation that the city of Chicago would become a scene of carnage.

Bonus: I got to use my mom's car while they were on vacation together this week. I was staying at Meagan's and we had wheels.

You'd think that after all of that a dragon girl would be able to spy the glimmer of gold in her hoard of possibilities.

But no. All I could think about—and dread—was the Valentine's Day dance this coming Friday night.

Derek had asked me to go with him. This wasn't a huge surprise. We'd gone to a few movies and hung out together over the past couple of months. He wasn't much of a talker but it felt comfortable being with him. We'd kissed twice and it had been sweet. I knew he wanted more than that, but I wasn't sure if that was what I wanted.

Inviting me to the Valentine's Day dance was big.

And I'd been avoiding him. It was serious finkdom on my part, but I just didn't know what to do.

The thing is, I like Derek. I even like him a lot. He's sweet and thoughtful and occasionally very funny. He's protective of me and pretty quiet; a bit intense. Plus he's a wolf shifter, so he understands the challenge of having two lives and keeping one part of your life secret from the other. We have the shifter thing in common and that makes it easy to be with him. I think it's wicked that he has the gift of foresight, that he can smell the future a couple of minutes before it happens. He calls it his early-warning system. I want some of that, but so far my Wyvern ability to see the future is nonexistent.

The problem is that I don't think I like Derek as much as he likes me.

And that worries me.

Does it matter? I think it does.

Derek is probably the guy I should go for. He's the one chance that could work.

Of course, I have this habit of falling hard for guys who don't fall for me. I did it first with Nick, another dragon shifter, and I'm pretty sure I've done it again.

For Jared. Who is older, elusive, hot, a rebel, and a member of a rock band. He rides a motorcycle, is never around when I want to talk to him, and possibly knows more about dragons than I do. He challenges me and dares me and makes me tingle right down to my toes—and that happened even before I scored my very first kiss from him. He jumbles me up and confuses me—and just the mention of his name makes my dad breathe fire and lock the doors.

I think I could have forgotten Jared—or at least let go of the possibility of seeing him again—until he sent me the only copy in existence of a book about dragon shifters. He had it and at first he said he wouldn't give it to me, so that I'd need to contact him regularly. He called me Dragon Girl then and his eyes were seventy million shades of green, his grip warm and tight on my hand. My heart did somersaults all over my chest.

Then he sent me the book last fall. What was I supposed to think? I thought he was done and gone and that was that.

I was still trying to reconcile myself to the idea of him being out of my life forever when he had called out of the blue. Then he got the tattoo I wanted, the one my mom had forbidden me to get on my back, on *his* back for *my* birthday.

I didn't sleep for three nights.

I've spent way too much time checking out the pictures he sent me of the finished tattoo on his gorgeous muscles.

Plus I still owe him a ride on my own personal Dragon Air.

So, should I hold to the dream, as crazy and unlikely as it sounds? Or should I accept that Derek is the more practical choice and agree to go to the dance with him? I don't want to be mean to Derek, and maybe love takes time to grow. Or maybe my instincts are right. Or maybe I'm just always going to yearn for guys that don't want me. Maybe that's part of what I like about them.

How twisted would that be? I like to think I'm more emotionally balanced than that.

Maybe Jared just likes the idea of having fan girls, of having me hanging on the line, waiting on him.

That really isn't my style.

At least, it shouldn't be.

I rounded the last corner and saw exactly what I'd wanted to avoid. Derek was leaning beside my locker, waiting for me and my answer. Meagan was at her locker, sorting her books, waiting for me and a ride home.

At least Jessica wasn't there. She and Meagan are still tight, tighter than Jessica and me. (Apparently their both being math whizzes is a stronger force than Jessica and me both being shape shifters and the wild cards of our respective kinds. Go figure.)

Derek's dark hair is straight and still a bit too long. It hangs over his eyes, but still doesn't disguise their pale blue hue. They are wolflike in color and intensity. I swear he has X-ray vision. He was wearing his usual dark clothes, a combo that the eye slides over easily and lets him blend into the shadows. He's so quiet that he could be made of shadow.

Of course, he wasn't surprised to see me and had even anticipated my direction. His gaze locked on me as soon as I turned the corner, his attention making my mouth go dry.

I'd have to give him an answer before I left today. But what would it be? Heart or mind? I had a feeling that there would be big consequences from my choice, but, of course, I couldn't even guess what they might be. My Wyvern powers of seeing the future could have helped me out here, but no such luck.

I was on my own.

"Hey," Derek said, a guy of few words, as always. His voice is low and rumbly, kind of like a growl. Sometimes it made me shiver. "How was art class?"

"Best class of the day," I said with a smile. "Makes the rest tolerable."

As I got to my locker, Meagan laughed, tapping her messenger to pull up a new message. She was laughing a lot more than she used to and no wonder; she'd finally gotten her braces off. Her teeth looked awesome and she was attracting a lot more attention. People saw how cute she was instead of her mouthful of metal. I was happy for her.

In fact, I had an idea that I knew what would make her happy if I could make it happen.

"It's Jared again," she said with excitement, scrolling through the new message.

"Again?" I asked as I opened my locker. I gave Derek a smile and tried to keep my tone neutral in referring to Mr. Incredibly Hot.

Derek didn't smile back.

He watched me closely. I knew that the big moment had arrived.

I dodged it just a little bit longer.

I nudged Meagan. "You two have something going on?" I teased, acting as if I didn't care.

Meagan laughed again. "He's sending me all these tips about spellsinging. It's amazing. I'm learning so much."

"Oh, so you hear from him often."

"Yeah! Like every second day. He's in Des Moines this week."

My heart stopped. Des Moines was comparatively close.

But he hadn't called me.

In months.

Meagan held up her messenger to show the image of some club on its screen. "That's where the band is playing tonight. They're sold out!"

"Great," I said, barely glancing at it. I felt a simmer begin deep in my heart.

She heard from him *every other day*?

And I hadn't had one *hello* since November?

I was so out of his life that he hadn't even told me that he'd gotten back with his band.

Even I know enough about guys to understand the implications of that. Jared had been messing with me. He hadn't called me because he didn't want to get in touch. Because he didn't care.

Just thinking that made me wince, but there was no point in ducking the truth.

I shrugged into my coat and met Derek's gaze. He was cautious, uncertain what I would do. "You still want to go to the dance Friday?" I asked him, my tone a little more challenging than necessary.

He straightened. "Only with you." He smiled crookedly and I was struck by just how cute he was. "I thought you weren't sure."

"I'm sure. Let's go."

His smile broadened then and I saw how much I'd pleased him. It is kind of amazing to have that effect on someone. Would it work the other way by Friday? Or after that? "I'll pick you up at seven, talk to your dad and stuff." He was big on the protocol of talking to my dad. Maybe it's a pack thing. A wolf thing. A question of respecting the hierarchy. Either way, my dad likes Derek a bunch.

Probably as much as he dislikes even the idea of Jared.

"They went to the Caribbean today. I'm staying at Meagan's this weekend."

Derek nodded. "Okay. I'll pick you up there." He glanced at Meagan. "You coming to the dance, Meagan?"

She pouted. "I don't have a date and I don't want to go stag. I've done it enough, and this year I really want to go with a guy."

"She's coming," I said to Derek, and Meagan didn't look that surprised. There's a casualty of her being a genius—it's tough to surprise her.

"But..." she started to protest.

"She's coming," I insisted, and slammed my locker. Derek looked between us, amused.

Meagan gave me a stern look. "You're not going to fix me up. I won't be a pity date."

"No, you won't be. But, yes, I am going to fix you up." I bumped shoulders with her, the way we always do, and smiled at her. "Trust me. I have a plan and you're going to like it."

I did and she would.

I just had to make it work.

ABOUT THREE MONTHS BEFORE, Meagan had gotten her first glimpse of the *Pyr*. That's the name for dragon shape shifters, or, at least, our name for ourselves. That's what I am, although I'm the only female dragon shape shifter in existence. There's only one female *Pyr* at a time, and she's the

Wyvern. I'm the Wyvern. And being the Wyvern means having a bonus pack of extra powers, some of which I'm still trying to locate.

But my point is that all the other dragon shifters I know, all of my buddies and the dragons I grew up with, are all guys. And they're pretty hot guys. I think the dragon business works in a big way for the males of the species: it seems to make them fill out and get buff more quickly than plain old human guys. So any female with a speck of interest in the opposite sex would notice them, even when they're in their human form.

In dragon form, they're breathtaking.

In November, Meagan had been targeted by the Mages because of her spellsinging talents. Spellsinging is innate: You're born with it or not. And if you are born with it, the Mages try to enlist you. They thought they could turn Meagan to the dark side, then maybe use her against me and my dragon pals. They weren't counting on Meagan the wunderkind figuring out their plan and deciding to go undercover to learn the real deal. It all culminated at a Halloween party at the house of an apprentice Mage named Trevor who goes to our school. Meagan had been crazy for Trevor forever, until she learned his nasty secret.

Even worse, Trevor offered up Meagan as the sacrifice for his initiation rite.

But then Garrett, one of my dragon friends, came to the rescue. Garrett is garnet and gold in dragon form, his scales like jewels, and just about as magnificent as a dragon can be. He scooped up this damsel in distress and Meagan has been talking endlessly about Garrett ever since.

Forget Trevor.

So, I can tease Meagan about Jared because I know she's totally nuts for Garrett.

The problem is that we're in Chicago and Garrett lives in Traverse City. Meagan and Garrett haven't seen each other since November. Rotten luck contributed to that—the *Pyr* got together at our place at Christmas, but Meagan and her family were on vacation in California at the exact same time. She was devastated.

And I think Garrett was a bit bummed, too.

He's got the same strong-but-silent-type intensity as Derek. I know Meagan and Garrett talked a bunch, because between the two of them they've managed to translate that treatise on the Mages that he'd found in his mom's used bookstore in the fall.

They didn't really need to do it, given the current state of the Mage population—the Mages who hadn't died had become incoherent messes, with no memories left—but it just seemed mean to take that away. They'd finished a month before and officially had no more excuses to talk to each other or see each other, at least not until the big NightBlade destruction we'd planned for April.

Which I'm sure seemed a very, very long time away for them.

So, that night, when I was supposed to be doing my homework at the dining room table at Meagan's house, I used my messenger under the table and invited Garrett to the Valentine's Day dance. Meagan watched me from the other side of the table, flicking glances toward the kitchen, where her mom was making dinner. Her mom is serious about homework, and if she caught me, she'd confiscate my messenger pronto.

I closed my hands over it in an attempt to muffle the sound as it chimed to signal an incoming message. I peeked between my fingers and grinned.

Ha! Garrett was coming.

"That had better not be a messenger I hear," Mrs. Jameson said from the kitchen. "We're going to eat in twenty minutes and I want to see that English homework done."

Who? Meagan mouthed.

I smiled as mysteriously as I could.

She wrinkled her nose at me, then glanced at her own messenger. It remained silent.

Geek, I mouthed back at her, and she wadded up a sheet of paper to throw it at me. We have an old joke that we're not geeky enough to message each other when we're sitting in the same room. (Even though we sometimes do.)

"I am talking to you, Zoë Sorensson," Mrs. Jameson added.

"Just finishing the last two questions, Mrs. Jameson," I answered, apparently the most dutiful student alive. Just so you know, I have nobody fooled on that one.

"Meagan?"

"Done, Mom." Meagan frowned and leaned closer to me, flicking another look at the kitchen. "Who?" she whispered.

“Wait for Friday,” I replied in kind, and winked. “You’ll love it.”

Meagan sat back. Of course she knew. Her mouth fell open and she raised a hand to her lips. *No!* she mouthed, clearly wanting me to say yes.

It is so tedious to try to surprise a brilliant individual, you know. Impossible, maybe.

I tried to act like I didn’t understand her, but we’ve known each other way too long for that. I’d been hoping to make her wait for it, at least until we went to bed, but no luck. Meagan was too excited.

She scribbled a note and shoved it across the table at me, interrupting my consideration of English lit question number 29.

Her expression was expectant as I read it.

Actually, she was bouncing in her chair, vibrating with such excitement that I knew I’d done exactly the right thing.

For once.

GARRETT!?!

I nodded.

Meagan snatched the paper back and scribbled some more. I smiled when I saw what she’d written.

OMG! WHAT AM I GOING TO WEAR?

THAT NIGHT I had a familiar dream. I am never really surprised anymore when I dream of snow. It’s Wyvern stuff. Snow means that I’ll have a dream visit from those two old ladies. I’ll see them sitting under that huge tree near a well, their world superimposed on mine, as if I’m standing on the cusp of another realm.

One is soft, like a sweet grandmother who knits and makes cookies and gives perfect presents—you know, exactly what you wanted before you even realized you did. I never knew my grandmothers, so maybe I’m mixing up my wishes with the dream, but I call this one Granny. She is always knitting, silently knitting a big white mound of something. I’ve thought that she was knitting clouds before. Or snowdrifts. She was the first to show up in my dreams, but she never says anything.

Last fall, when I started to dream about Granny again, she turned up with a friend. This one talks. She says her name is Urd and that Granny is really named Verdandi and that they're sisters. You'd never know to look at them; Urd has a face like a skull, while Verdandi looks like Mrs. Claus. There's a bit of edge to Urd. She pushed me down the well, for example—the dark, awful well that is right at their feet. I know it was for my own good, but still. I keep my distance from Urd.

So, when I felt cold in the middle of the night in the twin bed in Meagan's room and I opened my eyes to find snow drifting across my comforter, I was pretty sure what was going on. I rolled over, fully expecting to find Granny knitting and Urd spinning. I thought they'd probably turned up to tell me something important.

I doubted that it involved choosing between Jared and Derek, but I could hope.

I rolled over and my eyes just about fell out of my head in shock. Oh, Urd and Verdandi were there, and so was the big tree and even the well. Meagan's room had disappeared, and I was out on the tundra, just like usual.

The big difference was the blood.

It was everywhere. It was crimson and shone wetly against the snow. There was so much of it that my mind boggled. How could there be an ocean of blood? Where was it coming from?

Granny was knitting but her needles were flying with superhuman speed, as if she were trying to outrun something. Urd was spinning like a crazed woman, her drop spindle a manic blur against the snow and blood. Neither was looking around. Both seemed to be completely oblivious to the change in their surroundings, all that blood. Except, of course, for their speed and determination to ignore it.

I could even smell it and it made my bile rise.

I knew instinctively that what they were really pretending not to notice was the third woman. She stood between them with a huge pair of silver shears, slashing at the snowdrift that Granny had knit. She turned, laughing, and cut the thread that Urd had just spun with one vicious snip of those scissors. The drop spindle fell and rolled. Urd—who wasn't shy—

didn't say boo. She just ducked her head and went after it, rummaging under the cloud of white knitting. Granny continued to knit at warp speed.

And the third one turned her smile on me.

Uh oh.

She was young, this one, her hair hanging in a long gold braid over her shoulder. She had those scissors in one hand, while a knife gleamed in the other. She was tall and fit, a warrior princess dressed in a laced leather jerkin, jodhpurs, and black leather boots that rose over her knees. They had big, mean silver spurs on them. Her arms were bare and I could see her muscles, as well as the blue tattoos on her skin. Her gaze was steely and her expression was grim. I knew she could whup me without even trying.

I sat up and eased away from her.

Worst of all, there was blood spattered all over her. It dripped from the scissors and pooled on the toe of one boot, gleaming crimson against the black. She even had a few splashes on her cheek.

"I am Skuld," she said, her voice deep and rough. She sounded like she'd been chain-smoking for centuries. She took a step toward me, assessing me, brandishing that knife.

I'd done my research and thought this an ideal moment to show myself an apt student. "The third Wyrd sister," I said, trying to sound as if I wasn't worried. I'm pretty sure I failed. "Your name means 'what will be.'"

"No. It means 'what *may* be.'" Her eyes glinted and she laughed at me. I saw the gold crown on her one eyetooth and a hint of what looked like madness in her eyes. Then she flung out her hands, and our surroundings were instantly consumed in fog.

There was just Skuld and me and a whole lot of mist. I couldn't even hear Granny's knitting needles anymore. It was like she and Urd had vanished.

Or been banished.

The blood, however, was still there.

The mist wasn't normal mist, just so you know. It smelled wrong. Dirty. Like smoke. Blood. Trouble. There was also a glimmer to it, as if a red light was being reflected by the fog. Skuld didn't seem troubled by it. She shoved her knife into the holster on her belt on one side and the scissors into a second holster on the other. A bird screamed and there was the shadow of wings flying through the mist. She smiled.

You have to know that I was not thrilled when Skuld extended her hardened hand to me. "Come along, Wyvern. I've got something to show you."

There was a determination about her that had me on my feet in record time. I was pretty sure she'd just toss me over her shoulder if I didn't go with her. Nothing really bad had happened to me yet in these dreams. I was thinking I couldn't actually get hurt—even though the attitude of the other two sisters worried me. They clearly didn't want to mess with Skuld.

And I was a bit curious as to what she would show me. Urd had given me the key to the past. Verdandi had helped me claim my Wyvern powers in the present. Would Skuld give me a taste of the future?

Was she going to teach me how to claim the foresight that should be part of my Wyvern bonus pack? What about the Wyvern's supposed ability to send dreams? I would have loved to have had both powers, so I went with her.

But when I put my hand in hers, her skin was as cold as ice. Her touch sent a shudder through me, one that nearly stopped my heart. She glanced at me and shook her head, as if I wasn't good enough for her trouble, then leapt into the air, tugging me behind her. She became a pitch-black raven, her talons digging into my hand as she hauled me into the sky.

I was reminded of Kohana, the Thunderbird shifter who was sometimes my enemy, sometimes my ally, but her bird form was smaller than his. Her feathers had a blue-black gleam and her eyes were as dark as obsidian. His eyes, in contrast, were filled with the yellow fire of lightning. She didn't have any thunderbolts in her claws, either.

Just yours truly.

Skuld left the ground behind with dizzying speed, ripping through the fog with a speed and a confidence that seemed crazy under the circumstances.

It wasn't as if she had radar. I couldn't see more than six feet in any direction. Where were we? What else was out here?

I panicked then. I tried to shift to my dragon form, thinking I'd do better under my own steam, but apparently that ability didn't follow me to dreamland. Or maybe Skuld had shut it down. Either way, I couldn't shift. I couldn't free myself from her iron grip. I didn't know where she was going but I was getting the feeling I wasn't going to like it.

The glimmer of red light was getting brighter.

And it had started pulsing.

Maybe, just maybe, I shouldn't have been so quick to comply.

SKULD DESCENDED LIKE A ROCKET, heading straight for the vivid pulse of red light. As we got closer to the ground, I could see more details. It looked like we had arrived at a garbage dump, broken bottles and twisted metal in every direction I looked. The red light flashed over it all, like there was a cop car in the vicinity.

Except there wasn't.

Maybe it was a beacon, guiding us to Skuld's destination.

Skuld landed with a triumphant cry, shifting shape at the last minute and punctuating her arrival by kicking aside a pile of garbage. It toppled with a crash.

"What's that?" someone demanded. I peered through the mist and saw the silhouettes of three guys. They were standing together maybe thirty feet ahead of us. They seemed vaguely familiar to me, even though I couldn't see them clearly. My Wyvern—or maybe my dragon—sense started to tingle.

"They can't see or hear us," Skuld said. She blew at the fog and it dissipated, just like that. "You've nothing to fear."

Then she laughed in a way that implied exactly the opposite.

"They heard that." I pointed to the toppled trash cans.

She grinned at me. "But can't hear *us*."

It was clear she wasn't interested in arguing the technicalities. And, really, she would know the rules—such as they were—for this dream realm better than I. Paying attention was the best I could do.

I looked around the vacant lot. Now that we were on the ground, standing in the rubble, the red light was gone. It looked like we were in the real world. "What are we doing here?"

Her smile was chilly. "I like battlefields. I like my dead fresh." With that, she marched toward the guys, pulling her dagger on the way.

Like maybe she was going to get her own fresh kill.

I wasn't sure I wanted to see this.

On the other hand, I was in a dream. Theoretically, I couldn't get hurt.

Practically, the Wyrd sisters showed me stuff for a reason. I should pay attention. I might learn something useful.

The guys started to chant, as if they didn't see Skuld coming, but I have to believe that anybody with a pulse would have noticed her. She must be telling the truth, I decided. Or at least some of it. Either way, I followed her.

The chant was creepy. It made the hair stand up on the back of my neck, which gave me a theory about it. I looked closer and sure enough, I saw the dangerous orange light of a Mage spell. It erupted from their throats, then spun together into a kind of cord. It spiraled up into the air, getting thicker and brighter as it went, then widened into a sphere of molten gold.

So they had to be Mages.

No, they had to be apprentice Mages, who still had their own individual memory.

This was not good.

I looked back at the guys and realized I knew two of them. One was Trevor, the apprentice Mage from school who'd tried to trick and trap us shifters last fall. The other was Adrian, the senior apprentice Mage who had invaded our dragon boot camp the previous spring. I didn't know the third guy, but it looked like he was more junior than Trevor.

At least he looked more nervous than Trevor.

What were they doing? Trying to jump-start the old Mage plan for world domination?

The full Mages had been killed or gone crazy in that big battle in the fall. I'd pretty much assumed that cleaning up the dregs of their nasty group would be easy, since just the amateurs and the damaged were left. Trevor had been sickeningly nice to me at school, as if he were scared of me, which just reinforced my conclusion.

What is this spell for?

Is there something I don't know?

I moved closer, even without any urging from Skuld. The sphere they were creating with their spell became bigger and brighter. It was a golden globe, expanding in the air over their heads. Like a balloon. It looked more solid by the minute, like it was made of orange glass. And as their chant became a song, I saw shapes form within the sphere.

Human shapes.

Silvery human shapes.

ShadowEaters! I took a step backward, feeling like I was going to puke. The Mages had invoked these beings at that last ceremony, to feed them the shadows of their sacrificial victims. They'd creeped me out then, and didn't give a better impression this time around. There was something ominous and awesome about their presence, like they were visiting from another realm.

The thing was the Mages had invoked the ShadowEaters last fall using the NightBlade. How could apprentice Mages do this summoning? Kohana had the NightBlade, wherever he was.

There was, though, a full moon shining down on the scene, which had been part of the deal during our big battle in the fall. And there was no mistaking those shapes.

Or my dread at the sight of them.

The shapes in the globe became more substantial.

And more numerous.

So numerous that they strained at the constraints of the spell bubble, elbowing each other for space. Jostling and shoving. There was something aggressive about them this time, and I wasn't glad to see that change.

All the same, I didn't want to blink and risk missing anything.

As the guys chanted their spell, the ShadowEaters started to brighten. The orange light of the spell seemed to fill them, making their shapes luminescent, radiant with pulsing orange spell light.

This cannot be good.

The guys were staring upward, rapt at the results of their spell, even as they were fortifying it. The sphere became so crowded with shapes that it bulged. I saw fists and feet and elbows, as if the ShadowEaters tried to fight their way loose of the orb's constraint. The sphere looked to be stretched thin and I worried that it would burst. They struggled with more force. The guys sang louder. My heart pounded...

Then Adrian threw his hands up and shouted, "Be with us, O exalted ones!"

With a flash, the globe shattered into a thousand shards of gold. Hundreds of ShadowEaters leapt to the earth with purpose. Now they looked like menacing shadows, dark silhouettes with no features.

Except for their gleaming golden eyes. Their eyes were filled with spell light. They were silent but terrifying.

Adrian had time to laugh at his victory. "I told you we could do it!" he crowed to Trevor. "We made the Invocation of Destruction!" He turned to high-five Trevor, jubilant in his success.

But the ShadowEaters fell on the third guy like a pack of vultures. He screamed as they pulled him away from Trevor and Adrian, but there were so many of them that he couldn't fight them off. They snatched him and surrounded him and held him down. I saw their teeth flash as they bit and snapped.

When they retreated just seconds later, smacking their lips, he had collapsed on the ground. And he had no shadow.

I would have seen it in the light of that moon. They'd devoured it.

This cannot be good. When ShadowEaters ate a shifter's shadow, the shifter died. It was like the shifter ceased to exist, because he or she couldn't cast a shadow—or because in eating the shadow, the Shadow-Eaters stole the shifter's abilities.

Did it work the same way for apprentice Mages?

I took a deep breath, using my keen *Pyr* sense of hearing to check his vitals.

He wasn't breathing. And he had no pulse.

They'd killed him.

Without the NightBlade cutting his shadow free, without him being a shifter.

This was new—and horrible.

The ShadowEaters swirled around the two apprentice Mages like leaves dancing in a gusty fall wind, looking hungry and predatory.

"Holy shit," Trevor whispered. "What the fuck is happening?" Adrian was flipping through the book in a panic. Obviously, they hadn't invoked the particular destruction they'd anticipated.

The ShadowEaters pressed closer around the pair and I heard Trevor squeal like a girl; then the ShadowEaters swept into the sky. They soared like a golden tide, as if they'd been freed from some kind of captivity, a thought that didn't fill me with delight.

High above us, they disappeared into the night.

I saw the glow of their eyes shine longer, like nasty stars, until they winked out, as well. Where had they gone?

"You have to stop them!" Trevor shouted at Adrian, and I heard his fear.

"I don't know how." Adrian turned the pages of that book so fast that I thought they'd tear. He kept looking up, but the ShadowEaters were long gone from view. "It'll take me ages to figure it out!"

"We don't have ages! They're hungry and they're here," Trevor said, his horror echoing mine.

The two looked at the fallen kid, then at each other. I could taste their terror.

"I can't fix it," Adrian said quietly. He looked around, his eyes a bit wild. "Not yet. Maybe not ever."

Trevor swore. They stared at each other as a triumphant bellow echoed through the night. It came from above and sent shivers down my spine.

They pivoted and fled from the garbage dump, racing into the street. I heard two car engines start and tires squeal.

Did this mean that the apprentice Mages and the ShadowEaters weren't allies anymore? Had Adrian messed up, or had the ShadowEaters wrested control of the ceremony to serve their own purposes?

That was not an optimistic thought.

Who or what would they eat next?

I could only hope the ShadowEaters would feast on all the remaining Mages and apprentice Mages. They didn't look like discerning eaters, but it still seemed like a long shot that they'd do our dirty work.

Speaking of discerning eaters, Skuld was strolling toward the dead guy. He looked to be my age or maybe a year younger. She squatted down beside him, poked him, and then sniffed his corpse with satisfaction.

I supposed that this was as fresh as dead got.

"Wasted soul," she said with a shake of her head. "Oh, well." She sniffed again. "But a very nice liver." She cast me a look. "Hungry?"

I shook my head, unable to look away.

I watched in horror as Skuld shifted shape right before my eyes. She hopped onto his chest in her raven form and ripped his flesh open with her beak. When she tore into his body cavity, presumably looking for that liver, I couldn't stand it anymore.

I spun around and ran. I didn't know where I was or whether I could get back to the real world, but wherever I ended up had to be better than here.

2

I woke up with a start, my heart leaping around my chest and my breath coming in anxious spurts. Even when I closed my eyes, I could see the ShadowEaters falling on that kid, surrounding him and killing him. It was just as horrible remembering it as witnessing it. He'd been swarmed and overcome.

I had to think that he had been convenient. I had to think that they'd be more interested in continuing the Mage plan of eliminating all shifters than in snacking on their own kind.

Come to think of it, every ceremony of the Mages seemed to involve a sacrifice. So, Adrian had called down the ShadowEaters and someone had to die to finish the ritual. The kid had been in the wrong place at the wrong time. Maybe the ShadowEaters had done all the feasting they needed to do.

I had my doubts. I thought about the ShadowEaters leaping into the sky and disappearing. Like they'd run out of energy. Would they come after the shifters next?

But wait. Skuld said she was about the future. Had this happened already or not?

Was it going to happen—or was it just possible?

That calmed me down a little bit. I pulled out my messenger and began tapping madly. When we had interrupted the Mages' ceremony in the fall, it had been held on the night of a full moon. I found a lunar calendar and checked the dates. The next full moon would be Wednesday, February 12.

This week. My eyes fell on the clock in Meagan's room and I saw that it was two forty-five in the morning. Technically it *was* Wednesday. Had my dream come true yet? I went to the window and looked out, unable to see any golden spell light in the winter sky beyond Meagan's window.

"Scared?" a guy asked from behind me, and I nearly jumped out of my skin.

My older brother, Sigmund, was sitting on the end of the bed, looking as scruffy and disreputable as he usually did. That would be my *dead* older brother, Sigmund. He appeared to me from time to time.

He hadn't been there when I woke up. I would have noticed that.

I looked around the room, which looked perfectly normal as Meagan slept on her bed with the cat, King, curled up near her feet.

Had my brother come to help or to complicate things? With Sigmund, you never knew. "What are you doing here?"

"I'm not really here. Am I?" he asked, looking amused. "Being dead and all." He held up one hand and I could see right through it to the wallpaper on the wall behind him. He grinned.

"I can see you."

He leaned back, completely at ease. "So, do you usually talk to dead people?"

"Apparently, it happens sometimes." I watched him with some suspicion. Sigmund usually turns up to tell me something, but he never just drops the news. It's kind of irritating how I have to work it out of him. "What did you come to tell me?"

He smiled and got up, stretching elaborately. "Just checking on you, sis."

"Why?"

"Bad dream?" His eyes were glinting, as if he knew something I didn't—which wasn't exactly a long shot.

Two could play this game. "What makes you ask?"

"It's a Wyvern thing, you know." He bent and scratched King's ears.

Kincaid, that is. This cat shifter had adopted me in the fall, just as his pal—named Mozart by Meagan—had adopted Meagan. They were both vigilant sentinels in cat form, and good-looking—if enigmatic—guys in human form. They both seemed to prefer being cats. I'd only seen either of them as guys once, in that last fight with the Mages.

Maybe they hated school.

Maybe they'd run away from home.

I couldn't figure out why they didn't seem to have human lives, like we *Pyr* do, but they weren't telling.

Even though I'm not much for cats, there was no shaking King. I'd thought he'd move on after that fight, but he'd stuck to me like glue.

Never mind that he was a huge Maine coon in his cat form and had to weigh thirty pounds. He's no more enamored of dragons than I am of cats, so we have a relationship based on mutual respect and mild animosity.

Yes, I have been known to call him Fish Breath.

Usually when I have a bad dream, I wake up to find him watching me.

But he was sleeping on the end of Meagan's bed.

King didn't even move when Sigmund rubbed his ears. What was going on? Was this another, strangely realistic dream? The emergence of a new Wyvern power? Or was everything in some kind of flux?

Come to think of it, where *was* Mozart? Usually he and King crashed together on Meagan's bed.

I spoke with caution. "Casting dreams is a Wyvern thing, from what I understand."

"So is having them. It's the whole seeing-past-present-and-future-simultaneously trick." Sigmund shot a glance at me. "You can't do it yet, can you?"

I shook my head.

"Mastering it drives some Wyverns crazy, you know, so I thought I'd check on you."

Great. That was not news I needed to hear.

Sigmund arched a brow. "Feeling sane?"

"Pretty much."

He grinned. "Other than talking to dead people in the middle of the night."

I smiled back. "Other than that." Plus seeing ShadowEaters come to life, and talking to mythical beings who ate livers from corpses that were still warm. My platter of the strange and unusual was pretty full, and getting more so.

I glanced at King again, amazed that he was comatose.

In the blink of an eye, Sigmund disappeared, so quickly and surely that he might never have been there. King slept on, as did Meagan. The air hadn't changed temperature, the way it sometimes does when ghosts make an appearance. I looked in and under the bed for a frog—that's a typical joke of Sigmund's—but there was nothing. Just me.

But I had talked to my dead brother. I knew it.

Even though it seemed like he could have been an illusion.

Or a delusion.

Evidence that this Wyvern could go crazy.

You know I wasn't going back to sleep anytime soon.

I HAD to figure out the significance of what Skuld had shown me. It was like a riddle. Or a test. What were Adrian and Trevor going to do? (I'd decided to go with the assumption that the ritual I'd witnessed hadn't happened yet.) I trolled through that ancient document that Meagan and Garrett had translated—safely stored on my messenger in English—and composed a list.

I like lists.

You'll get used to it.

Six Things about Mages

1. Mages recruit humans with an innate musical ability. This power —called spellsinging—allows those gifted humans to enchant other humans with their music or their songs. (They naturally hold their audiences spellbound. Ha ha.) Not all born spellsingers choose to sign up for the Mage program. Meagan is a spellsinger and so is Jared. Both have passed on the invitation to use their powers for evil.

2. Those spellsingers who do join the Mages become apprentices and are trained in the art of casting spells. Like Trevor. Mages have a taste for shadows, and it seems to be an acquired taste—even apprentice Mages can bite shadows, as we learned in the fall when Jessica was captured.

3. There are at least two levels of apprenticeship in Mage Land, and

the ceremony to move from the lowest level to the next tier involves a sacrifice—presumably as well as some level of competence. Adrian must be more advanced, because he can do more things than Trevor—like voluntarily take on the shapes of all the shifter species eliminated by the Mages so far.

4. Full Mages shared a hive memory—or they did until last fall. Kohana and I burned this memory to oblivion, so the full Mages either died or became incoherent. Since then, we've had only apprentice Mages underfoot, and they've been twitchy, as if insecure about their future.

5. Mages had a plan to destroy all surviving shape shifters in order to assume their powers. They did this by cutting away their shadows in a ceremony that requires the NightBlade, a black knife. They invoked the ShadowEaters and offered the shadow of the victim as a sacrifice, which incidentally killed the victim, too. (Nice.)

6. There is supposed to be some kind of bonus energy surge available to the Mages when all shifters are eliminated, which is why they were actively hunting us last four kinds. Details are sketchy.

I looked over the list, tapping my fingers on the edge of my messenger. Essentially, each kind of surviving shifter has a new coming-of-age member with special powers. Kohana, the Thunderbird, calls us wildcards and says we're important. Of course, he won't say how. Derek, the wolf shifter, says his kind has a prophecy that we have to band together in a new pack and follow the dragon. As wild card of his kind, he transferred to my school to make that alliance with me, the wild card of my kind. Jessica, the jaguar shifter and wild card, also transferred to our school and insists that the future is in the hands of the four of us.

I initiated the alliance of the wild cards—and, by extension, the surviving shifter species—and led the fight in November. It seems to be working, even if Kohana is more of a wild card than the other three of us put together.

But what had actually happened in my dream? How had Adrian invoked the ShadowEaters without the NightBlade, or even any full Mages? What did it mean that they'd broken free? It didn't seem as if that had been Adrian's plan. Had he screwed up? Or had they taken charge?

I realized I knew very little about ShadowEaters, and that this might not be a good thing. I'd been thinking that without full Mages to invoke ShadowEaters and with the NightBlade safely in Kohana's custody, they weren't important.

Time to think again.

I STARED at the ceiling for hours, fretting, but must have finally fallen asleep again.

Because I woke up again suddenly to find Meagan's room still dark.

This time there was a large cat sitting on my chest, swatting my face with one paw.

King.

"There's a litter box in this house, too," I complained as I shoved him off my chest. I was cranky and tired and not interested in waking up to play catch the mousie. Predictably, I was covered in the hair he'd shed while harassing me. I'm convinced that he's always shedding, to a greater or lesser degree, which I guess is the price of a luxurious coat. It also means that everything I own, most of which is black, has been garnished with cat hair.

This does not work for me.

King doesn't appear to care.

He didn't care about what I said, either. He went to the door and waited, giving me a steady look. There's something regal about him, and even in cat form he has a commanding presence.

I got it. This was an order.

"Something's up," I guessed. He gave a meow of epic proportions and paced from left to right in front of the closed doorway.

Impatient for me to get a move on.

"Go out in the hall. No peeking," I instructed as I opened the door an increment. If a cat could grin, he did—but he did what I told him to do, as well. He slipped through the gap like a wraith. I knew he'd be waiting right outside. I could hear him pacing. I tugged on my jeans and a hoodie, then debated the merit of waking up Meagan.

I decided to go alone and crept after King, wanting to be sure I didn't waken the Jamesons. Once I left the bedroom, King made a beeline for the front door, moving faster than I'd ever seen him move. I winced as I turned the dead bolt, trying to do it as silently as possible, and he streaked out into the night at first opportunity.

I was right behind him.

"Should we fly?" I asked, intending to shift shape if it would help. I wasn't sure how far we had to go.

He didn't answer. He just leapt off the porch and into the shadows beside the step. One second he was standing in the snow, glaring at me, and the next he had hunkered down to peer into the shadows of the evergreens planted there. I could see only the swish of his tail.

I wondered whether he'd done some disgusting cat thing and brought me a "present" of a bird with its head bitten off. I had not come out in the night for that kind of token of his so-called esteem.

On the other hand, I was up so I might as well look. I bent and pushed the greenery aside.

Mozart was lying in the snow. He wasn't moving. He wasn't even rapidly rotating between forms, which is a sign of distress in a shifter. He's a soot-colored cat with a white bib and white socks. He was terrifyingly still.

"Is he dead?" I asked, wondering what had happened to him.

King narrowed his eyes, and then I noticed the faint whisper of Mozart's breath.

The subtle beat of his heart.

He wasn't dead, but he wasn't exactly in the prime of health, either. I crouched down beside King and touched Mozart's fur. His body wasn't as warm as usual, but the feel of his heart beating beneath his ribs made me feel better.

I looked at King. "You brought him here." He bowed his head regally. "But you couldn't bring him into the house without my help." King crouched down beside his friend's body, as if standing guard over it. It must have been terrifying to leave him alone, even for a few minutes.

No wonder he'd been so agitated.

"But what happened to him?" I still was thinking that this was some kind of cat-related injury. Cat shifters are more savvy about navigating the human world than regular cats, but still, their form has its risks.

King gave me an intent look, as if I was missing something really obvious. Then he batted at the snow beside Mozart with one paw, indicating something. At his gesture, I did see it. The porch light shone on Mozart, casting his shadow across the white snow.

But his shadow was wrong.

There was a bite out of it.

This was not the most encouraging sign possible. I looked around for spell light or apprentice Mages or even ShadowEaters but couldn't see anything.

King was watching me closely so I tried to hide that I was freaking. I didn't know what we could do to help Mozart or fix his shadow, but him lying wounded in the snow on a winter night—when his attacker could still be at large—couldn't be the right answer.

I scooped Mozart up into my arms and headed for the doorway, casting a glance at the night sky. I couldn't see any ShadowEaters, which had to be better than the alternative. King was right against my legs, slipping into the house when I opened the door. His eyes shone as he watched me lock the door; then he followed me to the bedroom on silent feet.

Mozart remained limp.

But alive.

I realized then that we had never learned his real name, that he just responded to the name Meagan had given his cat form, as if he were a cat. I knew so little about either of these cat shifters. They were mysterious to me, and maybe they liked it that way. Maybe they stayed in cat form to avoid discussion. To keep their secrets.

I had a feeling we'd have to find out more to help Mozart recover.

And one look at King told me they weren't going to like that.

Meagan was awake when we got back to her room and her eyes widened at the sight of Mozart. I shut the door behind us so her parents wouldn't hear that we were talking. She nearly tripped over the hem of her nightgown, coming to get him from me.

"What happened?" She cuddled him close.

"I don't know. King woke me up and took me to him." I turned on the light beside her bed, trying to sound calm. In charge. Competent even. "There's something wrong with his shadow."

Meagan gasped. "Mages! But how?" She sat down hard and chewed her lip as she cradled Mozart. "Or it could be apprentice Mages. But why now?"

I had to love having the brilliant student on my side. I told Meagan all about my dream as we tucked Mozart into the blankets on her bed. King immediately leapt up to sit vigil. He would have just hunkered down there to watch, but I wasn't having any of his mystery right now.

"No way," I said, shaking a finger at him. "You have to tell us what you know if we're going to help him."

"Absolutely," Meagan agreed. "We have to know how much of this has happened already."

He narrowed his eyes at me and looked hostile.

"Shift and spill it, Fish Breath," I said, sounding tougher than I felt. "What happened? What did you see?"

He gave a mewl of protest and glared at both of us; then there was a familiar shimmer of blue light. I closed my eyes to be diplomatic about it all, and when I opened them, there was a guy sitting on the end of Meagan's bed.

In human form, King has sandy hair and is built like a football player. He never says much, but he carries himself as if he owns the world. People step aside for him, even when he's a cat. He doesn't say much, and when he does, he's surprisingly soft-spoken.

"I woke up and he was gone," he said even more quietly than usual, flicking a glance at the closed door. He gently rubbed Mozart's chin as he spoke, but the other cat didn't respond at all. "I went looking for him, found him halfway down the block, dragging himself back here. He was exhausted. As soon as he saw me, he gave it up."

"He knew you'd bring him home," Meagan said, sitting down on the other side of the injured cat.

"I didn't know how else to bring him into the house," King said. "I had to shift to human form to carry him home, but couldn't enter the house that way. So I hid him and came to get Zoë."

"Thank goodness your parents installed that cat door," I said.

King's lips tightened. "He would have been better off if they hadn't."

"Did he tell you what happened?" Meagan asked.

King shook his head.

"Did you see anything? Was anyone else around?" I asked.

King frowned. "There was something strange in the air. Like electricity. I felt like my hair was standing up the minute I went outside." He shuddered. "It felt bad, like something evil was brewing."

I sat down, thinking, on the twin bed on the other side of the room. "Why Mozart?" I asked. "I wonder what he saw." You know I was thinking about ShadowEaters walking the earth.

"He can't tell us, not when he's like this," Meagan said, gently touching his ears. "How do we help him? How do cat shifters heal?"

"I can't tell you more," King said forcefully. His heated reaction surprised me a bit. "You need to ask Jessica."

I would have asked him more despite that warning, but he shifted shape, effectively ending the conversation. What had he been worried about? He gave me a lethal look in his cat form, then curled himself behind and around Mozart, his lush tail wrapping protectively around his friend.

Like a guardian.

One that wouldn't be bypassed easily.

Meagan was stroking Mozart's head with a care that King was prepared to tolerate. "My mom's going to want to take him to the vet in the morning."

"The vet isn't going to be able to do anything about this," I said. "We need to figure out how to heal his shadow, and I don't think they teach shifter physiology in college. Like King says, we'll have to ask Jessica."

King purred approval.

"Maybe we could hide him here." Meagan looked up. "Will you stay with him while we're at school, King?"

King lowered his head protectively. He seemed to enfold Mozart and I knew that the other cat shifter couldn't have a better defender.

Even if I wasn't sure what he could do against apprentice Mages or ShadowEaters on the hunt.

MEAGAN WAS sure that if my dream had already happened, then Mozart would have died. She had a point—the apprentice Mages nibbled at shadows, but the ShadowEaters consumed them. So, we knew two apprentice Mages, and we knew where one of them was.

"I have to talk to Trevor at school," I said. "Find out what he knows."

Meagan caught her breath. "It's dangerous."

"Not stopping them would be worse."

Meagan frowned as she reviewed my lists with record speed. She and I agreed that the ultimate key had to lie in the alliance of shifters we'd formed. Skuld had been warning me of pending disaster. We had to prevent it from happening.

I could see that Meagan was drooping, so I told her to get some sleep while she could. She curled up in bed with both cats, one hand on Mozart, and soon I was the only one awake in the room. I wasn't going back to sleep anytime soon.

First things first. I composed a message to Liam, Garrett, and Nick, my best guy friends and dragon shifters, too, briefly explaining my dream and asking them to come to Chicago ASAP. This was an emergency. Nick answered right away in the affirmative, I guess because he was awake. That made me feel a bit better. If there was fighting to be done, Nick was the dragon to call.

Next up, the other shifters. I'd see both Jessica and Derek at school in the morning, just hours away. I had no idea where to find Kohana, much less how to warn him, other than sending him a text message.

That got me to thinking about the alliance.

And King's reaction.

Wasn't it funny that we didn't know what the cat shifters even called themselves? Actually, we didn't know what Derek's wolf shifters called themselves, either, just that they had a prophecy to follow a dragon when "the stars stood still." That would be now, during the Great Lunar Standstill. There was quite a lot we didn't know about each other, so we'd better get started if we were going to solve this riddle.

By tonight.

No pressure.

I pulled out my messenger and sent another message to Garrett. I didn't think I'd forgotten those names for the other kinds of shifters, but it was possible. Garrett would remember if I had. Or he might be able to find out in his mom's bookstore. I asked him to score any details about shifters he could find.

I hesitated a moment, then sent a message to Derek, asking what the wolf shifters called themselves. It seemed suddenly important to define what was similar about us remaining shifters and what was different.

Were we four kinds the survivors for a reason?

One that Team Mage knew and we didn't?

Because there was exactly zero chance of my falling back asleep and it was only 5:14 in the morning, I made a chart on my messenger of what I knew about the four remaining kinds of shifters. It was pretty thin but looked like this:

Shape	Dragon	Thunderbird	Wolf	Cat
Name for Self	*Pyr*	*Wakiya*	?	?
Wildcard	Zoë	Kohana	Derek	Jessica
Origin	Europe	North America	?	?

I should have sent a message to Jessica then, but I hesitated. Meagan could do it.

Things weren't great between me and Jessica. I still felt that there was a barrier between us. I'd thought it was just the math proficiency that fed her bond with Meagan, but now I realized we hadn't talked about shifter stuff since discovering our respective powers in November.

Not at all.

And it was strange. I mean, having that in common had to be more important than sharing a talent for math. Both of us being wild cards gave us common ground, too. That was certainly rarer than acing math. Meagan had said before that Jessica was an only child, under a lot of pressure from her folks.

If she were the cat-shifter equivalent of the Wyvern, why didn't we have more of a bond?

I had tried to open the topic a bunch of times. But she always changed the subject, like she was avoiding my questions. And I was starting to think that she was avoiding me, too.

What didn't she want me to know?

I wished I could have not been suspicious of her, but given her behavior, I couldn't. That was partly because she'd been compelled to help the Mages in the past, but mostly it was because of her evasiveness ever since.

Were the cat shifters still aligned with the Mages?

Or were they just naturally secretive?

It was almost time for the alarm to go off, so I seized the opportunity and claimed the shower first.

When I came back into her room, Meagan was awake, sitting up in bed and typing on her messenger. The light from the handheld device was bluish and made her features look spooky.

Or maybe it was my mood.

"Jessica says something is going on," she whispered by way of greeting. I sat down hard, fighting my doubts. "She has to go someplace. Do you think it has anything to do with Mozart?"

"I don't know. Why don't you ask her?"

"She's not answering anymore." Meagan had her Einstein look as she surveyed me. "There's one part of your dream that doesn't make sense."

"What's that?"

"Trevor and Adrian don't have the NightBlade," she said. "Kohana does."

"Maybe they don't need it for the Invocation of Destruction ceremony."

Meagan shook her head. "No. When Garrett and I translated that old book of the Mages', it was clear that the NightBlade was needed for *any* ceremony." Meagan pursed her lips. "It must be that they'll do this on the *next* full moon. Not tonight's."

Instinctively I felt that it had to be sooner. I thought of Derek and his ability to see two or three minutes into the future. A month's warning seemed like too much, even for a Wyvern. "I think we four wild cards need to work together to solve this, like it's a test of the alliance, too. Can you ask Jessica to meet us before school?"

"You could ask her."

"You're already talking to her." It was an excuse and we both knew it.

Meagan frowned at her messenger. "She's not answering anymore."

I didn't much like the sound of that, but Meagan seemed untroubled.

"Don't worry, Zoë. We'll see her at school. Whatever she has to do can't take that long."

But I did worry.

It seems to come with the territory.

My mom's red electric Toyota didn't start right away that morning, which just figured. Meagan's parents were gone already, so we were on our own. If the engine didn't start, we'd have to walk, and I did not want to walk in this snow.

"I hate this piece of junk," I said as I opened the hood. I tried to look like I had a clue what to do, but, of course, I had no idea.

"At least you have a car."

"Not mine, really. Just a loaner." I sighed and frowned at the mystery of the engine. "I wish my dad had let me use the Lamborghini."

"Did you ask?"

I smiled. "Of course!"

"And?"

"He laughed and tossed me the keys to this one."

"Well, he is crazy for that car."

"He never even drives it anymore. It's like a shrine or something."

"What about that flashy new sedan he just bought? What is it, anyway?"

"Another Maserati," I said. "He says he likes Italian cars best."

"Well?"

"He drove it to the airport and parked it there."

"So you couldn't drive it?"

"I'm thinking so." I jiggled a pair of wires, then opened and closed the reservoir for the windshield-wiper fluid. You never knew.

"Is it charged up?" Meagan asked.

I nodded. That was one part I understood. I closed the hood, knowing there was nothing else I could do. "Let's try it again." We got back in and I turned the key. To my astonishment, the car started. Meagan hooted with glee. The engine wasn't running very well, but it settled into a choppy purr that was an approximation of its usual noise.

"What did you do?" Meagan asked. "What was that cap?"

"The windshield-fluid reservoir."

She laughed. "I thought you knew what you were doing."

"No idea." I counted off on my fingers as the car warmed up. "I know how to fill the wiper fluid, to top up the oil, to charge the battery, and lock the doors. Not that anyone would want to steal this heap."

"Maybe your mom will get a new car and you'll be able to drive that."

"Maybe." It was an optimistic thought, one that got me through the painful moment of driving into the school parking lot. It seemed as if everybody turned to stare.

And snicker.

I drove the battered and rusted red car through the array of shiny, beautiful luxury vehicles and felt like the poor country cousin. I could not figure out why my mom didn't want a new one, but she said she loved this one—and that it was more environmentally responsible to keep using it.

I just wished it looked better.

"It runs," Meagan insisted when I'd parked. "It's free and we get to use it." She gave me a look. "All good."

"All good," I agreed. "But the Lamborghini would be better. Just once, I'd like to drive it into this lot. Everyone would notice that!"

Meagan grinned and opened her door. "Sounds like your dad isn't the only one who likes Italian cars." She slammed the door as I got out. "My dad just likes Italian concertos, and you can't drive them anywhere."

We laughed together and headed to school.

She bumped my shoulder on the way. "You never know. Take care of this one and he might let you take your dream drive."

I didn't argue with her. It could theoretically happen. It would have had a better chance of happening with any other father and any other car.

Still, a dragon girl could hope.

Despite the fact that we were later than usual, there was no sign of Jessica. Usually, she was waiting for Meagan outside the doors, but not today.

I deliberately forced my suspicions out of my mind. Maybe Jessica was actually in danger. The Mages had nearly sacrificed her at Halloween.

Skuld had corrected me—not what *will* be but what *might* be. Could Trevor and Adrian save the third kid if they had another victim ready?

"We've got to find Jessica," I said. "Is she answering her messenger?"

"No, but she'll be in math class," Meagan said with a confidence I didn't feel.

"I really need to talk to her. Do you know where she was going?"

"Relax, Zoë. Maybe it's a family thing."

I couldn't relax.

"What's going on?" Derek asked. He was suddenly at my side, appearing with that silence that still unnerved me. His eyes twinkled a little when I jumped. I was pretty sure he did it on purpose, just to show off.

Or maybe to remind me that he had special powers, too.

"I smell trouble," he said when I didn't immediately answer. "And you're wearing the necklace I gave you."

On instinct, I had put on the silver necklace with a sterling hand of Fatima he'd given me for my birthday, and touched the charm now. "It seemed like a good idea. I had this dream."

I told him in an undertone about my nightmare. His eyes became brighter than usual, a striking pale blue, and his gaze danced over my features as I spoke. I wondered how much else he sensed.

"Find Jessica," he said to Meagan, an undercurrent of command in his tone. She nodded and loaded up her books with purpose. She gave me a smile, then headed off to class.

"She'll find her," I said, hoping it was true.

Derek watched her go; then he tugged a book out of his pocket. It was warm from being inside his coat. It was called *The Histories* by Herodotus. I read the title, then looked at Derek with surprise.

He had a secretive little smile. "As good a source as any." He shrugged. "You asked."

So this Herodotus guy had said something about the wolf shifters. Huh. I fanned through the book. It was pretty thick, but there was a bookmark in it.

"Any ideas where we can find Kohana?" Derek asked, glancing down the hall. His words recalled me to the moment and I shoved the book into my pack. When I slung it back over my shoulder and closed my locker, he took my hand in his. I wasn't expecting that, which maybe was why his touch made my heart skip. I liked the warmth of his grip.

Never mind the steadiness of his gaze. I stared at him, unable to look away.

His fingers entangled with mine, his thumb sliding across my palm very slowly, slowly enough to give me heart failure.

It certainly was slow enough to distract me.

"Because it would be good to confirm that he still has the NightBlade," he added, as if I needed the strategy explained to me.

I wasn't, actually, thinking about Kohana in that precise moment, or even the Wyvern's supposed ability to see past, present and future simultaneously. I was thinking about Derek, about how steadily he looks into my eyes and how slowly he moves. I was thinking about the warm caress of his thumb and I was thinking about Friday night's dance, and I was wondering just what he had planned.

A slow dance?

A slow kiss?

I am the worst dancer in the world, and I'm not sure I'm much of a good kisser, either. I have been kissed and I have kissed back some, but that doesn't exactly make me a pro.

Derek smiled and I wondered whether he could smell what I was thinking.

I blushed. You knew it had to happen.

"I've got my dad's car for Friday," he murmured, and that small piece of information seemed fraught with expectations.

I was well aware that Derek was watching me closely. It was becoming clear to me that this date wasn't anything casual. I was, in fact, remembering his words from the fall, about his taking the task in his pack to ensure the alliance with the Wyvern was made. Wolves are not the most subtle intellectuals, in my limited experience. They put more value in action than in words.

What particular action would secure the alliance, as far as Derek was concerned? Going steady? Doing more than sharing a kiss? I stood and felt his thumb caress my hand and had a pretty good idea that he wanted a bigger commitment from me.

Which meant that my dad wasn't going to like Derek any more than he liked Jared.

Before I could think of anything brilliant to say, the bell for class rang.

Derek squeezed my fingers, bolder now, then, to my astonishment, leaned closer and kissed my temple. "Later," he murmured in a low growl that made my stomach quiver. He gave me an intent look, then turned to lope down the hall.

Leaving me staring after him, my mouth dry.

"Sorry to interrupt a tender moment," Suzanne drawled from my other side, her tone snarky. "But Trevor wants to talk to you, freak."

I spun to find her glaring at me. I was as shocked by her words as her presence. Suzanne had never initiated a conversation with me—and Trevor never wanted to talk to me unless he was making trouble.

I had wanted to talk to Trevor. Suddenly, he wanted to talk to me. This was far too easy. Careful what you wish for.

To say that I was suspicious would have been the understatement of the century.

"Me?"

"At least you're as shocked as I am," Suzanne said. She jabbed her finger at me. "Do *not* get any ideas."

"Ideas?"

She leaned closer to whisper. "You're not his type. Don't imagine for one second that you are."

I laughed. I couldn't help it. The idea of me and Trevor becoming a couple was just that funny. He belonged to a group bent on destroying my kind forever, after all. "Don't worry. He's not my type, either."

She flicked a disparaging glance after Derek. "I guess not."

My temper flared that she was putting Derek down. "If Trevor wants to talk to me, why doesn't he?" I challenged. "Are you his minion now?"

Or was he afraid of me? Trevor did know what I was, after all, and we dragons had kicked major Mage butt in the fall.

Suzanne checked that there were other people at the end of the hall, then leaned closer, her eyes flashing. "Never call me that, freak."

She was always brave when others were around; it was when she and I were alone that her bravado slipped. "Then don't act like his minion."

"I am so going to get you," she muttered. "One of these days, I won't be the only one to see and I'll make sure to take you down."

I mocked a shudder. "Gosh, I'm afraid."

She didn't like that, not one bit. She opened her mouth to say something bitchy, but the hall was empty. I saw my chance and went with it, too mad to care about repercussions.

I let my eye change to a dragon eye just for a heartbeat.

Suzanne paled and retreated quickly.

"What's the matter?" I asked sweetly, knowing my eye was back to normal.

She looked away, then back at me, then shook a finger. "One of these days, Sorensson."

I pretended to tremble, then grinned at her. There must have been some dragon in that look, because she stepped back.

Suzanne jerked her thumb toward the parking lot. "Trevor's in his car." Then she arched a brow, more confident now that there was distance between us. "Unless you don't have the nerve to cut class."

If it had been art class, I might have hesitated. Science meant it was an easy choice. I pushed past Suzanne and headed out of the school, in search of Trevor.

I didn't have to look far.

3

Trevor's green MG was idling at the closest entry to the parking lot. It's a convertible, but he had the black ragtop up. I was surprised he was even driving it in February. Snowflakes tumbled out of the pewter clouds that filled the sky, and it was more damp than cold.

I bent down, cautious now, and he unrolled the passenger's-side window. "We need to talk," he said grimly.

I have to say that Trevor was looking less than his best. His hair was disheveled and I would have bet that he hadn't slept the night before. Maybe for a few nights. There were dark circles under his eyes and his skin was pale.

He looked a lot worse than he had in my dream. He is usually the squeaky-clean type, his jeans practically ironed and every hair in place. The contrast was startling.

Plus he couldn't stop fidgeting. His fingers drummed on the steering wheel, his agitation obvious. He kept looking around, scanning the parking lot, as if he expected boogeymen to jump him from every side.

Interesting. Was he really spooked or was it an act? I couldn't tell.

I actually had a moment when I wished I knew him better, just so I could assess his honesty, then realized how nutty a thought that was.

"So talk," I said, shoving my hands into my pockets. I would go with the bold Wyvern routine, I decided.

"Not here," he said. "Get in."

I laughed.

He stretched across the car and leaned out the window on the passenger's side. His eyes were wide and he looked terrified. Again I wondered, Is that the truth or an illusion? It seemed a smidge over the top, especially if my dream hadn't happened yet. He should still be cocky about their plan, at least the way I figured it.

"Look, Zoë, Adrian's got this crazy idea and I don't know how to talk him out of it. I need your help."

I leaned back against the fence beside the sidewalk, keeping my distance. "That has to be a first."

He shoved a hand through his hair. "He found this old book, and he thinks he can manage this spell, but I know he's not skilled enough. I'm worried that it will all go wrong and no one will be able to stop it. He won't listen to me!"

I straightened at that. "What kind of spell?" When he didn't answer, I guessed. "The Invocation of Destruction?"

He stared at me in shock. "How do you know that?"

I shrugged. "How can you do it, though, without the NightBlade?"

And how could I stop them from even trying?

Trevor averted his gaze and shoved a hand through his hair. "It's a special rite. I've never seen it done before. Adrian's sure he can nail it, but I'm afraid." He did look freaked. I felt a teensy bit sorry for him. "This isn't a joke, Zoë. You don't know what he did last night."

My Wyvern sense was on full alert. "Then why don't you tell me?"

Trevor looked from side to side, as if there would be anyone stupid enough to stand out here in the snow and eavesdrop on us. His voice dropped to a hiss. "He went out to eat shadows. He said it would build his strength."

"Whose shadows?" I thought I already knew the answer, but had to ask.

"Just get in. We have to stop him!"

"What makes you think I can change Adrian's mind?"

"Maybe we should be on the same side, Zoë. Maybe this is important enough."

Maybe Trevor wasn't bad to the bone.

"Look, Zoë, there's no time. The ritual has to be done tonight. If we're going to stop him, we have to do it now. Who knows what he's done while I've been gone? Just get in!"

"Do you have a plan?"

He nodded. "There's only one copy of the book, at this library, in the reserves. I want you to incinerate it so everything in it is lost forever."

"Can't you destroy it yourself?"

His lips tightened. "I've tried. I think it needs dragonfire." He looked at me. "Shifter power."

That was news. "Why?"

"Trust me on this. Get in!"

Trust Trevor. That was a stretch.

On the other hand, it sounded like Adrian had been the one who had attacked Mozart—and he might be stalking more shifters. He knew what enough of us looked like in our human skins to find us. I didn't trust Trevor to have my best interests at heart, but I did trust him to understand Mage lore better than me.

And I wanted to believe that he had some redeeming features.

I pulled out my messenger and sent a message to Meagan that I was going with Trevor and hoping to stop Adrian from attacking more shifters. She'd figure out that I meant Mozart.

"Come on!" Trevor said, revving the engine.

I still hesitated a moment more before I got in.

That was all the time it took for me to check for spell light. There wasn't any, so I figured that it would take Trevor longer to conjure a spell to trap me than it would take me to spontaneously manifest elsewhere. I had confidence in my dragon abilities—and also feared this might be my own chance to turn the tide and stop the ceremony. That was a risk I was prepared to take.

In hindsight, I can see that my decision was chock-full of assumptions.

. . .

Trevor's car was pretty plush inside, with leather seats and a dashboard that looked as if it had been carved of wood. (Did they ever really do that?) I felt as if I should be wearing mirrored sunglasses, or a swinging '60s Mondrian-inspired dress, go-go boots (white ones), or some other throwback fashion item.

Then he reached the main road beyond our school and I forgot about fashion statements. I was too busy hanging on.

Trevor drove like a maniac. Waaaaaaaaaaay too fast. I appreciated that he was worried about finding Adrian sooner rather than later, but wished I was under my own steam. Speeding was one thing, but he didn't seem to be entirely in control. This did not reassure me. Neither did his white-knuckle grip on the steering wheel.

I took this as a sign that he really was scared.

"You could slow down," I said, when he took a corner on two (squealing) wheels.

"No time to waste," he muttered, and, I swear, he drove even faster.

We left the part of the city I know really well, streaking into an area I'd never visited before. The buildings were neither new enough to be sleek nor old enough to have the grace of bygone days. They were all square and practical, made of brick and concrete, so similar that they could have been poured from the same mold. I saw a paved schoolyard with a chain-link fence around it, little kids running back and forth inside their cage, and was glad I didn't live around here.

Then Trevor took a couple of quick turns and screeched to a halt. He turned off the car engine and flung himself out the door.

He'd parked in front of a building with broad concrete steps and double doors. The sign over the doors said it was a public library.

I still felt that foreboding of doom, but it seemed to me that we couldn't get into too much trouble in a library.

Shouldn't hindsight have served me better? I'd assumed myself to be safe before and been wrong.

Misplaced confidence was the first sign of trouble.

"The book is in the reserved collection," Trevor said in a hushed voice. "They won't let it leave the building." He came around the car with purpose. "Come on!"

"You don't think people will notice if I shift shape and start a fire?"

He was dismissive. "I'll launch some spellsong. Don't worry about the details—just fry that book and leave the rest to me!" He leapt out of the car and came around to my side.

I took a good look at the building. What was wrong? I had a very, very bad feeling.

"I'm not sure about this," I said, just as the passenger's door was opened. "Maybe it's not a good idea."

Trevor smiled as he tugged me out of the car and I did not trust that smile.

Note sign of trouble number 2.

The street was deserted. Completely empty.

Portent of disaster number 3 present and accounted for.

Or was I just being chicken? Because if there was a book, I wanted to see it. I liked the idea of destroying a Mage tome. Breathe a little fire and terminate the possibility of anyone following those instructions ever again. It also sounded like there was something special about shifter power, something that worried the apprentice Mages, and I definitely wanted to know more about that. I didn't mind taking a small risk in order to get the job done and change the future for the better.

I knew I couldn't truly trust Trevor, but I'd beaten him before; even if Adrian was here, I'd thumped him a couple of times, as well. I rationalized that I could always spontaneously manifest elsewhere to get myself out of trouble. Even if I wasn't entirely accurate in targeting locations when I did that, all I had to do was be anywhere else.

Piece of cake.

"The book's inside," Trevor said. "Only copy in the world."

I was curious. You know what they say about curiosity and cats. I was pretty sure that didn't apply to dragons.

Trevor and I started up the steps; then the building did a very odd thing.

It wavered.

Like a sheet in the wind.

That was when I knew it was a glamour. Whatever it was disguising couldn't be good.

The book wasn't here.

It was all a ruse.

A trap.

I spun to run, but Adrian lunged out of the glamour and snatched my other elbow. He'd been waiting there for me, disguised by the spell. Now there were two of them, one on either side of me. Adrian pulled hard enough to make me stumble, and when I yelled in protest he laughed.

When I looked up, I saw the orange spell light dancing in his eyes. He could have been filled with it, brimming with it, the spell light boiling up inside of him to fill his eyes.

Oh, shit.

In the heartbeat it took me to process that new data, Trevor kicked my feet out from beneath me. I fell, skinning my hands. I shouted and tried to shift shape, but an orange bolt of spell light slapped me across the face.

I trembled, too stunned by its impact to even respond. The pair of them hauled me up those steps while I was disoriented. They weren't actually steps at all. They dissolved as we moved forward, disappearing as surely as if they'd never been.

Guess what the glamour was hiding?

You've got it. A vacant lot.

Unless I was very much mistaken, this was the same vacant lot where Skuld had brought me. That other kid from my dream was there, singing his Mage chant, holding a gleaming golden orb of spell light captive like a balloon on a string. It was filled to bursting with ShadowEaters and they pressed against the side closest to me as Trevor and Adrian carried me into the lot.

"It's not the full moon yet!" I protested.

"Sure it is," Adrian said. "You just can't see it in the daylight."

No! I couldn't screw up this badly. I couldn't be the reason their spell succeeded and my dream came true. I had to get out of there ASAP. I called to the shimmer, intent upon being anywhere else on the planet, but I couldn't find it. Somehow it had been shut down or turned off or blocked. I panicked and felt for it frantically, but no luck. I could only find a hard wall of orange in my thoughts.

A spell barrier that kept me from the power of what I was.

You can believe that I lost it.

I struggled and I twisted. I fought and I kicked and I swore and I screamed. None of it made any difference. Trevor and Adrian sang a nasty spell, one that I'd heard before and liked even less this time. As soon as they started, golden ropes of spells appeared in the air, growing longer and thicker as they wound all around me. I was trussed up in no time and powerless to escape, just like a shifter I'd seen sacrificed when I infiltrated the Mages' hive memory; just like Jessica and the guys had been in the fall.

And my blue shimmer was AWOL.

I didn't stop trying to summon it, even though I knew it wasn't going to answer. Meanwhile, Trevor and Adrian hauled me ever deeper into the vacant lot, the one that wasn't very vacant after all. They joined in the chant with the other kid, making the globe overhead get bigger and brighter, the silhouettes inside moving with greater agitation. The ShadowEaters pressed against the barrier of the spell orb, so close that I could see their eyes.

They glowed orange, just like in my dream. They had no pupils, no irises, nothing but orange spell light shining like beacons. The ShadowEaters could have been just skins filled with orange spell light. It was like the light in Adrian's eyes but a hundred times worse, and a thousand times more terrifying.

They were going to eat my shadow and destroy me, and there wasn't one thing I could do about it.

Except panic. I had that covered.

And my terror only increased when I saw Kohana.

The Thunderbird shifter who had tried to betray my kind to the Mages the previous spring, who had attacked me in the fall, and who had worked with me under protest to destroy the Mages' collective memory sauntered toward us, working his way through the broken bottles and discarded car fenders and busted furniture.

He still had dark hair and dark eyes, a secretive smile, and a tight pair of jeans. He was wearing a dark T-shirt this time, one that covered the feather tattoo I knew he had on his shoulder, and it seemed to me that his expression was a little bit mean.

Was he enchanted? I dared to hope, but there was no spell light around Kohana.

My heart stopped cold when I saw that he had the NightBlade, the weapon he had stolen from the Mages in November. He'd said then that he was going to destroy it, as it was the tool they used to cut the shadows away from the bodies of their victims, the better to offer sacrifices to the ShadowEaters. But he was back, he still had it, and it didn't look damaged in the least.

Plus he held it up, as if intending to use it.

This was how they were going to complete the ceremony—they *had* the NightBlade. Kohana had brought it to them.

No! Kohana's expression turned resolute, and my very bad feeling became forty-seven thousand times worse.

Because it didn't take much to figure out whose shadow was the *plat du jour*.

THE SHADOWEATERS clearly knew what was going to happen. Their forms were moving more quickly, shifting and shimmering, vibrating with excitement and anticipation. The orb was being stretched in every direction as they fought to become free. And there was a point in the orb where they strained toward Kohana, their fingers grasping in the direction of the NightBlade.

Even though they were still inside that orb of spell light that had conjured them, I could hear them salivating, licking their lips and clicking their teeth together. I swear their bellies growled—even though they didn't appear to have any.

They were the stuff of nightmares.

I struggled as I heard Trevor and Adrian and the other kid sing the spell of sacrifice. I knew I was next, that I was feeling the same horror and futility the other sacrificed shifters must have felt.

If they took me out, as Wyvern of the *Pyr*, I feared the rest of the dragon shifters would lose heart. My dad would be easy to trap then, in his grief, and he's the leader of our kind. I feared that all the dragon shifters would seek revenge, only to follow me and my dad to oblivion.

Because I'd been too cocky.

Big mistake.

I knew there was nothing I could do, but I still fought. I watched the mesh of spell light grow brighter and denser. Kohana's form was like a shadow falling over the spell light. He held the NightBlade high and called the invocation, the same invocation that Mages had sung in the fall.

It was obscene hearing that song fall from his lips, to see that spell wind out of his mouth to join the others.

I couldn't believe he would do it, but my eyes told me the truth. I saw the curved blade of the knife rise high. I saw its darkness silhouetted against the vivid light of the spell. I saw the ShadowEaters become frenzied. I saw the sphere get thinner in preparation for shattering. I felt Adrian and Trevor tremble in anticipation.

I struggled all the while, but I knew I was doomed.

"Now!" Kohana shouted. He leapt down toward me, and I squeezed my eyes shut.

But he sliced down the length of me with one savage stroke, severing the spells that bound me helpless. I leapt to my feet as he pivoted and sliced at Adrian, hacking off a big chunk of his shadow. Adrian screamed. The ShadowEaters sighed with lust and moved in new frenzy, licking and slurping and gobbling as they pushed at the spell that held them captive. The orb shimmered but held.

Just.

Trevor shouted in terror and tried to help Adrian, who had fallen to his knees.

I ran.

I heard footsteps behind me, and looked back to find Kohana closing fast, the NightBlade high in his hand. "You!" I shouted, once again unable to guess his allegiances. He'd lied to me and deceived me and helped me, and I never knew what to expect.

"Me!" he agreed, laughing.

I heard Trevor and the other kid singing and glanced back to see a spell being mustered.

It was shaped like a spear.

"Look out!" I shouted.

Kohana raced past me and sliced at the air. I saw a golden barrier before us part in a shower of sparks. As if he had cut a hole in the side of a balloon, the glamour that had disguised us from the world fell like sliced cloth.

Then the NightBlade did a strange thing. It wriggled in Kohana's grip, as if it had come alive, as if it were an eel or a snake. As if it were trying to work itself free.

Kohana swore and snatched at it with his other hand, but it sliced at him.

He yelled and it leapt from his grip, catapulting through the air toward Adrian and Trevor.

"Holy shit," Kohana said. "It's got a will of its own."

Trevor and the third kid stopped singing immediately and the spell they'd been conjuring fell to the ground, lifeless. They snatched for the NightBlade in unison, bumping into each other. The handle of the knife bounced off Trevor's head, rebounded—or leapt of its own accord—

And sliced open the orb that held the ShadowEaters captive.

They surged through the space, gleeful and frenzied.

Free.

"They called to it," Kohana said, his features ashen, and I knew he was right. The ShadowEaters spilled through the slash in the globe, milling on the ground, a great crowd of ravenous demons.

"How can we stop them?" I asked, but I knew the answer.

We couldn't. Not now, not when they were hungry and fervid.

As I watched in horror, Adrian got to his feet. He snatched the NightBlade out of the air, seized the new kid, and muttered an invocation. "Blood and shadow!" he cried, and slit his throat.

The kid gurgled. Blood spurted from his throat. Adrian laughed and shimmered.

Then, before our eyes, he became a ShadowEater himself. His features melted into shadow, and he turned into a silhouette, one filled with spell light. He hooted, and it was only by his position that I could tell which one of the ShadowEaters he was.

I was so stunned that I could have been rooted to the ground. This was an initiation rite. And Adrian had passed. Was this where all of these ShadowEaters had come from? Had they once been humans? Mages?

Kohana seized my hand and hauled me through the shattered glamour. I couldn't help looking back at the ShadowEaters. I had wanted my dream to be wrong. I wanted them to be benign, or easily defeated, or genies who happily went back into their respective jars.

No luck. They fell on the kid, just like they had in my dream, surrounding him and overwhelming him. He tried to run, despite the wound on his throat. There was nothing anyone could do to save him, and nothing could have stopped their feasting. I shuddered as he fell, buried beneath them.

There was something deeply wrong with the appearance of the ShadowEaters. They were shaped like humans but insubstantial. Their human forms had no real faces. Just those golden eyes and forms that couldn't be distinguished one from the other. They were all the same, interchangeable, all exuding menace.

And hunger.

Were they the next step in Mage evolution?

What came after that?

"Hurry up!" Kohana cried, and it was probably the first time I'd heard fear in his voice.

That was when I saw that Trevor had the NightBlade and was looking at us.

We raced forward together, and when Kohana yelled "Now!" I knew what he meant.

I hoped like hell I could do it.

We both shifted shape as soon as we were through the space. I was so relieved that my shimmer was back that I was trembling. Kohana was holding one of my claws tightly, as if he would have hauled me into the sky with force, regardless of whether I'd been able to shift or not.

I roared at the welcome power of my shift. That barrier was gone. I delighted in the unfurling of my wings and the majestic power of my tail. I pivoted, not twenty feet above the ground, and exhaled fire at the collapsing shell of the Mage glamour.

I had nearly died.

I would have died, without Kohana's help.

Just like that third kid, who was lifeless on the ground now, his blood staining the snow.

As we soared into the sky, the ShadowEaters retreated from his body. They were sated temporarily. They looked upward, all those golden eyes shining as they focused on us hovering overheard. I saw them leap into the air and didn't need any encouragement from Kohana to boot it out of there.

He took off like a shot, flying with terrifying speed in the opposite direction.

I was right on his tail.

I saw the ShadowEaters leap into the sky behind us and knew we wouldn't outrace them. They could fly through the air, too—I'd seen them do it in my dream.

There was only one way to save us. I tightened my grip on Kohana's claw, closed my eyes, and flung us both through space and time.

WE WERE INSTANTLY over a park beside the lake, one I recognized as being close to my school. Lake Michigan was choppy and pewter in color, and the snow was still falling lazily. There was about a foot of snow in the park.

And I was a white salamander clutched in Kohana's talons. It was one of two forms I could take as the Wyvern.

"Thanks," he said, exhaling as he ensured that his grip on me was firm but not too tight. (Newts squish.) He circled, choosing a spot in the middle of an open area, then landed with care. He shifted shape in the last instant, touching the earth in his human form, tossing my salamander self into the air.

His expression was expectant and I knew what to do. I shifted shape and landed beside him in human form, then took a deep steadying breath.

"That was close," he said, then flashed me a devilish grin.

His eyes glinted like jet, like he had a million secrets, and I wondered whether he really was about the same age as me or whether that was an illusion of some kind.

I looked at him, uncertain what to expect.

The thing was, I wasn't sure whether Kohana had saved me for good or just for now.

I certainly wasn't sure he'd tell me either way.

"Perfect, untouched snow in every direction," he said, surveying the field with satisfaction. "We walk away from here and the next person who comes along and sees the tracks will wonder where the walkers came from."

I watched him smile. "You like messing with people's perceptions."

"I like giving others something to think about." He gave me a hard look. "I guess we'll call it square, *Unktehila*." With that, he walked away.

"Square?" I said, astonished. "You just freed the ShadowEaters!"

"I did not." He cast the words over his shoulder, not pausing or turning back.

"You brought the NightBlade back to them."

He pivoted and flung out his hands, raising his voice for the first time. "Maybe it brought itself back to them."

"But it's supposed to be on the other side of the continent. In *your* safe-keeping."

"Ooops." Kohana turned to walk away again.

I raced behind him, catching up in about twenty feet. (It's possible that this was because he let me catch up. I'm tall but he's taller.) "Why didn't you just destroy the NightBlade when you had it?"

Kohana cast me a look. "Who says I didn't try?"

I remembered that wriggling and had nothing to say.

Kohana's eyes became impossibly darker. "The problem is that it's not easily shattered."

"King said that after you left with it," I remembered.

"I shouldn't have been surprised that it has a will of its own. That explains a lot."

"What do you mean?"

"I didn't know for sure until just now. But at home, it started to turn our elders against each other. I thought maybe I was seeing things that weren't there, but the disputes escalated and—" He frowned and fell silent.

"What?"

His lips tightened. "On the equinox, one elder was found dead."

I was shocked. "The NightBlade killed him?"

"No. It persuaded one of our own to wield it as a weapon."

"How could it do that?"

"I don't know," he admitted. "But I saw it. Things got so ugly so fast. They were arguing about who should be custodian of the NightBlade. You should have heard the things people were saying to each other—no. No one should hear that."

I thought of the effect of the Mage spells on the dragon-guys when we'd been at boot camp and Adrian had been messing with our thoughts. Even though I knew they hadn't meant what they'd said while under the influence of the spell, those words were hard to forget. "I've heard it," I said.

"I'd never seen such dissent among our kind, and when that elder was found dead, my grandfather and I both knew what had caused it. He hadn't liked my bringing it there, not from the start. I promised my grandfather that I would take the NightBlade away and not return until it was destroyed forever."

"You're an exile."

He nodded once. "A willing one. This weapon has to be smashed down to molecules." He spoke with such severity that I shivered.

"What were you even doing with Trevor and Adrian?"

Kohana frowned. "I can't break the NightBlade. I can't even scratch it. It seemed to me that the ones who made it would be the most likely to know how to destroy it."

"Maybe it made you think that."

His eyes glinted. "Maybe."

"Did you lie to them?"

His smile flashed, so irreverent that I couldn't help but smile in return. "Wouldn't you?"

"In a heartbeat."

He studied me and his smile faded once more. "They didn't believe me any more than you do," he said quietly. "They said I had to prove that I wanted to join them, that I had to participate in the ceremony to prove my intent."

"You had the NightBlade," I pointed out. "You had to know what would be part of the ceremony."

"Eliminate a shifter, preferably a wild card. Yes, I know." He nodded, his expression hardening. "I would have done it, too, because it might have given me the secret to destroy that weapon forever." His gaze locked with mine, his intensity making my mouth go dry. "If it had been any shifter but you, Zoë."

Before I could wrap my mind around that—not just what he'd said but that he'd called me by my name—Kohana bent and swiftly touched his lips to mine. His kiss burned against my mouth, even with the contact being as short as it was.

He looked deep into my eyes and spoke softly. "Remember, *Unktehila*, they get their power from eating shadows, and they like shifter shadows best."

Then he walked away, leaving me standing alone in the snow.

Astonished.

And shaken.

Which had nothing on my reaction when I saw the wolf watching us from the shrubbery that surrounded the clearing. The wolf was silvery gray and utterly still, unblinking, its expression that of a predator.

Derek.

Before I could do anything, the wolf disappeared into the undergrowth as surely as a shadow fades from view. Kohana, meanwhile, had also vanished.

I was alone in the middle of a snowy field.

Good. I glanced at the time on my messenger and took a deep breath. Excellent. I had English in ten minutes. A little spontaneous manifestation—arriving in one of the school restrooms—and I just might make it.

Derek was in my English class, but it would take me a bit longer than the trip over to figure out what to say to him about what he'd seen.

I MADE it to my locker, hyperventilating and desperately in need of a sugar hit (with no time to get any), only to find a note taped to it.

It seemed I had an appointment in guidance counseling.

And I was late.

Fantabulous.

The day just kept getting better.

The counselor, Muriel, was on the phone, so I took the seat outside her office and peeled off my coat. I sent a frantic message to Nick and Liam and Garrett, copying them all, explaining that the ShadowEaters really were raging through the world. I managed to send one to Meagan before my messenger started to chime with such urgency that I had to turn it off or else it would be confiscated. I'd have to tell Derek myself.

Where had Kohana gone?

Where was Jessica?

I had to hope she was with Meagan. I was getting really worried about her absence. I checked my messenger and found roughly forty-five thousand anxious messages from Meagan, including the update that Jessica still wasn't answering her messenger. She hadn't turned up at school, either. I quickly let Meagan know where I was, my concern for Jessica growing by the second. She was the one, after all, who had nearly been sacrificed to the ShadowEaters in the fall. That might make her more vulnerable.

I refused to give any more weight to the idea that she might be working with the apprentice Mages. That was probably what they wanted me to think, as it would divide us when we needed to pull together.

If only there was a way I could track her down. The Wyvern was supposed to be able to dispatch dreams. I hadn't had much luck with that, but it couldn't hurt to try again. I closed my eyes and thought about my fear for Jessica, focused it, then tried to send her an urgent alert, independent of modern technology.

I had no idea whether it would work.

When I opened my eyes, Muriel was still on the phone.

That was when I remembered the book that Derek had given me. I tugged it out of my backpack and opened it to the bookmark he'd inserted.

It couldn't be all bad to be found reading Herodotus.

Herodotus, it turned out, was a traveler who wrote up his adventures and experiences for other travelers or for the entertainment of those who stayed home. Fodor's for the B.C. era. For a guy who's been dead for a couple of millennia, he reads pretty well. This was the passage Derek had marked—4:105, in case you don't believe me:

> *The Neuroi practise the Scythian customs: and one generation before the expedition of Dareios it so befell them that they were forced to quit their land altogether by reason of serpents: for their land produced serpents in vast numbers, and they fell upon them in still larger numbers from the desert country above their borders; until at last being hard pressed they left their own land and settled among the Budinoi. These men it would seem are wizards; for it is said of them by the Scythians and by the Hellenes who are settled in the Scythian land that once in every year each of the Neuroi becomes a wolf for a few days and then returns again to his original form. For my part I do not believe them when they say this, but they say it nevertheless, and swear it moreover.*

Wolf shifters driven from their land by serpents.

You know I had a pretty good idea who those serpents might have been —and glimpsed another reason why some of the wolves were not so hot about making alliances with dragon shifters. Kohana's Thunderbirds had made a treaty with some reptiles they called *Unktehila*. It was an agreement that dragons would surrender North America to the Thunderbirds. That's why he'd called me an oathbreaker when we'd first met.

Had my ancestors really needed to piss everybody off?

Or did that just come with the territory of being a dragon shifter?

I wasn't doing a very good job of ensuring peace, love, and understanding myself. Maybe we're meant to be solitary and grumpy. But with apprentice Mages hunting shifters and ShadowEaters set free, we needed to keep this alliance with the cats and the wolves and the Thunderbirds to ensure the survival of all of us.

Regardless of our innate tendencies. I made a mental note to ask Derek if the wolves really did call themselves Neuroi, and closed the book as Muriel came out of her office.

She looked at the book.

She smiled.

I smiled.

But when she gestured me into the hot seat in her office, Muriel's smile disappeared.

It seemed that I was officially troubled, and my disappearance that morning was proof that I was unreliable in terms of attending classes. This was perceived to be a result of my parents' marital difficulties, a continuation of my bad attendance in the fall, and a natural if unfortunate emotional progression for a sixteen-year-old whose domestic life had become unmoored.

She did actually use the word *unmoored.*

Muriel didn't know the half of it.

Of course, I couldn't say anything in my own defense, even when it came to cutting class. *I had to leave school this morning in an attempt to stop the apprentice Mages from invoking the ShadowEaters, which is part of their plan to eliminate all remaining shape shifters from the world. Sadly, I failed so it's on to plan B.*

Uh huh.

Even better: *I was late getting back because the apprentice Mages trapped me, deceiving me with a glamour, then binding me with spells so they could cut away my shadow. Fortunately, a Thunderbird shifter saved me and we both flew out of danger to the park just around the corner. Phew.*

Or best of all: *The wild cards have been drawn to this school to make an alliance to ensure the survival of our respective kinds. Derek Black is a wolf shifter and Jessica d'Angelo is a jaguar shifter and I'm a dragon shifter. Suzanne really did see a dragon in the girl's bathroom last fall and it was me.*

Maybe not.

Trust me. It's much better to just hang your head and let them think you cut class to buy cigarettes.

Given the current absence of my parents and Muriel's unwillingness to compromise their last chance to rebuild their marriage (no, I have no idea where she got that interpretation of their vacation plan—ha) and her reluctance to draw Mrs. Jameson into this "disappointing situation," Muriel had a plan under which I'd check in with her before and after each class. My observation that this could, in fact, make me late for class made no difference. We were partners, Muriel and I, from this point forward, driven to ensure my attendance, which would henceforth be perfect.

The timing on this strategy completely bit.

I might as well be a poodle on a jeweled leash.

It's not my look. Just so you know.

4

So I was in a pretty crap mood when I got to English class late, one that was not improved by Derek glowering at me from the back of the room when I entered. I could feel his gaze boring into the back of my skull throughout the whole class, and he was ticked enough not to know the answer when he was called on.

I think that had to be a first. I hoped he'd be mad enough to ignore me afterward, but no luck; he followed me out of class and back to my Muriel check.

I was really not interested in getting chewed out, but Derek's heightened sense of smell apparently wasn't sharp enough to pick up on that.

Or else he didn't care.

"So what was that all about?" he demanded in his growly undertone. "Where did you go? And why were you in Trevor's car?"

"You saw that?"

"I had a feeling. I turned back to find you." He glared at me. "I saw you leave, but I couldn't catch up with you." His tone turned fierce. "You never should have gone anywhere with him. You know he's dangerous."

"He told me that Adrian had been eating shifter shadows. I went with him to try to stop Adrian." It seemed like a good idea not to mention—yet

—that I'd completely, totally, and utterly failed in that goal. I marched down the hallway and he walked beside me.

"Alone? Dumb, Zoë. Dumb."

That stung, because it had been dumb. It would have been nice for him to have had some confidence in me, though. "I told Meagan."

"Well, you didn't tell me."

I strode onward. I hadn't exactly had time to update everyone on the planet on my situation.

"We're a team," he said with force. "We have an alliance, in case you've forgotten. We're supposed to work together but you acted alone." I guess the fact that I didn't immediately defend myself made him even more angry, because he took a deep breath and a step back. "If you got yourself in danger, you deserved it."

Deserved it? I was with him until those last two words.

"Excuse me?" I halted in the hallway and spun to face him. I didn't care who saw me and I didn't care what my eyes did. I was feeling the need to breathe some fire.

"I *deserved* to be spellbound?" I demanded in an undertone. "I *deserved* to be cornered and nearly sacrificed to the ShadowEaters? Is that really what you think? Just because I didn't tell you what I was doing, I should *die?*"

Derek, to his credit, looked shocked. His eyes widened as he surveyed me. It was a bit late, to my thinking, to worry about the details.

"No," he whispered.

"Yes," I hissed with force. "The ShadowEaters are free. I tried to stop Trevor and Adrian, but I failed. Not only that, but they're hungry and they've already killed someone by eating his shadow."

Derek paled.

"Plus Adrian has become one."

Derek took a step back.

"Zoë!" Muriel called from the end of the hall. "You don't have time to socialize."

"No way," he muttered, but I could see his doubt.

"Yes! I would have been *lunch* if Kohana hadn't helped me."

His eyes flashed. "I would have helped you. You should have told me where you were going. I found you by scent, even though you disappeared. I would have followed you anywhere...."

"Obviously I made a mistake," I said, interrupting him. "But since I'm the one who was nearly sacrificed as a result, I'm not feeling like I owe you an apology."

Oh, he didn't like that. I saw the flash of anger in his eyes and the way his gaze dropped to my lips. That was when I knew that it was the kiss that really bothered him, not my leaving alone with Trevor or even endangering myself.

That made me see red. Because Kohana had kissed me. It hadn't been my choice, I hadn't invited it, and I sure hadn't drawn it out.

"You don't own me," I whispered, and Derek's features set.

"Coming, Muriel!" I shouted with false cheer, and marched toward the guidance office. She smiled at me, all sweet concern, but I nearly snarled at her. There must have been a little bit of dragon in my expression, because her smile disappeared in record time. She swallowed and marked the time on her sheet so I could sign it, then ushered me off to math class.

Standing in the hallway to make sure I went right there.

I was feeling, if you must know, a little bit pissed.

I BANGED open my locker at lunch and flung my books into the bottom.

"Bad morning?" Nick asked from right beside me, and I could have jumped for joy.

Then I practically fell on him, giving him a hug so tight that I nearly squished the stuffing out of him.

If dragons had stuffing. They don't, in case you aren't sure. All the usual blood and bones and guts inside. No sage-and-onion stuffing. Not even chestnut.

He hugged me back just as hard. "Okay, Z?" he asked, pulling back to look at me. He'd taken to calling me Z since my birthday. I'm not sure why, but I kind of liked it. The nickname had a buddy feel to it, which perfectly suited our friendship now that I'd abandoned my lifetime crush on him.

"Bad morning." I tried to compose myself, with—it must be said—mixed success. "What are you doing here?"

Nick smiled sheepishly. "You called."

I propped my hands on my hips to survey him. "I called you only an hour ago. Even you couldn't get here from Minneapolis that fast."

"So maybe I was here already."

What?

Nick flicked a glance up and down the hall. "I wanted to talk to you."

He had my undivided attention with that. "About?"

Nick's neck reddened but he didn't avert his gaze. "Isabelle." He said her name in a long whisper. Then he shoved his hand through his hair, leaving it all standing up, and looked unsettled.

Isabelle.

Well, the plot had thickened.

Just to fill you in on the gaps, Isabelle and I are convinced that she's the reincarnation of the previous Wyvern, Sophie. Sophie died with her *Pyr* lover, Nikolas, and once she died, I was conceived. Only one Wyvern at a time. The story is that they chose to sacrifice themselves because they couldn't be together, anyway—their love was forbidden stuff. Nick's dad was convinced that Nick was Nikolas reincarnated, and I thought it was incredibly cool that he'd been so determined to find his Sophie again that he'd started a new life just months after his last one had ended. Isabelle says she's been dreaming about Nick all her life, and that her dreams always come true.

Destined love? Sounds like it, in all its romantic glory—hopefully with a better ending this time around.

The trick is that Nick has been a little uncertain about all of this. Maybe more than a little. I know he likes Isabelle, I know he's not daunted by the fact that she's older than us, and it certainly doesn't hurt that she's gorgeous and kind and pretty much everything anyone would ever want in a girlfriend.

He just didn't want to promise what he couldn't deliver.

I respect that, even if it isn't the happy ending I—or Isabelle—might hope for.

"What about Isabelle?" I asked, pretending that I hadn't guessed.

"Well, you're a girl."

I had to tease him. He looked so earnest. "True."

He grinned and gave me a nudge. "Seriously." He pulled a jewelry box from his pocket. "Do you think this is a sucky birthday gift?"

"Her birthday's not for another couple of weeks," I said, taking the box. I didn't need to say that. Nick is one person who always remembers other people's birthdays. He's like a birthday calendar. He knows them all and makes sure he remembers everyone on their day.

It's quite sweet, and it's not just because he loves a party or loves to be remembered on his own birthday.

"Two weeks from Saturday." Nick grimaced. "I want to make sure I picked out something good while there's still time to fix it if I didn't."

He *was* worried about it. I opened the box and caught my breath. Inside was a pendant, set in silver, with two stones in the center. One was yellow and faceted, while the other was opalescent and rounded. They weren't huge stones but they were pretty together. The yellow one had a silver setting that made it look like it was the orb of the sun, while the opalescent one was set into a silver crescent of a moon.

"The sun and the moon," I said.

Nick and Isabelle, I thought. In his dragon form Nick has glorious golden scales and glowing amber eyes. Seeing him as a dragon is like looking into the radiance of the sun. Isabelle, meanwhile, is ethereal and a bit dreamy. When I'd dreamed of the past Wyvern, Sophie, her dragon scales had been so pale that they could have been made of moonbeams. I touched the pendant with a fingertip.

"Well?" Nick was practically bouncing in his anxiety. He swallowed visibly, obviously concerned that I wasn't saying more. "Do you think she'll like it?"

"I know she'll love it." I met his gaze. "It must have cost you."

He shoved a hand through his hair again and grinned, as nervous as I'd ever seen him. This was saying something. Nick does confidence like he invented it. "Yeah. I had the jeweler make it special. I wanted it to be right."

I looked down at the pendant, awed and wary, too.

I had to say it. "It's not a trinket, though, Nick. You shouldn't give it to her unless you're going to see her more than you do now." He looked worried when I said that. "Isabelle—well, anybody—would think this was a pretty serious gift. A declaration, maybe."

"Yeah, I know." He shuffled his feet again. "I guess that's what I really wanted to see you about. You know that night after the big fight with the Mages, before your birthday?"

"Yeah."

"I went back to her room at the dorm and we sat and talked...."

"Uh huh."

He grinned. "Really. We talked all night. It was awesome." He shoved his hands into his pockets and heaved a sigh. "It was easy but electric, too." He grimaced, but I knew exactly what he meant. "I don't know, Z. I don't know what to do. Can you see some future for me?"

That was not an easy question to answer.

The hall had emptied out and Nick's stomach growled right on cue. "You hungry?" I asked. "Let's get something to eat while we talk about it."

"Good idea," he said, and slung an arm around my shoulders. We headed to the cafeteria, grabbed some pizza, and sat in the corner together, talking—which gave all sorts of people all sorts of things to speculate about.

Nick is the kind of guy people notice.

No: *girls* notice him.

I felt every female eye in the place tracking us, even after we sat down. In fact, I felt more than one gaze boring into my back. I bit into my pizza—they actually had my favorite combo today, feta and green pepper, a sign from heaven that I was intended to eat lunch in the cafeteria on this day—and glanced over my shoulder.

Suzanne and her cronies were obviously talking about Nick. I knew this because Fiona and Yvonne were looking our way, Trish was snickering, and Anne was whispering something to Suzanne that made the Queen Bee smile. I also could hear what Anne said, courtesy of my sharp *Pyr* hearing.

Her comment made Nick and I smile, too. We exchanged a glance at the conviction that he must be my cousin to be seen eating with me.

"Right," Nick said with a teasing grin. "I should kiss you just to mess them up."

"Who cares what they think?" I said, dismissing them. "Anyway, a few months ago you were sure it wouldn't be fair to spend more time with Isabelle, in case you have a firestorm with someone else."

"In case destiny isn't on our side," Nick agreed, making a slice of pizza disappear in record time. He met my gaze. "But what if it is?"

"Something changed your mind," I insisted. "Was it really a night of talking?"

"I can't stop thinking about her." Nick flung out his hand. "It pisses me off a bit. I've never had this happen before."

"Could it be love?" I teased, and he flashed his usual confident grin.

"Well, doesn't it make sense to find out?" He leaned closer. "I mean, maybe I'm blowing a chance to find out for sure. She finishes her year here and goes back to England in two months, you know."

"It's not another planet. You could go there sometime."

Nick sat back and drummed his fingers on the table with impatience. "But I've got this feeling, Z, that I'm screwing up an opportunity. It just keeps getting stronger, like— I don't know. This sounds stupid."

"Tell me."

He looked right at me. "Like someone or something is trying to kick my ass before it's too late. I thought maybe it was you, since you're the Wyvern."

"Not me. Not yet." I smiled at him. "Maybe it's the Great Wyvern."

He rolled his eyes at that.

Maybe it was the last Wyvern. Sophie. Hmm.

"So, maybe you *should* find out. Go and talk to her." I nodded at the pocket where he'd shoved that jewelry box. "But I'd keep that in my pocket until I knew for sure."

He was cocky then, maybe because I'd convinced him that his instincts were right. "I've got two weeks to figure it out."

"Wait a minute. Are you cutting school for this?"

"You'd better believe it." He leaned across the table to whisper, mischief in his eyes. "But I told my dad I had to come and defend you while your folks are away."

"I am not your cover story!"

"Sure! It turned out to be true before I even got here. You've got to tell me all about this morning and those ShadowEaters." Nick cocked a finger at me. "But first, promise to cover for me." And he smiled at me, his auburn hair tousled, his amber eyes gleaming, and even though I didn't have a crush on him anymore, I still couldn't say no to him.

"All right, I'll cover for you." I shook a finger at him when his grin widened. "But you owe me big time."

"Tell you what. I'll get you another slice of pizza."

"More than that!"

He looked at me in mock horror. "You want *two* more? Z, you're not going to have a skinny butt for long if you eat like that."

I threw the wadded-up paper plate at him and he laughed all the way back to the line.

Then I smiled to myself. I knew this was going to work. Maybe not this month or even this year, but this would lay the groundwork for their future together.

Nick and Isabelle, together at last. It would be perfect.

The thing was that now I knew exactly what I'd give to Isabelle for her birthday. I'd wanted to give her the drawing I'd done of her and Nick at the lake the previous spring, but with Nick AWOL, it had seemed inappropriate.

I'd better get the final touches on that drawing before her birthday.

NICK INSISTED on going to check out the vacant lot after I finished school. Visit the scene of the crime, as it were, and see the evidence. He was adamant that everyone had to gather and hear my story right where it happened, as well as look for clues about the ShadowEaters. I was afraid Trevor and the ShadowEaters might still be there, but Nick was ready to kick their butts immediately if they were.

He was acting like a protective older brother and I couldn't argue with him very easily, especially after he got Liam and Garrett on his side. They wouldn't be here, but they agreed with Nick. Nick thought Isabelle's instincts would be helpful and I thought her presence would suit him well, so I pinged her and asked if Nick could pick her up. She agreed quickly, which I had to think was a good thing. My job was to tell Meagan and Derek and find Jessica before the end of the school day.

Overall, I was less than thrilled about this plan but could see the logic of it. At least we'd all be together. I was deeply afraid that we'd find a welcome committee there, one that wasn't very welcoming, but they couldn't take us all down at once.

Could they?

We'd beaten them before.

But I was afraid the rules might have changed.

Or was I just being chicken because I'd made one mistake already?

We'd go in with the full alliance, and see if we could save the day.

I took a deep breath when Nick took my car keys and went to get Isabelle, his heart obviously in his throat. We bumped fists before he headed out, and I was well aware of Trish watching from her locker on the other side of Meagan's.

Out of the corner of my eye, I thought I caught a glimmer of golden spell light. When I turned to look, Trish was whispering to Yvonne and sashaying down the hall and there was no spell light at all.

Great. I was so exhausted that I was hallucinating.

Belatedly, I tried to remember what homework I should have done at lunch. Being hunted was messing with my academic performance, that was for sure.

"Hey," Derek said, appearing silently beside me as he always did.

I ignored him.

"I don't want to fight with you."

I was still mad about his crack that I'd deserved to get in trouble.

I straightened and looked him in the eye. "How could I tell?" I asked, then bent to get my books.

But not before I saw him flinch.

"She's already upgraded," Trish shouted, taunting him from down the hall, and Yvonne giggled.

"If you change your mind, freak, you can toss the new boy to me," she said, rolling her eyes as she sighed. "What's his name?"

"Where does he live?" Trish added.

"What's he see in the freak?" they asked together, then collapsed in laughter and left.

"Their work here is done," I muttered, and dug for my books again.

"I'm trying to apologize," Derek said, sounding a bit hesitant.

"Try harder," I suggested, but my own tone had softened. "I made a mistake and I know it. I won't do it again. Don't you think tasting death was enough negative reinforcement?"

He folded his arms across his chest and leaned against the lockers, watching me intently. "What happened?"

I glanced up and down the hall. "It was a lot like my dream. Adrian conjured the ShadowEaters and they were trapped in an orb, like in my dream."

Derek didn't say anything.

"But the difference was that Kohana was there with the NightBlade, and they intended to sacrifice me. Kohana pretended to play along, but cut me free instead."

Derek's eyes brightened but he was still listening.

"We ran, but the NightBlade—this is going to sound weird—it struggled free and went to the ShadowEaters. It flew into the air and cut the orb and they swarmed out. They ate the shadow of a Mage recruit, then dispersed over the city." I grimaced, remembering the sight. "Hey, have you seen Jessica yet today?"

He shook his head, and I could tell he wasn't that interested in Jessica.

"So, you were saying thanks to Kohana?"

I met his gaze. "I didn't kiss Kohana. He kissed me."

"Why?"

"I don't know. Why does he do anything?"

Derek exhaled shakily. He looked up and down the hall, and I could almost hear him thinking. "Okay," he said, and I wondered who he was trying to convince. "Okay. Sorry I came down so hard." He fell silent as Meagan arrived at her locker beside mine.

"Hey, Derek," she said, then turned to me. "Have you seen Jessica? She's still not answering her messenger and I'm getting worried, since you said the ShadowEaters are free."

"How do you know that?" Derek asked Meagan.

"Zoë sent me a message."

"Really?" he said, giving me a hard look. I had a sense of a barrier solidifying between Derek and me. "When?"

"Before lunch." Meagan smiled and opened her locker, while Derek seethed.

I tried to make it better. "I couldn't send you one," I said to Derek. "I was waiting on Muriel, and after I told the guys, my messenger went crazy with incoming messages."

"The guys?" he echoed, clearly incredulous. "So you told Liam, Garrett, Nick, *and* Meagan, but not me?"

It did sound bad when he said it that way. "I told you in person...."

"An hour later and only because I asked." He folded his arms across his chest and glared at me. "Is this about getting even?"

I felt as if I were trying to hold on to something slippery, something that was wiggling out of my grasp despite my efforts.

"No! I just couldn't do it right then..."

Meagan looked between us, watching my total failure to win Derek's understanding. "Don't argue about details. We need to find Jessica and stick together." She turned to me. "I don't understand how they could free them without the NightBlade."

"Kohana was there with the NightBlade." I hesitated, knowing she wouldn't like this bit. "He was supposed to make the sacrifice, but he bailed on them at the last minute."

"At least he lies to everyone," Derek muttered. "Points for consistency."

"But the NightBlade pulled free of his grip and flung itself back at the apprentice Mages. It freed the ShadowEaters, like it had a will of its own."

Meagan's eyes widened in horror at that, and she pushed her glasses up her nose to peer at me. "Really?"

"The NightBlade was doing what the ShadowEaters wanted."

"Or Kohana threw it," Derek muttered. "Whose side is this guy on?"

"No," I said. "They summoned it."

Derek shook his head, apparently believing that I was covering for Kohana.

"We wild cards have to stick together—" I started, but Derek interrupted me.

"Convince Kohana of that first." He glared at me, and the air was charged between us.

Meagan cleared her throat, obviously trying to help me hold things together. "I don't understand why Kohana would even be here."

"He thought it was turning his elders against each other, so he exiled himself until he destroyed it."

"I'd say he failed," Derek commented.

I ignored him because I was having no luck changing his mind. "He said that he needed to know more about how it worked to find a weakness, because he couldn't even scratch it himself. He figured the apprentice Mages were the only ones who would know, so he tricked them."

"You don't actually believe this garbage, do you?" Derek asked.

Meagan was watching me closely and I knew she knew there was something more I wasn't saying. I thought about telling her, but didn't think it would help anything for Derek to know that Kohana would have happily sacrificed him in my stead if it had meant learning more about the NightBlade.

I was thinking, actually, that the NightBlade itself might have been twisting Kohana's thoughts in that arena, too.

"Do you think he's telling the truth?" Meagan asked.

"I do." I shrugged. "Even though he's been known to be less than straight with me."

"There's an understatement," Derek said.

I turned on him. "Look, it's not to Kohana's advantage for the Shadow-Eaters to be on the prowl, either. I don't think he expected that to happen. And I think he's in as much trouble as we all are...."

I saw very quickly that Derek wasn't really listening to me, but I kept talking all the same. I guess I was hoping that I'd say *something* he'd find persuasive.

But I realized suddenly that Derek was very still. It was more than not listening. He was looking at someone behind me and I swear his nostrils flared.

I turned, wondering who he disliked that much, and found a girl I didn't know standing behind me. No consolation that she, too, had appeared silently, without my hearing her.

Was I losing my dragon mojo completely?

Or just going crazy, as Sigmund had suggested?

Meagan started at the sight of her. "Hi," she said, scanning the girl, who ignored her.

This girl was beautiful, maybe in her early twenties, with that kind of long silky hair you see in shampoo commercials. It flowed over her shoulders like a dark river, so black that it looked like it had blue highlights in it. Her eyes, if anything, were even darker, like black velvet. She seemed mysterious and powerful all at once, sexy right to her bones, and I could guess why Derek was staring. My heart nearly broke with yearning to be so confident in my own skin.

And that was before she said anything.

"Jessica said you're looking for her," she said, and her voice was exactly as low and sultry as I would have expected.

Wait a minute. Had Jessica heard my plea? Or just finally turned on her messenger?

"Where is she?" I asked.

"Who are you?" Derek demanded. He took a step forward, as if to protect me.

She didn't even look at him. "Are you coming?" she asked me.

"Where is she?" Meagan asked, since the girl hadn't answered me.

The girl just started to turn away, glancing back over her shoulder at me with a question in those dark eyes.

Again, I was supposed to accept an invitation on trust.

It would have been smart to decline, but I really wanted to know that Jessica was safe.

As long as Meagan and I would be safe with this girl.

I took a deep breath and sensed feline. The girl met my gaze and smiled ever so slightly. There was something in that expression that reminded me of the way Jessica smiled—a secretive feminine allure, maybe—and I decided to follow my instinct.

It couldn't steer me wrong twice in one day, right?

"Okay, we'll come," I said. Meagan and I stepped forward, Derek right behind us, but the girl gave Derek a hostile glance.

"Not you," she said, the words low and hot.

Oh, this was not good.

Derek glared at her. "Why not?"

The girl smiled, then took Meagan and me by the hand, leading us out of the school. I glanced back, but Derek had already disappeared.

Was he following us?

I didn't think that would be a good idea.

On the other hand, after what I'd already faced today, additional backup was probably a good idea.

There wasn't much I could do about his choice, anyway. The girl had a strong grip on my wrist and was practically dragging me behind her. Meagan and I exchanged a glance, and Meagan shrugged. We were going to see Jessica, wherever she was.

Black Velvet was on a mission.

. . .

Black Velvet took us to a fancy apartment building downtown. I was kind of surprised. I knew that Jessica lived close to us—after all, she went to our school—but I'd thought her parents were tight for cash. Meagan had told me that they'd come from Argentina to improve Jessica's chances of getting into an Ivy League school, but that her dad wasn't able to use his license as a doctor here. He was driving a cab, which didn't lead me to believe that they were living in such fancy real estate.

Was Jessica sick?

Or in some kind of trouble? You know I was worried about her shadow.

Black Velvet wasn't answering any questions, so we stopped asking after a while.

The lobby of the building was magnificent. All Art Deco brass and dark stone, with a doorman in livery guarding the entry. His expression was stern, as if his face were carved of stone. I was a bit daunted by him, but he clearly knew Black Velvet. He just gave her a nod and summoned the elevator. He even knew where she was going, apparently.

Was she the one who lived here? She certainly would have fit in with the kind of glossy people who could afford this kind of real estate.

Yes, I did feel scruffy.

Just in case you were wondering.

The inside of the elevator was all mirrored, a bit of a dizzying effect, as there were hundreds of us extending to infinity in every direction. No missing the frayed hems of my jeans or the fact that my fave black boots could have used a buff.

Come to think of it, I needed a haircut.

Fortunately, my eyeliner was perfect.

A girl needs some constants.

Given that I'd nearly been a sacrificial victim today, I thought I was holding it together reasonably well.

Meagan flashed her killer smile at the doorman when we were on the elevator, just before the doors shut, and to my astonishment, he smiled back. I'd thought his face was made of stone.

But Meagan is really pretty. I couldn't help noticing that she seemed more at ease than I felt, maybe because she'd been to this kind of apartment before. With her dad being a concert pianist, the Jamesons did dip their toes into some different social circles than my family did.

Meanwhile, Black Velvet had hit the very top button.

The doors closed and we zoomed straight for the penthouse.

I know. It shouldn't have surprised me. Black Velvet was luxe all the way. She hadn't said a dozen words to me yet, but I had all these ideas about her. She must be a model. An heiress. A princess in exile.

There certainly was a feeling of security in this place. I felt safe, and more confident that Jessica was okay, which made no sense at all.

The elevator door opened, as smooth as butter and just about as quiet, and there was only one apartment door facing us. My eyes widened. The whole top floor of the building was a single suite? It would be like living in the clouds, with a full surround view. Meagan and I exchanged a glance, and now she looked a bit more impressed.

The foyer wasn't a whole lot bigger than the elevator, and there was only that one door opposite us. It was a nice door, painted a very shiny black, but a bit odd in that it had no knocker, doorbell, or keyhole. The knob was one of those you just push, but I didn't believe for a minute that the door was unsecured.

To the right, framed in heavy silver, was a square black pad, about five inches on a side. It had to be a scanner of some kind, but one I'd never seen before. On the other hand, this wasn't the kind of area where I usually hung out. The black square was too big for a fingerprint pad and really big for a doorbell, and I couldn't see the kind of light in it that iris scanners tended to have. There was no peephole in the door, either.

Black Velvet stepped forward and reached for the pad by the door as if she did it all the time.

So she wasn't going to knock.

She must live here.

I thought I had used up my daily allotment of surprise, but Black Velvet had one more for me.

Just before her hand touched the keypad, she shifted shape.

Black Velvet did shimmer blue, just before she made the transition, exactly the way all of us shifters do, but she changed really fast. Faster, actually, than any shift I'd ever seen—and we dragons compete on the basis of speed. I know from fast.

When she reached for the keypad, she cast a coy glance over her shoulder—that should have warned me—and then there was the blue shimmer and a sleek black panther holding one paw to the keypad.

A very large, sleek black panther.

She laid her paw on the black pad. There was a hum and a click; then she leapt forward and bumped the door with her shoulder. It was an elegant, easy move, once again making me think she did it all the time. She cast us a glance that seemed to be a challenge, especially as her eyes had become a vivid yellow, then she slipped into the apartment, like a shadow in the darkness.

Meagan and I took one look at each other, then followed. It was dark in the apartment so we moved slowly, waiting for our eyes to adjust to the shadows there. As far as I could tell, the apartment was spacious and luxuriously furnished. The carpet was really thick under our feet.

But dark. Dark like midnight. Dark like the windows that had to surround the penthouse had been draped. Sound was muffled, as well, as if there was a lot of fabric around us, and the darkness seemed to press against our ears.

Never mind that as soon as we stepped over the threshold, the door slammed behind us. There was that same whir and click, echoing loudly in the silence. I reached back immediately and grabbed the door handle, but it had locked. No surprise, there was no lock hardware on this side, either.

I didn't need to see the future to know that this was not good. I felt the pulse of several dozen heartbeats and panicked.

"You're all shimmery," Meagan whispered. "What's wrong?"

"We're not alone," I told her, because it was true.

I didn't say any more to Meagan because that was when a woman screamed.

5

My blue shimmer—generated because I was on the cusp of change and unable to do anything to stop it, not after that scream—illuminated the foyer of the apartment a little bit. It took me a second to hear the muffled murmuring of many, many women.

The ones whose heartbeats I'd heard first.

Black Velvet nudged open another door then, because we saw her silhouetted in a rectangle of bright light to our left. The woman screamed again and I could hear women trying to reassure her. Black Velvet disappeared into the room and the door didn't quite close behind her.

I took that as an invitation. I nodded at Meagan and we went to the door together. I peeked around the edge as the woman screamed for a third time; then someone hauled the door open wide to reveal us standing there.

There was a big bed in the middle of the room; that was the first thing I saw. And a woman was lying on it, her expression anguished and her knees up. She was surrounded by about a dozen women, and Jessica, too. All of them were focused on her, and the one who had opened the door indicated that we should be silent.

All of the women, even Jessica, were wearing red dresses. They were like tubes of sheer fabric, gathered on a drawstring at their shoulders and tied at the waist with a gold cord. They were all barefoot, and the cloth was sheer enough that I could see their legs silhouetted beneath. Even Jessica had abandoned her usual baggy clothes and baseball cap for the sheer red dress. She was clearly the youngest present, but the others treated her with deference. She looked as gorgeous and feminine as she had at Halloween, but more glam.

Was this some kind of ceremony? The bed was more like a platform than a bed you'd sleep on, or maybe like an altar. It had four large golden pillars, one at each corner, which actually connected to the gilded ceiling. I'd thought at first that the light emanating from the room must be sunlight, but it was candlelight reflecting on gold.

The walls were lined with cat sculptures. Most of them were gold, and most of them had red stones for eyes, like rubies. There were candles placed between them on the shelves, the flickering light making the cats seem alive, as if their red eyes were scanning the room.

The whole room shimmered gold and looked exotic. It felt to me as if there were many more present than just the women we could see.

I heard Meagan catch her breath when she saw Jessica, but I'm not sure Jessica knew we were there. Her attention was fixed on the woman on the bed and she looked a bit nervous. Why was Jessica here? Was she related to this woman? Or did she know her well? Black Velvet climbed on to the bed and lay beside the woman like a pet—or maybe a sentry.

"Push next time," advised one of the attending women. "It's close."

The woman on the bed was delivering a baby.

She had time to nod before the next contraction rippled through her body. She tipped her head back and bared her teeth but didn't scream. I saw her clench a fistful of Black Velvet's fur, and Black Velvet's eyes narrowed but she didn't move away or protest. One of the attending women reached to coax the baby into the world, and another firmly guided Jessica to the foot of the bed.

Jessica swallowed.

The baby's crown appeared, wet and dark.

"Push," advised the woman who must be the midwife. "Push."

The next contraction came; the mother pushed. The women leaned closer.

The candles flickered simultaneously.

Meagan and I grasped each other's hands.

And the baby surged forth in a rush. The midwife lifted the baby and cleared the mucus from its face. She cut the cord, and the baby cried out for the first time, its yowl nearly bouncing off the walls. The midwife tied it expertly, as if she'd done this a thousand times. The mother gasped with relief, smiling as the midwife put the child in her arms.

I'd never seen a baby born before. I wasn't sure whether it was gross or amazing.

The thing was that even though the baby seemed okay, tension remained in the air. The mother rose to her knees, her gaze locked on her baby, and the attending women gathered closer. Jessica looked as if she were facing down a terrible midterm.

What were they worried about?

One woman gave Jessica a nudge and she stepped forward. She reached for the child, who was still naked. It was a girl. The attending women watched with obvious anticipation; then one woman began to sing.

It was singing but not like choir practice. She made a wordless cry, kind of *lalalala*, one that reminded me a bit of Jessica's ability to scat. The woman beside her joined in, adding her voice. At regular intervals, another woman would join the cry. The ululation rose in volume as each woman added her voice to what became a chorus. It vibrated in my ears and made me shiver.

Jessica closed her eyes as if concentrating and held the child high. Every gaze was locked on the baby. What was supposed to happen? The song grew in intensity as the baby flickered blue and gold in her grip. The candle flames danced all around the room. There was a crackle of energy in the room, as if something had been summoned.

I gasped when I saw the cat sculptures on the wall move. At first I thought they'd come to life, but it wasn't that. There were ghostly cats between the sculptures, so many of them that the sculptures seemed to disappear in their midst. The golden ghost cats with red eyes mewled the same note as the women, watching Jessica.

In the same instant, a shape became visible in the haze of color around the child, a shape other than the child's own shape.

Superimposed on the shape of the child—or maybe coexisting with it—was the shape of a great golden cat.

The women gasped with relief and pleasure.

Meagan caught her breath. "She's a puma!" she whispered.

The chorus ended with a triumphant cry. The attendants smiled in relief at each other, then embraced as the mother fell back with obvious satisfaction. The candle flames stilled, flickering normally as they had before, and when I looked at the sculptures on the wall, there were no more cat ghosts.

The woman who had opened the door held up a finger for silence. "She *will* be a puma," she corrected, then she smiled at Jessica. "The new Oracle of Bast has awakened the ancestors to reveal the child's future. It is as all should be."

Jessica kissed the child, once on each cheek and once on her forehead. "Her name will be Safiya," she said with greater confidence, and I recognized that summoning the vision of the child's future had been a test for her. Or maybe the test had been awakening the ghosts. "Hold it sacred for Bast. May Safiya live long and bear many."

"May Safiya live long and bear many!" echoed the women.

Jessica handed the child to the mother, who kissed the little girl just as Jessica had.

Then she handed off the baby to the midwife and clapped her hands. An older woman brought her a golden box, like a little lidded casket. Jessica caught her breath at the sight of it, and the new mother smiled. She opened the box, revealing a golden necklace. It was made of linked squares, the hinges hidden so that the necklace appeared to be a solid gold band. It was more supple than that, though, because of the links. It was about two inches wide and there was a red gem mounted on the front square.

I saw that when she fastened the necklace around Jessica's neck. "Praise be that the power continues. Praise be that the ancestors have acknowledged a new oracle. Praise be that Bast continues to show her favor to her faithful." She gave Jessica the same trio of kisses, then spun her around. "Hail the new Oracle!" she said, and the assembled women cheered.

Jessica touched the necklace with her fingertips and bowed her head. I could see that she was both jubilant and overwhelmed.

Kind of the way I'd felt when Urd had first called me Wyvern.

The new mother guided Jessica toward us, her eyes glinting with purpose. I was amazed at her energy, given that she'd just had a child. "And so you have been permitted to enter our sanctuary," she said to Meagan and me.

"This is our Oracle," Jessica said, her awe obvious. From that and the attitude of the other women, I assumed this new mother was the Bastian equivalent of my dad.

She nodded, her gaze never leaving me. I felt interrogated before she even asked a question. "I allowed you to enter our sanctuary because of the depth of Jessica's concern. I needed her to be able to concentrate. But now you must tell me, Wyvern—why are you seeking Jessica?"

I told her and Jessica about Mozart's shadow and about King's instructions.

"He did as should be done. He kept his vow." She said with approval, then turned to Jessica. "You have the power to heal his shadow, and I am too tired to do it well. It must be done today, after sunset. He will be safe until then, but act quickly once the darkness falls."

"Yes, Oracle," Jessica said, and bowed.

I wanted to ask the Oracle a whole bunch of questions, but she spoke crisply, ensuring I had no chance. "And so you have witnessed one of the great mysteries of our kind, Wyvern. I allowed this because of the treaty between us, but you will not leave this sanctuary without making a pledge of secrecy."

Her gaze turned even more steely then, and I was pretty sure I didn't imagine the flicker of red in the depths of her eyes. She reminded me a little bit of Skuld, to tell you the truth.

"What do we need to promise?" Meagan asked.

The woman looked at Jessica, who squared her shoulders and spoke. "The mysteries of the vessels of Bast shall not be shared with any of the male gender. You must swear to say nothing of what you have seen to any man or boy of any kind."

The Oracle nodded approval of Jessica's words.

So that was why King had refused to talk. Either he didn't know more or it was smarter to keep what he knew to himself.

The problem was that I wasn't so good with this request.

"But there are other male shifters in our alliance," I began to argue, and the Oracle's eyes narrowed.

"We, the vessels of Bast, have endured for five thousand years," she said, her tone inflexible. "And we shall survive for five thousand more, alliance or no."

I thought it tactless to point out that the lion shifters, who were of their kind, had been exterminated by the Mages and that the cat shifters had been enslaved by them afterward.

But I thought it.

And she knew it.

"I have made an exception for you, because you freed us from captivity, but do not press me too far, Wyvern. We survive because of our ability to keep our secrets."

"But we all need to survive. I saw the ShadowEaters summoned...."

She smiled and her tone turned condescending. "And what should we care? Do you not know what the ShadowEaters are, Wyvern?"

I had to shake my head.

"They are Mages who failed." She sneered this last word. "They are Mages who tried to perform the final ceremony, to become pure spirit and merge with the universe, thereby turning all to malice. In that form, they would fill the thoughts of men with poison and hatred, inciting wars and strife and feeding greed. In the dissent, the remaining Mages could build their powers without interference, then ultimately dominate us all."

This was horrifying stuff.

Her eyes shone. "But they *failed* in making that critical transition. They are snared between our sphere and the realm of pure spirit, and this renders them harmless to anyone in either realm. Only the Mages can invoke them, and thanks to your efforts, the Mages are impotent, or close to it."

"But I saw them here...."

"You could not have." She shook her head firmly. "What ShadowEaters can influence is dreams. It is the highest form of spellcasting. They can give nightmares, Wyvern, and undermine your faith in what you know." She regarded me, her eyes glittering. "Do not believe everything you dream to be true."

I felt slapped down. Stupid. Like a kid.

That was the point.

The Oracle leaned closer to me, her eyes now shining with that red glow. I could see a golden cat shape surrounding her, like an aura or a ghost, and guessed that she was on the cusp of shifting shape. Which meant she either felt threatened or was mad.

Or both.

"Now promise," she hissed.

I couldn't just give in, not after she'd spoken to me like that.

"No guys? Absolutely none?" I asked. All the dragon shifters were guys, and they were my friends. How could secrets not divide us? "Not my counselors and friends or the wolf shifters? What about guy cat shifters, like King and Mozart?"

"No males may know of this divine secret," she said with resolve. "Those you call King and Mozart have accepted this truth."

Wow. Did they even have names in the realm of the Bastians?

The Oracle put out her hand. "Pledge your silence, Wyvern. Pledge it now." She smiled coldly, her gaze flicking to the cat sculptures on all sides of the room. "Or you will remain the guest of the ancestors forever."

I looked again and realized that the sculptures were actually jars. I could see now that the cat head on each one was a lid. What was inside them? She was talking about ancestors, and I was thinking about remains.

Was there a jar in this room with my name on it? I shuddered despite myself at the very idea. I could see them again, those shadowy cat ghosts, shimmering and gathering, slipping around our small group. The Oracle kept her attention fixed on me, her gaze unblinking. I thought about that door with no hardware. Jessica was watching, still fingering her necklace, and I could hear Meagan's heart thumping.

I did not have a lot of options.

"I pledge it," I said, not having any idea how I was going to make this work.

The Oracle's smile flashed. She kissed me then, with that same trio of kisses, and when her face was close to mine, she whispered. "Make no mistake: I shall know if you break your word."

There was a brilliant shimmer of gold and I saw those milling ghost cats on all sides again. They were all looking at me, their red eyes gleaming, and I knew they would be the ones to rat on me—ha—if there was cause to do so.

I had to hope she was right about the ShadowEaters.

But I didn't believe it.

With one last smile, the Oracle turned to her new daughter and the midwife, dismissing us from her attention. Jessica watched the other women for a minute, a kind of yearning in her eyes. She was one of the Bastians, I saw, but not really like them.

A wild card, just like me.

"Did you ever do that before?" Meagan asked.

Jessica shook her head. "Never." She glanced over her shoulder at the women. "The mother is the current Oracle, so she couldn't do the ceremony this time. I knew theoretically how to awaken the ancestors, because she taught me how to do it, but it's a lot different in real life. My mom was sure I could do it. I just hoped I wouldn't screw it up."

"No pressure," I said, understanding completely. She flashed me a smile. "You look like you could use a chocolate bar."

"Ice cream." Jessica grinned and nodded. "Definitely ice cream. Just let me get changed."

"And we've got big news," Meagan said.

"I figured that when I heard Zoë in my thoughts." Jessica gave me an intent look.

So that, at least, had worked.

"Can you really heal Mozart's shadow?" I asked.

Jessica nodded with confidence. She tapped her necklace. "I can, now that I have this."

That was good news. I had to think that things were finally looking up.

Relatively speaking.

IT DIDN'T TAKE Jessica long to get back into her usual clothes, complete with the baseball hat jammed over her ponytail. I couldn't even see the golden necklace under her T-shirt and hoodie, but I was sure it was there. It wasn't the kind of thing you just forgot and left behind.

The apartment was lit normally now, the women having opened the blinds and drapes. It was a beautiful apartment, decorated in black and gold with Art Deco furniture. There were big vases of flowers, everything so perfect that it looked like a photograph. I caught a glimpse of a fantastic view of the lake out the windows on the far side.

I wondered a bit about our exit, but as soon as we stepped into the foyer, the door opened, seemingly of its own volition. Jessica pushed the elevator button as the door clicked shut behind us. It looked as if she was used to this.

I had so many questions, I wasn't sure where to start.

Meagan didn't have that trouble. "Is this why you didn't answer me?"

"It wasn't up to me to tell you where I was. The Oracle had to decide, and she was a bit busy."

"But the panther girl," I said.

"The Oracle sent her," Jessica confirmed. "She asked me why I was worried, and I told her that you were concerned about me. She said I didn't have time for distractions."

Meagan pushed up her glasses. "Did you really call to the dead?"

Jessica nodded. "The ashes of all past Oracles are here in the sanctuary, and the current Oracle calls on them for guidance." She grinned. "Apparently, even an Oracle in training can get them to show up."

"How do you ask ashes for guidance?" Meagan asked as we got into the elevator.

"Because they're more than ashes," I said, understanding now what I had seen. "The past Oracles came alive, like ghosts, right when the baby was shimmering in your grip. They were there again when I had to promise."

Both of them looked at me in astonishment.

"You *saw* the ancestors?" Jessica asked. There was an edge to her tone, as if she didn't believe me, as if she thought I was making up that part.

As if maybe I was trying to steal some of her thunder.

But I had seen them.

The elevator zoomed toward the lobby, moving so fast that my ears popped a bit. It was a smooth ride, but the bottom of my stomach felt weird.

"I think so," I said, pretending to have more doubt than I did. "There were lots of gold cats, transparent ones with red eyes. They were walking between the sculptures, kind of weaving their way along the shelves, and meowing."

"That's them," Jessica said, looking at me in awe and maybe, just maybe, a teensy bit of resentment. "You shouldn't be able to see them. You're not initiated into our rites or one of our kind or anything."

Oops.

"Don't you see them?" I asked.

She shook her head.

"Not yet. But I've been told about them." She smiled. "I know what to look for."

"We both saw the puma," Meagan said.

Jessica nodded. "Everybody does. I never heard of anyone other than an Oracle seeing the ancestors before, though." She looked at me again, consideration in her eyes.

"If you can't see them, how do you know whether they come?" Meagan asked.

"I hear them," Jessica explained. "Today they told me the baby's name. And I felt their power surrounding her in that moment, revealing her future."

"Why does it matter?" I asked. "I mean, is it important what kind of cat the baby will be able to become?"

"Just that she can." Jessica exhaled and looked suddenly tired. "We never know, you know. A child might not have the power to shift and become one of us. It's not a gimme anymore, even for the child of an Oracle. Ever since the Mages—well, since we were their slaves—things have been erratic. This ceremony used to be just routine, but now it's really important. If the child will fully be one of us, the ancestors share that truth."

"And if they don't answer the summons?" I asked, sensing that she wasn't telling me the whole story. The Bastians sure were big on their privacy.

"Then the child will just be human." Jessica grimaced. "Or maybe the Oracle doesn't really have the gift to conjure them." She smiled wearily as the doors opened to the lobby. "I'm so relieved that they came today."

"You were great," Meagan said, giving Jessica a quick hug.

The doorman smiled at the sight of us, and it did not crack his face. He nodded at Jessica as if they were old pals, then swept open the door to the street. We walked through like queens, and I thought I could get used to living in a place like this.

Then Derek, looking ticked off, separated himself from the shadows to stride toward us.

"Remember your vow," Jessica muttered under her breath.

Derek gave me an electric look, like he'd heard what she said, and I wondered what I could tell him that wouldn't break my shiny new promise. I was thinking there was something to be said for my dad's skills with diplomacy and negotiation, and that maybe I should have paid a bit more attention when he'd explained all that to me.

"Did you tell her about the ShadowEaters this morning?" he demanded, flicking a look at Jessica.

"We didn't have time to talk about it yet," I said. I slipped my hand into his and he visibly relaxed. "Let's find Jessica some ice cream and bring her up-to-date before we get back to class." Derek's eyes narrowed and he looked closer at Jessica, but she held his gaze.

As if daring him to imagine she'd share her secrets.

I watched her and wasn't at all sure that the cat shifters *had* lost their royalty.

We scored some ice cream and claimed a pair of benches in a concrete park off Michigan Avenue. It was probably a busy little oasis in the summer, but in February, with the fountain turned off and the snow fluttering down, we had the place to ourselves.

It was hard for me to tell them about my experience with the ShadowEaters. It was gross to remember it, even though the Bastians' Oracle was sure it had been a dream even the second time. I thought she was wrong; the others weren't so sure. Again, I had that sense of things coming apart when they really needed to be together, but couldn't think of a thing to do or say to fix it.

Except maybe prove to them that I was right.

That was when we realized the time and that we'd be late back to school. We started to walk back together, moving pretty quickly.

"What about our alliance of shifters?" Derek asked, and I heard the edge in his tone.

"What about it?" Jessica asked, looking between us.

"Seems like it's not working," he said in a low voice. "Seems that some people would rather keep their own secrets and run their own plans than work together."

Jessica clearly took exception to that. She straightened. "Just because we're allies doesn't mean that I can betray the trust of my kind and share our secrets with everyone."

"We're not talking *everyone*," Derek argued. "We're talking about the four of us." His eyes snapped. "We're talking about trust and teamwork. Isn't that what an alliance is?"

Uh oh.

"You don't need to know everything about me to fight by my side," Jessica said.

"I think I do. I think that's the way it should be." Derek had even more than his usual intensity. I remembered his comments in the fall about wolves seeing the world in black and white.

"All or nothing," I murmured.

"Exactly," he said, punctuating the word with another hot look at me.

Jessica folded her arms across her chest. "You can believe whatever you want and you can tell me whatever you want, but we learned the price of trusting in the wrong place when the Mages took out the lion shifters. We keep our secrets, thanks. And let's remember that Mozart, one of my kind, has been injured already."

Derek—predictably—took exception to her tone. "Oh, so now you're assuming that I'm going to betray you!"

"Not you!" Meagan interjected, obviously trying to save the situation.

I wasn't sure it could be done.

"Who else, then?" Derek demanded. "Meagan and Zoë know whatever it was that you were doing, but I don't. Obviously you trust them."

"It's a girl thing," Jessica argued.

"It's a girl-*shifter* thing," Derek retorted, then glared at me. "You don't want wolves in the alliance. That's fine. We can take care of ourselves."

"That's not what's going on," I said, and his pale gaze locked on me.

"That's what you say, but you're not showing me anything that would make me believe you." He gave us each one last glare, then turned and trudged away.

Perfect.

I ran after him, but he pretended not to hear me until I caught his hand and pulled him to a stop. He looked at me with narrowed eyes, obviously wanting to be somewhere else.

Anywhere else.

The alliance was being destroyed and it was my fault.

All I could do was try to save it.

"Look," I said, talking fast and quietly. I knew he'd be able to hear me. "I made a mistake this morning. I'm sorry I did that, and I'm sorry I got mad when you challenged me about it. I really thought I could handle it."

"What happens if they get you?" he demanded through his teeth. "Our prophecy says that the only way forward is to follow the dragon. If there is no dragon to follow, there is no way forward. If you die because you're too confident, you're condemning all of us."

"Gee, no pressure," I said, trying to make him smile.

He didn't. "It's not a joke, Zoë."

"I know." I squeezed his hand. "I was wrong about that, and I won't do it again."

"I can only defend you if you let me go into danger with you."

"I know." I twined my fingers with his. "I promise not to go off on my own again."

"You just did it again!"

"Okay. You were right. I need to trust your instincts, too. I will. I promise."

That seemed to please him a bit. Or at least it calmed him. He took a deep breath and turned his hand so that his fingers tangled with mine.

"But you need to trust me, too," I said. "Secrecy is really important to the Bastians. They will leave the alliance over it, and I have sworn to defend it."

He looked at me. "That's divisive."

I grimaced. "It's the only way to keep them in the union. I can't lose them, or we're all goners. Come on, she's under pressure and worried about Mozart, too." I tugged at his hand, seeing that he was unconvinced.

But thawing. He was definitely thawing.

"Nick and Isabelle are coming after school. They want to go to the vacant lot and hear the whole story, see if they can pick up any clues. I think we should all go together. Will you come?"

He watched me, his eyes glittering with indecision.

I leaned closer to him, touching my lips to his cheek. I felt him melt. It was strange, realizing that I had some ability to affect his thinking with just a little touch, and it gave me an uncomfortable sense of power.

One I wasn't sure I wanted.

"Can you trust me?" I whispered.

Derek heaved a sigh, then turned to consider me. "The only time you ever kissed me back was on your birthday," he said softly, then pulled his hand from mine and walked away.

I watched him go, feeling like I'd blown it completely. I could have kissed him back any number of times. I could have initiated a kiss right this minute—well, two minutes before. I could have used that new power I'd felt to bring him completely to my side.

But it didn't feel right.

When I return someone's kiss, I'm going to mean it.

Which sounds really good and principled—except if it looks like that principle is going to trash the alliance that could save the last four kinds of shifters left in the world.

Did I care more about being honest with Derek? Or with ensuring the survival of our respective kinds? How much would I compromise for the greater good?

I knew Derek wouldn't have compromised anything, but it seemed that dragons saw more shades of gray.

Bonus.

Or not.

I DON'T KNOW how I got through the rest of the day. Muriel chewed me out for not telling her where I'd gone at lunch—never mind that I was late getting back—and I knew there was yet another black mark beside my name.

That I refused to confide in her compelled her to write a lengthy note in my file.

Meet Zoë the troubled teen, signed up for detention.

I hoped the others would wait for me.

They did.

Meagan and Jessica were still at my locker when I got free of Muriel and detention, but there was no sign of Derek. I figured he wasn't coming, even though I wished I could have had the chance to change his mind.

When we came out of school, Nick was waiting outside, leaning on my car and spinning the keys on his finger. I'd sent him a message and knew he'd give me a hard time about my detention. The three of us ran for it. Isabelle hopped out and gave us each a hug while Nick razzed me about being a troublemaker.

I had a feeling then and looked back, only to find Trevor leaning on his MG. He was surrounded by Suzanne and her crew, all of them flirting shamelessly with him. The spell light danced around them, giving me a sick feeling in my stomach.

I felt sicker when he turned to me and I saw the glimmer of spell light in his eyes. There was something odd about him, something that didn't look quite right, but I assumed my response was residue from earlier in the day.

I felt Nick beside me then, the weight of his hand on my shoulder. He glared at Trevor, who turned away quickly, as if intimidated.

I didn't believe it for a minute.

"He's going to follow us there," I whispered.

"Then we'll kick his ass," Nick said. "Let's go."

Let's face facts. My mom's car is not a big car. It's a teensy vehicle designed for commuters who travel alone, maybe with a briefcase and a bag of groceries. There were five of us. Five. Isabelle pulled the passenger's seat forward as far as possible. Meagan got into the back; then Jessica and I piled in after her. By some miracle, we managed to make room for Isabelle to put the seat back and shut the door, but I was glad we weren't going far.

There was still no sign of Derek as Nick drove away.

"Where's Derek?" Isabelle asked. Everyone looked at me.

"I'm not sure he's coming."

There was a heavy silence after that. I sensed that they blamed me for his absence, and, really, I did, too. The trouble was that I wasn't at all sure how to fix it.

It took me a while to direct Nick to the vacant lot, because the area had been unfamiliar to me. We went around a couple of blocks several times. The fact that there was no sign of the library—even though I knew it had been a glamour—didn't help me to get oriented.

"Are you sure, Z?" Nick asked for the forty-third time.

"Maybe it was another vision," Isabelle said. "Maybe it didn't really happen in this plane of existence."

"That's what our Oracle said," Jessica agreed.

"Don't you believe me?"

Isabelle smiled at me but it was forced. "You have such vivid dreams, Zoë, and the realm of the Wyvern includes dreams and possibilities."

"The Oracle says the ShadowEaters can't touch us in this realm," Jessica added.

"You could be confusing reality and your vision," Nick said. "It makes sense to me."

"It would make sense to me if you believed me," I muttered.

"What did it look like again?" Meagan asked, trying to be helpful.

Skepticism threw my game a bit and we drove around for another half an hour, the tension mounting in the car. I ignored Nick's deep sigh, as well as the way Isabelle reached out to touch him, ensuring his silence.

Finally, I thought I spotted it, and Nick parked where I indicated.

I got out and looked around, confirming my memories.

"Here?" Meagan asked, and I saw that she wanted me to be right.

I nodded. "I saw that convenience store when we arrived, when I noticed that the street was empty." I pointed. "And I saw that locksmith with the grates over the shop windows when Kohana and I took off."

"So, you see," Meagan said triumphantly. "Zoë did find it."

I didn't wait for a reply, just marched into the vacant lot. Yes, that was the streetlight that shone in my dream, and those were the boarded windows on the other side of the far street. This was the garbage can that Skuld had toppled over, still lying on its side. I headed straight toward the clearing I'd seen several times now, bracing myself for what we'd find there.

That kid might be there still, dead.

Or at least there would be his blood in the snow.

Even though I couldn't smell it.

I halfway expected apprentice Mages to leap out from behind the piled trash or ShadowEaters to pounce on us from the sky. Would Kohana reveal himself again? My heart was pounding as I walked to the clearing where the orb had been suspended overhead. I braced myself and looked.

But there was nothing there. There was nothing but discarded and broken bikes, bashed-up trash cans, dented car fenders, some barbed wire, and a lot of litter. The snow fell steadily and silently all around. The sky was a bright gray overhead.

It was just an empty lot.

With no body or blood.

Worse, the snow was pristine, as if we were the first ones to step onto this lot in a week. How could this be?

"Are you sure this is the right place?" Meagan asked. Even she was fighting to believe me now.

"There are no footprints," Isabelle said. "The snow is completely undisturbed."

"Like no one's been here all week," Nick agreed. "I don't think anyone's been here in a long time." He visibly inhaled, then shook his head.

He was right. There was no scent of anyone having been in this space.

No spell light, either.

How could that be? I turned around and around, staring at the lot, seeing the things that verified that I was in the right place.

And not seeing the really important things that would have proven it.

"So it was just a bad dream," Jessica said with satisfaction. She repeated what her Oracle had said about ShadowEaters. I could tell that the others liked this answer a lot.

"So they're just messing with Zoë," Nick said with approval.

"Or it could have been a vision," Isabelle suggested, maybe seeing that I was disappointed. "Something that *could* happen." She smiled. "You must be coming into your ability to see the future."

"That must be it," Nick agreed amiably. "It's not necessarily going to happen, but it could."

"And it hasn't yet," Jessica said.

But that wasn't it and I knew it.

I just didn't know how to convince them.

Again, I had that sense of the alliance weakening, and a growing sense that it needed to be more robust.

For...*something*.

"Maybe there's a glamour disguising the truth," I suggested, and I sounded a bit desperate even to myself. "The library was a glamour, after all." I turned to Meagan in desperation. "Can you sense any spell light?"

She shook her head. "There must be a lot of vacant lots that look pretty much like this one."

Nick nodded sympathetically. "We can drive around some more, if it makes you feel better, Z."

"I'm sure it was here," I insisted. "I'm *positive*. It happened right here, just a couple of hours ago." I looked around, scanning for evidence of the dead guy. That would prove that I was right.

No luck.

Isabelle dropped her hand on my shoulder. "There's no energy here, Zoë."

"They could have disguised it."

They all smiled at me, their false encouragement doing nothing to hide the fact that they didn't believe me.

"I think it happened," I insisted. "I think I dreamed it once, but then it happened for real. And I think the rules have changed, no matter what the Oracle says. I think that the ShadowEaters are here and..."

"Then where are they, Z? Here we are, fresh bait, and they're AWOL." Nick flung his hands skyward, cocky as ever. "Hey, ShadowEaters! Come on down! We're two wild cards, a shifter, and a spellsinger. Shadows all around! Lunch is served!"

"Nick!" Isabelle said in horror.

He grinned.

Because there was no reply. The sky looked normal. The hum of the city surrounded us. The snow fell steadily. Nick looked at me, and turned to go back to the car.

The others stood for a minute, then began to follow Nick.

"What about Mozart getting hurt last night?" I called after them. "That was real."

"That just means there are apprentice Mages around," Jessica said. "And we knew that already." She and Meagan came to me, each on one side, like they were going to help an invalid.

"You said that Trevor said Adrian did it," Meagan reminded me.

I looked at each of them in turn. "What about Trevor bringing me here in his car?"

Meagan grimaced. "You should know, Zoë, that he was in class this morning. I checked with a couple of people this afternoon when I was trying to find out what had happened to you. He was there. He didn't miss a thing."

"A glamour," I muttered. "He used a glamour."

We walked back to the car in silence, where Nick and Isabelle waited.

"I think you're seeing past, present, and future simultaneously," Isabelle said kindly. "That's supposed to one of the Wyvern's abilities and I'm sure it's confusing."

"I am not confused!" I shouted. "I saw the ShadowEaters invoked by Trevor and Adrian. I saw the NightBlade free them. I saw Adrian become a ShadowEater himself. I saw the ShadowEaters swarm that kid and eat his shadow."

"Twice," Jessica noted. "Who's to say that both times weren't dreams?"

"What we need to do is make a plan to ensure that your vision doesn't come true," Nick said firmly.

"Look at it this way," Meagan said. "Maybe the NightBlade does have a power of its own. Maybe it wants to be returned to the apprentice Mages for this very purpose. Maybe it's what is messing with your mind, so that you'll go to Kohana and get it." She linked her arm through mine. "Let's go home. Nick's going to keep vigil on the roof tonight."

I looked at him and he nodded. They'd made plans without talking to me?

They really were treating me like a crazy person.

"It's getting dark," Jessica added. "I have to take care of Mozart."

Nick pulled out his messenger. "I'll send a message to Kohana, confirm that we're still on for the spring equinox to destroy the NightBlade. Let's meet in the morning and make a plan."

"It'll all be just fine," Isabelle said.

Meagan smiled. "Don't worry, Zoë. We'll defend you."

But I was trying to defend them.

THE SUN HAD JUST BARELY SET when we got to the Jamesons' place. We'd dropped off Nick and Isabelle at the L because there wasn't much time left until dinner and we didn't want to be late. Mrs. Jameson immediately asked Jessica to stay to eat.

Then we headed for Meagan's room. King sat up when he saw Jessica, his tail thrashing at the air and his eyes bright with anticipation.

Just her presence seemed to improve Mozart's state. His eyes opened a little and he mewled, and that was even before she touched him. I had the feeling that she communicated with King on a different level than I could hear, but I sensed his reverence for her. She stroked Mozart and his breathing became more comfortable.

Like he knew she'd take care of him.

"Can you turn that light on?" she asked Meagan, who quickly did what she requested. The lamp was on the nightstand, so its light shone across Mozart, casting his shadow across the bed. Jessica traced its outline with her fingertip, murmuring softly. She looked to be in a kind of a trance. She winced as her fingertips passed over the bite in the shadow, and King shuddered.

Then she pulled out the necklace she'd been given. She kept it on, but left it on the outside of her shirt now, instead of hidden underneath. The red stone seemed to have a spark trapped within it, a glow that hadn't been there before. I could see the light reflecting off the opposite wall. Mozart opened his eyes to stare at her, and the light was mirrored in his gaze, too.

She murmured softly, maybe so that neither we nor the guys could hear her incantation clearly. The stone flashed red, making the cats' eyes look red.

I jumped when a dozen golden ghostly cats appeared in the room. Meagan shivered at the sudden chill in the air. I watched the ghost cats mill around Meagan's bed, their eyes flashing. They twined around Jessica's legs, and the stone's light got even brighter.

Jessica bent quickly and touched the stone to Mozart's forehead. The ghost cats leapt onto the bed and surrounded him tightly, circling with greater speed.

I thought I could hear them purring.

Then Jessica straightened with a flourish. The ghost cats were gone in the blink of an eye, and the stone could have been a piece of red glass. She tucked the necklace back into her shirt and stood up, just another math whiz come to do homework.

But the bite out of Mozart's shadow was starting to fill in. I could already see that it was smaller and that King curled around his buddy a little less protectively than before. Meagan followed my glance and her face lit.

"You did it!" she said.

Jessica smiled in obvious relief. "I started it. It'll take a couple of days to grow back. Don't let him outside until then."

"I'll secure the cat door," Meagan said.

"You summoned the ancestors again," I said.

Jessica nodded and smiled. "Second time in a row." Then she sobered. "Did you see them again?" I nodded and she studied me. "Careful, Zoë. You don't want to become one of those people who get lost in their visions."

Great. One more thing to worry about.

"What's the stone, though?" I asked. "Is it just for healing?"

Jessica smiled and looked a lot like the Oracle when she did. "I can't tell you its powers, but I can tell you its story." Meagan stopped on her way out of the room, turned back, and shut the door, leaning against it. "When we were enslaved, a plan was made for our escape. The Mages had a treasury, then, a collection of talismans they'd taken from different shifters when they eliminated them." She swallowed. "The story is that we stole from the treasury, hoping to bargain for our own freedom. We were caught, and the tiger shifters were eliminated to teach us the price of defiance."

She touched the stone. "But they didn't get everything back that we'd taken. This ruby was one of three hidden from them and passed in secret from Oracle to Oracle over the centuries. The cobra shifters filled these three stones with their powers and wore them on their brows."

She draped the necklace around her head so that the gem was on her forehead. She looked like a queen. "At least until the Mages eliminated them." She sighed and put it around her neck again, touching it with her fingertips. It had no spark in it now. "I can't tell you the secret name of this stone, but it is the one best used for healing."

"And the others?" I asked. "The Oracle must have one of them."

Jessica held my gaze, neither agreeing nor disagreeing. "They are hidden, as the ancestors wish them to be." She really reminded me of the Oracle when she gave me that look and when she left the room walking so regally.

At least one of us wild cards was getting it right.

The funny thing was that my doubts multiplied as the evening progressed. I wasn't sure what I'd seen or what to believe anymore. Was I right? Was everyone else right? Was this the road to insanity? I felt like something was eating away at me, devouring my confidence, something that festered in darkness and fed nightmares.

ShadowEaters.

No surprise that I wasn't particularly brilliant with my homework. I was just too twitchy. I couldn't keep my gaze from trailing to the big living room window and the square of night it framed. I couldn't stop thinking about my close call—and the possibility that the ShadowEaters might be hunting me. Kohana had warned me that they liked shifter shadows best. At night, the memory seemed even more creepy.

More real.

And that claustrophobic feeling of them drawing close, hungering for my shadow, isolating me and suffocating me...even the memory made me shudder.

What if the Oracle was wrong?

Was Jessica able to heal damaged dragon shadows?

I really wanted to talk more to Jessica and Meagan about the ShadowEaters and make a plan together, but Mrs. Jameson was hovering. We couldn't use our messengers because she'd take them away while we were doing homework. So I just fretted, which was just about the most ineffective solution possible. It did exactly zero for my confidence.

Mrs. Jameson kept checking on my progress with homework—of which there was little—so I knew that Muriel had found herself an ally. Meagan and Jessica sat on either side of me, periodically touching my hand. I guess they knew I was still freaked.

Mr. Jameson came home late from a rehearsal and was immediately assigned by Mrs. Jameson to drive Jessica home.

"I was going to do that," I said, but everyone shook their heads in unison.

"You're dead on your feet, Zoë," Jessica said, and Meagan nodded agreement. "You should crash."

I tried not to be paranoid. I wanted to think that they were being protective of me, not treating me like a wacko who shouldn't be driving—or a delusional person who couldn't tell the difference between dreams and reality.

"Everything will look better after you get some sleep," Meagan said.

"Maybe you should stay tonight," I said on impulse to Jessica. Mrs. Jameson gave me an odd look, so I made up an excuse. "Help me with this math question in the morning, before we go to school and have that test."

"You'll do fine. You know more than you think you do." Jessica smiled at me, and Meagan went to get her coat to tag along.

Don't go. They're out there, I mouthed to her when she looked back, unable to fully express my fear for her.

She must have seen it all the same. She flicked a glance at the window, then back at me. *I'll be fine,* she mouthed, as confident of the Oracle's perspective as I was not.

I exhaled, not liking the situation. Again I looked out the window. Was that the glimmer of orange eyes I saw in the shadows? I could hear my friends checking that they had everything and kidding around with Meagan's dad. I couldn't stop staring out the window. I had a feeling of foreboding, one I couldn't shake.

I wondered what Mozart had seen. I thought about doing my Wyvern trick of wandering through another individual's memories. I was pretty worn-out, but I was ready to give it a try.

I closed my eyes and concentrated, but I couldn't find a way into Mozart's mind, much less his memories. With the *Pyr*, I could follow the ley line that connected all of us. With apprentice Mages, I'd been able to follow spell light. But there was no conduit to Mozart, wherever his thoughts might be.

I checked the ley lines to the *Pyr* and was relieved to find them all pretty much where they should be.

"Milk and a cookie?" Mrs. Jameson asked, startling me so that I jumped.

I thanked her, begged off, and retreated to Meagan's room. I hadn't been physically injured during that encounter in the lot, but I felt psychically roughed up.

I left the curtains open and stared into the night sky, watching for...something.

I had a feeling I'd know it when I saw it.

But I had no idea what I was looking for.

That was probably exactly how the ShadowEaters wanted it to be.

Don't you hate when the bad guys are winning?

6

The sudden smell of toothpaste jolted me awake and alerted me to Meagan's arrival. She turned out the light that I'd left on and got into bed, making a fuss over both cats before she snuggled in. I kept my eyes closed, not really feeling like talking.

I *was* bagged.

Meagan cleared her throat, as if she were going to say something that was no big deal, but I didn't believe it for a minute. "So, are you still g-g-going to the dance with Derek?" she asked.

It was her stammer that got me.

What was *she* worried about?

I rolled to my side, turning to face her, and opened my eyes. I was just able to see her troubled expression in the darkness. "I don't know, actually. Why?"

"It seems like he's mad at you."

"Well, he is. He thinks I should have taken him with me when I went with Trevor. Or at least told him."

"Well, you did tell me."

"And you discovered that Trevor was still in class, when I said he was with me." I made a face.

Meagan, I could see, was thinking.

This could only be good.

"Well, it's weird, isn't it?" she said, patting Mozart as she frowned. "I've been thinking about it, and I didn't know Trevor could cast a glamour. I thought that was advanced stuff beyond his powers."

"Adrian did it at boot camp."

"Maybe he cast the one you saw today, too." Meagan grimaced. "But who cast the one of Trevor in school? Could Adrian do both at the same time? Or has Trevor learned more?" She turned on the light, pulled out her messenger, and began typing. "I'll ask Jared if there's a way to know for sure." A moment later, she smiled at me, and I ached that I couldn't just send a message to Jared like that, too.

Over. Jared was over.

Meagan turned out the light and put her glasses on the nightstand when she was done. "What else?"

"Derek's mad that I won't tell him what happened with Jessica today."

"You promised not to." She fluffed her pillow. "Isn't there something else? Derek's pretty loyal to you and you've explained all of this to him."

I fell silent, deciding how much to share.

But Meagan is my best friend, and she is brilliant, and the fact that she was staring at me in the darkness, waiting for me to go on, made me spill it. "Derek saw Kohana kiss me," I admitted.

"Whoa!" Meagan sat up, grabbed her glasses, and turned on the light. "When did that happen? And why didn't you tell me?"

"I didn't really want to talk about it in front of everybody."

She was excited. "But that means that Derek could confirm that Kohana was here, which would prove that you weren't dreaming...."

"I don't think he will."

"Just like Kohana won't tell anyone what *he* saw. Guys!"

To tell the truth, it wasn't guys who were frustrating me in this moment.

Meagan sensed as much. She looked at me hard. "What's the matter?"

Well, I was telling her the whole story. Wasn't I? "So, you don't believe me until I say that Derek saw Kohana; then you believe it, even though Derek hasn't said anything to you about it himself?"

"But that explains perfectly why Derek's so mad at you. I couldn't figure that out."

"You could have just believed me!"

"Okay, sorry." Meagan grimaced. "It's not that I didn't believe you. I wanted to believe you. I knew that you believed what you'd seen. I just thought that maybe you didn't have all the information."

"And now?"

"Maybe the Oracle's the one who doesn't have all the information." Meagan fell back against her pillows, thinking. "I mean, let's agree that it did happen and that we couldn't see that kid at the lot today because of a glamour."

"Okay."

"That would mean that the ShadowEaters weren't caught in their own realm anymore. They'd be here. Where?" I shrugged, but Meagan looked at me. "Seriously, why didn't they attack us at the lot today when Nick dared them?"

"I don't know. Maybe they're messing with us."

"No. They would have done it if they could. What's stopping them? And how do we find out?"

"Ask Trevor?" I suggested.

Meagan snorted, then pursed her lips. "Wait a minute." She was drumming her fingers on top of the bed, making enough vibration that King gave her a poisonous glance. She ignored him. "You see it, don't you?"

"See what?"

"Maybe they need more energy. They're using what energy they have to target you! If they'd shown themselves today, we would have all believed you. This way, they stay hidden longer." Meagan was excited. "That means you're the threat to their success." She sat up, her expression triumphant. "That means *you* can ruin everything."

She was right. She had to be right.

I felt invigorated again.

"I just have to figure out what it is." I smiled at her. "You know, it kicks butt having a genius for a best friend. Thanks." We reached out across the gap between the beds and brushed fingertips.

"You can do it, Zoë. You'll figure it out." She was smiling at me, exuding a confidence that fed mine. I felt again my happiness at her having her braces off, and took a good look at her. She frowned at me. "What's wrong now?"

I smiled. "Nothing. Just that when you get contacts, every guy in the world is going to be at your feet."

She dropped her gaze and pleated the sheet between her fingers. "Well, that's just it. Isn't it?"

I sat up, finally understanding. "Wait a minute. You don't think that if I'm not going to the dance with Derek that Garrett won't come."

She flicked me a look and blushed. "I'd really like to see him again."

"He'll come. He was totally bummed at Christmas that you were away."

"Really?"

"Really. I think you're the only reason he came to Chicago."

She was pleased by that—I could see it.

She settled down to sleep but I knew I had to fill her in on everything. "Hey, there's one more thing you need to know about Kohana and the NightBlade."

"What?"

"Kohana made a deal with Adrian and Trevor that he'd wield the knife for their ceremony, thinking he'd learn something from it."

"Yes, you said that he'd agreed to do the sacrifice. But he faked them out."

"He said he would have done it if they'd brought Derek or Jessica, just to learn more about the NightBlade, but that he couldn't do it to me. He saved me, then he told me all that; then he kissed me."

"So he knew they would sacrifice a wild card. That must be important." She turned to me. "Do you think Kohana is telling the truth?"

"I have no idea."

"But do you like Derek?" Meagan asked quietly.

"I like him," I admitted, "but I'm not sure I *like* him. I think I should be sure before...well, before anything more happens. I know he wants more commitment, but I want it to be honest." Now I was blushing like crazy.

To my astonishment, Meagan smiled. It wasn't like her to enjoy my discomfort. "What about Kohana? Do you like him?"

I shook my head. "I don't trust him. He'll probably turn up again, though."

"He's hot."

I shook my head. "Not really. I think he's just trying to mess with me."

To my astonishment, Meagan seemed delighted by this confession.

"What are you so happy about?" I asked.

"You're the Wyvern," Meagan said with a confidence that warmed my heart. "You're the key to everything, and you're my friend, and I know exactly what I need to do to help you out."

And with that, she went to sleep.

Leaving me in total suspense.

I TOSSED and turned for a while, maybe dozed off and on. I was both exhausted and jittery. Running through the sequence of events in the vacant lot over and over again was doing exactly nothing to help me get to sleep. I reviewed it for the umpty-gazillionth time, looking for clues—I wasn't sleeping, so I needed something to think about—when it hit me.

Kohana had been singing the invocation chant.

Kohana had been *casting spells.*

This was huge. It was epic.

And it had slid right past me.

"Kohana's a spellsinger!" I said, sitting straight up in bed. How could I have missed that? Was that his special power as the wild card of his kind? Was that why he thought he could destroy the NightBlade?

"Yes. I don't know. Yes and yes," said a man with a low, slow voice.

I jumped, then spun in the bed, knotting the sheets around my knees in the process. (Very elegant look, let me tell you.)

There was a guy sitting cross-legged on the floor, smoking a cigarette. He looked pretty old to be sitting like that, and his long dark hair was threaded with silver. His face was both tanned and lined, and so were his hands. He was wearing jeans and a red cowboy shirt.

And he was watching me.

Meagan was still sleeping, and King was out cold, too. (This even though I had pretty much shouted. I took this as a clue that I was in dreamland again.) The room looked completely normal, other than the guy on the rug.

This was like my conversation with Sigmund, chatting with a guy in what looked just like Meagan's room. It was reassuringly Wyvern-like, so probably not some ShadowEater nightmare.

So, who was this guy? I had a feeling he wasn't among the living anymore.

He took another drag, his dark eyes glinting, end of the cigarette glowing, and watched me as he exhaled. The smoke made a silvery plume, like a snake winding toward the ceiling.

Mrs. Jameson would have a fit that someone was smoking in her house.

That was my first thought.

I said my second one out loud.

"Are you dead?"

"She will. And yes again," he said, and this time he smiled a little. He twisted in place, showing me the bleeding gash in his back. It was a vicious wound.

"No blood on the rug, okay?"

He smiled and smoked. I realized now that I could see a second smaller tendril of smoke winding out of the wound. So his lung had been punctured. Nice.

I sat up, shifting around so I was sitting cross-legged on the bed facing him, the sheets wound around my lower body. He said nothing more. It seemed that I was going to have to start the conversation. "So, the thing is that when I see other dead people, they come to tell me something. Or give me a clue. Something like that."

I was ready for help—you can believe that.

He glanced at his back, then at me again, and took another drag.

Wait a minute. This guy knew about Kohana's powers. I guessed. "Are you the *Wakiya* elder who was killed by the NightBlade?"

He almost smiled; then he nodded slowly.

I was excited. Dead men might tell no tales but their ghosts might be able to help me out. "Can you tell me more about the NightBlade? What about the ShadowEaters? What do they want?"

He exhaled, launching three smoke rings in succession. They floated toward the ceiling, then slipped inside each other, changing order as he watched with a smile. I was amazed. "I suspected that there was a connection between the NightBlade and the ShadowEaters."

"I've seen it. It's true. They called it to them." I had a thought. "Is that why you died? Because you were figuring things out?"

He pondered that. "Possibly. It acted seemingly of its own volition, but now I wonder if the ShadowEaters dispatched it—and me. They feed on shadows, but shadows exist in our realm, not theirs."

"So without Mages to offer them shadows, they're hungry?"

"Impotent," he corrected. "Shadows give them power and energy. To be hungry is to be weak."

"And without Mages to offer them sacrifices, they were starving," I guessed. He nodded. "So, somehow they managed to use the NightBlade to free themselves." He nodded again. "So I *did* see the truth!"

He frowned then. "Kohana plays a dangerous game on behalf of our kind. You must help him. You must save him."

"But I don't know where Kohana is."

He looked at me steadily and I saw the vacant lot in my mind's eye, the snow falling steadily on it.

I frowned. "Why couldn't I see him when I was there?"

"Why couldn't you see the lot when you went to the library?"

Okay. It made sense that if ShadowEaters were Mages who had done a ritual wrong, as the Oracle declared, they would still have some Mage-like abilities. "They can cast glamours in this realm, too, then?"

He nodded. "The more they feed, the more powerful they will become."

"What do they want?"

He smiled. "What they have always wanted."

I remembered what the Bastian Oracle had said. They wanted to become pure spirit but had failed at the ritual. They were trapped between here and there, but still wanted to go *there*. "They came here for more fuel. For shadows."

He smoked calmly, and I thought he was considering this. Eventually, he nodded, then frowned. "You, too, are targeted, *Unktehila*."

I shivered at that.

I realized then that it must have been hard for this elder to come to me, given the broken treaties between our respective kinds. So there must not have been many other options available.

It was up to me to do something.

"What can I do to ruin their plans?"

He smiled and smoked.

I tried again. "Is there a way that I can undermine their glamours and spells, so we can see what they're doing?"

He pursed his lips and hesitated so long that I didn't think he'd answer me. "I can tear the veil of illusion and shred the glamours, *Unktehila*, but only at your command," he said finally. "You are the center of the web."

Well, that had to be a step in the right direction.

In fact, I was thinking that Meagan might be right, that this might be the one thing I could do to trash the ShadowEaters. Tearing the veil would mean that we would have more information to finish them off—instead of arguing about what had really happened.

Worked for me.

"Tear it, then. Tear it, please!"

He watched me for such a long time, just smoking without breaking eye contact, that I feared I'd asked for something terrible. More than I expected. More than he could do. Something was wrong with this choice.

"Zoë?" Mrs. Jameson called. "Who are you talking to? And is that a cigarette I smell?"

Was this a dream or not?

I glanced at the door in uncertainty, then back at the elder.

"Be warned that you must act swiftly, *Unktehila*," he said in an undertone. "You will see all possibilities and realities merged together, but still you must choose with speed."

What did that mean? I was on the verge of asking him for more information when his eyes flashed golden and he leapt straight up with incredible power.

I saw the cigarette drop and glow when it fell on the rug.

I saw the shadow of his Thunderbird shape.

I heard the rumble of thunder.

And I saw his claws shred my view of the room. It was as if Meagan's room had become a glamour. He tore away the wall with the window like it was a dark curtain, and all I could see was that vacant lot.

The vacant lot was right there, right *here*, two feet away from me.

With blood on the snow and the air filled with spell light and the dead kid on the ground. I crawled back on the bed in horror. It was as if the elder had torn the scales from my eyes. Was I here? Was I there? Everything was merged together.

How could I choose swiftly if I didn't know what was real?

Then Mrs. Jameson rapped on the door and pushed it open, crying out when she saw the burning butt on the carpet. The room reverted to normal in a flash, Meagan woke up, the cigarette was crushed and flushed, and much confusion ensued as I confessed to having snuck a smoke.

It wasn't like I could tell Mrs. Jameson the truth.

If dreams and reality were going to keep mingling like this, maybe I *would* end up going crazy.

HOURS LATER, everyone had settled down again but I was wide awake. Had anything changed? I was trying to figure out what I was supposed to do—I knew I had to do it swiftly—when I heard the faint sound of music.

The sound was distant, elusive, forcing me to strain my ears to catch the tune. I was tempted to open the window, but I was leery of that wall since the elder had ripped it. Everything looked normal, but I wasn't taking anything at face value.

It could be real. It could be a dream. It could be both.

I was already starting to see the downside of tearing the veil.

I got out of bed without really intending to, opened the bedroom door, and eased down the stairs to the front door.

I had a powerful urge to go outside, to follow the sound of the music.

No, I *yearned* to follow the music.

Like one of those rats following the piper to his death.

I opened the door, even knowing it was stupid. It was like I couldn't stop myself. The melody *was* haunting and beguiling, although I couldn't have named the tune.

It was in a minor key.

Wait a minute. Mages used minor keys.

It was a lure! I could see spell light dancing down the street toward the town house, swirling in the middle of the road, churning up the porch steps. To my surprise, Mozart and King were right next to me. I hadn't even noticed them leave the bedroom with me. But now they twined around my ankles.

I was glad to see Mozart on his feet, at least until he looked up at me and I saw that his eyes were filled with orange spell light. King was really agitated, circling around the smaller cat protectively like he'd hem him in.

No luck on that front. To my horror, Mozart slipped between my ankles and raced into the night. On the street, he rubbed his back against the golden ribbon of the spell at the bottom of the stairs. I snatched at King, guessing what he'd do, but was two seconds too late. My fingers slid through his fur as he yowled and peeled after Mozart.

No! I leapt down the steps, just as the pair of them ran down the street. They disappeared like shadows into the night.

No, they disappeared into a new barrage of spell light. It was headed right for me, like an orange tsunami.

I fled into the house, slammed the door, and locked it, my heart pounding. The music got louder and I watched in horror as tendrils of spell light rushed under the door.

They reached for my ankles.

No! I ran back up the stairs, the snake of light in hot pursuit. I slammed the door to Meagan's room and leapt back into bed, hoping against hope that this was all a bad dream.

Just a dream.

Just a nightmare.

Nothing really to fear.

No music in my ears.

I was nearly convinced when I felt something slither around my ankle.

Like a snake.

Or the tendril of a plant, one that was growing really fast.

It was cold and wet and moving up my leg.

Not real, not real, not real.

Heart pounding, I looked. I could see a golden spiral of spell light twining around my leg, making its way from my foot to my knee. It was like watching a plant growing, some kind of jungle plant that takes over the world in leaps and bounds.

And it was taking over me.

Or claiming me.

I sat up in terror and jerked my leg back. The spell tendril tightened around me convulsively, nearly eliminating circulation to my toes. Definitely real. I yelped and ripped at it, to no effect. I couldn't get a good grip on its slimy surface. It kept growing, too, capturing more and more of my leg.

I called to the shimmer and tried to change shape but failed completely.

Just like the spell light in the lot, this spell had the ability to short-circuit my shifter powers. The tendril of spell held on fast and kept getting longer. It was past my knee and up to my thigh.

And then it tugged, as if it would haul me outside.

I freaked.

I struggled.

It made no difference. It was just like being in that vacant lot, just like being bound by the spell light and powerless to do anything about it. I thrashed but it made no difference. I screamed but no sound came out.

I was already silenced.

Was this what it was like to become extinct?

I thought I could hear the sound of smacking lips and was terrified that the ShadowEaters would devour my shadow. I panicked at the prospect.

That outer wall disappeared again, just as it had when the *Wakiya* elder shredded it.

A heartbeat later, I was in that vacant lot again, still bound and helpless. I had to believe that the ShadowEaters had sent the spell to get me.

Because I was surrounded by them. There were hungry ShadowEaters on every side, slithering and salivating, their golden eyes gleaming with anticipation.

I felt the first lick, the first nibble, the first nip. It was nauseating. The spell kept tightening around me, trapping me and holding me captive. Struggling only made it worse, but I couldn't help it. I fought with all my might but it made no difference. I heard their dark laughter and smelled their anticipation. If they wanted to mess with my mind, they were doing a great job.

I screamed.

I still made no sound.

And there was a blinding flash, like lightning had struck me.

I WAS BACK in Meagan's bedroom, sitting up in bed with sweat running down my back. I was panting, but I couldn't see any spell light anywhere.

Believe me, I looked.

While I hyperventilated and my heart pounded so fast that I thought it might explode from the exertion. I had been sure that flash had been the result of my shadow being cut away, but I checked and it was intact.

Whoa.

Okay, so maybe that had been a dream. Or a Wyvern vision. Could it have been foresight?

More importantly, where was I now?

I still had to be in some dream realm—Meagan's bedroom was piled with snow, and the exterior wall melted into endless tundra. As in my typical Wyvern dreams—at least the ones I'd had in the past year—I could see a bough of that enormous tree bending over the room, its leaves young and green and rustling in a wind I couldn't feel.

I knew this place.

And it was—comparatively—safe.

Even if the old ladies were missing.

Wolves howled in the distance, and it says something for my state of mind that the sound of a hungry wolf pack was reassuring.

Then I saw that Skuld was crouched on the windowsill, watching me avidly. She was almost swallowed by the shadows, motionless, her eyes shining in the darkness. She looked like an action hero, ready to spring to action and slaughter the unworthy. Her eyes brightened, not unlike the eyes of a raven, and there was something sinister about her smile. I realized that her ponytail was bound with something that looked like sinew. I seriously didn't want to know what kind of sinew it was.

Or whose. She was spinning her scissors around one index finger, like a gunslinger playing with his revolver, as she watched me.

"Bad dream?" she asked, then started to laugh.

Her laughter was no better than that of the ShadowEaters. It was dark and malicious. If this was my ally, I had some kind of lousy company.

Maybe insanity would be a better choice. I could make friends with teddy bears and jelly beans.

"You could have helped," I said, hearing the accusation in my tone.

Skuld sobered and considered me. "How do you think you got back here?"

"*You* helped *me*?" Skuld might have looked like a warrior who got things done, but I wasn't at all sure that we were on the same side. I did not expect that she would do me any favors.

She rolled her eyes. "You didn't think you managed it yourself, did you?" There was nothing I could say to that because, you know, I had thought that.

And she knew it.

Worse, she thought it was funny. "Careful what you wish for," she said.

I blinked. "You mean that was my fault? Because I asked him to tear the veil?"

She nodded slowly and I was horrified. "Tearing the veil opened a portal." She gave me a hard look. "One that maybe should have stayed shut."

Oops.

"I thought it just removed the glamours."

"That, too." She turned her shears so that the moonlight illuminated one sharp edge. "Many weapons cut both ways."

Okay, I should have anticipated that a *Wakiya* person—like Kohana—might not have presented all of the truth. Or that a dead shifter—like my brother Sigmund—might have left out some important details.

"Is this the part where the Wyvern goes crazy?"

Skuld smiled. "Not all minds can bear to see the array of possibilities, all at once. Fewer yet can choose wisely among them."

Another test. Another riddle. Okay, I was on this like peanut butter on toast.

"What kind of portal?" I asked Skuld.

"A portal in dreams. They can find you in your dreams now, Wyvern, because you created the portal." She arched a brow. "And they can attack you there."

"I thought they already could influence my dreams."

She smiled. "Now they can kill you."

Shit. That was not great news.

"Good thing you have friends in high places." Skuld spun those scissors into her grip. She made an elaborate snip with them, then winked at me.

So that was how she'd done it.

I asked the obvious question. "That was the flash of light? You can cut spells with those things?"

She smiled. "You *are* paying attention, after all."

"I didn't know spells could be cut."

Skuld arched a brow. "There are a lot of things you don't know."

True. And if Kohana could slice binding spells with the NightBlade, it made sense that there were other weapons that could slash those nasty spells to bits.

Seemed like I needed a tool like this.

I knew Skuld wouldn't just give the scissors to me. I'd have to earn any gift she gave me. Or fight for it.

She turned the shears again, letting the moonlight gleam along the edge, just as she had done before, then gave me a hard look.

A clue.

I remembered what she'd said earlier, the other time she'd made that gesture.

"If it cuts both ways, there has to be something good about tearing the veil," I guessed. "Maybe something more than eliminating the glamours?"

She smiled at me and nodded approval. "They are still weak, but if the portal is open, they can be destroyed. Forever."

"The elder told me to hurry."

"They gain power with every shadow they devour." Skuld widened her eyes and said something I'd never have expected her to say. "Tick-tock."

On impulse, I put out my hand, palm up. A silent request for the surrender of the shears.

I thought she'd say no.

Or laugh.

Instead, Skuld's smile broadened, as if I didn't know what I was asking for or the price it would ultimately demand. She was that kind of a person, I could already see that, one who liked to test you by giving you what you thought you wanted. (Maybe all these dream people were like that.) I might have pulled back my hand then, but she dropped the scissors into my palm before I could.

I knew I couldn't just give them back.

For better or for worse, they were mine, along with the responsibility for eliminating the ShadowEaters. (Okay, maybe that had been on my plate all along.)

They were huge shears and heavy. The blades were wickedly sharp, gleaming silver. The handle looked ornate and was covered with symbols.

By the time I studied them, then looked back at Skuld to thank her, she was gone.

There was no more snow.

No tree.

Just Meagan's room.

No dead people.

But, yes, wolves howling at the moon.

That they had to be real was just icing on the cake.

THE MOON WAS FULL, hanging round and silver in the night sky. It was almost morning but not quite, the sky getting a bit lighter at the horizon. My dream hadn't been all dream: Mozart and King were still gone from Meagan's bed. And I still had Skuld's scissors in my hand. The cats could have been downstairs, but the scissors were too heavy to be a figment of my imagination.

In fact, it occurred to me that these babies could get me into serious trouble. The blades glinted, ferociously sharp steel polished to perfection, and when I touched them with a fingertip, I drew my own blood.

"Save me a liver," Skuld whispered in my thoughts.

It was like old-speak, the ancient language of the *Pyr*, so I answered her in old-speak. *"I thought you preferred souls."*

She laughed that dark cackle of a laugh. *"There won't be any of those where you're going."*

It was not the most reassuring thing she could have said. After all, she was the sister who held the keys to the future. I got up and peered into the park across the street from the Jamesons' town house.

Was there a glitter of golden eyes in the shadows? Maybe the Shadow-Eaters were the ones howling at the moon.

That was when I remembered that Nick was sitting vigil on the roof. He was a shifter and he had a shadow.

I was out of bed in a flash.

THERE WAS no easy access to the roof from inside the town house. There might have been one from the attic, but the trapdoor to the attic was in the ceiling of the linen closet, and Meagan had told me once that her dad had to take out all the stuff and the shelves in order to open the trapdoor. Her parents didn't go in the attic, ever.

I wasn't ready to go out the front door, not after I'd seen the spell light there, even though I was worried about King and Mozart. I was more worried about Nick. I called to him in old-speak but he didn't answer, which did nothing to make me feel better.

I had to go out there. I took Skuld's shears with me and went into the bathroom, moving as quietly as I could.

I'd have to use my ability to spontaneously manifest elsewhere. I could have used a chocolate bar for the energy surge but was afraid to make noise by going down into the kitchen. Mrs. Jameson always got up really early. Plus she'd already been up to chastise me over the cigarette. For all I knew, she was still awake.

I shut the bathroom door, turned out the light, and took a deep breath. I didn't know what I'd find on the roof, but I doubted it would be anything good. I tried to prepare myself for anything, to come out fighting if necessary.

Then I closed my eyes and wished myself on the roof.

It worked, worked so quickly that I staggered dizzily on the rooftop. The town house had a mansard roof, so the middle of it was flat. I was hoping to manifest right in the middle, to better ensure that no one would suddenly see me there. I was hoping to come out of the manifestation in dragon form, but tradition—or maybe exhaustion—prevailed.

I was a white salamander, as was usually the result when I manifested elsewhere. Of course, I couldn't hold on to the shears, which were bigger than me, so they dropped to the roof and skidded across the dusting of snow there, coming to a halt with a clatter against the metal lip.

I hunkered low instinctively, half expecting Meagan's parents to come out and check what the noise was.

The bonus of the newt form is that I can skulk without anyone much noticing, especially when my little white salamander body falls in snow. The snow was deeper than I was tall, but I followed the trail through the snow left by the shears and got my newty fingers on them again.

Then I looked around.

The snow was perfectly untouched in every direction.

Nick wasn't there.

In fact, Nick had never been there. I couldn't detect his scent at all. There was no tingle of dragonsmoke, except the faint vestige that still lingered from November's adventures. I heard nothing from the house or the neighboring houses.

I summoned the shift and changed to my human form, grabbing Skuld's shears.

I was alone.

Except for the faint echo of a spell. It was the same tune as my dream, the one that beckoned the listener to follow it. I remembered Nick being tempted by the Mage spell on Halloween and had a very bad feeling. I strained my eyes and saw the tendril of spell light wafting over the little park opposite.

Then it snapped like a whip, cracking over the park. The pack of wolves that I'd heard earlier were gathered in the park. The spell dove among them like a spear. I heard them bark.

I saw the silhouettes of the ShadowEaters riding that spell right down into the pack. It looked like a comet, an orange projectile followed by a cluster of ShadowEaters, hanging on tight.

It was true. By asking the elder to tear the veil, I'd made it possible for them to enter my dreams, attack me there, then follow me into the here and now when I awakened. They could harm shifters on earth without requiring an invocation from the Mages. Their glamours were destroyed, so I could see them—but they could see me, too. And chances were pretty good that there would be shifters in my company, no matter where I was.

Great job, Zoë.

While I stood there, grappling with my own responsibility, the spell whipped around the leg of a wolf. The wolf pivoted, snarling as the spell wound more tightly.

Just as it had in my dream.

The ShadowEaters fell on the pack of wolves, snatching and biting at their shadows.

Which told me exactly what kind of wolves they were, even before one of them turned to look at me with eyes of pale silver blue.

This was a colossal fuck-up on my part and I had to try to make it right.

I shifted to dragon form with a roar, leapt off the roof, and dove into the fray with Skuld's shears held high.

Wyvern time.

THAT ONE WOLF was bound by the spell, the light moving at lightning speed. I realized that the wolves could see the ShadowEaters but not the spell light. They leapt at the shapes of the ShadowEaters, snapping and snarling, ready to rip off a shadowed limb. Two of them were down already, ShadowEaters surrounding them and demolishing their shadows.

Meanwhile, the snared one struggled against a tether he couldn't see.

I bellowed and breathed fire, slashing at ShadowEaters with my talons and clearing space with my tail. I couldn't manage Skuld's scissors in my dragon form, though, and it was all I could do to hang on to them. Had Skuld been honest with me about them? I doubted it. What was the repercussion of using them? I couldn't guess, not without giving it a try.

As I hesitated, the spell wound around the wolf, choking the life from him. I figured he must be a leader if they wanted him so badly. The ShadowEaters clustered closer, making their nauseating noises, and I had no choice but to shift back to human form.

To get to the wolf I had to push through the ShadowEaters, brushing against their slippery, slimy forms, hearing their smacking lips. I felt one or two take a nip at me and my terror rose. It was way too easy to remember my dream. I lunged through them and slashed at the spell that held the wolf captive, as if cutting a leash.

It severed instantly, but the loose end flipped around like a snake.

Looking for another victim.

It quickly targeted me as the ShadowEaters pushed closer, chanting encouragement to their spell. I cut at it again and again, hacking it into bits in a frenzy, even as the other wolves snapped at the silhouettes of the ShadowEaters. The wolves leapt and bit, ferocious in their defense of their fellow. When the cut spell fell to the ground, like a dead thing, I turned Skuld's shears on the ShadowEaters.

The first one fell back with a howl. I saw the frisson of fear run through them, and wondered anew at the power of the shears. For the moment I just kept on cutting and slashing. The ShadowEaters abruptly leapt into the sky and scattered once more, leaving me alone in the park, surrounded by a circle of wolves.

And two badly wounded wolves. They shifted between their forms as human guys and as silvery wolves. That meant they were badly hurt. Several other wolves clustered around them; one shifted to become a man with a leather pouch on his belt. He acted like a doctor, and I assumed he was the healer of their kind.

The other wolves watched, their concern tangible.

It started to snow again.

Then he nodded and that one gesture sent a ripple of relief through the pack. The two injured shifters became wolves again and I saw one open his eyes. I was shaking with the aftermath of the fight and my relief.

The wolves turned as one to watch me, silent and wary.

I straightened, the shears hanging at my side. I realized a bit late that there were thirty wolves surrounding me.

Thirty predators.

The wolves watched me, motionless. I sensed that I was being judged, that an assessment was being made in a trial I couldn't hear, and I couldn't tell from the cold steadiness of their stares how the decision would fall.

It didn't look good, I have to say.

And I didn't blame them.

Then the one who had been bound by the spell approached me. He moved as if he were older and I saw that his snout was silvery. He shook thoroughly, as if ridding his coat of a bad smell, then bent and sniffed the dead spell. He could either see it or smell it now that it was broken. To me, it looked like a line of ash lying in the snow.

Until he peed on it, his disdain clear.

He watched me all the while, his eyes a clear blue. I had the sense that something had changed within the pack. Their eyes seemed to glitter more avidly and their attention seemed to have sharpened. I couldn't tell what they had decided, though.

I knew it was best to hold my ground.

The leader wolf came directly to me, his gaze locked on mine. He didn't blink. He stretched out and sniffed the shears, then folded his ears back. He gave me one more sizzling look, then lay down in front of me and put his snout between his paws. He kept his ears folded back and closed his eyes.

I knew enough about dogs to recognize that I was being acknowledged as his superior.

Alpha girl.

I smiled and bent down beside him, reaching to touch the paw that had been spellbound with my free hand. The fur was singed from the spell. His eyes opened and he stared at me, unblinking. I knew he would understand me. "I'm sorry. I will do my best to defend the alliance and ensure the survival of all of us."

There was a brilliant flash of light, and then an older man was crouched before me. His eyes were the same steady blue and his hand was in mine. We stood as one, then shook hands.

"As will we," he said, his voice a low grumble.

"I'm sorry."

"Much is unpredictable when the stars stand still. This is our teaching. What matters is your intent."

I swallowed, relieved that I had been forgiven.

I eyed the town house, so close behind us, and had to ask. "Why were you gathered here at all?"

His eyes narrowed. "We felt a threat. We came to investigate and possibly defend the dragon, to keep our pledge. When we were attacked, there were those who feared we had been betrayed." He smiled. "I thank you, Wyvern. We had doubt, but you have proven yourself." He gave my hand one last pump, his grip resolute and strong, and the wolves tipped their heads back to howl in unison.

The sound made the hair stand up on the back of my neck.

He gave a whistle and the wolves fell silent once more. I bowed my head at the telltale shimmer of blue, averting my gaze as he shifted shape. The healer and the leader were the only ones in human form, and they carried the two injured shifters out of the park. I glimpsed the shadows of the other wolves slipping into the last of the darkness, fading from the park as surely as if they had never been there, and felt honored by their trust.

That was when I realized there was one wolf left, standing by my side.

The one with silvery blue eyes.

He shimmered blue and Derek was standing beside me.

"Something else is wrong," he said, his gaze dancing over my features. I knew he could smell my emotions, but his powers of observation still surprised me. "Tell me."

"Nick was going to sit vigil on the roof, but he's gone."

"Where?"

I shrugged. "I can't sense him. I—"

Derek's eyes flashed and he muttered a curse about ShadowEaters. He tipped his head back to sample the wind and his nostrils flared slightly. I saw his eyes narrow, and appreciated that his sense of smell was even keener than mine.

He flicked a look at me, one that I couldn't read. "Remember that you were afraid for him."

I was confused by his tone. "What do you mean? The ShadowEaters must have taken him first...."

Derek shook his head. "He's with Isabelle."

I couldn't believe it, but Derek was so confident.

Had Nick broken his promise? I had to know for sure. I shifted shape to my dragon form and took flight, reaching down to snatch Derek out of the park. I saw the flash of his smile as I soared into the sky, Skuld's shears hanging from my other claw.

"Awesome!" Derek breathed.

But I wasn't feeling celebratory or even enjoying the marvel of being able to fly. If Nick was alive and well, if Nick had decided not to bother guarding Meagan and me because he didn't believe me, I might very well make him wish he were dead. I flew straight to Isabelle's dorm, probably setting a speed record on the way.

You know that I wanted with all my heart for Derek to be wrong.

You can probably guess that he wasn't.

7

When I landed and set Derek down outside the dorm filled with sleeping students, his face was alight. I'd never seen him look so excited.

"Wow, Zoë!" he said. "That was incredible!"

Derek is not an exclamatory kind of guy. But he was exultant. He enthused away for a couple of minutes about the wind and the feeling of freedom, and said more in three minutes than probably the whole sum of everything he had ever said to me.

And I am such a toad that all I could do was look at him and think how this was almost, but not quite exactly, what I wanted most in the world.

Yup. I still owed Jared that ride and I still wanted to see his face after I flew him somewhere. I wanted it to be Jared who was standing in front of me, looking expectant and in dire need of a kiss, and that made me feel like the lowest worm alive.

So, I turned to the door. "Let's go find them," I said, and opened it.

I heard Derek exhale slowly. I smelled his disappointment. I felt his sense of having been cheated.

And the worst part of it was that I knew he was totally justified.

I trudged through the hallways of the dorm, knowing the way to Isabelle's room, disliking that Nick's scent got stronger with every step.

That made me mad. He was here all right. They'd probably come into the building by the same door we'd used. And why? What was his excuse? Why hadn't he kept his promise? It was outrageous that I'd been worried about him but he'd just been goofing off.

Never mind that goofing off had saved his butt.

Was his promise to protect Meagan and me worth as little as that?

I was glad that Nick was safe from the ShadowEaters, but I was still pretty pissed by the time I rapped on Isabelle's door.

I didn't do it very quietly, either.

I heard voices whispering inside, and, sure enough, one of them was Nick's.

The other—no surprise—was Isabelle.

Derek and I exchanged a look. Derek had a glint of mischief in his eyes, and that was when I understood what Nick had probably been doing here.

Oh. Too late. I wished I'd just messaged him or chewed him out in old-speak.

There was the sound of rustling and whispered warnings—sometimes dragon hearing provides way too much information—the tread of feet, then the silence of someone looking through the peephole.

"Zoë!" Isabelle said, and opened the door just a crack. "What are you doing here?"

"That's what we came to ask Nick," Derek said.

Isabelle jumped a bit—she hadn't realized Derek was there—then glanced over her shoulder. She was gorgeous, her hair tumbling loose over her shoulders and her silk kimono held shut with one hand. Her feet were bare. She looked, if you must know, even more like a lingerie model than usual, given that she was wearing—right—lingerie.

But she blushed.

So did Nick—as he tried to scramble to his feet with some of his dignity intact, stammering as he struggled to think of an excuse.

He failed completely. The back of his neck was brick red.

He wasn't naked, at least. Maybe they were doing that talk-all-night thing again. Under any other circumstance I would have been glad that he and Isabelle were making it work. Not now, though.

Nick took one look at my face and tried to bluster his way out of the situation. "Z, do you know what time it is? What are you thinking, coming around here at this hour of the morning? It's not even five! People are trying to sleep."

"Sleep," Derek echoed, and both Nick and Isabelle turned more red.

"Only the ones who aren't fighting ShadowEaters," I said.

Nick rolled his eyes. "We went through that last night, Z. You just had a vision...."

"Then I had it, too, and so did my pack leader and two others in my pack when the ShadowEaters tried to consume their shadows," Derek interjected.

"What?" Nick said in alarm.

"When?" Isabelle asked, looking just as shocked.

"Not even half an hour ago." Derek shoved his hands in his pockets, looking big and formidable and pissed off. "We're here because Zoë was afraid that they might have gotten you. Kind of ironic that she wanted to save you. Don't you think?"

Nick looked between us with astonishment. "But I thought..."

"And you thought wrong." Derek eased past Isabelle and marched into her room, poking Nick hard in the chest. "You made a *mistake*. You broke your word and Zoë could have been hurt over it. Where would we be if she'd gotten killed?"

"Hey, now. Wait a minute. I didn't mean..."

"It doesn't matter what you thought you meant." Derek said, his tone hard. "It matters what you said you would do and what you *did* do."

"But there was no proof that Zoë's vision had come true," Isabelle interjected.

"Proof?" Derek repeated. He was furious enough to be shaken free from his usual near silence. I was in awe. "You don't need *proof*. You pledge to follow a leader and you do what that leader says. You believe what that leader tells you to believe. The effectiveness of the team relies on you doing what you're told to do." He scoffed. "You don't go changing plans for yourself and screwing it all up because you don't have all the information."

"But..." Nick tried to protest.

"But nothing! You left Zoë undefended when you had promised to stand guard." Derek looked Nick up and down, his disdain clear. "With friends like you, she doesn't need enemies."

"That's harsh," Nick retorted, his eyes flashing. "We agreed last night that she was wrong about the ShadowEaters, because nobody else had seen them."

"Nobody else but me and Kohana." Derek pulled out his messenger and waved it in front of Nick. "Funny, I don't see a message from you asking for my input." He shoved it back in his pocket and approached Nick. Nick took a step back. "You've got an interesting way of playing on a team. I'll have to make sure you're not the one who gets the job of watching my back."

Nick looked completely flummoxed by this.

Isabelle stepped between them. "But the Bastian Oracle said the ShadowEaters couldn't come into this realm."

Derek glared at her. "I guess she lied. Or maybe she's wrong. Are you going to believe a story or what Zoë and I just saw?"

Nick and Isabelle looked at each other, so obviously surprised that I felt bad for them. Never mind the part I'd played in the proceedings. None of this would have happened without my choice.

Guilt pang there. I opened my mouth to talk to Nick but Derek pivoted and walked back toward me. He grabbed my hand as he headed for the stairs. "Don't forgive him yet," he growled, and I shouldn't have been surprised that he'd known what I was going to say.

I was astounded, astonished, and a bit disoriented that Derek had defended me so thoroughly. I'm a dragon girl. I can fight my own battles.

Although it was nice to have someone take my side.

And be so articulate about it.

Especially when I wasn't innocent, either.

"Zoë!" Isabelle called after me. "Don't be so hard on Nick. You know why he's really here."

I did know. I was glad that they were together and that Isabelle's dream was coming true, even if Nick hadn't done what he'd said he would do. The fact that Derek was treating us like a team and acting like he was in charge also threw my game.

It was nice, but...

Derek flashed me a grin as we stepped outside, and the sight of his pleasure mixed me up even more. He held my hand tightly, his thumb doing that slow caress, and my heart started to thump.

I was amazed by the way Derek had defended me. He'd been so absolutely, totally in my corner. My own indecision seemed like loser thinking in comparison. In fact, his defense made me aware of how unfair I'd been to him. He was holding my hand so tightly—even though I'd just rolled out of bed to fight ShadowEaters and probably looked like it. He was loyal and strong and he had my back, better even than the guys I called my best friends.

Derek deserved better than what I'd given him.

A lot better.

By the time we stepped outside, I knew how I could start to fix that imbalance.

Derek walked me back to the Jamesons' town house. It was a bit after five in the morning and just getting light. There were delivery trucks and a few buses out on the roads, and not much else going on. I felt as if we were alone in the world.

And it was kind of nice.

Let's just understand here that I am not a morning person. Having spent the whole night racing around—fighting spells, kicking butt, and taking names—meant that I was exhausted right to my marrow. I could have curled up and slept through the weekend.

But for the moment, I was running on adrenaline.

And something else. Something that made me tingle when Derek took my hand in his.

I did see the occasional flicker of gray in the shadows and imagined that the wolf shifters were keeping close tabs on their wild card. I liked the way they all protected each other, and I liked that I had won them to my side, especially as it was a result of my doing what came naturally. I couldn't have stood by and watched those wolves lose their shadows, not for any price.

And that made me think about dragons. Specifically one dragon: my dad. Should I tell him about the ShadowEaters? I knew he'd have lots to say about my making a bad choice, but maybe he'd have some advice on making it come right.

On the other hand, all the rules had changed.

"What?" Derek asked.

"Your pack is following us, standing guard." I glanced at him and he nodded, unsurprised. "I'm wondering whether we should get some dragon backup, whether I should tell my dad what's going on."

Derek considered this. "What would he do?"

I smiled. "Charge in and breathe fire. Take command."

"Against an opponent he has never faced. You've already thwarted the ShadowEaters twice."

Well, there was that.

Derek gave me a look. "We are committed to following you, not your dad. If telling your dad would compromise your leadership of the alliance, maybe the news should wait."

I instinctively agreed with him, but decided I'd confer with Nick, Liam, and Garrett just to be sure. I squeezed his hand a bit, liking that we'd been able to talk about a question of strategy, and he squeezed my hand back.

It was snowing again, snowing more vigorously than it had before. The city looked kind of magical with all that white snow swirling across it. It was cold but not bitterly so. The snowflakes landed on my cheeks and the wind tossed my hair.

We walked along together in silence, just a hand's width of space between us. I could feel the heat of him beside me, which made my toes curl in my boots. I could smell his skin, the clean soap scent of him, and when I glanced up, his silvery blue gaze was fixed on me. He can be so still, as if he doesn't need to blink or to breathe, as if he doesn't miss one single thing.

My heart began to beat more quickly. I heard his pulse, courtesy of my dragon powers, and my heart did that dizzy-crazy thing of matching its pace to his. It's weird when that happens. It seems as if my pulse is redoubled, resonating throughout my body, overwhelming me with awareness of him.

Derek didn't say anything. He just studied me in that steady, unblinking way of his. It was as if he didn't want to affect the moment, maybe by saying the wrong thing.

In reality, I was the one who had said a lot of wrong things.

"Thanks for taking my side," I said, giving his hand a little squeeze.

"That's what I signed up for," he said, but didn't squeeze my fingers back. He looked ahead of us then, frowning a bit.

I had more work to do.

"I think it was my fault," I admitted. "I had this dream last night and was offered the chance to have the veil torn."

Derek turned to look at me, a question in his eyes.

"So everyone could see the truth of what the ShadowEaters are doing." I grimaced. "But that also seems to have given them more powers."

"Like?"

"Invading my dreams. Casting spells that snare us. Maybe even being able to target shifters through me."

"Then maybe it needed to happen," he said, stoic in his defense. "Maybe we needed to flush them out so we could defeat them."

"I'm sorry your leader almost got hurt."

"You saved him. It's square."

"Look, I wouldn't blame you if you were mad at me," I said. "But I'm kind of caught between what I want to do and what I'm supposed to do. I have to choose all the time, right in the heat of the moment, and I'm not even sure that I'm always making the right choice. All I can do is try my best."

He flicked me a look, his eyes gleaming. "You're not the only one, you know. It comes with the territory."

"Really?" Derek had to choose duty over desire? That surprised me.

But he nodded, smiling crookedly. "Something else we have in common."

"I'm glad."

His gaze dropped to the necklace he'd given me, the silver hand of Fatima on a chain, the one I was still wearing. His eyes seemed to shimmer the way heat shimmers above the pavement on a hot summer day.

I know I caught my breath at the sight.

He stopped on the sidewalk, then turned to face me.

"I know what you're supposed to do," he said, his voice all low and growly. I shivered at the sound of it, feeling my body respond to every word. He studied me, probably seeing every secret I ever had and—given his ability to see two minutes into the future—a good many of the ones I might have soon. "But I'm never sure what it is that you *want* to do."

And I saw how much I had hurt him. I knew I hadn't been as kind as I could have been, and I knew he didn't deserve my indecision, but I wanted to be straight with him. And that meant not pretending to feel something I didn't feel, even if it was inconvenient.

"What I want is to be honest with you," I said because it was true.

He dropped his gaze, shielding his thoughts from me. He touched the back of my hand with his other fingertip, the heat of his caress awakening an answering heat within me. "You never ask what I want," he murmured, then flicked me a hot look.

"Because I think I know," I said. He lifted one dark brow, inviting me to explain. "You want to go out together, to go to the dance, and— and, stuff."

The corner of his mouth lifted in a little smile. He flattened his hand over mine, his palm closing over the back of my hand. His hand was a lot bigger, big enough to engulf mine, warm and solid and strong. "What kind of *stuff*, Zoë?"

I swallowed. My thoughts were churning, descending into incoherence thanks to the press of his hand on mine. "Make an alliance?" I guessed.

"Secure an alliance," he corrected. He looked me right in the eye. "How are alliances secured, Zoë?"

I might have thought straight then, but he spread his fingers, spearing them between mine and locking his hand over mine. His grip was firm but not tight. "With treaties?" I suggested, hearing that my voice was higher than usual.

Derek shook his head. "That's for countries, not ancient species like us," he murmured, and my mouth went dry. His gaze dropped to my lips and his voice dropped even lower. "Maybe we should call it a union instead."

A hot flush rolled through my body at his intensity.

He was talking about sex.

"Eventually," he said quietly. "For now, we could go steady."

I thought I could probably manage that.

He looked down at our interlocked hands for a long moment. "Wolves are patient, Zoë, and we are loyal. I can wait. I just need to know whether it's even a possibility."

He wanted a commitment. Right here and right now.

I glanced across the deserted street, thinking as furiously as I could.

How much was I prepared to do to ensure the alliance between shifters, to ensure that all four remaining kinds had a future?

How long would Derek be patient?

And how could I know, without any real ability to see the future, whether there really was no possibility of that union occurring? I didn't know what I was going to want on Monday; how could I know what I wanted for the rest of my life? Especially since I was probably going to live for centuries? How could I know when I'd have a firestorm—the mark of a destined union for the *Pyr*—or with whom?

Maybe unions and alliances should be made where they could be made.

Maybe securing the future for four different species was more important than my own personal yearnings, given that my particular desire was unlikely to ever come true.

Maybe I'd been right that it would be smarter to like guys who liked me, rather than yearning after the elusive ones who never would like me.

"All right, I get it," Derek said, pulling his hand away. I reached out and stopped him, putting my hand on his arm.

He looked at me, all stillness and intensity.

"No. No, you don't." I swallowed and took a breath, knowing that in this moment, what I had to do and what I wanted to do were exactly the same. "I want to see the future. I want to know how everything is going to work out. I want to make the right choice every time."

"Nobody does that, Zoë."

"Wyverns are supposed to."

"Maybe that's just the myth. What you have is the reality."

He was right. All I could do was make the most reasonable choice in the moment and hope for the best. I looked into the shades of silver and blue and gray in his eyes and doubted I would ever know anyone more steadfast and true.

My heart clenched.

I remembered my resolution.

And I knew it was absolutely right.

"This is what I want," I said, and reached up to kiss Derek on the mouth.

I tasted his surprise and felt him jump a bit. His heart skipped as it never had before and mine matched that crazy pace. Although I made a clumsy start, the kiss rapidly improved from there. We melted against each other, and he angled his head so our mouths fit together better. I felt the weight and heat of his hand on my shoulder, the touch of snowflakes melting on my face, the press of his body.

And then his tongue met mine. I felt as if I'd touched an electrical wire and pulled back, my breath coming in gasps. I felt flushed and shivery at the same time.

That was only half what I felt when Derek smiled at me. "Okay," he said, and his voice was uneven, too. He visibly took a breath. "Okay."

I swallowed. "Okay," I said, and his eyes lit.

He smiled at me, a sweet smile that made my heart ache. "Do I get another ride?"

"Not just yet. I need some sleep." I was exhausted—not surprising given that I'd been dreaming and adventuring most of the night. I yawned, unable to help myself.

Derek grinned and flung his arm across my shoulders, turning to walk me back to the Jamesons'. It felt good to have the weight of his arm around me, the heat of him nudging against my side. I felt all squishy inside, warm from his kiss and stirred up, too.

And it was good.

IT SAYS something for my energy level that I did sleep. Hard. Despite everything I had to do and think about.

It seemed that I'd only just snuck back into Meagan's room and put my head down on the pillow when the alarm clock started ringing. I opened my eyes to find the sky was lighter and Mrs. Jameson was making coffee in the kitchen. Meagan went to the bathroom first, and I dozed off again.

The ring of Meagan's messenger woke me up, because she didn't answer it as quickly as usual. She came running from the bathroom and scooped it off the nightstand. "It's from Jessica," she said, then sat down on the edge of my bed to read the message. She made a face. "Mozart and King were at her door this morning. Mozart is even worse, so she's waiting for the Oracle to come, but then she wants to talk to you."

I was wide awake then. "I hope they'll be okay."

Meagan made a face. "Maybe two gems are better than one."

More fallout from my mistake. I had a feeling the day would only get worse.

By the time I was ready, Meagan was still making up her mind over what to wear—she was hoping that Garrett might turn up today, even though it was only Thursday—so I ended up leaving the bedroom first. It was knee-deep in discarded possibilities.

I could hear the television in the kitchen when I came down the stairs and could sense that Meagan's parents were riveted by the news. Something big was going on for them to be so attentive. There was a potent silence coming from the kitchen, as if neither of them dared to breathe.

"Any persons with information are requested to contact the police...."

I rounded the corner and Mrs. Jameson saw me right away. Her eyes were wide and she was pale. She gestured to Mr. Jameson and he killed the video feed before I could hear more.

"Good morning, Zoë," Mrs. Jameson said brightly—a little too brightly, if you must know. Her smile was definitely forced. "Did you sleep well after our little incident?"

"Yes, fine, thanks," I lied.

She fixed me with a stern look. "And we will not have a repeat of that incident. Right?"

"No. Not a chance. I just had the one and wanted to try it." I hung my head in shame. "I'm sorry."

"Everybody tries it once," Mr. Jameson said. "At least it wasn't dope." His wife shot him a glance that might have turned another man to stone. Mr. Jameson got interested in his breakfast.

The air practically crackled in the kitchen, and it wasn't about the cigarette.

"Something going on in the world?" I asked, glancing toward the television. The Jamesons exchanged a quick glance—which I didn't miss—then Mr. Jameson made a fuss about leaving the table.

"Nothing important," Mrs. Jameson said. "Yogurt this morning?"

You know, I've always thought I was the lousiest liar on the planet, but clearly I was going to have to surrender my number-one status to Meagan's mom. She was a completely crap liar. I'd have to have been kicked in the head by a team of mules not to realize that something *was* going on and that she didn't want me to know about it.

Which just meant that I would find out ASAP.

I agreed, she headed to the fridge, and I pulled out my messenger. I logged in and looked for headline news, and there it was.

LOCAL TEEN MURDERED.

And the picture was of that kid, the one I'd seen with Trevor and Adrian, the one who the ShadowEaters had attacked. Beneath his picture, it said his name was Steve Ford.

Here was the proof that I hadn't been making up that story yesterday, but it wasn't proof that I wanted to see. Even if this Steve Ford had been an apprentice Mage, I thought it was awful that he was dead.

Had his body been found because I'd asked to have the veil torn?

I read the article quickly, and it seemed as if he'd been found just as I'd seen him in my vision.

Pool of blood—check.

Slit throat—check.

Vacant lot—check.

Missing liver—check.

The article didn't mention anything about his shadow being gone. But would it?

I felt a curious mix of responsibility and relief—because how awful would it be to be dead and have no one realize you were gone? I could easily imagine that Steve had had a horrible death. I remembered the feeling of the ShadowEaters nibbling at my own shadow and shuddered. What an awful way to die.

Mrs. Jameson turned around and nearly dropped the yogurt tub in her shock. "Zoë! No messengers before school! You have a test today."

But it was too late and we both knew it.

I shut off my messenger and put it away. "I don't know him," I lied, then added a bit of truth. "He didn't go to our school."

Mrs. Jameson sat down opposite me. "No. He went to St. Joe's."

The Catholic school around the corner. I met her gaze and saw her fear.

"You have to be careful," she said, speaking hurriedly. "You and Meagan have to stick together and ride home together. Or maybe I'll pick you up instead of you driving yourself." She grabbed her own messenger and checked her schedule, her fingers shaking.

I reached out and took her hand, and she looked up at me.

I knew what I had to do. I summoned the flames of beguiling in my eyes and looked straight at Mrs. Jameson, willing her to believe me. She wanted to believe that Meagan and I were safe, so it should be easy to persuade her. "I'm sure it was a fluke," I said, dropping my voice to that low hypnotic tone.

"The police are afraid there's a killer," she said, licking her lips.

"He was probably just coming home late," I said, willing her to agree. "Breaking the rules."

"Breaking the rules," she agreed warily, then nodded. I could feel that I was losing her.

But then I was, after all, apparently a girl who knew a lot about breaking the rules. Maybe that hadn't been the most reassuring angle.

I went for simplicity on the next try. "Meagan and I are fine."

"Meagan and you are fine."

"We'll look out for each other and come home safely."

She smiled at me in relief. "You'll look out for each other and come home safely."

"We always look out for each other."

"You always look out for each other," she said, totally convinced of that.

"You don't need to pick us up. We're perfectly safe."

"Perfectly safe."

Our gazes held for a long moment and I sent her as many reassuring vibes as I could.

The thing was, I wouldn't be able to fix this, to figure out what to do and banish the ShadowEaters, if I got grounded. I needed Mrs. Jameson to be calm and confident.

"Everything will be fine," I told her, trying to believe it myself.

"Everything will be fine," she agreed; then Meagan came into the kitchen.

"I seriously need contacts," she complained, making yet another play to ditch her glasses. "The arm of my glasses is broken again...."

"I'll fix it," Mrs. Jameson said, leaping up and breaking the connection between us. She fussed over Meagan's glasses, Meagan impatient with the whole exercise. Her mother remained adamant that there would be no contacts in Meagan's immediate future.

That was when my mom called. Fortunately, it wasn't my dad, because he would have heard all the unspoken nuances in my news update, and I still had to confer with the guys about involving the older *Pyr*. Even my mom clearly had her suspicions—I could tell by her tone—and I thought she'd probably call Mrs. Jameson back later.

So she'd heard about Steve Ford and about me cutting class.

I felt bad about not sharing the news with my dad, but I knew that Derek was right. I knew this was our test to prove ourselves. We were the ones who had fought these enemies before. We had the data and I had the responsibility. We had to get rid of those ShadowEaters ourselves and we had to do it ASAP.

When I sat down to finish my breakfast, there was a news update on my messenger. Another kid had been found dead, throat slit, similar to Steve Ford. (He still had his liver, so Skuld must have missed out.) I didn't know him, either, but he'd gone to Central and played in the band.

Band. Was he another apprentice Mage?

One thing was for certain: the ShadowEaters were wielding the NightBlade in our realm—in a very icky and effective way.

Five Things I Know about the NightBlade:

1. It's an ancient ceremonial knife, supposedly made from a meteorite, used by Mages to cut the shadows away from the spellbound bodies of shifters.
2. Kohana seized the NightBlade intending to destroy it, but couldn't even scratch it.
3. The NightBlade appears to have a mind of its own, or a power of its own, at least under certain circumstances. Kohana believed the NightBlade turned the Thunderbird elders against each other, poisoning their thoughts with its own desires. I'd seen it leap out of Kohana's grip to cut the ShadowEaters free.
4. The NightBlade can cut spells like butter.
5. King had known immediately that Kohana wouldn't be able to destroy the NightBlade before he even tried.

I tapped the lip of my messenger, considering the list.

I didn't know where the NightBlade actually was at this point in time. I had to assume that the ShadowEaters had it, wherever they were.

Kohana might know more, but I didn't know where Kohana had gone. In my experience, I never could find him; he found me when it suited him. He also told me very little unless it suited him.

Where was Trevor and what did he know? Could I read his memory again? I'd done that in the fall. He was still functioning, so his memory hadn't fused with the Mage hive memory before its destruction. Still, it seemed like a long shot that I could poke around in his thoughts twice. He'd be on guard against me after the day before.

I considered number five again. Was the Bastians' knowledge of the NightBlade part of the reason Mozart had been attacked?

Talking to Jessica became much more important.

Updating Meagan would help, too. I'd tell her everything as we drove to school. You never knew—she might figure it all out before I could.

Checklist for a Typical Day in the Life of a Teenage Wyvern

1. Breakfast well. You never know what the day will bring or when you'll get to eat next.
2. Pinch an extra chocolate-covered granola bar from the kitchen, just in case you have to spontaneously manifest elsewhere and need a sugar hit to recover. Put it in your pocket, in case you don't have your backpack in the crisis du jour.
3. Ensure that Skuld's weapon is well wrapped and disguised. Under no circumstances reveal possession of said shears. Expulsion attracts parental attention and disciplinary measures, both of which interfere with the successful completion of all Wyvern missions.
4. Check in regularly with Muriel and smile frequently in these encounters.
5. Find out from Jessica whatever the Bastians know about the NightBlade.
6. In the quest to figure out how to banish ShadowEaters forever, begin by hunting down Trevor and getting the truth out of him. (Alternatively, score his liver for Skuld.)
7. Cram for math test, despite no real hope of getting more than a C.

. . .

Jessica was waiting at the entry to school and I could see from her expression that something was wrong.

"Aren't King and Mozart okay?" Meagan asked right away.

Jessica nodded. "The Oracle is treating them. She thinks they'll recover." That wasn't all of it, though. Her gaze kept flicking to me. Jessica peered at me from under the visor of her baseball cap, her eyes seeming darker than usual. "Did you have a dream last night?"

I had an idea why she was asking, but had to know. "Why?"

She shuddered. "Because I had an awful one. I was bound, helpless, just the way I was in the fall." She met my gaze with horror. "But worse, I couldn't shift."

"The ShadowEater spells block my shifter powers. I couldn't shift in my dream, either, but it was okay when I woke up."

Jessica shook her head. "I can't shift anymore."

Meagan and I exchanged a glance.

"Then how'd you get free?" I asked Jessica.

She licked her lips, glanced to the left, then the right before she answered me. "Kohana came into my dream with his thunderbolts," she admitted in a whisper. "I don't know how he did it."

"He can move in dreams. He's done it before."

"Well, he says I owe him." I could see that she was worried about what or when he might collect.

I tried to sound cheerful. "Well, I owe him, too. We're in it together."

"He's always keeping score," Meagan muttered. "I wouldn't be surprised if he'd set this up, just so you would owe him." She opened her locker and slammed the door hard. "I don't trust him "

"He's still part of the alliance," I reminded her. Meagan rolled her eyes, but I turned to Jessica. "Are you sure you can't shift?"

"Positive."

"There must be a spell bound to you still." I looked her over but couldn't see it. Would it be visible in her cat form? Visible to me in my dragon form? If it was there—and it must be there if she couldn't shift—I had to be able to see it somehow. "Good thing Skuld gave me her scissors. We'll cut you free."

Jessica looked confused so I explained to her, even gave her a peek. “Let’s find a place where you can try to shift.”

“It’s still early,” Jessica said. “We could go to the gym right now and get it over with before class starts.”

“No,” I said. “The gym’s too big. Anyone could walk in. Let’s use a bathroom.”

Meagan nodded. “Let’s go down to the other end of the hall to that one no one uses much.”

As we walked down the hallway, I was struck by an unexpected sense of foreboding. Theoretically and intuitively, our plan made perfect sense. I knew it was the right thing to do. But the idea of Jessica deliberately attempting to shift at school made me squirm. I rationalized that I was still spooked from the day before.

How was I supposed to know that my foresight had finally arrived on the scene?

You’d think I could have gotten a formal announcement or something.

8

The girls' bathroom we'd chosen was deserted, just as expected.

It smelled strongly of bleach and faintly of both cigarettes and perfume, which was also as expected. They'd removed all the dead bolts from the doors after my shifting incident in the fall, which didn't exactly inspire confidence in our long-term privacy.

"Just be quick," Meagan said. "I'll be the lookout."

Jessica took off her baseball cap and shook her hair out of her ponytail. It's funny, but I forget how gorgeous she looked at Halloween in that costume that emphasized her curves. It almost seems like she's a different person, or one who lives in her brother's discarded baggy clothes. But just that act of shaking her hair free made her look sensual and feminine. It seemed that the curve of her lips was riper and sultrier and that her gaze turned knowing. She unzipped her hoodie and I saw the gold necklace lying against her skin like the precious and ancient relic it was.

She was suddenly exotic and beautiful, at ease with a femininity that she kept hidden away. I thought of her at the birthing the day before and felt young and awkward in her presence. I was pretty sure she could sense it.

I pulled the shears out of my backpack and unwrapped them carefully.

We exchanged a look, Meagan confirmed that the coast was clear, then Jessica flung out her hands and tipped back her head.

I knew she was summoning the change.

I knew what to expect.

But nothing happened.

Her eyes widened and she swallowed and I heard the nervous skip of her heart.

"Don't think about it too much," I said. "Breathe deeply; don't question or doubt your powers. I'm sure you can do it."

She nodded and brushed her fingertips across that necklace. I saw her lashes flutter and heard her murmur something in another language. Maybe it was a prayer.

Then she tried again.

And this time, I saw the golden silhouettes of a hundred cats swirling around her ankles. They took form out of nothing, just long enough that I caught glimpses of them, then faded from view so quickly that I thought I was imagining them.

I saw that faint electric shimmer of blue dance over Jessica's skin, like she'd been touched by lightning. I narrowed my eyes as it grew brighter, wanting to see the moment that her shape changed.

But the blue light was suddenly extinguished. It fizzled and died in a way that I knew wasn't natural.

Jessica blinked.

She frowned.

Our gazes met for one instant and I knew what she was thinking.

Just like in the nightmare.

Just like the moment of being spellbound.

"Holy shit," she whispered, her fear obvious. "Can you see the spell that's blocking me?"

"Not yet. Try again." I tightened my grip on Skuld's shears, ready for action.

Jessica touched the necklace with her fingertips again and swallowed her fear, murmuring that prayer one more time. The shadowy cats grew brighter and more substantial before my eyes, and I knew they were answering a summons from her.

And this time when that blue shimmer danced over her skin, the cats rubbed against something that was locked around Jessica's ankle. It must have had a glamour on it to disguise it, but the ghostly cats pushed the glamour aside to reveal it. I saw the golden tendril of spell light clearly, thanks to them.

But I saw it only for a heartbeat before it was hidden again.

This time, the shimmer just sparked off her fingertips before it died to nothing. It didn't even travel up her hands, let alone over her whole body.

The sight was terrifying.

Would I be able to see the spell better in my dragon form? My keen *Pyr* senses were even sharper when I was a dragon girl. It was worth a try.

I had to hope that whatever had touched Jessica wasn't contagious.

But I knew the ShadowEaters were hungry.

My adrenaline was pumping when I flung out my hands and called to my own shimmer. I felt the power of the change slide through my body. I saw the brilliant blue light pass over my skin. I felt the tide of the shift, terrified all the while that it would stop before it was done.

But it didn't. They didn't have me yet. I felt the surge as the change was completed, raised my wings to beat them hard, and tipped my head back with joy.

Jessica hooted and applauded. Meagan did, too.

I wanted to shout. I wanted to roar. I wanted to breathe fire. I thrashed my tail, fiercely glad to still be what I am, and stretched to my full size.

Jessica tried to shift and the spell tendril glimmered more vividly on her ankle. It looked luminescent to me now. I locked my dragon gaze on the spell. Even now I could see it swelling. I could see it sucking something away from Jessica, like a parasite draining the life force from its host.

And there was a small one snaking toward my own foot.

It was spreading. Finding her through the dream portal, then extending into real life to target the shifters around her.

That was enough. I lifted the shears and hacked at the spell closest to my own claw first, slashing it to oblivion. It fizzled and hissed and died, shooting little golden sparks in every direction as I consigned it to oblivion.

Then I went after the one that had claimed Jessica's ankle. It was more substantial, this one, thicker and more robust and harder to cut. I had a tough time with the shears, given my lack of dragon dexterity.

"Let me help," Meagan said, and abandoned her post. She seized the shears and started to snip, glancing to me for direction.

"Right here!" I directed. I bent and caught one end of the spell, holding it out so that she could guess where it was. "Cut harder!" I said. "Faster!"

It wriggled and writhed in my grip, like a boa constrictor that would have preferred to eat me alive. I held fast and Meagan snipped with all her might. As soon as the spell tether was severed, it spewed sparks, like a high-voltage cable severed while the power was still on.

One landed on Jessica and I saw it take root, growing a tendril that began to wind around her arm. Every spark was alive, a possible cause of our destruction.

"Stay back!" I bellowed, and protected both Jessica and Meagan from the onslaught of spell chunks. I grabbed the shears and sliced with abandon, then loosed a torrent of dragonfire on the scattering spells. To my relief, that seemed to work; they fell to the ground like ash when I fried them. I got busy and went after every last one.

When I turned to chase the final stray spark, I saw that the bathroom door was open.

Suzanne stood there, smirking. "I knew you losers were up to something," she said, then lifted her messenger and took a trio of shots.

"No!" I bellowed, and lunged after her. I shifted shape on the way, acting on instinct, but it was exactly what she expected me to do. The flash made me stumble and I lost precious momentum. She must have nailed images of me in transition and in human form, as well, her camera clicking like mad as she backed out of the bathroom.

My heart, just so you know, had fallen right through the floor.

I wasn't even going to survive long enough to catch hell for breaking the Covenant. My dad had chewed me out before for revealing myself in both human and dragon form—the Covenant sworn by all the *Pyr* was intended to protect our privacy, and he hated when I broke it. I had no idea what Suzanne and her friends would do to me, armed with those images, but I knew it wouldn't be good.

I had to make sure that proof was destroyed.

ASAP.

. . .

Suzanne bolted down the corridor, trying to lose herself in the crowd of kids getting to class—or dawdling not to get there too soon. She kept looking back at me, and I smelled that she was surprised that I didn't give it up. She shoved the messenger into her purse, pretending she didn't have it. She dove into a cluster of her cronies—Trish, Anne, Yvonne, and Fiona—nudging Trish as if to set her on guard.

But none of them could keep me away from this.

Even the spell light that swirled around them couldn't keep me away from this.

Two of the teachers were coming down the hall together—just my luck, it was Mrs. Mulvaney and Mr. Zacharias. Mrs. Mulvaney is older than God and big on discipline. I'd had her for homeroom the year before. I swear she would have failed me in homeroom for drawing during the announcements if she could have figured out a way to do it. Mr. Zacharias is one of those people who lives in his own world. That he could walk alongside Mrs. Mulvaney, calmly sipping his coffee as she ranted about something or other, pretty much said everything about his complacent nature.

I sensed Meagan and Jessica behind me, watching, and knew that the whole school would hear about this within five minutes. Mrs. Mulvaney would happily have my hide as a souvenir if I broke any rules, too.

But the stakes were high. I needed to erase those images.

I shoved past Trish easily and caught Suzanne's elbow, as kids milled all around us.

Just two girls, not getting along.

"Girls!" Mrs. Mulvaney shouted, and I heard her heels clicking faster. "What's this about, girls?"

Of course, everyone ignored her.

Suzanne's pack started to taunt me as they surrounded me, and if I'd been anything other than a dragon-girl, I might have worried about my own welfare. Right then and there, I didn't care. I'd shift if I had to—although that would defeat the purpose. Suzanne must have guessed how intent I was because I could feel her shaking. I let my fingers dig into her arm and smiled, letting her think about talons and fire and big sharp teeth.

It was tempting to beguile her into believing she was being fried alive.

She caught her breath.

"You have something that belongs to me," I said softly.

She threw back her hair. "As if I'd want anything of yours, Sorensson," she said, but there was an undercurrent of fear in her voice.

"Why don't you just give me the messenger?" I said. It was a long shot, but I had to try.

Suzanne laughed. Her friends jostled around us and that seemed to give her confidence. Either that, or it was Mrs. Mulvaney's proximity. "I knew you were a freak," she whispered, her eyes shining with malice. "And now I have proof."

I snatched her purse then, moving so fast that she didn't anticipate my move, and dumped its contents on the floor. Lipsticks clattered and bounced. A hairbrush fell. A notebook and four pens scattered in all directions.

The messenger never hit the floor. I grabbed it out of the air, threw aside her designer purse, then ran.

"Zoë Sorensson!" roared Mrs. Mulvaney.

"No!" Suzanne shouted, coming after me. The kids in the hall parted before us like the Red Sea. I felt Suzanne snatch after me and miss. "That's *mine*. You can't steal it from me!"

I kept running, right to the end of the hall. I had to buy myself a bit of time.

"Zoë!" Mrs. Mulvaney shouted after me. "What's this about?"

I poked open the back of the camera and removed the memory card as I ran. I shoved it into my pocket, then pivoted at the end of the hall. I slammed my back into the lockers at the end of the hall, smiling at Suzanne.

The smile slowed her down.

She wasn't that stupid. I held the messenger behind my back while I replaced the back panel.

Mrs. Mulvaney was marching toward us, pointing her finger and lecturing about rules.

I held up the messenger between us. "Sorry. Thought it was mine." I tossed it at Suzanne.

She barely caught it, then scanned it for damage. It took her a minute to figure out what I'd done; then her eyes flashed. "Bitch!" she snarled, but I dropped the memory card on the tile and slammed the heel of my boot down to destroy it forever.

Suzanne squared her shoulders to glare at me, ignoring Mrs. Mulvaney. "You owe me, Sorensson," she said.

"Less than you owe me," I replied.

"Suzanne Moore!" Mrs. Mulvaney said. "Such language is inappropriate."

Mr. Zacharias trailed behind Mrs. Mulvaney and glanced down at the smashed memory card. He was probably assuming that Suzanne had taken nude pics of me in the bathroom. Mrs. Mulvaney had missed my move with the memory card. She was too busy organizing and ordering, shooing people this way and that. Suzanne and I simply glared at each other.

"She wrecked my messenger," Suzanne said. "She did it on purpose."

Mrs. Mulvaney looked at me.

"I didn't wreck it. I just thought it was mine."

Our excuses were so thin and so lame that even Mrs. Mulvaney knew that they were only a fraction of the truth. "You have it back, though," she said to Suzanne.

Suzanne nodded. "But she owes me." She mouthed the word then: *freak.*

I smiled my confident dragon smile, liking that she shivered just a bit.

"All right, everyone. Get to class," Mrs. Mulvaney said. She pointed at me. "You're coming down to the principal's office, Zoë." Suzanne only had time to smirk before Mrs. Mulvaney pointed at her. "And so are you, Suzanne. Let's get this argument sorted out, girls."

We were walking down the hall when Meagan came to my side. She handed me my bag and I knew from the weight of it that she'd hidden Skuld's shears inside. "Your messenger is in the side pocket," she said, slanting a glance at Mrs. Mulvaney.

I made a show of checking, then feigned relief. "How weird. I never put it there before. Thanks, Meagan!"

"An honest mistake, then," Mrs. Mulvaney said, a triumphant conclusion, but Suzanne snorted.

And I looked back to see Derek scooping up the smashed bits of memory card. I flashed him a smile of gratitude. Jessica was standing beside him, back in her usual sloppy clothes, but looking much more serene. This was the alliance in action, each of us guarding each other's backs and succeeding as a team.

I should have known it couldn't last.

THEY SEPARATED us to get our stories without collaboration.

I insisted that Suzanne had bumped into me and I thought she'd taken my messenger, although, gosh, I couldn't imagine why she would play such a trick on me.

I have no idea what Suzanne told them, but the interrogation team went back and forth between us for a good twenty minutes. Then they had to confer with each other for another twenty. Then they decided to call our parents. Suzanne pitched a fit about this, because apparently she was worried about having her freedom limited right before the Valentine's Day dance.

It took them another fifteen minutes to reason with her and explain that they were doing this for her own good. Suzanne wasn't buying it, but her attitude gave me some time alone in my designated corner: the principal's office. The office had windows on all sides and so did the door, like it was command control—or a lookout tower. This worked for me, because I could see everything that was going on and, thanks to my *Pyr* senses, hear it, too.

What was the deal with the spell light surrounding Suzanne and her friends? I thought I had seen some the day before around Trish and Yvonne, then later with Trevor in the parking lot. Were they being targeted by the ShadowEaters? Or was Trevor up to something?

Suzanne and her cronies were all human, with no shifter powers and no spellsinging powers—at least not that I knew of. While they certainly thought themselves special, I couldn't see what the ShadowEaters would want with them.

I knew I wasn't imagining the spell light, though. It had to be Trevor's doing, but I couldn't figure out his scheme. It was a puzzle.

"Mr. Sorensson is waiting on two," the principal's secretary said from the reception area.

"Thank you." The principal came into her office, shut the door behind her, and picked up the desk phone. She looked pretty grim. She pushed for the second line, while I sat there with my mouth hanging open.

They'd called my parents.

In the Caribbean.

Why hadn't I guessed that would happen?

And welcome to the inner circle of hell. Remember that my dad is a dragon shifter—he can supply the fire, if not the brimstone, on demand.

I doubted this exchange would end well.

I OFFICIALLY LISTENED to one side of the conversation, eavesdropping shamelessly and secretly on the other side.

The principal's tone had that mix of honeyed sweetness and iron will that characterized all of my dealings with her. (Probably everyone's dealings with her, come to think of it. She is not someone you would ask for a hug.) "I'm very sorry to trouble you on your vacation, Mr. Sorensson, but there has been an incident at the school and I knew you'd want to know about it."

My father made conciliatory noises.

She discussed the incident in question, distaste in every syllable she uttered.

My father made sympathetic and faintly outraged noises, which only encouraged her. He didn't defend me, not one iota. Between the two of them, I was judged and convicted in a matter of moments. The principal repeated most of her points, seeming to enjoy her moral triumph, then handed me the phone.

I stared at the receiver and gulped. All I had to do was ace a math test, check in at regular intervals with Muriel, find the NightBlade, banish the ShadowEaters, and persuade my dad that I shouldn't be on his Incinerate Now list.

No pressure.

IT IS some kind of cosmic joke that when everything seems to be going to hell, the most unlikely things come easily.

My dad doesn't like me drawing attention to myself for any reason. It makes him think of dragons being nearly hunted to extinction in the Middle Ages, and generally moves him into high-octane, take-no-prisoners, Protective Parent mode.

This is much worse with a dragon dad. Just so you know. I know because we've been there and done that.

Would I be grounded?

Exiled?

Roasted?

The principal's eyes narrowed as she watched me.

I decided to take the initiative and grovel for mercy. "I'm really sorry, Dad. I didn't mean to get into trouble...."

"We shall have to talk about this when your mother and I get home!" he shouted sharply, and I winced. "You had better behave yourself for the next week, Zoë. Frankly, I expected better of you, and if one more thing happens while your mother and I are away, you will be..."

The principal smiled with satisfaction, then left me in the office alone.

My dad stopped in mid-tirade. "Is she gone?" he asked, his voice low and silky. Conspiratorial.

"Yes," I said carefully.

"You were caught," my father said easily, as if we were talking about my sneaking a granola bar before dinner. His tone had changed completely and I didn't trust it one bit. He was softening me up, faking me out before he went for the kill. I had broken the Covenant again, after all.

I nodded, then remembered he couldn't see me. "Yes." I swallowed.

"Excellent choice," he said. "Almost intuitive in its speed, which is always the key to containing any incident in which you are revealed. Did you destroy the memory card in the messenger?"

I straightened. "Yes."

"Very good. I assume that you had a good reason for shifting as you did, and that it was unavoidable?"

"Yes."

"Also that you cannot tell me about the details now?"

I glanced at the principal hovering outside her office door. "Not really, no."

My dad mused for a minute while I sat blinking in astonishment that he wasn't roaring at me. "It's entirely possible that no one will believe this Suzanne person this time, either, but for the sake of insurance, if you can be alone with her, it might be wise to beguile her. As soon as possible."

I had to fight my smile of triumph. The principal was still lurking. "Yes, Dad. As soon as possible."

"And I think a reward is in order for your deft handling of an unavoidable breach of the Covenant. What do you say to having your own car?"

"What?" I asked, barely daring to breathe.

"Your mom wants a new car. You can have the Toyota. I'll pay the insurance, but all other costs will be yours to cover. Deal?"

I was being rewarded.

I slanted a glance toward the principal, who was talking to her secretary and suitably distracted. If goodies were being distributed, I knew which one I wanted—and it wasn't the Toyota.

"You could give me the Lamborghini," I suggested softly.

My dad laughed, a throaty dragon chuckle. "That insurance I'm not going to pay. Besides, it's sold."

I was shocked. "Sold?"

"A collector of vintage cars. He's going to pick it up after we get home, which will make room for your mom's new car in the garage."

Sold? Before I even sat in the driver's seat?

Sold?

"Can I drive it just once?"

"No." He was succinct and firm. There was no wiggle room on this. "It has been sold in its current pristine condition and will be delivered the same way."

Rebellion rose hot in my chest. I wanted to choose my reward, and it wasn't the bashed-up red Toyota. "But..."

"Have you been maintaining the dragonsmoke boundary at the loft?" he asked crisply. "It may be starting to wear down already, and I don't want anything to happen to that car."

"I'll go after school to check."

"Excellent." His voice dropped to a warmer timbre. "Well done, Zoë," he added, then he was gone.

It says something for my state of mind that I stared at the receiver for a minute before putting it back in the cradle.

My dad was proud of me.

I had a car of my very own.

And, you know, I was thinking the Toyota wouldn't be so bad.

Suzanne's call wasn't going nearly so well, from the sound of it. I was excused, and headed off to math class late and without having managed to spare a minute to cram for the test.

But the math test was easy.

So easy that I was sure there was a mistake. Had I gotten a different one? The wrong one? Like maybe the one I should have gotten a year ago? No one else seemed to be surprised by it, so maybe I was channeling some Meagan and Jessica brilliance.

Speaking of which, Meagan wasn't in class. Her seat at the front of the room was empty. I might have been more worried about this if Jessica hadn't been there, acting as if nothing was wrong at all.

You will be less surprised than me to realize that no one noticed Meagan was gone.

I saw a teensy shimmer of purple spell light dancing around Mrs. Dawson's head. It swirled around her head like a glittery blindfold. Apparently, Meagan *was* learning more about spellsinging—and her spell ensured that Mrs. Dawson didn't notice the empty seat in the prime A-student zone.

I could have used a bit of that for Muriel.

I had to wonder, though, how exactly Meagan was going to conjure up the test she wasn't taking.

Never mind where she was.

I surreptitiously checked my messenger and saw that there was a message from her. I might have gone for it, even against school rules, but I saw Trish watching me. There was venom in her eyes—as well as that twinkle of golden spell light—and I understood that she would be more than happy to rat on me in vengeance for Suzanne.

Who was not in class.

I smiled at Trish, dropped my messenger back in my bag, and focused on my test.

Even having started ten minutes late, I was done fifteen minutes early and itching to accomplish something before art class. When I finally got out of there, I had a plan.

First things first. I needed backup.

Dragon backup.

I sat down by my locker and tugged out my messenger again. The message from Meagan was pretty enigmatic—she just said she had something to do and would see me at lunch. I decided on a meeting at my fave tofu-burger place and sent her an update. I composed messages to the guys, my fingers and thumbs moving in a blur as I brought them up-to-date and asked them to come to the restaurant.

I was sure that if we all put our heads together over lunch, we could come up with a ShadowEater Elimination Plan.

Of course, I wasn't counting on the fact that Meagan already had one.

The red Toyota had improved remarkably in its appeal during the morning.

The news that it was mine, all mine, made it look infinitely better.

I walked around it in the school parking lot, admiring its color and its signs of experience. It started right away when I turned the key, as if it, too, liked that we were going to be a team.

"Nice of your dad to let you use the car," Derek said when he got in.

"It's mine now," I said with a thrill of pride. I'd already told him that Jessica had said she was going to meet us at the restaurant. I was assuming that she was with Meagan.

He looked impressed. "What are you going to do to it?"

"What do you mean?"

"You could repaint it. Black."

"Purple," I said. "Lime green."

"Or install a better stereo," he added a minute later. We skidded a little bit on a corner. "Get bigger tires for the snow."

His suggestions got me excited about the possibilities. Just because my mom had liked the car being minimal in terms of luxury didn't mean I had to keep it the same way.

It was mine and I could change it. I felt the power.

"Paint a dragon on the side," Derek said with a grin. "That would get attention."

"That would get it taken back!" I argued with a laugh.

He grinned. "Let me look under the hood later. Maybe we can soup it up a bit."

"Really?"

"Oh yeah. Engines can always get a bit of a nudge."

I was really excited about the car by the time we got to the restaurant. I parked it with new pride and couldn't help looking at it, imagining the possibilities.

It turned out that Derek and I got there first. We ordered and claimed a big group of tables in anticipation of the others arriving. Derek sat right beside me, doing this proprietary thing that made me blush. Then Nick and Isabelle arrived and gave the nonexistent gap between us a significant look.

Before I could comment—or think of how to do it—and before things got awkward (again) between the four of us, Liam arrived, as good-natured and easygoing as a ray of sunshine. He gave me a big tight hug and it was only after he stepped away that I saw he was growing a mustache.

Or trying to.

At least, I assume that was the plan. There was a weedy little auburn thing on his upper lip.

I wasn't going to say anything, but I looked at it too long and he noticed.

"What is that thing on your face?" Nick demanded, then began to tease Liam about it.

Liam blushed. "Forget about it," he said to Nick, who (of course) did not.

"Let me help you wash it off," Nick razzed him. "A little dirt like that will just take a wipe. We've got napkins right here."

"Leave it!"

Nick and Liam started to mock box over it, the two of them getting so rowdy that I thought they'd get us tossed out.

Then Garrett sauntered in, his gaze dancing over the people gathered at the table already. The other two dragon-guys straightened up at the sight of him, maybe because Garrett always seems so serious.

Although he tried to hide it, I saw his disappointment. "Meagan said she had something to do. She'll be here in a couple of minutes, and I think Jessica must be coming with her." He smiled then and ruffled my hair as if I were six instead of sixteen, so I poked him in the gut to get even.

So, they ordered and we all sat down, leaning over the center of the table to talk in (comparatively) hushed voices about what had happened so far. The guys had some questions and I answered them, Derek nodding periodically.

"What about these kids in the news today?" Nick said.

"That Steve Ford guy is the one I saw in my dream—and again yesterday." They nodded, not surprised now. "I wonder if the other one was an apprentice Mage. It said he was in band."

Isabelle pulled out her messenger. "I saw on the way here that there were two more bodies found this morning. These were two homeless people with mental problems." She frowned. "They had jobs until November. As music teachers."

"Let me guess," I said. "They had no history of mental problems before November, either."

"Mages," Liam said, and we all nodded. "They couldn't function after the hive memory was destroyed."

"That's what must have happened to the survivors," Nick said.

"So the ShadowEaters must be targeting surviving Mages and apprentice Mages," Isabelle said.

"Well, that's not a bad thing." Nick shrugged. "Saves us the trouble of hunting them all down."

I shook my head. "That's how they're building their power. They must be taking on the spellcasting power of every Mage or apprentice Mage they kill." I told them about tearing the veil and how the *Wakiya* elder had told me that I had to act quickly.

"But do what quickly?" Liam asked.

"That's the million-dollar question," Derek said.

Jessica arrived then. Alone. She looked flustered and a bit annoyed. Liam stood up and smiled at her, making space for her beside him. She smiled warmly at him, holding eye contact longer than I might have expected.

And Liam blushed a bit. Hmm.

"I thought you were coming with Meagan."

"No. The Oracle wanted to talk to me." She made a face and that surprised me. I thought she revered that woman.

What had changed?

"There's a problem," she said. "I can't stay."

"You've got to eat," Liam protested. "Let me get you something."

We sat in restless silence while he was gone, impatient to find out what was going on but not wanting him to miss anything. When Liam came back, we leaned forward for Jessica's story.

She took a bite first, nodding approval at Liam over his choice. "So, this morning, when I told the Oracle about my dream, I thought she was going to lose it completely. She said that was proof that someone tore the veil, eliminating the barrier between the ShadowEaters and us. She says it's proof of meddling." She looked me right in the eye. "*Your* meddling."

Yeah, well, there wasn't a lot I could say to defend myself there.

"Is it true, Z?" Nick asked.

I had to nod. "I told him to tear the veil."

"There has to be an upside to it," Isabelle murmured.

"Are King and Mozart okay?" I asked.

Jessica grimaced. "They're not better; just about the same."

That wasn't good news.

"But that's not the worst of it," she continued. "There were more Bastians hurt during the night and three of them aren't going to survive. Their shadows are completely gone."

Derek caught his breath and took my hand. I knew he was thinking of those two wolves.

"The Oracle says you're dangerous company. I'm not allowed to be in the alliance with you anymore or even talk to you. She's monitoring my messenger and my mom's covering the phone." She frowned at her burger. "I don't know how else she learns things, but she always does. I can explain being here by saying I had to tell you."

"But then you have to go," Isabelle said, grimacing.

"But we have to stick together," Liam said.

"Why wouldn't she ask Zoë to explain her actions?" Derek said, with some annoyance. "Why do the Bastians always have to pull away like this?"

Jessica shot him a look. "I tried to change her mind. I told her about Zoë destroying the spell that was keeping me from shifting. She said it wasn't enough."

"But there has to be something good about tearing the veil," Isabelle said, looking at me.

"It destroyed their glamours," I said. "And it means we can destroy them."

"We just have to figure out how," Nick said with a nod.

"And fast," Liam agreed.

"I've got to go." Jessica looked at me again and there was a mutinous glint in her eyes. "But Derek's right. The Bastians can't pull back on this issue. I think you're right. The Oracle doesn't have to know that I'm still on your side."

"Really?"

She nodded at me. "You cut me free. They would have had me otherwise. I'm in and I'm staying in."

Derek grinned approval of that.

"Do you want me to pass messages between you two?" Liam asked.

Jessica touched his arm briefly, then shook her head. "Thanks, but it won't work. They're expecting something like that." She smiled and there was a gleam in her eyes. "But what they're forgetting is that Zoë can send me messages telepathically. Like she did yesterday. And they can't monitor that."

"No way!" Nick said. "Sending messages! That's full-power Wyvern stuff." He gave me a high-five across the table. We all grinned at each other, and I was glad I had given it a try.

"You'll have to be sure you don't seem distracted," I warned Jessica. "The Oracle picked up on your concern yesterday."

"Only because she was so focused on my needing to concentrate. If I'm not with her, I don't think she'll notice." Jessica's lips set. "Especially if I try to hide my feelings from her." Then she stood up. "But I have to go now, before she figures out I've been here." She gave me a look. "Let me know where I have to be when, and I'll be there."

"I'll tag along," Liam suggested, but Jessica shook her head. He kept talking. "I'll keep watch over you or fight ShadowEaters if necessary. She can't have a problem with you being defended." He held Jessica's gaze and something about his expression—pure puppy dog with muck on his lip—must have changed her mind.

"You just want the rest of my lunch," she teased, and he grinned.

"Well, if you're not going to eat it..."

Jessica smiled and handed him the last of her fries.

I didn't like our group separating, but the idea of Jessica being with Liam was better than her being alone. "But what else do you Bastians know about the NightBlade?" I asked Jessica, and she shrugged. "Because King knew that Kohana wouldn't be able to break it right from the start."

"I didn't," Jessica said. "But I'll tell Liam our story about the origin of the ShadowEaters."

"She called them failed Mages."

"I'm not sure if it's important or not, but it might give you a clue." Jessica nodded, then tugged on her coat, Liam close beside her. The others started to discuss ShadowEaters as Isabelle's messenger rang with more updates on the murders.

I heard a motorcycle engine and the bottom dropped out of my universe.

I had a sudden idea what Meagan had needed to do.

The motorcycle engine grew louder as the bike came closer.

There was no way it could be a vintage Ducati.

Ridden by the hottest guy on the planet.

The spellsinger who was corresponding with Meagan, teaching her how to develop her innate skill, and ducking me big time.

The oh-so-sexy rocker rebel who got my dragon drawing tattooed on his back for my birthday when I couldn't get a tattoo myself.

Jared Madison.

No. It couldn't be him.

It *wouldn't* be him.

Jared had bailed on me.

I was never going to see him again and I knew it.

But that bike was pulling into the lot...

And Meagan had insisted that she had a plan. Was it this one? I turned to look out the window, unable to stop myself. Derek inhaled sharply. Nick looked like he was fighting a grin. Isabelle covered her mouth to hide her smile. Garrett looked between Derek and me. Jessica and Liam looked up on their way out of the restaurant.

And Jared roared into the parking lot, looking leaner and sexier and roughly ten zillion times better than ever, with Meagan hanging on to the back of his bike.

My heart stopped.

Then it fell through the floor, popped out in China, did a gleeful somersault, and charged back through the earth's core to slam into my chest again. No wonder I couldn't breathe.

Jared parked, then helped Meagan off the back. Just the way he'd helped me off his bike a couple of times. My knight in black leather.

I was sure my mouth had to be hanging open. Smooth—that's me.

No. He was not *my* knight in black leather. I reminded myself of his silences and unresponsiveness. Assuming he was here for me was just plain dumb.

Had he come to help Meagan? I had to consider the possibility, given that she'd been in contact with him and I hadn't.

Meagan tugged off her helmet, revealing her jubilant expression. She waved at me, racing toward the restaurant as Jared parked the bike to his satisfaction. He took a lot of care with it, just the way I remembered.

"Hey, Zoë!" Meagan shouted as she entered the restaurant. "I thought we needed a secret weapon! What do you think?"

I could not say one word.

I watched Jared saunter toward the restaurant, his eyes gleaming as he smiled at me. He knew his effect on me so precisely that he could have measured it out. I doubt anyone else missed it, either. My gaze was locked on him, as if he were the only person in the universe.

In that moment he was.

Me, I couldn't say a single word. I couldn't even *think* of a single coherent word. Even *hi* would have been a stretch.

Instead I thought about the way Jared had teased me, the fact that I owed him a ride, the way he kissed, the way he provoked me and challenged me, the way he made me feel simultaneously excited and confused.

Like I was feeling right then and there.

It would have been nice if time had diminished his effect on me. Or if absence had made the heart forget. No luck. Mine was beating double time while I thought about the song I was sure he'd written for me last year and the tattoo—my dragon drawing—he had on his back.

I itched to see it.

Or maybe just to see him half-naked.

Of course, he had bailed on me. He hadn't been in contact at all. And I was sitting right beside the most loyal and helpful guy ever. I slapped my impulses down and fought them, hard.

I believed I'd made the right choice.

I'd believed it more five minutes earlier, but I'd work with what I had.

Isabelle moved and Jared eased into the seat beside me, pressed the length of his thigh against mine and leaned closer to steal one of my fries. His eyes were glinting with mischief and still appeared ten thousand shades of green. He bit the fry, so obviously enjoying my awareness of him that I thought I would spontaneously combust.

"Hey, dragon-girl," he murmured in that low sultry voice of his, the one that gives me palpitations. "Miss me?"

Then he winked at me, and I was a goner.

Again.

Or maybe still.

I barely noticed Derek shoving out of his seat to leave. In fact, I wouldn't have noticed at all if he hadn't sworn under his breath and slammed the door.

Even so, it didn't seem important.

Which was a very big problem.

Sadly, it wasn't my only one.

9

Garrett smiled at Meagan and moved to make a place for her to sit. Meagan blushed and sat down beside him, looking radiant and happy.

So at least something was going right.

"You want something to eat?" Garrett asked her quietly.

Meagan looked at me, grinned at my reaction to Jared's presence, then stole the other half of my tofu burger. It wasn't as if I was going to manage to eat it, not while I was sitting there gobsmacked. She and Garrett shared a smile and he sat back down beside her.

I tried to focus on job number one, which was keeping the alliance together.

One member of which was walking away. "We have to stick together," I reminded them all, looking at Derek's retreating figure.

Yet not wanting to leave Jared.

Now I needed to be in more than one place at a time. I wanted to be here. I should go with Derek. I should stick with Jessica and Liam. I needed to check in with Muriel in sixteen minutes. All the while, I was keenly aware of Jared close beside me, listening and watching as my carefully built alliance shattered into shards.

Isabelle took a napkin and started to write on it. "Okay, we have a bunch of issues," she said, starting a list. "It might make sense to split up to solve them. We need to find the NightBlade to destroy it. We need to figure out how to destroy the ShadowEaters and why we need to hurry. It would be good if we could find Kohana and find out what he knows." She glanced up with concern. "You don't think they've captured him, do you?"

"We never know what side that guy is on," Nick said, eyeing the menu as if he wanted another round.

"Nick and I will look for the NightBlade and Kohana," Isabelle said firmly. "I'll bet one will lead us straight to the other."

"Don't you have class, Zoë?" Garrett asked.

I nodded. "And a detention afterward." I snapped my fingers as I remembered something. "Which happens at the same time as Trevor's jazz-band practice."

"Good," Jared said. "You can show me where and I'll corner him, see what I can learn."

"He's not going to want to talk to you," I protested.

Jared grinned. "Don't underestimate my charm."

His confidence annoyed me. "You're not part of the alliance," I said. It sounded rude the way I blurted it out, but it was true.

"So maybe I'm joining up." Jared glanced pointedly over the table. "Doesn't look like you have much of a team left, anyway."

It was too much.

First he ignored me.

Then he showed up and confused me.

Then he implied criticism of what I was doing, even though he wasn't doing anything. In fact, if he hadn't arrived, Derek would still be at the table.

"And whose fault is that?" I demanded of Jared. "You just show up, out of the blue, and screw up everything. Why? Because you like to mess with me?" I pushed to my feet, really angry. "It's not funny. Jessica and I were nearly claimed by ShadowEaters in our dreams last night. They're free, and the veil between their realm and ours is destroyed. We have some kind of limited-time offer to destroy them but I'm not sure what it is. I know in my gut that it's going to take every one of us to pull it off. We don't have time for screwing with people's feelings just for fun." I hauled on my coat and zipped it up with a savage gesture.

To Jared's credit, his cocky smile was gone, but I was too mad to let it go.

"Did you see the news?" I demanded. "That kid, that apprentice Mage, is dead. They sacrificed him. This isn't a game!"

"He was an apprentice Mage, Z," Nick said.

"So what? Maybe he didn't know what he was getting into. I doubt he knew that he was going to be sacrificed before it was too late to save himself. I understand what he must have felt in his last minutes, and it's not funny."

I turned on Jared before I lost my nerve. "I'm glad you think it's entertaining to mess with people's lives," I said to him, my tone snarky. "Thanks for your help. I'll have to put you in my will."

Then I pivoted and marched out of there. I might not have been breathing fire, but I was pretty sure there was steam coming out of my ears.

Nobody came after me.

Big surprise.

Trevor fell into step with me as I was walking back into the school. I spared him a look and kept walking. He looked nervous—again—but I was pretty sure he was putting it on. There was a shimmer of spell light around him, but it wasn't very bright. It was just enough to ensure I didn't forget what he was.

"Zoë, I need your help."

I glared at him. "Be serious. We've been there and done that."

He shook his head. "No, this is different! Didn't you see the news?" He dropped his voice to a horrified whisper. "They're hunting apprentice Mages!"

I stopped and turned to face him. "So you invoked them but the ceremony went wrong. If they were eating shifters and I came to you for help, what would you say?"

His gaze locked with mine, then danced away.

"If I ask you now to tell me what they want and how they can be stopped, will you tell me?"

"Zoë, I just need some help...."

"Bullshit. Clean up your own mess." And I marched into the school, leaving him staring after me.

I had my locker open before I thought of it. The ShadowEaters were hunting Mages and apprentice Mages, eating their shadows and taking on their power. They were building their strength with spell power from their own kind.

But what had traditionally given Mages a burst of energy was the elimination of a species of shifter. And what was supposed to give them the big final surge was the elimination of all remaining shifter species. I'd asked the *Wakiya* elder what they wanted, and he'd said they wanted what they'd always wanted.

To become pure spirit and poison the universe with the strength of their malice.

The ShadowEaters would stop only when they destroyed all of us—unless we destroyed them first.

The question was how.

I GOT through the rest of the day somehow, even though Meagan and Jessica didn't come back to school, nobody sent me a message, and Derek had disappeared without a trace. I even survived my stupid detention.

I was feeling like a total loser at my locker afterward when I packed my books up for another riveting night of homework and nightmares. I could not solve this riddle and it was the most important one ever.

Then I saw denim in my peripheral vision. Dark jeans and biker boots.

I knew who was wearing those jeans.

"Still pissed?" Jared asked. His eyes were glinting, as if he were on the verge of laughter.

That annoyed me. I'm not funny when I'm mad.

"Didn't anyone stop you from coming into the school?"

"Some woman. She was intense."

"Muriel."

"Perfect name for her." His grin widened. "You probably didn't even know that I'm your cousin from Philadelphia."

I straightened and didn't look at him. "Shouldn't I be pissed with you, *cuz?*"

He leaned against Meagan's locker, apparently thinking, and folded his arms across his chest. "It wasn't quite the reaction I'd hoped for."

"Then you shouldn't have screwed up everything when you got here."

I saw the flash of his irreverent smile. "True."

I made the mistake of looking at him when he made that concession and the warm glint in his eyes confused me all over again.

"Maybe I just didn't think it all through, Dragon Girl."

"Maybe you just like to make an entrance." I slammed my locker.

He fought a smile. "I do." Then he leaned closer, his proximity making me dizzy. "But maybe, Dragon Girl, you mess me up just about as much as I mess you up."

What?

That made me look at him. The notion of me having an effect on any guy, especially a guy like Jared, was radical enough to stop me cold.

He must have seen how it surprised me, but he just held my gaze steadily.

Willing me to believe him.

It took me a minute to find anything resembling coherence.

I glanced down the hall and saw Muriel watching.

Was Jared just telling me what I'd longed to hear?

"But notice that I haven't screwed up your life over it," I said, although my tone wasn't as frosty as planned.

He laughed. "Haven't you? I just bailed on my band again to come here and help you fix this *issue*. Trust me, they are not happy. There was some manager coming to hear us play tonight, and Angie nearly ripped my heart out when I said I wouldn't be there." He grimaced. "It's entirely possible that they are no longer *my* band."

I stared at him in shock. He'd trashed a chance for his band just to be here. I could understand Angie's frustration in a big way, but in a bigger way, I was impressed that he'd done that to help me. I shouldered my pack, well aware that my resistance was melting pronto. "You did that to come here?"

"I did that to help you, Zoë."

Why did he have to use my name? It was easier to keep my guard up when he called me Dragon Girl.

Okay, everything is relative. I still can't keep my guard up completely but it's still in the vicinity.

"I thought you didn't answer to anybody."

"I don't." He glanced up and down the hallway and I swear he looked surprised by what he was going to confess. "But I help the people I care about." He looked me in the eye, dead serious. "Like you."

I opened my mouth to argue, but the astonishing thing was that he was right. He had helped me solve the riddle, each and every time. He'd prompted me to try harder when we'd first met, then returned to help me fight the Mages. He'd sent me that book the second time, leaving a note in it to guide me to the answer.

Maybe he'd help me with this one.

I watched him warily. "That could be true only if you know the way to destroy the ShadowEaters."

His grin lit his features. "Bingo, Dragon Girl. I think I know how to get rid of them for good." His eyes glinted with satisfaction at my evident surprise; then he turned and strode down the corridor.

I ran after him like some besotted fan. "When exactly is it that you plan to start helping me?"

"Now."

"Are you going to tell me what you know?"

"No," he said, and I could have swatted him. "I'm going to *show* you."

"What about the NightBlade? Do you know how to break that?"

"First things first." He held the door for me, and stepping into the cold air made me catch my breath. It had nothing to do with my elbow brushing against his chest. "Let's go for a ride."

Riding with Jared on his motorcycle was every bit as exhilarating as I remembered. If anything, it was more exciting in the city, as he cut in and out of traffic with elegant ease. I halfway didn't want to bother him with questions, but there was so much I needed to know.

"How do you know this?" I asked finally, taking advantage of the fact that there were microphones and headsets in the helmets.

"There has to be some benefit of having been courted by the Mages for an apprenticeship."

Right. Jared was a natural spellsinger, like Meagan, and the Mages had tried to recruit him. That's why Derek didn't trust him at all. He said it wasn't clear how far Jared had progressed in the training and that we only had Jared's word on the fact that he'd declined to continue. And Jared had acknowledged that the Mages had been using him to get to me, even without his agreement.

I had a funny feeling then that maybe coming with Jared hadn't been the smartest choice.

That feeling redoubled when he parked the bike in front of that vacant lot.

It was the very same one. Same streetlight, trash can, locksmith, convenience store. I thought back to being trapped here by Trevor and Adrian, of the ShadowEaters biting my shadow, and shuddered in recollection.

"Not here," I said.

"Here," Jared insisted, and turned off the engine.

Before I could ask more, Jared marched to the edge of the sidewalk. He looked up, as if he were looking up the stairs of that library glamour I'd seen before. Then he propped his hands on his hips and began to hum.

It was a coaxing melody, as if he were enticing something to come out of the shadows, to reveal itself to him when it would have preferred otherwise. I could see the silvery light of his spell, like fireflies dancing amid the falling snowflakes, winking and glinting, tempting something to follow them.

And when I looked back up, the library was there again, just as substantial as it had appeared before.

"You summoned the glamour again," I said, astounded that he'd been able to do this. "How?"

"Spellsinging 201." He reached back and grabbed my hand, then started for the stairs.

I halted, fighting his grip. "Where are you going?"

"Inside the glamour."

"You can't do that. It'll ripple and disappear. It's not real." I pointed. "And what's behind it is dangerous. I nearly was consumed back there...."

Jared looked pointedly between me and the glamour. "Don't you want my help?"

I was way out of my depth, no matter which way you measured the distance to the shore. It wasn't much consolation that I knew it. "Yes, but not like this."

He tilted his head to study me. "I thought you trusted me. That's what you said before." His words were soft, as if he were surprised by the possibility of my not trusting him.

As if my not trusting him could change everything.

I was torn. I did trust Jared. I had told him that I trusted him, and I wanted that still to be true. But he wanted me to do something that I knew was dangerous.

And I wasn't nearly ready to attack the ShadowEaters. I had no plan. No understanding of their weakness. It was dumb to just leap in and hope for the best.

I extricated my hand from his and took another step back. "I do trust you," I said. "But you don't have all the information here. I've been in that glamour and I nearly died, and I'm not going to go in there willingly again."

His eyes narrowed. "Even if it might be the only way to accomplish what you seek to do?"

"Even then."

"Even if you didn't have all the weapons you needed last time, but you do now?"

I sighed. I swallowed.

I took a step back.

He half smiled and glanced away, then looked back at me, his eyes bright. "A dragon girl shouldn't be afraid."

"I'm not afraid. I'm learning from experience."

He lifted a brow, skeptical, and I knew we'd never agree on this. Probably because it wasn't strictly true. I was afraid. No, I was terrified. I had learned that from experience and I didn't think it was a bad thing to recognize when a choice could cost me my life.

But Jared was daring. Jared was reckless.

Maybe Jared had less to lose.

Or less to live for.

I felt that we were on opposite sides of an abyss, that there could be no middle ground. There was only one thing I could say.

"I'm sorry." I turned and walked away from him, past the bike and down the street, feeling the weight of his gaze as he watched me.

And when he finally started the bike again, its sound faded from earshot.

He rode in the opposite direction.

That was that.

But this time, I'd sent him out of my life.

Funny, but it didn't feel like much of an accomplishment.

I FEARED I couldn't go into that glamour and survive, not without a better plan, and I resented that Jared had expected me to do it at his request. On the other hand, I had a niggling sense that I'd made a big mistake by turning him down. I walked back to school to get my car, arguing both sides of it in my mind until I was sick of myself.

Eventually I heard the faint hum of a motorcycle, cutting in and out. I was sure it was the Ducati and I suspected that it was trailing behind me, even though I never caught a glimpse of Jared. The engine was throaty, maybe a bit unhappy to remain in a low gear. It both irritated me that Jared was following me and pleased me that he was sticking with me.

As usual, he was mixing me up in a very big way.

It was getting dark, though, and I was starting to glimpse the golden glint of the eyes of ShadowEaters in the periphery of my vision. When I looked straight at them, they faded from view, as if they'd never been.

As if I were imagining them.

But I could feel them.

And I could hear spellsong.

Faintly.

Hauntingly.

How many apprentice Mages did they have to divest of their shadows before they could attack me outright? Were they mustering power? Or waiting for an opportunity?

It took me a while to realize there was another song on the wind, mingling with the throaty purr of the Ducati's engine.

It was Jared. He was humming that song of his, the one called "Snow Goddess," the one I thought was about me.

That's what he was doing: trailing behind me and defending me with his spellsong. Keeping the ShadowEaters at bay.

Maybe I hadn't ditched him after all.

My heart did that stupid lurch thing where it leaps and practically sticks in my throat.

I finally reached the school, only to discover that the little red Toyota was parked all by its lonesome in the lot. It seemed to look particularly ill used, battered and sad. But it was mine. I was feeling a bit bashed up myself. Maybe we belonged together.

I got in and started it, turning up the heater to full blast. My fingers were too frozen to even compose anything on my messenger. I sat there, letting the ice in my veins thaw, and watched the spellsong swirl around the car. Orange, viney Mage spell light, interspersed with flickering purple Jared spell light. Jared's spells looked like barbed wire, with big nasty spikes. I had to like that.

I was so busy looking that I didn't see Suzanne, not until she rapped on the passenger's-door window. I nearly jumped out of my skin at the sound.

What she said astonished me even more.

"Hey, freak. Give me a ride." She yanked open the door and flung herself into the passenger's seat, treating me to a vicious glare. This made me wish I had locked the doors as soon as I'd gotten in. "Let's go already."

"Excuse me? I never offered you a ride."

"But Trevor is a no-show and I'm freezing my ass off, and you owe me big time."

I didn't move. "I don't owe you anything."

"Oh no? I could make your life miserable in so many ways, and you would deserve it. But give me a ride and we'll be friends."

I laughed. "With a friend like you, I wouldn't need enemies."

"Listen, bitch," she began, and pivoted to face me.

But I had had enough of Suzanne for one day. I turned on the beguiling flames pronto and she forgot whatever she was going to say.

Her mouth dropped open a little bit. "What's wrong with your eyes?" she asked, her voice already a bit dreamy. She was pretty suggestible, which worked for me.

"There's nothing wrong with my eyes," I said in my beguiling voice.

"Nothing wrong," she echoed, then shook her head and looked away. "This is some kind of freaky dragon trick you're trying to pull on me and it isn't going to work."

She reached for the door handle but I hit the power locks, glad yet again that my dad loves his toys. This car had nothing on the new sedan he'd parked at the airport.

Even with all its gadgetry, I didn't lust for the sedan, though. It was the ancient gas-powered Lamborghini that snared my heart and held fast.

"Hey!" Suzanne shouted, then turned to look at me again. I had the flames in my eyes turned up, ready for her, and smiled when she stared.

Caught.

"You didn't see anything in the bathroom today," I said, low and enticing.

Suzanne licked her lips, fighting the notion.

I tried another tack. "You got a shot of me naked."

"Naked," she echoed with satisfaction.

"Just to humiliate me."

Her eyes shone. "Just to humiliate you."

"But there was nothing strange about it."

"Nothing strange," she echoed softly.

"Just a skinny butt."

"Just a skinny butt." She said that with malice, savoring her advantage in the curve department over me.

I was tempted, you know, to shift shape in the car when she was trapped with me, to compel her to watch me make the change, just to find out whether some humans really could be driven insane by the sight of the transformation. I'd never done it really slowly, never lingered in it so there could be no doubt of what was happening, but wanted to now. Just for the sake of gathering evidence. Proving theories. For the better of *Pyr* and mankind.

But I stuck with beguiling.

Who says I'm not a good kid?

I dropped my voice an increment lower and made it softer. "There are no dragon shifters in our school."

She closed her eyes and I thought I'd lost her. Then she shuddered from head to toe and I saw how much that lie relieved her. "No dragon shifters in our school," she said, as if the weight of the world had slipped from her shoulders.

"Arty kids, losers, math whizzes, jocks. The usual variety."

She smiled. “The usual variety.”

“Nothing special at Ridgemont High.”

Her lip curled and she glanced at the school. “Nothing special at Ridgemont High.”

I let my voice become normal again. “So, you want a ride?”

Suzanne started, as if awakened from a long sleep, then glanced at me. “Well, there’s no one else around, is there? Beggars can’t be choosers.” She gave me an address on Riverside Drive.

I was pretty sure it was where Trevor lived, where we’d gone for the Halloween party. “You live there now?”

“No, freak. Trevor does. I’m going to find out who he thinks he is, leaving me standing in a snowstorm.”

I had to razz her a bit, make our exchange seem authentic. “Does he usually forget about you?”

Suzanne was annoyed with me and him. “He was supposed to meet me after his jazz session and give me a ride home, but there’s no sign of him.”

“Funny he’d do that. Maybe he’s got another girlfriend.”

“Be serious. I’m the best thing that ever happened to him.” She punched savagely at her messenger. “He’d better have a good excuse. I left my car at home today because of him, and passed on a ride from Trish in her new car.” She flicked me a look. “It’s not like I’d volunteer to be seen in this heap.”

“You have an interesting way of saying thanks,” I noted as I made to turn down Riverside Drive.

“Don’t go all the way to the house!” she instructed. “The last thing I need after this day is for Trevor to see me in this car with you.”

“You’re welcome,” I said tartly after I stopped at the corner.

She got out of the car, leaning down for one last taunt through the open door. “You should be thanking me,” she said. “I’m probably the most popular person you’ve ever had in your car.”

“So what?”

“So I have the Midas touch. This could change your social fortunes, Sorensson.”

“Not if no one sees you,” I smiled. “But it’s okay. Let’s keep both of our reputations intact.”

She slammed the door then, content that she’d won a round. Meanwhile, I was feeling triumphant that I'd secured my cover according to the Covenant.

One more item off my To Do list.

Too bad there were still so many more.

There was no chance of that depressing me. I watched Suzanne walk down the street, swinging her backpack onto her shoulder. To my surprise, a wraithlike shadow separated itself from the shadow beside a house. Suzanne started; then I overheard her greet Yvonne.

They walked together and I had time to think that they deserved each other before Yvonne glanced back at me. Her eyes shone gold as she smiled.

Then I blinked and she looked normal again.

I looked in my rearview mirror and caught a glimpse of a guy on a bike tagging behind me. I saw the gleam of Jared's protective spell and the sight of both made my heart skip a beat.

It was true that he didn't have all of the information, but neither did I. I knew just about nothing about spellsingers.

Maybe if we pooled our data, we could find a solution.

Maybe it was just an excuse to talk to him again.

Maybe I didn't care.

I WALKED into the little park opposite the Jamesons' town house after I'd parked the car, relieved to be within shouting distance of dinner. I wasn't quite ready to go in, not when I had questions for Jared. I could hear the thrum of the bike trailing behind me still and see the wispy tendrils of Jared's spell wafting around me. It was like a gossamer net, spun out of sapphires and amethysts, protecting me but not confining me.

There was so much I didn't know about spellsong, so much I would probably never understand. His spells could be so many different colors and shapes. All I knew for sure was that Mage binding spells were orange.

I turned to face him, staring at the silhouette of his figure on the motorcycle at the end of the block. He didn't move closer, just braced his heels on the ground. Waiting. Giving me space. Not expecting me to answer to him, either.

Could he read my thoughts, even at this distance?

"What are they?" I asked. "The ShadowEaters?"

He took that as encouragement to ride the bike closer, then turned off the engine when he was beside me. He didn't get off the bike and he didn't have his helmet on.

"They're Mages who took the last rite."

So the Bastians had it right. "Their book calls it metamorphosis."

He nodded, scanning our surroundings even as he listened to me, humming when he wasn't talking. He hummed a little harder before he answered me, buttressing his spell, then spoke quickly. "By eliminating species of shifters, they assume the powers of the shifters that are no more. They also strengthen their own ability to shift between forms." He glanced around us, looking worried, so I tried to fill in the gaps.

"I've seen Adrian rotate between forms," I said, and Jared hummed some more. "He can take the shapes of all the eliminated shifters. Or he could until he became a ShadowEater."

"But he couldn't hold any of those forms for long. It was a fleeting transformation."

I nodded. "He held the other human form for a while at boot camp."

"A sign of his prowess. The more proficient the Mage, the longer he or she can hold a form. They all max out around a week, and it completely wears them out."

"And the metamorphosis?"

"Is an advanced rite for full Mages to move to the next stage. They were supposed to become immortal and move beyond the constraints of the physical realm."

"But that's not what happened."

He shook his head. "They did it too soon, I think, before they had mastered all the necessary skills. Instead they got stuck halfway between human and immortals."

"Can they take other shapes?"

"No. They have only their former human skins, filled with spell light." He grimaced, hummed a bit more. "I don't think they understood fully what it meant to fulfill the rite. The ritual talks about joining the divine and becoming divine."

"But it's not very divine. They're predators, always hungry for more shadows, at least from what I've seen."

Jared smiled. "It wouldn't be the first time that the advance publicity oversold the attraction."

I smiled back, unable to help myself. "But was there just one group who did it? Is that where they all came from?"

"The story is that there was a mass rite several hundred years ago. All of the full Mages participated, thinking they were going to change the world. And all of them transformed into ShadowEaters."

"You never told me that part."

"I thought it was a bullshit story—you know, the kind of thing they'd made up to make being a Mage sound cool. I never really believed that ShadowEaters had been created from human Mages."

"But I saw Adrian do it."

He nodded ruefully. "So it was true. Which explains why all you shifters thought they weren't an issue. Essentially they would have disappeared, all at once."

I nodded. That made sense to me. "So, the power surge from eliminating all shifters would catapult the newer Mages into that divine immortality, as well as the Mages already trapped as ShadowEaters. So what happens if they succeed in becoming pure spirit?"

He exhaled. "A universe filled with powerful malice, instead of striving toward goodwill and peace." He met my gaze. "Probably one without shifters."

Right.

He frowned at the bike. "Not a place I want to visit, much less live."

It didn't sound as if I'd have a chance to live there.

Jared's expression was grim. "There has to be a way to beat them, Dragon Girl."

It would have been nice to have known how.

The glint of golden eyes was clearer now in the shrubbery at the perimeter of the park, and even with Jared's spell enfolding me like butterfly wings, I shivered at the sight of them. It seemed to me that I could hear them salivating, and felt them drawing closer. I could see tendrils of spell light inching toward me, easing along the ground like thick vines. One dared to breach Jared's spell and sparks flew from the point of contact. The Mage spell fell back, singed, but three more tendrils took its place, edging closer.

I knew I would dream of them enfolding me, snaring me, squeezing me, sucking the life out of me and offering my shadow to the ShadowEaters.

"I should go in," I said.

"No lock can protect you from them." Jared was serious. "Should dragons be afraid of what needs to be done?"

"I'm not afraid," I insisted, but we both knew it was a lie. "I just need more information before I risk my life. I need to have a plan."

He watched me, humming, cutting me no slack.

I threw out my hands. "I'd built a team. I had everyone working together. Then you came along and scared Derek away, made it sound like I have to do everything myself. That's not leading. That's sacrificing."

"Don't Wyverns sacrifice their self-interest for the good of everyone else?"

"That's what the last Wyvern did," I said, my tone bitter. "I'm not quite ready to die."

Jared said nothing. He held my gaze for a long moment, then bent to start the bike. "Suit yourself," he said quietly. "You don't have to answer to me."

I knew I'd disappointed him, but it wasn't as if he hadn't disappointed me a few times. I stood there and watched him ride away, knowing I was safe—for the moment—within his spell.

But as soon as he rounded the corner, I ran for the house. I was sure there were Mage spells pursuing me, but when I locked the door and looked through the peephole, all I saw was a cloud of golden eyes gleaming in the darkness.

MEAGAN AND GARRETT and Liam were at the dining room table. Mrs. Jameson was in the kitchen, and dinner smelled good. Vegetarian lasagna, maybe. Even though I hadn't thought I was hungry, I realized I hadn't eaten much all day. The looks of relief on their faces reminded me that I hadn't checked my messenger, either.

"You okay?" Liam asked, getting up when I appeared. "We were worried about you."

"I know. I'm sorry."

"You're late," Meagan said, her expression filled with concern.

"I was with Jared," I admitted, shedding my coat and taking a seat.

"I knew we had to trust you," Garrett said. "That you'd let us know if you needed help."

"But the thing is, we've found something," Meagan said. "We broke the code on that book!"

"Not we—Meagan broke the code," Garrett corrected.

"You mean the book about Mages and their spells that you found in the fall?" I asked. "The one that was in Latin and in code, too?"

"Right. We'd translated the Latin, but never broke the code. Until today." Garrett nodded and nudged Meagan, his expression filled with admiration. "Tell her."

Meagan blushed, pushed her glasses up her nose, flicked a look at Garrett, then back at me. "It's about music, just like we thought, but it's specifically about *musica universalis*."

"Should I know what that means?"

"The music of the spheres," Liam contributed. "Pythagoras wrote about it originally. For him, the harmony of the spheres was about celestial sounds emitted by the planets, each one harmonic with the others because their orbits were in proportion."

"You know that?" I asked him, surprised.

He grinned. "I've learned it today."

Garrett continued. "The idea is that there's perfect harmony in the heavens and that we should emulate that here on earth."

"Okay. But I don't understand the *harmony*."

"Pythagoras is the one who discovered the mathematical relationship between pitch and the length of the string on a stringed instrument, which led him to conclude that harmonious sounds can be mathematically calculated."

I was lost and it must have shown on my face.

Garrett grabbed a sheet of paper and drew a sine wave. I remembered that from math class. Then he drew vertical lines, one at the beginning of the wave and a second where it started to repeat. "That's one interval," he said, and I nodded. Then he drew a second sine wave, one that had two repetitions in the same linear distance.

"That one's half as long," I said.

"If it's exactly half as long, these two notes will be in perfect harmony."

"But these are graphs," I protested.

"Which represent tones." Meagan went to the piano. She played a note, then a second one. When she played them together, I could hear the way they vibrated together in a very sweet kind of harmony.

"Wow. But what does this have to do with ShadowEaters?"

"The Mages figured out that if you have four harmonic tones in unison, it invokes power," Garrett said. "Their book is all about those four perfect notes, how to sing them purely, how to add them together, then what to do once you have that chorus."

Liam leaned closer. "Even better, it's how they made the NightBlade out of the stone from a meteorite."

"It's the weakness Kohana was looking for. It's how we can break the NightBlade," I guessed.

They all nodded. "As long as the power we summon isn't stolen by the ShadowEaters for their own purpose," Meagan added.

Cheerful thought.

"Do you know what the notes are?"

Meagan shook her head. "It's obviously a secret passed down orally through the generations. It's never defined in the book."

"Or at least we haven't found it yet," Garrett added.

Meagan frowned. "It'd be hard to get pure harmonic notes with the human voice and to hold them for long enough to achieve anything. I'd think they'd each train for one note."

"We'll figure it out," Garrett said.

I had a thought and leaned across the table. "Isn't your mom surprised to have the guys here?"

They all clearly thought this was funny, because their eyes danced with mischief. Meagan grinned. "Garrett told her that we had an assignment together, that he and Liam were new here and needed extra tutoring."

"You beguiled her," I accused Garrett, and saw the truth in his quick smile.

"Just a little. For the greater good."

"But what about later?"

"We'll guard from the roof," Liam said.

I shook my head. "You'd better ask Jared for some spell protection.

They're out there and they took other shifters last night. I don't want to lose you guys."

"I'll ask him," Meagan said, and pulled out her messenger to do it. "He can teach me the spell and we'll weave it together."

"Does Jared know the four notes?" I asked. "Or one of them?"

Meagan shook her head as she kept tapping. "I already asked."

"That part is up to us," Garrett said.

It was like a riddle, but one I had very little chance of solving on my own.

There was an optimistic thought to end the day.

"Has anyone heard from Derek?" I asked, ever hopeful, but they shook their heads as one. Everyone had messaged him, so now I tried, too.

I seriously hoped I hadn't offered up the next sacrificial victim.

I SLEPT with Skuld's shears under my pillow, one hand locked around them.

Just in case.

10

I shivered in the night, feeling the cold chill of snow slip down the back of my shirt. I tugged the comforter up higher, trying to block the icy fingers of the wind, and squeezed my eyes shut. I held on tight to the shears. I really didn't want to visit Skuld and her sisters. I thought maybe I could ignore the whole dream interlude.

No luck. A finger poked me in the shoulder. Hard.

"You think I can't tell when you're awake?" There was a thread of humor in Skuld's tone. "Come on, Wyvern. You have work to do. No ShadowEaters will get you on my watch."

I felt her move away, obviously expecting me to follow. The absence of her presence was as formidable as the weight of her gaze on me. I felt a huge yawning void behind me, dared to be relieved that she was gone, then caught a whiff of carrion.

It wasn't her absence that made the air seem still.

It was that the wind had completely stopped. I sat up and looked.

Skuld *was* gone.

I think. The thing was that I couldn't see very much very clearly. I was surrounded by a blanket of white fog, fog that glistened slightly, as if illuminated by a source I couldn't see. I stood up with reluctance, the hairs standing up on the back of my neck. That smell of rot was pervasive and troubling. I recalled Skuld's affection for battlefields and had an idea where I might be.

I looked down and yelped. I was standing on a pile of corpses. There was blood staining the ground, the smell of putrefaction in my nostrils, gaping wounds and spilled guts and eyes staring at nothing everywhere I looked.

Suddenly, being without Skuld didn't seem like such a good idea. I thought I heard something ahead of me and to the right, so I ran that way. I winced as bits crunched under my feet, knowing they were bones and teeth and skulls.

For once in my life, I wished I'd worn boots to bed.

My bile rose along with my panic. My state was such that spotting Skuld striding through the detritus as if she were going to pick up the mail was a relief. I raced after her and she must have heard me coming, because she paused and turned to watch me approach. There was humor in her eyes, as if I were the crazy one.

I gagged when I saw the eyeball impaled on the end of her knife.

She laughed at me, then ate it off the tip of the blade, chewing with gusto. "Thought you were too tired after your day of doing nothing," she said, arching a brow.

I had to look away, look anywhere but at her with her gleaming eyes and those squishy pink eye bits between her teeth as she smiled.

"I didn't do nothing today," I protested, trying to defend myself. "I fought the ShadowEaters even before the sun was up."

"But not when you could have beaten them," Skuld said, giving me a significant glance.

"They could have captured me with their spells if I'd gone into that glamour. It would have been reckless and stupid."

"Bold," she said, bending to examine a corpse. The person had been decapitated and Skuld showed a keen interest in the severed head. She slit the rotting skin, poked her knife into a fissure between the bones, and used it to widen the gap. I nearly retched.

"It would have been stupid," I said.

"It's stupid to forget your assets." She gave me a steady glance, munching on a treat from the decapitated body. The corpse's staring eyes seemed to look at me, too. "I'm going to stop giving you gifts if you forget to use them."

"Where are they now?"

"Hovering." She peered into the distance, chewing. "They prefer to hunt when you're all asleep, but that will change as they get stronger." She finished her snack and tossed the head like a baseball before turning to stride on. I glanced after the discarded head and caught my breath.

Because it had landed beside a corpse that looked just like Derek.

I charged through the debris with purpose, needing to know for sure. I dropped to my knees in front of the body, not caring about the muck anymore.

It *was* Derek and that truth made me whimper. His pale blue eyes were wide open, staring up at the sky. His heart was silenced. I touched his shoulder, unable to believe my eyes, but his skin was cold. His hoodie was torn and I looked down to see that his chest had been ripped open and his guts were spilled on the ground.

Then I did puke.

"You'll know this one, too," Skuld said with an ease I wasn't nearly feeling. She seized my shoulder when I didn't move and dragged me through blood and bodies to another corpse.

Garrett, frozen forever in a grimace of pain. As still as a sculpture. His body was shredded, just like Derek's. I saw with horror that he cast no shadow.

"No," I whispered.

"Sure," Skuld corrected me easily. "Take a good look at the future, Wyvern." She strode away then, content to leave me to take it all in.

They were all there. It didn't take me long to find them. King and Mozart and Jessica, Liam and Garrett and Nick, Derek and Kohana. They were all mixed up, their bodies tangled with each other and various parts torn away. There were other corpses mingled with them and I guessed that these were the shifters of their kinds, the ones I didn't know. I saw the kid brothers of Liam and Garrett and Nick, too, the *Pyr* who were just coming into their powers. I saw all of the older *Pyr* I knew and loved, every single one of them slaughtered and dead.

So many dead shifters. The future was a battlefield covered with fallen shifters. It had to be all of them, really, except for me. I had to put my head between my knees for a minute at the prospect of being all alone.

When I opened my eyes, I saw a dragon talon severed from the claw. It was so covered in blood that I couldn't even identify the original color.

I pushed to my feet and shouted after Skuld. "Why? Why are you showing me this?"

My cry echoed and I realized that the air was ridiculously still. There was destruction in every direction, fog obscuring the distance, but the only movement came from me and Skuld.

The only life.

She turned to peruse me, still chewing. "Because you let it happen, of course. Do you think I show you these things for my own amusement?"

"I wouldn't put it past you. There are a lot of livers here."

She smiled and sighed, nudging a body with her boot. "And more than one good soul." She gave me an intent look, as if I were missing something important.

That was when I saw that the corpse she considered seemed to be me.

Impossible!

I marched to her side in terror and denial, forcing my way through the fallen, needing a closer look. It *was* me, wearing my fave black jacket and boots, silver rings on my fingers and my earlobes, my body ripped open and my guts spilled on the ground.

Utterly still.

One hand was missing.

That had been *my* dragon claw I'd found twenty feet away.

"What did I do?"

She shook her head. "No, Wyvern. The question is what *didn't* you do." With one last intent look, she spun on her heel and walked away. She moved really fast, covering distance in a major way with her long strides, but I tried to run after her.

"But what was that?" I shouted. "Does this have to happen? What can I do to prevent it? You have to tell me!"

Skuld was a hundred feet away, on the verge of being swallowed by the fog. "I don't have to tell you anything," she said softly, her words carrying to my ears with a ghostly echo. "But let me ask you this: What would you die for? What would you die to save, Wyvern? Is there anything that matters that much to you?"

Then she was gone, her marching figure swallowed by the fog. I yelled and raced after her, squinting my eyes shut as the fog took on a brilliant radiance. It shone on all sides of me with fierce white light and turned hot, as if I had stepped into the middle of the sun.

And with the heat, the ground beneath my feet softened. I sank down, knee-deep in corpses and blood. I tried to shift shape but my shimmer was AWOL. I tried to manifest elsewhere but no luck.

Meanwhile, the muck was pulling me down. It was like quicksand, sucking at me, dragging me deeper. The more I struggled, the faster I sank. Everything I could reach to grab for support was part of a body, soft and putrid.

The smell of rot assailed me. I fought as I sank deeper and deeper, to my waist, to my shoulders. In no time, the sickly soup of corpses was right beneath my nose and I knew my next breath would be disgusting.

How long could I hold my breath?

How could I escape?

Why couldn't I shift shape?

I shouted for Skuld, fearing she wouldn't help me.

I was right.

I WOKE UP, panting and terrified in Meagan's room, my fists clutching the sheets.

I was safe, but that was by no means a permanent situation or a guarantee, given what Skuld had shown me. Meagan was sleeping soundly. I looked out the window and I saw the glimmer of purple spell light spun by Meagan and Jared, wound around the house.

I thought I could see zillions of ShadowEater eyes gleaming in the darkness behind it.

I got up, shut the drapes, and perched on the side of the bed. What would I die for? I thought of my afternoon adventure with Jared and knew that I had chosen wrong. I hadn't entered the glamour because I'd been afraid, afraid for my own survival. I'd been more worried about myself than for my friends and the world around me.

Yet Meagan and Jared had spun spell light to protect me while I slept.

Thanks to Skuld, I now knew what I'd die for.

I could only hope I hadn't missed my only chance to get it right.

Meagan's mom was freaking by the morning. The body count was up—four more bodies had been found. Meagan was surreptitiously checking her messenger, trying to determine whether they were all Mages and apprentice Mages, or whether the ShadowEaters had gotten any shifters, too. Nick and Liam were okay, and headed off to guard Isabelle for the day.

I didn't want to send Jared a message, even though I was determined to see him. Actually, it was because I was determined to see him that I didn't ping him. Experience had taught me that Jared blew me off when I sent him a message. I didn't want to warn him that I was looking for him and have him disappear.

Again.

It's entirely possible that this time would be different, that this time he would hold his ground and wait for me, but there was too much at stake for me to bet on that. Jared came to me when it suited him, or he disappeared. I needed to find him before he could take off.

So I asked Meagan where he was staying and she told me that he was crashing at a hostel popular with musicians. It wasn't that far away, so I decided to go there first thing.

I'd chosen my acid-green wrap, the one I'd been wearing the first time I'd met Jared, and knotted it around my neck. I told myself that I'd grabbed it because it was warm but I also knew it makes my eyes look greener.

Black jeans, black jacket, black sweater, black boots, black eyeliner, purple gloves, lots of silver jewelry, and I was ready for anything. Pretty much. At the last minute, I rummaged in the bottom of my overnight bag and got the red rune stone Granny had given me in a dream almost a year before. Who knew if I might need it again? Skuld's shears had place of pride in my backpack.

Meagan nodded when I met her at the door, and I knew she knew what I was up to. We drove in silence together.

At least until Sigmund showed up.

"Message for you," he said, suddenly leaning over the seat from the back. His head was right between us, and I was so surprised that the car swerved.

"What's wrong?" Meagan asked, reaching for the wheel.

"You need to stop doing that," I complained.

"What do you mean?" Meagan asked. "We'll end up on the sidewalk!"

"Not you. Him."

Sigmund chuckled.

Meagan shrank back, leaning against the car door as she stared at me. "Who?"

"Sigmund."

Then she took such a careful survey of our surroundings that I knew she couldn't see Sigmund. "And where exactly is Sigmund?"

"In the backseat." I had to lean around his head to make eye contact with her. Meagan flicked a glance at the road, and I focused on driving.

"There's nobody else in the car, Zoë," Meagan said with care.

As if she were talking to a crazy person.

Sigmund chuckled. "Told you," he said, gloating.

I could have slugged him, but I spoke to Meagan. "I'm not losing it. My dead brother, Sigmund, is here, in the backseat, trying to make me think I'm going nuts."

Meagan looked pointedly at the backseat. "Did you get enough sleep last night?"

"No. But that doesn't change the fact that he's here."

Sigmund was killing himself laughing by this point—no pun intended.

"Do you often talk to dead people?" Meagan asked.

"Just Sigmund. He's kind of irritating like that." I thought for a minute. "And the *Wakiya* elder."

Meagan nodded, thought about it, and clearly decided to go with it. "So, is there a point to his being here?"

I had to think about it for a moment, to remember what he said. Also, I was changing lanes. "He has a message, apparently." I stopped at a red light, then turned to Sigmund, ignoring the triumphant glint in his eyes. "You'll notice that she doesn't think I'm crazy."

"Yet," he acknowledged with a grin.

"Who's the message from? And what is it?" We were about a block from school, at the corner where I'd have to turn left to go to the hostel. Meagan would go right to the school, which we could see. Kids were arriving slowly, some being dropped off at the curb by their parents, others driving their own cars into the student lot.

I stopped at the curb, parking there for Meagan to get out, then turned to look at Sigmund. Meagan watched me, expectant.

"This is so good," Sigmund said. He winked, then got all gooey. Really, he looked as if he were melting. His hair and his eyes and his nose dripped like wax from a burning candle. I couldn't help but stare. Everything about him dripped and morphed and slid into something else.

Right before my eyes, he became Kohana.

"Well, if you're not going to tell me, I'm going to class," Meagan said, and opened the car door.

I kept staring into the backseat, fascinated and horrified. Sigmund-Kohana grinned, that provocative grin so characteristic of Kohana, his dark eyes glinting. "Hey, *Unktehila*," he said, and waved two fingers at me.

Was this another glamour? Was I talking to Sigmund or Kohana?

If it was a glamour, who had created it?

Or was Kohana dead, too?

I must have looked shocked at the idea, as shocked as I felt.

"Zoë?" Meagan asked, concern in her tone as she leaned back into the car. "Are you okay?" I didn't know what to say, not until Sigmund-Kohana delivered his message.

To my astonishment, he tipped his head back and sang a single note with all his might.

It vibrated in my ears, so resonant and clear that I knew I'd never forget it. The glass globe on the exterior light of the apartment building next to us exploded suddenly, and Kohana's singing stopped.

He winked and disappeared.

Just like he'd never been there.

"Oh, my God!" Meagan shouted. "How did you do that?"

"I didn't." In fact, I couldn't believe it had even happened. I turned off the car and got out, going to the lamp. The glass was broken, all right, shards all over the concrete walk. I looked at the matching light on the other side of the apartment building doors. It was still vibrating slightly. When I leaned close, I could even hear it moving in the fixture.

"Is that cool or what?" Sigmund whispered in my ear. There was no sign of him or of Kohana, and Meagan was looking at me as if I were bonkers.

Maybe I was. I was a bit freaked myself by the way Sigmund had changed into Kohana.

No. Meagan had heard it, too.

"But you heard it, right?" I asked Meagan. She nodded, then looked determined. She pushed up her glasses, eyed the broken light fixture, then emitted a perfect echo of the note Kohana had sung. She held that note as I watched the globe on the second fixture vibrate with greater and greater intensity.

Then the light shattered just as the first had done.

I was no less shocked the second time.

"It's mathematics," Meagan said matter-of-factly. "The result of creating a sine wave that induces a vibration. The oscillation can be too much for the physical item that is echoing the frequency, like that old bridge video we saw in physics class. The wind set up a resonance that vibrated the bridge apart."

I did remember that vaguely. I'd thought it was faked.

She smiled, seeing that I didn't entirely follow her explanation. "What happened? What didn't I see?"

I told her and was relieved—if surprised—that she believed me.

"Don't be ridiculous, Zoë," she said, noting my surprise. "I heard it, too, and I know you can't sing, let alone hold a note like that. Do you think it was really Kohana?"

"I don't know what to think. Sigmund tends to be enigmatic, but pretty much everything he has told me has proven to be true." I frowned and made the inevitable observation. "I'm wondering whether Kohana is dead."

"Why? Because Sigmund is dead and Sigmund brought him along?"

I nodded.

Meagan frowned at the ground for a moment and I could almost hear her thinking. "But you've dreamed of Kohana before. You said before that he could move in dreams."

"Maybe he's in trouble. He was trying to trick the apprentice Mages and he was determined to get the NightBlade back. Maybe they caught him."

Meagan pursed her lips. "Maybe Kohana's giving us one note of the harmonic sequence to destroy the NightBlade."

"Maybe. But there has to be more to it than that," I said. "Just playing or singing those notes can't be enough, or Kohana would have done it himself." I squared my shoulders and looked back at the car. "I need a spellsinger. Wish me luck."

"Luck," Meagan said with a smile. "Let me know if you need help. I'll keep working on this and see what I can come up with. Maybe I can figure out the other notes."

We parted ways. She headed on to school and I took my detour to the hostel.

I wouldn't think about Muriel or what might result from my choice to cut class. I wouldn't think about what my dad might have to say about me choosing to seek out Jared. I wasn't going to think about how I'd blown it with Derek, or fret about the plans that the ShadowEaters had for destroying us.

I had to save the world instead.

IT WASN'T SNOWING for once, and the sky was a clear crisp blue. The air was cold enough to freeze your lungs in one breath, and once I got off the main streets, the snow squeaked under the tires. When I parked and got out of the car, I saw that the driveway to the hostel hadn't been shoveled. I was glad to have my black boots with the serious treads, not just because they look awesome but because they give great traction.

The hostel was in an old house, what had once been the grande dame of the block but was now showing some neglect. It had three stories and stood apart from its neighbors. There was a driveway down one side and a carriage house at the back of the lot. The carriage house had a definite lean to the right.

It was so quiet that the house itself might have been slumbering.

I realized a bit late that Jared was probably a night person and might still be asleep. My imagination busily conjured images of Jared bare chested, my dragon tattooed on his back. From there it was easy to imagine more, but I'll spare you the details. Suffice it to say that I didn't find it that chilly any longer.

I had climbed the ancient steps to the front door and raised my hand to the bell when I heard the sputter of a motorcycle engine. Then there was a clanking sound, a definite obscenity, and the clatter of tools. I could smell oil mingled with Jared's scent.

You know my heart skipped at that.

The sounds were coming from behind the house.

I peered around the house, down the driveway, noting that there was a single line of bike tracks in the snow as well as a trodden-down footpath. It looked like people used the back door, which was why I'd had to break a trail up the steps. As I walked down the driveway, the smell of oil grew stronger, as did the sound of muttering.

I rounded the corner to find Jared there with his bike, glaring at it. He had a wrench in one hand, and his hair was standing up in spikes. He was wearing jeans and a long-sleeved T-shirt, despite the cold, and he looked mad enough to spit. There was a cloth spread across the snow and lots of what must have been engine parts spread across it.

"Mechanical problems?" I asked, savoring the way he jumped.

It's easy to forget when you hang with shifters that humans don't have such sharp senses as we do. We're harder to surprise or sneak up on—although Derek manages to do it to me—and I found it pretty satisfying to have surprised Jared.

For once.

Then he surprised me with the warmth that lit his eyes. "You changed your mind," he said, admiration in his voice. It had to be a guess, but there was no doubt in his manner. "I knew you would, Dragon Girl."

"How'd you know?" I came around the back porch of the house, sizzling as I stepped closer to him, pretending to be fascinated by his bike. It was safer than meeting his gaze, especially if he was going to be saying nice things to me.

"You have more strength than you realize, but sometimes you spook when I surprise you. I thought you'd come around with a bit of time." He flicked a glance at me. "Took less than expected." I caught his grin, saw pride in it, and got interested in my boots.

"Thanks for the spell light."

He nodded once in acknowledgment, then crouched down beside the bike, his expression rueful. "I hate gears. I've had problems with third ever since I got this bike. Doesn't matter how many times I replace the parts or reassemble it."

I crouched down beside him, relieved to be talking about something else. "Have you asked Donovan?" I asked. Nick's dad had sold the bike to Jared. "I mean, it was his bike before. Maybe he knows the trick."

Jared grinned. "He said he wondered whether it would give me trouble, too. He said it had always been that way, as long as he'd had the bike, and he'd been starting to think it had something personal against him."

I laughed. "That doesn't make sense."

"No. Especially as it has the same grudge against me." He surveyed the array of parts and chose one.

"So, you know how to put all this back together?"

"It's like a jigsaw puzzle, Zoë. And now I've done it so often I could do it in my sleep. I keep hoping the next time will be the trick."

Who would have guessed he was so persistent?

Jared started to work then, frowning in concentration as he fitted the parts together. I sat down on the back steps of the house, brushing off some of the snow first. From the look of them, the wooden steps had been painted a couple of hundred times, but all the layers were peeling. It was strangely peaceful in the backyard, only power lines and telephone poles breaking the view of the backs of other houses, their windows blank.

I propped my chin on my hands and watched Jared work. He moved decisively and worked quickly, so certain of each choice. He had clearly done it a lot, because the reassembly was almost choreographed.

"What changed your mind?" he asked softly.

"I had a dream of what the future might be if I didn't act."

He flashed me a smile. "Hey, Wyvern."

I smiled back, but only for a second. "Well, I almost died there on Wednesday."

"What?" He pivoted to look at me, his work forgotten.

"Trevor lured me there, saying he wanted my help to stop Adrian from performing a ceremony he didn't understand. But they did perform it, and they needed a sacrifice, and..."

"They tried to make it you."

I shivered and nodded, then told him the rest. He was thinking more about the story than his gears; I could see that.

"How'd you get away?"

"Manifesting elsewhere."

He nodded slowly, although I wasn't sure whether he was thinking about what I'd said or the gear box. "That's uncommon among shifters, you know. I think you might be the only one who can do it. The other species must have forgotten."

"Maybe they didn't ever know. We wild cards seem to have different powers, both from our own kind and from each other."

He bent down beside the bike again, and it wasn't my imagination that his brow was even more furrowed. "That has to be important," he murmured. "No wonder you didn't want to go in."

I told him what had happened the next night, and he asked to see Skuld's shears. Jared surveyed the shears. He didn't touch them; just had a good look then went back to the bike.

"The answer has to be something about us wild cards," I mused, drumming my fingers on my knees. "They seem to be targeting us but waiting for something."

"Maybe all of you to be together. Maybe the effect is even greater if you're all finished off simultaneously."

I stared at Jared, hearing the resonance of truth in his words. "Do you know that?"

"Just a guess."

But it was a good one.

"There's a lot of old lore about the entrapment of shifters," he said quietly. "I should have paid more attention to it when they were trying to recruit me."

"Why didn't you?"

He shrugged. "I like my own freedom too much to ever want to snare anybody." He turned and looked at me, his eyes filled with invitation. "I like it better when shifters come to me."

Our gazes locked and held then and I felt the temperature rise in that yard. I could have fallen into his eyes forever, with all their umpty-gazillion shades of green. My heart started to do that wild dragon thing of matching its beat to his, and I felt our breath synchronize, too. It makes me dizzy when that happens, although I realized then that it wasn't a sign of kismet as much as it reflected my own attraction.

And I could—apparently—be attracted to more than one guy at a time.

The feeling was more powerful with Jared, though, and I wondered whether it was just that I didn't know him as well or whether we really did have a stronger connection. I wondered whether I was ever going to know, and sighed as I deliberately looked away.

"What's bothering you?" he asked, focused on his bike again.

"What do you mean?"

"Something's bugging you. I noticed it yesterday. Come on, spill it. The bike won't be fixed for a few minutes yet."

"We could go in my car."

"It'll wait a few minutes."

"Are you afraid, too?" I asked on impulse.

His gaze flicked to me and back to the bike, so quickly that another person might have missed it. I heard his quick intake of breath, too, and felt the jump in his pulse.

He wasn't certain of what would happen.

Maybe this was an opportunity to learn more. To go in armed with more data. I watched Jared for a minute and remembered that he was the one who seemed to know the most about dragon lore—well, other than my dead brother, Sigmund. That was probably because he'd had Sigmund's book on the *Pyr* for a while and read it repeatedly.

Maybe he knew something more about Wyvern stuff.

"It's this Wyvern thing," I admitted, shamelessly fishing.

"Sounds like you've been working at it."

"It's the future part that isn't happening. Plus Sigmund says that this part of a Wyvern's evolution or development can drive a Wyvern insane."

"That's not very encouraging."

"No. It's not. But he's like that."

"Wait a minute. Sigmund who?"

"Guthrie. My older brother." Jared glanced up, surprised. "Yes, the dead one who turned *Slayer* and wrote that book you had, mostly to piss off our dad."

"Probably worked, given what I know of Erik."

I nodded.

"So, you're talking to dead people, then?"

"Only Sigmund. And only when he feels like it." I left out the bits about the *Wakiya* elder and Kohana's appearance this morning. I'd noticed before that there was something electric between Kohana and Jared. No need to spoil the moment.

He straightened and flashed me a grin. "That's reassuring."

"Is it?"

"It's got to be better to talk to a limited group of dead people, in terms of your sanity, than all the dead people ever."

I threw a snowball at him. Jared laughed and ducked.

I stretched out my legs, trying to explain my frustration to him. "The thing is that I'm supposed to be able to see the past, the present, and the future simultaneously, but I never really know what's going to happen."

He cast me a glance. "Never?"

I blushed then and looked down. "Well, not about important stuff."

Jared smiled. "So you're in good company. Nobody else can see the future, either."

"But I'm supposed to be able to! I'm the Wyvern."

"I don't understand why you'd want to see it," he countered, surprising me a bit.

"Doesn't everybody want to know what's going to happen?"

"Only superficially." He straightened and faced me, gesturing with a greasy motorcycle part in one hand. "I mean, if you could see your whole future, every choice and its consequence, every seemingly random event, every single thing that was going to happen to you before you die, then what would be the point of living? You could just look at it all, like watching a movie, then say, 'Oh, that's that,' and die."

"Not funny."

"I'm not joking." He bent down beside the bike again. "What if you can't see the future because it's filled with a thousand possibilities? What if it's a network of choices influencing events? What if choosing one path closes off another? What if it's not a fixed destination but a realm of possibilities?" He glanced up. "What if the only way to see the future is to live it?"

"Then what about this Wyvern ability?"

"Maybe what the Wyvern sees is the array of possibilities that can result from a single choice." He shrugged. "Maybe she can see where this decision will lead, based maybe on the other decisions being made simultaneously. Maybe it's a very short-term thing, this vision of the future."

"Two minutes' warning, max," I said, thinking of Derek.

Jared glanced up, apparently recognizing my reference. "That's the wolf's gig, isn't it?" I nodded, and there was suddenly a bit of tension between us.

"So, are you dating him?" Jared was trying to sound indifferent, but he blew it completely. He was deeply interested. I heard it in his voice, which was thrilling.

Once again, I felt a strange sense of personal power, an inkling that my choices were part of whatever resulted from this discussion. Was Jared right? I stretched out my legs, acting casual about it, knowing I was anything but. "Sort of." I took a deep breath. "He's a good friend and a nice guy. He's here and he's intense and there are no games."

Jared smiled. "That future is clear?"

I bristled at his tone, thinking—rightly—that he was criticizing Derek for being predictable. And that irritated me because Derek was predictable and it wasn't one of the things that attracted me to him. I did like Jared's adventurousness.

"He's direct," I said, hearing my own defensiveness. "I like that."

Jared straightened then and turned to confront me. His eyes flashed with unexpected annoyance. "Direct? That's what you like now?"

"It's better than not having a clue what someone is thinking. It's better than never hearing anything at all!"

"I told you about Donovan's warning!"

"I don't believe that you would change your mind about anything you really wanted to do, regardless of who told you not to do it. Even Donovan." I stood up. "I believe that you didn't call me because you didn't want to see me."

Jared didn't like that. He didn't like it one bit.

His lips tightened for a minute; then he pointed at me. "You want direct? Here's direct. You're sixteen. I haven't been for a while. That makes you jailbait, and I'm not going to have any more dealings with cops ever again. And if you don't think that changes my choices, then you can think again." He pivoted to crouch down beside the bike, his body vibrating with anger.

Why hadn't I thought of that?

I watched him for a few minutes, the silence charged between us, and knew he wasn't going to speak first. "You never told me what you did."

"Because it doesn't matter." He spoke quickly and with heat. "I was full of hell when I was sixteen. Nothing major, but I got the attention I wanted—then found out it wasn't worth having. They sealed the records, so I'm not going to be the one to spill the whole sordid story."

It bothered him. I could see that.

I could have been graceful and let the conversation die.

Instead I pushed him. Call it making the future.

I went to his side and crouched down beside him. He didn't look at me. "So, what does this jailbait comment really mean? Since you're being direct?"

"You want me to tell you the future? The one you can't see?"

"Give me your version of it."

I didn't think he would, not in a million years, but Jared surprised me one more time.

"That I'll be turning up for the next two years. Just checking in, keeping in touch, helping you out when I can." Jared stepped closer and his eyes brightened as he turned to face me. We were almost nose to nose. He arched a brow, his expression completely intense and I knew I never wanted him to be any other way. "But once you're legal, the only way you'll get rid of me, Dragon Girl, is to tell me to go away forever." He smiled crookedly, smiled enough that that deep dimple made an appearance. "I'm hoping that by then, you won't do that."

My heart thumped.

My breath caught.

He'd said exactly what I'd wanted to hear, and even better, I knew that wasn't why he'd said it. Jared had said it because he meant it.

And this was my chance to push my future in a specific direction.

So I leaned forward, eliminating that little sliver of space, and kissed him.

It felt, just so you know, every bit as good as it had the other times.

Plus it just felt right.

II

My messenger rang, and I was so absorbed that I almost didn't realize it was mine. It was in the pocket of my jacket, the sound muffled a bit. It was Jared who pulled back, then caught his breath.

"For you, I think," he said, and his voice was rough.

He straightened and cleared his throat and turned his attention back to his bike.

It was Meagan and she was freaking out. "Derek's gone," she said as soon as I answered. "Trevor's not here today and neither is Suzanne. I can feel spell light in this place like crazy. It's like the school is filled with spell-song. It's enough to make me feel sick, and I can't even make a dent in it."

"Where's Jessica?"

"She's right here and really worried about you."

"I'm okay. I'm with Jared. We're going after them."

He glanced up at me, and I saw that there were no more bike bits on the cloth. He tightened a nut, threw his leg over the bike, and started the engine. It caught and ran with a throaty throb, and he grinned in triumph. He fiddled with the gears, nodded with satisfaction, then revved the engine for emphasis.

"Keep us posted," Meagan said.

"I will. Take care of Jessica. You're the spellsinger."

"Got it," Meagan said. "And, Zoë, be careful."

Right. I was, after all, getting on Jared's bike.

WE GOT to the vacant lot and the glamour of the library that Jared had summoned was still there.

I slanted a glance at him, wondering at the power of the spells.

This time, though, it was swirling with orange Mage light. I could see the spell pressing against the windows from the inside, as if it were full of the chaotic power of spells, spells so potent and vibrant that they couldn't stay still for a moment. They couldn't just glow—they had to zoom around like manic fireflies.

"Can you see the spell light?" I asked Jared quietly.

"I can feel it." Even though we were both wearing helmets, I could hear how grim he was through the microphone. "It's only going to get worse," he added, which was probably true.

I got off the bike, liking that he offered me his hand, and tugged off my helmet. I watched with some amusement as he parked the motorcycle carefully.

He glanced up and caught my smile, took offense a little. "What's so funny?"

"I'm not sure you're ever going to need it again." I glanced at that spell light and knew it would be some kind of miracle if we went in there and returned alive.

On the other hand, we didn't have a lot of choice.

"Think positive," he said.

I nodded and tried to do just that.

Even though I'd never seen spell light so vivid or frantic.

"Is it true that they mostly hunt at night?"

"Until they get stronger."

"Can we tell how strong they are yet?"

He gave me a look and I got it. Not without going in.

Jared fastened the helmets to the back of the bike and came to stand, just looking at the glamour of the building, beside me. He reached out and took my hand, gave my fingers a squeeze.

"What did you get busted for?" I asked, and felt his surprise.

He glanced my way. "What difference does it make?"

"Probably not much, but I'm thinking I might not ever have the chance to ask again." I shrugged, my gaze compelled to watch that orange spell light. "Do me a favor and get rid of one distraction."

"Just one?" I heard the smile in his voice before I saw it.

I squeezed his hand back. "Just one."

He heaved a sigh and considered the glamour. I knew he wasn't really looking at it. "It was a guitar. I really wanted it. My dad could have bought it for me, but he'd never buy me a guitar."

"Why not?"

"He thinks music is a waste of time." Jared pursed his lips. "My dad is really successful. He makes a lot of money and he buys a lot of stuff. That's important to him. The stuff and the way other people admire his stuff." He shook his head. "It was never very important to me. He thinks that because we don't want the same things, I'm just not ambitious. He thinks the music is an excuse, a way to be lazy." He turned to look at me, his eyes glinting. "I asked him about the guitar. We had a huge fight, not just about the guitar, but about everything. He had a lot to say about my being a disappointment and not being worthy of being his son."

"Ouch."

"I was mad and I was done. I went and took what I wanted. The owner knew me, though, because I'd been in to admire that guitar so many times. It didn't take a brilliant cop to follow the breadcrumbs to me." He grimaced. "I was stupid."

"Why didn't you just get a job or do something to earn the money to pay for it?"

"Impatience. I wanted to impress some people, some people who didn't deserve to be impressed."

He wasn't looking at me, but his words made me remember my own act of theft. I'd stolen the carrier for a pizza to impress Adrian, the apprentice Mage. I'd returned it, but still.

That gave me an idea. "Were the Mages trying to recruit you then?"

"What difference does it make?"

"Well, their spells can make people do things they wouldn't do otherwise. They can make you think things and act in ways you wouldn't usually...."

Jared squeezed my fingers. "Thanks, Dragon Girl, but you don't need to find an excuse for me." He released my hand, then held up his right hand. "This is the hand that broke the store window." He looked at his left hand. "And this is the hand that took the guitar from the display." He looked at me, his expression resolute. "It doesn't really matter what influenced me to do what I did. I did it. I had to answer for it. And I can never change the fact that I did it."

"Did you go to jail?"

"No. My dad knows people. He tried to fix it, the deal being that he'd be rid of me forever in exchange. I had to work in that store for six months for free, and give back the guitar. It turned out to be the best thing that ever happened to me. The owner was really cool and encouraged me to learn to play better. That's where I met my band mates and where I realized what I wanted to do with my life."

"Did you tell your dad?"

"No point. He'll always think I'm a loser with no ambition." He shrugged and glanced at me, cautious. "Besides, he doesn't have a son anymore."

"I don't think you're a loser."

He considered me and I saw the glint of hope in his eyes. He spoke softly then, his words making me shiver. "Maybe dragons do see beyond the surface."

"Maybe."

"Donovan was the only one who stood by me. He sold me the Ducati cheap, because he knew I loved it and would take care of it. Dragons have always been there for me. Which is why I wanted to meet you, to meet the only dragon girl there is." He turned to face the glamour while I tried to deal with the lump in my throat, and he took my hand in his once more. "Maybe this is what it's all about, Zoë. Maybe finishing these ShadowEaters—and by extension the Mages—is why we met and why we connect."

"I don't think so. I don't think that's good enough."

He smiled at me. "Saving the last four kinds of shifters isn't enough for you?"

"Not nearly."

"Maybe that's what I like about you, Dragon Girl. You're not one to go with the easy choice."

"I'm a dragon," I said with pride. "We don't do subtle."

"No, I guess not." He looked at me and my heart nearly broke with yearning. But that spell light was dancing and tugging at my attention, so strong that it drew my gaze even from Jared.

"So, what do you say?" I said, acting all cavalier. "Shall we kick some butt and save the world?"

"It's too early for lunch," Jared said with a grin. "We might as well do it."

And we marched up the steps, hand in hand.

This time, the glamour didn't waver.

It glowed.

I refused to think that it was a glow of anticipation.

The windows were so filled with golden spell light, it appeared as if the interior of the building was on fire. Even though it was an illusion, it felt foolish to be walking closer. Once again, the street was completely vacant. We could have been the last two people left on the planet.

Maybe that was the effect of the spell. My heart was pounding, not just because Jared was holding my hand so tightly and his shoulder was brushing against mine. I could feel a beat, one that resonated through my whole body and shook my bones.

Jared started to hum. I saw a purple and blue spell unfurl from his lips, sweeping around us. It was small, a gossamer net, and I wondered whether he was trying to fake them out by pretending to be a less powerful spellsinger than he was. I had to assume that he could buttress that filigree net and be quick if necessary.

I hoped he was quick enough.

We reached the double doors. I took a shaking breath, uncertain what we'd find inside. Jared gave my fingers one last squeeze, then released my hand and opened the door.

At his touch on the door handle, the glamour collapsed into nothing.

We were falling—right at the same moment that the ShadowEaters swarmed us. There were thousands of them, snapping and licking and biting, pressing against us on all sides. They were more powerful than I'd expected—they'd let me underestimate them until it was too late.

Jared shouted, losing the rhythm of his spell, and I couldn't tell whether he could see them or just sense them. It didn't matter. They were blinding in their brilliance and their sheer quantity. They snatched at us as we tumbled, and I felt teeth on my shadow. The spell light danced around us like a web, and there was only one thing I could do.

I called to the shimmer and, in a flash of pale blue, I shifted to my dragon form. I snatched him up and leapt into the darkness, soaring high in the air. A wind erupted, swirling around us like an angry hurricane, and the ShadowEaters leapt after us, shouting and salivating. Jared began to sing, brilliant purple spell light spilling from his mouth to surround us like a cocoon.

Jared gave a shout of triumph as I flew higher and I cleared both the turbulence and the ShadowEaters. I turned then, looking down at the ground. They were there, their golden eyes gleaming in the darkness, and I wasn't really surprised when the first one leapt to snatch at us.

"The first guard," Jared said.

He was right. They were a distraction.

I peered into the shadows beyond them. With my sharper sight, I could see a nexus of spell light far below. It was leaping and sparking like a bonfire lit in a trash can.

If I wasn't completely disoriented, it was at the same spot where Trevor and Adrian had summoned the ShadowEaters.

There was a spellbound figure beside the bonfire.

Was it Kohana?

"Sing," I said to Jared, then dove toward the flickering golden light. He sang with vigor, throwing out his hands as he conjured an impressive shell of purple and blue spell light. He wove it around us, shaping the spell with such dexterity that I knew he'd been practicing for this moment. We were inside a mesh cocoon of his spell light that repelled the assault of the orange spells. Jared's spell wove and sheltered. Theirs were all spikes and points and lightning bolts intended to cause as much damage as possible.

The ShadowEaters howled in anticipation of a feast, leaping toward me and snatching at my claws and wings. I soared through them like a fighter jet, protected by Jared's counterspell and targeting the bonfire. It might be a lure, but it was where the prize could be found. Those spells seemed to respond to my proximity, and the flames leapt higher as I dove toward them.

I saw Trevor. I saw the book that he was consulting, reading it like a songbook. I saw Kohana bound on the ground before the bonfire, shifting shape rapidly between human and Thunderbird form.

I chose to believe that this wasn't a trick, that Kohana really was in danger. It was a risk, given his history, but I couldn't do otherwise.

As I dove toward them, the ShadowEaters pressed behind us, pushing us closer in a way that did nothing for my confidence. Trevor suddenly and triumphantly pulled the NightBlade from his sleeve. They hooted and clustered near him, anticipation making them vibrate in the air. I raced toward him, talons outstretched. That was when I saw two more figures spellbound on the ground.

Nick and Isabelle.

Motionless.

And Suzanne was sitting beside them, as if she had been frozen in stone.

"The sacrifice," Jared whispered, and I knew he was right. Trevor intended to join the ShadowEaters, too. "Put me down," he instructed tersely.

"But..."

"I need to brace my feet to sing properly, and you don't need the deadweight."

I chose not to think about the literal meaning of what he'd said. I set him down as easily as I could without slowing down very much, and he gave me a thumbs-up.

Just as he'd said, his spellsong became suddenly brighter, swirling up to surround me like a protective cloak.

Trevor continued his invocation, then pivoted with a flourish. "Shadow and blood!" he cried, and reached for Suzanne. I watched in horror as he slit her throat and she tumbled to the ground, like a doll. He laughed, turning toward Nick and Isabelle with glee. I plummeted toward the earth and snatched the NightBlade out of his hand, the sharp edge still dripping with blood.

"No!" Trevor shouted, not releasing his grasp on the handle. His eyes were radiant gold, as filled with spell light as those of the ShadowEaters.

I soared high, but he hung on with superhuman strength.

I had the NightBlade but wasn't sure what to do with it. I didn't want to use it, because I was afraid it would twist my impulse to its own purposes. I wanted to ruin it. But I had no idea how—and there was no guarantee that any plans I made with it in my grasp would be my own.

They might be the will of the NightBlade.

I tried to sing the note that Sigmund had delivered in that message, well aware that I am officially tone-deaf. It couldn't have been the right note, or maybe it didn't matter, because it made no difference to anything.

Then Trevor began to snap at my shadow. His features dissolved as I watched, his clothes disappearing and his body becoming an anonymous skin filled with light. If I hadn't been staring right at him as he morphed, I wouldn't even have been able to tell which of the ShadowEaters he was.

I thrashed, flying haphazardly in an attempt to shake him off. He finally locked his teeth on my shadow and ripped a bite free with such savage force that I felt as if my soul was being torn. He laughed again, exultant, then threw himself into the air to join his fellows. I was stunned that he left me in possession of the NightBlade, as if it didn't matter.

I looked down to see a ShadowEater taking a bite from Kohana's shadow, delighting in ripping it away from his body. I heard Kohana cry out; then the ShadowEater joined its fellows. They swirled in the sky, mingling and whirling, potent and disgusting.

Then they circled and prepared to dive toward the bonfire to finish what they'd begun.

They were going to have a feast.

On Nick and Isabelle.

Over my dead body.

Jared had taken advantage of their momentary absence. He sang with all his might, widening the cocoon of spell light to protect the three captives. He could have been weaving a bubble over them, one that defended them from the ShadowEaters' assault. I felt their indecision like a tangible force, then knew their decision a heartbeat before they made it.

They turned on me, thousands of hungry beings, and lunged toward me. They were intent on ensuring that I was surrounded and trapped, their spell light flying through the air like ropes and grappling hooks cast at the walls of a medieval fortress.

I held the NightBlade high and shouted a taunt, then dove through them. It was my best impression of a football play. In the scrimmage, I lost my grip on the NightBlade and felt it wrenched out of my hand. Afraid of that import of that, I bolted. I flew toward my pals without thinking about landing, just descending as fast as I could. I burst through Jared's bubble of spell light, almost certainly because he let me, then shifted shape.

In human form, I skidded to a halt. I put my hand down to brace myself, and felt something sticky and warm.

I chose not to look at Suzanne just yet.

I was glad that I still had my backpack. I hauled out Skuld's shears and cut Nick free with a savage slice. He shifted shape, leaping skyward in dragon form to rage dragonfire at an approaching golden tendril of spell light. I cut it away, as well, chopping it into tiny chunks. It writhed as I did so, like a snake that simply would not die.

When it was still and blackening to ash, I would have gone to Isabelle and Kohana. But I felt heat and I turned just as the bonfire leapt suddenly high. I thought the ShadowEaters were calling to it, because it fired straight up in the air, making a tall plume of flame.

Which burned right through Jared's carefully constructed spell wall, the way a flamethrower might incinerate a piece of tissue paper.

I pivoted to see that Jared was ashen from his efforts. All the same, he cried out to them. "Can't even take out a novice Mage? What a useless bunch of spellsingers!"

I cried out when the ShadowEaters surrounded him, their spell light wrapping around him like a thousand heavy ropes. Jared sang a defensive spell, but he was ferociously outnumbered. He cast me a hot look, one that told me he'd drawn their fire on purpose.

For me.

"No!" I cried, and would have gone after him, but Nick shouted a warning.

"Now, Z!" I looked up to see the net of spell light closing around us, as it had once before.

Nick soared down and snatched up spellbound Isabelle, grimacing as the spell light tried to wind its way around him, too. I reached with Skuld's shears to cut it back and heard Jared's song become louder.

"Go!" he roared, just before they surrounded him and took him down.

"No!" I screamed, and would have gone after him.

But Nick snatched me up, letting me cut Isabelle free as he shot into the sky. He flew straight toward the closing wall of spell light, holding fast to both Isabelle and me. She was unconscious in his grasp and I could feel his tension.

I was crying for Jared, knowing they'd finished him off. Grief gave me power, though. I held the shears open and used them like a sword, slashing at the rapidly closing net of spell light. Nick slipped through like he was greased, then raged ever higher in the night sky.

Isabelle didn't stir.

Jared was lost far, far behind us.

And the air was brilliant gold with the frenzy of ShadowEaters at their feast. I was tempted to lean my head on Nick's powerful shoulder once we had escaped and cry my heart out.

I'd failed.

Miserably.

But I felt his anxiety and fear for Isabelle, and knew that showing my terror wouldn't help him at all. It was my job as leader to give him hope and inspire him to go on.

I'd do my best and we'd fight right to the end.

Even if the chances of winning seemed more slim by the minute.

Jared was dead.

"Go to the school," I said in old-speak. *"Meagan and Jessica might be able to help Isabelle."*

"Good idea," Nick agreed, then looked down at me. *"What about you?"*

"Just take care of Isabelle. I've got an idea."

It wasn't true, at least not yet, but Nick didn't need to know it. I felt his heart skip with hope.

Then I closed my eyes, knowing exactly where I wanted to be.

Alone.

· · ·

I SLAMMED into the driver's seat of my car, panting and perspiring and trembling. I looked around with some trepidation, but the street outside the hostel looked just as it had earlier in the morning. There were a few pedestrians, one woman pushing a baby carriage, another walking a dog, and a couple of older kids with backpacks, maybe going to class at the college. The snow was still falling lightly.

It was astonishingly normal.

I took a deep breath and looked at the house, which also appeared to be the same. The driveway wasn't shoveled and the paint on the porch was peeling.

Had I dreamed it all? Or had it really happened?

You know what I wanted the answer to be.

I took a deep breath and opened the car door. My heart was pounding, but I had to know for sure. I went down the driveway, noting the single tread from a motorcycle and a line of footprints. Were they mine? They matched my boots perfectly, which was not a good sign.

There was silence behind the house, no tinkling with motorcycle parts, and I pretty much knew what I'd see when I came around the last corner. There was a mark in the snow where a motorcycle had been parked. The sheet where Jared had spread out the gear parts was folded and jammed under the railing of the back porch, right where he'd left it. And there was a circle of melted snow where the bike's exhaust had heated the ground.

No motorcycle.

No Jared.

It had happened.

I tipped back my head, fighting my tears, wishing I really was going insane, because then Jared would be safe and I wouldn't be the biggest failure of all time.

Insanity was the much better choice.

After a few moments, I pulled out my messenger. The in-box was chock-full of messages, but I didn't have the heart to sit and read through all the news. Kohana and Jared were dead. Nick and Isabelle were headed to the school, and Jessica and Meagan would be there. What about everyone else? How much of a team did we have left? I sent Garrett and Liam messages to come to the school, too.

Most importantly, how much power had the ShadowEaters gained in that ceremony?

I might as well find out the worst of it, live and in person.

I turned around and trudged back to the car, then drove to school, my heart dragging behind the exhaust pipe. I was sure things couldn't get any worse, but, naturally, I was wrong.

One look told me that the ShadowEaters had really scored.

The school could have been one of my dad's pyrotechnics displays, but an interactive one. It was surrounded by a halo of brilliant yellow and gold Mage light, so bright that I could hardly look straight at it. The building seemed to radiate golden spell light, the binding spells weaving around and above it in such frantic patterns that the sight made me sick.

I'd probably made the school more of an attraction by having everyone gather here. But I needed them all together.

Still, I had major trepidation about going into the school. I parked the car and watched the spells dance for a minute, dreading whatever I would find inside. Never mind what would happen to me when I got in there. Maybe we were all doomed. Maybe the ShadowEaters had already won.

Maybe this was it.

Maybe I was going to go down easy.

I pulled out Skuld's shears and tucked them inside my coat, wanting them closer than in my backpack.

Then I got out of the car, my mouth as dry as sandpaper.

The first ShadowEater appeared beside me when I'd gone only ten steps. Its eyes glowed with that luminescence. I turned to look at it, shocked that it would be so overt about stalking me in broad daylight.

It bared its teeth and snapped in my direction.

I pulled out Skuld's shears and snapped back, chopping off its hand with one savage gesture. It howled and retreated.

Victory was fleeting. I watched in horror as spell light poured from its severed wrist. It swelled up like a cloud of animosity, a miasma of sizzling spell fury. The spell light inside the ShadowEater was spilling out of his skin, and as the orange cloud became bigger, his silhouette deflated like a balloon. In a heartbeat, there was a towering cloud of spell light before me, crackling like a bonfire, lit with interior sparks.

And a flat, dark skin on the ground, discarded.

It looked a lot like a shadow, actually.

The cloud swirled and joined the display surrounding the school. I knew it made the existing spells burn brighter and move more agitatedly.

When I looked back at the ShadowEater's skin, it was gone.

So I had eliminated a ShadowEater, but its energy had strengthened the spell surrounding the school. This couldn't be a good thing. I hid Skuld's shears beneath my coat again and walked warily toward the school.

How could the ShadowEaters be dispersed and the spell light extinguished? It was a riddle and I reminded myself that I was good at solving riddles.

If somewhat short of sleep.

To my relief, there was a tendril of purple spell light slipping through the barrage of brilliant swirling gold. I knew that had to be coming from Meagan and followed it with purpose. There were lots of kids in the halls, so it must have been between classes. I looked at the time on my messenger, not sure what class I was missing.

I didn't even have a chance to find Meagan.

Muriel stood by my locker, a sentinel with a sour expression. "You're late," she said, scanning me with disapproval.

"I, uh, had car trouble," I lied. "It wouldn't start."

"You should have just walked."

"I thought I could fix it but I was wrong." I forced a smile. Muriel, she of the many merry smiles, did not smile back. "Sorry, Muriel. I should be in English class, right?"

"Art class," Muriel corrected.

"Bonus!" I feigned enthusiasm.

She watched me with suspicion. "You never miss art class, Zoë," she said quietly. "Would you like to tell me the real trouble?"

The real trouble. I was tempted to tell her, just to see her reaction.

I watched Trevor murder Suzanne this morning in order to convert himself to a ShadowEater, a being of spell light and malice. There wasn't anything I could do about it since I was fighting binding spells myself at the time. The worst part is that the guy I'm crazy for let himself be killed by the ShadowEaters to give me a chance to escape, and I have no idea what the point of living is with him dead.

No. The truth had no place in this discussion.

I glanced up and down the hall, relieved to see Meagan closing in fast and Jessica right beside her. Both looked freaked, but both were surrounded by a glistening blue halo of Meagan's spell light. I sent Jessica a thought about Meagan defending Garrett, Liam, Nick, and Isabelle, who should arrive soon. She nodded once and bent to whisper to Meagan.

Meagan's gaze was locked on me and her eyes were wide with horror. Best-friend radar never fails. She knew something really bad had happened, something bad enough to shake me to my marrow.

I couldn't send the news about Jared through Jessica.

And then there was Muriel. "You should know, Zoë, that the police wish to talk to you."

"The police?" I was genuinely shocked and Muriel knew it.

She beckoned with one finger and a police officer strode down the hall toward us. He was trying to look friendly and pretty much failed. He was older than Muriel, a bit stocky, and looked as if he'd seen a lot of nasty things.

Because his eyes were dancing with spell light.

Good. He was going to keep me busy while the ShadowEaters slurped up the last bits of Kohana and Jared. I appreciated their concern for my schedule.

I would fry them all—as soon as I figured out how.

I shot a look at Meagan and Jessica, but they were heading down the hall. Going to defend the others. At least something was going right.

"This is Detective Smith," Muriel said. She preened a little, as if she thought he was hot, which was just about the most revolting idea I'd had all day. (Which is saying something.) "He wants to ask you a few questions."

"Okay. Are you going to stay with us?"

Muriel flushed and smiled and gestured to the empty classroom adjacent to my lockers. Detective Smith got out his digital notepad, and the interrogation began.

He asked my name and address, my age and my grade, even though he must have known all of that already. I understood that these questions were supposed to help me relax.

They didn't.

He asked about my car and my parents, then gave me an intent look.

That golden spell light dancing in his pupils gave me the serious willies, but I held his gaze. I knew he'd think I was lying if I looked away.

"Suzanne is missing. I believe you know her."

"Everyone knows Suzanne."

"Someone saw her get into your car last night, but no one has apparently seen her since."

"Yeah, I gave her a ride."

He scribbled with his stylus. "Why?"

I shrugged. "She asked for one. It was snowing and she said Trevor hadn't picked her up like he was supposed to."

"And what was her destination?"

"Trevor's house."

He flicked a look at me. "And that's where you left her?"

"No. She wanted to be dropped off at the end of the block." Detective Smith arched a brow, and I smiled apologetically. "She didn't want to be seen in my car."

His attention sharpened at that. "Why not?"

"It's too old and beat-up to be cool."

He flicked through his notes with a fingertip. "But doesn't Suzanne have her own car?"

"Yeah. A new Interceptor convertible."

"Then why did she need a ride from you?"

"Her car wasn't here. Maybe because Trevor was supposed to give her a ride."

He impaled me with a brilliant yellow glance. "Isn't it true that you and Suzanne had a fight yesterday? Isn't it true that she didn't have her car because she was being punished by her parents for that fight?"

"I don't know why she didn't have a car."

"But the fight?"

"Yes, we fought. Muriel saw it."

"And what was the reason for that fight?"

"She took a picture of me in the bathroom. It was embarrassing and she was going to show it to everyone."

"So you took her messenger?"

All of this was public knowledge. I saw no point in denying it. "I asked her to delete the picture. She refused. I took the messenger and deleted it myself, then gave the messenger back to her."

"In fact, you removed the memory card and destroyed it."

"That deleted the image forever."

His nostrils flared. "Yet despite this, you gave her a ride."

I shrugged. "We had settled it. What was done was done."

"You weren't afraid she might try to get even with you?"

I looked at him. I had had enough. "No," I said, and there was a bit of dragon in my quiet tone. "I'm not afraid of Suzanne."

Our gazes locked and held. The spell light in his eyes danced with greater intensity, becoming brighter as he tried to stare me down.

I wasn't daunted.

Maybe there was more dragon in my look than I'd realized, because Muriel looked flustered.

She even forced a smile.

"And why were you in the parking lot alone last night in the first place?"

"Because I'd just gotten out of detention." It was half of the truth, anyway.

The detective glanced up at Muriel.

She nodded, ever helpful.

"Why were you late today?" the detective asked. "Didn't you have class this morning?"

"I did, but I had car trouble," I lied. I held the detective's gaze, and funny enough, he ran out of questions then.

Muriel effectively ended the interview. She made encouraging noises about my being willing to start fresh with Suzanne.

The detective got fed up and excused himself.

But Muriel had a full head of steam. She spouted a lot of stuff about ensuring that I did what would make my parents proud, that I kept a positive attitude and ensured my grades were good. It was imperative that I not develop any habits that could imperil my academic record, and surely I knew that Muriel would be there for me whenever I wanted to talk more.

I nodded and even managed to conjure up a tear of heartfelt gratitude. Muriel gave me a hug, which astounded me, and promised to talk individually to my teachers about my attendance. Then she smiled at me and told me not to be late for my class right after lunch.

Lunch.

Right.

I was starving.

Meagan, the best friend in the whole world, was waiting by our lockers for me, protective blue spell light at the ready.

"So?" Meagan demanded as soon as Muriel was gone. "What did the police officer want?"

"Did you hear about Suzanne?" Jessica asked. "She's missing."

"No," I said. "She's dead." I heaved a sigh. "So are Kohana and Jared."

They were both shocked. "Trevor isn't here today, either," Meagan said.

"Because he's become a ShadowEater," I said grimly.

They both started to ask questions, their voices hushed, but I held up a hand. "I need food."

We headed for the cafeteria, wading through the dizzying golden cloud of spell light. I could practically feel Jessica sweat, and reached out to take her hand.

Sadly, the daily special was some mystery meatloaf that would have looked revolting even if I wasn't vegetarian. I went straight for dessert and got myself a chocolate sundae with chocolate sauce.

It might, after all, be my last meal.

We took a table in the corner and huddled over our lunches.

"Where are the guys?" I asked. "I sent them here."

"I sent them to Isabelle's place with Nick," Meagan said. "They wanted to stay, but I could see how the spell light was getting to them."

"Safer for them not to be enchanted if we have to fight for our lives," Jessica said.

I tugged out my messenger and pinged Liam and Garrett and Nick. They were all freaked, but they were together and with Isabelle.

Who was still comatose.

Like King and Mozart.

At least the guys were together.

"You can see the spell light, right?" Meagan said. "Is it really bad?"

"It feels really bad," Jessica said. "And watchful."

I glanced over my shoulder at the light swirling in the cafeteria. I could see shapes within the cloud of light and knew that there were Shadow-Eaters among us, choosing their prey. Meagan's light was protecting us, but I wondered how many other kids would lose their shadows before nightfall.

Never mind after that.

"They're everywhere," Derek said quietly. He'd slid into the seat on my other side when I'd been looking the other way. I jumped, just the way I always did, then I hugged him in my relief.

"I was afraid...."

He hugged me back after a moment's hesitation, as awkward as I'd expect. "We had to convene," he said gruffly. "Vote."

I pulled back to look at him, fearing what he would say.

He held my gaze, his own expression wary. "They're with you," he said, then dug into his meatloaf special.

I couldn't help but notice that he said *they* instead of *we*. I supposed I had that coming.

As we ate, I recounted the whole sorry story of my morning, including what had happened when I took out the ShadowEater in the parking lot. Meagan hummed quietly, buttressing the protective spell that surrounded us.

"What else happened here?" I asked, eating my sundae before it completely melted.

"Suzanne's friends are missing," Jessica said, nodding at Meagan to keep humming.

Meagan beckoned to me, indicating that she wanted the notebook I always carry. I use it to sketch dragons, but Meagan turned to an empty page. She wrote quickly, without stopping her spellsinging, and Jessica read what she wrote to us.

"Meagan used that note you heard this morning as the beginning of a harmonic sequence. She says it could be the tenor part in a harmony." Jessica looked up, her eyes bright. "It's in a minor key."

"Which we know that Mages like." I nodded, feeling as if Meagan was supplying the clue we needed. Jessica frowned as Meagan drew a musical staff and sketched in the notes, her gaze dancing over Meagan's rapidly drawn notes.

"So this would be the first note," Jessica said, singing the note I'd heard from Kohana this morning in a single clear *Ah!* "The soprano part to go with it is this." She sang another, higher note, then did the same with the bass and the alto parts.

"Theoretically, if we sing them all together, that would make the harmony that might vibrate apart the NightBlade," I said, and Meagan nodded with enthusiasm. "But only two of you can sing." I had an idea then, and recorded Jessica's singing into four different music files on my messenger. It wouldn't play all four concurrently, so we shared the files and queued up our messengers to play them all at the same time.

I turned to watch the spell light as the harmony began, thinking I'd see something in the motion of the spell if this resonance was powerful to it.

It made no difference at all.

I was disappointed, and so was Meagan. "That can't be it."

She frowned and scribbled that she'd look for alternatives.

Was she wrong? Or were we just missing a critical piece of the puzzle?

"What's next?" Derek asked, and I understood that he was saying that he was still following the dragon. I smiled at him with relief and saw a wary gratitude dawn in his eyes.

"I need to reinforce the dragonsmoke at our loft. I promised my dad." I shrugged. "Maybe I can find something in my dad's hoard or in that book to solve the riddle."

"I'll come with you," Derek said immediately, and got to his feet.

He looked purposeful, which didn't bode well for any discussion we might have on the way.

On the other hand, I was glad to have his company.

It was forty-seven kinds of bizarre to enter the loft where I lived with my parents, knowing they weren't home and yet I was bringing a guy with me.

On the one hand, Derek was adamant that he had to defend me.

On the other hand, this was breaking every household rule I knew.

Plus it gave me a funny feeling.

Not only was he in my home, not only was he crossing the dragonsmoke barrier with me, but he was going to see me breathe smoke. I felt incredibly self-conscious about that.

My dad's dragonsmoke barrier had begun to erode, just as anticipated. It touched my skin like quicksilver, the chill of it making all the little hairs on my body stand up in unison. I shut the door behind us and locked it. The loft was still and echoed with its emptiness. There were no fetid smells coming from the kitchen, which was a good thing.

I gestured to the room. "You might as well come in and sit down. I don't think there's anything much to eat."

"It's okay," Derek said, and perched on the end of one of the black leather couches in the living room. "Kind of stark." The room was austere, almost monastic in its strict simplicity, which was precisely how my dad liked it. The ceilings were high in the space and the rooms uncluttered—which left lots of room for dragons to gather.

"My dad does black and white in a big way."

Derek smiled. "I like him already."

I sat down opposite him, not really settling back into the couch's squishy comfort, either. "Look. About yesterday..."

"There's nothing to say. I saw how you feel about Jared." He looked away from me and his throat worked a bit. "And now that you've told us the whole story, I think maybe I was wrong about him."

"What do you mean?"

Derek looked back at me, his pale eyes seeming unnaturally bright. "He let them take him this morning so that you could get away."

I nodded, sadness welling inside me again because I hadn't been able to save him.

Derek cleared his throat softly. "As much as I'd like to hate his guts, I respect what he did for you."

I looked up, astonished by this.

Derek didn't blink as he watched me. "Wyvern, lead us."

I had to walk through this with him to make sure I understood. "But you were the one who wanted to ensure the alliance, who wanted commitment from me in order to follow me."

Derek grimaced. "Didn't I tell you that I understood about having to do your duty instead of doing what you wanted?"

"But I thought you liked me."

"I do like you." Derek swallowed. "I'm not sure it's enough, though."

I stared at him.

"I know I don't like you as much as you like Jared. I understood that yesterday."

"But you left like you were mad...."

"I *was* mad. I was trying to do what I was told to do, and you were messing it up." He swallowed visibly. "And when I saw the way you looked at him, I knew that you could only ever give me a fraction of that." He heaved a sigh and looked away. "If you can't look at me the way you look at him, I don't want half measures."

"Black or white," I murmured.

"All or nothing," he agreed. He almost smiled. "I said I'd follow the Wyvern, and that means that the Wyvern's agenda is my agenda."

I was glad I was sitting down. Relief would have buckled my knees. All of the wolves were in, despite my choices.

I still needed a plan. I settled onto the floor, kicked off my boots, and cracked my knuckles.

"Anything I can do?" Derek asked.

"Just be quiet. It's kind of a meditative thing."

He watched, his eyes glittering as I summoned the shimmer and let my body shift shape. The surge of power ripped through me with explosive force, compelling my body to take its alternate form. I loved the sensation of it.

In a heartbeat, I was a massive white dragon, my tail unfurled across the floor and my wings resting against my back. I opened my eyes to find that Derek had braced his elbows on his knees and was leaning forward to watch.

That did just about nothing for my self-consciousness. But I knew what I had to do. I let quiet slide through my body, although the exercise was a little more difficult than usual. I breathed slowly and deeply, letting my eyes drift closed, persuading my heartbeat to slow to a fraction of its usual pace.

And I breathed smoke, a long glittering tendril of gossamer dragon-smoke. It wound from my lungs through my nostrils and into the air of the loft like a vein of quicksilver. I directed it toward the exterior, letting it slide beneath the front door, weaving it back and forth across the doorway, entwining it with the thinning remnants of my dad's dragonsmoke barrier.

Once the interweaving began, I slipped into a familiar rhythm, focusing on the dragonsmoke and the protective barrier it made. I forgot about everything except breathing smoke in a long steady tendril.

Breathing smoke can't be fascinating to watch, especially to someone who can't see the smoke. I noticed that Derek got up and looked out the window of the loft after a while. I kept breathing, focused on my task, but a bit curious as to what he'd do.

A few moments later, he bent down and unzipped my backpack, then removed a book. His book. Herodotus. He waved it at me to show me what he'd taken, turned on the reading lamp at the end of the couch where he'd been sitting, and settled in to read a few travel tips about the ancient world.

To each his own.

I breathed smoke.

Sometime later, I heard a guy walking around my dragon form.

Derek and I had been alone; then suddenly there was someone else in the loft. No doors or windows had opened.

My eyes were watchful slits. Dragons never truly sleep, you know. We doze. We slumber. We might look comatose. But on some level, we are always vigilant. Maybe our interior alarm systems are preset to a more sensitive level.

I heard the guy in the loft, even though his footfalls were silent.

Derek was still reading on the couch opposite me. He looked pretty engrossed and utterly unaware of the intruder.

That was odd.

The loft had fallen into the shadows of early evening.

The intruder walked around my tail. I felt him looking at it, as if he'd never seen the like. He wasn't afraid—his pulse was too slow for that. He was more curious. But wary. He walked slowly around my back as I remained motionless, feigning sleep. I could practically feel the weight of his gaze as he studied my folded wings. I felt the air move as he lifted a hand, then dropped it again, deciding against an exploratory touch.

He smelled like wood smoke and the outdoors. Was he a vagrant or a street person? How had he gotten into the loft without setting off the alarm system that deterred human invaders? He could have passed through the dragonsmoke barrier easily. It didn't trouble humans, but there were no doors or window open.

He took another step, coming around my left shoulder. I tingled with the awareness that he was checking me out; braced myself for whatever he might do. I was prepared to roar to life, to pivot and fry him to cinders, no questions asked. He had invaded my parents' home and my father's lair.

We dragons have no sense of humor about uninvited visitors.

My dad's hoard was here and I was in charge, left to defend our earthly possessions and personal security.

I was ready.

He took another step, and I saw his silhouette in my peripheral vision.

I smelled blood. Old blood. Dried blood. It awakened something primal within me. Who knew what this guy had done? Who knew what he planned to do next? I was ready to defend everything I cared about.

I braced myself, waiting on that next step that would bring him more clearly into my range. One more step. One leap and breath of dragonfire. There was no explanation he could give to justify his presence, nothing he could say to save himself.

He took that step, he crouched down to look into my eyes, and he whispered the one thing that evidently could stop me cold. "*Unktehila*, we need your help."

There was only one person who called me by that name, by the name the Thunderbirds had given to the dragon shifters. Kohana called me that, but Kohana was dead.

I raised my head and looked at him. It was the *Wakiya* elder from my dream, the one who had dropped his cigarette on the rug. His dark eyes glinted as he watched me, and I guessed that he had known all along that I wasn't really asleep.

And I should have known that this was another Wyvern vision of the possibilities. Both real and not real. Okay.

"I told you to hurry," he said. "And Kohana gave you the clue you need."

"It doesn't help if I don't understand it."

Derek kept reading as if I hadn't spoken.

The elder reached into the pocket of his jeans. With one hand, he withdrew a stone.

It was a piece of red rock, rounded and small enough to hold in one hand. I knew it had a rune scratched on one side and a circle etched on the other.

How had he gotten it?

How long had he been creeping around the loft?

"Hey, that's my rune stone!"

"And it holds the answer." He lifted it up so that the circle was facing me and gave me a hard look. Then he sang the same note Kohana had sung. He tugged his other hand out of his pocket and tossed a handful of what looked like snow into the air. It glistened and glittered—maybe it was a handful of starlight—and then aligned briefly into a musical staff.

I was reminded of what Meagan had drawn at lunch.

The circle on the stone looked like a note.

I still didn't get it. Meagan had already theorized that Kohana had given us the first note in a harmonic sequence, but the harmony she'd come up with hadn't made any difference to anything. "We tried that already," I said, but the elder smiled.

He tossed the rune stone in the air and caught it again. By the time I followed the trajectory of the stone and looked back at him, we were standing on the red rock that I'd visited before, snow swirling all around us.

"Here the earth speaks her secrets. Here the truth of the riddle is revealed." He bent and brushed the snow away from a section of the rock that was covered in carvings. He touched one of a bird, a figure that repeated over and over on the rock face.

"*Wakiya,*" I said, remembering both that this was a term for a place sacred to the Thunderbirds and the name they used for themselves.

The elder nodded, then tipped back his head to sing. He sang that note, letting it ululate in the back of his throat. Other men stepped out of the flying snow, forming a circle around him and creating a chorus. They were ghostly, there but not there, their voices the most material sign of their presence.

It was potent, that singing. It made my body tense and my pulse quicken. It was summoning a kind of energy.

The dead elder who had brought me here stopped singing, letting his fellows carry the note as he turned to me. "Four kinds left," he said. "Four notes."

"Each one is characteristic!" I said with excitement. "Each of us has to provide our note to destroy the NightBlade."

He smiled and stood, extending his hand to me. "Let us defeat the threat together."

I shifted shape and stepped forward in human form to shake his hand. His skin was papery, just like Sigmund's. Was it progress to be shaking hands with more dead people as well as talking to them? I really didn't have time to think about it.

"You have to help," I said to him. "I can't do this alone."

"I have just offered my assistance."

I knew instinctively that this wasn't enough. "No, you have to come with me. We have to defeat them all together. You have to sing the note, live and in person, to do the *Wakiya* part, since Kohana can't."

"I am not alive, though."

"You can still sing."

He frowned and shook his head, looking back at his ghostly fellows. "My time in your world is done. I have done what I can, but I cannot go back there again. The portal is secured against me."

"Then I'll just take you with me," I said with a confidence I didn't quite feel. "I'll make a portal." He looked surprised, but I gripped his hand and smiled. "Here we go."

Worst case: he'd be right and it wouldn't work.

Best case: I'd have the fourth surviving kind of shifter present and accounted for.

You know which option I was hoping for.

I took one last look at the red rock in the snow, not at all sure I'd ever see it again. It was tranquil and powerful, a wonderful place but not one necessarily for me. It had been an intersection for our kinds to negotiate our differences, but I had a feeling that now that was achieved, the *Wakiya* would secure it for themselves.

Which meant I had to make this work.

I closed my eyes, holding fast to the elder's hand. Spontaneously manifesting out of a dream—instead of just waking up—felt like the right answer, but I wasn't at all sure it could be done. I couldn't think of another way to take the elder with me, though, and I was going to trust my gut.

I wished with all my heart and soul to be back in my parents' loft, back opposite Derek, and hoped I'd be in dragon form. I felt the tingle that always accompanied my attempts to spontaneously manifest elsewhere, felt my body begin to make the transformation, and tightened my grip on his hand.

Holy hoard. It worked.

. . .

When I manifested in the loft, I gave a hoot of joy. I was in my dragon form, exactly the way I wanted to be. And—bonus—the elder was still with me, clutching my talon. I had time to see that he was as impressed as I was, then Derek shouted in surprise.

He sat up, his eyes wide. "Zoë, what are you doing?"

"Solving the riddle!" I cried, triumphant, and shifted to my human form in a glorious tide of shimmering blue light. The elder nodded approval. "And bringing help."

Derek looked pointedly around the loft. "What help?"

"Him." I gestured to the elder, who seemed mightily amused.

"Uh, there's no one else here, Zoë."

"Don't worry about it. Trust me." I hauled out my messenger and checked the time. It was eight thirty already. "We've got to get to the dance."

Derek was looking at me like I'd completely lost it. "I thought you didn't want to go anymore."

"We have to go. The ShadowEaters will be there. They'll have the NightBlade and will try to take out at least one wild card. We're all supposed to be there, and the school is already filled with spell light." I was hauling on my boots as I talked, grabbing my keys and my backpack. Excellent—I still had Skuld's shears. "If Jessica's there, she's in trouble already. Let's go!"

I bolted out the door, and Derek came after me. I ran down the stairs to the parking garage, trusting the ghostly elder to keep up. Meanwhile, I messaged Meagan, my fingers flying. She'd gone to Isabelle's place with Jessica, so I told them all to come to the school together and meet us there.

I was through the door to the parking garage when she called. I quickly explained the issue, then remarked, "You said there were four parts to the harmony."

"Soprano, alto, tenor, and bass," she agreed.

"Which one was that note of Kohana's?"

"Tenor."

I got into my car, scrolling through the recorded notes stored on my messenger. Derek got in the passenger's seat, looking a bit shaken. Like he'd been startled awake to find the world shifting hard. I smiled at him and delegated a task. "I need a sound, characteristic of the Neuroi, that matches one of these notes. A powerful sound for you, or a ceremonial sound."

Derek's eyes shone with purpose as he took my messenger, scrolling through the audio files as I turned the key in the ignition. The car sputtered but didn't start. I tried again as he worked through the three remaining notes.

Nada. The engine was dead.

No, the battery was dead. It should have had enough juice for the week, but I'd taken that extra trip downtown to Jared's hostel and run it dry. Stupidly, I hadn't thought to plug it in when I got home. There was no time to charge it up because we had to get to the school before the others were hurt.

I could have shifted shape and flown there in dragon form, carrying Derek. But I was afraid that I would need every crumb of my dragon powers for the fight ahead. Plus I might end up needing to beguile a whole bunch of innocent bystanders who saw me in dragon form (don't we love the Covenant?) and I just didn't have time.

But there was another choice.

I slanted a look across the parking garage to the car carefully covered with a tarp and protected for all time. Or at least until its new buyer came to collect it in a week or two. My heart skipped a beat at the boldness of my idea.

The Lamborghini was here.

Its gas tank was full.

And I knew where the keys were.

It seemed that this was the night that some dreams could come true.

"Be right back," I said to Derek, and raced upstairs. I grabbed the Lamborghini's keys and was back in the garage in record time, moving practically at the speed of light.

Derek was gone.

My messenger was emitting one of those notes, the sound echoing around the parking garage in a decidedly eerie fashion.

I panicked for a second, certain the ShadowEaters had gotten him.

But no. Derek was in wolf form. I exhaled in relief when I saw him. His paws were braced against the pavement in the space that was usually occupied by my dad's new sedan. My messenger was on the ground beside him, holding that note.

When he saw me, he tipped back his head and howled, loosing the howl I'd heard the wolf shifters make when we triumphed over the Mages in the fall. It was a sound that made me shiver.

And it perfectly matched the note emanating from my messenger.

The elder lounged against the fender of my car, nodding approval. "That's two," he said, and I laughed.

"Help me get the tarp off," I said to Derek, snatching up my messenger on the way past him. I saw the blue shimmer of his shifting shape, then he was beside me again. In no time at all, we had the car unwrapped, and we both stopped to stare.

The car was perfect. Utterly black, polished to the gleam of a dark mirror, sleek and powerful, and apparently untouched by human hands.

My heart did a trio of backflips.

Was I out of my mind?

"Pretty much," Sigmund said, and I could have smacked him.

If I'd been able to see him.

I was not happy that he was adding the disembodied voice to his repertoire of dead-guy tricks. He would choose this moment to change his rules.

"You know, in some cultures, it's believed that people who see the dead do so because they'll soon be dead themselves," Sigmund said conversationally.

I was sure he was referring to my dad's reaction to me driving the Lamborghini.

"Thank you very much for that," I said. "I'll keep it in mind."

"Keep what in mind?" Derek asked.

"Don't worry about it." I forced a smile, feigning confidence, and hit the button to unlock the doors. The car beeped and the lights flashed. I heard the locks disengage.

"You know how to drive this thing?" Derek asked, his uncertainty clear.

"I guess I'll learn," I said, and his eyes widened. I opened the driver's-side door. I was more terrified of damaging this car than I'd been of anything ever in my life.

Which was saying something, given that I lived with dragons and fought ShadowEaters on a daily basis.

On the other hand, I was thrilled.

And I told myself I didn't have a choice.

There were, of course, really only two seats in the car, the backseat pretty much big enough for just an umbrella or a purse. I realized suddenly that I was the reason my dad had had to set aside his precious automobile.

No room for a baby seat.

I glanced at the elder, who moved his arms to mock flying. I gave him a thumbs-up. Derek looked between me and the place where the dead elder stood, with an expression that told me he couldn't see our companion.

I got in, was swallowed by the leather seat, and was amazed that my dad had given this up for me. It was completely deluxe, and so antique that it could have been from another planet. Slick, though.

I looked at the dashboard in awe and uncertainty.

Derek visibly swallowed and I wondered what he saw two minutes in his future. "You think your dad will be cool with this?"

I didn't need dragon powers of perception to hear his worry.

"No," I admitted, and Derek looked alarmed. "He'll be furious enough to spark an inferno." I smiled. "Unless we save the world tonight."

"No pressure," Derek said, gritting his teeth and fastening his seat belt.

I felt for the seat adjustment. I'm tall, but my dad is taller, and I couldn't quite reach the clutch.

"There," Sigmund said, and I felt his fingers on mine, even though I couldn't see him. The rearview mirror moved, seemingly of its own accord, and I was relieved that Derek didn't seem to notice. Ditto on the side mirrors.

Sigmund set me right up. "Look like you know what you're doing," he advised. "It'll inspire confidence, even when you're putting it on."

I turned the key and the engine roared to life. I said a quick prayer, then looked at the gearbox, mystified. I knew how to drive a standard, but the gearbox was different.

"You'll find reverse over here," Sigmund whispered in my ear, and I was really glad to be hearing dead people. He walked me through the gears in order, up to fifth and back to first. An older brother teaching me to drive.

That thought made me smile. "Easy on the clutch, sis. It's pretty punchy. This baby is made to race, after all."

"Right," I said. "Thanks."

"And if you fry the clutch, neither one of us will be safe from Erik."

"I could blame you," I teased, seeing how Derek was staring at me.

Sigmund laughed. "And I'd blame you. Who would he believe? You're the only one who has a physical form."

He had a point. I put it in reverse, feeling where the clutch engaged, and backed out of the spot with care. Derek was looking at me as if I'd lost my mind, but was probably thinking it would be smarter to not distract me.

"So, what do you see two minutes in our future?" I asked.

"Nothing good."

"Skeptic." I grinned at Derek, probably looking like a maniac, and touched the gas.

The car surged forward like a cheetah let loose.

In precisely one half second, I knew that this car was made for me. I knew that driving it would be more fun than anything I'd ever done.

Me in this car was kismet.

Just like I'd always believed.

THE TIRES SQUEALED as I rounded the corner to the exit. Derek was pale but I didn't care. Our spaces were at the back of the garage, so I had another corner to go. I took the second corner in a harder turn, thrilled by how responsive the car was.

Derek audibly gulped.

"Time is of the essence," I informed him.

I heard Jared in my thoughts. *A dragon girl should be bold.* I blinked back my tears and focused. I'd have plenty of time to mourn later.

First I had to make his sacrifice count.

The parking garage had a sensor that lifted the door. As soon as we passed it and the door mechanism clicked, I knew we were going too fast. The garage door was old and clunky and took forever to ascend.

I hit the brake. The Lamborghini squealed to a halt, skidding a bit on the pavement and sliding toward the opening door.

"Shit!" Derek shouted.

The Great Wyvern was with me. The door was no more than two inches over the hood of the car as we slid beneath it and came to a stop. The door continued to crank upward. I was so relieved that I took my foot off the clutch.

And stalled it. The cheetah lurched forward another foot and came to a choking halt.

I knew the garage door would reach the top, remain open for a timed interval, then close again. Was there a sensor to detect a car or anything beneath it? I wasn't sure and it seemed a bad time to find out. I turned the key hard in the ignition and the engine ground in complaint.

Derek swore some more and peered through the windshield at the garage door.

It hit the top and stopped.

"Easy, easy," Sigmund said. "Don't flood it."

Right. Deep breath. Stay calm. I put on the emergency brake, put the car in neutral. I could feel the seconds ticking down and the sweat rolling down my back. I squared my shoulders, ignored Derek's agitation, depressed the clutch, and tried again.

The engine started, settling into a throaty purr. I would have hit the gas, but Sigmund shouted.

"The brake!" he sounded more agitated than I'd ever heard him.

Too late. I stalled it again.

The door started to descend.

Sigmund swore with enthusiasm.

Derek watched the door descend and I could hear his breath quickening. "Hurry up, Zoë."

"You'd think it was your car," I muttered. I went through my routine again—neutral, clutch, ignition—and the car choked for only a moment before the engine started again.

"Maybe it likes abuse," Sigmund muttered, but I ignored him.

I had things to do. I could see the shadow of the garage door coming closer and knew there would be no other opportunity. I disengaged the emergency brake, put it back in first, and touched the gas.

"Move it already," Derek shouted, and I floored it.

The car shot out into the night. It is possible that the garage door scraped the roof of the car. Or touched it. I'm not sure. But I saw it ascending again in the rearview mirror. Then I saw a vivid flash of yellow light in that mirror, and a massive black bird swooped out beneath the descending door. He disappeared from my view and I knew he'd be flying above us.

I had one heartbeat to think myself a success before Derek screamed a warning.

The car bounded onto the road—I swear it took flight at the end of the driveway. It was a fast beast, faster than I expected.

Too late, I saw I'd neglected to check the road for oncoming traffic.

"Left!" Sigmund roared.

"Right!" Derek cried.

I swerved hard to the left to avoid a van that had been moving along the street, minding its own business, until I'd decided to occupy the same physical space. The other driver honked as I skidded. I realized there was a bit of ice on the road, too. There was an oncoming car and I was in the wrong lane. Sigmund reached over and jerked the wheel hard to the right.

The Lamborghini fishtailed with glorious drama. Derek swore again and tightened his seat belt.

"Steer INTO the skid," Sigmund shouted.

"I'm trying!" I shouted back.

"Try harder," Derek complained.

After about ten thousand years of sliding around, the tires found their grip. We were at the end of the block, the light was green, and I saw no reason to take it easy. Time was wasting. I rocked it into second and left the honking van in my dust.

"Help me with your foresight," I said to Sigmund.

"Do it yourself, sis," Sigmund murmured.

I might have argued with him, but something opened in my mind. I saw a network of possibilities, an array of scenes emanating from this point in time like a glorious web. It was the future, in all its myriad possibility. I put the engine in third, accelerated through an intersection before the light changed to orange. The display in my mind's eye changed, some possibilities falling by the wayside, others becoming visible.

It made me think of driving down a highway and seeing all the choices available from the next exit. If I passed on that exit, the options at the next one became visible. If I took the exit, there were more options created as a result of my choice.

Exactly as Jared had said.

The future was mutable.

And we made it ourselves.

But this vision in my mind's eye made driving the car like a game or a simulator. I could see all that was coming, and the result of all possible choices—at least in the short term. That fed my confidence in a very big way. It wasn't two minutes' warning. It was much, much more than that.

"Don't dig your nails into the upholstery," I told Derek. "It'll tick my dad off."

"There's a truck coming into the next intersection from the right," he said grimly.

"I know."

"He's not going to stop and we're going to take it head-on!"

"I don't think so," I said, and pushed the gas pedal to the floor.

I swerved hard to the left while entering that intersection. The light was green, I was on the right, and there was no other traffic. The truck honked, leaping into the intersection from the right. Derek swore. I zoomed right around that truck, rocketing into the next block, leaving us unscathed.

I swear there were flames coming out the back of this car. We were one, Dragon Girl and Italian sports car, its performance an extension of my own abilities.

I got us to the school so fast that it was almost disappointing.

I DELIBERATELY SKIDDED the car to a halt at the front door of the school, almost but not quite bumping the tires against the curb. I turned off the ignition with some regret and we turned to look at the school.

It was glittering with spell light like a Christmas tree.

Worse than that, it was surrounded by ShadowEaters. They milled outside the school. They mingled with the kids who were attending the dance. They were inside, too, and I suspected that any kid foolish enough to wander away from the larger group might not come back. They'd taken out apprentice Mages individually already, after all. Now the ShadowEaters pushed against the kids, exuding menace, vibrating with frenzy.

I sensed they were waiting for something.

Enough power for a full and final assault.

I had a feeling that I knew where they'd get that surge of power.

"Can you see them?" I asked Derek.

He shook his head, looking—it must be said—a bit green around the gills. "Feels really bad but I can't see anything."

"There are ShadowEaters everywhere. I'll bet the NightBlade is here, too."

"Big finish," he said, nodding. "What do we do?"

"Let's act as if everything's normal and see what we can learn."

He exhaled, clearly not liking my plan but not having another, and got out of the car. There were a group of cool kids approaching, drawn to the car and obviously wondering who was driving it.

Were they ever going to be surprised.

Derek bent and kissed the ground, deliberately giving me a hard time. The kids laughed, razzing him about his ride. I saw that there were ShadowEaters following the group of kids, their eyes shining with malice. They nibbled at them, pinched them, considered them as if they were choosing from a buffet. Even though the kids couldn't see them, they eased away from the ShadowEaters instinctively, sensing something they didn't like.

I got out of the car and they were suitably astounded. "It wasn't that bad," I said to Derek, blushing furiously as they encircled the car, talking about Zitty Zoë's deep secrets.

Derek gave me a look. "Next time, I'll walk."

The kids laughed aloud and I pretended to be insulted. I locked and armed the car, then came around it to Derek's side.

That was when I heard the music drifting out of the doors of the school. I had seen the golden spell light churning around the building from the moment we arrived, but now I saw a tendril of blue and green spell light winding through it. The golden spells surrounded the blue-green thread, containing it and feeding off of it but still letting it grow.

Because it was Jared singing "Snow Goddess."

I stared in shock, my heart thudding. Was it a recording?

I watched the blue and purple spell light swirl upward, knowing I'd never seen it emanate from any recording of Jared's before.

"He's alive," I whispered, my heart thudding.

Derek swore under his breath. "They saved him for this."

I nodded, my throat tight. "They baited the trap."

"That means you can win, Zoë."

I wasn't so sure of that. I thought it just meant they needed me for their ritual.

Or my shadow.

A taxi pulled in beside us and squealed to a halt; then Jessica, Meagan, Liam, and Garrett spilled out. Jessica shuddered as she looked at the school, and Meagan gasped when she obviously recognized the tune.

I whispered to Meagan about Derek's howl when I gave her a hug and saw when I stepped back that her eyes had widened. Then she got her Einstein look and I knew she had the solution.

She immediately typed a message and my eyes widened when I read it.

THE KEENING NOTE THE BASTIANS USE TO SUMMON THE ANCESTORS MUST BE THE SOPRANO.

I looked at her and she nodded furiously. It made sense. We last four kinds held the secret to the four notes that could destroy the NightBlade. We wild cards hung out with spellsingers, which meant we could figure it out.

That explained why they wanted to finish us off so badly.

And the note had to be distinctive to our respective kinds. That left the *Pyr* with the bass note. I played the note and couldn't think of anything we did that echoed that sound.

"What are you doing?" Liam asked in old-speak.

"Solving the riddle that can destroy the NightBlade," I said, and told them what I was looking for. Liam looked thoughtful but Garrett frowned.

"If Jared's alive, we have to save him," Garrett added, glancing toward the stage. *"No time to mess around with games and riddles."*

Meagan's eyes lit as she looked between us. "Is that old-speak?" she asked. She grinned and tapped madly on her messenger, which then emitted a tone so low that everyone in the room looked skyward.

Thinking it was thunder.

"One octave lower!" Meagan said, triumphant. "That's it!"

"But how do we know when to make the sound?" Derek asked, turning toward the stage.

"I'll give Meagan a signal," I said. "Watch her for your cue."

We nodded at each other, exchanged looks, and I probably wasn't the only one who took a breath. I offered Derek my hand; then we marched toward the doors together.

There was no way that I could turn away from Jared, even if he was spellbound.

No matter what the consequences might be.

13

I could see a thousand possibilities extending from this moment as we walked into the school. Very few of those options for my future ended well. I suspected that Derek was silent because he could see a subset of the same thing.

Some things were as expected. There were red streamers hanging over the doorways and signs for the dance. Red hearts were plastered on windows and walls. There was smoke in the air and it wasn't all cigarette smoke. A bunch of the teachers were on patrol, watching over us and trying desperately to look young and cool. (They failed. Every one of them.) Lots of people were dressed in red or red and white, and there were many couples holding hands. Music was playing, sending out a strong bass beat.

That the same song was being played over and over again didn't seem to bother anybody.

That it was Jared singing "Snow Goddess" sure bothered me.

There were ShadowEaters everywhere. The other kids didn't seem to see them, although they shivered periodically and glanced over their shoulders as they talked and laughed in their groups. The ShadowEaters eased back to let Derek and me pass, growling and biting as we moved through the throng of them. I was sure one licked me, and I tried not to shudder.

They let us pass because they thought we were stepping into their trap.

They thought they were going to have their big slaughter, taking all of us out at once, and get their power burst to make it to that pure spirit form.

What they were going to get was a surprise.

There was a lot of spell light, too, winding around our ankles, the tendrils so thick that they hid the floor. We waded through a maze of spells, like explorers in a hostile jungle. I felt the spell snakes slide over my boots, never really binding me but making sure I understood that they could.

I cradled the weight of Skuld's shears beneath my jacket with my free hand, glad to have them.

There was a trickle of sweat running down my back.

I saw some apprentice Mages in the hallway, although there were a lot fewer of them than other times we'd squared off. I knew which ones they were because they were flickering between the forms of the species they'd conquered. There's something about a merman becoming a basilisk, then becoming a butterfly that catches the eye. (Trust me.) They were agitated or excited, maybe worked up in anticipation of whatever waited ahead.

That couldn't be a good sign of anything.

It was interesting that the apprentice Mages were here, given that the ShadowEaters were here. The ShadowEaters had been hunting surviving Mages and junior apprentice Mages, after all. Did this bunch think they were the top of the class? The ones who could join the ShadowEaters? They might just be stupid, but the fact that they could move between forms indicated that they were at least as adept as Adrian.

They might have the same false confidence as Adrian, too.

I could hope.

We stepped into the cafeteria, and I was startled by how many unfamiliar people were there. Not that we hadn't been introduced—I'd never seen most of them in my life. The dance floor was thronged with hot guys and gorgeous girls, none of whom looked familiar.

Were we at the wrong school? An alternate universe?

Then two of the guys turned to Derek and made a single nod of acknowledgment. When he nodded back once, they returned to their dancing, and I guessed.

"They're yours," I said, and he gave me a slight nod.

I was relieved and worried that the wolf shifters had come. Was this part of the ShadowEaters' plan—to ensure that as many shifters as possible were present, to improve the shadow feast?

I didn't want to look at the stage. My heart was so filled with hope that Jared was okay that I didn't want to lose that possibility. I didn't want to see him spellbound or injured or turned into some kind of zombie.

I just wanted to close my eyes and listen to him sing, in case it was the last time.

"Want to dance?" Anne asked suddenly. We all started to find her right behind us, smiling as if we all were actually buddies.

I saw the glimmer of spell light in her eyes. She smiled at Garrett.

"It's a trick," I warned him in old-speak.

"I know, but also an opportunity," he said. Then he smiled at Anne, took her hand, and headed for the dance floor. I could see two of Suzanne's other cronies, Fiona and Trish, and both of them had eyes of glowing gold like Anne's. Trevor and the ShadowEaters had spellbound them.

Converted them to staff.

Like Suzanne, they were probably going to be sacrificed.

"Great idea," Liam said, feigning enthusiasm as Garrett and Anne started to dance. "Let's dance," he said to Jessica, and they followed Garrett.

"I don't like this," Meagan said, worry in her tone. "They're waiting for something."

"It's going to get worse," Derek said, folding his arms across his chest as he stood between us. Sure enough, the spell light seemed to be swirling with greater intensity, becoming brighter by the second.

Liam and Jessica took to the dance floor, and I was surprised at how smooth a dancer Liam was. He guided Jessica through the crowd with ease, following her slight nods to pause in the vicinity of one attractive girl after another. Dancing made it easy for her to spread the word.

I looked at Derek and he looked at me. There was a weight of expectation between us, a moment of what might have been; then he turned to Meagan. She looked between us but I nodded, relieved that she would have a wolf standing guard over her. They did the same thing, sliding through the throng of dancers. Derek exchanged a word with this wolf and that one, and I turned to look at the stage.

When I saw Jared, I caught my breath.

He was snared in a golden bubble of spell light and looked to be lost in his own world. He played the same song over and over again, crooning the words, making love to his guitar. As I watched him, I realized that he was trapped in a sequence of moments, doomed to repeat them over and over and over again.

Was he aware of his fate?

Did he know I was here?

Was he still in there?

I had so many questions, but two were the most important: Could I save him? And if I did, would he ever be the same?

He was surrounded by ShadowEaters, as if they were his backup band. Their eyes shone a brilliant gold as their ranks parted suddenly. They pushed forward a guy who looked like he'd rather be anywhere else in the world.

Kohana.

I gasped. He wasn't dead, either.

No, they'd saved him so they could eliminate all four wild cards at once. They really wanted the energy boost to be as big as possible—and they were that confident that they'd win. That simultaneous execution was what was going to give them the power surge they needed.

I had to stop them!

Just as when I first met Kohana, there was a noose of spell light around his neck. His hands were bound before him. The music stopped. The dancing stopped as everyone looked around, uncertain.

I had a really bad feeling.

Then everything happened very fast.

THE SPELL LIGHT swirled in a golden frenzy, taking on a pulsing energy that was faster than the beat of Jared's music. I heard a different song become ascendant. The ShadowEaters converged on the cafeteria, pressing in from the perimeter with obvious hunger.

That was when I saw that the scene had frozen.

At least, all of the normal kids were frozen, trapped in a single moment of time.

Which meant that all the shifters and spellsingers were revealed, because none of us were frozen.

The ShadowEaters laughed and grabbed. They surrounded Liam and Jessica, closing around them like an ardent swarm. They isolated Garrett, and Anne helped to push him away from the group. He fought her, but the ShadowEaters had him outnumbered.

Meagan understood immediately what was happening and started to sing. Derek shifted shape when the ShadowEaters surrounded him and Meagan, with only Meagan's determined spellsinging giving those two a buffer. I could see that she was losing the battle, though, even though she was determined to keep singing.

Derek leapt and snapped, his hostility helping to keep the ShadowEaters back. They retreated, maybe acting instinctively, because his bite had no effect. His jaws closed on empty air and spell light, but he kept snarling all the same.

Meagan kept trying to ease them toward Garrett, and I knew she wanted to get him inside the influence of her spell light.

Then I heard Trevor laugh. How could that be?

There was a ShadowEater on the stage, one that burned a particularly vivid shade of gold. He was singing a spellsong, one that pulsed and caressed his silhouetted form. As the song grew louder, I saw his dark skin take on detail again, his features appear out of the shadow and brilliance.

The ShadowEater became Trevor, right before my eyes.

His eyes still shone the vivid gold that characterized ShadowEaters, but he'd moved back to the physical sphere.

How long would the spell last?

Why had he done it?

Trevor held the NightBlade high over his head, its dark knife gleaming with evil intent, and I knew exactly why he'd done it. This was it!

A ripple of excitement passed through the cafeteria. The ShadowEaters pushed Kohana closer to Trevor and the stage, moving faster although he struggled against the spell. Anne and the ShadowEaters kept Garrett at the perimeter of the room, isolated from all of us. A group of ShadowEaters pushed Liam and Jessica toward the stage.

Meanwhile, the mood in the cafeteria was turning frantic. The Shadow-Eaters vibrated more rapidly in anticipation. They pressed closer, gnawing on the captives they surrounded. The apprentice Mages spun more quickly through their forms, adding their voices to Trevor's song.

When I looked back toward the stage, I saw something that made me sick. Nick and Isabelle were there, surrounded by a net of spell light. Isabelle's eyes were golden and glazed, and she was completely entranced—as was Yvonne, who held their spell tethers. Nick was struggling, without success, against his spell that had him tightly trussed. I was both relieved to finally see them and terrified that they were spellbound. Meagan's protective spell had been destroyed.

Jared played and played, lost in a world of his own.

This couldn't get worse.

I saw the ShadowEater Trevor hold up the NightBlade. I saw him begin the invocation and target Nick and Isabelle.

They weren't going to be sacrificed again.

Even if they were bait for me, and even if I was going to die, I was still going to win.

Because I could see that Trevor's spells were once again feeding on Jared's music.

All I had to do was silence him.

Before anyone was sacrificed.

THE GOLDEN MAGE spell light became blinding in its intensity as someone's hand locked on the back of my neck. I turned to find Trish behind me, her eyes shining gold. She pushed me hard toward the stage, tripping me when I resisted her.

The spell snakes locked around my ankles, binding them together with lightning speed. I fell to the ground. I hauled out my shears and hacked at the spell snakes. I heard the others shout out and knew they were in trouble, too. The spell snakes grew faster and faster, replicating and replacing themselves, locking around my legs, binding me to the hip so fast that I knew I didn't have much time.

Trish laughed as I hacked at them in desperation.

I stabbed down a bunch of snakes, slashing with a violence I didn't know I had in me. (And I'm a dragon. Think about it.) The spell snakes obscured my vision, and the shears caught on something more substantial.

Trish.

The spell light poured from the cut, revealing her to be a ShadowEater. I didn't have time to think about when that had happened or why, because she snarled and leapt at me. Spell light spilled from her mouth, targeting me.

I ripped the shears through Trish in self-defense. She collapsed like a rag doll, spilling spell light all over the place. It rose into the air, a renewable resource, and made the ShadowEaters pulse with new vigor.

Her skin turned dark and empty, like a deflated black balloon.

Ick.

I shifted shape with a roar, calling to the others to do the same. Liam shifted, becoming a glittering malachite and silver dragon. I thrilled at the sight of him, and was awed when Jessica changed into a jaguar and they fought back-to-back.

Garrett shifted into his garnet-and-gold dragon form with a roar and breathed dragonfire on every ShadowEater foolish enough to get between him and Meagan.

Meagan sang her heart out, and soon had both Derek and Garrett within her bubble of spell light. The trio moved with purpose, surrounded by her song, making steady progress toward the stage.

Trevor lifted the NightBlade high over Kohana. "One more species possessed for all time!" he cried.

"One more triumph!" cried the apprentice Mages. The ShadowEaters kept us from the stage through sheer numbers, their dark menace keeping us from saving Kohana.

I didn't have time to mess around.

"No way!" I shouted, and spontaneously manifested right behind Trevor.

In human form.

I had surprise on my side. I seized the NightBlade and retreated. He came after me with a snarl, but I slashed once at him with Skuld's shears. The sharp blade cut his side and spell light spilled through the gash. He shouted in rage.

I expected him to collapse, but he began to sing with fury.

I didn't have time to free Kohana, not yet. I tried Skuld's shears on the bubble that held Jared captive, but it bounced off the golden sphere.

When I looked back, I saw that Trevor's spells were attacking and binding every note that Jared made. Trevor milked each one dry, using Jared's power to heal his own wound, twisting Jared's spells to his own purpose. I watched in horror.

Then he came after me.

I retreated around the bubble that imprisoned Jared. It looked like spun glass and I had to believe I could break it, even while dodging Trevor. The NightBlade was humming in my hand, filling my thoughts with darkness. I didn't trust it one bit, but instinct told me that it could be used against this spell.

What would be the price?

I didn't know, but I had to try. I stabbed it into the bubble of spell light, which exploded on contact into a flurry of golden stars.

Jared fell lifeless to the ground, his song silenced.

Maybe forever.

He was completely still.

I stared in horror at what I'd done; then I heard Trevor snarl behind me.

I SPUN TO FIGHT, hoping I could fix everything else once we survived. The NightBlade wriggled in my grip, trying to get away. Who knew what it wanted to do next? I sure wasn't going to use it again.

I leapt over Jared and slashed at Kohana's bonds with Skuld's shears. He was free in a heartbeat, tossing aside the noose. He shifted shape and flew high, obviously glad to be free.

That was when the *Wakiya* elder began to sing the note from the Thunderbirds. I realized that no one could see or hear him because he was dead.

No one but me.

And the NightBlade. I saw it quiver when he started to sing.

In fact, it vibrated in my hand, acting like a tuning fork.

Trevor snatched at it, but I stabbed at him with Skuld's shears again. He didn't back down and I was soon slashing at spell snakes as fast as he could make them.

"Now!" I cried, and Jessica began to sing the keening note that the Bastians used to summon the ancestors. The other cat-shifters at the dance joined in, and soon the air was filled with the eerie cry that gave me goose bumps. I saw the golden ghostly cats appear and begin to mill through the crowd on the dance floor, their eyes glowing hot red.

The NightBlade vibrated harder.

Derek tipped back his head and howled, the signal for his fellows to join in. There was a dizzying flash of brilliant blue as a quarter of the guys on the dance floor changed shape, becoming wolves. There were big wolves and small wolves, silver ones and white ones and charcoal ones, wolves with blue eyes and wolves with eyes of pale green. Every single one of them tipped back his head and howled that same note.

"No!" Trevor shouted. They targeted me then, apprentice Mages and ShadowEaters and minions pouncing. I shifted shape to dragon form, hiding the NightBlade along with my clothes. I could feel it shaking beneath my scales, twitching as it responded to the notes being sung.

"Old-speak, old-speak, old-speak," Garrett began, repeating the same words over and over again in that deep note. I saw Meagan shake her head and tap her messenger, and he changed his words to her suggestions. He let loose a long low stream of *"Ooooooo."*

I stumbled over the stage, cutting Isabelle and Nick free. Isabelle was out of it, but Nick shifted shape. He became a fearsome dragon of vivid orange and yellow, his scales gleaming so brightly that looking at him was like looking into the sun. He roared and breathed dragonfire, apparently in relief, then took up the note that Garrett was singing. Liam and I joined in, and the NightBlade resonated so hard that it shook itself loose of its hiding place.

It fell on the stage.

I leapt after it.

Trevor pounced on it and held it high, triumphant that he'd caught it. He pivoted to face me, his intent clear. I breathed some fire, just to let him know I wouldn't go down easily. We squared off, and I kept singing that bass note.

Before he could do anything with the NightBlade, it shook hard. He could barely hold on to it, and I meant to snatch it from his grasp.

But it shattered, shattered into a thousand thin shards.

They scattered across the stage, a thousand thin slices of darkest night. I thought it was my imagination that they looked like shapes as they fell to the stage.

The ShadowEaters gave a horrible cry; then they faded to nothing so abruptly that they might never have been. The spell light winked out. The cafeteria, instead of being bathed in the sickening hue of spell light, was pretty much normal again.

"No!" Trevor shouted and fell to his knees, trying desperately to gather up all the broken bits.

I stepped forward like an avenging angel and changed back to my human form. I raised Skuld's shears and he looked up at me, fear in his golden eyes. I slit him in half, loosing the spell light that had filled his skin.

This time, there was no spell light for him to use to save himself.

Like the others, he deflated. Unlike the others, he made a low moan as he ceased to exist. The spell light that had filled him rose into the air, seeking to join more energy of its kind. Finding none, it winked out.

Like someone had flipped a switch.

I STOOD THERE, shaking in the silence that stretched afterward. I was dimly aware of the crackle of blue light, the shimmer of the wolves and Bastians changing back to human form and the dragons doing the same. I stared at the empty shell that had been Trevor, incredulous that it was finally over.

The spell that had snared the normal kids was broken, as well. I heard the music start again—although it wasn't Jared singing anymore—and the laughter of people flirting. I looked at Jared, who didn't get up or wake up.

What had I done to him?

"Those would be mine," Skuld said from beside me. She put out her hand for the shears. I was pretty astonished to be able to see her when I was awake, but she smiled and winked at me. "Good job."

So I'd passed another test. I looked between her and the shears. "Thanks. I guess I don't need them anymore."

"No, you don't." She shoved them into the holster on her belt and tossed her braid over her shoulder, then bent to pick up the pieces of the broken NightBlade. "I hate a mess," she muttered, but I sensed there was more to it than that.

I didn't much care. I dropped to my knees beside Jared, knowing that if the cost of destroying the NightBlade and eliminating the Mages was his death, it had been too high of a price. I couldn't feel a pulse and his skin had become very pale.

I felt Nick behind me, the weight of his hand on my shoulder. I saw Isabelle kneel beside me and take my hand in hers. She was still pale and looked unsteady, and there were tears in her eyes. "It doesn't have to be this way, Zoë," she whispered.

"Maybe all Wyverns are doomed to lose at love," I said. "Or to sacrifice for it."

"No," Isabelle said with such conviction that I wanted to believe her. She reached into her purse, always prepared, and pulled out her deck of tarot cards. She shuffled it once and then offered it to me.

Our gazes met.

I didn't want to shuffle them. I didn't want to touch them. I halfway didn't believe they'd respond to me. But I reached over and I cut the deck, turning it over in my hand to show the card.

THE MAGICIAN.

I looked at Isabelle. She smiled.

"Number one," she said, indicating the Roman numeral at the top. "The prime mover, the card of artists and of people who make things happen by directing energy and resources."

"People who make the future happen," I said, remembering Jared's ideas about that. "People who choose."

Isabelle nodded and put the deck away. She straightened and stood beside Nick. I saw her slip her hand into his and I glanced up to meet her gaze, and realized that she was wearing the necklace he'd had made for her.

The last Wyvern had made herself a future.

I'd make myself one, too.

I eased closer to Jared, realizing that we could have been in a little bubble of privacy. The dance went on around us, a tight circle of shifters and select humans and a spellsinger hiding Jared and me from view. Liam and Garrett were there, Meagan and Jessica, Isabelle and Nick, Derek and Kohana. They were my friends and they were all on my side.

Well, except Kohana. I was never sure about him.

He smiled at me, maybe guessing the direction of my thoughts.

"This one's for you, *Unktehila,*" he murmured, then sang a trio of notes.

I saw the vivid green of his spellsong. It danced like a feather on the wind, then settled over Jared's heart. I realized that Kohana was helping me, that he was repaying the debt between us.

Mostly I knew this because the dead *Wakiya* elder watched with obvious satisfaction.

Meagan watched Kohana, listening to him with care. She then added her voice to his in a simple harmony, the two of them jamming softly together.

Meagan's spellsong was red this time, and I liked how it twined with Kohana's. The two threads of spell light wound together like plies of yarn or snakes on a caduceus or a DNA string.

Jessica improvised some scat. She didn't make spell light but it sounded pretty.

I loved that they were trying to help me.

To help Jared.

That gave me hope.

The entwined spell light wound toward Jared, making a vortex over his heart. I felt as if it were showing me something. On impulse, I put my hand into the middle of the swirling spell light, putting my finger on the eye of the hurricane.

And Jared's heart pulsed hard beneath my fingertip.

He wasn't dead. He was injured.

Maybe he was lost.

Maybe he just needed someone to call him back from wherever they had banished him.

I flattened my hand, putting my palm against his chest. My mouth was dry and I was nervous, uncertain. But I'd learned to fly without a manual and I'd learned to become the Wyvern without any instruction book.

I had my instincts to guide me and they were pretty good.

On impulse, I touched my lips to his, keeping my hand flat against his chest. It was a sweet kiss, a chaste touch of my lips to his, but I exhaled a tiny breath against Jared's mouth.

And his eyes flew open, those gazillion shades of green nearly stopping my heart cold. He studied me, probably reading my thoughts, and I held his gaze, letting him look.

He must have liked whatever he saw.

"Hey, Dragon Girl," he murmured, and his voice sounded rough. Then he smiled crookedly at me, the sight of that dimple making my own heart skip. "Would this be the happy ending?"

"Not quite," I said with a grin. "I still owe you a ride."

"You're never going to deliver on that," he teased, his eyes dancing.

"Get it in gear, Madison," I retorted. "We're going right now."

I stood up and imperiously offered him my hand. He got to his feet under his own steam and visibly shook off something. The others hugged him or pumped his hand or thumped his back. He checked his guitar, then entrusted it to Nick, congratulated Meagan on her spellsinging, thanked Kohana.

Then he took my hand in his and smiled just for me.

"So, I was thinking, Dragon Girl," he said, looking down at our hands.

"Always the better choice," I teased him, and his grin widened.

"I kind of like this town."

My heart leapt in anticipation as he glanced toward my friends.

"Since I don't have a band anymore, would it cramp your style if I found a job in town?" He shrugged, avoiding my gaze. "Maybe hooked up with another band." He looked me in the eye. "Met your dad."

My heart stopped cold. "Wouldn't cramp my style at all."

"Good. Good." He smiled, getting that wicked glint in his eyes, the one that made the world seem full of possibilities. He slid his arm around my shoulders. "Because the way I see it, I've got a couple of years to fill and this would be a good place to do it."

This time when I smiled at him, he bent and kissed me. Hard. It was every bit as thrilling as the very first time.

And I had a feeling it always would be.

We turned as one and walked out of that cafeteria together as if we owned it.

And, you know, I think we did.

You had to guess that when it was all over, I had a dream.

I felt the snow landing on my face and heard the click of knitting needles. I rolled over to find the three Wyrd sisters busily at work, just as usual. Granny was knitting with superhuman speed, Urd was spinning wool for her so fast that her hands were a blur, and the snowdrift that

Verdandi knit swelled over their knees. Skuld was leaning back against the trunk of the tree, cleaning her nails with those massive shears. The tree was in full leaf above them, and the sky was full of stars.

(It made no sense that it was snowing when the sky was clear, but there you go. Dreams follow their own rules.)

I watched as Urd and Verdandi did as they had once before. There could have been a silent signal, for they both moved in the same instant without saying a word. They put aside their work and Urd reached for the bucket, the one she sent down the well. I knew that Verdandi would pull a ladle out from under the snowdrift and that they would water the great tree.

It was soothing to watch their quiet and efficient routine, so I settled back to doze. This was a mark that all was right with the world.

But this time, they surprised me. When Urd pulled the full bucket out of the well, she set it on the ground. A bit of water sloshed over the edge of the bucket; then the three sisters gathered around it to peer into its depths.

There was no ladle. I frowned and sat up to watch.

Skuld shoved her shears into that holster on her belt. She reached into the snowdrift and pulled out a handful of items that reminded me of sugar cookies or gingerbread cut into shapes. But these shapes were black.

They were the remains of the shattered NightBlade.

Urd chose one from the collection in Skuld's hands and held it up. She blew on it, as if to blow away the black dust on it, and I smelled ash.

But it stayed black, whatever it was.

It was shaped like a griffin.

Granny did get her ladle and she filled it with water from the bucket. Instead of pouring it on the tree, she carefully poured it over the shape that Urd held in her hand. It seemed to be very important that Urd's own bony fingertips weren't touched by the water.

To my astonishment, the shape swelled. It rounded. It grew. And by the time Granny poured the third ladle of water over it, it had become a griffin that towered over the three sisters. It could have been a black sculpture, a griffin carved of dark marble.

All three sisters blew on the griffin and the blackness that covered it fell away like soot.

It was beautiful. It had the head and wings of an eagle and the body of a lion. Its coat was all in shades of gold and black, an elegant and beautiful creature. I could see the fur on its sides and the gleaming ebony of its nails. Its eyes were as dark as bittersweet chocolate. Its beak could have been made of hammered gold and it shone like the fierce weapon it was.

But its wings were astonishing. They shaded through every color of the rainbow: yellow at the tips, then orange and red and violet and blue, and green where they joined its body. Each feather glistened and each one was tipped in gold.

Then Skuld clapped her hands. My eyes nearly fell out of my head when the sculpture came to life. It was like it thawed or awakened from a long sleep. The griffin flapped its wings; it stretched and let out a fearsome cry. That cry could curdle the blood of anyone. And those wings were even more stupendously beautiful when they were spread wide. Just when I thought nothing weirder could happen, it shimmered blue.

A familiar pale blue, a blue light that illuminated its perimeter and danced through its veins.

And the griffin shifted shape into a woman with long dark hair and elegant strength. She embraced the three sisters, then turned to face me. I saw the tears glisten in those beautiful dark eyes as she bowed low and touched her forehead to the ground before me.

"Thank you, Wyvern," she said, the words resonating in my thoughts like old-speak. She blew me a kiss, changed back to her griffin shape with a roar of delight, then launched herself into the air. She circled once over the great tree, dipped low in triumph, then gave that fearsome cry before she flew into the starry night.

"Always liked them," Skuld mused with satisfaction. "Even if I did have to wrestle one once in a while over a choice morsel."

"I'm glad they're back," Urd said.

Granny gestured with her ladle, returning her sisters' attention to the business at hand. Urd chose another shape, a shape I now realized was a shadow, the shadow of the one of each kind. The extinction of each kind of shifter had added to the NightBlade, strengthening it, creating new layers like mica and made of shifter shadows. We'd broken the bonds that enchanted them, and the Wyrd sisters were setting all those kinds of shifters loose in the world again.

I watched the sisters work, my mind filling with questions and possibilities. How many kinds of shifters were there in total? How would we all get along? It looked like I'd be learning a lot from my dad about making alliances and treaties.

I thought of the chart I'd made just days before and envisioned it becoming a massive spreadsheet. Did these other shifters live openly among humans or hide themselves? The *Pyr* were charged with defending the earth and its treasures. What were the quests of all these other shifters? What could we shifters do together to make the world a better place? What would humans think of so many myths coming to life among them?

No doubt about it—the world had become a much more interesting place.

I'm ready for the adventure.

Are you?

ABOUT THE AUTHOR

Deborah Cooke sold her first book in 1992, a medieval romance published under her pseudonym Claire Delacroix. Since then, she has published over fifty novels in a wide variety of sub-genres, including historical romance, contemporary romance, paranormal romance, fantasy romance, time-travel romance, women's fiction, paranormal young adult and fantasy with romantic elements. She has published under the names Claire Delacroix, Claire Cross and Deborah Cooke. **The Beauty**, part of her successful Bride Quest series of historical romances, was her first title to land on the *New York Times* List of Bestselling Books. Her books routinely appear on other bestseller lists and have won numerous awards. In 2009, she was the writer-in-residence at the Toronto Public Library, the first time the library has hosted a residency focused on the romance genre. In 2012, she was honored to receive the Romance Writers of America's Mentor of the Year Award.

Currently, she writes paranormal romances and contemporary romances under the name Deborah Cooke. She also writes medieval romances as Claire Delacroix. Deborah lives in Canada with her husband and family, as well as far too many unfinished knitting projects.

Learn more about her books at her websites:
DeborahCooke.com
Delacroix.net

ALSO BY DEBORAH COOKE

The Dragonfire Novels:

Kiss of Fire

Kiss of Fury

Kiss of Fate

Winter Kiss

Harmonia's Kiss

Whisper Kiss

Darkfire Kiss

Flashfire

Ember's Kiss

Kiss of Danger

Kiss of Darkness

Kiss of Destiny

Serpent's Kiss

Firestorm Forever

Here be Dragons: The Dragonfire Companion

The DragonFate Novels:

Maeve's Book of Beasts

Dragon's Kiss

Dragon's Heart

Dragon's Mate

The Dragons of Incendium:

Wyvern's Mate

Nero's Dream

Wyvern's Prince

Arista's Legacy

Wyvern's Warrior

Kraw's Secret

Wyvern's Outlaw

Celo's Quest

Wyvern's Angel

Nimue's Gift

The Prometheus Project:

Fallen

Guardian

Rebel

Abyss

To learn more about Deborah's paranormal and contemporary romances, visit her website:

DeborahCooke.com

To learn more about her Claire Delacroix historical and fantasy romances, visit her website:

Delacroix.net

www.ingramcontent.com/pod-product-compliance
Lightning Source LLC
Chambersburg PA
CBHW020533310726
48979CB00014B/2319/J

* 9 7 8 1 9 9 0 8 7 9 5 0 0 *